Diedre is the first in her family to go to college. She's about to start law school when she meets Mitch at a party. Diedre doesn't believe in love at first sight, but the passion in his glance stirs her heart.

Treva is happy as stepmother to a teenager who can't decide if she wants to be a rap star or the next Brandy—but there's an empty place in her arms that aches to be filled by a new baby.

Pepper struggles to make her luxury lingerie boutique a success. She's too old to fall in love, she thinks—until she is swept off her feet by a millionaire. Despite his ardent claims of love, she fears that Gray sees her only as a trophy wife.

When Mitch reappears in Diedre's life, she discovers that there is far more to him—and to their relationship—than an uncaring one-night stand. When Treva's husband learns of her endangered health, he so fears losing her to death that he drives her from his bed and nearly from their marriage. When Pepper sees Gray's relationship with his adult son, she wonders if Gray understands that people are not perfect, and what that will mean if they have children together and her youthful beauty fades.

From warm holiday gatherings to the harshest of custody battles, *Choices* illuminates the complicated landscape of the modern family.

CHOICES

ABIGAIL REED

A TOM DOHERTY ASSOCIATES BOOK
NEW YORK

This is a work of fiction. All the characters and events portrayed in this book are either products of the author's imagination or are used fictitiously.

CHOICES

A Forge Book
Published by Tom Doherty Associates, LLC
175 Fifth Avenue
New York, NY 10010

Forge® is a registered trademark of Tom Doherty Associates, LLC.

ISBN: 0-812-54528-1

First edition: September 1999

Printed in the United States of America

0   9   8   7   6   5   4   3   2   1

Acknowledgments

Every one of the characters in this book is a figment of my imagination. If I have used the name of a real person, it was through accident only, and not intentional. The antiabortion group No Genocide is a product of my imagination, as is the clinic depicted in this book, an amalgam of several abortion centers. Thousands of women visit such clinics each day, facing the same sorts of choices as the women make in this book. None find it easy.

My depiction of Ann Arbor, Michigan, also includes fictional locations, and in some cases I have taken liberties with various real settings.

Special acknowledgments go to Sue Hertz, author of *Caught in the Crossfire: A Year on Abortion's Front Line*. Her vivid picture of daily life at the Preterm Health Services clinic in Brookline, Massachusetts (where later an abortion murder would take place), is "must" reading for anyone interested in the abortion issue.

Also Roni Moncur; Beth de Baptiste, assistant prosecuting attorney, Oakland County; Alfreda Menlove, attorney-at-law; Lynn Albertson; Janet Smigielski, Rochester Hills Public Library; Toni Shears, editor, *Law Quadrangle Notes*, University of Michigan Law School; Planned Parenthood; and the Hôtel Plaza Athénée.

Deepest thanks to my literary agent, Cherry Weiner, who helped me brainstorm this idea while sitting in a restaurant having coffee before a writers' conference. And to my wonderful editor, Melissa Ann Singer, whose suggestions challenged me and spurred my enthusiasm for yet another draft. Also, Jennifer Hogen, who believed in the book, and Ginger

Clark and Pamela Loeser who helped fine-tune. Any mistakes are mine, not theirs.

And to all the others I love: my children, who make life worthwhile; my husband, whose love is like a rock; and my parents, whose support has always been there.

CONCEPTION

DIEDRE

PARTY NOISES THROBBED IN THE HUMID JULY NIGHT.
Yells of laughter and the pounding rhythms of Nine Inch
Nails, the shriek of a girl being thrown into the lake, the
buzzing of Jet Skis. Moist, water smells mingled with the
smells of beer, wine, barbecue smoke, and cigarettes.

Diedre Samms stood on the redwood deck that overlooked Orchard Lake, feeling at once high on wine and removed from the noisy life that reveled around her. She
didn't really belong here. She was willowy and slim, with
butterscotch-colored hair twisted into a French braid. That
part was fine, but she was also twenty-three, several years
older than most of these partying kids.

And her feet ached. She had waitressed a full shift today
at T.G.I. Friday's, wearing a T-shirt with BREW CREW emblazoned on the back and a set of red suspenders with a
bunch of slogan buttons pinned to the elastic. Now here she
was, in a blue and yellow flowered sundress with spaghetti
straps, and blue, high-heeled sandals, stranded at this party.

She didn't know the hostess, Amber somebody, whose
father was a rich Bloomfield Hills builder who specialized
in strip malls and shopping centers. Nor did Diedre know
most of the guests, undergrads from the University of Michigan and Michigan State, who were celebrating the Fourth
of July one day early. It was Danny Preskin who had invited
her, and he was out front, lying on the beach in a chaise
lounge, playing full frontal kissy face with an old girlfriend
he'd run into.

The girl in the lake had torn her bikini top off. She was
still shrieking.

Diedre took another gulp of wine from a clear plastic
glass, wondering if her date was going to totally desert her,

or if he'd remember to drive her home. Was she just supposed to stand around and wait for him? Apparently. Unless she wanted to get tossed in the lake, an option Diedre thought briefly about, then discarded. Besides, by the sound of it, about ten guys had jumped in after the topless, drunk girl, not exactly Diedre's idea of fun.

Fun. Her sister, Pam, accused her of not having enough of it, and Diedre thought Pam was probably right. She *wanted* to let loose and play, but this year had been way too focused for that. She had been waitressing thirty-five hours a week, in addition to carrying a full load of classes at Wayne State and getting nearly straight A's. In what spare time she did have, Diedre filled out scholarship applications, trying to write dynamite "personal statements" and optional 250-word essays.

If she got the scholarship she wanted—a very, very big *if*—it would be a full, free ride. The going rate at the U. of M. law school these days was twenty-eight thousand dollars per year for all expenses. And it took *three* years. Diedre had gone from praying to making bargains with God, and had even taken to wearing her lucky earrings, real sapphires that had belonged to her grandmother. She'd vowed not to take them off until she heard the news.

More yelling and Jet Ski noise came from the lake, punctuated by screams as more girls jumped in the water. Diedre saw flashes of white skin.

She upended her plastic glass, draining the remaining wine, and drifted toward the far end of the huge deck overlooking the lake, where several long redwood tables held two kegs of beer and three or four picnic coolers crammed with sodas and bottles of wine. Beer was puddled on the decking, emitting a sour reek, and had been tracked everywhere. Diedre felt it creeping up the soles of the high-heeled sandals she wore, wetting her bare toes.

"You're not skinny-dipping tonight?" said a voice beside her. Diedre turned to see a guy she'd noticed earlier when everyone was scarfing down the barbecued chicken and baby back ribs. He was tall, with a shock of glossy, dark hair, and wore a blue chambray shirt open at the throat, khaki shorts, and a pair of Top-Siders.

"Didn't bring my skinnies," she joked, laughing a little too loudly.

"Hey, it's really noisy here. I think the neighbors called the police, but everyone is yelling so loud nobody noticed. Did you see a flashing blue light in the driveway?"

"Oh, that's what it was. I thought it was the party decoration." They both bent over, laughing hilariously as if she'd said something amazingly funny. *Man,* Diedre thought. She was getting a little hammered here.

Diedre sneaked another look at the guy—his name was Mitchell, something like that. No, Mitch. There was a white scar on his smooth-shaven chin about a half inch long, marring his looks just enough to make him interesting. He'd probably gotten it white-water rafting or snowboarding, she decided, some cool sport that girls like her, counting every penny, couldn't indulge in, at least not often.

Diedre pulled a bottle of Sebastiani out of one of the coolers, watery ice chips dripping from it. "Ooops," she said, slurring her words slightly. "This one has a cork."

"Hey, I'm an Olympic cork remover," he said, grabbing a corkscrew from the tabletop, the sophisticated kind with two winglike stainless steel handles. At home, Diedre's mother used a twisty attached to a can opener, or she jabbed with the point of a kitchen knife. The wine always had brown bits and pieces of cork floating in it.

Mitch inserted the point of the corkscrew and in two deft motions had extracted the cork. With a flourish he refilled Diedre's glass. He poured another glass for himself, then lifted it in her direction. "Cheers," he said, raising his voice to be heard over the tumult of party noise. "Are you a friend of Amber's?"

"I don't even know her."

"Good." He grinned at her. His teeth were white and straight, the kind that had gotten that way with braces, and his eyes were that pale blue that looks transparent. "Amber's life's ambition is to be a publicity director for Northwest so she can get free plane flights. What's your life's ambition?''

Diedre smiled. ''I'm still waiting to hear about mine. Either I get a big scholarship, and I achieve it, or I end up, oh, maybe taking a job as assistant manager at Friday's. You know, hiring bussers, firing bussers, ordering napkins and swizzle sticks, a really exciting career.''

Actually she had planned to lower her sights and go to Wayne's less prestigious law school, burdening herself with thousands of dollars in debt that it would take her years to repay, but for some reason she didn't feel like telling Mitch this now. It revealed too much about her.

''Oh, by the way,'' he said, ''I'm Mitchell—but people call me Mitch.''

She pretended she hadn't already heard his name. ''Glad to meet you, Mitch. I'm Diedre. My friends call me Deeds.''

They each drank another eight-ounce tumbler of wine. His smile was as sweet and dazzling as Donny Osmond's had been, back when Diedre was a child. Once, she'd been half in love with Donny Osmond. Mitch told her he'd just graduated from the University of Chicago and was living at home with his parents, working as a fill-in security guard at Chrysler Corporation in Highland Park while he decided what he wanted to do.

''A security guard?'' She giggled.

''Uniform and all. I do important stuff like stand by the gate so the hourly workers can't leave early. Let's see, are you one of those women who go for guys in uniforms, I hope?''

She flirted with him a little. ''Maybe, if you were wearing one.''

''I can always drive home and get it.''

They bantered for a while, laughing, leaning closer to each other. Diedre found herself wondering, did the sundress she was wearing look sexy enough? Was the hem too long? Did her skin look too pale? She'd hardly been in the sun all summer. *He* already had a great tan.

''Did you come with anyone?'' Mitch asked her.

"Not really," she said, thinking it would be too complicated to explain that her date was now lying in a beach chair rubbing up to a former girlfriend named Alyssa.

"Then let's go. I've got my dad's Le Baron convertible, and it's incredible with the top down and the wind blowing through your hair. And I know a good beach on the other side of the lake—one that will be quiet and not full of all this noise."

Oh, she should have known this would happen. Should she go? But of course she was going to. In the first place, Danny wasn't driving her home, that was clear, and she would be reduced to begging for a ride from strangers, or a girlfriend, or even her mother. In the second place . . . well, there was something about Mitch. He made her skin feel hot, he made her want to lean over and touch him.

Diedre walked into the house to fetch her shoulder bag from the big, curved leather living room couch where she'd dropped it. The room was crowded with expensive furniture, a group of people sitting on the floor. No one even looked at her. When she went back to Mitch he took her hand easily, as if it belonged to him.

They walked through the party roar and out the front door of the house to the street side. The night was hot, still eighty-five degrees, and it swam with a hundred summer odors. Barbecue smoke, grass clippings, the seaweed smell of lake, a tang of gasoline. Cars and vans were parked everywhere, lined bumper to bumper in the circular drive, pulled up on the lawn, double-parked on the street. A couple leaned against the fender of an Aerostar van, the guy's hand exploring underneath the girl's white halter top.

"Where's this great Le Baron?" Diedre demanded.

"Would you believe parked down the street about a mile away? I got here late and had to hike it."

Party sounds followed them. There was a halo of shimmering light around everything, and all the cars, trucks, and vans had tiny dewdrops of moisture on them.

The sight of those shimmering dewdrops caught Diedre like a hit in the stomach. Life was so beautiful, and where had she been the last four years? Studying until her eyes ached, agonizing over tests and exams, waitressing every spare minute—sometimes thirty hours a week in addition to her classes. It seemed as if she had recklessly squandered her days and now she had to catch up.

"Wait—wait," cried Diedre, grabbing Mitch's arm. "There's something caught in my shoe. A stone."

"Then take it off," said Mitch.

So she did. She stepped out of her strappy sandals that smelled of beer, and carried them by their heels, walking barefoot.

When they reached his Le Baron, a chromed and sexy black car with the top left rolled back, Diedre saw the little droplets of dew all over the luxurious leather seats. Mitch pressed her against the side of the car and slid his arms around her. He deposited soft, butterfly kisses on her cheeks and eyes.

"You're different than the others," he murmured. "None of that silly screaming. I like you."

The kisses grew deeper, mouths open, hungry tongues exploring. Diedre's skin burned and her breathing was shallow. For a moment she wondered if he wasn't carrying a hammer in his pocket, and then she stifled a nervous giggle: it was his erection. Several cars drove past them, a horn beeping while Mitch scooped Diedre so close that she felt the living heat of him.

She'd only had two boyfriends, and a half-fighting sex experience with one other guy in high school, making a total of three lovers. There was no man currently in her life, and she wasn't carrying a condom, hadn't even thought of bringing one.

Oh, she had to stop this right now; it was already getting unsafe. How had this happened so fast? Her genitals felt heavy, moisture seeping onto her panties. She started to move away, but then he kissed her again and helplessly Diedre melted against him, stifling a small moan.

"Let's go," he said suddenly.

"What?" Wrenched out of the piercing sexual desire she felt, Diedre could only stare at him.

"That beach I told you about."

In the moonlight Mitch's face was outlined in silver, his cheekbones sculpted by shadow. Much better than Donny Osmond, he looked like a fantasy, some guy from a rock video, all surface, all sex.

"I can't," she whispered.

"Why not?"

"Because—I don't do things like this. Really. I don't."

"Neither do I." Mitch grinned, his straight teeth flashing white in the darkness. His beautiful, pale eyes locked on hers. "That's why I want to do it. Will you, Diedre?"

She started to say no, heard the word blow out of her lips like a small gust of wind, but somehow Mitch didn't hear it or maybe she hadn't really said it aloud. Sensing her ambivalence, Mitch pressed himself against her, rocking his pelvis into hers. Diedre uttered a shuddering sigh.

"Just—just for a while. I can't go all the way," she whispered.

"I won't ask you to."

"Guys lie."

"Not me, not about this, not unless you consent, Diedre. I'm not promiscuous, I'm not a stud."

Diedre had a few seconds of sanity when she recalled the heavy-breathing high school encounter, the boy struggling to pin her down. She hadn't even known it was called date rape.

But then she felt Mitch's fingers splayed along the curve of her buttock, slowly, slowly pulling her dress up.

"Oh, please," she begged thickly. "*Not* all the way."

"I'll take care of you," he promised.

It was past all controlling now, roller-coastering like the rides at Cedar Point; she could no more have stopped matters than she could stop from screaming at the top of a 150-foot drop.

They drove to the "beach" he'd found, really a public-access site for boat launching, only about fifty feet wide and flanked on either side by expensive homes. A corrugated cement ramp sloped down to the water, which was glassy-flat, a swath of silver spilled across it. Mitch drove the Le Baron down to the water's edge and doused the headlights. Across the lake drifted shrieks and music from the party they had just left, punctuated by the revving, aggressive motors of the Jet Skis. Diedre'd had no idea that sounds carried that clearly across water.

"Let's get in the backseat," Mitch suggested, hugging her. "There's more room back there."

Oh, Diedre thought. *Oh.*

They both got out of the car, Diedre half stumbling again, Mitch steadying her as he helped her into the backseat. The fine-smelling leather, covered with a fine slick of night dew, creaked under their bodies as they sat down.

What was she doing? She didn't even know Mitch.

They came together again, pelvis to pelvis. The creaking of the seats became gradually more rhythmic, taking on, perhaps, the rhythm of the blood beating inside them. Diedre wanted to giggle at the sound, but she couldn't, because Mitch's mouth was pressed on hers.

The full moon floated above them, striated with craters and valleys. Far out on the lake a boat motor chugged, and the party noise came in on the lapping waves.

Mitch began stroking her flanks, his heated fingers running up and down her body. Finally he had the dress at her waist, and hooked his fingers in the elastic of her bikini panties.

Her heart thudded.

Please, I really can't.

The protest was born inside her throat and died there as Mitch slowly pulled down her panties, his hand cupping, caressing, her pubic mound. His finger caught in a wiry curl and Diedre almost cried out . . . or maybe she did cry out. Suddenly she felt fierce, frantic with her need. She brought her knee up, wrapped it around him. She felt wild, she wanted to tear away her clothes, climb on him, lower herself on him, feel the slick, juicy slide of flesh . . .

Mitch pulled away. "Diedre," he whispered. "This is as far as I can go without having to go all the way. I'll stop now—if you want me to. But I do have a condom in my wallet. It'll be safe, and we both want this."

She nodded, unable to speak. Of course they had to have a condom, but the rubber seemed too real, a reality that interfered with the sweet, tumultuous feelings she was having.

Mitch took a Ramses package out of his billfold, trying to unwrap it in the dark, laughing a little, his breathing raw. Finally he managed to get it open. Immediately the familiar odor of rubber and lubricant filled the car. Diedre winced, trying to hold on to the romance. Did rubbers have to smell so horrible? They took away the sweetness and put sex on the level of a bodily function.

"Put it on me," ordered Mitch hoarsely, guiding her hand. "Quick."

Diedre hurried, unrolling the condom as far as she could, sliding it up Mitch's average-sized but rock-hard organ. Then his hands were on her again, all over her. She urged and eased and positioned herself to give him access, and then she just gave up and clutched him, moaning low in her throat like a small jungle animal.

"Sorry—car's kind of cramped—" Mitch breathed.

The leather creaked, and the car shook back and forth. He moved her on top of him so that she straddled him, impaling herself. She gripped him so fiercely with her fingers that he would probably have black and blue marks the next day.

She whimpered as the pleasure rippled up from her vagina, ecstasy that kept flowing until her mind emptied and she cried out something—she didn't even hear what.

"Ah . . . ah, God," he cried out, and he kept thrusting, coming, too, and overhead the moonlight bathed them like the finest sheen of perspiration.

Afterward they struggled back into their clothes and wiped the moisture off each other's faces, and Diedre found a comb in her purse and they both used it. It felt so warm, both using the same comb; it was the most intimate thing she had ever done. She had hardly seen much of his body; now she wanted to touch him all over, explore him. But it was too late because they were already dressed.

"I should keep this comb," Mitch said. "Just because it's been in your hair. Unless you have cooties."

"Only a few," she said. She wasn't hammered anymore, she'd passed beyond that, and now she just felt soft, gentle.

"I want your phone number."

She rummaged in her purse again and found an old T.G.I. Friday's pay envelope, tearing off a piece of it to scribble down her number. She tried hard to write legibly, not to reverse any of the digits. If she made even one little mistake, he'd probably never find her again.

"Diedre Samms," she said. She spelled out the last name. "Two m's. Don't call after eleven," she told Mitch. "My mom goes to bed at eleven and the phone wakes her."

He tucked the scrap of paper into his shirt pocket. "I'll call."

Diedre looked at him. Some clouds had blown over the moon, and the shadows on Mitch's face were in deeper relief now. The curve of his mouth seemed tender and sweet.

He started the engine and Diedre began giving him directions to the apartment house in unfashionable Madison Heights, near John R. and Eleven Mile, where she lived with her mother.

"Wait, wait," protested Mitch, laughing. "I'm not that quick, especially at four in the morning. You just tell me left, right, north, south, and we'll get there."

He *would* call, she told herself as Mitch drove the Le Baron out of the boat-launch site onto the two-lane blacktop, heading toward West Long Lake Road. Of course he would call.

PEPPER

THE SHOP HAD BEEN CLOSED FOR HOURS.

Pepper Nolan sat cross-legged on the floor, her tongue thrust between her teeth as she dabbed with the little paintbrush, trying to make inconspicuous repairs to the four silver mannequins she'd purchased last week at a going-out-of-business sale at a bridal shop in nearby Ypsilanti. Overhead the fluorescent tube was buzzing and flickering again, as it always did late at night, and even Pepper's cat, Oscar, was sleeping in his wicker basket in the front window of the shop.

Damn ... the touch-up paint didn't exactly match. She was going to have to break down and spray-paint the mannequins, a messy job she hadn't planned on.

She got up, stretched, and padded over to the small refrigerator that sat on the floor of her cluttered back-room office, next to a desk that held her computer. Hanging on the wall was an ironing board and a steam iron. There was a cat fur–covered couch and a table covered with hangtags, boxes of lavender shopping bags with the Pepper's logo on them, and other supplies for her struggling lingerie boutique in downtown Ann Arbor, Michigan.

No, not struggling, Pepper mentally corrected herself. *Succeeding.* All she needed was about six good months and she'd be in the solid black.

Pepper took a can of Diet Pepsi out of the fridge, popped the top, and was halfway through her first long, icy swallow when she heard a pounding noise at the front of the shop. Someone was at the door.

She choked down the cold liquid, her heart fisting inside her chest. This was downtown, not a nice little mall location. She shouldn't have stayed here so late ... All of her friends had warned her. At this hour the bars were letting out, and all sorts of night people wandered the streets.

The banging continued. Pepper emerged from the back and stepped onto the shop's floor area, scented with rose potpourri and ranged with elegant displays of lingerie, gowns, and slip dresses in candy-box colors.

Standing behind a display rack of shorty robes, Pepper peered cautiously toward the door. A man was standing there—through the antique, etched glass she could see the flash of his light-colored polo shirt.

"Pepper!" called a familiar voice.

"Oh, God . . ." She hurried toward the door and released the dead bolt, flinging it open. "Jack!"

"Hi, sweetums."

"Jack, what are you *doing* here at almost two in the morning?" Pepper ushered her ex-husband into the shop, rebolting the door. He brought with him the odors of cigarette smoke and bourbon. "You scared the living hell out of me."

"Oh, I was in the area, you know how it goes. Knowing you, I thought you might still be here. You workaholics never quit." He gave her one of his dazzling smiles that charmed landladies, waitresses, and just about every other woman under the age of seventy-five.

Pepper walked with her visitor to the back room. She still loved Jack, maybe always would, but his total irresponsibility had killed their marriage. Jack was the type of man who'd leave the house to go buy a magazine, and be gone two days. He would spend ninety dollars on a candlelit dinner for two, then bounce six checks the following week.

"Want a Pepsi?" she offered.

"Pepsi is what I have for breakfast. Jack Daniel's is what I have at this hour of the night. I don't suppose you have any of that."

"Sorry."

They sat down on the back-room sofa, Pepper brushing aside some of Oscar's splendidly long, white cat hairs. Then they just looked at each other and laughed.

"The last time I saw you was when we went to Cedar Point," Jack said. "You nearly broke my fingers on that ride . . . What was it called?"

"Demon Drop."

"You screamed and screamed," he said.

"I was afraid I would leave my stomach somewhere in the air and never get it back again."

They exchanged news. The rock group Salt-N-Peppa had been in the shop while doing a concert in town, and bought fifteen hundred dollars worth of bustiers, bras, and panties. He'd been skydiving, taking a one-day class near Tecumseh, south of Ann Arbor. She'd been written up in the *Ann Arbor News* as an up-and-coming local entrepreneur.

Pepper showed him the clipping, which contained a very flattering photo of herself, her black, curly hair piled on her head and secured with antique barrettes, her figure model-slim. Even in black newsprint, her face was unusually striking. Beautiful, many said, although Pepper usually brushed this away if they said it directly to her.

"Yes," said Jack, looking at it. "Those cheekbones. You still could put a few cover models to shame. You dating anyone right now, Pepper?" he asked her.

She bit her lip. "Not really."

"That translates to no, right?"

"Well . . ."

"What happened to that airline pilot guy?"

She looked down at her knees. She'd spattered a drop of silver on her trousers. "It broke up."

"And why, might I ask, did that happen?"

"Scheduling problems," she admitted. "Between his runs to Chicago and me at the shop, well, we just barely saw each other. We had to make appointments to make phone calls."

"Maybe you're too scheduled," he told her.

"And maybe you're not scheduled enough!"

Then they sat quietly for a few minutes, each waiting until the flare of emotion died. "Oh, babe," he began. "It's really not an accident that I'm here tonight."

"I wondered."

"It's—well, I've got a one-way ticket tomorrow to La-La Land."

"One way? Los Angeles?" Pepper felt a sudden wrench of loss. Her relationship with Jack during the past four years since their divorce . . . well, it hadn't been the usual acrimonious, bitter squabble. There'd been phone calls, spur-of-the-moment dinners, usually to someplace practically off the map that served a special kind of fish available nowhere else. That crazy trip to Cedar Point. Occasional arguments. Yeah, a few of those. Old habits died hard, but Jack had been special in his way.

"Remember Tommie Curtis? Well, I'm going in with him. We're going to start a talent agency, we're going to specialize in ethnic character actors. We're going to call the agency Rainbow Characters."

"It sounds crazy, Jack, just like something you'd do. Oh, Jack," she sighed. "You're really doing this, pulling up stakes?"

He slid closer to her on the couch, smelling of Jack Daniel's, tobacco, and orange spice aftershave mixed with musk. "You're going to miss me then?"

"Yeah."

"Pep? This sounds really crazy, but you wouldn't want to fly out there with me, would you?"

"Fly out with you?"

"And, well, maybe we could make a stop in Vegas first."

"Vegas?" She stared at him.

"Yes, snookums. As in one of those gaudy little wedding chapels. I hear they've got a couple of new ones, very glitzy . . . We could test one of them out."

"Jack. Are you asking me to *marry* you? I mean, remarry?"

He smiled gently, and laid his arm across her shoulder, the heat of his flesh pressing into her. "I knew you wouldn't go for it. Now, why did I ever think you would? Little wedding chapels aren't exactly your style, and I'm not either. But I do love you. I always have and I always will.

There's something about you . . . well, you're so special you make all the other women seem like imitations.''

Somehow hearing this was so sad that Pepper had to fight the tears that suddenly pricked her eyelids. ''Jack.''

''Ah, God, Pepper . . . I can't believe I could still feel this way about you.'' Jack was smiling. ''How about a good-bye kiss? One kiss, or three or four, maybe more than that.''

''Oh, Jack.'' But she wrapped her arms around him, feeling as sorrowful as if he'd suddenly announced he had cancer. What would he do in L.A., really? The agency wasn't going to work out because Jack would only stay interested in it for five, six months, then he'd suddenly get this wild urge to drive to Oregon and he wouldn't show up for a week. He'd wine and dine customers, then not return their calls. His checks would be returned and his creative excuses after awhile would not wash.

''Baby . . . oh, baby,'' he murmured into her neck.

They held each other, the feel of Jack's body so familiar that Pepper felt her eyes moisten. He was one of those tall, lean men who have almost no fat on their bones. She could feel the bony bump on his shoulders, the stringy hardness of the muscles in his upper arms. They kissed, the kiss instinctively deepening, like a reflex they couldn't break.

''Pepper . . .'' Jack tightened his grip around her, murmuring her name several times. ''I need you tonight,'' he whispered. ''Do you need me?''

''Jack—''

''Please,'' he begged. ''It's a damn lonely life and you're the only woman who ever made me feel alive. Why couldn't we have made it work? Were we ill-fated, two lovers who got their stars all fucked over?''

''We never even had any stars, Jack.''

''Then tonight. One night, Pepper. Call it anything you want, call it a mercy fuck. Just hold me.''

For a quick moment Pepper thought of pulling away, of jumping to her feet and telling Jack that no, she couldn't, she might be lonely but not that lonely, and he'd better get home, get some sleep before that flight.

"I'm not going to sleep at all tonight," he said as if reading her mind. "Make love to me, Pepper."

"I haven't—I mean I'm not on anything. Not right now."

"I had a vasectomy a month ago, honey, so it's safe."

He'd had a vasectomy? For whom? Or was it just a general safety measure, making children impossible no matter who he was with? They knew each other so well and yet now they were strangers, too.

She was *never* going to get divorced again, Pepper told herself. She sighed, and reached out to her left, where a rheostat switch controlled lights for the back room. She dialed it down until only a faint glow lit the room.

"Ah, baby . . . babe . . ."

Like everything else about him, Jack's lovemaking was creative, erratic. Once they had made love in the swelling waves outside their hotel on Maui, and had nearly drowned in the incoming afternoon surf. Tonight Jack was in his tenderness mode. His hands gently pulled away the black silk blouse she wore, then her bra.

"You haven't changed," he murmured, tonguing her. "Your nipples are just as insouciant as ever."

"Insouciant." She laughed low in her throat. "Whoever uses that word?"

"I do. It's my favorite word this week. I had a very insouciant dinner tonight, and my car was definitely insouciant until I smashed up the fender a little bit."

"You smashed up your car?"

"Not noticeably. Let's just kiss, Pepper."

So they did, and then they stretched out on the couch, laughing because his feet hung over the edge. "I . . . just . . . love . . . you," Jack said as he pushed in and out of her, the rhythm as familiar as her own breathing. Smells rose around them, leafy and spermy and body-hot, the reaction of their combined fluids, creating a scent as unique as DNA. Men and women might come together all over the world, but they would never be Jack and Pepper. No one ever again would be Jack and Pepper.

He climaxed but she didn't, the sadness got in her way

again, the sense that somehow their "stars" had screwed up, and so had they, and there had been a secret they might have learned if only they'd tried harder.

"You okay?" Jack finally said, sitting up. He brushed away some cat hairs.

"I'm fine."

"You don't act fine."

"Maybe it's just—well—maybe this wasn't a good idea," she admitted.

He began adjusting his clothes. So, after a moment, did she. She'd been wearing a hot pink, embroidered bra from the shop, and Jack murmured when he saw it. Apparently he hadn't noticed it before, in the heat of sexual need. She went into the tiny bathroom cluttered with supplies, with a little hole in the wall where the pipes came out. She washed herself off, blotting away her ex-husband's semen. In the mirror Pepper saw that her face was pale, with lavender circles under her eyes. Not for the first time, she wished she had a shower here at the shop. She felt sticky, and full of sudden, sharply realized regret.

Why had she done this? Sex with Jack had relieved the loneliness, yes, for fifteen minutes. Now she just felt empty.

She went back into the other room. Glancing at her watch, she saw that it was nearly 3:30 A.M. Incredible. She'd have to get to the boutique tomorrow by nine-thirty so she could open at ten. Jan Switzer, her close friend and assistant manager, didn't come in tomorrow until noon.

Jack was looking at her, easily assessing her mood. "I guess this was a mistake, huh? I admit it was a wild hare of an idea. I just wanted to see you."

She nodded. "I think I need to close up and go home, try to catch a few hours of sleep."

"I can't interest you in a walk? We could hold hands, go window-shopping, look at the moon, smell flowers if we can find any. If we find any, I'll pick you a bouquet, Pepper. The store owners will all be snoozing and they'll never notice."

She felt her heart tighten. Jack, Jack. He would never

change, would he? He'd always be a romantic who could never get it right. "I'm sorry," she said, inexpressibly tired. "Please, I really do have to close up now."

"Okay, honey." Jack got to his feet and suddenly turned, pulling Pepper to him, putting his forefinger underneath her chin and turning her face up to his. "Look me in the eye and tell me this didn't affect you."

"Of course it affected me."

"You've got to go on with your life, Pep. Stop these lonely mercy fucks with ex-husbands and idiot airline pilots and find some guy who really loves you, who'll give you what you need. It won't hurt if he's rich, either."

She nodded, although the rich part meant little to her.

"And when you find him, go for it, hon. Don't make the same mistakes you did with old Jack. Start fresh, start with a clean sheet of paper, and write a beautiful love letter on it, write that love letter in gold."

"Jack," she whispered.

"I mean it, Pepper." Jack's voice cracked a little, and he pulled away. "Oh, shit. I've gotta go, maybe I'll get some eggs at Denny's."

She walked him to the front of the shop and went through the process of unlocking the dead bolt. Their voices had awakened Oscar, and the animal jumped lightly down from his bed in the window, stretching like a tiny, white lion. He wore a blue satin bow around his neck, his long, white fur soft and brushed.

"Good old Oskie," said Jack, who had given her the cat just after their divorce.

"Oh, yes."

"Does he claw furniture like he used to?"

"A little, but I got him two scratching posts, one for the shop and one for home. He's a lot better now."

"Good-bye, sweetheart," he said, kissing her gently. "Remember what I said."

He left, a lonely figure walking down the sidewalk, the streetlights catching his shirt and making it look washed out.

"Oscar," said Pepper, scooping up the cat and holding

him in her arms, his silky tail drooping like a white feather boa. "Oskie . . ."

She walked through the shop, flicking off all the lights except for the one she used as a security lamp. She loaded Oscar into his carry-cage for the trip home, collected her purse, and then went to the security keypad on the wall, hidden by the curtains. She punched in the code that would arm the system. This was her life; she was happy running the boutique, exhilarated by the challenge. Jack had made her forget that for a while.

When she stepped outside the shop, the moon was blazing over downtown Ann Arbor, illuminating the familiar shop windows, the sign for the Italian *ristorante* next door, the geraniums in tubs. The heavy silver light made the hoods and windshields of the few remaining parked cars seem molten.

TREVA

TREVA CONNOR WAS STILL IN THE BATHROOM WHEN SHE heard the stereo coming on in the bedroom—the deep, sexy voice of Luther Vandross, Wade's favorite, singing about "She's a Super Lady." She knew her husband would be putzing around the bedroom, lighting two or three dozen candles, until the room flickered with romantic light. She was a sucker for candles, always had been, and Wade teased that for her, candle wax was an aphrodisiac.

She took one of her high-blood-pressure pills, swallowing it down with water, and then she inserted contraceptive foam, finally gazing at herself in the mirror, feeling a burst of pleasure. Turning from side to side, she admired herself.

She *loved* that little lingerie shop downtown, on Liberty.

It was the most luscious satin gown that Treva had ever seen, its color pale celery. Its straps were made of matching lace and there were wonderful embroidered medallions set along the long, sexy slit that ran from hem to thigh. A slit that showed *plenty* of long, brown leg and—if she turned just right—hinted at other treasures as well.

The gown had cost her a week's pay, but even in the dressing room at the boutique, Treva had known that Wade would absolutely die when he saw her in it. And the shop owner, a tall, beautiful woman around thirty or thirty-one, had confirmed that Treva looked sensational. "And I always tell the truth to my customers," she'd assured Treva.

Now Treva stood caught, thrilled by the way the gown made her look. She had combed her hair out in a silky cloud of black, and added a bronzy blush to her cheeks, bringing out their caramel glow.

Not bad for forty-one, she thought. In fact, she was *damn* good for forty-one.

Treva laughed to herself. Her sister, Rhonda, thought she and Wade were crazy because they celebrated more than eight "anniversaries," ranging from the day they'd met (at a boring university function) to the occasion of the first time they'd made love. However, "ring day" was still her favorite. Ten years ago Wade had given Treva her half-carat engagement ring neatly sandwiched in the middle of two scoops of vanilla ice cream with crème de menthe poured on it. Now each year they vied to hide a gift for each other in the most surprising, startling spot. This year Treva had purchased a diamond pinky ring for Wade, and had taped it to his toothbrush.

She giggled, wondering what Wade had for her, and where he had hidden it.

"Treva," called her husband. "Trev . . . what's taking you so long? I've got so many candles lit that I'm afraid I'm going to burn the bedroom down. And Luther is definitely wondering where you are."

"It's not Luther I want," she said in a sultry manner, making her entrance with a hip-jutting, butt-curving walk, like a stripper she'd seen years ago in Chicago, back before she married Wade, a professor in the University of Michigan's School of Social Work. The bedroom was ablaze with light that flickered and moved along the walls, as mysterious as if she were entering the palace of the Mountain King.

"Hey," said Wade, his voice thickening. "Baby . . ."

Treva got into the spirit, swinging her hips with greater abandon, and causing the slit of the celery-colored gown to fly out. The movement revealed indecent amounts of thigh.

"Oh, woman," breathed Wade.

Treva felt herself melt. There he was, the color of coffee mixed with just a little cream, his height nearly six five. Twenty-five years ago he'd been a running back for Purdue and he still had the look of a man who could run one hundred yards without even panting for breath. Flecks of gray in Wade's black, curly hair made him distinguished, and laugh lines around his mouth made him endearing.

"Hey, there, Mr. Hunk," she murmured.

"I'm Mr. Hunka Hunka Burning Love, that's who I am. Do you want to sample me?"

"I'm going to do more than sample," she told her husband lasciviously. "Much, much more."

They eyed each other, pleased with themselves, knowing they had all night and there was no reason to hurry. Their repartee might not be very witty, but it was their repartee and it was an integral part of lovemaking for them.

"Come here," Wade invited, patting the bed. "I've brought up a snack for us—see, I've fixed a nice plate of hors d'oeuvres."

It was a plate of low-salt crackers, a favorite dip, and a veggie plate containing everything from artichoke hearts to sweet red bell peppers, plus a wedge of Havarti cheese, which Wade liked. Sometimes Treva nibbled on it, too, and tonight she knew she was going to.

Treva sank onto the bed, crossing her legs so that plenty of thigh showed. "Oh, ho," she said. "Am I going to have to be careful of my fillings when I eat that nice cheese?"

"Maybe. Or maybe it's that dip, it could be dangerous." Wade's grin revealed square teeth with a space in the center.

"Or maybe it's not any of those," she accused. "Maybe

you just brought up that tray because you knew I'd wonder what was in the food. Oh, you're getting sly, Wade Connor. You're giving me decoys now.''

Wade's brown eyes danced as he slid his arm around Treva, easing it over her nearly bare flesh. "Maybe you should plump up the bed pillows a little, fix the bed, get rid of those wrinkles in the mattress. I don't know why we have wrinkles in our mattress all of a sudden.''

Treva darted a swift hand underneath her pillow, then probed all around it, searching for telltale lumps and bumps that might indicate some object had been hidden inside. One year Wade had given her a little Japanese netsuke, hiding it in her tissue box. She'd had a cold that year and was constantly sneezing; she would always love Puffs because they reminded her of finding that netsuke.

"Nothing," she said. "And the mattress is as flat as glass. You're just teasing me, Wade . . . Where have you put it?''

He laughed, stretching out beside her. He wore only low-slung Jockey briefs, a bright red pair she'd bought him several months ago. "Find it," he challenged her.

Treva laughed low in her throat. "Oh, I know where to look," she said. "Oh, yes, I think I know where you've hidden it this year . . .''

They laughed and wrestled and teased, their shrieks of laughter whooping so loudly that Treva was afraid someone passing outside on the street might hear. Two middle-aged social workers acting like a pair of high school kids, but oh, the hell with it. She began to heat up as Wade started stroking the satin gown. His hands were big, and gentle, and he was in no hurry, caressing her flanks up and down, up and down, until Treva's nerve endings melted in pleasure.

"Treva . . . oh Trev." His voice thickened. "God, I love you. I wish I'd given you ten rings that day. You'd deserve every one of them—you could wear one on each finger of your hand . . .''

Ten rings? Was it a clue? Treva's mind became distracted, and even as she was moaning, she was wondering just what the phrase "ten rings" might mean in terms of hiding a gift.

Gloves had ten fingers. But which gloves? She began running over the list of gloves she owned. A pair of pink plastic dishwashing gloves, some driving gloves, some well-worn gardening gloves, and one long, elegant yellow pair she'd worn once with an evening gown.

No, she thought, not gloves.

Wade had his hands inside the slit of the gown now, his searching fingers finding that warm nub of her flesh that could cause such piercing ecstasy. Treva's brain blurred with soft, loose pleasure, and she forgot all about the gloves. Her breathing quickened as she opened herself to give her husband more room to maneuver, feeling as sensual as an odalisque, as treasured as Cleopatra.

She came first with his fingers, ripples of exquisite sweetness spiraling up through the center of her body. "Ah . . . ah . . ." she gasped, knowing this was just the beginning. She clutched him, rocking under the force of her orgasm, then finally lay there perspiring, still in the gown, both straps fallen off her shoulders, the satin skirt rucked to her waist.

The numb satiety lasted only for a minute or so, then Treva felt a harder, stronger wave of desire flow over her, as if she'd swum out of a tributary stream and met the thundering Mississippi.

"Now let's take that gown off you," said Wade in a thick voice.

An hour later, they lay side by side, letting the perspiration dry on their skin. Treva stirred, turning on her hip, and slid her hands lightly down her husband's body, toying with the smoothness of his chest, finding the curly whorls of hair that marked his groin.

They talked quietly, about nothing really, the usual kind of pillow talk, comfortable and inconsequential. Did he want her to buy more lingerie from that great shop? She'd spent so much on the gown—she'd really splurged. Maybe she'd spent too much . . .

"I want you to open a charge account there," said Wade

firmly. As he spoke his breath blew over her chin and shoulder, as sweet-smelling as clover.

A grin spread across Treva's face as she again remembered what day it was. "Honey . . . I don't know how to say this . . . but I'm gonna say it," she said.

"Uh-oh."

"Babe, your breath is just a tiny bit sour," she whispered with wifely candor.

Wade immediately sat up and padded naked across the room into the bathroom. She heard the creak of the medicine cabinet door as her husband took out the plastic toothpaste container. Treva lay still, waiting and listening. Then she heard it, his wild whoop of laughter.

He'd found the ring.

But he continued to laugh, hilariously, as if there was a joke only he knew about. "Honey?"

"Yeah?"

"I'm not the only one whose breath smells, well, a little off."

Treva squealed and jumped out of bed, rushing to the ceramic duck with the holes in it where they kept their brushes. She snatched out her well-used, green bristly brush from the holder. Nothing, just some dried white foam in the bristles.

Wade raised an amused black eyebrow. "Don't you think that toothbrush holder's a bit tacky? I mean, ducks . . ."

Treva grabbed the ceramic duck and shook it. She heard a rattle. She shook it again, crowing with delight, but the object, whatever it was, was too big to come out through the toothbrush holes. She began tugging at the rubber seal on the bottom of the holder.

"Ah, Wade . . ."

It was an antique ring guard, a circlet of diamonds designed to surround her solitaire wedding ring, augmenting its glitter. Treva stared at the ring guard, too stunned to move. She'd been wanting one of these for several years.

"Put it on," said Wade huskily. "Happy ring day."

SIX WEEKS LATER

DIEDRE

AN AUGUST SKY ARCHED OVERHEAD, ALMOST WHITE with humidity. A nearby Little Caesar's pizza place was releasing odors of yeast and pepperoni, the smell vaguely sickening.

Diedre Samms hurried across the parking lot of the strip mall, her heartbeat pounding in her throat. The Rite Aid drugstore was sandwiched between the Little Caesar's and a dry cleaner's, and usually she came here to buy mundane things like birthday cards, aspirins, or tampons.

Now she was here for an entirely different reason, and it did *not* have to do with tampons.

She couldn't believe it . . . couldn't believe that she had not gotten her period this month.

Maybe I'm just late, she told herself desperately. *I have to be late.*

The timing could not have been worse. Four days ago she'd received her letter from the Detroit law firm of Halsick, McMurdy and Toth, telling her she'd won their full, three-year scholarship to the University of Michigan Law School.

It was almost as good as Ed McMahon coming to Diedre's door.

She'd laughed. She'd cried. She'd grabbed up her mother and whirled her around until Cynthia Samms begged for mercy. Then she'd jumped up and down with such vigor that she nearly beaned herself on the hallway light fixture.

Twenty-eight thousand a year, a free ride. She wouldn't have to go into debt, saddled for years after her graduation with humongous loan payments.

Nervously Diedre pushed open the door and walked inside the big drugstore. *Please, let me be just late.* Except for that first high school sex experience, she'd always insisted the guy use a condom. She'd had irregular periods before, but she'd never been this late, and she'd never had such a strange, stomach-sickening feeling about it before.

Mitch's condom must have had a hole in it, she thought for the dozenth time. *One of those little pinholes they get from the guy carrying them around too long in his wallet. Oh, God . . . I hate him!*

The drugstore was laid out in the usual fashion, with a big August back-to-school display. A woman with three young children was pricing three-ring notebooks, while one of the children begged and whined for stickers. Diedre came to a halt, swiveling her eyes over the aisle signs, searching out the one for women's sanitary goods.

There—there it was, two aisles over.

She glanced nervously around her, to make sure no one she knew was in the store, then began sidling toward the sanitary aisle, her footsteps slowing as she approached it. Her thickened heartbeat was now drumming in her ears like a tom-tom, and heat burned on her skin, causing her to perspire slightly.

Pregnant. Oh, God, what if I am?

It would be a disaster, total and crushing. It might mean— But Diedre couldn't allow herself to think of what an unwanted pregnancy would mean, not now. She couldn't get it fully in her mind yet, not unless she really had to.

She found herself standing in front of the shelves that held such "feminine" items as panty shields (of all shapes, both perfumed and odor-free), tampons (including her own favorite, O.B.), and various douches that featured sentimental, floral scenes on the packaging. Plus there were jellies and foams, even something called Replens that was supposed to replace natural vaginal fluids.

Oh, God! Diedre closed her teeth on a frustrated scream. Where were the pregnancy test kits? They had to be here somewhere . . . but they weren't. She did another scrutiny of the long aisle, carefully reading labels, thinking she might have overlooked them.

Nothing!

Finally she straightened up, realizing she was going to have to ask. Why did they have to hide the kits? Fighting her humiliation, Diedre searched for a clerk, but the only one she could find was a man unloading boxes of Hallmark cards. He was about eighteen, with owlish wire-frame glasses, and had scraggly peach fuzz on his upper lip. Diedre shuddered at the idea of confiding in him.

Finally she had to walk back to the prescription counter and wait until a red-haired woman in her sixties had finished waiting on an elderly couple.

"Could you tell me where the . . ." Diedre unconsciously lowered her voice. "Where the pregnancy kits are?"

"Right behind you." The woman motioned to a small display that held condoms.

Near the condoms? Sort of the "before" and the "after"? Diedre stifled a nervous giggle. Condoms were what had gotten her into this mess.

No, it was me. I got myself into this mess. No! Not that either. We did it. Mitch and me.

The pregnancy kits had been placed near the floor, underneath the colorful array of Sheiks and Ramses, each with their pictures of romantic, pretty couples.

Diedre squatted down, reading the advertising blurbs on the pregnancy kits. *Virtually 100% accurate. Use any time of day. The same test used in doctors' offices. Only 1 minute waiting time. Fast—results in 5 minutes.*

She was breathing hard through her mouth, her mouth tissues dry. She realized she'd read all the labels and didn't remember a single thing they said. She forced herself to slow down and read the package labels again. She didn't even know which kit to buy . . . Was one better than another? She'd heard her girlfriends talking about several tests, but couldn't remember the names now.

A teenage boy with his hair shaved up over his ears was hanging around a few feet away, pretending to look at cough syrups. Diedre knew he was waiting for her to leave so he could look at the condoms. She grabbed one of the pregnancy kits at random and got to her feet.

It seemed a very long walk to the front of the store where the checkout was. Diedre clutched the kit against her chest so it wouldn't be as visible to staring eyes. She wanted to cry and she wanted to giggle. This made her feel like she was thirteen again, trying to buy Kotex for the first time. She was even starting to break out in hives again, just the way she'd done that day.

She got in line. Fortunately the man ahead of her, wearing a T-shirt that said WARREN STAMPING, didn't even glance at her. *Please,* Diedre prayed as she handed the clerk a twenty-dollar bill and waited for change. *Please let this be just a scare. It can't happen now . . . not when I'm going to law school in two weeks.*

Diedre decided to wait until the next morning to test herself. She'd heard that if you drank too much liquid during the day, your urine could be diluted and the test wouldn't work.

She spent the evening in her room, reading over the seventy-two-page student handbook the law school had sent her in the mail. Its cover picture showed ten or eleven students lounging on the steps of the beautiful, Gothic-style "law quadrangle," which looked as if it belonged in sixteenth-century Europe, although it had been built back in the 1920's.

Inside were pages of instructions on everything from the various law school clubs and organizations to dropping courses to finding a printer.

In Room 160 Legal Research, there are 20 IBM-compatible computers, 5 Macintosh, and 5 laser printers. There are also 10 portable IBM computers on a first-come, first-serve basis. In Room S236, Sub2 of the Library, there are . . .

Her fingers shaking, Diedre dropped the handbook. Would she ever have the chance to use those computers, sit on those law quad steps, too? She felt as if her life had been compressed down to one small, black tunnel opening. She either went through the tunnel or she did not.

Car headlights flashed on the ceiling of her bedroom, flaring and then disappearing, as the busy traffic on Eleven Mile Road drove past her apartment building. The headlights illuminated Diedre's old pine desk, the two wall bulletin boards she and her sister had kept since high school, the space where Pam's twin bed used to be, before she took it to Ann Arbor.

Mitch, Diedre thought dully.

He'd never even called her. She'd spent her day off after the party waiting to hear from him, never roaming far from the telephone. All the following week she'd waited, praying he would call, continually asking her mother if she'd had any messages. The week after that she'd still waited, only now she was angry. Suppose he had lost her number. But that was an old, crummy excuse. Still, she'd thought that Mitch was different.

Finally at the end of the third week, it occurred to Diedre that even if Mitch had lost her phone number, he still knew where her apartment building was because he'd *dropped her off here,* and that was when she'd given up hope.

Mitch was a jerk; that was all he was.

And she'd been equally a jerk, impulsively going to his car with him, getting in the backseat, having sex with him. A one-night stand. She *never* did crazy stuff like that. She didn't even know why she'd done it this time. She'd drunk too much wine, she'd fallen in love with summer, she'd wanted just once to be carefree like everyone else.

Well, she would never be careless again, Diedre promised God, if only her test would come back negative.

The portable radio in the kitchen was playing FM morning drive-time, and two or three disc jockeys were laughing and telling jokes about weird things to do in an elevator if you got bored. Diedre emerged from her bedroom, dressed for her waitressing job at Friday's and carrying her shoulder bag.

"Hon? You okay? You're looking a little bit pale," said Diedre's mother. Cynthia Samms, a receptionist for an engineering firm in Troy, was blond and pretty, a forty-four-year-old version of Diedre, so good at answering phones and pushing a gate buzzer that it took two women to replace her at breaks.

"I'm great," lied Diedre. "I just haven't got my makeup on yet, is all." She had her purse because she didn't want her mother to see the test kit, which she'd hidden in one of the zipper pockets.

"I'm still so excited about your scholarship, honey," her mother went on proudly. "I've told everyone at work. I guess I've been boasting just a little. They're all very impressed."

Diedre tried to smile, and went into the small bathroom, closing the door behind her.

The room was designed for basic utility, apartment style. For ten years the overhead fan had sounded as if it were gargling. Still, Diedre's mother had installed a wicker shelf over the commode, which held pink, fluffy towels, pots of silk flowers, and bottles of conditioners. More towels hung from the two towel racks, and there was wallpaper purchased at The Home Depot, put up by her mother. Always, Cynthia made something out of nothing.

Running from their abusive father. That had been their life for three years, back when Diedre and Pam were in grade school. They even lived in a car for two months. They'd used a gas station bathroom then, and Cynthia had scrubbed the filthy women's bathroom with bleach, every day, and bought air freshener to fill it with a strawberry smell.

When Diedre graduated from law school, she intended to buy her courageous mother a house, and new furniture to fill it, and wallpaper that was hung by someone else. And *two* bathrooms plus a powder room.

Diedre took the pregnancy kit out of her purse and tore it open, forcing herself to read the directions. There was a little plastic cup inside the test kit. Gingerly she sat on the commode, releasing a stream of urine, managing to splash it all over her fingers as well as getting some in the cup. Ugh. She set the damp cup on the white Formica next to the sink and washed her hands, her heartbeat thudding.

All she had to do now was dip the plastic tube in the urine.

Killing time, anything to put off the telling moment, Diedre reread the printed directions, noticing that the instructions on the reverse were written in Spanish. She read those, too, knowing she was just putting it off—finding out. The little plastic dropper looked so tiny and flimsy. And the plastic test cassette with the tiny windows looked too small to be so important.

Her entire life, that was what this pregnancy test held.

Oh, Diedre wanted babies, *someday*. She pictured herself having maybe two girls, giving them sweet canopy beds, new books instead of library books, ballet and gymnastics lessons, giving them all of the "extras" her mother, Cynthia, had never been able to buy for her and Pam.

But not now!

It was the exact wrong, impossible time for her to have a child. Law school was supposed to be incredibly hard. You were supposed to prepare three hours for every hour spent in class. Every bit of your time would be sucked up, and there were all kinds of extracurricular activities, too— everything from Campbell Competition to law review and all kinds of law student clubs and organizations.

In college she'd often been brilliant, but Diedre held no illusions about law school. *Everyone* would be brilliant, and she might end up only average which meant she'd have to struggle twice as hard. As she stood at the bathroom sink, Diedre's eyes dampened with tears. It wasn't fair, it just wasn't! Mitch Sterling deposited a few million sperm and drove his car away, leaving her with all of the consequences.

Diedre could hear her mother's high heels clacking across the kitchen tile as Cynthia straightened a few breakfast things before leaving for work. Diedre cringed at the idea of her mother's disappointment.

Finally she picked up the tiny little plastic tube, dipping it into the container of urine, pulling up a small amount of liquid. The instructions were to deposit ''no more than three drops'' into a little well in the plastic piece.

Diedre's hands shook as she followed the directions.

There. One, two, three. Diedre stared down at the cassette, waiting for the blue control line to show up. If the line was just blue, she was okay. But if there was another, second line, shaded pink to purple . . .

Diedre glanced nervously at her watch. She was supposed to wait exactly three minutes for the results. Should she watch the plastic piece, watch while the colors changed? That would be totally nerve-racking. She heard a loud, sucking sound and realized it was her breathing.

She glanced away, taking a tissue out of the box that sat on the wicker shelf and blowing her nose. She hadn't realized she was crying. Oh, God, she wanted one blue line. She wanted it more than anything.

She stared at the tiny window, waiting for it to change.

I can't have a baby now.

I can't.

Please.

The blue line began slowly to materialize and then another line started forming, too, below it . . . a line shaded with pink and lavender.

''Diedre? Are you all right, sweetie? I've got to run,'' called her mother outside the bathroom. ''The traffic report says there's a big tie-up on I-75 near Oakland Mall. A rollover accident, they said. Traffic's backed up for six miles—not that that's any big surprise.''

''I'm fine,'' called Diedre dully.

''You've been in there over thirty minutes.''

''Have I? I was . . . shaving my legs,'' Diedre lied, hastily stuffing the test kit and all of its parts back into her purse. She rubbed her hand over her abdomen, trying to picture just what was inside her now. A tiny thing, about the size of half a pea, she knew from college biology classes. With a primitive, pumping heart.

She couldn't think about *that*. What was she going to do? What could she do? But she knew . . . she'd known ever since she bought the kit, what she would have to do. She hadn't said the word aloud to herself yet, hadn't even wanted to think it. But all along she had known.

After Diedre's mother left, saying her cheerful good-byes, Diedre sat hunched on the living room couch, listening to the increasing roar of cars and vans out on Eleven Mile as rush-hour traffic took over the world. She tried to cry, but no tears ejected from her lids. She felt so numb . . . If she did have any tears, they were frozen to ice.

A thought came into her mind and she acted on it, her hand shaking violently as she went to the kitchen wall phone with the extralong cord and dialed the information number.

"What city and state?"

"B-Bloomfield Hills, Michigan."

But there were six Sterlings listed, the operator told her, plus there could be many unlisted ones as well.

"Then . . ." Diedre had to try twice before her voice would hold. "Try Highland Park, Michigan. The—the Chrysler plant."

"Which number, ma'am?"

"The main number, I guess."

There was a chime, then a computerized voice giving her the number, speaking maddeningly slowly. Numbly Diedre copied it down with a ballpoint pen.

Chrysler . . . where Mitch worked for the summer. The only way she knew to get in touch with him.

Flushing, Diedre tried to picture herself getting Mitch on the line, assuming she even could. It would probably be some semipublic phone with a lot of other security guards or hourly employees hanging around. Maybe he wouldn't even remember her name.

Suddenly Diedre hung up, and then she just sat there, staring down at the slip of paper. Finally she balled up the bit of paper and thrust it behind one of the couch cushions.

What was she thinking? She must be crazy. For her to call Mitch Sterling . . . It was total idiocy. *It was just a one-night stand.* He'd never called her back, he'd never returned to her apartment building, he'd just erased her, and if he'd left a few reproductive cells behind, well, would he even care? Obviously he did not. She was on her own, baby.

For the first time, the word entered her mind and materialized there, taking form as slowly and inexorably as the pink and blue lines had done. Diedre tried to push the word back, but then it came again.

Abortion.

PEPPER

YELLOW SUNLIGHT STREAMED IN THE SECOND-FLOOR window of the old Victorian house, filtering through a Battenberg lace curtain that had been first hung in the late 1980's when Pepper's landlady, Mrs. Melnick, started renting to students. The lace made a pretty pattern on the hardwood floor, scarred from furniture-moving and student shenanigans.

This morning Pepper Nolan was going through her usual juggling act, trying to get her cat, Oscar, to enter his carry-cage so she could take him to the boutique. Even though they did this every day, the beautiful, long-haired, white Persian always acted as if he'd never seen the cage before, and couldn't possibly deign to ride in it.

"Oscar, Oscar," she crooned, trying to hide her irritation. "Come on, baby, don't you want to sit in the window and soak up all that nice, hot sunshine?"

A yowling meow told her that he didn't.

"Oscar . . . Oskie . . ."

Another yowl. *Drat.*

She scooped up the heavy animal and held him for a few minutes, stroking his back and behind his ears, and then slid him into the cage, quickly latching the door. Oskie was purebred, a descendant of show cats, and her customers loved him. He was Pepper's best advertisement. People exclaimed about him all the time, often entering the shop just because they'd seen him. She usually put a blue satin bow around his neck, and at Christmas, of course, he wore red and green. Fortunately he wasn't much of a wanderer, having been neutered, and once he arrived at her shop, spent most of his time snoozing happily in the center of her window display.

Quickly Pepper moved around her one-bedroom apartment, preparing to leave. Her Mr. Coffee machine off. Curtains pulled. The antique lace throw that covered her couch neatly folded. The stack of bills ... well, she'd wade through them when she got home tonight.

Anxiously Pepper gazed at the pile. Because her first business, a costume jewelry shop in Detroit's Trapper's Alley, had gone bankrupt, she couldn't get a conventional bank loan, so she had borrowed not only from her mother, but also from her uncle Ned, responsibilities that now weighed heavily on her.

Picking up the cat cage, Pepper let herself out of her apartment door and locked it, emerging into the creaking upstairs hallway decorated with a much-worn Oriental carpet. The Victorian, once a gingerbready showplace, had gone downhill, and now held five apartments. This morning the hallway smelled of its usual eclectic mix of odors: pizza, Murphy's Oil Soap, some spicy Thai concoction, and a slight fustiness of old wood and carpeting. Usually the combination of stinks amused Pepper, but this morning they only made her feel sick.

"Pepper, you always leave *so* early," said her landlady, Noreen Melnick, emerging from her own apartment opposite Pepper's. Mrs. Melnick was seventy-five, a tiny doll of a woman, and wore her frosted blond hair as perfectly, tightly

coifed as a wig. Today she had on purple sweats and Reeboks with purple, plaid shoelaces in them.

Mrs. Melnick could be nosy and much too chatty, but
Pepper smiled politely. "Have to open up the shop early. I
have a lot of stuff to unpack and put hangtags on."

"If you get in any really pretty robes, let me know."

"Oh, I did get in a couple, they're in sea green and sage
purple, and I'll let you . . ." Pepper's words trailed off as
she was attacked by a strangely wobbly sense of wooziness.
White dots surrounded her, switching to black, then white,
like some eerie special effect.

Whoa, she thought.

She blinked her eyes, trying to force her vision back to
normal, but now everything became black velvet . . .

"Honey? Honey, are you all right? Oh, honey, you scared
me so."

To her shock, Pepper realized that time had somehow
passed, and she was now lying on the hall carpet, her head
near the cat cage, her feet extending toward the stairs. She
could see some water marks on the ceiling and the bottom
half of her landlady's wrinkled chin.

"Honey? You fainted. You just keeled right over. I was
afraid you were going to hit your head. You just went down
with a crash. Are you all right?"

Mrs. Melnick hovered over her, extending her blue-
veined hands, which were jammed with rings on every finger, anxious and clucking.

Fainted? Pepper lay still, feeling very comfortable here
on the rug. Nothing hurt, everything felt fine, except that
the smell of her landlady's cologne was making her feel
nauseous. Beside her in the cage, she could hear Oscar indignantly meowing, switching his feathered tail back and
forth.

"Oh, should I call a doctor?" inquired Mrs. Melnick anxiously.

"I . . . I'll be okay." Slowly Pepper pushed herself to a
sitting position. She hadn't fainted in years, not since she
was thirteen and first got her period.

"*I* think you should turn right around and go back in your apartment and get some rest. You young girls work such inhumanly long hours, no wonder you passed right out."

"I'm fine," repeated Pepper, breathing in deeply as if to sample herself, see what parts of herself ached and which felt fine. Did she feel a twinge of nausea in the center of her stomach? Yes. Her head was buzzing just slightly, as if an electrical wire were caught inside her skull. She felt a slight sense of anxiety, as if something were missing. Something that should have happened but didn't.

"You're *all right,* aren't you?" Mrs. Melnick emphasized the *all right* in a significant manner. "I mean we are all adults here, aren't we? I remember when I was pregnant with my second son, I passed out three or four times, once while I was shopping at the downtown Hudson's. You probably never went in the downtown Detroit Hudson's, did you? They said I had low blood pressure."

Pregnant? Pepper stared at her landlady and felt her stomach muscles clench like fists. She remembered that night six weeks ago with Jack. "Oh, no, I'm sure not," she managed to say.

"Well, good, good," responded Mrs. Melnick, cheerfully dismissing the matter. She bent down to poke a finger through the wire mesh of the cage door. "Poor Oskie had a fall, too, didn't he? Good thing he has nine lives. He wants some catnip to make up for his discomfort, doesn't he, Oskie? Oh, yes, he deserves a big, big helping of catnip."

"That's fine, because I have some at the shop."

"Well, you give him some, hear?"

"I certainly will."

Pepper got to her feet and gathered up her purse, picking up Oscar's cage by its handle. She felt slightly bruised from her hard landing. There was a sensation at the back of her throat that told her that with just a little urging, something might come up.

She walked downstairs, let herself out the front door, and walked across the wide porch where the beautiful, curlicued gingerbread, a work of art, was disgracefully peeling in big flakes. Mrs. Melnick had been trying to scrape the paint, but at the rate she was going, it looked like a lifetime job.

Pepper lugged the cat carrier to her six-year-old Ford Tempo. It was parked on a gravel area that used to be lawn, next to Mrs. Melnick's van and the Ford pickup belonging to Billy Ip, the engineering student who rented the first-floor apartment immediately beneath Pepper's. Apparently the other residents had already left for the morning.

When she started up the Tempo it began making a faint rattling noise which was probably her exhaust system, starting to need replacement. Pepper'd been putting it off, investing instead in new Laura Ashley wallpaper for her boutique, believing that if she poured her money into her shop, it would eventually pay off big dividends and she could get a new car.

Pregnant. Oh, God, could it be possible? In a sense of growing panic Pepper realized what was missing, her period. She hadn't had one in . . . how long? Certainly not since Jack's visit. Christ, why didn't she keep better count? She'd been so absorbed in her boutique. Struggling so hard to show a profit. Loving the struggle, exhilarated with it, so focused that she hadn't even thought about her body.

In her car, Pepper arranged Oskie's cage on the seat beside her. He had settled down a little, and was beginning to emit his machinelike purrs, staring at her through the mesh with his slanted green eyes, his irises contracting and expanding.

"Oh, Oskie," she said.

Beginning to be frightened now, she drove toward downtown Ann Arbor. Her shop was located on Liberty Street, only a short walk from campus, in one of the historic old redbrick buildings that dotted the area. Pepper shared the building with a trendy new Italian eatery, and over that was a photography studio. Oh, what if she was really pregnant?

She would be *so* screwed, literally and figuratively.

She swallowed again, the nausea becoming much sharper. Gripping the steering wheel, Pepper wondered if she was going to have to pull her car over, open the door, and throw up right on the road. No . . . no . . . *Christ* . . . Gulping, she fought the nausea and won.

Morning traffic clogged the downtown streets, but Pepper managed to get a parking space in the structure she usually used. She had a monthly card, and it was only a short walk to her boutique.

Getting out of her car, she locked it and began carrying Oscar to the shop. All of the store windows were so familiar she barely saw them. A futon place, a new bead shop that probably wouldn't last long. Many of the merchants had flowers in wooden boxes, and a big Akita was chained to a tree outside Zev's Coffee Shop, which was jammed with its usual breakfast crowd. Even on the sidewalk, Pepper could smell *huevos rancheros*.

The Akita pricked up its ears and jumped to its feet alertly when Pepper walked past with the cat. The dog growled low in its throat.

"Whoa, boy," she said.

Safely inside the carrier, Oscar hissed, trying his best to look mean.

As she approached her own shop, Pepper couldn't help pausing to admire the appearance it made. The brick building had been sandblasted several years ago, so it looked very rosy and fresh, and the shop door was made of etched glass, its floral pattern intricately whorled. In the window, two of the silver mannequins wore wonderful chiffon and lace gowns, sexy and outrageously expensive. Both of the gowns were white. When Oscar began snoozing in the window, his fur would exactly match them.

Pregnant. Oh, it was impossible right now. It simply could not happen. Pepper Nolan set down the cage and fumbled in her shoulder bag for her keys, then unlocked the heavy, original old door. When she walked in, the scent of the potpourri she kept in a low bowl on a table hit her like too much perfume.

It was one of those rush-rush days, when Pepper had to be in six places at the same time, greeting, chatting, fetching garments, offering advice, running up sales, answering the phone. She'd had to put the potpourri in a drawer, because the smell bothered her too much.

By midafternoon Pepper had no doubt that something was wrong. When she went out for a sandwich, she had to turn around and leave the deli because the spicy odors of pastrami and rye were so strong that they made her sick to her stomach. At three o'clock, as she was on the phone to a customer, she felt clammy perspiration spring out on her skin, and another surge of the nausea.

She made an excuse, hung up, and rushed into the bathroom, where she was violently sick. Heaving and gagging, she closed her eyes so she wouldn't have to stare at the sight of the toilet, which only made her feel sicker. This was how she'd thrown up when she was seventeen, when—

No . . . No . . . not a second one.

"Pepper?" said Jan Switzer, her assistant manager, a round-faced, freckled, forty-five-year-old law professor's wife. Jan had once worked in marketing at Jacobson's headquarters, and was a real treasure—not to mention a close friend. "Pepper, are you sure you're all right? I don't mean to pry, but I couldn't help noticing . . . well, I did have to use bathroom spray."

"I don't know," admitted Pepper. Moisture glazed her eyes. "I have to go out and buy a pregnancy kit."

"Oh, Pepper."

"I don't even have to buy it to know," admitted Pepper miserably. "Oh, Jan. You know how much I'm living on the edge here. I'm living in a little student apartment, I can barely pay my bills. I work twelve, eighteen hours a day sometimes. I'm all wrapped up in this shop, and if I go bankrupt again, my mother and my uncle Ned are going to be the losers, they're going to lose their retirement nest egg. I can't let that happen to them. How can I . . ." She stopped, her voice shaking.

"Pepper, it might not be pregnancy. You might just be coming down with something, there's been a bad stomach flu going around. Or maybe it's just food poisoning. People do get that, too.''

Pepper flushed. "Jack and I . . . well, he was in town in July . . . He came over here to the shop around one-thirty in the morning. He . . . we . . .''

"Oh, dear.''

"He said he'd gotten a vasectomy, Jan. Only the idiot must not have had it tested. And I trusted him . . . again.''

They gazed at each other with the long look of a friendship that had gone on for two solid years, being together for hours daily. A look that said what fools men could be, and why did women long so desperately to trust them?

Again Pepper's eyes watered. "I can't take care of a baby right now.''

Jan reached out and Pepper went into her friend's arms, shaking with sobs. "I want a baby! I really, really do! But someday. Not now. Oh, not just now, Jan. Why does it have to happen now? Why did I have to listen to Jack? A *vasectomy*? I should have known he'd screw it up!''

Four days later, she still had not gotten her period.

Walking into her shop, Pepper drew a deep breath, breathing in the faint, subtle smells of silk, satin, and lace. The shop was as glamorous as money and a lot of hard work could make it. The carpeting was sink-your-toes-in thick, a beautiful robin's-egg blue that Pepper prayed would hold up through the following winter. On the walls were white grids from which hung the gorgeous silk pajamas, slips, body-suits, chemises, bustiers, bras, and panties, not your average Victoria's Secret stuff, but a step above that, expensive and special.

How would an infant fit into all of this?

She had a cat in the window; would she now have a baby sitting in an infant seat behind the counter? Would she be rushing to make a sale, then mix formula? Could she lug *both* Oscar and a baby in a stroller to the shop every day? Did she want to? Didn't she owe her child a lot more than that, a real life instead of being just one more obligation? Not even really wanted?

"You look awful," remarked Jan when Pepper approached the cash register, where Jan was sorting sales slips.

"I feel awful," said Pepper hollowly. For the past days, she'd eaten almost nothing except toast and dry cereal, and had been sick on the average of four times daily. She was becoming agonizingly familiar with the visual appearance of the inside of her toilet bowl. It was just the way it had happened before, when she was seventeen.

You were big enough to get yourself p.g., now be a big girl and stop blubbering about it, an angry-sounding nurse had said to her, in the small clinic her mother had taken her to in Miami. Pepper winced at the unpleasant memory.

"Why don't you go home early? I can handle the register," offered Jan. "Business is a little slow right now anyway."

"No," said Pepper. "I need to work."

She waited on a few customers, helped a college student pick out some bridal lingerie, then drifted into her back office and sat down at her computer screen, flipping it on and waiting while Windows 95 came up on the screen.

She had a ton of work to do—accounts to prepare, phone calls to make. *Oh, God.* Pepper stared helplessly at the screen, images of a baby entering her mind. She'd held a cousin's three-week-old baby a few years ago, and the tiny, fuzzy skull had been so fragile that she could see the fontanel pulsating. The infant had tried to suck on her finger, and Pepper had felt such a sudden, powerful wave of love that it had amazed her. For those few seconds, she'd *wanted* that baby. Wanted it with all her soul.

But that was then, before the boutique, before all her responsibilities.

Troubled, Pepper touched her stomach, which was just as flat as ever, as yet giving no sign of her pregnancy.

She had several IRA accounts, one of which she could cash out to pay for the procedure. She would not have to call on Jack for financial help, thank God. He'd been a jerk,

an asshole, blithely assuming his vasectomy was effective
. . . or maybe he'd never bothered to get one at all, it occurred to her. Maybe he'd lied to her that he had. It was so
like Jack, that kind of irresponsibility. So *maddeningly* like
him.

She should call him, of course, tell him what had happened, tell him about the futile vasectomy, get angry with
him. But did she really want to listen to Jack begging her
to marry him again, promising her that he would be a good
father, that he would change, become something he was not?
Maybe she would send him a card, she decided reluctantly.
After she'd had the abortion.

Pepper picked up the mouse and double-clicked on the
Excel icon, then selected a spreadsheet she'd been working
on yesterday. Her baby, when she finally had one, was going
to be special, cherished, totally loved.

That was the way all babies should come into the world,
not as a mistake, a disaster.

TREVA

OUTSIDE THE MASTER BATHROOM WINDOW, A FLOCK OF
blue jays in the ravine were uttering their raucous morning caws. Next door, three men working for a garden service were simultaneously running a leaf blower, a Weed
Whacker, and a lawn tractor, creating a nerve-edging racket
that blasted away any remaining suburban peace.

Wearing only a camisole and panties, Treva Connor
barely heard these annoying neighborhood sounds.

She stared at the plastic test indicator, her heart slamming
so wildly that it was in danger of thumping right out of her
chest. She couldn't believe it . . . Two tests, and they'd both
come up positive! Should she go out and buy a third test?

No . . . God . . . she really was pregnant. Two tests could not be wrong.

She sank down on the edge of the whirlpool bathtub with plants aligned along its edge, her breath coming raw in her throat. The ''ring anniversary,'' that delicious night of the celery green satin gown. Her dear, ''hunka hunka burning love'' husband.

And now this. It seemed so unbelievable . . . so terrifying.

God, what if it was another miscarriage? Early in her first marriage, Treva'd had a pregnancy that ended in a miscarriage at eighteen weeks. She'd been totally devastated, and then she'd lost another fetus, which had affected her even more emotionally. She still thought about those babies, wondering how old they'd be, what they'd be doing now. She had followed both of them through a succession of birthdays and graduations.

Married to Wade now for ten years, she'd hoped . . . But now with her chronic hypertension, often not fully controlled, pregnancy wasn't desirable. At least four doctors had told her that, their various warnings rushing into Treva's mind now.

Resolutely she pushed away the half-remembered warnings. The important thing was, what should she tell Wade?

Treva rubbed her temples with her fingers, trying to smooth away the headache that had begun to prick her skull, like delicate needles. She wanted to rush to the phone right now and call him at his office at the School of Social Work, bursting out with her wonderful—and scary—news.

He'd be so thrilled . . . wouldn't he?

Maybe not.

She stroked her hairline with her fingertips, gradually moving them around to the middle of her forehead, which also had begun to throb. Maybe she wouldn't tell Wade yet, not for another day. She needed a little more time, Treva told herself. Time to adjust to this fantastic thing that had happened to her body . . . time to muster up a persuasion for her husband.

Maybe she'd arrange to have lunch with her sister,

Rhonda, today. She *had* to have someone to talk to, someone who would understand and not lecture her.

Quickly Treva went into the large master bedroom and got dressed for the women's clinic where she worked, putting on a pair of dark green drawstring pants and a yellow T-shirt that said IF YOU REALLY WANT IT DONE, ASK A WOMAN on it. She slid on comfortable leather shoes and applied bronzy makeup, which highlighted her large eyes and full mouth, her caramel coloring.

They were all supposed to wear Kevlar vests, but Treva was damned if she would wear one in August, and had always believed that no one would harm her. She was just a phone counselor, she helped people. It was just not in her stars to die, shot down by some crazed abortion activist.

The humid summer morning made the air seem misty, sunshine caught in it, like light seen through white wine. Waiting to turn left into the clinic parking lot, Treva felt her whole body pulsating with the exhilaration of her strangely exalted mood.

Another pregnancy—after all these years. *Oh, girl.*

An empty space appeared in the traffic flow, and Treva drove her Pontiac Grand Am into the lot. The Geddes/Washtenaw clinic looked like any prosaic doctor's office, a one-story brick building with white, colonial-style shutters and a cupola roof. Its windows, however, had been filled in with reinforced glass bricks to discourage fire-bombing, and a uniformed security guard paced back and forth in front of the door. Discreetly placed video cameras surveyed the entrance parking lot.

As Treva parked, a middle-aged woman suddenly jumped out of a parked car, lugging a professionally printed poster that said SAVE A BABY.

"Hi, Treva . . . *don't* go in there today," called Bobbie Lynn urgently, trotting up to within about fifteen feet of Treva, then stopping. "*Don't* do it. Turn around and go home. Quit your job. Just quit!"

Treva sighed. No one knew Bobbie Lynn's last name, or where she lived, but she had shown up every day for the past five years, working as a "sidewalk counselor," handing out leaflets and trying to convince patients to leave. In rain Bobbie carried an umbrella, in snow she wore a long down coat and fake fur hat. Today she had on a gray business suit, white blouse, and sensible midheel pumps. A plastic name tag on her lapel said MY NAME IS BOBBIE LYNN, WORKING FOR THE LORD.

"You know I have to, Bobbie. How are you today?"

"Oh, fine. You know." Bobbie's voice became more intense. "*Don't* kill a baby today, Treva."

As always, the accusatory words made Treva feel as if she'd been hit by stones. She wanted to talk back . . . but they'd been told it was useless and futile to get in a parking-lot argument. Shouting matches could easily escalate into full-fledged demonstrations, bringing the police on scene and scaring all the arriving patients. Which, of course, was exactly what the demonstrators wanted.

Treva hurried past the demonstrator, greeting Bill, a forty-year-old security guard, who had recently injured his hand on a table saw. "Hi, Bill, and how's your hand?"

"Better and better. That therapy is something else, man. But I'm getting almost full movement now from my thumb."

Treva made warm conversation about his injury. She knew everyone who worked at the clinic, their hopes, politics, children, and personality quirks, and also their abortion histories. Seven of the nine women on staff had had abortions, several back when it was still illegal. Mei Rosario had nearly died from her botched abortion, in a motel room in Detroit in the late sixties.

The security guard pressed the keypad that would work the electronic door, and escorted Treva inside.

"Hopefully she's all the demonstrators we get today," he told her. "That Bobbie Lynn, I wonder how she can do it, week in and week out. I heard she was here on Christmas day. She's gotta be, you know, three slices short of a loaf."

"She believes in what she does," said Treva gently. "Just as we do, Bill."

They walked through the vestibule (which had another video camera installed in the ceiling) into the huge waiting room, crowded with chairs. In a staff meeting last year, they'd decided that the place was too clinical, too sterile and cheerless, so now there was cheerful floral wallpaper, dusty rose carpeting, and a large-screen TV set. They'd even splurged on a gas-log fireplace, believing that women facing abortions needed to get away from the ugly hospital image.

Treva turned to her right, entering the door to the office area.

"Hey, Treva," Annie Larocca greeted her, looking up from one of the five computers that were arranged in a row behind the reception counter. A freckled woman of fifty-two, she was a physician's assistant, and a close friend of Treva's. Annie had worked at a clinic in Worcester, Massachusetts, before coming to Michigan.

"Hi, Annie . . . How many have we got today?"

"Oh—thirty written down. Who knows how many'll show?" The clinic always overbooked because about 10 to 15 percent of the women who made appointments did not keep them.

"Great. Keep 'em coming."

Annie grinned and glanced at her watch. "In twenty minutes they're gonna be *here,* and we need those extra chairs. I'm calling that furniture place again. I'm going to demand they make the delivery this morning. You going to be around for lunch, hon?"

Treva couldn't help the wide smile that split her face. "Not today. I'm having lunch with my sister. Then I have a doctor's appointment."

"Hmmmm?"

Treva blushed. "We'll talk."

She went into the coffee room, poured herself a mug of decaf, then carried it back to the bank of phones. Already the phones were ringing, but the clinic's answering machine was still picking up the calls.

Treva plopped herself in her chair, setting down the cup and reaching for her call log. She turned the pages to a fresh

day. Also on her desktop were pads of admitting forms and
a plastic disk divided into weeks and months to help her
calculate gestation dates. She also had a little Dilbert calendar someone had given her.

Pregnant! She still could scarcely believe it. Thank God
for foam and condoms that didn't work, the 3 percent or
whatever that simply slipped past no matter how careful you
were. If only her health would permit it. If only her forty-
one-year-old body could manage it. If only it wouldn't be
too dangerous.

A call rang through. Treva picked up the phone. "Geddes/
Washtenaw Women's Clinic, this is Treva speaking. Is there
a way I can help you?"

"I don't know." It was a mature woman's voice, raw
from crying. "It's my daughter . . . Do you . . . that is, do
you . . . I mean does your office do abortions?"

"We offer a full line of services to women," Treva explained as she always did. "Breast exams, mammograms,
birth control information, sterilization, Pap smears. Abortion
is one of those services, yes."

"Oh!"

"How old is your daughter?"

The woman started to cry. "She's . . . fifteen. A b-
baby . . ."

"Slow down, now, ma'am. We're here for you. Can you
tell me what's wrong?"

More sobs. "She's missed three periods! She was afraid
to tell anyone, she's kind of heavy and nobody noticed, she
just hid it from all of us. Is it too late for her? Four months?
Do they still . . . you know . . . do it then?"

Treva sighed. A "second tri" abortion, done in the second trimester of the pregnancy, was more painful and complicated, as well as being emotionally rough on both the
patient and the staff.

"Yes, there are options available, but you'll need to bring
your daughter in to talk about them. What's her first name?"

"Kelly. Kelly Irene. Oh . . . we've been so upset. We're
both crying our eyes out."

Treva set up an appointment time, reassuring the woman that her daughter would receive counseling and would not be forced into any decisions. The initial intake session would be prorated on ability to pay, or free if they could not afford it. She also warned the woman about the sidewalk counselors, telling her that if the prospect of being heckled was too unnerving, a volunteer in a van would pick them up and bring them in to the clinic.

"Thank you . . . oh, thank you."

At ten-fifteen Treva walked down the hallway past the rows of exam rooms—most of them full—and the classroom where groups of women were counseled. This was not a quiet place. Phones rang. Soft music played over a PA system. She could hear voices from the classroom, the blare of some morning show on the waiting-room TV set, and also rock music in some of the individual exam rooms, where Dr. Rosenkrantz always had the patients pick out CDs to play while they were having their procedure. Counterpoint to this was the whirring roar of the vacuum extraction machine.

Dr. Ellen Rosenkrantz's office was the last one on the left, its walls covered with photographs and diplomas. Some were photos taken of Ellen during the 1960's, when she'd been a Vietnam protester who'd worked alongside Tom Hayden. Other pictures were ones taken of her at a women's clinic in Haiti, where she'd spent ten years delivering babies and treating everything from prolapse of the uterus to breast cancer. At seventy-three, she was aging, as most abortion doctors now were—the few that were left. Only the older doctors remembered the days when women were brought to emergency rooms with perforated uteruses, massive hemorrhages, or killer infections.

"Well, Treva, we've got the final go-ahead for the abortion study, the funding is in place, and all systems are go."

Dr. Rosenkrantz's tiny, bony face was wreathed in smiles. She wore her long, white hair braided in a coil at the base of her neck, and despite her age, exuded energy.

Treva uttered a crow of delight. The four-year grant would provide money for them to study 250 postabortion patients. The women would fill out two-page questionnaires and take the Rosenberg Self-Esteem Scale, a standardized test that measured overall well-being. Participants would also give once-yearly personal interviews, either by phone or in person, that covered their current lives, feelings, and problems.

Although another, larger study had covered this territory, some researchers, including Dr. Rosenkrantz, challenged that other study's techniques and believed that the self-esteem scale failed to measure all the characteristics of "postabortion syndrome" and still left questions.

"This is fantastic! I almost forgot we applied," Treva cried excitedly.

"Fifteen months. Well, the Feds move exceedingly slow, but I guess they do move. Dr. Tallchief and I will finalize the questionnaire and send out bids to some market research firms to mail them out and tabulate the results. You ready to start interviewing? We'll bring in Mei to help, maybe some others if we need them."

"You bet."

They talked for a while about the study. Thus far they had 155 permissions, a good start. Treva would write the interviewing section of the final report, which would be authored by Dr. Rosenberg, Dr. Charles Tallchief, and Treva, and later they would try to work the results into a laymen's book, using any publisher's advance they received as a donation to the clinic. Treva and any other interviewers would receive per-interview stipends.

Finally Treva walked back to her phone, settling in again to the steady stream of calls. *Is this the place where . . . ?* Many of the women were upset or crying; a few were angry. No one could calm frantic patients like Treva could. She listened and counseled, letting the anger flow easily away from her. She knew the women were angry not at her, but at the situation.

She loved these women, their courage, their struggles to

do what was so difficult. For some of the younger women, this would be their first adult choice ever.

The restaurant where Treva was to meet her sister, Rhonda, was on busy Stadium Boulevard about a half mile from the recently refaced U. of M. football stadium, which held more than one hundred thousand screaming fans on football Saturdays in the fall. The restaurant specialized in Greek and American food, and smelled deliciously of lamb, beef, and the flaming cheese that was their specialty.

Treva arrived early and sat with a copy of the *Ann Arbor News*, her eyes flicking over the headlines. They were working on a new, undetectable, virus-killing vaginal foam that women could use to guard against HIV, one article said, explaining that men controlled condom use and women had to negotiate for the man to wear one—one reason females around the world were getting AIDS.

Treva was interested in the topic, but she didn't ingest one word of it. She couldn't. She was just too hyped.

"Hey, Sissy." Rhonda slid into the booth opposite her, a tall, pretty, brown-skinned woman who worked as a respiratory therapist at Mott Children's Hospital, part of the huge, U. of M. hospital complex.

"A lot of traffic on the way?" inquired Treva, bursting with her news.

"Just a few senior citizens going at thirty miles per hour, that's all. I passed them like Michael Jordan. One old guy gave me the finger. He must have been at least eighty. Whatever happened to polite senior citizens?"

"Rhonda!" Rhonda had a heavy foot on the accelerator and had racked up several speeding tickets in the past few years.

"Well, I can't help it if I only had an hour to see my Sissy."

They smiled at each other with the warmth of sisters born only a year apart, who had often been mistaken for twins when they were growing up. Their lives were vastly different. Treva was the happily married wife. Rhonda was the "professional single" who never spent Friday night alone in her apartment. Yet they met twice a month for lunch, phoned each other three or four times a week, and shared most of their secrets, except for the private marital ones that Treva would not share, even with her sister, out of loyalty to Wade.

"What are you ordering?" asked Rhonda, rattling the printed menu. "I'm thinking spinach pie."

Treva grimaced. "The usual. Broiled chicken, no salt in cooking, no sauce. I've got to be extra careful right now . . . with what I eat, I mean."

Rhonda looked at her. "Your BP's up again."

"No. I mean, it's—I really should wait to talk to Wade about this."

Her sister looked more closely at Treva and then gave a little squeal.

"Oh, no," said Rhonda. "No *way* you don't. Who's the one played Barbie dolls with you and helped you paint her so we got a *black* Barbie instead of old white-bread Barbie? Who's the one told you all about Wade Connor and how if you'd just start going to some of those dumb university *meetings,* you might meet someone interesting? Who's the one who—*Tell me your secret, girl.*"

"All right, all right," laughed Treva, grinning. "You win."

"Tell me, then. Tell, tell."

Treva couldn't hold the news in any longer. "I'm pregnant, Rhonda."

"You're what? Pregnant, as in . . . stomach way out to here? Pregnant, as in . . . baby?"

"That's the general idea."

"Oh, Treva. Oh, God."

"You sound underwhelmed," Treva remarked dryly.

"I'm—Treva, are you sure? I mean maybe the pregnancy test lied or something."

"One might have lied. Two tell the truth."

"You took two tests?"

"Yeah, just to be sure. They were both positive!" exclaimed Treva, the smile wreathing her face now, splitting it from ear to ear. "I sat there in the john and I looked at that little plastic thing and this line started to get darker and it was the *pregnancy line,* and I just stared at it for a long time, and then I started to shake. I just shook and shook. I did, Rhonda. I just shook."

"And you didn't tell Wade yet?"

"He'd already left for class. No, I'm saving that—I want to do it in some special way. I want to make it special for him, something we can both remember. Maybe I'll, I don't know, blindfold him and drive him to a baby-furniture store, take him in and show him a crib. They have gorgeous cribs now, really beautiful, not like when you and I were babies."

"That would sure freak him out. Another of your anniversaries," sighed Rhonda. "Oh, Treva. It sounds great, but maybe you shouldn't do that yet. Not just yet."

The college-student waiter was heading their way. Taking their orders, he tried to convince them to order the flaming cheese. Both women shook their heads.

When he had left, Treva's smile faded. "I'm going to have this baby, Rhonda."

"But you know you shouldn't. Haven't you been trying all these years to avoid having another pregnancy? Honey. We black women have a lot of strikes against us, and one of them is this damn hypertension. You've been up, down, up, down, for years. What makes you think you can have a smooth pregnancy? And your age, Jesus, Treva, you're what, forty-two?"

"Forty-one. Don't add a year on me. I've been good for six months, I've been stable. I *have,*" declared Treva. "I'm going to the doctor's office and then I'm going home to tell Wade."

"Don't tell him yet. I mean it. Not until you've really thought this through."

Couldn't Rhonda give her anymore moral support than this? Treva's face flamed as she grabbed up her purse, the newspaper falling to the floor. She put several bills on the

table to pay for both of their lunches. "I am thinking it out,
Rhonda. I *am* thinking it through."

Then she was marching out of the restaurant, past tables
full of people scarfing down grape leaves, lamb kebabs, and
other salty dishes Treva hadn't been able to eat in years.
Rhonda hurried after her, her white uniform pants and jacket
swishing as she walked fast on her hospital shoes.

"Girl, I didn't mean to hurt your feelings—"

"My feelings are not hurt. They are not hurt at all. I'm
going to the doctor's office now. Maybe Dr. Haugh can see
me early and then I can just get back to work."

Treva stalked through the lobby, pushing open the door
and heading across the lot to her car. The sun was at its
noonday zenith, the air wet-feeling. It broke out a sweat on
Treva's skin as Rhonda trotted after her.

"Treva . . . I *said* I'm sorry . . ."

By the time Treva reached her car she was shaking. Oh,
just what she didn't need, pregnancy emotions. She leaned
against the hood, while tears rushed out of her eyes and
mucous streamed from her nose, as it always did when she
cried.

"Honey," said Rhonda anxiously.

"Have you got a damn *tissue* or something?" Treva
choked.

"Yeah . . . somewhere . . . this stupid purse . . ." Rhonda
fumbled in her bulging shoulder bag, producing a rather
crumpled-looking white hospital tissue. "You want me to
come to the doctor's with you? I promise I'll keep my
mouth shut. I won't say one word. I swear I'll just sit with
you and be there for you."

Treva wiped her nose and then she blew it loudly. More
tears flowed, and she blew again.

"You're such a honker, girl."

Treva's giggle had tears in it. "*You* honk twice as loud.
And you snore, Rhonda. Like a Skil saw."

"Oh, *you* don't snore?" Rhonda put her arm around
Treva, steadying her. "I've heard you snore a time or

two . . . Oh, Treva. Where's Dr. Haugh's office, over on Washtenaw?''

''Yeah.''

''I'll drive us.''

''No, I can drive . . .''

''No, you can't. You're expecting. And you're still leaking, girl. Look, I've got a whole box of Kleenex in my car—it's just enough to get us to the office, if we're very careful and we conserve tissues.''

The waiting room was filled with women in all stages of pregnancy, from barely showing to enormous. One woman looked as if she were going to deliver any hour now. Treva couldn't help eyeing these women enviously. She wanted to be big, too. She wanted to be so huge that she waddled, joking about her backaches, her hemorrhoids, and not being able to see the tips of her shoes.

''Mrs. Connor?'' A nurse called Treva's name.

Treva's heart did an immediate flip-flop. Both she and Rhonda jumped up, then they both laughed.

The nurse looked from one to the other. ''Which of you is Mrs. Connor?''

''Me,'' said Treva, nervousness coloring her voice.

Rhonda hugged her and said, ''Go for it, I'll be waiting right here,'' and gave Treva a small push. Then Treva was walking through the door into the examining-room area, which was dominated by a huge board display plastered with hundreds of newborn photos, of the type that were taken in the hospital.

Treva couldn't help pausing to look at all the squinched-up, Kewpie faces, some crying, some puckered, some asleep, some bald, others with heads of dark, fuzzy hair. Newly minted human beings with all colors of skin, too new and scrawny to have that round baby cuteness yet—which made them somehow even more touching.

''We're going to have to start a new board pretty soon,'' said the nurse, noticing Treva's interest. ''That one's about used up.''

''So cute,'' Treva said, swallowing.

* * *

The exam room was like all the ones Treva'd ever been in, immaculately clean, hung with bland pictures and a wall poster showing the pregnant uterus at various stages. Narrowing her eyes, she tried to pick out what stage she was at. Yeah, maybe the one where the woman's stomach was totally flat.

The room smelled of the Hibiclens hand-washing disinfectant hanging in a dispenser by the sink, and the talc from inside rubber gloves. A red container for biohazardous discards sat near the sink.

She sat on the end of the exam table, feeling uncomfortably bare in the blue paper gown they'd given her, which flapped open in the back. The internal exam had gone well, but now she was shivering, goose bumps rising on her skin.

"Mrs. Connor, I don't want to alarm you, but you may want to think long and hard before you continue this pregnancy." Dr. Richard Haugh, forty-five and homely, was seated on a stool near her, looking at her with an anxious expression that created triple rows of wrinkles in his forehead.

Treva hugged the blue gown to her chest and shook her head. "But my BP's been stable for months. I'm feeling great, really."

"I know, and we want you to keep on feeling great. But, Mrs. Connor—"

He went on to give her a lecture about the hazards of hypertensive disorders during pregnancy, which could lead to a condition called preeclampsia or even full-blown eclampsia, which was apparently very dangerous and to be avoided at all costs.

Scare tactics, Treva thought, unconsciously moving her hands down to protect her stomach. People sued their OBs so often these days that malpractice insurance rates had shot through the ceiling. Some doctors had left the field. Some of the others painted bleak pictures just to protect themselves.

". . . If the condition worsens, the liver can become enlarged. There can be vision problems . . . blurred vision, sometimes detachment of the retina and blindness.''

Blindness? Whoa, Treva thought in horror.

''The patient can have bleeding in the brain, she can have repeated seizures, she can have—''

''Stop,'' whispered Treva, tightening her grip on her stomach area. ''I know you mean well, but you're really frightening me.''

''Mrs. Connor, have you told your husband about this pregnancy yet?''

''I . . . no . . . I haven't.''

''I think you should bring him in and we'll discuss this with him. I want both of you to see the risk, the seriousness of this.'' Dr. Haugh leaned forward, his expression grim. ''Hypertension occurs in a certain percentage of normal pregnancies, even when the mother didn't have a problem before. But with your health and age and unstable blood pressure, you really are at a much higher risk for serious problems. Very serious problems. You should consider a therapeutic abortion, Mrs. Connor. Of course, that's entirely your decision.''

Abortion.

The word jolted Treva right in the uterus; that was exactly what it felt like. She could feel herself cramping. ''No!'' she cried.

''Mrs. Connor, believe me, I know how upsetting this is. Please, just go home and think about this. Out at the desk, I want you to make an appointment for tomorrow and bring your husband. I'll tell my assistant to work you in.''

''A-all right,'' Treva mumbled.

After Dr. Haugh left the room, Treva fumbled into her street clothes, so anxious that she found herself putting her shoes on the wrong feet. Hastily she corrected the ridiculous mistake. She wanted to cry, but no tears came.

She made the appointment for herself and Wade, and wrote out a check for the day's visit. She had to do it twice; she'd written in the wrong amount and date.

Rhonda was sitting in the waiting room and she jumped

up immediately when she saw Treva's stricken face.

"Honey? Sissy? You okay?"

"Let's go," said Treva, her voice unsteady. "Let's just drive. I called and told them at the clinic that I might be a little late. I—I have a big problem."

Rhonda stopped at a pay phone to call her supervisor and say she'd be late, then they drove west on Scio Church Road toward the village of Chelsea. Ann Arbor's burgeoning housing market was spreading out farther every year. New housing developments flashed past them, along with still-remaining stretches of woods and fields. A couple of small boys were riding dirt bikes in a field, yelling like baby road warriors. They were so cute that Treva had to look away from them.

"What *is* it?" cried Rhonda.

Treva managed to stammer out the gist of Dr. Haugh's scary lecture.

"Oh, honey. Oh, God, baby. What are you going to do?"

"The only thing I can. I'm going to have it."

"But, baby, didn't you listen to the man when he told you that stuff, warned you about the medical problems?"

"Of course I listened. But I didn't want to hear, Rhonda. I work in that clinic and every day women want to get rid of fetuses and I want to keep mine, and where's the sense, where's the reason?"

Treva grabbed for the box of tissues and blew her nose, making the honking sound that Rhonda teased her about. "It's so complicated," she went on dully. "How am I going to tell Wade? I'll have to do it tonight because the appointment's tomorrow. What will I do if he doesn't want me to be pregnant?"

"Honey . . . don't borrow trouble now. You haven't even been back to the doctor's office yet, Wade hasn't even heard what Dr. Haugh has to say."

Treva nodded, blowing her nose again. In a few minutes Rhonda turned the car around and started toward the city again. They both had to be back at work.

*   *   *

When the last patient had left the recovery area, Treva drove home, still trying to decide how to break the news to her husband.

She turned off Huron Parkway in to their subdivision, which had been built on a series of rocky hills formed by the last glacier to hit Michigan. The homes were affluent and big, with walk-out basements and decks that gave ravine views. Many had pools. Treva, who had grown up in Detroit in a big, shabby home split into apartments, had fallen in love with the neighborhood. She especially loved the fact that she and Wade were not the only minority homeowners. She would not have wanted to feel isolated or a ''token.''

They'd paid for their own huge, Tudor-style house with three college textbooks that Wade had written, each of which was still selling vigorously.

She let herself into the house, allowing its warm colors to surround her like an emotional balm. The brick fireplace was huge, its mantel lined with some of the original pottery Treva had been collecting for years. Over it she'd hung a wonderful painting of an African woman in traditional dress with a huge basket balanced on her head, the lines of her facial features beautifully serene.

The living room was her favorite room, with its cathedral ceiling and bank of windows gazing out at sun-dappled tree-tops. Over the hardwood floor Treva had laid down some Chinese rugs in warm brick reds and pottery blues. A big, curved brick red couch loaded with pillows picked up the color scheme, a favorite spot for Treva and Wade to sit and watch the large-screen TV in their entertainment center.

Okay, she thought. Now she had to figure out what to do, how to break the news to Wade.

They had some New York strip steaks in the refrigerator, a treat for Wade, and Treva decided they would cook them on the grill. She would serve baked potatoes and garlic-and-herb sautéed mushrooms, Wade's favorite. Maybe by the time they were done eating, she'd have an inspiration.

Her husband arrived home tired, his short-sleeved, striped

shirt crumpled from a long day of classes, seminars, and committee meetings. But still Wade had a kiss for Treva, and a long back rub with his big, dark, strong hands.

"You seem tired, babe," he said.

"Yeah. I am."

She stood out on the back deck beside the gas grill with him, watching while he turned the steaks and tested them with a fork. The odor of the cooking meat, mixed with the smell of the hickory chips that Treva had thrown onto the lava coals, was pungent.

"How long since we had these?" he asked. "And my sautéed mushrooms, is this some special night?"

"I'm pregnant," Treva blurted.

"Say what?" Wade had been in the act of forking over a piece of meat, and it fell off the fork onto the grill, creating a smoky spray of burning juices.

"I took a pregnancy test. I took two tests. I'm pregnant. And Dr. Haugh confirmed it."

Wade put down the fork and turned to her, letting the meat burn. "Babe?"

"I *know* I shouldn't," Treva said, tears in her voice. "We must have somehow screwed up with the foam and all. But now it's happened and I'm happy about it. I am. I'm just—Wade, aren't you happy, too?"

Burning meat juices smoked as her husband enfolded his arms around her. "I am . . . I . . . I don't know what I am."

Tears sprang to Treva's eyes because her husband's reaction wasn't what she'd expected. He was supposed to be half crying with joy—laughing and happy—Oh, she didn't know! Instead he was just holding her, rubbing her back, his breathing irregular.

"Aren't you *happy*?" she repeated.

He didn't respond directly. "Treva, you said you'd been to the doctor."

"Yes," she responded defiantly. "Yes, I have, and he wants us both to come back tomorrow—we have an appointment at ten forty-five—because he wants to tell us about all sorts of terrible, horrible problems." She was an

honest woman; she couldn't keep this from him. "He says
it's very risky," she finished. "He had a lot of scary stories,
but I think it's mostly scare."

The burning steak smelled awful, dark and bitter.

Wade held her close to his chest, and she could hear the
deep rumbling of his heartbeat. "Oh, God," he whispered.

"What's wrong?"

He pulled back a little, so they could look into each
other's eyes. His were brown, solemn, moist. "You *know*
what's wrong, Treva. Didn't we talk about this, ten years
ago and five years ago and last year? You know you can't
afford to be pregnant. This isn't the first doctor who's told
you it could be dangerous. Damn," Wade added, rubbing
the corner of his mouth the way he sometimes did when he
was upset. "Why did this have to happen?"

Her eyes felt as if they were being prickled by tiny, hot
needles. She had to turn away from the smoke. "It happened
because it happened."

"You know I want a baby with you. I want it in the worst
way, I always have. But, Trev, I don't want it enough to
lose you."

"You're not going to lose me."

"I can't take the chance—*we* can't take the chance.
Honey, you know what has to be done. You know you can't
carry it. Now, babe, you know that."

"Wade—"

Wade's voice cracked. "No, listen. You're everything to
me. You're the sun and the moon and the stars and the
goddamned universe to me, Treva. I need you. *I need you.*
I know men aren't supposed to need women, but I guess
they never had you before, and I . . . I can't . . ."

He stopped, and they held each other, both of them shaking, Treva struggling a little in Wade's arms as he steadied
her. Neither of them smelled the charred dinner anymore,
or heard the dog next door, which had started barking, probably at the smell of the meat.

"You can't carry this baby to term," he said hoarsely.
"You can't risk everything we have, you can't risk *us,*

Treva. You're going to have to call the clinic in the morning, make an appointment. For the abortion. You know it's the only way.''

"It's *not* the only way."

"Yes—it has to be, for your health."

"Damn my health! I hate my health!" Treva bent her face into her husband's chest, fighting him now, twisting and pummeling him with her fists. Working in the clinic, she'd seen all the charts, read the books. Already the fetus had a head with a heart bulge in the body, and a curved tail. It had limb buds, and the contractions of its heart had begun. She hit and hit, her fists landing softly on Wade's chest. She heard a loud voice and realized it was her own angry sobbing.

Wade was crying, too. "Treva . . . Treva . . . don't . . ."

"I want my baby!"

"I know, and I want it, too, but, babe . . . your BP is so far out of whack. You know what all the doctors have said, and you *promised,* Treva, you promised you would never carry a baby to term. You promised me. You swore to me that if you ever became pregnant, you would get a therapeutic abortion."

Had she? If in fact she had made that promise, it seemed far away, part of a dim and misty past, a promise made before she had full knowledge of herself and her own body. *A promise made before she was pregnant.*

"That was before!" she cried.

"And this is now," Wade said gently. "Treva, *you have to.*"

PEPPER

A CHAMPAGNE-COLORED LATE AFTERNOON SUN WAS CASTing long rays over downtown Ann Arbor, creating shadows on the sidewalk where the buildings cut off the light.

Spicy odors of garlic, basil, and oregano drifted from the Italian restaurant next door to Pepper's shop. Patrons were already standing in line, a few spilling out onto the sidewalk, laughing and chattering.

Pepper Nolan turned the sign on her shop door so that it said CLOSED and switched on her security pad, coding in her four-digit number. As she did this, she nearly stepped on Oscar, who had chosen that moment to stalk a scrap of lavender tissue paper that had fallen out of a package. The cat played and pounced as if the bit of paper were a live mouse.

"Get 'em, killer," said Pepper, trying to smile over the sensation of queasiness that was always with her now. The smells of lasagna and manicotti from next door were making her stomach do funny wobbles.

"All right," said Jan Switzer, when Pepper had returned to the back room, Oscar bounding behind her. "I've got the wine, plus I picked up some appetizers from the deli. And a carton of strawberries! We can dip them in powdered sugar. I got that, too."

Jan had laid out the small repast on top of Pepper's desk and had already begun to munch on a huge, red berry the size of a plum. "Mmmm," she said cheerfully. "I don't know anything better than strawberries, they are positively sinful."

Thank God for Jan Switzer, who had given up a faculty dinner with her husband to sit with Pepper tonight, and who would accompany her tomorrow to the clinic.

Pepper picked at the feast, not telling Jan that even the huge, luscious strawberries turned her stomach. At her intake interview she'd been told that pregnancy nausea could disappear within minutes after the abortion. She'd bet hardly anyone knew about that one, little-known advantage. But they'd have to finish their "feast" by midnight, because after then she wasn't supposed to have anything to eat or drink.

An hour later they'd finished half of the bottle of wine and were sitting on the couch, Oscar purring on the cushion back behind them, shedding a few more of his beautiful, silky hairs as the two friends talked.

Men, life, procreation, sex. Admirable topics for the night before an abortion.

"Well, I learned about sex by eavesdropping," declared Pepper, after Jan had regaled her with a long story about sneaking a marriage manual off a bookshelf hidden in her parents' basement.

"Eavesdropping?"

"My mother had her bridge group over, and I was supposed to be in bed, but they kept laughing and waking me up, so I crept halfway down the stairs. They were talking about some man who couldn't get totally hard and so his wife would have to just take his penis and stuff it inside her. I remember listening, and I was just amazed. But it was funny. It was like I instantly *got* it . . . what the purpose of it all was."

"So what did you do?"

"The next day I asked my mother about it. She just freaked. And then she finally did sit me down and tell me. Erect penises. Sperm. Ten million of the things all swimming up you . . . and then she went into the whole toilet-seat thing. For years I thought there were gangs of sperm on toilet seats just waiting to wiggle up me."

They both laughed and told a few more hilarious stories about motherly sexual advice.

Then the mood went downhill as Pepper sighed. "Things changed so fast, Jan. Almost before I could comprehend them. I had my first abortion at seventeen, well, I told you about that before."

"Yeah . . . , poor Pepper."

"I was pretty damn rebellious and one Saturday night I ran off with this twenty-year-old guy and married him. My mother found us two weeks later and she forced me to come home. When I missed my period she was the one who took me to Miami for the abortion. Would you believe I never even knew what an abortion *was* until then?"

"Ah, God," said Jan, being supportive.

"I cried and told her I wanted to keep the baby, and she told me not to be a total fool and ruin my life. No man would ever want me if I already had a baby. So I had it. I'd never even had an internal exam before . . . It was like being raped. I cried through the entire thing and this awful nurse chastised me."

"How terrible."

Pepper blinked teary eyes. "And now I'm having another one."

"But this one isn't the same," Jan pointed out. "For one thing, you're not a teenager now, and your mother isn't making you do it. You're choosing it, it's a pro-choice act, it's something you're doing for yourself, Pepper. This time you're in control."

Pepper set her wineglass on the floor. She was feeling nauseous again, and wondered if she would be forced to jump up and run to the bathroom. Would she feel better if she threw up, or worse? She gave a hiccuping laugh.

"Oh, Jan. I've been through a few men. Do you suppose I'll ever meet a guy who is gentle and kind and keeps his promises? Someone who respects you and doesn't use you? Someone who could even be man enough to want his child? Damn that Jack. If he wasn't such a—if he wasn't—I might have married him and kept this baby."

She bent her shoulders and cried, sobbing until her throat hurt, while Jan patted her shoulders, uttering .murmuring sounds, and offering tissues and drinks of water.

"Honey, it's not so bad," said the loyal, freckled Jan. "You'll survive, and survive well."

"It *is* that bad. I'm getting an abortion tomorrow morning, Jan. How's that for the exact opposite of *romance*? The exact, total, fucked-up, messed-up *opposite*."

"It'll happen to you, Pepper."

"What, romance?" Pepper dabbed at her eyes, reaching up for Oscar and lifting him into her lap, just so she could hold his furry warmth. "I doubt it. I really doubt it."

Jan stared at her in surprise. "The way *you* look—your

gorgeous looks—Jesus, men stare at you when you go to the mall without any makeup.''

"What do looks have to do with it?" asked Pepper pensively. "My mother was beautiful, but what did it get her? A condo on Sanibel, alimony payments, a marriage clause. If she ever remarries, she loses her alimony. Take my advice, Jan," she went on. "Don't even *expect* romance. Then you'll never be disappointed."

Her face flushed with wine, Jan reached for one more big strawberry, dipping it in white sugar. *"Aha!"* she said.

"What does that mean, *aha*?"

"It means you're going to have romance, plenty of it. People always say they don't want romance and then they're the ones it happens to. Mark my words, Pepper."

"Oh, you're really plastered," slurred Pepper. "Shut off that woman's wine supply, and make her stop reading romance novels."

DIEDRE

DIEDRE LAY AWAKE, LISTENING TO THE TRAFFIC ON Eleven Mile Road and gazing at the photo of the magnificent Gothic law quad which she had hung on her bulletin board. The picture had been taken in early spring, a hint of green just starting to show on bare tree branches. The eleven huge, arched stained-glass windows that lined this side of the structure glowed with a soft, orange light.

In her mind she went over the two big reasons why she had to do it.

Law school.

The rest of her life.

About 4:30 A.M. she felt thirsty, so she got out of bed and went into the bathroom, where she started to pour herself a Dixie cup of water, then remembered she wasn't supposed to drink anything after midnight. She poured out the water, watching it go down the drain, like her fetus would in the morning.

Oh, God!

Lifting her eyes, Diedre blearily stared at her face in the vanity mirror. Ravaged blue shadows were etched underneath her eyes. She'd been so tired the past few weeks, she'd dragged herself to her waitressing job, dragged herself home again. She just wanted to fall asleep everywhere, and her breasts felt sore and tender. Even her nipples were bigger, browner, hurting when they rubbed against her bra.

Still, all these symptoms meant that she was able to have a child, if she wanted one. She had already proved it—she had gotten pregnant.

Oh, God, what was she thinking? She was too tired, that was all, way too stressed. There were still a few hours left, she had to try to get some sleep. In about six hours she wouldn't be pregnant anymore, and her life could go on. Diedre had another wild idea about calling Mitch Sterling in the middle of the night, but then she pushed it back. Crazy, to think of calling him now. He wouldn't want to hear from her.

Padding barefoot back to her room, Diedre encountered her mother coming out of her bedroom, slim and young in a blue terry cloth robe, her blond hair sleep-rumpled.

"You're up at this hour, Diedre? I heard you moving around. Everything okay? You usually sleep like a log."

"I . . . I can't sleep."

"Come on in the kitchen, baby, and we'll talk about it. I've got some decaf coffee. I'll make you some."

"No . . . I can't have any," admitted Diedre in a low voice.

Cynthia Samms looked at her. "Well, into the kitchen with you anyway. A little talking never did anyone any harm."

The kitchen was constructed railroad style, counters and appliances facing each other across a narrow aisle, so the two women sat down in the nearby dining area, which was

furnished with a gray, Formica-topped table Cynthia had
bought used more than ten years ago.

"Something is bothering you," prodded Cynthia gently.

"Yeah." Diedre slumped in the chair, rubbing her eyes
tiredly, then rubbed her hands through her blond hair until
it was practically standing on end. By the time she finished,
tears had begun to spill out of her eyes. "I'm getting an
abortion tomorrow morning, Mom. Pam is driving me. I
have to do it or I can't finish law school, so please, *please*,
don't try to stop me."

Cynthia's face showed first surprise, then grief, then com-
passion. "Honey . . . honey." She reached across the table
and took her daughter's hand, enfolding it between her own
capable fingers, which could type over eighty words a minute and run a 150-line phone system, fingers that had painted
and wallpapered, changed the oil on the 1987 Ford Sunbird
she drove, clipped coupons, and written out rent checks that
grew higher each year.

"Mom . . ." Diedre choked. "I didn't want to disappoint
you."

"Diedre, you'll never disappoint me, no matter what you
do or whatever happens," said her mother. "That's a given.
You're my daughter, my special girl. Until the day I die,
that's what you'll always be to me."

Diedre's eyes stung and now the tears did start to flow,
hotly. "I got crazy," she wept. "At this stupid party in July.
Everyone was drunk and skinny-dipping in the lake. I . . . I
drank a lot and this guy . . . we drove across the lake to the
other side . . . He had a Chrysler Le Baron."

"Darling, sweet dear, you don't have to give me all the
details," said Cynthia quietly. "Have you thought about this
long and carefully, honey? Have you considered all of the
alternatives? Getting an abortion is a very final thing. You
can't change your mind later."

"I know." Diedre's voice cracked. "Mom, it's not the
right time for me. It's *not*. He never called me, he just
dumped me, and I—I can't have a baby and go to law
school. I'll never make it through if I do."

Cynthia nodded, not releasing Diedre's hand. "It's a rough choice, isn't it?"

"Y-yeah."

"All women have tough choices to make sometimes," her mother went on slowly. "I told you how I stole that woman's purse that time, in the fitting room at J.C. Penney's? I had to have the ID, I had to fix it so your father wouldn't find us. He had beaten me many times and I could tell he was going to start beating you and Pam if I didn't do something."

"I know, I know, Mom." Cynthia had sent back the purse with all the money and credit cards intact, keeping only the driver's license and other ID, which she had used for four years until their father finally died in a car accident while driving drunk.

Cynthia glanced at her watch. "It's still only five A.M. You still have an hour or so to sleep, or to think, whatever you want to do, Diedre. So I'd better let you go back to bed. Look into your heart, Diedre. I know you'll find the right answer there. And whatever choice you make, I *will* love you. Always remember that."

So Diedre stumbled back to bed and crawled under the covers. A siren screamed past the apartment complex on its way to William Beaumont Hospital, but she barely heard it. Her eyelids were already falling shut, so heavy she could not have pried them open.

For an hour and a half, she slept without dreams.

TREVA

THE AFFLUENT NEIGHBORHOOD LAY STILL, NOT EVEN THE sound of a dog's barking to intrude on its nighttime somnolence. Only the wind was active tonight, blowing through the trees in the ravine and raising a huge susurration of leaves and branches being pushed and rubbed. Usually Treva loved that kind of wind, loved to listen to it.

Tonight the wind seemed lonely, isolating, as if they lived on some island off Newfoundland, Canada, instead of in pleasant Ann Arbor, Michigan.

Treva and Wade lay in the center of their king-sized bed, tangled in each other's arms. Wade had been snoring for hours, taking deep, rattling, indrawn breaths that he expelled into Treva's shoulder. She'd always loved the sound of his snoring, the way it made her feel safe, protected.

But now the snoring was keeping her awake. Or maybe it was just her thoughts, flaying her mind like whips, with no way to get away from them, no way to be at peace.

They'd lain awake talking for hours. The pros, the cons, the risks. Treva had listened and agreed, but part of her had not agreed. The talking had settled nothing. She twisted restlessly, putting her finger on her husband's upper lip, hoping the pressure would cause him to turn over and stop snoring.

"Cupcake," he muttered, turning several inches to the left, and uttering a series of slightly less loud snorts. "Love . . ."

Treva sighed, turned over, and snuggled her hip into the angle formed by Wade's bent knees. In the past ten years, Wade had always been there for her, always emotionally available; she'd been the luckiest woman in Ann Arbor.

Almost the luckiest.

She stared, dry-eyed, into the darkness, listening to the lonely wind.

The phone rang and Treva picked it up before it would wake Wade.

"Girl, it's Rhonda. I'm thinkin' about you."

"I'm fine," whispered Treva, hoping her husband would not stir.

"Just know that God doesn't give us anything we can't handle," said her sister.

"I'll handle it. But God better step back."

"What does that mean?"

"I don't know," admitted Treva, rubbing her burning eyes.

"Well, I love you, hon. You sure you don't want me to be there with you and Wade tomorrow?"

"No, Rhonda, he wants to take me. Probably to make sure I get there," said Treva bitterly.

After she hung up, she lay in bed again, staring into the darkness and listening to the sound of the wind, imagining it full of spirits and souls, restless hearts that could not find peace.

ANNIE

SUNRISE HAD PILLOWED THE SKY IN PUFFS OF PINK, salmon, and fuchsia, but the colors were beginning to fade as Annie Larocca drove her Dodge Shadow into the women's clinic lot and parked in her usual spot. A wide-bottomed, insulated mug sat on her dashboard, still emitting delicious coffee odors despite her twenty-minute ride from home.

As usual, Annie was the first one to arrive this morning. Glancing around the parking lot, she saw with satisfaction that no "sidewalk counselors" or demonstrators had arrived yet. Which was a good thing, since Annie'd forgotten to wear her Kevlar vest again. Annie's husband, Carl, nagged at her about wearing it, when he wasn't nagging her about quitting her job altogether.

"The place gets death threats, for God's sake, Annie," he'd say. "That Dr. Rosenkrantz, how many threats has she got on her answering machine now? Five? Ten?"

"A few," Annie'd admitted. "Just regular death threats, though—you know, 'die, you nasty abortion doctor.' Nothing *really* hairy."

It was like battlefield humor; she had to joke about it or

she'd go freaky. Over one fourth of the abortion clinics in the country had received death threats, including theirs. At some clinics the death threats had been carried out, with staff members murdered. And now there were those horrible sites on the Internet listing the names of abortion doctors—

Still, Annie made it to work every day. In 1958 Annie's older sister, Linda, had aborted herself with a coat hanger carefully bent into a loop and thrust up into her uterus. She'd died of a perforated uterus and raging infection, a tragedy that still caught up with Annie sometimes, causing tears to spring to her eyes. People today had forgotten. They no longer remembered the tragedies, the thousands of women who had died like Linda. And who would die that way again if abortion was outlawed.

Annie got out of her car, locking the door and starting toward the clinic. Today would be an especially rough day because Treva Connor was on the list of procedure patients. Everyone would be more tense than usual.

"Hey, Annie," said Bill, one of the security guards, hurrying from around the side of the building where he had been doing a perimeter walk. The bandages were off his hand now. "You're some early bird. Always here before anyone."

"I like morning."

"Me, I can't get going until I have at least three cups of coffee," said Bill, punching her in on the security keypad.

"Me, I have about a dozen by the end of the day," admitted Annie. "I've been trying to cut back, but it gives me the jibby jabbers."

Annie walked inside, flicking on the row of light switches, breathing in the smells of new carpeting, disinfectant, air freshener, yesterday's coffee. And yes, the faint odor of fear and anxiety.

The first thing she did was head for the coffee room. In a few minutes Dr. Rosenkrantz would arrive, followed by Dr. Tallchief, who worked two days a week, trailed by the others, and she wanted to have several pots of coffee going by then.

Annie took packets of coffee out of a storage drawer, slitting them open with a pair of scissors and releasing their deep-roasted aroma. Dropping coffee into two pots, one regular, the other decaf, and then adding water to both, she began thinking about Treva Connor.

She was worried about her friend.

Annie had been startled two days ago when she'd seen Treva Connor's name on the list of appointments. As supportive as Treva was of pro-choice, as much work as she'd done for the clinic, Annie happened to know that the woman badly wanted a baby. If it hadn't been for the hypertension, Annie knew that there would be at least two little Connors crawling around the Connors' living room rug right now.

Now an abortion . . . Poor Treva. Women having therapeutic abortions went through a whole different kind of hell than women having regular abortions, Annie knew. The guilt—It was like losing a full-term child.

When both coffeemakers were dripping coffee, Annie let herself behind the long Formica counter and found the appointment book, opening the wide, double pages to today's date. Yes, there was Treva's name, along with others whose names she didn't recognize.

Then she moved along the row, turning on computer terminals, bringing five screens to humming, green life. Minutes from now, clerks would be sitting at those screens, the phones would start ringing, the counselors would begin fielding calls.

Treva, Treva, Annie thought.

And all the other women who were scheduled for today? Many must be leaving now for the clinic, or already on their way. What were they thinking, feeling? But at least they were going to be safe, Annie told herself strongly. Abortions were very safe nowadays, safer than childbirth, and their clinic's safety record was one of the best in the country.

DIEDRE

PAM WAS LATE. GROGGY FROM THE LONG, RESTLESS night, which had been capped by an hour and a half of strangely deep sleep, Diedre Samms glanced at her watch, then paced to the window of her bedroom, which faced the apartment parking lot. Damn . . . it was already past eight o'clock and her sister should have been outside in her old Toyota, beeping her horn, more than fifteen minutes ago.

Diedre paced back and forth, her pulse fluttering nervously at the hollow of her throat. Her stomach felt unbearably clenched. She knew Pam had to drive all the way from Ann Arbor. Had her sister overslept? Had there been a traffic tie-up on I-275? Would the clinic save her appointment time if Diedre arrived late, or would they just cancel her and tell her to come back next week?

Diedre didn't think she'd have the courage to go through this ordeal twice.

The phone rang and she snatched it up, thinking it was Pam.

Instead a strange female voice said, "This is Judith Matsumura from the U. of M. law school."

Diedre recoiled in surprise. She'd been so absorbed in her immediate problem that she'd forgotten that registration day was coming up fast.

"I'm just calling to confirm that you'll be enrolling in class in two weeks. We're mailing you some papers to fill out regarding your scholarship, and we need you to get them back to us as soon as possible, preferably before you register."

Register. Diedre had already received the printed list of the first-year courses—along with dates, times, professors, sections—and she'd studied it avidly. But this morning registration seemed about three thousand miles away, something distant that she could barely picture in her mind.

"I'll get them back," she heard herself promise.

The woman went on, listing a few other requirements, including the expectation that Diedre would meet several times, on an informal basis, with Rodger Halsick, a partner of the Detroit law firm that had awarded her the scholarship. Halsick, she said, was involved in a pro bono student group on campus that did unpaid legal work for indigent women.

"Of course I'll meet with him. I'm so grateful for everything," Diedre breathed, recovering some of her equilibrium.

Judith Matsumura terminated the call, and Diedre lowered the phone onto the cradle, her stomach again curdling. Where *was* Pam, dammit? She wanted to go to the clinic and get this over with, get on with her life.

"Honey?" called her mother from the hallway.

Diedre opened her bedroom door.

"Morning, Mom."

"Baby—my DeeDee," said Cynthia, using Diedre's baby name. Her mother was dressed for her job at the engineering firm, wearing a navy cotton jacket, navy and red scarf, and beige, cuffed trousers, her blond hair pulled back neatly. Cynthia Samms looked fresh, neat, and competent—the exact opposite of the way Diedre felt at that moment.

"Will you be all right?" her mother wanted to know.

"I'll be fine."

"I take it you've decided . . . to go ahead with it."

"Yes. Mom, I—"

A blast on a car horn interrupted her, and with relief Diedre pulled away. "Hey, there's Pam, Mom—gotta go."

She rushed back into the bedroom and grabbed the little packet of things they'd told her to bring, the sanitary pads, the urine sample, and stuffed it into one side of her canvas tote. Then she rushed back and hugged Cynthia, trying not to cry.

"I haven't disappointed you?"

"Never, as long as you're sure you're making the right

decision. Diedre—call me as soon as it's over and let me know you're all right."

A quick, emotional hug and then Diedre was running down the stairs to the main door of the building.

"Sorry," said Pam as Diedre ran across the parking lot and threw herself into the front seat of Pam's six-year-old, run-down Toyota, which lacked two hubcaps. "The damn alarm clock stopped—we must have had one of those little power outages."

"Of all mornings."

"Hey, we're not that late." Diedre's sister was ten pounds heavier than Diedre, but had the same snub nose and wide blue eyes. However, Pam had colored her hair ash blond, and wore it big and curly.

Pam went on, "And they're still going to take your money . . . our money . . . if you're a couple of minutes late. Trust me on that."

Diedre leaned back in the passenger seat, too dispirited to think of anything to say back. Pam had loaned her the money for the procedure, and Diedre had promised to repay her after graduation.

Her hand unconsciously drifted to her stomach, and she splayed her fingers over her abdomen, down where she thought her uterus was. She wished it were all over with. She might not have disappointed her mother, but she had deeply disappointed herself.

PEPPER

PEPPER NOLAN WOKE THAT MORNING WITH A CHOKED scream. She'd been dreaming that her boutique had caught on fire, and she was racing to save the expensive lingerie. Desperately she rushed among the racks and shelves, snatching up the beautiful things, trying to pile all of them in her arms at once. But she was holding too much; chemises and bras kept falling out of her arms. Then she saw Oscar, his white tail flying like a banner as he walked directly toward the flames.

"Oscar! Oskie!" Her screams gave way as consciousness slowly returned.

Blinking open her eyes, Pepper saw the familiar lace curtains on her window, the ivory-colored antique throw she'd splurged on two years ago, a novel by Anne Rivers Siddons that Jan had loaned her. There was a heavy, warm weight on her thigh—Oscar, still asleep. Maybe his feline body heat had triggered her odd, scary dream.

She moved, and the cat sprang lightly down from the bed. Then he returned to rub himself back and forth against her hand, brushing his silky fur against her. Pepper buried her fingers in his softness, trying to forget the ugly dream. If anything ever happened to Oscar, she'd be devastated.

"You cats have such a darn easy life," she whispered, getting out of bed. "Hungry, Oskie? At least you get to eat this morning. Me, I don't think I could even if I wanted to, which I don't. Ugh. I'm *definitely, seriously* queasy."

Pepper walked to her small closet, bulging with thrift-shop finds and a few designer splurges, and tried to decide what to wear. They'd told her she had to wear a two-piece outfit, since she'd only strip from the waist down.

Finally she spotted some blue cotton leggings and a faded Celine Dion T-shirt she had bought at a concert and worn to run in about a hundred times. Comfort clothes. She selected a pair of Nikes and some clean, white socks, laying them all on the bed.

Oops, the urine sample. Her cramped, rectangular bathroom had once been a closet, Pepper felt sure. She had papered it in a lush, lavender bargello pattern, and had put in an antique mirror, which didn't change the size but made it more bearable. She went through the messy ritual of peeing into a small plastic jar. Then she turned on the shower. But instead of stepping under the spraying water, Pepper walked closer to the mirror.

She narrowed her eyes at her naked reflection, wondering what she'd look like if that flat stomach was swollen out like a fleshy, bulbous watermelon. Putting both hands on her stomach, she thrust it forward. Hmmmn. Would she carry high or low? Probably high, she decided, taking a guess.

Well, she wasn't going to find out for real, was she?

A wave of sorrow ran over her, catching Pepper off guard.

She showered, then dug a comb into her tangled, black hair until it was reasonably well tamed. She scrubbed her face, rinsed the morning-after wine taste out of her mouth. The queasiness became active nausea, and she fought to keep it back. This time she didn't win.

Finally, pale-faced, she dressed and put out food and water for her cat, then walked back into the living area, feeling suddenly restless, at loose ends. There was no point in putting on makeup. She hadn't phoned her mother in Florida or any of her other friends; she couldn't eat breakfast, of course. All she had to do now was wait for Jan.

Restlessly Pepper flipped through a fashion magazine, trying to concentrate on an article about Julia Ormond. Then just as she'd begun to feel another small surge of nausea, the doorbell rang.

Relieved, Pepper ran out of the apartment. Fortunately Mrs. Melnick's door was closed, a morning TV news show emanating from underneath her door.

Jan was standing on the porch, wearing jeans and an embroidered denim shirt, holding a small gift bag from one of the shops on West University. "I brought you something."

Pepper thrust her hand into the sack. Her fingers met something soft and furry. "Whaaat?"

"I thought you might need these to keep your feet warm. For today, you know. They say your feet get terribly cold."

Pepper pulled out the contents of the gift sack, stunned to see a pair of sock-slippers, made of some silky polyester fiber that almost exactly resembled Oscar's long, white fur. Each fuzzy slipper had two cat ears and two green-glass eyes. Where had Jan ever found them? They were perfect.

"These look just like Oscar," said Pepper numbly. She brought one of the slippers to her face. The soft fur tickled her cheeks and lips. She felt absurdly touched; she fought sudden, weak tears. "Oh, Jan."

"I just wanted you to have something to take with you," declared Jan. "The little gift shop on campus—they had doggy slippers, too, but I thought you'd like the Oscar slippers the best."

"Oh, I do. They're so—" Holding the absurd, furry slippers, Pepper felt totally undone.

"Honey?" said Jan.

Pepper tried to hold back the tears, but they kept on burning her lids, sliding past, spilling fast down her cheeks, dampening her T-shirt. Fiercely she brushed them away. She'd chosen this, she told herself. Crying wasn't going to help now—it would only make her feel worse.

TREVA

A FLOCK OF CANADIAN GEESE WAS TRYING TO CROSS HUron Parkway, the big birds waddling across four lanes as if they owned them, probably headed toward several manmade lakes in a nearby condo development.

"Little buggers," said Wade, who disliked the green droppings the birds left. The numbers of Canadian geese were multiplying all over Michigan, drawn to anywhere that had water or even a small pond, and some city fathers were trying to figure out how to make the birds fly elsewhere.

Wade slowed the car for the parade of birds, as he and Treva tried to make normal conversation in the face of what had to be the worst day of Treva's life.

"Shanae called yesterday," said Wade.

"Oh?" Shanae was Wade's pretty fifteen-year-old daughter by his first marriage, who lived with her mother, Wanda, north of town in nearby Brighton, attending high school there.

"Yeah . . . she wants a guitar for her birthday," said Wade glumly. "And lessons, singing lessons, too. I put her off, Trev. Singing lessons? For a beautiful black girl? It's like a license to join the rock 'n' roll life and get totally fucked up."

Treva nodded. Shanae's latest "thing" was wanting to be a rock star, and she had already started dressing the part. Her punky "lock" hairstyle and trashy, form-fitting clothes were a constant source of worry to Wade.

"If anyone hurts that girl, I'll . . . rend them limb from limb," he growled now. "I'll tear their gonads off. And I told her that. Was I being a little too strong?"

"Not unless you think Drano is a soft drink," said Treva dryly, coming out of her shell a little.

"Well, she's driving me crazy. I always thought I'd have a sensible kid."

"She will be sensible—when she's forty."

"But can I wait that long?" Wade groaned.

As they drove into the clinic parking lot, Treva could feel her head begin to pound. *Oh, dearest Lord . . .* Cars and vans filled the lot, and Bobbie Lynn was there, lugging around a poster depicting an aborted fetus being cradled in a physician's rubber glove, which looked huge compared to the diminutive size of the baby. Treva, who had seen the emotionally affecting poster many times before, swiftly averted her eyes. *Please,* she thought. *Don't let Bobbie bother us today.*

"You okay?" asked Wade anxiously.

Treva forced a sad smile.

Wade took her arm, escorting her to the clinic door, where the security guard buzzed them in. They walked inside, meeting the cool chill of air conditioning. Wade hesitated at the sight of the waiting room, already packed with women and their husbands, lovers, mothers, girlfriends. A few of the patients were crying; others looked dazed or grim-faced. A large-screen TV set blasted out a news segment on another disaster movie that would be in theaters soon.

"Babe," announced Wade, eyeing the crowd and holding on to Treva's arm. "I'm going to be right there with you as long as they'll let me. If they don't have any chairs, I'll stand."

Treva knew clinic rules permitted him only in the waiting room. "Waiting room's as far as you get, honey. The place gets so packed in there, none of the relatives can go back. Everyone knows me and I'll be just fine."

"What about recovery? Ask them," urged Wade. "Ask if I can be with you in recovery."

"I wish you could, baby, but they barely have room enough for patients."

A girl got up, summoned by a nurse, and Treva took her chair, Wade taking the vacant seat next to hers, his hand automatically reaching for Treva's. Their fingers naturally linked, finding the most comfortable position, the rings they had given each other on "ring night" bumping together.

"I love you," whispered Wade, leaning close. "Never more than today, Treva."

DIEDRE

THEY STARTED DOWN I-75 TOWARD I-94, PAM NERVOUSLY chattering, giving Diedre a running monologue about her boyfriend, Bud, and a knee injury he'd suffered the previous week in a volleyball game, and her own problems with her boss, Dean Moss, at the university, where Pam worked as an administrative assistant.

"So he goes, I want you to work until eleven on that presentation. The *geek*. He knew all day he had those overheads coming up, and he doesn't even bother to give me the work until four. I don't know how somebody so dumb can make it so high up . . ."

Scenery flashed by, lots of Dearborn exits, then Garden City, Westland, the big, ugly, fifty-foot Uniroyal tire sign, Detroit Metro Airport. A 747 was making a landing just as they drove by, a silvery metallic shape caught in the morning sun glare. Dully Diedre watched it aim down toward a distant runway. She had never flown on a plane. If she had a baby in seven and a half months, it would probably be years before she ever did.

Finally they were in Ann Arbor, a university town dominated by the huge University of Michigan, the majority of the population under thirty.

"Fifteen minutes," announced Pam. "Then we'll be there."

Diedre felt her body tightening up.

It's not too late, she thought feverishly. She could still cancel this. Just tell Pam to turn around and drive back to Madison Heights. They'd go to a Denny's they'd passed on the way, have breakfast, try to figure out how she was going to manage a killer study schedule and a pregnancy.

I'll have to give birth, then get up and go to class in two days so I don't miss anything. Learn to study with a baby in one arm and a book in the other. Get by on three hours of sleep a night. Yeah, or drop out of law school.

As they drove into town, Diedre shut out Pam's chatter and concentrated on her own fear. Others had done it, she knew—had babies and gone to college. She'd seen tired young mothers all over Wayne State. But that was mostly undergrad school, and those women could afford to get Cs. They didn't have a twenty-eight-thousand-dollar-a-year scholarship to hold on to . . . and Diedre was under no illusions about her scholarship. If she didn't maintain a B-plus average, *minimum,* then she was out. The law firm had made that very clear to her in their acceptance letter.

"Diedre?" asked Pam impatiently. The chattering monologue had suddenly stopped, and so had the Toyota. "Well? Are we going in? We've been sitting here for five minutes with the motor running."

Diedre shook her head, feeling dazed. Looking around at

the packed parking lot, she saw that they were already at the Geddes/Washtenaw clinic. Somehow time had passed, like a tape fast-forwarding. God, she'd been so upset, so self-concentrating, that her mind had blanked out whole minutes.

Pam cleared her throat, her blue eyes anxious. "This is it, Deeds. You still want to, you know . . . do it?"

Diedre tried to speak, but no sound would issue from her lips. Law school . . . or this baby. To her the choice seemed either/or. But why should she spoil her life just because of a pinhole in a condom that Mitch had been carrying in his wallet for too long?

"Deeds? Say something."

"We—we'll go in," she decided painfully.

PEPPER

I T WAS WAITING-ROOM HELL. CROWDED, NOISY WITH THE sound of the TV, and full of the odors emitted by upset, scared women.

"You okay?" asked Jan, who had brought a quilt square to appliqué while she waited. The pattern was symmetrical, entwined rosebuds with curved green leaves.

"I've been better," admitted Pepper, holding the shopping bag with the furry Oscar slippers in it, slipping her fingers inside to feel the silky fur. Maybe she was crazy, but she would have been happier if Oscar himself could have accompanied her.

"I guess that wine last night wasn't such a hot idea."

"Food hasn't been a very hot idea, not for the past couple of weeks. Oh, Jan . . ."

"Hang on," said Jan, touching Pepper's hand.

Pepper noticed the middle-aged black couple sitting with their hands tightly locked together. The woman looked vaguely familiar; was she a customer at the shop? The big man was whispering to the woman, comforting her. Pepper felt a twinge of envy. His loving concern radiated toward his partner, spilling over to fill up the rest of the room, too.

Would any man ever hold her hand like that? Be so *there* for her?

Oh, God. Please let them call my name, Pepper thought. *Let this be over with soon.*

A freckled woman wearing green surgical scrubs finally came to the door of the waiting room, carrying a clipboard. She read off a list of first names. "Keisha . . . Diedre . . . Treva . . . Amber . . . Donna . . . Pepper . . ."

When she heard her name, Pepper jumped, her movement so awkward that her purse fell off her lap to the floor. She fumbled for it, scooping it up and picking up her tote bag. Her hands were terribly cold, her fingers as icy as if she'd been making snowballs with her bare hands.

"Go for it," whispered Jan, hugging her. "Good luck, Pep. Don't forget to wear those fuzzy slippers."

She followed the others into a big reception area.

The interior office section was big and a bit intimidating, with its row of women sitting behind a counter at computers and phones. Soft rock music emanated from a stereo system—and also, it appeared, from a few of the exam rooms. Pepper heard a familiar vacuum-cleaner sound that caused her stomach to clench.

"I'm Annie, I'm a PA," said the red-haired woman who looked soft, freckled, and friendly. "That's short for physician's assistant. I know you're all a bit anxious, so we've scheduled a short group session for all of you to explain the procedure. It'll be in Room Seven, down the hall and the second door on your right."

The room was papered in a cheerful stripe pattern and had a long, Formica conference table in the center. The window was filled with wavy glass bricks, letting in the light but no view. Posters on the wall showed the intricacies of the female reproductive system—ovaries, uterus, fallopian tubes, vagina. Pepper averted her eyes. She didn't want to think about her insides right now. She just wanted to think about getting through this.

The women all took seats, and Pepper couldn't help looking around at the others. There was a frightened-looking girl about sixteen, and another girl in her early twenties, blond, pretty. The oldest was the black woman, who appeared to be about forty. She *was* one of Pepper's boutique customers, Pepper realized, looking at her more closely. Their eyes briefly met, then Pepper politely looked away.

Annie, the PA, walked to the head of the table and smiled at them. With her freckles and snubby nose, she looked as friendly as a Welcome Wagon hostess. "This procedure you're having today is a *lot* safer than having a baby, and this clinic has a terrific safety record, so that's one worry you can put right out of your heads—if you follow instructions, of course."

There was a slight nervous murmur.

"I'm going to fill you in on the procedure today. Afterwards I'll answer any of your questions."

Procedure, Annie had said. Not abortion. That was to make it seem less terrifying.

She began talking about IV lines, the sedative they would be given, a combination of Valium and Sublimaze. There'd be blood drawing, a pelvic exam, and a gonorrhea and Pap smear culture. They were all given consent forms to sign. Then Annie reached into a drawer and began pulling out instruments.

"This—you may have encountered it before—is a speculum. It might feel a little chilly when the doctor inserts it, but it doesn't hurt."

There were dilators, tapered chrome rods about nine inches long, the smallest about the circumference of a drinking straw. A plierlike instrument called the tenaculum. And the cannula, which looked like a clear plastic tube.

Pepper stared at these instruments, unable to imagine them penetrating her body.

"When you leave here you can expect to have some bleeding, which might last from a couple of days to about two weeks. That's why we told you to bring the sanitary napkins. We're going to prescribe an antibiotic for you— seven days worth, and we want you to take the entire prescription even if you feel well. You aren't to put anything into your vagina for two weeks. No tampons, no fingers, no douches, no penises.''

At the word *penis,* a ripple of nervous laughter circled the room. The sixteen-year-old laughed the hardest, and almost couldn't stop. She clapped both hands over her mouth, like a child giggling in school, and finally managed to subside.

There was more—a listing of possible complications, a discussion of various birth control methods, their pros and cons.

''We don't recommend the sponge,'' said Annie, smiling. ''It only comes in one size, and women's vaginas aren't made in one-size-fits-all. We see a lot of sponge patients here,'' she added. ''Not to mention pill patients and condom patients. Oh, yes, and rhythm patients.''

Pepper was a vasectomy patient; Annie hadn't mentioned that. Her mind started drifting. Was the abortion going to hurt as much as it did last time? No, it was called a procedure. God, she was scared. She could smell her own hot, acrid body sweat.

TREVA

TREVA CONNOR LISTENED CAREFULLY TO THE RECITAL OF what was going to happen to her. Annie had told her she didn't have to put herself through the orientation since she already worked at the clinic, but Treva had wanted to attend the group session.

She wanted to get a full, realistic look at what she was going to do. She wanted to face it unblinkingly, the reality

of the abortion. And she would not use the clinic's euphe-
misms of "procedure," "termination," or any other such
cowardly words.

She forced her eyes to linger on the ugly instruments that
would suck out life. *Baby,* she said to the tiny scrap of
humanity that was floating in amniotic fluid deep within her,
next to its yolk sac. *I am with you and I will stay with you
as long as I can.* For some reason her mind conjured up a
few verses from Eric Clapton's song "Tears in Heaven."
She wondered if the soul of her baby would be there in
heaven to greet her when she herself died. Several years
back, when her BP had skyrocketed while she and Wade
were on a trip to Jamaica, Treva had faced the reality that
she probably would not live to be eighty. In fact, even living
to sixty might be a stretch.

She had high blood pressure, she was already forty-one.
What had she done with her life so far? What had she given
to the world?

"Treva," someone was saying. "Treva."

Treva glanced up, stunned to realize that the session was
over and the other women had already filed out of the room.
She and Annie were the only ones left.

"Oh, Treva," said Annie, her freckled face wrinkling
with sympathy. "I know how bad this is for you. I just feel
for you so much. When I saw your name on that appointment list—"

"I'll get through it," declared Treva.

"Would you like me to stay with you? I can get Mei to
cover for me—"

Treva shook her head. "I just want to be alone with my
baby for a minute."

Annie squeezed Treva's hand. "We all love you, Treva.
We're here for you a hundred percent."

Annie left the room, closing the door gently behind her.
Treva leaned forward, bending at the waist until her forehead was resting on the conference tabletop. The brown Formica felt cool on her fevered skin. She brought her hands
around in front of her and clasped them.

Softly she began to pray. Prayers from her childhood in Detroit when they'd attended Mt. Sinai Baptist Church and seventeen-year-old Treva Jones had set the gospel choir aglow with her impassioned, fiery voice.

PEPPER

THE EXAM ROOM WAS AIR-CONDITIONED, ALMOST TOO cool, fitted with an examination table, the standard chairs and cabinets, and a tall, white box with a steel top from which protruded a long, plastic hose. Pepper had seen such a box before, back when she was a terrified teenager, and now she tried to push away the unwelcome memories.

You're thirty-one, you're not a kid anymore. It's going to be different this time. You're in control.

"We'll need you to undress from the waist down and cover yourself with this sheet," said the nurse who had escorted her in, a thin young woman wearing white pants and a turquoise lab coat.

Pepper waited until the woman had left the room, then pulled off her loose leggings and the pair of expensive, cinnamon-colored bikini panties she had chosen to wear. She wrapped herself in the sheet, remembering to pull on the furry Oscar slippers. Immediately the slippers began to warm her feet, calming her fast heartbeat a little.

This was only going to take six or eight minutes, she knew from past experience. She'd stood it once. Surely she could endure it one more time.

She lay gazing upward at the clean, white, perforated tiles of the ceiling, wishing she hadn't slept with Jack. She almost wished he were here with her, though. Holding her hand. Murmuring his silly jokes into her ear. If anyone could ease the next eight minutes, it would be Jack, and that was such a horrid irony.

Tears filled Pepper's eyes for all the lost things in her life, the love that had never come to fruition. Ah, Jack . . . Why had she always selected crazy men like him?

DIEDRE

DIEDRE LAY TENSELY, THE IV NEEDLE AND PLASTIC TUBE taped to the back of her left hand. Her feet were thrust into stirrups which were covered with terry cloth mitts, presumably to keep her feet warm. She needed them. Her extremities felt like blocks of ice; it could have been February instead of a sunny morning in late August. Why? she thought. Why had she gotten in the backseat of that car? She had behaved crazily; she had allowed herself to become intoxicated by wine and a summer night and a cute guy. Now she was paying the price.

A doctor strode into the room, in her early seventies, tiny and white-haired, crackling with energy. A blond nurse followed her.

"I'm Dr. Ellen Rosenkrantz," the doctor introduced herself, smiling. "And you must be Diedre."

"Yes."

"Everything is all right, Diedre? You still want to be here?"

"Yes."

"What sort of music do you like?"

Diedre jerked her head, startled.

"We have a nice CD collection and it's always good to concentrate on music for about six to eight minutes. Let's see . . . a little Michael Bolton for you, hmmmm?"

Diedre couldn't help smiling at the idea of Michael Bolton accompanying her through this. She bet he'd die if he knew he was being used in an abortion clinic as a sedative. "He'll be just fine."

Dr. Rosenkrantz put on plastic gloves, sending a talcumy whiff into the air, and examined Diedre internally, making kind little jokes about the coldness of the speculum. "Just relax and let your legs fall apart," she instructed. "Yes . . . wider . . . You're doing fine, Diedre. Excellently."

Diedre had had only one vaginal exam before in her life, and she'd hated it. However, she did as she was asked. She felt the metallic chill of the speculum as it penetrated her. *Oh, God,* she said to herself. *Oh, God.* Dr. Rosenkrantz stuck a syringe in the IV line and about ten seconds later Diedre felt a rush of light-headedness, a kind of ringing, singing in her brain.

Michael Bolton's rich, ripe, sexy voice filled the exam room.

"Now you're going to feel a little bit of a pinch," Dr. Rosenkrantz said. "Just a couple of pinches. We're injecting the local anesthetic into your cervix."

Diedre gasped as the needle entered this most tender spot.

"Now she's putting in the dilators, Diedre," said the nurse-assistant. "You should feel some cramping now as your uterus contracts."

The cramping progressed from mild, period-like pains to twisting, grinding cramps that felt like what she imagined childbirth to be.

"Oh—" Diedre gasped. She gripped the side of the table, her clammy fingers slipping on the metal surface. She struggled not to cry. Oh, she would never have this done again ever.

"Almost finished, you're doing very, very well," someone said. "You're a real trouper."

Diedre was breathing heavily through her mouth, her entire body clenched. Where was the sedative? Why wasn't it working? Why couldn't they have knocked her out, given her something stronger?

"Relax, relax, please," said Dr. Rosenkrantz. "You're

doing excellently, Diedre. Listen to the music. They say music soothes the savage beast. Do you think they ever played CDs for King Kong?''

She was inserting something into her—the cannula. A cramp clawed Diedre's stomach. Out of the corner of her eye she saw the nurse attaching the hose of the aspiration machine to the tubelike cannula. Dr. Rosenkrantz stepped on the foot pedal.

A roaring sound filled the room, like the sound of a vacuum cleaner, but Diedre didn't have time to think about it, for it felt as if all of her insides were being sucked out. King-sized cramps ripped at her. She uttered a choked scream. *''Oh,*'' she wept. *''Oh, my God.''*

"Hold my hand," said the nurse. "Squeeze. Just squeeze my fingers, Diedre. You won't hurt me."

Diedre squeezed, grateful for this human contact. The suctioning roar stopped. The tube was being pulled out of her. It was over.

"You did super," said the nurse. "How do you feel, a little weak? The cramps should be gone in a couple of minutes. You'll rest for a while and then you'll go into recovery."

Diedre sagged against the tabletop, falling into it, all the energy seeping from her as if suctioned out along with the tissue she had been carrying. The fetus was gone, she realized for the first time. A few bits of cells. She started to smile and the smile became a laugh, which became half laughs, half sobs, rippling out of the center of her. She laughed and laughed and couldn't stop. It was awful, laughing like that.

The relief. It was so incredible.

TREVA

Exam Room 4 seemed to spin around Treva, hard white light speckled with black dots. Was she going to faint? Oh, no, she couldn't. She had to think. She realized that she hadn't yet lain down on the exam table, but was still sitting in a crouched position, arms wrapped around her knees as if she could protect her fetus for just a few minutes longer.

"Treva, how are you holding up?" asked Annie, in a worried tone, tucking a clean examination sheet around Treva's shoulders. "Here, this will warm you a little."

"I'm . . . fine," whispered Treva.

"Are you sure?"

"I don't know anymore, Annie."

A few minutes passed, or maybe it was hours; the passage of time had become distorted for Treva. The air conditioning had chilled her to the bone, although Annie seemed comfortable enough. Treva tried to fight the shivering.

"Maybe you should lie down," suggested Annie, touching Treva's hand. "Doctor Rosenkrantz has finished her other procedure and is scrubbing. I'll start your IV right away with the sedative—that should help."

"Please, I don't want a sedative."

"But it would really smooth things out for you."

"I don't want to be smoothed over! I want to feel!" Treva sat forward, the sheet dropping from her body. Her voice rose. "I want to feel what's happening to my baby!"

"Treva." Annie looked upset. The door had opened, bringing in a drift of Michael Bolton, and Dr. Ellen Rosenkrantz entered the room, crisp-looking in her green surgical coat.

"Treva?" she said, observing Treva's agitation. "Is there a problem?"

"Yeah." Treva slid down from the table and hurried over to the chair where she'd placed her jeans and undergarments. She snatched up her panties and began throwing them on, getting them on wrong side out but not stopping. Then the jeans. She was panting.

"Treva? Are you okay?" Both Annie and Dr. Rosenkrantz were asking it now.

"Home," blurted Treva. "I'm going home."

Annie and the doctor looked at each other.

"Then it's the right decision," said the tiny doctor, her voice gentle. "For you. So go with it, Treva. You won't be sorry." It was what they always said when a woman changed her mind—they never tried to persuade—but now the words touched Treva unbearably, and she had to force back a sob.

"Thank you—Ellen—Annie—"

"Go with God, dear," said Dr. Rosenkrantz. "There is always a purpose."

Treva finished dressing and fled down the busy corridor, emerging in the waiting room, her eyes finding Wade at once as he sat nervously in front of the TV set watching a commercial extolling Bathroom Duck. His eyes widened as he saw her.

"Let's go home," she said thickly.

Wade rushed over to her and put his arm around her, shepherding her out into the vestibule. They exited into the parking lot, where two demonstrators were walking up and down, the legal fifteen feet away, singing hymns. The whitish, humid sky had turned solid blue and the August heat burned down, at last warming Treva's skin.

"I told them no," Treva announced. "I said no."

"Are you all right?"

Now that she was out in the sunshine, Treva felt suddenly free, exhilarated and powerful, more in control of her destiny than she'd been in forty-one years. "Now I am."

Bobbie Lynn and a skinny man called Lou came charging

toward them, and Wade tightened his arm around Treva, shouting, "Get away! Get away!"

He helped Treva into the car, closed the passenger door, ran around to the driver's side, and got in, punching the electronic door locks. "Treva, Trev. It's okay. You're upset, it's understandable, this place can get to you. We can come back tomorrow morning. I'll call when we get home and reschedule the—"

"I am *not* rescheduling!" Her voice rang out. "I am not. I am going home and I'm going to have this baby, Wade. That decision is made."

He started the car, revving the engine too much in his agitation. "Treva, you shouldn't have a baby, we've known that for years. We've been over it and over it. *Any* baby, *any* time."

"The decision is made."

"No, it isn't!"

"It is, Wade," Treva said. "I will give birth."

"*I* have a share in this, too, in case you've forgotten! I'm your husband. I don't want to buy funeral flowers for you, Treva! I am not going to go to your goddamn funeral!"

Treva gazed at her husband's dark, angry face. They fought only rarely, usually only once or twice a year, about things like her not balancing the checkbook, or his habit of leaving stacks of newspapers and books all around.

"Everyone ends up having a funeral," she said softly. "Even me. Everyone in that clinic, everyone in Ann Arbor, everyone alive now, will eventually die."

"But not yet! Treva, what is wrong with you?" Wade's voice rose. "Haven't you got the picture? Weren't you listening? Dr. Haugh said you could have seizures, go into a coma. You could have a heart attack. You probably wouldn't carry the baby to term and it could die, too. *Why are you being such a stubborn ass?*"

"I'm a stubborn ass and proud of it!" she yelled.

They drove for ten minutes in tight, simmering silence.

"I'm sorry I said you were an ass," he said. "But I don't believe you want to die," Wade added tiredly. "I know you too well. You embrace life, you always have.''

Treva felt some of the exhilaration recede from her, like a wave returning to sea. ''Wade, what have I been put here on earth for? I haven't done much. Oh, I worked those years as a caseworker, I work at the clinic, I have friends, I have family, I have you and Shanae and Rhonda. But why? What has it all been for?''

''It's been to stay alive,'' Wade whispered. ''It's been to love, to be loved. Don't you tell me that dying for the sake of a fetus is going to make your life worthwhile. Don't you tell me that.''

''I'm not going to die for the sake of a fetus,'' Treva said calmly. ''I'm going to give it life. Life! There's a hell of a huge difference, Wade. I wish you could see it.''

DIEDRE

LYING IN THE RECOVERY ROOM, HER SPELL OF HYSTERI-cal laughter gone now, Diedre dozed for several hours. Her dreams were tangled, voices crying out, Mitch Sterling taking his hand and rubbing it in circles on her stomach. *Go away!* she cried to him in the dream. *You're nothing but a one-night stand.*

She awakened slowly, to find herself pulled up by voices and sounds. A radio was playing the new Sheryl Crow single. Two nurses were talking about *Miss Saigon,* which they'd seen at the Fox. One of them laughed, the sound wonderfully carefree.

''How are you feeling, honey?'' someone asked. ''A teeny bit groggy?''

Diedre fluttered open her eyes. The relief was still with her, as strong as a triple spritz of perfume, almost pouring out of her skin. She looked around. She was in a room filled with six or seven hospital gurneys, each one with a woman lying on it. The sixteen-year-old she'd seen in the conference room was lying curled up on her side, her dark hair tangled, looking like a baby herself.

Diedre said, "I'm fine. Can I sit up?"

"Let me take your BP and then we'll raise your head a little. If you don't feel any faintness, you can sit up and then you can try to urinate. If that works, if you're still okay, you can go home. Remember, you can shower, but no tub baths for a week. Don't drive a car. Nothing in the vagina for two weeks, no tampons, no douching, no soaking in the tub. No sexual contact."

"Okay." Sexual contact? There wasn't going to *be* any, Diedre thought. She wasn't going to date in law school; there wouldn't be time. This was never going to happen to her again.

The pressure cuff tightened on her left forearm, and Diedre lay flat, listening to the whooshing sounds it made, then the slow release.

"One twelve over seventy-five," announced the nurse. "Not too bad."

The Sheryl Crow song finished, and a bubbly-voiced female traffic reporter began chattering about a three-car pileup on Ford Road in Dearborn. A disc jockey bantered with her, then began offering Lyle Lovett tickets to the thirty-ninth caller.

The winning caller came on the air and squealed, "Oh, my *God*," when she heard she'd won.

All the while Diedre had been having her insides suctioned out, the real world, foolish and fine and energetic, had been continuing on as usual.

It's over. I won't think about it anymore, Diedre told herself. *I'm free now.*

Thirty minutes later she was back in the Toyota with Pam, heading for I-94 again. The old car's air conditioning barely worked, and heat seemed to throb in through the windshield, but Diedre barely cared. She just wanted to get back home. As soon as they got back to the apartment, she would phone her mother at work.

"Was it really awful?" asked Pam in a low voice.

Diedre nodded. "I wouldn't call it a picnic."

"I hope I never have to have one."

Diedre sighed. "You won't if you use about three kinds of birth control all at once—or forget guys altogether. That's going to be my birth control choice, abstinence."

"Oh, yeah, right."

"I mean it, Pam. I don't care who comes on to me, I don't even give a shit. I'm getting through law school and nothing is stopping me."

PEPPER

LUNCH?" SAID JAN SWITZER WHEN SHE AND PEPPER were finally driving out of the clinic parking lot, the deed done, Pepper still blinking with surprise that her nausea was gone—just like that.

"*Lunch?* Oh, I couldn't."

"But you haven't eaten in days, hon. Crackers don't count. And you barely touched those strawberries last night, I noticed."

"I know, but . . . it seems so . . . crass . . . to be eating lunch when I've just—"

"You aren't planning to starve yourself as a guilt thing?" asked Jan dryly. "Pepper, you made a careful, thoughtful decision, one you had a legal right to make. Now, don't punish yourself for it, please. You need to get some food in you; you're starting to waste away, you know. You've got hipbones like knobs."

"Knobs?"

"Well, I'm exaggerating only a little. Where to now? A restaurant? Home? The shop?"

"The shop," Pepper finally said. "I won't really work,

I'll just lie on the couch, but I want to be there for a while.
And then maybe later I'll order something from the deli.''

Lying on the back-room couch, which was liberally sprinkled
with Oscar's long, white hairs, Pepper drifted into a deep
sleep that took her to a place where she had no cares or
problems.

But she still woke up with tears wet on her cheeks.

She brushed them away, sat up, and reached for the phone
to order her favorite turkey club from a nearby deli, which
delivered. She'd get just half a sandwich. Oh, and some of
their potato salad with dill. Her appetite still hadn't come
back fully, but this would be the first real food she'd actually
wanted in days.

"Honey?" said Mrs. Melnick the next morning as Pepper
was leaving her apartment with Oscar, on her way to her
boutique. A long nap, some deli food, then a night of sleep,
and Pepper felt better. "Honey, you weren't coming down
with the flu, were you? The way you fainted that day . . .
but now you look fine.''

The landlady's eyes were sparkling with curiosity. It was
obvious she suspected. The old bag, Pepper thought. Just
itching for a tidbit of gossip.

"It's my new makeup," insisted Pepper, smiling and
making her escape.

And as the days slid past, she *became* fine. Her memories
of lying on the exam table, with that horrid, wrenching sucking sound of the machine in her ears, gradually faded. Her
mind wanted to forget, and soon the images became vague.
Pepper slipped into her regular work routine, absorbing herself in her usual problems, like late shipments, mistakes in
orders, customers who returned worn merchandise.

She was fine, she assured herself. And this month's profit
was 1.2 percent bigger than last, even in the city's slow
summer season when students still hadn't come back to
school.

After a harried Friday, Pepper felt a longing for some of Zev's famous chili.

Zev's Coffee Shop was one of Pepper's favorite workday routines. Now that she wasn't nauseous all the time, she started going back.

Today, as soon as Pepper walked in, the famous Zev's odor hit her—a rich mélange of freshly ground coffee mixed with jalapeños, cardamom, and the heavy chocolate of Zev's renowned Decadent Chocolate Cake. Pepper breathed in deeply, almost religiously, thinking that you could gain weight in Zev's Coffee Shop even before you ordered.

Although it was 10:00 P.M., the coffee shop was nearly full, groups of noisy U. of M. undergrads lounging at the closely packed tables, along with businesspeople who'd stopped in for a quick bite. Zev himself, a popular Ann Arbor character, was standing at the antique cash register, his big belly pushed up against the money tray.

Pepper went up to the window and gave her order to a young man in an apron with Zev's logo on it. Chili, Tex-Mex style, hot enough to make you sweat. Then she moved on down the line, adding a small salad and a double order of garlic rolls to her tray. She finished up with a cup of strong Kona coffee. She was starving. She hadn't eaten since breakfast, fifteen hours ago.

She carried her tray to a table near the window and began dipping up spoonfuls of the prizewinning spicy chili, which Zev frequently took to chilifests around the country. He had a whole wall behind the register hung with blue ribbons he'd won.

A tall, silver-haired man wearing a business suit filled his tray and sat down at a table partially facing Pepper's. Pepper gave him a cursory glance, then returned to her meal, beginning to plan her work schedule for tomorrow. She had a dozen phone calls to make to suppliers and she needed to reorder the glossy, lavender shopping bags with the blue Pepper's logo that were her trademark.

Suddenly a big group of students all got up to leave at once, noisily scuffling as they crowded past her table and the businessman's. Pepper felt a flash of movement to her left, and then something warm splashed all over her shoulder, arm, and front.

She looked down at her clothes and groaned aloud as she saw the big gobbets of tomato, shredded beef, onions, and jalapeño peppers all over her, grease already soaking into the silk blouse and tunic she wore. *Oh, shit.* These were clothes she wore in the shop—and they hadn't been cheap. Now she was covered with so much chili it looked like she'd been participating in a food fight.

"I'm sorry—those kids—someone must have elbowed me. That's my chili all over you." She looked up to see the silver-haired man, his face reddened with dismay. He looked almost as appalled as she felt. "Oh, sweet Lord, I've covered you. Are you burned?"

"I don't think so," she responded dryly. "Fortunately for my skin, that chili appeared to be fairly cool."

"Chili . . . all over you. I can't believe this happened. I'll pay your dry-cleaning bill . . . Oh, shit, will dry cleaning even fix this? I'll pay for new clothes."

He looked so penitent that Pepper quelled her anger. Anyway, it wasn't his fault; the kids had bumped his tray. "You're right about the dry cleaning; once chili and silk have made contact, I don't think silk is ever the same again. I'm going to accept that kind offer," she said.

"Good." He fished in his pocket, bringing out a sterling silver money clip, and peeled off three hundred-dollar bills. "Will this be enough?"

Pepper looked at the money. He'd managed to estimate within ten dollars the cost of her outfit.

"This will be more than fine."

"I'm really sorry. Believe me, it was totally an accident. I don't usually drop chili all over a woman in an attempt to meet her—although I admit it was a desirable side effect. Maybe I could buy you a drink or something to make up for the inconvenience."

Pepper looked down at her ruined outfit. "Not in these clothes. I'd probably be trailing droplets of chili. The only thing I want to do right now is run home and change my clothes and take a long, hot shower that doesn't smell of jalapeños."

"How about doing that, and then meeting me afterwards? Name me a place close to your home and we'll have a fast drink. Oh, by the way," he added, extending his hand. "I'm Gray Ortini."

"Pepper Nolan," she said, wondering where she'd heard his name before. "I'm sorry—I'm not sure about the drink. I think once I get home I'm probably just going to feel like crashing."

He continued to smile, but his disappointment was so obvious that Pepper found herself relenting. He *was* attractive, in his early fifties, with that gleaming, prematurely silver hair, blue eyes, and very young looking skin. "Well," she said, "if you really mean a fast drink, I could meet you at eleven." She named a nearby hotel bar. "For just a little while."

Before she could leave, however, Pepper was forced to go to the ladies' room, where she sponged away the worst of the chili mess with water and a paper towel. What remained was a greasy, red-orange stain. The garments definitely were going to have to be thrown out.

"You okay, honey?" said a young waitress, perky in a Zev's T-shirt, entering the room. "That's some mess."

"I think I've got the worst of it out."

"Well, at least the guy who spilled it on you is pretty sensational. I like that older, *Fortune* magazine type," said the woman, a pug-nosed blonde. "If you don't want him, give his phone number to me. I'd take it in a heartbeat."

"Whatever," said Pepper.

Pepper walked back to her shop, picked up Oscar, and drove back to her apartment, her whole car now reeking of Tex-Mex spices. Had Gray Ortini spilled the chili on her in an attempt to meet her? If he had, she wasn't sure she wanted to see him even for the few minutes it would take to order one drink. And yet he certainly had done the right thing, paying for her clothes without a moment of hesitation.

She didn't usually date older men . . .

Inside her apartment, she let Oscar out of his case and the white cat meowed and crisscrossed in front of her, obviously intrigued by the smell of chili that was still all over her.

"Smell good, Oskie? Do I smell like dinner?"

A begging meow.

"We're lucky we didn't run into that Akita you hate so much. He would have taken one sniff of me and I would have *been* his dinner, and you would have been dessert, Oscar Cat."

She shed her clothes, rolling them into a ball and tossing them directly into the kitchen wastebasket, then padded naked into the bathroom, where she turned on the shower and stepped inside the stall.

Turning under the spray of water, Pepper rummaged through her memory banks, wondering where she had heard of Gray Ortini before. Then it came to her. He owned an Ann Arbor software company called GrayCo that was beginning to make a national name for itself selling CD-ROMs, computer games, and other software. In fact, a few weeks ago the *Ann Arbor News* had called him "Michigan's answer to Bill Gates," as well as "Ann Arbor's most eligible bachelor," she remembered with a grimace.

"Eligible" bachelors weren't usually her thing, either.

She stepped out of the shower, ran a comb through her curly, black hair, then climbed into a pair of stovepipe black jeans. She finished off the outfit with an eggplant-colored silk blouse and a spill of 1950's-style silver pendants that she'd picked up at several antique shows, one slung on over the other.

The high-rise hotel on Main Street was crowded with physicians in town for a conference on childhood cancers, a big sign on a tripod welcoming them. The doctors congregated in the lobby and filled the bar, talking shop, but Gray had managed to secure them a booth in the bar.

He must have gone home and changed, too, because he was now wearing a pair of new, crisply pressed jeans. A blue chambray shirt was open at his throat, its color almost exactly matching his eyes.

"I really didn't think you'd show up," he told her, smiling. "I'm glad you did."

"I promised I would and I don't stand people up."

"Well, that's very nice to hear."

The bar was buzzing with activity, doctors and their wives bellying up to the bar, a woman laughing loudly, emitting a brassy, beery shriek.

As Gray spoke, Pepper began to notice more details about his appearance. His eyebrows and lashes were black, the lashes thick and curly. His nose was straight, patrician, his jawline nice and square. She had to admit he was sexy . . .

They talked for a while about Zev's, which they both had been frequenting for some time. Gray told her a couple of Zev stories she hadn't heard, and Pepper told him about the time she'd seen Aretha Franklin eating there with her entourage.

"I must admit I did think about speaking to you tonight, trying to pick you up," admitted Gray. "But then you looked so preoccupied I decided not to. I guess I'm lucky that kid bumped my elbow." He paused, wrinkling his forehead as if for comic effect. "He didn't tell you that I paid him to do it, did he?"

Pepper laughed. "So that's your secret of meeting women? Pouring chili all over them?"

"It worked, didn't it?"

"You didn't really—I mean *really* do it on purpose?"

His smile faded. "Of course I didn't. Only Steve Martin does stuff like that to meet women . . . Oh, by the way, you haven't told me yet that I look like him. Most people tell me that within fifteen or twenty seconds after meeting me; you have remarkable self-control."

She eyed him, cocking her head to one side. "Hmmmm. There is a superficial resemblance . . . You definitely have good hair. But I rather think you're much more distinguished looking.''

"Distinguished looking?'' Gray uttered a groan. "Oh, what a kiss-of-death word. Now, why couldn't you have told me I looked macho . . . hunky . . . compelling . . . charismatic . . .''

She giggled. "Now you do sound like him.''

They continued to talk, bantering easily.

"So what do you do?'' Gray finally asked. "How do you earn a living in this crazy town?''

"Guess,'' she responded lightly. "A hint—we're within a short stroll of my workplace.''

He pretended to look puzzled. "Well, you don't own this hotel, do you?''

"No . . .''

"Or work here?''

"No.''

"Then you must be a retailer, right?''

"Yes.'' Her eyes teased him. "Can you guess which shop?''

"Oh, that's a tough one. I'm not much of a shopper. Aren't most boutiques tax shelters anyway?''

"Tax shelters? Not mine!'' she cried, stung. "Mine is a legitimate business, in the black, I'll have you know.''

"Sorry.'' He smiled. "I guess I put my foot in it.''

"It's *Pepper's,* '' she cried. "The lingerie boutique. I'm turning a profit. That might not seem like much to you—''

"No, no, I admire your abilities,'' he protested. "Truly.''

His smile was dazzling, mollifying Pepper's irritation at his implying that her shop was a "tax shelter.'' She started asking him about GrayCo, the company he owned, and Pepper swiftly began to realize that its profits were tens of thousands higher than hers each month. Not that he pointed it out to her . . . she just began to realize it.

When Pepper glanced at her watch, she was startled to see that more than forty-five minutes had passed. "This has been great, but I've put in about an eighteen-hour day, and frankly, if I don't go home and crash, I'll pay for it tomorrow.''

Gray Ortini smiled. "The same for me. I'm in the office by six-thirty or seven and usually I'm still there by nine or nine-thirty at night. Which qualifies me as a certifiable workaholic; I hope you don't mind that.''

She smiled back, not to be outdone. "By those standards, I'm one, too. Thanks for the drinks, Gray—and I'll forgive you for being a klutz with the chili.''

"I'd like to see you again." He leaned forward, fixing his eyes on hers. "Pepper, you're a very beautiful young woman and I'd like to know you better.''

Until that moment, Pepper *had* been considering going out with him, but something about the way he'd said it— "you're a very beautiful young woman"—put her off somehow. Maybe it was because that phrase reminded her of an older, executive man coming on to a younger woman, the smarmy, clichéd things those types of men usually said.

"Well . . ." she began, rummaging through her mind for an excuse.

"Did I say something wrong, Pepper?"

"Of course not," she said, flushing.

"May I call you this week? I haven't had a woman's company in more than six months," Gray went on. "Not on a serious basis. Please believe me when I say that. Chili-dropping is not a regular ploy of mine.''

"All right," she agreed, pushing aside a strange feeling of reluctance. "We could have dinner, I guess—later in the week.''

"I'll call," he promised.

She handed him one of the business cards she'd had made up for Pepper's, sleek and understated on lavender stock, writing her home number underneath her business and fax numbers. He didn't comment on the appearance of the card, and for that she was grateful. If he'd called it "pretty," she would never have wanted to see him again.

TREVA

SHE'D SAID NO—AND MEANT IT. WADE AND TREVA
drove home from the women's clinic, into a humid August morning that threatened to reach ninety degrees by late
afternoon. However, inside the car, the air conditioning kept
the air a cool seventy-two degrees.

Treva stared out the car window, her emotions seesawing.
It felt so right, what she had done, refusing the abortion.
And yet—she could not get rid of the tiny drift of fear.
Dangerous. But she couldn't think about that now, and did
it really matter? She'd already made the decision and it felt
as final as anything she had ever done.

By the time they reached home, Wade was hoarse from
arguing, and Treva had become progressively more stubborn, her arms crossed over her chest. Finally they just
stopped talking; it seemed as if they were both on the verge
of saying too much, words they'd both regret.

Their house waited for them, gracious with the plantings
and flowers Treva had put in, impatiens and miniature rose-
bushes growing in tubs on a side deck, where she'd placed
a wrought-iron table and four matching chairs. On the other
side of the house was the rock garden she'd spent many
hours designing and tending, getting professional advice as
to what plants to use.

Wade pulled the car onto the broad driveway apron,
pressing the garage door opener. In silence they waited
while the double door rumbled up. A third, single door led
to their boat and trailer which they occasionally took up to
Elk Lake, in northern Michigan.

"I have to go back to campus, I have a curriculum meeting," Wade told her hoarsely. "I didn't think I was going
to make it, but now I can, so I'm going. Afterwards I might

stop at the racket club for a fast game. I need some physical activity.''

''All right,'' she agreed equally stiffly. ''Exercise, then.''

''Treva, while I'm gone you *have* to think about this. We've got to call the clinic again and rebook you. I know how tough it is but—''

''I told you, I am not going to do it. Didn't you hear me? Didn't you listen to any one of my words?'' she snapped.

Treva pushed the door open and got out of the car. Wade got out, too, and came around the side of the car, taking her into his arms in the stiff, almost reluctant manner he affected on those few occasions when he was angry with her.

''Love you,'' he said briefly, giving her a kiss. It was an air peck, just barely landing on her cheek, as far apart from his usual kisses as an ice cube is from a steaming cup of coffee.

''I am not going to call the clinic,'' cried Treva. ''So please, can you support me in this?''

He didn't respond, instead jumping into the car and slamming the door shut. As Treva stepped into the utility room, she could hear the rev of the engine, a screech of tires as Wade backed out, his wheels kicking up pieces of driveway gravel.

She shook her head, hoping he'd slow down before he reached Huron Parkway. He was the one who needed time to think, she thought. She prayed that when he did, he'd want the baby as much as she did.

She walked into the kitchen, a huge space warmed over with hardwood flooring, oak cabinets, paintings, and pottery they'd purchased over the years at the Ann Arbor Art Fair. A large skylight positioned overhead spilled sunlight down. Wade's breakfast dishes were still on the counter, everything the way they had left it two hours ago.

Treva loaded the dishwasher. She would have to call Dr. Haugh, she decided, get a recommendation for a specialist in problem pregnancies. Or maybe Rhonda knew someone. Rhonda knew tons of medical people.

She didn't have to be afraid. She lived in Ann Arbor, site

of one of the finest university hospital systems in the country. The hospital had more than 740 physicians, 11,500 employees, 750,000 patient visits in a year. Doctors here performed miracles routinely. So why shouldn't Treva and her baby be one of the miracles?

She picked up the phone and had a long talk with Rhonda, spilling everything that had happened.

"You mean you went *home*?"

"Yeah."

"Oh, girl," Rhonda said. "Well, I'll stand beside you, lovie, and I'm sure Annie will, too. All your friends, baby. We love you."

Treva started to sniffle, touched at this support she was not getting from her own husband. Why did he have to be so stubborn and angry about it? He was spoiling what could be a happy, joyful moment.

As soon as she and Rhonda finished talking, the phone rang again.

"Treva? Hi. It's me, Shanae."

"Hi, honey," said Treva warmly. Wade's fifteen-year-old daughter had been five when Treva had married Wade, a skinny, pretty child with cornrow braids. Shanae and Treva had formed an instant bond, and now—despite various teenage moods and problems—that bond still existed.

"What are you doing?" asked Shanae, her voice bright.

"Oh, I'm loading the dishwasher."

"I thought you'd be at work."

"I . . . I took some time off today." Treva drew a deep breath, feeling the almost uncontrollable urge to share her news with someone else. The more people she told, the more real the baby felt. "Shanae, we have some very good news."

"Yeah?" But before Treva could respond, there were noises in the background, a woman's voice speaking angrily.

Treva heard Shanae saying, "I'll *do* it, Mom, I'm on the *phone.* I'm talking to Treva. Yeah, I—*Mom* . . . Oh, all *right.*" There was a pause. "My mom is such a butthead," whispered Shanae, returning to the phone.

"Oh, now," began Treva. "Your mother is a very nice, bright woman who works very hard at her business."

"She's such a *dick.* She went through my room yesterday and read all of my song lyrics. Then she tore them up! And she won't let me have singing lessons or guitar lessons either. I've asked and asked and I even said I'd get a job to pay for them, but she says no. She says only sluts become singers," the girl went on bitterly.

"Shanae," said Treva. "You are no slut."

"I'm not, but she thinks so. I want to visit you and Dad this weekend—can I? Can Dad come and pick me up tomorrow night?"

Treva hesitated, thinking that she and Wade had a lot of talking to do this weekend, a controversial pregnancy to get used to. Then something squeezed deep within her stomach. Wade adored Shanae. Surely seeing his daughter would make him think again about the deep pleasures of having another baby to love, instead of seeing only the risk.

"Of course," she responded warmly. "Ask your mother, sweetie."

Wade and Wanda had a very casual, loose visitation arrangement, built on flexibility, cordiality, and good manners. It didn't hurt that Wanda was currently dating now, and enjoyed her free weekends. In a few minutes Shanae was back, her voice happy. "Mom says it's great. She's got a date anyway with that engineer guy she met."

"Good," said Treva.

"Tell Dad I want to come right after school on Friday and I want to stay until Sunday night late."

"Fine. And, Shanae . . . there is something I wanted to tell you."

"Yeah?"

Treva just couldn't stop herself. "You're going to have a half brother or sister."

"What? A half . . . ? Does that mean . . . ?" The girl's voice rose in a squeal of excitement. "*Does that mean you're gonna have a baby?*"

Treva laughed. "It means exactly that."

"Oh! Oh, Treva!"

"It's going to be a tougher pregnancy than most, maybe," she told her stepdaughter. "Maybe with some risk involved. But think what we're going to get out of it—another little Connor."

"Let's hope she looks like you and not Dad," giggled Shanae.

"Or he. What if it's a he? Then he'd *better* look like Wade."

"I think it's gonna be a girl," announced Shanae. "Oh, I can't wait! Can I help you choose a name? Can I baby-sit it? Can I give it a bottle and all of that?"

"You can do everything," said Treva happily. "In fact, you can be not only its big sister but also its godmother. Would you like that?"

Shanae seemed thrilled. "Can I really be the god-mother?"

"You really can."

"I'm going to buy it those little, tiny running shoes that are so cute. And a Britney Spears T-shirt if I can find one little enough."

They talked for a while longer, Shanae bombarding Treva with a dozen questions. Shanae's pure, unadulterated, teen-age joy was so genuine that her pleasure lifted Treva, too. She answered all of the questions at length, loving the girl's enthusiasm. It was balm for her troubled feelings, actually the first enthusiasm that had been expressed for this child.

A baby, Treva thought. She was going to have a baby. And it felt wonderful.

Night had fallen in a rush of purplish light amid scents of freshly cut grass clippings. The thermometer Wade had hung outside the kitchen window said that the temperature had hit ninety-three degrees. Clouds of tiny insects circled in the air.

Treva could tell that Wade was still angry because he had arrived home after a punishing racquetball game, deciding to mow the lawn with the riding mower. Then, in a grim push of further activity, he had trimmed all of the front shrubs and bagged the cut branches. Physical activity was always his answer to emotional stress.

Now she could hear the whine of the weed cutter.

But he would adjust to the pregnancy, Treva assured herself. Having Shanae around, with her bubbly enthusiasm, was sure to help.

She drew herself a bath and stepped into the large tub, lowering herself carefully into the warm water. She soaped herself, feeling with pleasure the contours of her nice, round abdomen, wondering when she would start to show. She was six weeks along. Would she waddle around like some pregnant women did, her belly leading, everything else following behind? Treva chuckled to herself at the mind-picture this presented.

If only Wade would change his mind—stop being angry. She wanted to share this joy with him; she wanted the baby to be for both of them, not just her.

Weariness suddenly swept through her, as pervasive as a syringe full of medication. Her upbeat mood suddenly drained away, and Treva lay back in the tepid water, too tired to think anymore. Tomorrow, she decided. Tomorrow she'd figure it all out, figure how to make Wade accept her decision. For now, she'd just go to bed early. It had been a hellishly long day.

Lying in bed, Treva heard the Weed Whacker stop, then the garage door roll up. Wade's car pulled out, its tires making noises on the driveway gravel. The door hummed down again and she could hear Wade's Ciera driving down the street, headed toward Huron Parkway.

She couldn't help stiffening, hurt. They didn't have the kind of marriage where one just drove off without telling the other. Wade *always* told her when he went somewhere; it was part of their sharing, each always wanting to know where the other one was.

She lay alone in the king-sized bed, where they had made so much love, and where they had conceived the fetus she now carried, feeling abandoned. She needed Wade right now, needed his arms around her, his comfort and reassurance that yes, she'd done the right thing, and yes, they'd get through it, and there would be a healthy baby. Instead she was getting nothing, and Treva stifled a stab of fear that this was the way it was going to be—her struggling through the ordeal alone.

Well, not alone. She had Rhonda, and Annie, her friends at the clinic, Shanae . . . but she wanted her husband.

Around 10:00 P.M. Treva must have drifted off, for she was awakened by the movement of the mattress as Wade slid into bed beside her.

"Honey?" she murmured, turning to him, automatically reaching for his hip. "Wade?"

"Trev." He held her briefly, pressing her to the length of him and caressing his hand along the curve of her body. But it was a different kind of holding, she noticed at once, seeming both slow and sad. Treva felt a thrill of fright. *What have I done? Is this baby going to ruin our relationship?*

"Don't you want a drink of water?" Wade whispered.

"Water?"

"You must be thirsty, Trev."

Treva mumbled something, half sitting up in bed, and then she felt the coolness as her husband pressed a water glass into the palm of her hand. Treva closed her fingers on the glass. She heard something clink inside it.

"Drink it," Wade ordered. "Drink all of it."

Obediently Treva began to swallow. When she had the glass half empty, she again heard a clink at the bottom of it.

"Reach in," said Wade.

Treva reached her forefinger and second finger into the water, poking around on the bottom of the glass. Her fingers touched something small and hard.

She laughed a little, through tears, as she shifted the glass around, trying to pull out the object through the water. Droplets of liquid spilled on her stomach and on the bed.

"You don't have to soak us," whispered Wade, laughing a little.

Treva finally managed to get her fingers on the object and pull it out of the glass. She held it in her palm, staring at it in shock. It was a tiny, sterling silver teddy bear charm for her bracelet.

"It's for the baby," Wade explained. "I had to drive all over town to find a jewelry store that was open."

"Wade. Oh, Wade." The little teddy bear had been depicted in meticulous detail, and wore a tiny bow around his neck.

"Look on the back," said Wade.

Treva turned the charm over. BABY CONNOR had been engraved on the other side, in tiny letters.

"I had a hell of a time getting engraving. I had to bribe the clerk and give her my great, big Connor smile. And promise her I'd write a nice letter to her boss praising her to the skies."

"*Wade.*" Treva started to cry. She held the charm clutched in her fist, and the tears just spurted out of her eyes. Blindly she reached out to the bedside stand for the box of Puffs, and then she felt one being placed in her hand.

"Blow, darling. Cry all you want, honey. Whatever you want, I want."

"The . . . the baby?" she sobbed.

"Especially the baby. Treva, you know I don't agree with your decision, but I'll support you a hundred percent. You're my wife, you're my love, you're everything to me, and now that's going to include our child."

Treva turned to her husband, fitting her body to his, her arms wrapped around him, tears streaming down her cheeks.

DIEDRE

PAM DROVE OVER TO MADISON HEIGHTS AND HELPED Diedre pack for the move to Ann Arbor, where she would share Pam's two-bedroom apartment off Pauline

Street, not far from the U. of M. football stadium. Pam's roommate had moved out in July, the timing perfect.

"Now, don't lift anything heavy," her sister cautioned.

"I won't. I'm not. I feel fine," Diedre insisted. "In fact, I feel great."

"You sure?"

"I'm sure."

They continued to pack, hanging Diedre's clothes in clean plastic trash bags, stuffing her books, toiletries, and mementoes into cardboard boxes they had begged for from a nearby Kroger's. Bud Clancy, Pam's boyfriend, would help them carry Diedre's bedroom furniture into the small U-Haul trailer they had rented, Diedre paying for the rental with her last paycheck from T.G.I. Friday's.

Fortunately, the law firm had already sent her first living-expense check, so she'd been able to write Pam a check for her share of the rent and utilities.

"What's this?" said Pam, rummaging on Diedre's dresser and finding the letter that Rodger Halsick, from the Detroit law firm of Halsick, McMurdy and Toth, had written to her advising her that she had won the scholarship.

Pam read aloud. " 'Your superb grade point average and high LSAT scores, together with glowing recommendations from your professors, are very impressive.' Wow, I wish someone would say that about me," she said, her voice slightly tinged with envy.

Diedre flushed. She knew Pam did not have the energy or desire to attend night classes after working forty to forty-five hours during the week—or maybe it was just that Pam was more interested in dating Bud right now than she was in trying to finish her associate's degree, for which she had accumulated only eight credits.

While Pam was in the other room, Diedre read the glowing letter again, before tucking it into one of the cardboard boxes. That high praise . . . If the year started going badly, she intended to pull the letter out and reread it, just for courage.

Pam poked her head into the room again. "Mom wants

to talk to you—she has a gift for you, I think.''

Diedre went into the small living room of the apartment, where Cynthia Samms, dressed in Saturday jeans, sat in front of the TV set watching CNN and looking a bit sad.

"Diedre . . . I'm really going to miss you,'' Cynthia began, starting to choke.

Diedre's eyes blurred, as well. "I'll miss you, too, Mom.''

They went through the please-call-me and don't-you-forget routine and Diedre faithfully promised to call her mother at least once a week.

"I have a little something for you, honey," said her mother, handing Diedre a small envelope. "Actually, it's not little.''

Diedre tore it open and pulled out a gift certificate for a local computer store. Shocked, she stared at the amount, twenty-five hundred dollars. "Mom, what does this mean? Twenty-five *hundred*? This is way, way too much money.''

Cynthia smiled triumphantly. "No, it isn't. I had a little windfall last month, my aunt Rose left me eight thousand. I've given Pam her share. But I want you to go out and buy a computer, honey, one with all the software you need. And be sure to get plenty of memory. I'm sure you can use it at law school for your studies. It might give you an advantage.''

Struggling not to cry, Diedre just stood there with the certificate in her hand. Eight thousand dollars was a fortune to her mother, enough to buy her a decent used car that wasn't always needing repairs. Instead she'd given most of the money to her two daughters. "I love you, Mom, but I can't take this. Get the transmission fixed on the Sunbird.''

"I already have, dear. Aunt Rose wanted each of you girls to have a share. I'll be so proud of having a lawyer in the family. I want you to have every chance and then some.'' Cynthia went on, smiling. "So go to Ann Arbor and knock 'em dead, honey. I mean that. Don't let *anything* stop you.''

*   *   *

It was a hot, muggy afternoon when they finally pulled into
the apartment complex where Pam had been living for the
past two years. Newer, classier developments in town had
long ago surpassed this one. The complex, built in the
1970's, looked outdated, each unit with its brown-shingled
mansard roof and untrimmed shrubbery that threatened to
engulf the lower floors. The swimming pool was postage-
stamp small, and currently closed for repairs. The biggest
asset the complex had was that the rent was cheap.

Today theirs wasn't the only U-Haul in the parking lot—
there were five or six. This was because Ann Arbor was
beginning its annual fall population explosion. From now
until June, the cheaper apartment complexes would be
packed, with long waiting lists, street parking would be nonexistent, popular restaurants jammed. Football Saturdays
would be wild and woolly, with drinking in the streets and
an occasional beery riot.

Pam's apartment was on the second floor of Building G,
furnished with futon couches and furniture Pam had picked
up at the Salvation Army and repainted. She'd framed big
squares of fabric, giving the walls a bright, eclectic look.
Prominent were a new television set, VCR, and microwave—Pam's purchases with Aunt Rose's money. The rest
she had spent on repairs to her Toyota.

When they had finished unpacking and had arranged the
old pine dresser and single bed in the small second bedroom,
Bud Clancy left, saying he had promised to play basketball
with some buddies.

"Let's drive over to campus," suggested Pam to Diedre.
"We can walk around the law quad, gloat now that you're
finally in. See what the first-year men are like."

"Oh, I don't want to meet any guys."

"Well, get used to it, Deeds—they are definitely in abun-
dance at law school, if you like the smart, aggressive ones.
And if you marry one of them, well, you can look forward
to a big house in Barton Hills, diamond rings, maybe a
vacation condo, trips, designer clothes, maid service—"

Diedre laughed. "Whoa, whoa! Pam, you sound just like

Ed McMahon. Not all lawyers make that kind of money—''

"Plenty do. I heard of a guy who was making eighty-five thousand dollars as a *starting salary*."

Diedre only laughed. "Now can we shut up about men and money, and just get in the car? I want to go and see the place that's going to eat up all of my time for the next three years."

The University of Michigan campus had sprung to life again after a slow, deserted summer. Knots of incoming freshmen, here for orientation, thronged the sidewalks, many wearing GO BLUE or U. of M. shirts purchased at campus bookstores. A young man in a motorized wheelchair buzzed along State Street, his face eager with anticipation. Students played Frisbee on the green campus lawn crisscrossed by a sidewalk called the "diag." By December these same students would be agonizing over finals, but for now it was lighthearted and idyllic, the sun beginning to sink in a soft, golden splash.

The parking situation was awful. However, Pam had a coveted staff sticker on her car, so they were able to find a space in the faculty parking lot she used. In fact, since Pam worked at Angell Hall, only a short walk away from the law school, Diedre planned to ride to campus with her sister in the mornings. This would save her the cost of a car payment, and Pam would loan her the Toyota occasionally, in exchange for gas money and financial help with repairs.

The previous spring Diedre had toured the law buildings, of course, and she'd pored over their photographs in the catalogs she'd been sent. But nothing compared to actually being here again, as a legitimate, admitted student.

She couldn't help drawing a quick breath at the sight of the place where she'd be spending the next three years. The "law quad," as it was called, Gothic and splendid, looked as if Henry VIII might come riding out at any moment on a caparisoned steed. There were arches, towers, buttresses, stained-glass windows, and magnificent stone walls covered with climbing ivy.

She and Pam walked through a curved stone archway into the grassy courtyard where six or seven male law students were playing touch football underneath the windows of the Lawyers Club, the law students' dormitory.

"This place seems like another world, even from the rest of the campus," commented Pam. "The law library is, like, right out of a movie or something. I can't believe that law firm is really giving you twenty-eight thousand dollars a year to come here. That's a lot more money than I make in a year."

Diedre nodded, uncertain how to respond.

"You *are* going to forget about it, aren't you?" Pam added sharply. "The abortion, I mean. You won't dwell on it, and spoil everything, I hope."

"Of course not," Diedre breathed.

"Because you'll be a big asshole if you do."

Within several days, Diedre was plunged into a heavy schedule of demanding classes. Civil Procedure. Contracts. Torts. Introduction to Constitutional Law. Legal Process. It was what she'd dreamed of, and now that she was actually here, waves of adrenaline poured through her system. This was it—what she had prepared for. This was why she had waited tables at Friday's for four years. She just felt so revved up. . . .

She sat in her Torts class, along with ninety other students, scribbling notes as fast as she could, terrified she would miss something. Hutchins Hall, part of the quad, was old, the acoustics echoey, and the air smelled distractingly of dozens of competing aftershaves, colognes, and perfumes, mixed with the heady scent of late summer.

A tort, Diedre had immediately learned, was a wrongful act, injury, or damage for which a civil case could be brought, and could cover everything from product liability, to slip-and-fall, to airline crashes. Professor Desmond Cury taught the class. He was about fifty, short and pudgy, with a New York accent and a habit of speaking very fast.

He also regularly pointed at some unsuspecting student,

rattling off a complex question, creating class amusement if the unlucky person stammered his or her way through a lame, unprepared answer.

Diedre felt ashamed, but she laughed, too, her laughter tinged by nerves. Sooner or later it would be her turn and how would she perform?

One day Professor Cury called on a statuesque black woman who gave an answer so inaudible that her words faded and died before they had traveled two rows. A few people snickered. They knew what was coming.

Suddenly Professor Cury pounded his fist on the lectern.

"People! Bright, talented people! One day you're going to be in a courtroom arguing cases worth millions—but not if they can't hear you. When you speak up in class, you've got to speak loudly. These rooms are large and the acoustics aren't that great. No one will hear you if you whisper or mumble. Mumbling gives the impression that you don't know what you're talking about—and it can help lose a case for you." He pounded again. "So loudly, loudly, *loudly!* Even if you're wrong."

"I'm not wrong," shouted the black woman, speaking up in a rich contralto that traveled to the chairs in the last row. Everyone laughed, and Professor Cury repeated the question, and class went on.

But Diedre took swift note of the incident, cataloging it in her mind. Never mumble. Always speak up. She had to remember this and every other thing her professors said—if she expected to graduate with honors.

That night Diedre sat curled on the twin bed in her room, propped up on three pillows, her Constitutional Law textbook spread open over her knees. The intimidating book weighed about eight pounds and was densely packed with complex case descriptions and judges' decisions.

"Boooring," Pam insisted, coming into the room and glancing over her shoulder. Pam was giving her blond hair a hot-oil treatment tonight, and smelled of coconut and other oils. "God, look at all that tiny print. They'd have to tie me down and pay me big bucks before I'd read stuff like that."

"No—not boring. It's just confusing," admitted Diedre. "I'm not supposed to just memorize and regurgitate, I'm supposed to keep reading over and over, until I understand the principles behind the cases. I have to learn how to reason in a legal manner. That's the big thing here."

"Well, I don't know how you can stand it. It makes me yawn just to look at one page of that big book."

Diedre glanced up. "I'm not bored; I'm too scared to be bored. Most of these classes have only one final exam, Pam. *One*. It's not like college where you have tests and midterms so you know pretty much how you're doing. Here it's all or nothing. You just keep going, and hoping that the final exam won't shoot you down. If I fail even one class, then I've just blown my scholarship."

"No way," said Pam, shaking her head. "That's scary."

"Yeah."

The next afternoon Diedre walked into the law library and, as she always did, stood in the entrance, entranced by the reading room, which looked more like a medieval cathedral than a twentieth-century library. Whoever had built this room had been thinking of the days of illuminated manuscripts scribed on parchment. Tall, arched, stained-glass windows let in prisms of diffused light. Carved half-paneled walls suggested monasteries, and beamed, arched ceilings contained more intricate carvings. Dozens of two-tiered chandeliers hung down, each fit to hang in a castle.

Rows of tables filled the room, each table equipped with a rectangular study lamp and lined with students bent over their books.

Diedre selected an empty spot at a table near the back, trying to be quiet in the high-ceilinged, echoing room as she set her book bag on the floor and extracted her thick Torts and Contracts casebooks. She sat for a minute just enjoying the atmosphere, then opened the Torts book and began reading the pages she'd been assigned.

"Well, hello, law student," teased a male voice beside her.

Startled at the interruption, Diedre turned her head.

"Aren't you even going to say hello?"

Tall, blue-eyed, a forelock of coal black hair hanging over his forehead. And a half-inch white scar on his handsome chin. At first Diedre couldn't speak. All she could do was open her mouth, while shock waves rolled through her.

"*Mitch,*" she whispered.

Oh, God, Mitch Sterling, her one-night stand, the father of her child. After all these weeks. She had forced herself to put him out of her mind. Now here he was, like a bad dream coming back to life.

"What are you doing here?" she managed to whisper, even the whisper seeming to echo in the spaces of the vaulted, Gothic room.

"Studying, obviously. At least, I intend to." Uninvited, Mitch set a stack of law books on the table and sank into the vacant chair next to Diedre's. As he sat down, his chair legs scraping loudly, she caught a whiff of his lime-scented aftershave.

"But I didn't know you went to the law s-school," she stammered.

"I was on a wait list. Believe me, it was suspenseful, but I got the call about two weeks ago, and here I am. Graduation or bust."

He smiled cheerfully at her, making her remember the hot July night, the hasty, awkward lovemaking in the backseat of his father's Le Baron convertible. Suddenly Diedre felt a wave of such anger that it left her dizzy. He'd had sex with her and dumped her to face the consequences. And now here he was, cavalierly sitting down beside her as if nothing had happened.

"I don't want to talk to you," she snapped, gathering up her books and dropping them into the book bag.

"But Diedre—Deeds—"

"*Don't* call me that." She jumped to her feet, slinging the bag over her shoulder, and started off down the aisle between the tables, ignoring the annoyed looks of other students who were trying to study.

"Diedre," said Mitch, hurrying after her. "Wait! I want to apologize," he continued as they reached the stairs that led to the newer, modern lower level called the Smith Library addition. "And explain."

"Oh, *really*." She catapulted down the stairs.

"Yes—I mean it. Look, will you stop running? My mother died. She died four days after we saw each other."

Diedre slowed up, wondering if he was telling the truth, then began walking faster again. "I'm sorry, but it's been months now, Mitch."

Mitch walked fast beside her. "She was scheduled for double bypass surgery, and she died on the table. She—I—" His face looked stricken. "And then I lost your phone number, if you can believe being that dumb."

Diedre stopped. "Look—I'm sorry about your mother. But you did know where my apartment building was, you drove me there, remember? You could have found me if you'd really tried."

"But I—"

Diedre wasn't in the mood to hear excuses. He got lost? Didn't remember the street? Bullshit! She turned on her heel, entering the lower-level reading room, leaving Mitch to stare after her. Her skin felt fiery and her heartbeat was thudding. She wished Mitch Sterling had chosen a law-school somewhere in Australia—not here.

Although she opened a book, Diedre was too angry to concentrate. As soon as she judged that Mitch was gone, she fled the library, hurrying upstairs into the crisp fall afternoon. Four or five students were playing football in the courtyard, yelling "hut-hut" and behaving like high school jocks. Diedre recognized one of them as Allen Huber, a guy from her Torts class. He'd tried to be friendly, but Diedre had not reciprocated. She needed a man right now like a trout needed a bicycle.

She had calmed down a little by the time she reached State Street, down by the main campus, a portion of which was lined with shops, bookstores, an art movie house, and popular student eateries.

A small restaurant sold gourmet pizzas by the slice. Diedre reached into her shoulder bag and checked her wallet, deciding that she had a few extra dollars. She went inside, sitting down at a table and breathing in the heavenly odors of cheese, peppers, ham, pineapple. Crowds of students chattered noisily, giving the place a party atmosphere.

She splurged on a slice covered with grilled chicken, apple butter, cilantro, Neufchâtel cheese, and pineapple, a combination that to her untutored tastes sounded exotic and adventurous.

Waiting for her pizza to arrive, she gazed out the restaurant window at the street, where a parade of students trekked back and forth, all skin colors and ethnic costumes, plus the standard uniform of jeans and T-shirt. Then her heart jumped. Was that Mitch, walking past with an Asian girl on his arm? But when the couple got closer, she saw that it wasn't Mitch at all.

Her pulse continued to beat irritatingly faster than normal. What rotten luck that he should turn up here. The law school was a small community within the bigger university. She was bound to run into him again and again—all of the classes were held in Hutchins Hall—which would make matters very inconvenient. Well, if he talked to her again, she'd just walk away, she decided. She would brush him off as he had done her.

"How's law school this week?" Cynthia Samms wanted to know, phoning that night after Diedre had gone back to the apartment.

"Oh . . . great," said Diedre.

"Do I hear a hesitation?" said her mother.

"No, really, it's just so challenging. And the computer you gave me, I'm already starting to type up my course notes on it. We're supposed to have course notes for each class—it'll help us at exams, and when we study for the bar exam. Which right now seems about a thousand years in the future.''

Diedre began telling her mother about her classes, characterizing all of the law professors for her, trying to sound as upbeat as possible, and saying nothing about seeing Mitch Sterling. She didn't want her mother to worry.

It was in her Constitutional Law class where Diedre was called upon for the first time.

"Miss . . . ah . . . you in the fourth row. Woman in blue,'' said Professor Cloris Kovaks, a tall, black-haired, dramatic-looking woman who always wore black or gray, and who had sold several mystery novels with a law professor as a protagonist. Professor Kovaks was witty, often cutting, and cut laggard students absolutely no slack.

Diedre flushed scarlet as she realized that she had a blue blouse on, was in the center of the fourth row.

"Me?"

"Yes, you, if you're wearing blue, and you seem to be. Give me a thumbnail description of *McCulloch v. Maryland*—in three sentences if you can.''

Diedre rose, her cheeks burning. She'd studied this last night—she knew it—but in three sentences?

"It—it took place in 1819,'' she began.

"One," said Kovaks, holding up a finger. Everyone laughed.

"Chief Justice John Marshall ruled 'that the constitution and the laws thereof are supreme; that they control the constitution and laws of the respective states, and cannot be controlled by them.' '' Diedre was terrified Kovaks would interrupt her by saying "two." "It was all about whether the State of Maryland had the right to tax a branch of the Second Bank of the United States . . . The defendant was the cashier of the bank, James McCulloch, and—''

"I'd say you got past two and three and were starting on four, well on your way to five, connecting everything with 'ands,' '' said Kovaks. But Professor Kovaks was smiling. She went on to make her point about the case, while Diedre sank back in her seat, her cheeks burning. Still, no one had laughed, and Kovaks herself had even smiled, which meant . . . she'd done well.

That afternoon Diedre had two hours between classes, and as was becoming her habit, she went into the law library to try to catch up on her reading. She had only been sitting at the table for twenty minutes when she glanced up to see Mitch Sterling again sliding into the chair beside her.

"Can't you find another place?" she murmured, her cheeks turning hot.

"All the rest are taken—look," he said, pointing to the full room. "Lots of eager-beaver law students and no chairs."

Diedre sighed. He was right, and she'd already been down to the Smith addition in the lower level to use the copier and found it crowded with second- and third-year students researching papers for advanced seminars. "All right," she agreed reluctantly. "But it goes like this. You study and I study and we don't talk to each other."

"Fine," he agreed pleasantly.

"Shhh!" hissed a man across the table.

Flushing, Diedre bent her head over her Constitutional Law book, picking up a yellow highlighter to mark a few important sentences.

"You want a breath mint?" Mitch whispered.

Diedre jumped in annoyance. "No, I do not want a breath mint."

"How about a pizza slathered in pepperoni and Italian sausage and five kinds of veggies including black olives?"

"Oh, *please*," whispered Diedre, her concentration shot.

"You don't like pizza?"

"I really don't."

"I can't believe that. Everyone likes pizza. Maybe you like pizzas covered with shrimp and sun-dried tomatoes . . . I can get you one of those if that's what you want. I know a nice little place over on State Street."

Probably the same place she'd gone by herself the other

day, Diedre thought irritably. Why did Mitch have to fill up all the air around him with his presence? And she could smell the sexy aftershave again . . . bringing back memories she did not need.

"Not tonight," she sighed.

"Then when? If not tonight, then that must mean another night, right?"

Diedre put down her book, preserving her place with the marker. "You don't get it, do you? I am not interested, Mitch. So please stop hitting on me."

"Oops, I've offended you," he said, giving her that quirky grin again, the one that had so dazzled her in July that she'd gone into the backseat of his car with him. It still dazzled her, too, although she would never indicate that to him.

"Look," she sighed. "Didn't anyone ever tell you that libraries are for reading, not talking? Especially this library."

"Yes, I believe someone did. Her name was Elsie, and she was a librarian about a hundred and eight years old. She had gray hair she wore in these little, tight curls and a white blouse with lace on the cuffs. And horn-rimmed glasses."

"Well, you should have taken her advice," Diedre snapped.

They both started reading again, but now Diedre couldn't concentrate. Out of the corner of her eye she was acutely aware of every move that Mitch made. The way he pushed back the forelock of clean, glossy, black hair. His fiddling with a Magic Marker cap. The way the denim of his jeans clung to his muscular thighs . . .

When Mitch looked up, Diedre jumped, accidentally banging her book against the table. The noise reverberated through the high-ceilinged room and six or seven people glanced up in annoyance.

"Didn't your librarian ever tell you that books aren't for banging around?" whispered Mitch, grinning. "Mine certainly did. Miss Elsie. She was a real terror."

"I'll bet she was."

His smile appealed to her. "Diedre, my stomach is rumbling. I'm amazed you haven't heard it. Please would you accompany me to the pizza place? I promise it will just be a fast slice or two, with no further commitments."

"Shhhh!" snapped the man across from them. "Really! So go and get pizza."

Diedre couldn't help it; she began to giggle.

"Good advice, sir," said Mitch, making a show of tipping an invisible hat to the irritated man. "Thank you, thank you."

Outside, it was another idyllic fall afternoon. The campus trees were dappled gold and green, with students riding bikes or strolling past in groups. A young mother was changing her baby's diaper on a plastic pad that she had laid out on the grass. The baby wore a tiny T-shirt that said GO BLUE. Diedre noticed that Mitch turned to smile at the wriggling infant as they passed.

They walked along South State past the ivy-covered Michigan Union, their bodies positioned far enough apart that their shoulders didn't brush. Diedre thrust her hands deeply into her pockets, so there would be no chance of those touching him either.

Already she was regretting this sudden impulse. Mitch Sterling was a *one-night stand,* that was all he was. He'd created a big problem in her life, a huge, unpleasant decision. How could she have forgotten, even for a few seconds? Now she was committed to this stupid pizza.

A dark-skinned youth wearing an African costume zoomed past them on a bicycle.

"I love this place," remarked Mitch. "It's not all white bread, like Bloomfield Hills, where I live. It's got some life. What do you think of Cury?" He named Diedre's Torts professor.

With relief, Diedre plunged into a typical law-student discussion about professors and courses. At least she and Mitch did have law school in common.

The pizza place—the same one as before, saturated with the same mouthwatering fragrances—was again crammed with students, and they had to wait fifteen minutes for a table. Diedre became aware that a group of women in sorority sweatshirts were staring at Mitch's dark good looks.

Mitch rattled the menu, apparently not noticing his admirers. "They have a wonderful stuffed pizza here, you really should try it."

"I want to pay for my own food," Diedre said rashly, thinking of the gas money she owed Pam. Still, she didn't want to be obligated to Mitch financially.

"All right, you can pay for the beer."

"I pay half of everything."

"Agreed."

"We'll have a pitcher," Diedre told the waitress, then excused herself to call Pam at work, to tell her sister she would be late and would not be needing a ride home.

"Whoa, you have a *date*?" remarked Pam, laughing. "I thought you were never going to date law students. I thought you wanted to send men to the planet Mars—for about a hundred eighty years."

"It's not a date-date. We're just getting pizza."

"That's a date in my book. Who is he?"

Diedre hesitated. "Just—just a guy from law school. It's a study thing."

"Oh, a *study thing*," Pam teased. "Is he cute?"

"Average," lied Diedre, going red.

"What's five hundred average-looking lawyers buried at the bottom of the ocean?" Pam wanted to know.

"A hell of a good start," sighed Diedre, saying goodbye.

Dodging waitresses with pizza trays, she threaded her way back to their table, seeing Mitch's dark handsomeness with fresh eyes. Good heavens, more women were staring at him, and one looked as if she were getting up her nerve to walk over and hand him her phone number.

What was Diedre doing with a good-looking, rich boy like him? He was a distraction, a guilty memory that she didn't want or need.

Well, she wasn't going to be with him long. How long

did it take to wait for a pizza and eat it? About an hour and a half, Diedre told herself. Then the sorority sisters could have him.

"I honestly wanted to call you," Mitch explained when she had returned to the table. "I mean after the party this summer. But it was really rough when my mom died. My dad kind of lost it, he really fell apart. I had to be there for him. It was—" He stopped, swallowing, his Adam's apple moving up and down his throat. "It was pretty bad. We're a close-knit family."

"I'm sorry," she said, meaning it. "If I lost my mother, I know I'd feel terrible."

Mitch nodded. "I was sure I'd put your number in the pocket of the shirt I wore that night. But when I went to look for it, the housekeeper had already washed the shirt and I guess she must have thrown the note away. And by then it was a couple days later . . . I didn't remember the exact street you live on . . . I was so hammered that night I could hardly remember the *town* . . . Oh, hell, it's not much of an excuse really. I really do apologize."

Diedre froze a little, then nodded. She couldn't help thinking that Mitch's family had a housekeeper, while she, Pam, and her mother sometimes had to struggle just to find the piles of quarters for the washer and dryer in the basement of their apartment building. And he lived in Bloomfield Hills, one of the richest suburbs not only in Michigan but in the whole country. The per capita income was sky-high. Whereas she, her mother, and sister came from low-rent Madison Heights, a working people's suburb. Which made him a little out of her league, right?

"Anyway, we did meet up again," Mitch went on, a smile breaking across his face. "So it turned out great. And this time I'm going to give you *my* number, all right? The responsibility for keeping it is going to be in your hands this time."

"No—please . . ."

He scrawled something on a scrap torn from a notebook page and handed it to her.

"We're going to run into each other over and over," he said easily. "I'll probably see you in Hutchins Hall a dozen times a week. In fact, I'm in your Con Law class. I just transferred in, I had a scheduling problem."

"No," she said involuntarily.

"I usually sit in the back row, you sit in the fourth or fifth."

"Then you heard it today—when I got called on," Diedre blurted.

"Yes, and you were great—at least I thought so. Those constitutional cases are so boring they're hard to wrap your teeth around. Kovaks pushed you a little, but that's her style. She pushes you, but she doesn't mean it in a really sarcastic way. She's basically sincere."

Diedre narrowed her eyes suspiciously. "How do you know all that?"

"She's my aunt."

"Your . . ."

Mitch laughed, throwing up his hands. "My mother's sister. I go over to her house about once a month and she serves a fancy buffet and everyone talks about the law. Sometimes she invites mystery writers. I met Carol Higgins Clark there one time."

"I'm sure it's very interesting."

"Maybe you should come with me sometime."

"Maybe," said Diedre in a way that meant just the opposite.

Their pizza arrived and they demolished all of it, combining their money to pay the check and leave the tip. Diedre reluctantly calculated that she'd have to be extra careful the rest of this week, to make up for her extravagance.

They walked out of the restaurant and stood on the street. While they had been inside, dusk had fallen, full of leaf smells and the greasy waft of cooking odors coming from campus fast-food places. The parade of students had increased, several carrying boom boxes that emitted loud alternative rock. Someone was strumming a guitar. It was still fun-and-games time for undergrads.

Mitch asked Diedre if she had a car, and she said no.

"I got incredibly lucky and managed to park not too far from here. I can drop you off."

Nervously she pictured them saying good night in the parking lot of Pam's apartment complex, perhaps an attempt at a kiss—or a lot more. After all, the last time they'd been together, they'd had sex. What if he expected the same thing again?

"No, thanks," she responded quickly.

Mitch looked surprised. "But it's getting dark. How will you get home?"

"It's a nice walk, just a few miles." Diedre hugged her book bag to her chest and looked Mitch straight in the eye. "Mitch, the pizza was nice, and I'll probably see you in class sometime."

She walked away, full of her pride, leaving him standing there.

It *was* a long walk home, several miles in the dark. Several cars honked their horns at Diedre, the thumping beat of rock music from souped-up sound systems trailing as the vehicles passed her. But Diedre stepped up her pace, her thoughts confused. The problem was, Mitch still attracted her.

"So you walked home?" said Pam in disbelief, as Diedre finally let herself into the apartment, footsore because she'd been wearing the wrong kind of shoes.

"I needed the air."

"But I thought you had a pizza date."

"I did."

"And he couldn't drive you home?"

"Look—I didn't want him to drive me, Pam." Tiredly Diedre put her book bag on the futon couch, then threw herself down beside it.

"Was he an asshole, then? You know, slobbering all over your neck?"

"I didn't notice any slobbering, but I didn't want there to be any, okay?"

Pam shrugged. "They all eventually slobber, kiddo. If

you don't want them to, then don't get pizza with them, and don't smile and don't flirt. Wear real baggy jeans and a T-shirt that says 'I've Got PMS and I've Got a Gun.' That's what this woman at work does. Oh, and only put on deodorant about once a month if that often—''

Pam ducked as Diedre picked up a couch pillow and hurled it at her. "Don't worry about me," Diedre said, laughing. "I can handle this guy. And I can still wear deodorant while I'm doing it."

Four days later, after class, Diedre hurried to the basement lounge in Hutchins Hall, where crowds of law students gathered every noon to "brown bag" their lunches. Six or seven people were lined up at the microwave, their frozen lunches in hand, while the odor of some rather vile chicken-and-rice concoction filled the room, mingling with the smells of lunches past.

Diedre bought herself a Diet Pepsi from a vending machine, and a bag of chips from another machine, then took her bag lunch over to a battered table and sat down.

She unwrapped her ham-salad sandwich and had just started to eat it when she felt something clutching at her jeans. Startled, Diedre looked down and saw a brown-skinned toddler about two years old, his head covered with soft-looking black frizz. His tiny fingers dug persistently into the fabric of her pants.

"What's your name?" she asked, charmed.

"I Tarik. I a big boy," he told her.

"Well, I guess you are."

"I gots Reeboks. See?" The little boy lifted up one foot to show off a brand-new pair of running shoes that made his feet look adorably huge.

"Tarik, don't bother the lady," said a voice. Diedre looked up to see a woman named Lashonda Robinson, who was in several of her classes. In fact, Lashonda was the woman who'd mumbled too softly in Professor Cury's class, then amused everyone by speaking up extra loudly.

"I hung'y," announced the little boy. "I *starved*. What you eat, lady?"

Diedre couldn't help grinning. Tarik was certainly cute.

"Just a minute, baby, I'll go to the machine and get you something," said Lashonda. "Hey," she said to Diedre. "Could you watch him for a minute while I go buy him some food? I hate bringing him, but he's got a cold and day care won't take him. Thank God he's quiet most of the time. I brought him in class and no one said anything."

As Diedre lifted the toddler up onto a chair, he offered her a beatific smile that showed tiny, white teeth. "I want candy. I want choc'ut."

"First a healthy sandwich," announced Lashonda, returning. "Then maybe *one* piece of candy. If you promise to sit still." She sank into the remaining empty chair and began unwrapping a cheese sandwich for her son, another one for herself, and two cartons of milk.

Lashonda was tall and curvy, her full hips and buttocks encased in tight stretch jeans. She wore her hair in small braids that framed her pretty, chocolate brown face.

"How on earth do you manage with a small child?" asked Diedre, feeling a strong burst of shame because Lashonda was going to law school with a baby, doing the very thing that Diedre had thought she couldn't do.

"This helps." Lashonda pulled a beeper off her belt. "With this the day care can always get me. My last year at Wayne State, I paid another student to watch Tarik in the halls while I was in class. I'd check on him during breaks and take him to the library. He'd play with his toy cars and I'd study. A couple of times they kicked me out when he cried, but mostly they let him stay."

"Are you . . . I mean, are you on scholarship?"

Lashonda laughed. "Honey, I've got itty-bitty scholarships from about four places plus a government loan, and my granny owns the house I live in. Hey," she added. "Want to join a study group?"

"Well, yes—" Study groups were being formed among the first-year students anxious to seize every advantage.

Abigail Reed

"Our group, it's all women, we didn't want any guys in it. That okay with you?"

"Sure," said Diedre.

"About three quarters of us are black, and have kids—that bother you?"

"No, as long as we stick to studying."

"Good," said Lashonda. "First meeting's at my apartment. It isn't big, we'll have to sit on the floor, and the kids might yell a little, but bring all your textbooks. We're going to map out a study plan. We've got a real big goal. Straight A's for all of us. We want to ace our first-year exams."

"All *right*." Diedre and Lashonda looked at each other, and then they raised their hands and gave each other the high five.

Lashonda lived in a first-floor apartment in an old frame house on Felch Street with a sagging front porch that hadn't been painted in fifteen years. Four mailboxes were nailed up next to the front door. A child's red and yellow plastic Big Wheel was parked on the sparse lawn.

Lashonda had the right-hand apartment, its rooms cluttered with toys, law books, stacks of dirty and clean laundry. It smelled of recently heated Spaghettios. Still, Diedre sensed the hope here. A sign saying J.D. SUMMA CUM LAUDE had been made with black Magic Marker and tacked to the living room wall.

"Hey, ready to get down and dirty?" asked Lashonda, grinning. "We are gonna put a few people to shame when we are done here. We are gonna *rock and roll*."

The study group consisted of eight women besides Diedre, five African-Americans, two Hispanics, and another Caucasian, Eileen, hugely pregnant. They all seemed welcoming, and told her incredible stories of the lengths they went to, to go to school and care for their babies as single women.

"That's my baby, Rashida," said one black woman, Belinda, pointing to a baby about eight months old, snoozing in a car seat. "I make tapes of the lectures and play them at night. I read aloud to her from my Torts book. By the time I graduate, she'll know as much law as I do.''

"I'm gonna deliver next week and then I'm back in class the next day," boasted Eileen.

While the three babies napped in car seats, and several toddlers watched cartoons on television, the women sat on the floor, mapping out their battle plan and arguing about legal cases. One baby started crying and its mother took out a bottle of juice and fed it while continuing to talk.

"What does it mean when the court said that the defendant demurred to the plaintiff's complaint?" asked Belinda.

Three women tried to answer at once, and they all ended up arguing. It was noisy and exhilarating, and here, in her own apartment, Lashonda's voice wasn't timid and mumbling, but loud and confident. How strong these women were, Diedre found herself thinking as guilt assailed her. That Eileen, delivering one day, in class the next? Could she really pull that off? They had twice as many obstacles to overcome as she did . . . and look how cheerful they all were.

After the others left, Diedre lingered for a few minutes, watching as Lashonda lifted up the sleeping Tarik, divested him of his clothes, and put him to bed in a tiny, closetlike room wearing an undershirt and his little white Huggies.

"Ma," whispered the boy, briefly awakening.

"Hush, Tarik. Mama's here. You go to sleep and dream of stegosauruses. Great big green steggies.''

"Stegosauruses?" asked Diedre as they tiptoed out of the room.

"This boy is crazy about dinosaurs. Has been since he was eighteen months old, can you believe it?''

"What do you do with Tarik if you have to, you know, study at the library or something?''

"I get sitters wherever I can find them. Belinda sits for me, and Granny drives over from Detroit. Or I just bring him. You're not interested in sitting a little, are you? I can't pay you much.''

"Sure, I'll sit, as long as I can bring my books.''

"Honey, you be sure and bring your books. I've had my books *arc welded* to my hands, that's how often my books go with me. Books and Tarik, that's about all I'm gonna think about for the next three years."

The next day, when Diedre was on the phone to her mother, she told Cynthia about the study group, and all the things the women did to cope with both children and law school. "I felt . . . well, as if I should have been that brave, too."

"Yes, darling, they are very brave women," said Cynthia. "But this is only the first semester of three long, grueling years. Some of them might find the struggle too much. What if a child gets sick, and the mother can't keep up her grades? What if it's just too hard to juggle all that studying and the demands of a baby, or what if some of the women get pregnant again?"

"God . . ." said Diedre.

"Honey, I know you feel guilty about the decision you made, but it was the right one for you, so I think you should just drop your guilt and concentrate on your work," said Cynthia quietly.

Two weeks later, Diedre was sitting in class when she experienced a familiar grinding sensation in the pit of her pelvis. A crampy ache . . . As soon as the class was over, she rushed to the women's room and discovered blood on the tissue.

She had her period!

She sat on the commode, surrounded by the sounds of female chatter and flushing toilets, a thrill of relief shaking her. Usually she'd found her period annoying, and she, her mother, and sister had sometimes referred to it as "getting a visitor named Flo." But now, as she found a tampon in her purse and inserted it, all Diedre could think of was what the period meant. It meant she wasn't pregnant. It meant that her uterus was cleansing itself, preparing for another month when she *could* get pregnant.

Diedre frowned thoughtfully. Before the abortion, she'd

never had these kinds of thoughts. But she'd grown up some, Diedre realized. She would never take her body—her life cycle—lightly again.

Nearly every day Diedre glimpsed Mitch Sterling on campus. She found herself scheduling lunch in Hutchins Hall a little later, because she knew Mitch ate earlier. She sat in the front row of her classes, because she knew Mitch liked to sit in back. And she made sure she was talking with a couple of the women from her study group whenever she did leave the classrooms.

It was taking a lot of work to avoid him, she realized to her chagrin. In fact, she was actually spending time *planning* how she could stay out of his orbit.

"I hope you haven't lost my phone number," said Mitch a few days later, catching her as she was leaving her Constitutional Law class. Students crowded the hall, heading for other classes or the library. He was wearing a blue cotton sweater that picked up the sand-washed blue of his eyes. "Because if you have, I've brought along a replacement. I'd really like to see you again, Diedre. I mean that."

She didn't know what to say. Everything was so wrong. *We almost had a baby together—and he doesn't even know.*

Unable to find words, she started toward the nearest exit, but Mitch lunged after her, planting himself in front of her so that she would be forced to push past him in order to continue.

"Why?" he demanded, looking her in the eye. "You liked me before—a lot. And I liked you. Now you act like you hate me. Why?"

She found that her mouth had gone suddenly dry. This was awful—he was demanding a truth she was in no way prepared to give. But she had to say something or he would pester her forever.

"I was hammered," she admitted in a low voice. "That night. I'd worked a full shift and it was a hot night and my date was with another girl and I didn't think he was going to drive me home. I—I don't usually do things like that."

"Well, neither do I. I'm not a stud. Is that it?" he demanded. "You resent me because we had sex. You think I have sex with lots of women and you were just a—a notch on my belt."

A swift one-beat memory entered her brain, Mitch's face in the moonlight that night as she straddled him, his head thrown back, his eyes shut, perspiration glistening silver on his skin . . . the wild shudders of his body as he climaxed. In that moment she had loved him . . .

"Yes," she replied, because what else was there for her to say? She could hardly say that she resented him because he'd impregnated her and she'd had to get an abortion. She did not want to say that now. She should have told him that time they'd had pizza. Now it felt much too late.

"But you acted like you wanted to. All you needed to do was say no and I would have backed off right away. I didn't hear you say no," he accused. "You were a willing participant."

Shame heated Diedre's face as a group of students clattered up the stairs, laughing and talking about the upcoming Purdue game. "I know. Oh . . . please, Mitch, just let me pass, will you? I don't want to talk about it."

"Fine. I won't impede you. I hurt you and I'm sorry. But, Diedre, we don't have to have sex again, not if you don't want to. And I promise I will always call when I say I will. I'll take your phone number and tattoo it on the back of my hand if that's what it takes. There's a tattoo shop on Main over by Kerrytown," he went on. "I could go there. You could come with me. You could watch me getting the tattoo, bearing pain . . ."

"Oh, please." But she couldn't help sneaking a look at him; his blue eyes were sparkling, full of cheerfulness. His height . . . the way he leaned close to her . . . She was annoyed to discover that her heart had begun to pound, just as it had in July.

He went on, "Anyway, my aunt Cloris is having a little get-together at her house on Sunday afternoon. About fifteen law students, mostly third-year students, and a few professors. Maybe some local writers if we get lucky. And us, if you want to go. Could I pick you up?''

A soiree at Cloris Kovaks's house? Surrounded by professors who, around the law school, were petty gods with enormous power. And third-year students who were light-years, eons, away from her in expertise. Diedre felt a jolt of adrenaline, mixed with dry-mouthed fear. Yes, she wanted to go, and no, she didn't want to. If only Mitch weren't the one who'd be taking her.

''I take that silence for consent,'' declared Mitch. ''Give me your address and I'll come and pick you up at one-fifteen on Sunday.''

Diedre was about to refuse, but her mouth opened and somehow she heard herself give him the address of Pam's apartment.

He grinned at her, the smile sweet. ''Now, you only have to see me this one time, Diedre. If you don't like it—if you still hate me after Sunday—then we're history, all right? I'll stop bugging you and leave you alone. Anyway, this legal gathering is part of your studies, in a way. An extra part of law school you really shouldn't miss.''

Diedre nodded, her face hot.

''Sharpen up your verbal skills, you're going to need them,'' Mitch told her. ''Aunt Cloris and her friends love a good debate. Hey—I'll see you later, okay? Oh, dress casual on Sunday, all right? Jeans.''

He jogged down the hallway, pushed open the door to the quad, and was gone.

Diedre walked over to Angell Hall to meet Pam for the ride back to the apartment, her cheeks blazing hot. She had a date . . . just what she'd told herself she wasn't going to do. And with Mitch Sterling, the man who'd fathered her child. And he *attracted* her. He made her feel excited inside, caught off guard.

What was she thinking of?

PEPPER

W HEN PEPPER ARRIVED HOME AGAIN FROM THE HOTEL
bar where she'd had the drinks with Gray Ortini, the
alcohol from the two glasses of wine she'd drunk was swimming in her veins. It had been a long day—then meeting a
new man, that whole chili fiasco. She felt as if her entire
body was leaden.

In her bedroom decorated with lace throws and pillows,
Pepper stripped down to her panties and crawled into bed.
As Oscar jumped up and settled himself near her right hip,
she thought again about Gray Ortini.

Rich. Good-looking. Sure of himself. Maybe a little patronizing. She realized that she had very mixed emotions
about the man. Many women would find Gray extremely
attractive, Pepper knew. The only trouble was, she didn't.
Well, yes, she did, but . . .

She'd always dated men her own age or a little younger.

Charming, bad-boy kind of men, guys like Jack, who
could sweep you off your feet, break your heart, then apologize so deeply that you trusted them again . . . until they
broke your heart one more time. Oh, she'd had her share of
men like Jack, and Gregg, the airline pilot she'd dated for
a while, and a few others, equally charming and undependable, and usually financially strapped.

Now here was Gray, the exact opposite of all that. *Definitely* not financially strapped.

Her eyes fluttered shut.

The ringing of the phone awoke her. Pepper uttered a
curse and shot out her hand. What the hell time was it? She
forced her sleep-gummed eyes open, seeing a soft, pink-
tinged light streaming through the lace intricacies of her

curtains. A glance at her clock radio told her it was 6:38 A.M.

"Yeah, this is Pepper," she growled.

"Are you still in bed?" said her mother's contrite voice. "I thought you'd be up—I tried to wait until I was sure you'd be awake. Oh, dear. If this is a bad time, I'll call you at the shop later."

Toni Maddalena was calling from Sanibel Island, Florida, where she had lived in a condo for the past thirty years, turned into one of Florida's bitter, leather-skinned women, never remarrying for fear of losing her alimony check.

"I'm up. Is everything all right, Mom?" said Pepper, struggling to wake up.

"Oh . . . fine . . . I was up at five and started watching some movie on cable. Why are cable movies always so boring? This is about some stupid girl photographer who falls in love with a Mafia man. I mean, *really*. Couldn't she have guessed what he was all about? He has two bodyguards and carries a gun, for pity's sake."

Pepper threw Oscar off her stomach, groping for an extra pillow to put behind her back. It was obvious her mother was settling in for a long conversation about her TV programs, her women card friends, her complaints about her doctor, and the dearth of interesting older men in Florida.

Still, she listened as best she could. Her mother had been generous, loaning Pepper start-up money for her boutique when the bank refused her because of her past bankruptcy, and charging her less interest than a bank would. Besides, her mother really was lonely, Pepper knew.

Thirty-three years ago, Toni Maddalena had been a stunningly beautiful young woman, too full-figured to model any type of clothing but lingerie. But that type of modeling she had done exceptionally well, and then she'd met Pepper's father, Mason Maddalena, a businessman thirty-five years older than she. A restaurateur who owned more than fifty restaurants, he was so wealthy that he claimed he did not even really know how much money he actually possessed, because interest kept accruing on the interest.

In those days, they still called it "marrying a sugar daddy."

The marriage only lasted a year, long enough for Mason Maddalena to become repelled by his wife's advancing pregnancy. It turned out he just did not like full breasts and rounded, protuberant bellies. When Pepper was only eight weeks old, Mason divorced Toni, lavishing a large settlement on her, generous child support, and awarding her an even more generous alimony, with the clause that if she remarried, the alimony payments would cease.

Mason Maddalena occasionally got around to seeing his little daughter, Pepper—maybe three or four times a year— but when he was not available he sent her flowers and expensive gifts . . . Pepper forced her mind away from her father. He'd died of a heart attack when she was twenty-two, and her memories of him were contaminated by all the anger her mother had felt toward him.

"And men?" probed Toni now, beginning her usual quiz about Pepper's life. "What about men in your life?"

"I met a new one," admitted Pepper reluctantly.

"I suppose he's one of your usual airline pilots or photographers." Toni managed to make this sound like "your usual janitors and busboys."

"Actually, he owns his own company, Mom."

"What kind of a company?

"They make software and CD-ROMs."

"Is it a big company or just a little fly-by-night thing?"

"Big," responded Pepper shortly.

"Well, that's a very nice change," said Toni. "I've always told you, there's no sense wasting your time with a man who hasn't got four twenty-dollar bills in his pocket, when you can have one who flies his own airplane and could buy and sell Donald Trump."

Pepper couldn't help it; she laughed. She laughed so long and so hard that she fell back against the pillow, the phone nearly dropping out of her hand as Oscar yowled and jumped out of the way.

"What's so funny?" demanded Toni indignantly.

"Mom . . . Mom . . . you'll never change, will you? Not everyone wants Donald Trump, believe me. Have you ever noticed that the really rich men—the ones with lots and *lots* of money—always seem to have these fat, pouchy cheeks like Donald Trump does? Fat-cat cheeks. Even when the rest of the man is well conditioned, there is just that extra padding on the face."

"Just like your father," remarked Toni softly. "He had those kind of cheeks. But on him they looked good."

After her mother had hung up, Pepper struggled out of bed and took three Excedrin, washing the pills down with orange juice, while Oscar crouched on the Formica counter, waving his silky white tail and regarding her with emerald-eyed interest.

"Don't look at me that way, Oscar," she told the cat. "I'm not hungover, I'm sleep-deprived. Between Gray Ortini and my mom, I only slept about four and a half hours, thank you very much."

Oscar meowed.

"Now, don't you give me any trouble this morning getting into your carry-cage, Mr. Oscar Cat," she told him. "I might not have the patience."

Another meow.

"Well . . . I could bribe you, I guess . . . What about these?" She rummaged in a cupboard for a box of cat treats and tossed one to Oscar, who pounced on it daintily.

"Piggy kitty," said Pepper fondly.

In ten minutes she was ready, and for once, Oscar went meekly into his cage for the trip downtown.

Despite her monthly ticket, the parking structure was almost full and Pepper had to cruise up and down the levels to find a spot. Then she discovered that some rusted-out old GM van had hogged more than its share of the space, barely leaving room for her to lift out Oscar's cage.

She let herself into her boutique, relocked the door until official opening time at 10:00 A.M., and let Oscar out of his cage. The Persian headed straight for his usual window spot, curling up in the morning sunshine, a living advertisement for the shop.

Pepper was already preparing some papers for her accountant when Jan arrived at 9:55 A.M. carrying a huge floral arrangement wrapped in green florist's wrap.

"I ran into the florist delivery guy out there on the sidewalk . . . Wow, this is huge. What's the occasion, Pepper?"

Pepper stared at the arrangement. Even through the floral wrapping it emitted a honeylike, spicy fragrance. There was only one person who could have sent it.

"I suppose we ought to unwrap it," she said reluctantly. "And see if there's a card."

"Do you mind?" Jan tore off the paper, revealing a stunning bouquet of pink tea roses arranged in a white ceramic cachepot on which more roses had been hand-painted. "Gorgeous!" raved Jan. "All these roses . . . There has to be three dozen. And this cachepot is beautiful. All this must have cost a small fortune."

Pepper said nervously, "The card. Where's the card?"

"I don't—Oh, here." Jan pulled out the tiny envelope and handed it to Pepper.

She tore open the little envelope. *I am definitely looking forward to our dinner together* had been written in a spiky, masculine-looking handwriting, that definitely did not belong to some floral clerk. *Until then, something to brighten your day. Gray Ortini.*

"Well? What does it say?" demanded Jan.

Pepper handed her the card.

"Gray Ortini? Jesus, Pepper, you know Gray Ortini?"

"As of last night. We had a little chili-spilling thing." Pepper told her about the incident.

"It's a good thing he spilled it on you instead of the reverse," teased Jan, smiling. "Guys definitely do not like gooey things spilled on *them*. I'll bet he would have sent you dead weeds instead of these gorgeous honeys."

Pepper had always been funny about flowers. She'd received her first bouquet at age six, from her father, when he couldn't come to pick her up one afternoon. It was supposed to be an apology. But to her six-year-old mind it had said, *I don't love you, so I'm sending these flowers.*

Now she checked the bouquet to see if it had enough water, then placed it on a low table, moving it several times to ensure that it looked its best. At least her customers could enjoy it.

"I wish in a way that he hadn't sent such an elaborate arrangement," she said to Jan.

"Any blossoms are good blossoms, in my book."

Pepper began rearranging a display of push-up bras. "I don't know if he's my type, Jan."

"He doesn't have to be your type, does he, for you to have dinner with him?"

"No . . ."

"Is there something wrong with him? I mean, did you see a facial mole the size of the Goodyear blimp, or smell BO that made you pass out in disgust?"

"No . . . no . . ." Pepper gave a snorting laugh.

"I've met this man at parties, I've seen his picture in the *Ann Arbor News.* Gray Ortini is the most eligible bachelor in Ann Arbor, Pepper—he's *seriously eligible,* didn't you know that?"

Of course she did. She'd read the *News,* too. Pepper stood holding a champagne-colored satin stretch push-up bra, her mind still on this man who had come into her life with literally such a gaudy splash.

"I'm probably not ready for this," she muttered.

Jan laughed. "Oh, come on, Pepper. What's wrong with you? Loosen up! You need to get out in the world again. And Gray Ortini isn't a bad way at all to start."

"Isn't he?" said Pepper pensively.

Their date was set for Thursday, when Pepper usually closed the shop at 6:00 P.M. She bundled up Oscar and rushed home to change, forced to run the gauntlet past her landlady, Mrs. Melnick, who was sitting on the front porch of the old Victorian with a group of her women friends, all of them dressed in sweats or brightly colored running outfits. If she wasn't mistaken, these women in their sixties and seventies were dishing about men.

Upstairs, she let Oscar out of his cage, fed the cat, cleaned out his litter pan, and then rushed around trying to decide what to wear. Something slinky and black? But she didn't want to come on that strong. She sensed it would be a mistake with a man like Gray.

She finally settled on a white blouse lavishly embellished with cutwork embroidery, and a long, pencil-thin navy skirt, worn with three-inch DKNY heels. Piling her coal black hair up on her head, she fastened it with several antique pearl clips, which she had collected at antique shows. She fastened antique pearl studs in her ears.

She worked on her face for half an hour, thickening her lashes, blending eye shadow, putting on her lipstick with both a pencil and a brush, widening her lips just a fraction.

Then, gazing at the results in the oval mirror she'd hung in the bathroom, Pepper made a face. Too Rachel Hunter, just what a man like Gray Ortini probably expected. Damn. That wasn't the impression she wanted to give at all. So she washed everything off and started over again, using only the minimal makeup she usually added for work. She tugged out a few stray hairs from the pearl clips, pulling the locks down untidily.

Pleased, she regarded herself again in the mirror. She looked more like herself . . . like the Pepper she wanted to be.

The doorbell rang. Pepper rushed downstairs, where Gray Ortini was standing on the porch, apparently unembarrassed by the scrutiny of Mrs. Melnick and her friends.

Seeing him, Pepper could understand why the older women were eyeing him with such intense interest. Gray looked as if he'd stepped straight from a corporate boardroom. He wore a well-cut, gray business suit that emphasized his wide shoulders. His tie was tasteful and expensive, his silver hair gleaming in contrast to his young-looking face.

"You look wonderful tonight," he murmured to Pepper.

"And, baby, so does he," one of Mrs. Melnick's friends muttered under her breath, then the whole group laughed delightedly.

Pepper blushed, feeling unnerved by this unasked-for commentary. He *was* much sexier than she had remembered—trust Mrs. Melnick and her cohorts to notice.

Had she locked her apartment door? She couldn't remember if she had. She didn't want to show Gray up to her apartment, not so early in their relationship, and not with six or seven lively elderly women watching their every move.

She excused herself to hurry upstairs and lock up, then returned to find Gray casually chatting with Mrs. Melnick. He was asking the landlady all about the history of her house, and the older woman, obviously flattered, was responding at length.

"You come again, hear, Mr. Ortini? I can show you the original house blueprints, and I have photographs that were taken right after the house was built, of the senator, his wife, and their eight children and three dogs, all right here on this very porch."

"I'll look forward to that," said Gray warmly.

"I see you made a friend," Pepper said, smiling, as they walked to Gray's car, a silver Infiniti, which he'd parked on the street. It was freshly washed, the chrome glistening.

"Mrs. Melnick reminds me of two or three aunts out of my childhood," said Gray. "And her friends were priceless."

They began the hour-long drive to Detroit, where Gray said he was taking her to a restaurant on some of the newly developed riverfront property. Gray had brought along a CD carrier and asked Pepper which music she would prefer. She finally decided on some Bonnie Raitt. His sound system was top of the line, the best she'd ever heard, bringing out nuances in the recordings that Pepper hadn't heard before.

However, for some reason, she balked at complimenting him on the fine system. In fact, conversation began to seem awkward.

"I suppose you worked all day long in your pretty shop," he said politely. "I drove past it the other day. That cat in the window is a nice touch. I saw people gathered outside just to look at him."

"That's Oscar," Pepper explained. "He's my mascot."

He asked her questions about her boutique, and Pepper began telling him about the big bridal show at the Silverdome, coming up in February, where she was thinking of staging a runway show.

"You'll model in it?"

Pepper frowned. Now, why had he said that?

"No, it's too stressful trying to be both in the dressing room and on the runway," she said quickly. "The goal is to show off the garments, and I can do that a lot better if I'm totally in control without distractions."

"But you have modeled before," he probed.

"A little—when I was in college."

Now Gray began peppering her with questions. Why had she never gone to New York to pursue modeling there? She would have been such a natural. How had she ended up owning a lingerie boutique? Had she thought of opening several stores, or even franchising her boutique?

Pepper formulated a response, feeling a bit annoyed by these typically male questions—it was not the first time she had been asked them. It seemed most men felt that if one boutique was great, fourteen ought to be even better.

"I like my shop exactly as it is," she heard herself telling him, a bit sharply. "If I franchise it, it won't be unique anymore."

They had to wait for construction traffic to clear, and by the time they reached downtown, it was dark and the city of Detroit glittered, the curved towers of the Renaissance Center aglow. Pepper had been here many times at night, especially when she'd had her shop in Trapper's Alley, but she loved the city lights and the sense of magic they always conveyed.

Gray turned his Infiniti in to a riverfront area with office towers and condos under construction. The restaurant was a modern building with its second floor cantilevered out, so that it seemed as if it were right on top of the river. On the Canadian side of the river, rows of lights glimmered like a flung necklace.

"This place just opened three months ago and already the reservation list is booked solid for the next five months on Friday and Saturday nights," Gray told her. "Fortunately, I know the owner, so he slotted us in."

Pepper nodded. Powerful men usually did "know someone" so they could get the best tables, tickets, or other items. Her father had been given all of the perks, being comped at Vegas and treated like royalty by maître d's.

Gray went on, "Wait until we get inside. You'll feel like you're practically on the water."

They walked into an elegant lobby, and Gray gave his name to an obsequious maître d'. They were immediately seated at a table on the upper level, next to the soaring bank of windows that projected over the water. From up here, the glittering, far-off Canadian lights were even more spectacular.

"This *is* beautiful," gasped Pepper. "You almost feel as if you're in a boat."

"I thought you'd enjoy it," said Gray, seeming satisfied at her reaction. "And wait until a freighter goes by. They're huge and at night they're all strung with running lights. You feel like you could reach out and touch them."

The other well-to-do diners in the restaurant were a mixture of Detroit's races and cultures, along with suburbanites who had driven down for the ambiance. Gray pointed out Detroit's Mayor Dennis Archer to Pepper as well as a couple of local television celebrities.

They ordered drinks, and a waiter brought a leather-covered menu that featured such pricey items as smoked salmon with terrine of avocado, and medallions of beef with foie gras and black truffle sauce.

Pepper ended up ordering grilled yellowfin tuna, and then dutifully began to devote herself to the work of making conversation.

And work, she realized, was what it probably would be. This man was not a Jack Nolan who could joke and jump his way around a dozen topics, until you were dizzied and laughing.

"How did you get started with GrayCo?" she asked.

"I'd had a software company for a number of years, specializing in SPC, which is statistical process control for manufacturing companies. Then I began hearing about CD-ROMs and I realized immediately the moneymaking potential that could be involved. Right now the CD-ROM market is in constant flux, but I think it's going to bottom out at about twenty to thirty publishers eventually, the ones who now are earning ten million or more in total sales."

Pepper listened, asking further questions, just like a date was supposed to, but part of her mind had begun to glaze over. This was beginning to feel like a business dinner, she told herself, forcing back a yawn. Oh, shit. And their salads hadn't even come yet.

Finally a freighter passed by, studded with hundreds of lights, its black bulk so huge that it blotted out the Canadian skyline as it passed within eighty feet of them. Pepper dutifully exclaimed over it, glad to have a relief from GrayCo.

Several couples came up to the table to greet them, the men giving Pepper quick, interested looks. Even the restaurant owner, a man named Sam Riga, stopped by to greet Gray, and ask how they were enjoying their meals.

"The food is wonderful—just as we expected. And this beautiful woman is Pepper Nolan," Gray introduced her, his eyes burning briefly on her.

"I own a retail business in Ann Arbor," she put in, not wanting to be seen only as "this beautiful woman."

"That's great, Pepper," said Riga, but he didn't ask her what it was, and turned his conversational efforts back to Gray. Pepper sat there, annoyed. Both of the men were acting as if she were only a decorative device, rather like the tall, glorious urns of fresh flowers that adorned the restaurant's lobby.

Then, after Riga had wandered on to other tables, it was back to Gray's monologue on GrayCo. It seemed he wanted to talk about every product the company made, how it was conceived, programmed, and marketed. If she'd wanted to know that, she could have gone on the Internet, Pepper thought irritably. GrayCo had a very interactive Web page, as Gray was quick to tell her.

Finally Pepper excused herself and strode back to the ladies' room, which had a floor-to-ceiling window in its front lounge area, also giving great river views. She repaired her makeup, wondering how she could cut this evening mercifully short. They hadn't connected at all—not on any emotional level. Gray was coming across as a boring businessman.

When she walked back to their table, Gray didn't see her. He was staring pensively out the windows, a look of disappointment on his face. But as soon as he spotted Pepper, he smiled again, and his eyes fastened on her with evident pleasure as she sat back down at the table.

"This has been a lovely meal," she began, preparing the way for their early departure. "Everything has been superb."

He looked at her, raising one black eyebrow. "I'd say this has been an unsuccessful meal," he told her quietly. "Pepper, what happened? What's gone wrong with this date? Let's fill in the blanks."

Startled by his honestly, she could only stare at him.

"Everything's wrong," he said. "Here we are, two people who were brought together by a bowl of chili, and I thought—yes, I really did think—that there were some sparks between us. Now those sparks have definitely fizzled. Is it anything I've said or done?"

She moistened her lips, trying to think of a polite, face-saving response, but nothing came to her. This was the downside of dating—when a man actually was bold enough to ask why things weren't clicking.

Gray motioned to their waiter, and asked for the check. He put several bills in the leather folder, telling the man to keep the remainder. "Let's go for a walk," he suggested to Pepper. "Let's go look at those sparkling lights."

Outdoors, the air smelled of river water and traces of gasoline from boat wakes. The sky overhead was velvet black, studded with glittering star points, a ruffle of silver clouds stitched to the east. Across the water Pepper could see the flashing blue lights of a police car or ambulance, somewhere in Windsor, Canada.

They walked across the jammed parking lot to a wooden walkway that had been built to stretch for fifty or sixty feet in either direction along the concrete seawall, so patrons of the restaurant could stroll along the river. Water lapped against the concrete, and they could hear the engine of a big motor cruiser somewhere out on the water, people laughing.

Hunching her shoulders against the chilly wind that blew over from Canada, Pepper wished it had been different. She had wanted to like this man. There was something nice in him, underneath all of the rich-man traits, the show-offiness and business talk.

"Take my jacket," said Gray, shrugging out of his suit jacket.

"I'm not that cold—"

"Of course you're cold. You just have that little blouse on—by the way, what are all those holes in it?"

"It's cutwork embroidery," explained Pepper, putting on Gray's suit coat, which still held the cozy warmth of his body. "Cutwork is a dying art these days; I bought this at an antique market. Originally it was a tablecloth, but I made it into a blouse."

"It's very beautiful," he said. "About as beautiful as you are."

Pepper stopped. "I *wish* you wouldn't keep saying things like that."

"Saying what? That you're beautiful? But you are. Pepper, you could have had a major modeling career in New York if you'd wanted it."

"I've got a major career right here in Ann Arbor," she responded. "Oh, sure, I inherited a certain body and bone structure, and I'm grateful for them, of course. But they don't define me," she told him intensely. "I'm not just a set of cheekbones and some lips and some eyes. I'm a business owner. I make my living every day selling beautiful things and doing what I love. I may not be big-time yet, but I'm working on it, and I hate being patronized. You called my shop pretty, Gray! *Pretty?* You acted like it was a—a hobby, or a toy. Something I just play around with. Well, my business is not a toy to me and I am not a toy either!"

"Oh, Jesus," Gray said. "Oh, shit. So that's it. I've been very offensive, haven't I?"

She nodded. "To me, certainly."

"I'm sorry. I'm very sorry." He said it in a low, penitent voice. "I haven't been around many women as frank and honest as you are."

"I love my business," she said firmly. "It's part of me, a big, big part, and you'll have to accept that and respect it."

Gray took her cool hand, enveloping it in his warm one. "Of course I will. Again, I apologize." He went on. "Pepper, there are a few things you should know about me. I'm a wealthy man, I'm divorced, and a lot of women consider me a legitimate target—money on the hoof. Even the *Ann Arbor News* implied so with that silly article about 'most eligible bachelor in Ann Arbor.' Sure, I've dated a few women since my divorce. Most of them seemed very much interested in me, but I've never known for certain, was it me that they wanted, or was it my business, my wealth, my position?"

They stood looking at the running lights of a large Chris-Craft buzzing its way toward Belle Isle.

"In a way, that's like being too pretty," commented Pepper. "You can't escape it. You can't separate it from the rest. You always wonder, what if I got fat? What if I had to have a breast removed? Would he still care?"

"Pepper, I'm in a position in life where I'm *never* going to know, not a hundred percent, if a woman wants me for myself or my money. And I suppose you'll never know, either, how much of an effect your looks are having. You just have to trust.''

His perception was so accurate that it seemed to hit Pepper like a tiny punch in the midsection. ''Yeah.''

Still holding hands, they gazed out over the black and silver water. For the first time since she'd gotten into Gray's Infiniti under the eyes of Mrs. Melnick and her friends, Pepper felt herself begin to relax.

''I dressed down to go out with you,'' she admitted. ''I mean I had a lot of makeup on and then I took most of it off.''

He nodded. ''I'm sorry that you felt you had to do that.''

''I'm me,'' said Pepper. ''Me, inside this face.''

''Hello, me.'' He leaned close to her and kissed her temple so gently that it might have been a kiss of the wind. She thought he might kiss her on the mouth, but then he pulled away, smiling.

''I don't want all this glitz, not all the time,'' said Pepper, indicating the upscale, cantilevered restaurant behind them, filled with prosperous diners and local celebrities. ''I mean it's nice, and I enjoy being pampered, and it's fun looking at a menu where I can't pronounce half of the items, but I like simple things, too.''

''Like what?''

''Like going for long walks, and playing with my cat, and running, and going swimming. And antique shows,'' added Pepper. ''I collect embroidered fabrics. A lot of them I use in my shop and I have them all over my apartment, too. I sew some of them into pillows. Some I make into clothes for myself.''

''Then we'll do those things,'' promised Gray, pulling her closer to him. ''Antiquing, swimming, long walks. *But* I want you to do some of my things, too.''

''Like what?''

''An occasional black-tie dinner. Tickets to concerts. Trips to the Caribbean or maybe Aspen, where my son lives. And flowers. I like to send flowers, Pepper. I hope you like to receive them.''

"Occasionally," said Pepper.

Water plashed and lapped at the pilings below them as they stood silently, their hands linked together, some kind of an electricity binding them.

"Does this mean that we're going to keep on seeing each other?" asked Gray, his voice husky.

"I . . . I guess it does."

TREVA

TREVA WAS EAGER TO GET STARTED ON THE ABORTION study, and Dr. Rosenkrantz provided her with a computerized printout of the women who, at their intake interviews, had thus far agreed to participate in the study. They'd been collecting these permissions for a year, hoping the study would be funded.

The first woman Treva called was a young law student named Diedre Samms, who'd had her procedure—Treva glanced at the printout—the same day she herself had gone in.

Diedre wanted to know more details about the study, and its funding, and Treva went over it with her, giving her the same explanation other participants would receive, emphasizing the methods the researchers would use to ensure confidentiality. The questionnaires would be "blind," that is, there would be no "match-back" number, and the personality tests and interviews would be coded with a first name and a number only. The clinic would keep the participants' full names locked in a file, and would destroy them when the study was published.

"When can we set up the first personal interview?" Treva asked quickly. A percentage of participants would back out at the last minute, and she was hoping Diedre would not be among them. "We could meet for coffee if you like. I know it isn't easy discussing personal things with a stranger, and we want to put you at your ease as much as possible."

"Could it be a coffee shop away from the campus?" Diedre asked. "I don't want anyone I know overhearing anything."

"You pick the restaurant and the time," said Treva. "Or I could come to your home."

"No—my sister would be around, I share an apartment with her."

Diedre named a restaurant on Stadium and said Treva could meet her there the following night at seven-thirty. "I'm blond and I'll be carrying a big stack of law books."

Pleased, Treva thanked her and hung up, then spent several hours organizing her thoughts and her notes, rereading the study proposal and the basic interview questions they had decided to ask. Mostly the interviews would be loosely structured, allowing each woman to express her feelings freely.

The small coffee shop only a few blocks from the stadium had a bakery bar that sold several varieties of Danish, small tarts, and bagels, and smelled deliciously of yeast and exotic coffees. The walls were hung with dozens of old U. of M. football team photos, some dating back to the 1900's, and football mementoes hung from the walls and ceiling. The only other customers were a couple seated in a booth at the front, drinking coffee and reading the *Ann Arbor News*.

It was "seat yourself," so Treva found a booth at the back, facing the door, and waited.

Diedre was ten minutes late, and when she finally did rush in, she hurried to the back of the restaurant, then stopped dead in her tracks, staring at Treva, before finally sliding into the booth.

"You were there that day," she said in wonderment. "You were in that room . . . you know . . . I saw you."

"Yes," Treva said quietly. "I was there. Is that a matter of concern for you, Diedre? If it is, I can arrange for another interviewer."

"No . . . no . . . I just . . . Did you get an abortion, too?"

"No, I didn't. I changed my mind," Treva answered honestly. She never lied to patients and she would not lie now to this pretty, concerned-looking young woman. "I have a high-risk pregnancy and the doctor and my husband felt I should abort, but I decided to take the risk."

"Oh." Diedre began fussing with the stack of books she'd brought in, finally putting them on the seat beside her. "What made you decide not to do it?"

Treva moistened her lips, speaking carefully. She didn't want to antagonize this young woman or make her feel guilty.

"The point of these interviews isn't to cast blame, Diedre, or to make a woman feel as if she made the wrong choice. Every woman who was in that clinic that day—or any other day—made the choice she felt was right for her at that time. We respect that. That's why the clinic exists, so that women can have those choices."

The waitress came and they both ordered *cafe lattes*. Treva decided to break the ice by asking Diedre about herself and her background, and if she minded if there was a tape recorder on the table. Diedre hesitated, then gave her consent. "But no names mentioned," she said. "I'm adamant on that. On that paper I signed you promised I'd have my privacy, and I'll hold you to it."

"Absolutely, and you have my personal word as well."

Diedre began telling Treva about the study group she'd joined, the young women who had kept their babies and were managing long study hours and the demands of child care. "I see them struggling. They baby-sit for each other, they eat cereal for dinner, they read law books to their babies, they somehow get aunts and mothers and grandmothers to help them, they live in shabby little apartments or even in one room, and they . . . they're making it. They even laugh about their problems. One woman had a baby on Saturday night and went to class on Monday afternoon."

"Wow. How does this make you feel, Diedre?"

"I guess they were stronger than I was."

"Every woman is in a place that is unique for her," Treva commented. "We all make decisions based on where we are then, at that exact spot. And that's all right. God understands. He sees us and loves us always, I'm sure He does."

Diedre was holding her coffee cup in trembly fingers, her eyes shining moistly now. "Treva... Can I call you Treva?"

"Of course you can."

"Does God love the baby I gave up? Even though it never was born?"

"Of course, Diedre. His love encompasses everyone who is human, from fetuses to old, old men and women. Let me tell you a secret, Diedre. A few of the women who come to us for procedures tell me they believe that God took the soul from their fetus and put it in another baby, a baby who was destined to be born. This gives them comfort."

"Oh!" Diedre rubbed two fingers underneath her wet eyes. "Oh, Treva... I guess I'm still kind of emotionally rocky from having the—from having it. But I'm so glad I came here tonight. I thought you'd be all cold and efficient—you know. Instead you were wonderful. You made me feel more peaceful. But I guess I didn't give you much of an interview, did I?"

Treva smiled gently. "It takes time to build up trust for a good, deep interview, Diedre. If it's all right with you, how about us scheduling another one, maybe in a few weeks? We can meet here at this same coffee shop if you want."

"All right."

They finished their coffee and Treva paid the check—the study covered such expenses—and they walked out to the parking lot together. The fall night had turned cool, wind skittering dead leaves through the parking lot, piling them against the curb. Distant band music filled the air—the U. of M. marching band must have been rehearsing at the stadium.

"I'm going to be studying tonight until two A.M.," confided Diedre.

"That's a rough schedule."

"I don't mind."

They smiled at each other, and Treva felt as if she'd begun to establish a strong rapport with Diedre. "Do you need a ride?" she asked.

"No, I have my sister's car. Treva . . . thank you. I do want to talk to you again. I think this study's going to be worthwhile. That's why I signed up for it. If it can help some other women . . ."

The next day Treva drove to the University of Michigan hospital complex, an enormous, rambling medical center that contained dozens of hospitals, medical schools, and research institutes and centers. She entered the East Medical Center Drive, driving into the huge parking structure that gave patients access to the confusing sprawl of medical buildings.

Parking was a big problem here, but Treva got lucky when a van with an Ohio license plate pulled out of a space. A door led directly into the Taubman Center, the huge, three-story office building where gigantic waiting areas on three floors were packed with patients who had come from all over the state to see specialists.

Turning toward the second floor area where Dr. Ruth Sandoval, the specialist recommended by Dr. Haugh, had her office, Treva couldn't help staring at her surroundings in disbelief.

It was like entering a city of sick people. Patients thronged everywhere, the elderly, people in wheelchairs, women in creative chemotherapy head scarves, old men clutching big manila envelopes containing their own X rays—hundreds of patients. In some hallway seating areas, as many as sixty or seventy people waited.

If she had not been on such a hopeful errand, Treva might even have found this sight depressing. But this place was going to help her have a healthy baby, she reminded herself. She would certainly put up with any amount of crowding, parking problems, and other hassles to achieve that.

She had to wait over fifty nervous minutes to see Dr. Sandoval, during which time she had her blood and urine taken by an on-premises lab.

"You'll be in Room Ninety-five, Mrs. Connor," said a young, African-American nurse, escorting Treva down a long corridor lined with an intimidating number of doors. There were more exam rooms in this one section than many motels had rooms. Entering Room 95, Treva began to worry that she was going to be merely a number.

"Please, take off your clothes and put on this gown, with the opening in back," said the nurse, smiling.

Treva put on the inevitable paper gown, and wished she'd had the sense to bring a magazine. Were they going to keep her waiting another fifty minutes?

But five minutes later, a resident came in and began taking Treva's blood pressure and other vital signs, as well as a detailed medical history that included every illness and operation she'd ever had, and her entire reproductive history from her first menstrual period on.

Then another thirty-minute wait. Finally Dr. Ruth Sandoval strode into the room, a six-foot-tall woman with tortoise-colored hair neatly pulled back, and hooded brown eyes that matched the color of her hair. On her white physician's coat she wore a sterling silver teddy bear pin.

"I apologize for the long wait. I had an emergency that I had to take care of. You can call me Ruth or Dr. Sandoval, but please don't call me Dr. Ruth," she joked, regarding Treva with warm, intent eyes. "For one thing, I'm much too tall."

"And you can call me Treva."

They talked for a few minutes, getting acquainted. Treva found herself warming up to this kind woman who wore no makeup and had pleasant smile lines.

"I'm here because I want to carry my baby to term," Treva said quietly. "I need someone to help me do that."

"Well, Treva, I've looked over your history, but maybe you can review it for me in your own words."

Treva found herself telling Ruth Sandoval everything

again, about her fluctuating blood pressure, the various attempts to control it, the miscarriages she'd had, the abortion that almost was.

"I couldn't do it. I just felt that this baby has a chance."

"It isn't hopeless," said Ruth, causing Treva to feel an immediate surge of her pulse rate. "There are many things we can do to help you, Treva. I can't give you a promise of a hundred percent favorable outcome—it isn't possible to make those kinds of promises in any pregnancy. Working in a women's clinic, you yourself know that. But I can tell you that we'll do everything we can to give you a healthy baby, and keep you healthy, too. That's our goal. But you're going to have to do most of the work, not us."

"Oh?"

"Bed rest. For the duration of your pregnancy. I want you to start as soon as you go home today."

"Bed rest?" Treva was dismayed. "For the next six months or so?" Her voice rose. "But I have a job, I'm doing a survey—I have a house to take care of—my husband—"

"Your husband will adjust, and you can take family medical leave—I'm sure the clinic will support you all the way. Call them today, and I'll fax them my recommendations." The physician went on, "Bed rest is safe, and time after time we've seen it work. In your case, because it reduces physiological strain, it may reduce your blood pressure or stabilize it—in fact, bed rest may be the single most important thing we can do for you, Treva."

"Of course," agreed Treva, shaken. It all seemed so sudden. *Today? When I get home?* But who would prepare dinner? And she had to pick up some things at the dry cleaner—

"Now," began Ruth briskly. "There are certain specific instructions you'll need to follow. You do have bathroom privileges—that is, you can get up three or four times a day and go to the bathroom, and you can take a shower if you have a downstairs bathroom, but other than that, you are to be in bed or on a couch, lying on your left side, with your head elevated."

Treva stared at her, surprised. "You mean I can't lie on my back?"

"Sorry. Lying flat on your back for any extended period of time causes the uterus to press against your major blood vessels, reducing the blood flow to the placenta, which could be dangerous."

"Fine," agreed Treva.

"No sitting up straight, even to eat. Don't lift anything heavier than a paper plate with food on it that *someone else* prepares for you."

"Whoa."

"I hope your husband is a good cook."

Treva laughed. "He's going to learn to be. Anything else?"

"I'll have my nurse give you a printed list of dos and don'ts. When you come to your doctor appointments, someone should drive you, and you should adjust the car seat so that you're lying back as horizontally as possible."

Oh, Lord, Treva thought, beginning to realize just how hard this was going to be. Lying on her side for five or six months! The boredom was going to be immense. What would she do with herself? And how would Wade manage? An indifferent cook, he'd have to prepare all her meals. Microwave dinners weren't an option for her, not with all the sodium they contained. Wade would have to vacuum, fetch things . . .

The physician began telling her about the antihypertensive drugs that she would use with Treva. They'd start with diuretics, then if those weren't effective, they'd proceed to drugs such as beta-blockers or methyldopa, which wouldn't harm the baby.

Treva listened to the recitation of side effects she might experience with these drugs. She was very familiar with them from past experience. Her mind drifted, and then she heard Dr. Sandoval say, "Treva, I don't mean to scare you, but you absolutely *must* keep all your prenatal appointments so I can check your blood pressure and check your urine for protein."

She began explaining what protein was, but Treva only half heard the lecture, her mind unable to focus on more than a few phrases here and there. She was still reeling from the shock.

Bed rest. It was going to be worse than being in prison. At least prisoners got to exercise.

Arriving home, Treva lay down on the big, brick red sectional couch in her living room, grabbed the portable phone, and began making phone calls. She tried Wade at the School of Social Work, but only got his voice mail, so she dialed Dr. Rosenkrantz at the clinic.

"Honey, I was expecting this," said the tiny, white-haired physician. "Of course you can have medical leave for as long as you need, and we'll fix you up with that disability insurance the clinic carries. Up to twenty weeks at sixty-seven percent of your regular pay. I'll fax Ruth Sandoval the forms she'll need to fill out."

"Oh . . . great . . ." Treva felt too excited and anxious to concentrate. "What about the abortion study?"

"The proposal specifies the personal interviews can be done by phone or in person, so I don't see why you can't get started on that at home if it isn't too taxing. Do you want a hospital bed?"

"H-hospital bed?" Treva stammered.

"For your bed rest."

Treva shook her head vehemently. "No . . . a hospital bed would be way too depressing. I like our couch, it's got great pillows, it gives great nap, and it will help prop up my back when I have to lie on my side."

"All right. Just remember—we all care, Treva. Anything you need, anything, you just call, all right?"

Treva's next call was to Rhonda. "Whoa, whoa, whoa, just slow down, Sissie," her sister said. "You're gonna *what*? Be on the couch for *months*?"

"Yeah, I'm going to become a real couch potato."

"Well, it won't be that bad. A woman I know at work did it, and she had her whole life down to a science."

Rhonda launched into a long list of the creature comforts
that Treva could surround herself with, including items such
as a cooler full of sandwiches, fruit, bottled water, and
juices.

"I don't think we even have a real cooler, just one of
those cheap Styrofoam things," said Treva dubiously.

"Well, I've got a picnic cooler big enough for a whole
football team," said Rhonda. "I'll be over with it tonight,
girl—and I'll bring you a bunch of other goodies, too. Oh,
God! We're really having this kid, aren't we?"

"*We* are, yes," agreed Treva, laughing.

Finally Treva managed to reach Wade at his office at the
university and told him the gist of what Dr. Sandoval had
said, reading him some of the instructions from the folder,
which, as she read them again, seemed intimidatingly strict.

"Seriously?" Wade said. "You really have to be on the
couch twenty-four hours a day?"

"That's right."

"Oh, baby."

"I'll survive it. But I can't do it alone."

"I'll be there for you, Treva. Do you want me to drive
home right now?"

"Would you?" she said, relieved.

"Look—I have to teach a class in two minutes. I'll go in
and cancel it. Then I'm on my way."

As soon as he hung up, Annie called, and Treva had to
tell the news again. Telling it over and over was beginning
to exhaust her, but at least Annie, too, was positive, promising to visit Treva often and keep her cheered up.

Treva lay on the couch on her left side, propped up by
several pillows. She had only been doing this for twenty-
five minutes, but already she felt very cramped. Perversely,
she wanted to stretch her legs, jump up, run in place, vacuum the rug—anything to be active.

Months of this? But she knew she'd endure it because she
had to. She would follow the bed-rest instructions to the
letter, no matter how onerous it was.

A few minutes later she heard the garage door going up and Wade rushed into the house, lugging a briefcase and a stack of textbooks and papers. His face was anxious.

"You're already on the couch," he said, surprised.

"As of twenty-five minutes ago, I'm an official bed-rester. Oh, and Rhonda is coming over tonight with a big picnic cooler and who knows what else."

"Treva . . . honey . . . are you sure this bed-rest stuff is okay? You can't even sit up straight to eat?"

"I'm going to be curled up like a shrimp for the foreseeable future," she said, trying to joke.

"You'll go apeshit."

"I'm going to try not to. But if I do . . . just wrap me up in a sheet and tie me to the couch. Don't let me ride the exercise bicycle and don't let me vacuum any dust bunnies. Do not let me go up and down stairs and don't . . . well . . . don't let me start babbling in weird voices."

Wade didn't laugh at her lame joke. He knelt down beside the couch, sliding his arms around her. "What about love-making?"

"Um," said Treva. "I think we're just going to have to save up our passion."

"You mean no sex?"

"No anything," she sighed.

"Oh, baby. And I only know how to cook three things."

Treva couldn't help it; she started to laugh. "I'm *not* going to eat pancakes for six months, Wade."

"Not even if they have chopped-up bananas in them?"

"Not even then."

"Or blueberries?"

"Well, maybe . . . but I won't eat grilled steak, not every day. As for peanut butter and honey sandwiches, that other culinary delight of yours, forget it."

He teased, "Oh, I thought I'd give you steak and pancakes for breakfast, peanut butter sandwiches for lunch, steak for dinner, a little cold steak for a midnight snack . . ."

"No way," said Treva, but she was laughing uncontrollably. "I'd die of a cholesterol attack. And by the way, we're calling a maid service, or maybe one of your students wants to earn some extra money. Oh, and when our little darling is born, I want to work only three days a week, all right? Or maybe just two.''

"Let's just get that far," said Wade with an anxious smile. "Getting him born, I mean. Anything, Treva, any amount you want to work. I'll just write another textbook and that should keep us going just fine."

Wade disappeared into the kitchen while Treva fussed with the TV remote, clicking through channels and finding nothing good to watch but CNN. She'd led such an active life before this. She'd worked a full-time job, taken care of a house, entertained her stepdaughter, Shanae, on at least two weekends out of four, gardened, ridden her exercise bike, belonged to several professional groups, and attended church.

Now her life was going to be constricted to one sectional couch. One *comfortable* couch, she reminded herself.

She got up to use the downstairs powder room, realizing she would have to have Wade bring all of her cosmetics and personal items downstairs. Since there was no downstairs shower, it would be sponge baths for her for a while. Treva was going to miss her baths very much. Still, she preferred being in the living room in the central part of the house, rather than imprisoned upstairs in the bedroom.

"Honey?" Wade came trudging back into the room carrying a white wooden tray with feet that they occasionally used for breakfast in bed on Sunday mornings. He had arranged the tray with a blue linen place mat, a dinner plate, a bowl of freshly cut fruit, and a rose in a bud vase.

"Wade!" She started in surprise. The tray looked like a cover illustration from *Family Circle* magazine.

"I have red snapper . . . steamed green beans with un-salted butter and rosemary . . . and a little spinach salad."

"Beans with *rosemary*? Spinach *salad*?"

Wade grinned. "Actually I called Shanae and she talked me through it. I told her what was in the fridge and she told me how to cook it. Then she told me to go out and pick a rose. We didn't have too many left. Did I cut the stem the right length?"

"You cut it exactly the right length. It's so pretty. And the food looks delicious."

Wade brought his own dinner plate into the living room to eat with her, and then he went upstairs and brought down Treva's computer and printer from her study, setting them up on the coffee table. She could move the keyboard to her lap as she worked, he figured. He rummaged around for stacks of magazines she hadn't read yet, and collected the John Grisham and Terry McMillan novels she'd been hoarding.

"There. More reading than you'll be able to do in a year. And no excuses about falling asleep, either."

"Treva! Are you really going to have to stay on the couch for nine months?" Treva's stepdaughter wanted to know, calling a few minutes later.

"Not nine months, I sincerely hope," said Treva, smiling. "Maybe six, though."

"Six *months*? Ewwww . . ."

"I plan on surviving it."

"I'm going to teach Dad to cook," Shanae announced. "I already helped him with one dinner."

"And it was wonderful," Treva raved. "Shanae, I didn't know you cooked that much."

"I do . . . Mom gets this *Gourmet* magazine with a lot of pictures in it of food, you know, food that looks like art, and one time when she was out serving a banquet, I started fussing with the recipes. I made this white mousse with raspberry sauce," said Shanae. "I drizzled it all over the plate, it was so cool."

"Well, I see that I'm going to be eating extremely well," said Treva, her voice bubbling with laughter. " I'm going to get fat and happy."

"Oh, no, I'm going to watch the fat content of the meals I teach Dad. Treva, can I come over this weekend? Can we start, you know, painting the baby's room and all that?"

"Maybe in a few months we'll have someone paint," said Treva. "Or you can help paint. Yes, you can come over, if your mother agrees. I think you're really going to cheer me up, Shanae."

Sleeping. It was a whole new world, trying to get to sleep on a living room couch instead of in their own comfortable, king-sized bed. Treva lay bolt awake for half of the first night, feeling stiff from the unaccustomed sensation of not moving around. She was afraid if she actually fell asleep, she'd change position and endanger the baby.

She lay in the darkened living room, her eyes gradually becoming accustomed to every nuance of the big room, the glitter of the pottery and a glass hurricane lamp on the mantel, the red light on the cable box, the cut-glass gleam of a vase of roses Wade had brought her earlier in the day.

The drapes were opened, and through the bank of windows, the outside floodlights illuminated the treetops of the ravine. Through a clear space in the trees Treva could see the perfect, silver circle of the moon. A few lacy clouds blew past it, then the clouds thickened and extinguished the moon, like a hand going over a candle flame.

And the eerie sounds . . . a branch banging against a window, blown by the night wind, a distant click as some timed thermostat in the house activated. Then a sudden crack in the walls that made her jump. Wood stretching or shrinking or something like that, she guessed.

"Seeing any ghosts yet?" said Wade, coming downstairs about 2:30 A.M. in his pajamas.

"I'm beginning to wonder if we don't have some," Treva admitted. "I never knew the house could make so many weird noises."

"Yeah . . . I was hearing them upstairs, too. Look, hon. There's an old air mattress upstairs over the garage, the one I used to use for camping before I met you. I'm going to go get it and make it up so I can sleep on it."

"Down here, with me?"

"Yeah. That big old bed is too damn big without my

Treva in it." Wade sat down on the couch beside Treva and ran his hand over her hair, caressing her back gently. "I can't let you sleep down here alone, baby."

She blinked back sudden, hot tears. God, she loved Wade—so much. How lucky she was to find a man like him on the second time around. She only hoped she could give him a healthy baby.

On Friday night Wade drove the twenty-five minutes north on US-23 to Brighton to pick up his daughter and bring her back to Ann Arbor. As always, the teenager arrived in a flurry of activity.

"I brought you a present." Shanae came bouncing over to the couch with a small shopping bag. Tonight the teenager had on a tight black vest with orange flames coming up the front, ending in yellow, and a pair of hip-hugger black plastic pants. On her feet she wore high-heeled, cloggy-looking shoes.

"A present?" said Treva, surprised, and hoping Wade wouldn't comment on the outfit his daughter wore.

"This—a CD."

Shanae fished in her shoulder bag and retrieved a plastic compact disk case emblazoned with bright colors. "This is by Porsha Morgan. She's my age, she lives in L.A., and she's already got her own video and she opened for Queen Latifa."

"Shanae," began Wade warningly. He stood behind Shanae holding the girl's overnight bag, which Treva hoped contained at least one pair of blue jeans.

"Well, she did, Dad! She's already on her way to being a star, and Brandy *is* a star, and look at me. All I do is go to school and listen to my mom nag me. I could sound as good as Porsha, I could, if I could only get some lessons. You can't make it in the singing world without professional help."

"Shanae," said Wade even more firmly. Apparently they had been arguing in the car about this topic before Shanae's arrival.

Treva glanced up at her husband's stony face, then tactfully turned to her stepdaughter. "I've been wishing for some music. The CD player's upstairs in my study, on the bookshelf. And maybe you can run some other errands for me, too, Shanae, while you're here this weekend. I desperately need someone to go buy me some crossword-puzzle books."

"Sure," said the girl, turning and heading for the staircase. They could hear her heavy shoes clunking as she took the steps two at a time.

"I wish you wouldn't encourage her in this music craze," began Wade.

"I'm not encouraging her, I'm just going to listen to a CD she gave me."

"It would be disastrous for Shanae to try to become a singer," he pointed out. "You know how tough the music business is. They'll eat her alive, you know it, Treva. How many girls do you see in your clinic who've gotten caught up in that kind of shit?"

"Well, my listening to one CD isn't going to hurt."

"You encourage her, Treva. It's the last thing she needs."

Treva looked at her husband. "Lighten up, honey," she said gently. "This is the girl that's teaching you to cook, remember? Believe me, she's going to make a big culinary difference in our lives."

"No peanut butter sandwiches, you mean. And I thought you rather liked them."

"Dream on," said Treva.

Wade took Shanae's overnight bag to the upstairs bedroom the teenager preferred, and said he was going to correct some papers. Treva stretched out on the couch, remembering to stay on her left side. Already she'd accidentally turned several times. It was hard work remembering to stay always in one position.

"I'm back, I found the player," said Shanae, returning to the living room. The teenager opened the plastic jacket and took out the CD, balancing it with the tips of her slim, brown fingers. ''Play the number four track first,'' she urged. ''That's her best one.''

Treva manipulated the buttons, then a voice washed over her. She sank back, listening to Porsha Morgan singing about a lost boyfriend. Only—she began listening more closely—the singer of this song wanted to ''track him away, get down to the killing line.'' Aware of Shanae's eyes scrutinizing her reaction, she continued to listen to the track, then pressed the stop button.

''She's very, very good, Shanae.''

''Isn't she?'' Shanae glowed.

''The lyrics are powerful, almost violent.''

''She writes her own stuff. *I* write some things, nobody's ever seen them or heard them—I want to sing my own music when I get to be famous,'' Shanae hurried on.

''You want to be famous,'' repeated Treva cautiously.

Shanae frowned. ''Yeah . . . yeah, I guess . . . but my mom thinks rock music is cheap and slutty, especially for black women. She says we get treated different. Unless we sing gospel. Ugh! I'm never gonna sing gospel.''

''I see.'' Treva tried not to show her amusement. At age twelve, Shanae had been the light of her church youth gospel choir, which had gone on many trips all over the state and entered several contests, which they had won.

Shanae's eyebrows knotted together, an expression of gloom tightening her features. ''I just want to *sing*,'' she burst out. ''I don't really care about being famous. Oh, I mean I'd like it, because it would mean I was good, but I just—I can't explain it—I want to make people happy with my voice.''

Treva looked at her stepdaughter, thinking that this was the most mature thing she'd ever heard the girl say.

''Maybe someday you can.''

''I doubt it. No one is going to let me.''

''Maybe not now—''

''Not ever,'' Shanae insisted bitterly. ''I told you, my mom hates the idea. And so does Dad. And I have to do what *they* tell me. My life really sucks. At least that part of it.''

Treva felt a pang. "Oh, Shanae, you're only fifteen, there's still so much time—"

Shanae stared at her. "No, there isn't."

The weekend was over. Wade collected Shanae's overnight bag, putting it in the trunk of his Cutlass Cierra. Then he walked around the car, holding the passenger door open for his daughter, who was now wearing baggy jeans and a Salt-N-Peppa T-shirt.

"Hop in, beautiful."

"Oh, Dad—I'm not beautiful."

"I'll be the judge of that. I'd say you're the most beautiful girl in Ann Arbor, certainly Michigan, and probably the whole damn United States. Even in that flaming vest thing. You sure it didn't burn your skin?"

"Dad," she giggled.

"Did you have a nice weekend, chickie?" he said to his daughter as Shanae settled herself in the seat.

"I did. Thanks for the CD-ROM, Daddy. I love it." They had gone to Egghead Software and Shanae had picked out *Myst*.

"Good. Take care of it. You didn't mind that we had to rent movies? And ate in the living room?"

"No, it was fun. And, Dad, I *loved* giving you the cooking lessons. I'm going to fax you a bunch more easy recipes, and I can talk you through them over the phone."

"Today broiled fish, tomorrow cheese soufflé, next week I'm Paul Prudhomme," quipped Wade, starting the engine.

As Wade put the car in gear, Shanae turned to him. "Daddy, is Treva going to die?"

The sudden question jolted him. "No," snapped Wade without thinking. Then he softened his voice. "Nothing is going to happen to her. Believe me, Shanae, when I tell you that."

"But—"

"I don't want you worrying about it, cupcake."

"But there was this girl at school," his daughter persisted. "And her mother had a baby and she started bleeding and they couldn't stop it—"

"Please, don't worry. Those kinds of things hardly ever happen. Treva has the best doctors, and if they aren't good enough, we'll get more. She's going to be just fine."

They entered US-23 north.

"I don't want Treva to die," Shanae repeated pensively.

"And I've told you, Shanae—she's not going to."

A few days later, Treva lay curled on the couch, a CD playing quietly in the background as she used the new speaker phone, which Wade had brought her. It had proven to be much easier since she was on the phone so much.

The clinic interviews—she could do them from home and they were saving her sanity.

"I couldn't believe it," said Janina, a thirty-one-year-old artist whose abortion procedure had taken place the previous July. "We'd gone in for a second ultrasound. When the doctor told me . . . well, my mind just sort of froze down, I could not understand what he was telling me. Anencephalic. What was that? I kept shouting that they were wrong, they'd done the reading wrong. My baby was *not* going to be born without a brain . . . It was all a horrible mistake. But I was crying so hard the doctor couldn't understand me."

Treva nodded and murmured, letting Janina talk it through, replaying all of the emotions she'd felt.

"I didn't want the abortion," said Janina. "I fought it, I cried and raged for two days. But I felt there was no choice. She'd be institutionalized—if she even lived. She'd be worse than a vegetable. I . . . I couldn't stand that thought. The night before I went in, I named her. I had to do that, I couldn't imagine her going to heaven without a name. I called her Summer."

"Summer. What a pretty name."

"She was never going to see summer. I wanted her to have—" Janina's voice again broke. "I think she's an angel now, Treva. In fact, I know she is. I carried her for five months and I felt that I got to know her, she became part of me. She'll always be part of me. Until I die.''

Later, Treva got up for one of her permissible bathroom breaks, then returned to her couch to resume her phone calls. She'd needed the brief break. Janina's story about Summer had affected her deeply.

Fetal testing, Treva knew, could sometimes bring pain, not joy. Some studies showed that 95 percent of women whose amniocentesis revealed the abnormal chromosomes of Down's syndrome elected to have abortions. Around 90 percent of women whose children were diagnosed with spina bifida also chose to abort.

What most people didn't know, however, was that approximately one-third of all pregnancies naturally and spontaneously abort before the end of the eighth week, sometimes before the woman even knows she is pregnant. Even Mother Nature—or some would say God—regularly aborts fetuses.

It was a thought that sometimes kept Treva awake in the night.

Her own lost babies . . . In medical parlance, the miscarriages she'd had were also called spontaneous abortions.

DIEDRE

DIEDRE HAD RECEIVED A PHONE CALL FROM TREVA CONnor saying she would not be able to meet her in the coffee shop as planned, because Treva was now on bed rest for a high-risk pregnancy.

Would Diedre mind coming to Treva's house for the interview, or would she rather wait and be interviewed by someone else? Or they could do it over the telephone. Diedre had liked Treva and decided she'd take a break from her studies and go to the woman's home.

Following the directions Treva had given her, Diedre wondered why she felt such a strong attraction for this black woman in her forties. Maybe it was the big, rich, warm laugh. Treva had helped her feel better about the decision she'd made ... Treva really cared about people. Diedre would like to be just like her someday—helping women.

The home was huge, set on a beautiful, wooded ravine lot, just the type of home Diedre would like to buy for her mother someday, or live in herself, although realistically she didn't expect to make great amounts of money in her career. Helping indigent women wasn't exactly a profit-making enterprise.

Treva had told her that she should go around to the side of the house and enter through the mudroom door, which had been left unlocked. Diedre followed these directions, ringing a small bell that had been left on the counter to warn Treva she was entering the house.

"Diedre! It's good to see you," Treva greeted her warmly. "Come in—and pardon the junk. I've kind of spread out."

The older woman was lying on her left side on a couch in a living room so big that it would contain practically Pam's entire apartment. She wore maroon and gray sweats, and gold hoop earrings that complemented her clear, caramel-colored skin. Two large coffee tables had been drawn up to the couch area, each stacked with items that included a computer, piles of books, papers, and magazines. A huge picnic chest sat on the floor, while a stereo played a popular Ann Arbor radio station that featured soft rock.

"So this is bed rest," said Diedre, smiling. "You look as if you have all the comforts."

"Everything except chocolate, and I can't get fat or I'd have that, too, believe me." Treva motioned to a small, overstuffed chair which had been moved close to the couch. "Have a chair, Diedre—that's my visitor's chair. I can offer you bottled water, or various kinds of diet sodas, or freshly squeezed orange juice—help yourself from my cooler."

Feeling comfortable and at ease, Diedre did so.

"How are you feeling?" she asked, sipping from a can of Diet Pepsi.

"Well—fine, actually."

Diedre asked more questions about the bed-rest rules and regulations, finding herself amazed at how restrictive it was. Lying on one side—for months? Diedre told Treva she didn't know if she could ever have the patience.

"A couple times a day I start to feel stir-crazy and want to climb the walls, yelling. Then I remember this little one—" Treva rubbed her stomach. "It all feels very worthwhile. Anyway, I'm committed to it and my husband has come around very nicely, thank God. For a while I thought we were going to have a serious difference of opinion."

They began talking freely, each one thinking of something interesting to say, and finding themselves laughing, more like two girlfriends than a young woman and a woman nearly old enough to be her mother.

Diedre began telling Treva about her classes and how much her study group was helping, and then she burst out, "Something's happened . . . I mean . . . I didn't tell you last week, but the man who fathered my baby has transferred into the law school! He's asked me for a date!"

"Whoa," said Treva. "Does this man know about your pregnancy?"

"No." Diedre nervously began playing with the can of soda she had selected.

"He doesn't know?"

"I never told him. We had a one-night stand, Treva. I would have told him if he called me back, but he never did and I thought, what right does he have to know?" She flushed. "He says his mother died and he lost my address. Then he said he couldn't find my apartment building because he'd had too much to drink and couldn't remember the exact street."

"But now he does want to see you."

"Yeah . . . and I accepted a date to go to a party at his aunt's house. She's a professor at the law school." Diedre leaned forward. "Treva, this is just bugging me, driving me crazy. I'm attracted to him. Under other circumstances I could even . . . but how can I really see him when there's this whole big thing he doesn't know, a thing that has to do with him?''

Treva's smile was gentle. ''You could see him for this one date . . . see how it feels.''

Diedre sighed. ''Yeah . . . one date. That's all it's got to be. Because I can't picture myself saying, look, we had this one-night sex, you deposited about fifty million sperm in me . . . and our cells divided, and now those cells are gone. I had them vacuumed out. Ugh! How awful that sounds.''

Restlessly she got up and walked to the big wall of windows that looked out on treetops now covered with rust-colored and yellow leaves, some of the branches bare.

''Your house is so pretty,'' she heard herself say, changing the subject. ''Up in the treetops like this.''

''I can watch the woods at night while I'm in bed,'' said Treva. ''It looks very different, almost magical, at night.''

With a jolt of surprise, Diedre realized that the woman slept all night on the couch as well. She said regretfully, ''Oh, Treva. I've really got to go and get some studying in. I'm so busy all the time—and we didn't even really finish the interview.''

''You can stop by again any time you want,'' said Treva kindly. ''We can do the interview in pieces, if you like, Diedre.''

Diedre lingered for a few minutes, and by the time she left, she felt—just as before—much more at peace. What was it about this woman that was so soothing?

Next time, she decided, she would bring Treva flowers or maybe a gift for her baby. She wanted this woman's friendship.

Later that afternoon, Diedre sat curled up with her Torts textbook, studying a case in which a longshoreman employed in the port of Philadelphia allegedly sustained serious injuries while unloading bags of cocoa beans from the ship's hold. He had slipped and fallen on a sheet of plastic that had been placed under the bags.

The phone rang, interrupting her concentration.

"Hello?"

"Is this Miss Diedre Samms?"

"Yes . . ."

"I'm Rodger Halsick, of Halsick, McMurdy and Toth."

"Oh!" Diedre gasped. Halsick, McMurdy and Toth was the Detroit law firm that had awarded her scholarship. She had been told that a partner would call.

"I want to thank you," she blurted. "This scholarship . . . it means everything . . . I won't let you down."

"No need to thank me again, your beautifully written thank-you letter was more than adequate. I take it you are happily enrolled in law school and are getting along quite nicely," said Halsick.

"Oh, yes."

"Well, the reason I called is that I'm in town for some meetings at the law school and I'd like to arrange to take you to lunch tomorrow, if you're free. The firm usually offers personal contact with its scholarship winners; we feel that it is beneficial for both parties."

Yes, they'd emphasized that in the acceptance letter.

"I can be free tomorrow at noon," said Diedre.

"Good. I hope you like seafood. I'll meet you in the Lawyer's Club Lounge. It'll be easy to recognize me—I'll be the one with white hair."

After she'd hung up, Diedre flung down her textbook and hurried to her closet, where she began rummaging on the rack and the overhead shelf, trying to decide what to wear the following day. A business suit? But that would be too dressy. Ann Arbor was definitely a casual town. Finally she settled for a tan herringbone trouser suit with a darker silk shell, and some clunky tan leather shoes with two-inch heels she'd bought last year. She would pull her dark-honey hair back from her face, and as for makeup—she would wear only what a woman lawyer might wear in the courtroom, she decided.

* * *

The Lawyer's Club, part of the law quad, was the residence hall for around three hundred law students. It offered meal services, meeting rooms, periodical subscription service, even a commercial dry-cleaning service with pickup and delivery at its busy main desk. In the dining room there were even special language tables for students wanting to share mealtime conversation in French, German, or Spanish.

Today the lobby was full of law students trooping in for lunch or utilizing "brown-bag passes," which allowed nonresidents of the club to eat bag lunches in the dining room with a complimentary beverage.

It was easy to spot Rodger Halsick, a slender man in his mid-seventies with upright posture and a shock of white hair complemented by matching bushy white eyebrows. He was standing by the main desk, wearing a tweedy jacket, open-collared shirt, and jeans.

"I'm Diedre Samms," she said, walking up to him and extending her hand.

"Ah . . . Diedre . . . our star scholarship student." A smile creased Halsick's wrinkled face, lighting up his features. "I hope you don't mind this last-minute invitation, but I had several committee meetings to attend and I didn't know until yesterday whether or not I would be free."

They walked outside to his car, which Halsick had parked in a staff lot near the law school. "I understand student parking these days is a total hassle," he remarked. "If you can even get assigned a commuter spot. In my day we lived in the Lawyer's Club and we walked everywhere . . . Of course, that was about a thousand years ago, my dear. Well, actually, right after the war. I felt damn privileged to be at law school at all. So many of my friends never came back from the Pacific."

He rambled a little, but was so warm that Diedre didn't really mind, and the ride downtown passed pleasantly, with Halsick reminiscing about his law-school days on the GI Bill. "And I hate to confess this, but it was nearly all male students at that time," he told her. "Women were a distinct rarity then. I'm glad that aspect of law school has changed, and I'm even more pleased that my law firm has worked to encourage more young women to enter the profession.''

The restaurant was located on Main Street, a popular seafood place that Diedre had walked past several times but never been inside. Enticing odors drifted out to the sidewalk.

"Do you like lobster? Crab? Scallops? Order anything you want," said Halsick, when they were seated in a booth. "You might as well take advantage. I suspect your usual lunches don't begin to match this."

Diedre smiled. "Peanut butter and jelly, that's my usual lunch. And tuna or ham salad once in a while for variety. Believe me, this seems wonderful."

At Halsick's suggestion, Diedre ordered the crab legs, and a waiter trotted over with a plastic seafood bib to put around her neck, an experience that made her feel slightly foolish, wishing she'd ordered the crab salad instead.

As their entrées arrived, the law partner began asking her questions about her courses.

"It's exciting," Diedre admitted, picking moist crab meat out of a pink shell with a tiny fork, and hoping the juices didn't spray. "I feel a rush of adrenaline every time I go into class."

"Yes, I remember that so well. Will you be called on? Will you make a fool of yourself or will you manage to perform adequately, or even better, brilliantly?"

"Yeah . . . I'm learning to think on my feet."

"Which is three quarters of what being a lawyer is all about. I'm glad you're grasping that important point, young lady."

"I *have* to be good," Diedre told him intensely. "There's so much at stake. I'll be the first person in my family to have a law degree—or any degree."

Impulsively she began giving him some of her mother's background, details she'd never written on any law school or scholarship applications.

"My father stalked my mother for years, calling her as much as sixteen times in one day, and showing up at her job to shout at her and threaten her. Once he pulled her into his car and tried to strangle her. She lost two or three jobs because of him, but when she went to the police they told her there was nothing they could do.''

"Ah," said Halsick, nodding. "This was way before current stalker laws."

"She went to a lawyer, but when he told her his fees— well, she came back home. So we moved," explained Diedre. "Three months later he found us and we moved again. That's when my mother happened to find a purse that had been left in a fitting room at J. C. Penney's. It had identification in it . . . Well, she returned the purse and money but kept the ID. And that's how we really got away. She began using the name in the purse, Kowalchik."

"Your mother sounds like quite a survivor."

"Yeah . . . Eventually my father died in a drunk-driving accident and my mother could go back to her own name. She'd had years of worry and stress because she was being hunted, and because she was using someone else's name illegally. I made up my mind that I was going to help women like her, women who had no money and nothing but their own courage."

"Brava, Diedre. I'd like to meet your mother sometime, she sounds like quite a lady."

The conversation turned to Halsick's own legal career, and he told her that when he turned seventy he had hip-replacement surgery, and decided to devote the bulk of his time to pro bono work. He was now faculty adviser for a law student group called Women's Law Services Club, which helped local women with legal problems.

"I've heard of the group," said Diedre. "Isn't it for second-year students?"

"First and second, yes. Second-year students are legally eligible, in Michigan, to advise an indigent person and appear for them in court, if they conduct themselves under the supervision of a state bar member, and if they have completed a passing grade in law school courses. Our first-year students don't have courtroom privileges. You would work one-on-one with clients, help plan case strategy and draft your own pleadings, motions, and orders. But you're closely supervised by an attorney who appears in court for your cases—that attorney being me. Sound interesting to you, Diedre?''

''Oh, yes!''

''Good, because we're having a meeting on Thursday, and I already have a case I think you might be very much interested in. She's a young graduate student who worked as a topless dancer at a club in Detroit in order to care for her four-year-old son. Now her ex-husband is suing for change of custody, claiming she is an unsuitable mother because of her unconventional lifestyle. He's refused Friend-of-the-Court arbitration and is going directly for the jugular. In other words, the case is going to court, and there's going to be an evidentiary hearing.''

''Is she still dancing?''

''I believe she has quit that. Her husband is still using it as evidence, however, to support his contentions that she's morally unfit to have custody of the child.''

''I would love to take on the case,'' said Diedre excitedly.

''Good—I thought you would, Diedre.''

Halsick began talking about the laws and ramifications of child custody, including the eleven factors that had to be examined by the court to determine the ''best interests of the child,'' items such as the mental and physical health of the parties involved, the home, school, and community record of the child.

He went on, ''Even the preference of the child as to which parent he or she wants to live with—and courts have accepted that children as young as four do have a right to express some preference. So you see, it's not just one thing that determines custody, but a whole slew of factors, and we'll have to prove that our client meets every one of them, or we could lose our case or have it go to appeal.''

There was a lot more. Diedre listened intently. She wished she'd brought a notepad with her to take detailed notes.

* * *

On Sunday Diedre spent twenty minutes scouring her closet again, trying to decide what to wear for her date with Mitch Sterling.

Mitch had said jeans, so she decided to pair them with a hunter green silk blouse and high-heeled, clunky shoes. Pam braided Diedre's hair for her, weaving a green velvet ribbon into one thick, honey-colored plait.

"Very sophisticated," Pam said, assessing the results.

"But is it right for a party with all those professors and third-year students?" Diedre fretted.

"Who cares? You'll be the prettiest one there," Pam declared. "Trust me. Anyway, it's Mitch you have to look good for, not a bunch of professors."

"It's only a first date, not even really a date, it's not that important," insisted Diedre.

"No? Then why are you acting so nervous?"

"I'm not nervous."

"Then why are you pacing around like that? You're going to wear a track in the carpeting," Pam said, giggling.

At exactly 1:15 Mitch arrived, dressed in jeans and a white cotton sweater. His black hair was glossy-clean, still showing comb marks, and his eyes traveled over Diedre in her jeans and beribboned braid, obviously liking what he saw. Diedre flushed under his scrutiny, angry at herself for letting him make her nervous.

"Ready for a little verbal sparring?" he asked. "I'm telling you, Aunt Cloris's parties are almost as good as moot court. And if there are any writers, it can get quite interesting."

"I'm ready."

They drove out of town on US-23, exiting within a few miles onto Whitmore Lake Road, a pleasantly rural road with trees nearly meeting overhead in places, lined by homes that ranged from old, rural farmhouses to an occasional new, big home. Diedre stared out the car window, trying to quell her growing unease.

This was insane. Wasn't it? *Mitch is the father of my baby.* What was she doing here with him? But it was too late now, they already were on their way to his aunt's house. She could hardly tell him to stop the car in the middle of the road and let her get out because she had changed her mind.

Mitch began telling Diedre about some volunteer work he was doing. "I'm sort of a coach to a bunch of handicapped kids. They play wheelchair basketball."

As he described one spunky eight-year-old girl named Jalessa, and her efforts to overcome the effects of a crippling automobile accident, Diedre heard the note of deep caring in Mitch's voice.

"You really love kids, don't you?"

"Always have. Someday I'm going to have about seven or eight, and maybe I'll even adopt a few, too. I wouldn't mind having ten kids. There're too many kids in this world that no one wants."

With every word, Diedre's stomach twisted into a tighter knot. Mitch loved kids, wanted them. Not just one or two, but *ten*. News that he'd already fathered one would certainly blow him away, she thought guiltily.

Professor Cloris Kovaks lived in an old, white-painted frame farmhouse surrounded by overgrown blackberry bushes and ancient apple trees that still bore stunted fruit. Apples lay on the ground, emitting a sweet, fruity odor. Several dozen cars were parked in the gravel driveway or on the grass, which needed cutting and raking.

They walked inside and were greeted by their hostess, who had abandoned her usual classroom drab blacks and grays for a melon-colored silk pantsuit and silver ethnic jewelry.

"Welcome, Diedre—come—the group is in the sunroom and they're already in a shouting match about that California immigration dispute. Come and join the melee. And please, do share your opinion with us. We expect it."

The farmhouse was crammed with bulging bookcases that contained everything from law books to current literature and mystery novels, including the three or four that Cloris herself had written.

She led them into a long, glassed-in porch that looked out over a large garden plot that still boasted stalks of desiccated corn and sunflowers. People were sitting around a table and lounging on window seats, everyone talking loudly. Nervously Diedre recognized several of her law professors, including Professor Cury, who taught her Torts class.

She and Mitch joined one of the debating groups, talking about immigration laws, and after a few nudges from Mitch, Diedre offered her opinion, then hotly defended it against attack from the other guests.

"You were definitely brilliant," said Mitch as the guests finally dispersed to raid the buffet table, consisting mostly of purchased salads and a spiral-cut ham, served with pitchers of sweet Michigan cider. "I could tell even Aunt Cloris thought so, and she's hard to please. It's easy to see you're a natural lawyer, Diedre. The way you analyze facts—no wonder you got that big scholarship."

"How did you know about my scholarship?"

"No big secret, the announcement was in the *Detroit Legal News*."

Flushed with triumph at her success, Diedre was riding high on adrenaline, almost forgetting she had wanted to stop the car and get out on the way over to the party. She had acquitted herself well today, and in front of her law professors.

"Do come again, Diedre," said Professor Kovaks when they were getting ready to leave. "And bring this big lug with you. I think you bring out the best in him. He actually behaved for a change."

Driving home, Diedre felt relaxed, happy. The party had been fun, challenging. She had argued well. Now she had the Women's Law Services case to look forward to. Even Mitch had been fun, and certainly he'd been extremely attentive, bringing her glasses of wine, making sure she met everyone.

"Did you enjoy yourself?" he asked quietly.

"Oh, yes."

"Enough to want to make a repeat experience out of it?"

"Another party, you mean?"

"If you want. But I was thinking more along the lines of a law-student date—you know, that exciting evening where both people hunch over their law books and take a break at eleven o'clock for a cup of coffee, then go back to two more hours of studying."

Diedre felt the blood rush to her face. Oh, God, she should have known he would want to see her again. Now what would she tell him?

She managed, "You make it sound positively thrilling."

He turned his face toward her, grinning. "It can be very intense, two people poring over casebooks, muttering to themselves in legalese, occasionally stopping to say, please pass the legal dictionary."

She couldn't help laughing. "I don't know," she hedged.

"Tomorrow night? Law library. Six o'clock."

"I'm not sure—"

"Of course you're not sure. But with or without me, you're going to *be* there studying, aren't you? And at least I can offer a pizza break . . . with sun-dried tomatoes, hmmm? And maybe a pitcher of beer. This time I'll pay."

She wanted to. She found herself caught by his logic. She would be there anyway, wouldn't she? Besides, how intimate could a library date be in a room full of a hundred people?

"Maybe one time," she said.

There were twenty law students who showed up in the Cook Room of the Lawyer's Club for the meeting of the Women's Law Services Club. Ninety percent of them were women, about what Diedre had expected.

The students gathered around a battered twenty-cup coffeemaker, talking, as law students always did, about classes, cases, and professors. Then Rodger Halsick appeared, again wearing a sport jacket and jeans, his white hair flying. He carried a stack of legal-sized manila folders and looked quite pleased with himself.

"For those of you who are new, welcome, and we intend

to work your butts off, so I hope you're prepared for that. Your reward is going to be practical legal experience, the kind you can't get anywhere else, at least not right now in your first year of law school.''

He went on at length about what would be expected of them, and the legal regulations involved in their helping indigent women; then he began handing out case folders.

Diedre opened hers with interest. Marcie Hertz was twenty-six, a master's degree candidate in psychology.

''Uh-oh,'' Diedre thought, reading the long, technical title of Marcie's master's thesis, which turned out to be a report on sexual acting-out behavior among children under the age of ten who had been physically abused. She went on to read that until a month previously, Marcie had been employed at a topless club called the Booby Trap on Eight Mile Road in Detroit. ''An establishment of lewd and lascivious behavior,'' stated the ex-husband's petition for a change of custody.

''You're going to find this case interesting,'' said Rodger Halsick later, as the group was drinking more coffee before dispersing.

''Almost every aspect of her life seems to be oriented to sex in some fashion,'' remarked Diedre. ''The thesis—the topless dancing job. No wonder the ex-husband has freaked out.''

''And yet she's quit the dancing, and the topic of her thesis, approved by her adviser, should hardly be used as a means to punish her,'' said Halsick.

''I agree. I'm going to call her tonight and make an appointment to see her.''

''She may just surprise you, Diedre.''

Her first case. Even if she couldn't personally try the case, and would have to sit in court behind Halsick, Diedre was terribly excited about it, wondering what Marcie Hertz would be like and whether or not she'd be able to do anything for her.

She went to the library and began reading up on child

custody cases, digging into the case literature. *Williamson v. Williamson*, for example, involved a court ruling that "a mother's acts of adultery do not necessarily preclude her from having custody of her children." It was all fascinating when she had a real person to think about, who would be affected by such previous rulings.

"She was a topless dancer?" said Pam, when Diedre told her about the case.

"Yeah . . . but the operative word is 'was.' She doesn't dance anymore. She's working at a restaurant now—the Red Caboose. That's a respectable place."

"But she did dance. Deeds, have you ever been to one of those topless places?"

"No," said Diedre. "Have you?"

"Once, yeah, I went once last year with Kenny Ventimiglia, before I started dating Bud. He was drunk and wanted to show it to me. The lap dancing is really obscene. Well, you saw *Showgirls,* didn't you? And *Striptease*? The women squat right over the men, sticking their crotches in the men's faces, or rubbing them down below . . . trying to get them to come in their pants."

"Just great," groaned Diedre.

"Oh, and that's not all," Pam went on. "Some of the women, well, they do private parties, and God only knows how 'private' it really is, if you catch my drift."

"You mean they're prostitutes."

"Well, maybe some aren't," admitted Pam grudgingly.

"Just because you're a topless dancer doesn't mean you're a whore."

"No? But a lot of people sure think so," said Pam.

That night Diedre called her mother and told Cynthia all about the case she'd been assigned.

"A topless dancer? But will you have time for your regular work?" her mother asked anxiously.

"I can do it, Mom. I just have to concentrate. This law firm wants to see how I can perform under pressure. They're looking me over, that's what Mitch says. Besides, I can't pass up the great opportunity. This kind of experience is worth more than reading ten law books.''

But her mother had zeroed in on the name she had mentioned. ''Mitch?''

''A—a guy I'm seeing,'' Diedre stammered.

''This isn't the same Mitch you waited all summer for a phone call from, is it?''

''Yes.''

''Honey—'' But then Cynthia Samms stopped whatever she'd been going to say. ''Oh, Diedre, you're so young and strong it boggles my mind sometimes. The world is going to be yours if you're careful.''

Careful. Diedre flushed, knowing exactly what her mother meant. The abortion, men . . . That was what Cynthia was referring to. Diedre tried to allay her mother's fears that she would wreck her law career before it even got started.

''I will, Mom—and there won't be any cause to be 'careful,' because he's just a casual study date and I'm going to keep it that way. I'm not going to get serious with him, Mom.''

''Just . . . please be careful,'' Cynthia couldn't resist saying.

They talked for a while longer, Cynthia sharing the news that her company had given her a fifty-cent per hour raise. Diedre congratulated her, trying not to show her anger that the company hadn't been more generous—receptionists like her mother were among the lower-ranking clerical workers, paid next to nothing. Finally Diedre said good-bye and hung up.

I am strong, she thought. *I can handle the custody case and I can handle Mitch Sterling, too—if I keep it real casual.*

Diedre's library date with Mitch turned out to be exactly that—a marathon study session with textbooks, followed by a pizza, then more studying. Diedre was painfully aware of Mitch sitting next to her, his movements as he shifted in his chair, the occasional warm smile he directed her way.

"Exciting, huh?" said Mitch as he drove Diedre back to the apartment. "I really loved it when we looked in the legal dictionary together."

She had to smile. "Well, it certainly went exactly as promised."

The apartment complex was alive tonight with the excesses of Saturday night in a university town. Several units had windows silhouetted with people holding beer cans, rock music pounding loudly. Inebriated guests spilled out of doorways, yelling and laughing. Someone's car alarm had gone freaky. A Hungry Howie's pizza delivery man was trying to carry three big insulated vinyl pizza carriers into a building.

Mitch pulled into the parking lot, parking under one of the covered structures in a space that belonged to Pam's neighbor. "Diedre," he whispered as he shut off the engine. He slid both arms around her and leaned toward her, his dark eyes luminous in the parking-lot lights. "I've been wanting to do this for weeks."

His lips were every bit as soft, mobile, and sexy as Diedre remembered.

"Mitch . . ." She attempted to pull away, but it wasn't much of an attempt. "Please . . ."

"Just a kiss, one or two kisses. I swear, nothing more than that, Diedre. I promise I won't jump you."

She was past thinking, past common sense. Almost of their own volition, her arms looped around his neck as she breathed in the musky, exciting scent of Mitch's body, the clean smell of his shampoo.

He held her tightly. "Diedre . . . ah, God . . ."

The kiss seemed to last for hours, the deep kind that left her mind fuzzy, her heartbeat hammering, one kiss merging into another one even more compelling. Her eyes, her cheekbones, her jawline, her neck, all received warm, almost worshipful kisses while Mitch murmured over and over again how beautiful she was.

Somehow the gearshift knob was knocking her in the hip

. . . Her knee hit the dashboard. In another world, Diedre barely felt the pain.

Then some partygoer walked across the parking lot with a can of beer in his hand, pausing to thump on the trunk of Mitch's car with the flat of his hand. The loud noise jolted Diedre back to reality.

"Please . . . we have to stop," she managed to say, pulling back. *Christ.* They couldn't have sex. No way. She certainly didn't have a condom and she wasn't trusting herself to his, and . . . she had promised not only her mother but herself. "Pam's waiting up for me," she went on quickly.

"Why, do you have a curfew?" he teased.

"We have an agreement," she blurted. She grabbed up her shoulder bag and pushed open the passenger door. "It— was a great study date, Mitch," she added, then hurried across the parking lot before he could follow her.

On the doorstep, she grabbed her building key from her purse and quickly let herself into the downstairs hall. Thank God no parties were going on in their building tonight. All she could hear from the closed apartment doors were TV sets, not drunken screaming.

"Well, *you* have a nice case of whisker burn," announced Pam when Diedre came in, grinning as she looked up from a movie she was watching on Channel 7. Pam was comfortably dressed in a long, baggy T-shirt and leggings, her buttery blond hair piled on her head and secured with a pink plastic clip. It was her "at home" mode, for the nights when Bud didn't visit.

"I do not," said Diedre, touching her hot cheeks.

"Your lips are whisker-worn," observed Pam, laughing. "Is he a good kisser?"

"He's—we only kissed a little."

"A little? Honey, you look like you've been at the drive-in movie for six hours."

"Really, Pam!" Holding her spine straight, Diedre walked into the kitchen and found a Diet Pepsi in the refrigerator, carrying it through to her bedroom. "I'm going to bed," she announced.

Immediately she glanced in the dresser mirror and was appalled to see that her lips *were* raw-looking, her cheeks reddened. And that red scrape on her neck . . . maybe it was whisker burn. Maybe they'd kissed a lot more than she'd thought.

Diedre sighed, feeling a warm melting in her stomach. Glancing at her watch, she saw to her shock that it was 1:15 A.M. She and Mitch had been parked in his car, kissing and necking, for over forty-five minutes.

Diedre had promised to baby-sit for Tarik the following morning while Lashonda had a meeting with her law school adviser. Tarik again had a cold, and his day care center would not take him.

"You give me cookie, DeeDee?" he asked her, smiling brilliantly despite his snuffly nose and shiny eyes.

"Only if Mama says you can have one."

"Don't let him seduce you into the cookie thing," said Lashonda, laughing. "He tries that with everyone. Usually he ends up with cookies, too. I think Tarik is going to be a great persuader when he grows up. At the very least a politician."

After Lashonda left, Diedre settled the toddler in front of the TV set, where he lay listlessly watching a cartoon, and she opened her Contracts textbook, beginning to study.

She couldn't concentrate. All she could think about was Mitch, his kisses, his sweetness. Most of the other guys she'd dated would have been begging for—or demanding— sex, but Mitch had been true to his promise not to "jump" her.

Still, she'd come close, so close, to giving in to him sexually. Again. What was it about him? Did he have some personal PIN code that gave him access to her specific sexual vibrations? Every time she saw him, even that first time . . . He was dangerous, she realized. He made her want to do things she had vowed not to do—*sworn* not to do.

No way, Diedre thought grimly. She was not going to have sex with the man, she wasn't even going to come close to it again. She was not going to risk what she'd worked so hard to get.

Restlessly she got up, wandering toward Lashonda's kitchen. The room was thirty years out of date, its worn plywood cabinets cracked and peeling. The kitchen counters were made of linoleum, not Formica. On the floor, faded linoleum tiles were practically worn through in places. A stack of bills was piled carelessly on the counter. Some of them were stamped OVERDUE. PLEASE REMIT AS SOON AS POSSIBLE. Diedre bit her lip, thinking how close to the edge Lashonda really lived, despite her scholarships and her granny's help.

Again the shame rolled over her, that she hadn't followed Lashonda's path, that she'd been lacking in courage.

When Lashonda returned, she fished in her purse for money to pay Diedre, but Diedre shook her head, waving away the bills.

"Hey, I didn't ask you to sit for free."

"I had to study somewhere," said Diedre, flushing. "Please—it was a privilege to be with Tarik for a little while. He's really a cutie."

PEPPER

GRAY AND PEPPER WALKED HAND IN HAND ALONG THE paths of a park that straddled both sides of the Huron River. It was a warm day in mid-October, the indigo water flashing with light reflections. All around them, picnickers sprawled on blankets, enjoying the day. A young man was doing Frisbee tricks with a beautiful golden retriever that leaped in the air to make every catch, while a group of people stood around cheering the dog on.

Pepper sighed with contentment. "This is my kind of day," she told Gray. "It reminds me of one of those scenes by the Impressionist painters, everyone so relaxed and happy. You could almost think that nobody had any problems.''

Actually, this was the first time that she and Gray had slowed down since they'd met. Over the past month and a half, they'd managed to fit a busy social life into their varying schedules. Wonderful, expensive dinners that had taken them to every fine restaurant within twenty miles of Ann Arbor. Tickets to the Purple Rose Theater in Chelsea, the Fox Theater in Detroit. They'd also seen every top-rated movie and taken in several concerts at Hill Auditorium. It was as if Gray opened up the entertainment section of the newspaper every Thursday to see what he could tempt her with that week.

The Frisbee dog made a spectacular catch, leaping high into the air.

''That dog is working so hard he makes me think of all the work I have piled up on my desk at the office,'' said Gray ruefully.

''Whoa! Don't think of that today.''

His laugh was gentle. ''I told you I was a workaholic. I'm just being honest. But for you I'll stroll in the park and I'll even have some of that picnic you brought. What's in the basket?''

''Croissants stuffed with ham and cheese, fresh grapes and peaches, and some apple tarts I made myself. Oh, and some fresh cider I bought at Kerrytown.''

''Sounds wonderful.'' He pulled her to him, putting two fingers on her chin and tilting her face up so that her eyes met his. ''It's the first meal you've prepared for me. I think I'm going to love just about anything you cook, Pepper. And everything else you do. I didn't know a woman could charm me as much as you do.''

Pepper gazed into Gray's seemingly honest blue eyes. *Charm* wasn't a word that really appealed to her; it sounded false, like a woman trying too hard to impress a man.

''Why do I charm you so much? I certainly haven't gone overboard. I've just been myself.''

"Pepper, you are one of the most alive women I've met. You just shine with life and energy . . . it exudes from your every pore. I suppose I'm trying to soak up some of that, trying to make some of it mine."

Pepper looked away. "Race you back to the picnic basket," she declared, speeding up her steps.

"Ho—no you don't!"

They began running, Gray at first in the lead, then Pepper, and finally they were abreast as they approached the old Hudson's Bay blanket they'd left lying on the ground, along with their woven-wood picnic basket.

"Dead heat," declared Gray, dropping onto the blanket. He began opening the picnic lid, taking out plastic forks and red-checked cotton napkins that Pepper had bought at a garage sale.

They ate companionably, speaking about casual things, books, music, a new CD-ROM game that Gray's company was developing for girls. Computer games mostly attracted boys, and Pepper gave Gray several ideas on games she thought girls might enjoy.

When they were finished Pepper produced some moist towelettes and they washed off their hands. Gray took Pepper's hand in his and carefully sponged off her fingers, attending to the creases between her fingers in a way that was sharply erotic.

"Don't," she said, pulling her hand away. Sex had not been a part of their relationship up to this point. Pepper had firmly told him that she was not ready for that kind of intimacy. She knew it was looming on the horizon, though—in fact, Gray had begun to pressure her in subtle ways such as this that he was ready for their relationship to become physical.

Gray did not comment on her pulling away.

"My son called this morning," he told her.

"Oh?" Pepper knew that Gray had a twenty-six-year-old son named Brian, but he had not talked much about him, other than to say that he was married and lived in Colorado, and he and Gray did not get along all that well.

"They've already had some snow in the mountains, and Brian and his wife and the kids they hang out with are waiting with bated breath for ski season."

"Your son skis?"

"He's a ski instructor, Pepper. He's taught at Loveland, and now he's teaching at Buttermilk, that's the teaching mountain at Aspen. In the summertime he does construction or works as a surveyor. This is a kid with a one thirty-five IQ, Pepper—a kid who could have been a highly paid professional if he'd wanted. Now he just scrapes along financially, drifting from one ski resort to another."

Gray spoke with such bitterness that Pepper couldn't help reaching out and covering his hand with her own.

"Are you disappointed in him?"

"Disappointed? Yes. I agonized over his decision to drop out of high school his senior year, certain that he was doing it to spite me, to hurt me. It took me many, many months to let it go, and I'll confess, sometimes I still wake up in the night wishing that Brian wanted to realize his potential."

Pepper thought of her own relationship with her distant, cool father. The gifts, the tennis camps and dude ranches, when he could fit them in; the bouquets of roses that were supposed to make everything all right if he canceled at the last minute.

"I guess all kids engage in battle with their parents at one time or another," she remarked.

"Pepper, I've decided it isn't that important to battle with my son. I had a mild heart attack about eight months ago . . . It's healed completely, and they tell me it was more of a warning than an actual heart attack. But it taught me a lot of things. I had to change my ways." Gray smiled at her. "I don't battle so much anymore. I try to smell the roses along the way. Sometimes I just sit in the park with a beautiful woman and look at the light shining on the water."

Gray slid his arm around Pepper's back, and she leaned into his embrace, feeling suddenly comfortable in a way she had not before.

"Were you afraid when you had your heart attack?"

"Not really, because I thought it was indigestion. But later they had me on sedatives. Only after I was home from the hospital did I realize I could have died. Died with so much left unfinished. With my life still a tapestry of mistakes."

Pepper fell silent. She was thinking of her own "mistakes," her two failed marriages, the bankruptcy of the jewelry shop she had owned four years previously, her two abortions.

"We all make mistakes," she muttered. "I have. I've made many mistakes."

Gray hugged her tighter. "I can see it in your eyes, sometimes, Pepper . . . the hurt. I want to fix things for you. I mean that, Pepper."

She didn't know what to say—what she could or should say. No man, certainly not her father or Jack, had ever wanted to be there for her "all the way." They had all used her, shown her off, neglected her or smothered her, pleasing her only if it suited their agendas.

"I've always taken care of myself, Gray," she finally said. "I'm good at it. I've always solved my own problems."

She began cleaning up the picnic ware, loading everything back in the basket, moving briskly, efficiently, knowing that she had broken the mood. Gray frightened her a little, with his declarations, his increasing indications that he was falling in love with her. Did she really want that?

"More roses just came," announced Jan Switzer the next week, one busy morning at the boutique. "A great big arrangement, as usual. I've put them in the back room on your desk until we can get them open."

Pepper was in the middle of waiting on a customer, showing her several pairs of sand-washed silk charmeuse boxer pajamas. She rang up the sale, convincing the woman to add her name to Pepper's growing mail list.

"I just *love* your shop," the woman raved as she was preparing to leave. "And your beautiful white cat. I don't suppose you've ever considered selling him?''

"Oscar? He's my family," said Pepper, smiling and shaking her head.

After the customer had left, Pepper walked into the back room to unwrap the florist's wrap from the delivery. The roses were white today, kissed with pale salmon at the tips of their lush petals. Pepper happened to know that they came from a special grower and were very expensive.

As always, she smelled the roses' unique, spicy scent, trying to take pleasure in them, but something inside her also wished that Gray would drop the blitz of flowers. She'd dropped hints that he was sending too many, too often, but he'd thought she was merely being modest.

Well, at least the magnificent roses added to the decor of her shop, and customers frequently commented on them. She carried the arrangement to the front and placed them near a display of nightgowns she wanted to draw attention to.

"He's really wooing me," she remarked to Jan.

"You don't like being wooed."

"I've never *been* courted before, not like this. You know how it's been. Candlelight dinners, tickets . . ." Her voice trailed off.

"The bottom line is, do you like him?" said Jan.

"Yes, I—I more than like him. He's every woman's dream, I know that." She went on, "But he's also—I don't know. Old-fashioned. In a lot of ways he reminds me of—" Pepper bit off the word, clapping one hand to her mouth.

"Reminds you of who, Pepper?"

"My—" But she couldn't say the word. *My father.* That was who Gray reminded her of.

At six o'clock Pepper said good night to Jan and locked up the shop, putting the CLOSED sign on the door. She put on her running shoes, going jogging around the downtown streets as she often did after she closed the boutique. *My father.* Now, why did she have to think about him now?

Oh, Mason Maddalena had taken Pepper on some memorable vacations. They'd gone skin-diving in Hawaii. Dude ranching in Montana. He'd taken her with him to a tennis camp one year, and Pepper had been forced to play tennis six hours a day, becoming a reasonably good player in the process.

It was nearly dark, the short days of winter almost upon them. She swung down Liberty, passing the familiar shops where she knew every display item in each window almost as well as she knew her own. A lesbian couple strolled ahead of her, holding hands. A man walked a huge Great Dane. Inside Zev's Coffee Shop, where she'd met Gray, she could see people sitting at the small, crowded tables.

She'd wanted to love her father. Sometimes she *had* loved him, especially when he paid attention to her without the current blond wife or girlfriend.

But then she'd return home after the visit to face her mother's jealous questions. *What did you do? Who was Daddy with this time? Was she beautiful? Did she have on a lot of jewelry? Did Daddy give her a necklace, a bracelet, a watch? What did he give* you, *Pepper? You should have asked him, he would have given you more . . .*

Sometimes, after Pepper arrived back from one of these vacations, Toni Maddalena would keep her up half the night, talking to her about men, and particularly her father.

"When they're finished with you, then they throw you aside like used Kleenex," Toni said bitterly. "Used Kleenex! They just toss you away into the wastebasket! So you better get what you can from them. If your father takes you into a jewelry store, I want you to point to something and tell him you want it, hear? He'll give it to you . . ."

Now Pepper ran hard, punishing herself until her breath heaved in and out of her throat and a stitch jabbed into her rib cage. No wonder Gray's elaborate courtship made her feel so uneasy.

In so many ways, Gray did act like her father, Pepper told herself, as she slowed down and gasped for breath, swinging her arms back and forth. The flowers. The candy. The expensive dinners, the theater tickets—all of it. Even the damn roses.

Pepper returned to her shop and was unpacking a shipment of jacquard lounge shirts when the phone rang. She grabbed the phone and said hello while continuing to unfold the garments.

"Is this Pepper Nolan?" It was a woman's rich, contralto, African-American voice.

"Yes . . . this is Pepper."

"Well, my name is Treva Connor, and I'm a licensed social worker, a counselor at the Geddes/Washtenaw Women's Clinic."

"Oh! Oh, yes." Pepper belatedly remembered she had signed an agreement to participate in an abortion study. "Is it about that study?"

They discussed the study for a few minutes, while Treva assured Pepper of her total privacy. "I'm on bed rest," Treva explained, "for a problem pregnancy, so I've been doing the interviews by phone. Will that be a problem for you, Pepper?"

"I have no problem with that," she responded. "In fact, since I'm so busy with my business, it might work out very well."

"Wonderful," said Treva warmly. "Did you want to start now? With the basic stuff, I mean. We'll probably need several phone calls, especially during this first interview phase. There'll be an interview each year for four years."

"Now would be fine." Pepper drew a deep breath. She would do this, for herself. Maybe she could learn something from the abortion, maybe she could grow in some way. Maybe it would not have been for nothing.

Gray had invited Pepper to a black-tie benefit dance for the Make-A-Wish Foundation, which provided last wishes for dying children. Every year his company sponsored a table.

Pepper stood in front of her small closet, pawing through a succession of black separates, some of thrift-shop origin, all of which had already done yeoman duty in her busy social life with Gray Ortini.

"Nothing," she cried in exasperation. "If I wear any of this stuff again, I'm going to feel like Wanda the funky witch."

"So what's so bad about funky?" Jan Switzer was perched on Pepper's bed, cradling Oscar in her lap. "Pepper, you know you wear clothes fabulously. I don't care what you put on, you'll look great in it."

"Yeah . . . but I just don't have *enough* clothes." Pepper heaved a sigh. "Not for Gray's lifestyle, anyway. Wives of men like him think nothing of spending two thousand dollars on one outfit, and here my closet looks like a resale shop."

"I should find a resale shop that looks half as good as your closet, woman."

Pepper uttered another sigh of exasperation. "Oh, Jan. I spend ten to twelve hours a day at the boutique. I never even thrift-shop anymore, not with Gray in my life. I don't have time. And now this black-tie dance comes along. I want to look great, but I just haven't got the money to spend two thousand dollars or more on a dress."

"So don't," said Jan.

"What do you mean?"

"You already have something to wear, Pepper. I'm surprised you haven't thought of it. You must be too close to your boutique to really notice what you have for sale."

"What are you talking about?"

"Slip dresses, my dear. We have at least eight of them in the shop right now, and you know lots of the stars are still wearing them, or variations of them. Rachel Hunter, Halle Berry, Sofia Coppola, Goldie Hawn, Demi Moore . . . I could go on and on naming names. Pepper, you have a body just as good as any of theirs. And I seem to recall a smashing little eggplant-colored number you could shimmy right into."

"The one with the double spaghetti straps?"

"The very one."

Pepper sank down on the bed and began to laugh. "Oh, God, Jan. You're right, that's exactly what I should do. Go glam in a slip. Do you think it would be too sexy?"

"Trust me, Gray's not going to complain. One more thing," Jan added after a pause.

"What's that?"

"It's just a little hint, Pepper. You've been having a merry old time with this man for quite a while now. He's been marvelously patient, but you and I both know what men eventually want, no matter how patient they are."

"Hmmmm," said Pepper.

"Well, I don't want to accompany you to anymore clinics, darling Pepper, so why don't you call your gynecologist, if you haven't already?"

Pepper flushed. She'd already done that, getting a prescription for Lo/Ovral. She told Jan this.

Jan paused. "Your feelings aren't hurt that I said that, are they?"

"No . . ." said Pepper. But she was hurt, just a little.

"Oh, lady," said Gray when he picked her up on Saturday evening at her apartment. "Oh, *lady*."

His eyes flicked appreciatively down Pepper's slim body, taking in the long, eggplant-colored gown with its stunning lace inserts that revealed hints of skin, and its low-cut sides that barely held her in. With it Pepper wore some antique garnet jewelry she'd picked up at an antique fair several years previously, and funky, black high heels.

"You like the dress?" At his frank, almost electric admiration, Pepper felt a warm flush spread all over her skin.

"I love the dress. I love you. You're simply the most stunning woman I've ever laid eyes on."

I love you. It was the first time he had said it, the words just slipping out. Pepper decided to act as if his comment referred to the dress, not her.

"Well, I hope this mansion we're going to is heated, because I can tell you one thing right now," Pepper said, nervously smiling. "Spaghetti straps are definitely on the chilly side."

"I'll keep you warm."

"I imagine you will. But just in case you don't, I've got a lace shawl."

However, as they were leaving her apartment, Pepper stopped to adjust her shawl in the wall mirror, and recoiled. *Oh, God . . . too much cleavage showed!* And the sides of the dress were cut way low, revealing too much of the curvy sides of her breasts. She stared at herself, appalled.

Gray glanced at her, his expression gentle. "Pepper, you're thinking about running back in the bedroom and changing . . . aren't you? I can see the urge written all over your face."

She jumped guiltily. "How could you tell I was thinking that?"

"Because I'm beginning to know you. You're a very private woman, Pepper. Honey, you look beautiful in that dress, but if it's too much for you, I'll be happy to wait while you go change into something else. Honest."

It was one of the kindest things he had said to her, and if he hadn't said it, she probably *would* have gone to change.

"I'll wear it," she decided, smiling. "But I'm hanging on to this shawl."

It was a cool evening suffused with tiny droplets of mist that glowed in halos around streetlights, as if a cloud had drifted down on Ann Arbor, blanketing the university town. The black-tie dinner was being held in a Victorian mansion on Washtenaw. Formerly owned by a lumber king, the house was reputed to contain nearly forty rooms, including a spectacular ballroom.

They pulled into a circular driveway, behind a line of cars dropping off guests in evening wear. A valet parker in a blue jacket came racing out to take Gray's car and help Pepper out of the passenger seat.

Pepper pulled her lacy shawl over her shoulders as Gray escorted her underneath the elegant, white-pillared front portico. Several men standing inside the entrance turned to stare at her in the skimpy slip dress.

Gray squeezed her arm reassuringly. "Don't mind them," he said. "You're the most beautiful woman this mansion has seen in ninety years. I'm sure there're going to be more than a few envious ghosts."

Inside, a string quartet was playing. A bar was serving mixed drinks, and Gray went to fetch Pepper a glass of wine, while she stood watching the parade of elegantly dressed people. She'd attended parties like this before with Jack—when they'd had money—and she'd always enjoyed the people watching. She nodded to a few women she recognized, most of whom had bought lingerie at her boutique. It gave her a feeling of pride, that her customers were among Ann Arbor's wealthiest, most civic-minded citizens.

Her eyes fastened on Gray standing at the bar, his stunning silver hair gleaming in the lamplight. Even in repose, his mouth seemed to curve slightly at the corners, a smile waiting to happen. He was a man who had grown into himself, she saw.

"Happy?" said Gray, returning with her drink. "You look happy, Pepper. And very relaxed."

"I suppose I am. I've just seen eight women who've spent more than a thousand dollars at my shop."

"Good. Now let's wander around a bit, see if we can find some of the people from GrayCo who're going to be at our table. I'd like to introduce you."

It was after 2:00 A.M. when Gray finally drove Pepper back to her apartment. The cloudy mist had turned into a light rain that pattered down, coating the street with glistening water.

Pepper still felt suffused with pleasure from the gourmet dinner in the huge ballroom adorned with antique chandeliers and gilded, carved ceiling molding. Later, they'd danced to two alternating bands, one a rock band, the other an eight-piece orchestra that played more conventional dance music and some swing music from the 1940's.

Swaying to a slow, dreamy fox-trot, being held close in
Gray's arms, Pepper'd felt unadulteratedly happy, wishing
the evening could continue for hours longer.

Now the big apartment house owned by Mrs. Melnick
was mostly dark, except for some lights still glowing in the
first-floor apartment belonging to Billy Ip, an engineering
student who usually studied most of the night, even on
weekends.

"Well, I don't see your landlady's lights on," whispered
Gray, holding on to Pepper's hand as they reached the
porch. "So I guess it means I don't have to run the landlady
gauntlet again."

"I thought you wanted to see the original plans for the
house," Pepper teased.

"I do—only not now when I have a gorgeous woman at
my side."

They tiptoed upstairs, still holding hands, and Pepper unlocked her apartment door. Oscar came strutting out to greet
them, his beautiful white tail waving. He meowed and
rubbed himself against Pepper's expensive slip dress, shedding a few white hairs in the process.

"Hi, guy," said Gray genially to the cat.

The apartment was dimly lit, mysterious shadows falling
across the floor, cast by the patterns in Pepper's lace curtains
filtering the glow of the yard lights that Mrs. Melnick always
kept burning.

"Coffee?" Pepper whispered. "Or some wine?"

"Neither," said Gray. "I've had enough wine. The only
thing I want is you. Pepper . . . ?"

She felt a moment's fear, then she drew in a deep breath
and whispered, "Yes."

Her double bed was draped with embroidered cloths, and
held seven or eight pillows, all covered in white embroidery
or lace. Pepper led Gray over to it, and they stood next to
it, locked in each other's arms.

"Pepper . . . ah, God . . . are you sure you're ready?"
Gray said, kissing her face, her neck, finally her lips.

"Yes."

"I've wanted you since that first night I saw you at the coffee shop. God, how I've wanted you. It's been so hard to hold back."

She wrapped her arms around him, giving herself up to the softness of his kisses, which quickly heated up until they were clinging together, breathing rawly, their hands caressing backs, hips, thighs. He had a solid, firm butt, she discovered to her great pleasure. She'd always loved the look of a well-muscled male rear.

Gray slid the spaghetti straps down over her shoulders, pulling the slip dress down until her breasts were exposed. Pepper felt a brief flicker of nervousness—her slimness extended to her B-cup breasts—but that quickly disappeared as Gray whispered, "Such lovely breasts. You're perfect, Pepper . . . you have a perfect body."

Now he kissed her shoulders, her nipples, the sides and undersides of her breasts, his breath warm on her skin, heating her flesh. Shaking, obviously very moved, Gray pulled the slip down over Pepper's sides, peeling it away from her until she stood only in her panty hose.

"Panty hose," said Gray, half laughing, his voice burred and husky. "They always faze me . . . What do I do with them?"

"You wait while I take them off," she whispered, her skin hot all over as she stepped out of the hose, dropping them on the floor. She stood before him naked.

Gray was throwing off his own clothes now, tossing them to the floor, starched white shirt and bow tie falling beside the cummerbund, expensive jacket, and evening trousers. "Ah, Pepper . . ."

In the lacy glow of the outside yard lights, Pepper looked at Gray's body, still well molded despite his fifty-one years. A tangle of black hair on his chest, streaked with silver, traveled down toward his stomach and a patch of darkness at his groin. He was erect, his penis thick in circumference and urgently rock-hard.

"I wish I could be thirty for you again," he whispered as he took her in his arms and laid her down on the bed.

"But I want you now, the way you are," she said into his mouth. "But I also want you to wear a condom. I went on the pill, but I'm not a hundred percent sure it's safe yet, and besides—we need to be safe."

Even in the dark, it felt so intrusive to be forced to say this.

"I have to tell you," said Gray, briefly pulling back after he put on the condom. "I reversed my vasectomy after my divorce."

"You reversed it?" she couldn't help saying.

"I made many mistakes in child rearing and I thought maybe—someday there'd be a second chance—a chance to rectify things . . ."

He meant he wanted a baby! But Pepper was too much aflame with sexual desire and need; her mind would not concentrate. She wrapped her arms around him, caressing his back and firm butt.

"Ah," he said, rolling her over after a few moments and positioning her so that she was on top of him. Slowly, sensuously, his hands reached and stroked, lingering here, exploring there, roaming like molten fire over her hips, then back to her buttocks and then to the crease between them.

Finally he explored the most intimate and delicate part of her, stroking her clitoris from behind with his fingers until Pepper moaned, close to orgasm.

"There isn't any part of you I don't want to know, Pepper," he said hoarsely. "I am going to love every inch of you—over and over and over."

He was true to his word, and Pepper returned the favor, exploring his maleness with lips and tongue and hands, tasting the sweetness of his most private fluids, smelling his intimate scents. He was gentler than Jack, yet stronger, sexier, making her feel worshiped and special.

He brought her to three climaxes, until she lay spent and exhausted, laughing and insisting that she could not take it anymore.

*   *   *

Gray left at five-thirty in the morning, explaining that he had to go home, shower, and change. Even though it was Sunday, he planned to go into the office today to work most of the morning.

"But I'll think of you all day, Pepper. And if I can't concentrate, it'll all be due to you."

He kissed her good-bye, the kiss lingering and sexual, threatening to have them both in bed, all over each other again. "I'll call you later," he promised.

Pepper let him out of the apartment, relocked the door, and walked back to bed where she fell on the mattress and was instantly asleep, as if drugged. When Oscar came out from behind the living room couch and hopped up beside her, nestling in the curve formed by her bent knees, Pepper didn't even feel him.

TREVA

SUNLIGHT STREAMED THROUGH THE FLOOR-TO-CEILING living room windows, illuminating a bird feeder that Wade had installed on the back deck so Treva could watch the robins, cardinals, and jays, and the feisty red squirrels with their creative efforts to steal the birdseed.

Wade was in his study writing a chapter for his new textbook while Treva lay on the couch, restlessly flicking through the cable channels. She was now in her second trimester, seventeen weeks along, and bed rest had rapidly lost its allure. Even the abortion-study phone interviews didn't seem to keep her busy enough, because most of the calls had to take place in the evening when the women were home from school or their jobs. It was going to take her and Mei, and maybe another interviewer, to complete the first year's interviews on time.

She aimed the clicker. Zap. Zap. She'd never realized

how boring TV really could be when you were faced with huge, indigestible chunks of it.

She channel-surfed up and down, trying the premium movie channels, then hesitating on the previews for Pay-Per-View, but nothing appealed to her.

Then a program caught her eye. It was a talk show on one of the PBS channels, and appeared to be about the medical problems of black women during pregnancy. They were interviewing a woman who'd had hypertension, culminating in eclampsia.

"I was in a coma," a woman in a bright red pantsuit was saying. "I was in and out of consciousness, and when I woke up I had a respirator down my throat. They said I'd been on life support." Treva stared at the screen, transfixed.

"So this was full-blown eclampsia," said the host, a thin, dark-skinned woman in blue.

"Yes . . . only I was too out of it to know what it was."

"Sharelle, can you tell us some of the other things that happened to you?"

Sharelle moistened her lips, seeming nervous.

"Actually, my husband told me what happened. I . . . I had several seizures. He said I foamed at the mouth, I stopped breathing, I bit my own tongue so badly that blood was running down my face. I threw myself off the bed and broke my arm . . ."

Horrified, Treva zapped the channel button. In a second, gravel-voiced Bea Arthur was on the screen, in a rerun of "Golden Girls."

Treva sank into her pillows, her entire body shaking. Her first thought was of Wade. Thank God he was upstairs working and hadn't seen this program. She must never tell him this. He was already hyperanxious about her pregnancy, and he didn't need to be further stressed about something that might never happen.

Of course it wasn't going to happen.

They just brought extreme cases to TV—that was what created ratings, Treva told herself, trying to stifle her anxiety.

However, all the rest of the morning, she found herself in a blue type of mood, very unusual for her. She couldn't eat the tuna sandwich and fruit cup that Wade brought her before he left to teach his one o'clock class.

I foamed at the mouth, I stopped breathing . . .

Annie Larocca came that afternoon to visit, ringing the bell they kept in the mudroom to signal her arrival, then walking in, so Treva didn't have to get up. Annie carried a shopping bag from Borders bookstore, and brought a chatter of cheerful gossip about clinic staffers.

Treva tried to act enthusiastic as she tore open the bag, finding three glossy new hardcovers. "Annie! You know what hardbacks cost."

"Well, we all chipped in. And here's something from Bobbie Lynn. She heard you were on bed rest and wanted to give you something, too."

Bobbie Lynn was the "sidewalk counselor" who haunted the clinic parking lot. Annie handed Treva a slim paperback titled *Pro Life Answers to Pro Choice Arguments.*

Treva had seen the book before and she leafed through it, then put it aside. "I saw this really awful TV program, Annie."

"Yeah? What was it about?"

"Bad stuff," admitted Treva. "About black women, and hypertension in pregnancy. They had this woman on who'd been through it, and it was pretty harrowing."

Annie leaned forward. "Babe—of *course* it was harrowing. If it wasn't, they wouldn't have put it on TV. But, Treva, you have to remember that every woman is unique. The heavy-duty problems may never happen to you. You do have a great doctor. Ruth Sandoval has pulled off some major miracles. There're kids—and women—who wouldn't be alive if not for her."

Treva tried to pull herself out of her blue funk. "Oh, Annie, I know that . . . most of the time. But then I see a TV program like this—"

"You don't *have* to watch scare TV, you know. Believe me, there are some Montel and Jenny Jones shows that would bring up your blood pressure by about two hundred points. And CNN is just as bad, sometimes. Protect yourself. Don't watch any of that shit, babe. Don't allow anything that'll spike your BP.''

"In other words, bury my head in the sand.''

"If it works, do it.'' Annie grinned.

"Oh, Annie . . . it's so hard to stay brave day after day,'' Treva admitted in a low voice. "I put on a good front for everyone, especially Wade, but . . .''

"Honey, honey,'' said Annie, patting Treva's hand. "Bed rest is one of the toughest things a pregnant woman can go through. You wouldn't be doing it if there wasn't a problem. You have a ton of free time to worry, and you feel guilty that you can't vacuum the floor and make dinner. You have to lie in one position until you could just scream, and you can't have sex . . .''

Finally Treva laughed. "I guess that describes it, all right. Especially the sex part.''

"Hey,'' said Annie, grinning. "Speaking of sex. Did I tell you that Dr. Rosenkrantz has a boyfriend?''

"No . . .''

"Yeah, he's a doctor who just came back from Haiti where they both used to work. He's about sixty-nine, I think—a younger man. Apparently they've had a thing going off and on for years.''

The idea of tiny, white-haired Dr. Rosenkrantz in an ongoing romance with a "younger'' lover struck Treva as great, and she laughed richly, deep in her throat.

"That's more like it,'' declared Annie. "That's my Treva.''

After Annie left, promising to return in a few days with more prime gossip, Treva heard the mudroom bell ringing again. It was Pepper Nolan, arriving for her interview. Pepper had decided that she really would feel better if they talked in person rather than on the phone, explaining that her shop closed at six and she could return to the shop later to work on some displays.

"Anybody home?"

"Come in, come in," called Treva as she heard the bell. "Through the kitchen and dining room, then turn right."

When Pepper appeared in the living room—a tall, strikingly beautiful, dark-haired woman wearing black silk pants and a silk T-shirt, and minimal makeup—Treva let out a laugh. This was the first time she'd seen Pepper Nolan face-to-face . . . or had she seen her before someplace else? Oh, God, the clinic . . . that day . . . She'd been too upset to really look at anyone's face.

Pepper, too, looked startled. "You're the customer who bought the green gown."

"Yeah, and what a night it was. It got me where I am today," Treva explained, rubbing her rounded stomach.

Both women started laughing.

"Honey, that lingerie of yours ought to be declared off-limits to anyone who isn't wearing contraceptive foam."

More laughter, dissipating the last of Treva's funky mood of earlier in the morning. She motioned for Pepper to sit down. "I can't believe I'm laughing so hard. I think we're gonna be friends."

Pepper obviously felt the same way, and both women were relaxed as they got down to the interview. Finally Treva turned off the tape, but the two women continued to chat. "So how did you get started at the clinic?" Pepper asked. "I mean, to be an abortion worker."

"I'd been a member of a pro-choice group for years. Dr. Rosenkrantz visited the group and I met her. I really admired her for all she'd done in Haiti, and now she was at this clinic here in Ann Arbor. When they had an opening, she called me," Treva explained.

"Do you like it?"

"I get a tremendous amount of satisfaction when I see how we've helped women deal with a really stressful, important time in their lives. Some of the younger women are making their first adult decision ever. Many of them hug us and thank us with tears in their eyes."

"But the stress," said Pepper. "I mean, the danger. I've read horrible things in the paper."

"Yeah . . . there are moments. Like the time a protester sneaked into the clinic, posing as a boyfriend of one of our patients, and chained himself to the urinal in the men's room."

"What happened?"

Treva gave a throaty laugh. "Well, the police had to come in and saw him off. We took our time in calling them, though. In fact . . . well . . . we waited a good nine hours, actually. He was in the clinic way past closing, until Dr. Rosenkrantz got fed up with his hymn singing and finally called the police. One thing, he certainly was conveniently close to bathroom facilities."

Pepper roared with laughter. "That's too funny."

They traded stories, Pepper telling Treva about a woman at her boutique who'd gotten stuck in a nightgown while she was trying it on.

"She was crying and telling me it was the Reuben sandwich she'd eaten for lunch. I mean, really. Then she told me it had to be because the sandwich had given her gas. I never heard of gas jumping you up from a size three to a fourteen, did you?"

They laughed and laughed.

"If I wasn't on bed rest," Treva finally said, "I'd have come back to your boutique and bought about five more gowns *and* gotten put on your mailing list. I don't suppose you have a catalog, do you?"

"As a matter of fact, I'm printing a small sale catalog and I can put you on the list. Or better than that, I can drop by sometime with a selection of gowns."

"Much as I'd love it, I can't ask you to go out of your way."

Pepper smiled. "Well, how about if you invite a few of your friends over as well, and we'll have a mini lingerie party? I only do it for a very few customers. In fact, you'll be the first."

Treva laughed richly. "You're on, Pepper. How about

next Thursday around seven? I promise to have about ten or fifteen women here, maybe more. Just don't bring any gowns so small that my friends get stuck in them, okay? A couple of them are size fourteens and sixteens. As for me— I'm a size twelve when I'm not with child.''

The following week, Pepper arrived at Treva's house carrying two large suitcases. One of Wade's students, a woman named Danica, had been hired to greet the guests and serve the salads and desserts that Wade had purchased.

"I've brought a ton of goodies," Pepper told Treva, beginning to unpack. "I have the most mouthwatering jacquard gowns, and I brought a lot of them in bigger sizes. The fourteen might fit you now, and then you could still wear it later, after the baby is born."

Rhonda was next to arrive, bringing a plate of sweet 'n' spicy chicken wings she'd made, followed by Annie Larocca and Dr. Rosenkrantz. Other clinic employees came, plus several women from Treva's church, Sally, Wade's departmental secretary, and several of the Connors' neighbors.

"Pepper . . . this is Annie Larocca. And Dr. Ellen Rosenkrantz. And this is Gina Eklund . . . and Freddie . . . and Carole, Kyla, Cherise . . . oh, and Mei.''

Several of the clinic workers did double takes when they saw Pepper, who was wearing a white jumpsuit tonight with a long, matching embroidered vest that looked like it had been made from antique cloth. Everyone wanted to know where she had got the vest, and when they heard she had made it, several suggested she ought to make the vests for her shop.

Gales of laughter and ribald comments rose as the women modeled the expensive, sensuous gowns, or held them up to their bodies. Rhonda bought three matching sets of bras and panties, declaring her boyfriend was gonna propose after he saw these. Everyone bought at least two items, and Treva splurged on both of the jacquard gowns, plus some bras and panties for after the baby was born.

"Of course, first there's gonna be a *major* diet," she declared, holding up a sexy little racer-back lace bra.

Later, after the women had left, each carrying a ten-dollars-off certificate Pepper had printed up specially on her computer for the party, Pepper lingered over coffee with Treva. The talk turned serious again. She began telling Treva about Gray Ortini and her mixed feelings about him.

"He sends too many roses, if you can believe it," Pepper said, shaking her head. "He spends more on theater tickets than some families do on food for the month. He's too focused on my looks."

As Treva raised an eyebrow, Pepper went on, "No, really. It's like sometimes he can't see past my face. And that—it scares me a little."

"What, specifically, are you scared *about*? What do you think is really happening? Can you verbalize it, Pepper?"

The other woman sighed, running a hand through her mane of dark, carelessly curled hair. "I'm afraid of being used," she admitted. "Does that sound strange? All my life . . . well, I've looked like this. And men wanted to use me for my looks, did use me. I don't want it to happen with Gray Ortini. I want it to be—more special than that."

Treva frowned. "But how do you separate pretty face, pretty body, from all the rest of it? They are part of you, aren't they? A gift from God?"

"Yeah . . ."

"And isn't his money a part of Gray?"

"Well, yes, but I don't care about his money!" cried Pepper.

"Well, then, maybe he doesn't care about your looks, not the way you fear he does. Pepper, we women all know that men are much more heavily fixated on looks than we are. That's because they respond sexually to visual stimuli." Treva chuckled. "Mother Nature is making sure that men give their genes to a woman who's healthy and strong, and can bear good babies."

Pepper grimaced. "So *that's* it?"

"From the perspective of about a hundred thousand years of humanity, yes. You'd be surprised what kind of tidbits

Wade brings back from his social work classes." Treva patted her rounded rump. "Only I have a feeling that in the case of my ancestors, bigger bottoms were considered a sign of good health, and that's why I've got mine now. Evolution sucks sometimes, doesn't it?"

Both of them laughed.

Pepper left, and the student finished cleaning up the party dishes and loading the dishwasher. Wade came downstairs and wrote the woman a check, then began getting out his air mattress to sleep on, which he kept in the front closet when it was not in use. Treva had worried that it wasn't comfortable, but Wade assured her that it was.

"Makes me feel like I'm camping up in the Upper Peninsula," he always said, laughing and kissing her. "Only instead of a bear at the campsite, I've got my gorgeous Treva."

"You okay, Treva?" he said now, snacking on a leftover chicken wing. "You're not too tired after all that partying?"

"Maybe a little. It was such fun having everyone over . . . I miss that . . . and I bought two dynamite gowns," she added. "Maybe I should model one for you tonight, assuming you can exercise a little self-control."

Wade reached out and found the Pepper's sack, whistling as he pulled out the ivory jacquard gown with a dangerously low neckline.

"This is heavy-duty, Treva. I don't know if you should put it on. I might not have *any* self-control."

She eyed him underneath her lashes. "We could just cuddle. And I could, you know, do a few things for you. The doctor said I couldn't have any orgasms, but she didn't say anything about you, baby."

"Honey." Wade sank down on the couch beside Treva and pulled her into his arms, as much as he could without changing her prescribed left-side position. "I know you're generous to think of me sexually, but I can't be selfish and satisfy myself when I know you can't do anything. How about if I just give you a nice back rub, hmmmn?"

Treva shifted slightly, and Wade climbed behind her, peeling away the velour sweatshirt she wore and unfastening her bra. "You have such smooth skin," he murmured, stroking her back, his fingers working rhythmically.

"Mmmm . . . ah . . . a little further up," Treva sighed ecstatically. She'd always loved having her back rubbed and kneaded.

"Here?"

"Yeah . . . ah . . ."

Wade stroked her back for nearly twenty minutes, while Treva's muscles relaxed and her eyes fluttered shut, her entire body suffused with a feeling of well-being. "Did I ever tell you that I love you?" she murmured.

"Not in the past hour, no."

"Well, I'm telling you now. I don't know what I'd ever do without you, Wade."

He smoothed her skin with his fingertips. "Well, you're not ever going to have to face that possibility," he told her. "You and me, Treva—we're in it for the long haul."

"And our baby," she sighed. "The three of us."

"You and me and Squirt," agreed Wade.

"*Squirt?*" drawled Treva.

"I had a feeling you'd hate that one. How about Horace?"

"Horace?"

"A little far out?"

"Ugly," laughed Treva. "No class at all."

"Newt?"

Treva giggled. "That sounds either like a lizard or a politician. Where are you coming up with these awful names?"

"Well, we might go in for the cold-cash names. You know, Barclay or Cash, or maybe Fortune. Or if it's a girl, we could call her Mercedes, or maybe Sterling."

"*Sterling?*" Treva hooted with laughter. "Since when is a pretty little black girl called Sterling? We might as well name her Muffy."

"Quanisha?"

"No way."

"How about Shakira? Ebony?"

"Those are pretty, but let's keep on thinking. Oh, and could you rub my back a *little* more?"

DIEDRE

HER FIRST REAL CASE.

Diedre was excited as she drove to nearby Ypsilanti, an old, redbrick town that housed Eastern Michigan University and was the site where World War II fighter planes had once been manufactured at Willow Run Airport, thousands of workers imported from the South to do the labor.

The neighborhood where Marcie Hertz lived was run-down, the street filled with homes that had probably been built before the war. She lived in a typical shabby student rental house, the porch listing noticeably to the left. There was an old couch on the porch, half its stuffing coming out, on which snoozed an orange tabby cat. Stickers in the windows advertised REFUSE & RESIST and GAY MEN & LESBIANS' ALLIANCE, plus several other stickers put out by the National Rifle Association. The stickers would probably inflame a vengeful ex-husband, and would not look too great to a Friend-of-the-Court investigator, either.

Diedre rang the front bell and was welcomed by a young black man wearing baggy, yellow pants and no shirt or shoes. He had the prominent musculature of a bodybuilder, and was swigging from a can of some protein beverage.

"Marcie? She's upstairs. 2A."

Diedre walked upstairs and knocked at the door of 2A. Behind it she could hear the sound of a TV set playing morning cartoons.

"You're my lawyer?" said Marcie, answering the door,

staring dubiously at Diedre, who was about the same age she was.

"I'm a first-year law student assigned to your case," said Diedre, getting it all straight up front, as Rodger Halsick had advised. "I will advise you and help with pretrial meetings, and I'll do some of the paperwork, but when we're in court, a lawyer will be present and I'll assist him or her."

"Okay." Marcie did not look totally like the sexpot Diedre had imagined. She did have thick, white-blond hair pulled back into a ponytail, but her face was narrow and foxlike, her nose too sharp, her lips a little too thin. Most people would say her face had only average prettiness. However, Marcie's figure more than made up for any facial defects. She had large breasts and a tiny waistline, assets even loose jeans and a baggy T-shirt could not conceal.

"Come on in," said the graduate student, leading Diedre into an apartment that was as clean and neat as the rest of the building was scruffy. The walls were scrubbed clean, taped with art posters and childish drawings. Several board-and-brick bookcases bulged with books. More books were stacked on the dining room table where an Apple computer had also been set up, its screen filled with dense-looking type—probably Marcie's master's thesis.

An angelic-looking four-year-old boy with blond hair lay on his stomach in front of the TV set, watching Big Bird and Elmo. His hair had been cut in a modified bowl, cascading partly down his head to form a line below which the rest of the hair was clipped short at the nape. He was wearing a pair of little jeans, a U. of M. T-shirt, and high-topped Adidas that made his feet look gigantic.

"I hope you don't mind instant," said Marcie, starting toward the kitchen. "Making a whole big pot is so wasteful when it's only me, so I don't buy regular coffee."

"Instant is great," said Diedre. "I drink it all the time."

"I hope you can do something," said Marcie in a low voice as they drank coffee at the kitchen table. "I mean, I'm getting desperate. If I lose Evan . . ." Her voice shook. "If he gets custody, Jerry is going to take Evan out of state,

I know he is, even if the state says he can't.''

"That's parental kidnapping and there are laws against that," said Diedre. "He could go to jail if he does that, Marcie.''

She had brought a steno notebook with her, and now she took it out, preparing to make detailed notes. She asked about Marcie's new job as a waitress at the popular Red Caboose restaurant, opened in an old train station. Marcie said the job was going well and she was becoming one of the top earners in tips. She showed Diedre a little chart she had kept, where she wrote down the tips she had received for each night she worked. "Of course, as soon as I get my master's, I can get a decent job, and Jerry knows that. He knows the restaurant is only temporary. He's such a jerk!''

"Maybe you could tell me a little about your ex-husband. What does he do for a living?''

"He's a salesman. His company sells medical equipment. He travels all over the country . . . I'd say he's out of town thirty, forty percent of the time. Even if he had Evan, he'd have to leave him with a sitter most of the time. Whereas I can be with Evan every day. That's one reason why I danced at that club, so I'd have days with my son. The other reason was, Jerry hadn't paid child support in months," said Marcie bitterly. "We got tired of eating cereal for dinner.''

"Was there a lot of animosity during the divorce?''

"Animosity?'' Marcie gave a hard laugh. "That doesn't begin to describe it. The key word is *hatred*. The man hates me because I dared to object to his drinking and his womanizing.''

"Womanizing?''

"Yeah . . . another big irony, isn't it? He had women all over the place, he's a prime candidate for HIV, but all the flak comes down on me because I danced in a G-string. He told me he was going to crucify me as a table-dancing whore.''

Diedre bit her lip, remembering what Pam had said about activities that went on at places like the Booby Trap.

"You say you table-danced? What does that entail?''

Marcie reddened. "I went to the table with a step stool and I stood on the stool and danced. It was ten dollars plus any tips. The men put the money in my garter. They weren't supposed to touch me—the club had bouncers to keep them from doing that."

"And lap dancing? Did you do that, too?"

Marcie looked unhappy. "Yeah—I did once or twice. I needed the money so badly and that's where the big tips were. You can't really take home the big money at those places unless you lap-dance. But then . . . well, this really drunk, crazy guy tried to attack me. It was horrible, they had to pull him off me. I got really scared, so I stopped lap dancing."

"Did they ask you to do private parties?"

Marcie sighed. "Yeah, they asked. But I heard what went on at some of those parties. Bachelor parties, the guys would get so drunk and wild. I wanted no part of it."

Diedre plowed on, unable to believe she was asking these intimate questions of a stranger.

"Are you sexually active, Marcie? I'm sorry, I have to ask these kinds of questions if we're going to fight your ex-husband in court."

"No—I've been celibate for nearly two years. And I *never* did private parties, I mean never. You can ask anyone at the Booby Trap, they'll tell you."

"But Jerry is saying you're promiscuous. Does he have anything specific, any proof to back it up?"

Marcie again flushed. "Maybe it's this building. A couple of the other women do see men regularly—maybe Jerry saw one of them coming or going. He became so vicious. He called me a prostitute. And now I'm so afraid . . . well, that some judge is going to believe him."

Diedre drew a deep breath and began explaining to Marcie about the eleven factors the courts considered when judging the best interests of the child in a child custody case.

"And every one of them has to be examined by the court. Not just your sexual behavior, but all the factors—the type of home you provide, your capacity to give love to Evan, your willingness to encourage a close and continuing relationship between your child and the other parent—''

''Whoa,'' said Marcie. ''That'll be a hard one. Jerry is—''

''But he is Evan's father and it's going to be part of the whole picture, Marcie, your showing your willingness to do what's best for Evan.''

Diedre went on firmly, ''Jerry *isn't* taking custody away from you. Because we're going to work like hell to make sure that he doesn't. And another thing. If you can afford it, move to a better neighborhood and rent a very neat house with green grass and trees, preferably with a nice grade school within walking distance. In a place by yourself, just you and Evan, even if you have to borrow money to do it. Make sure Evan has a nice, clean room, and decorate it like a little boy's room—posters, pictures, bookshelves—you know what I mean.''

Marcie nodded. ''I did save up a little and I might be able to get my brother to loan me enough for the security deposit. Do you think that will help?''

''Marcie, it will. Believe me, if he has a smart lawyer, they will use this apartment building against you. You want to present a picture to the judge that you are a good, fit, loving mother, providing a suitable home for your son in every way imaginable.''

Marcie rubbed her blond hair, her face defiant. ''I'm giving Evan a good home now. He's happy, he's well adjusted—he already knows all his letters and can read some words. What you want is for me to put on a show for the judge, a charade.''

''It's not a show if it will help you keep your son.''

''Oh, please,'' said Marcie, her voice shaking. ''I love him so much, it would just kill me to lose Evan.''

''I'm going to help you, Marcie. It's going to be all right.''

Driving back to Ann Arbor, Diedre gripped the steering wheel of Pam's old Toyota, adrenaline shooting through her veins. She'd made a lot of promises she hoped she could fulfill. And now Marcie was depending on her.

"So how'd it go with the Booby Trap woman?" asked Pam that night when the two sisters were preparing themselves macaroni and cheese from a box, and a tossed salad. Later, Pam was going out clubbing with Bud, and she already had dressed for the occasion in black, shiny plastic pants, a matching black vest, and clunky shoes. Her lips were outlined with dark pencil, filled in with nearly black lipstick, the groove of her upper lip exaggerated. Diedre didn't have the heart to tell her sister that she looked like Morticia.

"I can handle it," said Diedre. "And don't call her the Booby Trap woman . . . She doesn't even work there anymore."

"But she was a sexy dancer."

"Not anymore, she isn't. She's a hardworking waitress and she's got great prospects once she gets her M.A. degree. I just hope I can convince the judge he should overlook those few months that she danced."

PEPPER

GRAY HAD INVITED PEPPER TO FLY OUT TO ASPEN, COL-orado, with him to visit his son, Brian.

"Well," she began dubiously, thinking of her shop. They had met for a quick lunch at Zev's, and she had to get back to work. "Saturdays are usually my busiest day. Sometimes we're really swamped."

"Can't you get Jan to take charge?" Gray wanted to know.

"Yes, but she can't be in the shop by herself all day. She has to take time to go to the bathroom and have lunch."

"Then just have her close up at noon."

"Close *up*?" Pepper was annoyed that Gray acted as if her business was something she could easily and casually drop when something more interesting came along. "Gray, I have customers who set aside part of their time on Saturdays to stop by my boutique. In a peripheral way, I'm part of their lives. I can't let them down, and I'm amazed you would think I'd do that."

His smile was contrite. "Sorry. But you do need another clerk. My secretary happens to have a daughter who's a sophomore at the university, and I'll bet Mandy would be more than happy to help out whenever you want her, Pepper. It certainly would make our Aspen trip possible, and you could have a little more freedom."

Pepper fought another burst of annoyance, thinking how much Gray was taking over her life these days, but then she gave in. She did need more help, dammit. Her business *had* picked up, and those days when Jan was unable to come in, Pepper usually went without lunch all day and had to pee when there was a lull in the parade of customers.

"I'll call your secretary tomorrow," she agreed.

"Good." Gray's smile was delighted. "And pack some warm things for Aspen. Brian said they're getting some snow flurries already."

The small commuter plane seemed to bounce up and down, shuddering as it flew over snow-dusted foothills of the Rockies. As they approached Aspen, it seemed to a nervous Pepper that the plane flew *between* great bulks of mountains, rather than over them.

"Don't tell me you're a white-knuckle flyer," said Gray, amused.

"Sometimes—when there's turbulence—oooh—" She gasped as the plane again began bucking.

"It's all right, this always happens in the mountains." Gray took her hand in his.

Pepper clutched him nervously. "Turbulence scares me ever since my father and I were flying back from Maui one time, and the plane suddenly dropped hundreds of feet—it was like we were in an elevator. People were screaming and crying, it was awful.''

"What did your father do?''

"He told me that I never had to fly again if I didn't want to—we would take trains and sleep in sleeping compartments.''

"Very romantic.''

"Except that we never did. About four months later he sent me plane tickets and I had to fly out to L.A. to visit him,'' Pepper finished the story. "By myself. Thank God for flight attendants, and a nice lady sitting next to me . . . I guess I'm boring you with all this talk about my childhood.''

"No, you're not boring me. Those stories are you, Pepper.'' Gray drew a long breath. "And I guess Brian is me . . . Well, you'll see when you meet him.''

When they deplaned at the airport in Aspen, Pepper was startled to see a young man come hurrying up to the gate, his face almost an exact replica of Gray's except that his hair was black instead of silver, and Brian's skin was tanned a deep mountain brown. Pepper couldn't help a sudden, reactionary thudding of her heart. It was like looking at Gray thirty years ago. Except that there was an arrogant look to this young man, a pout of discontentment.

"Dad,'' said Brian Ortini, reaching out a hand to shake Gray's just as Gray was reaching out to hug him. It made for an awkward greeting, but Gray made a fast recovery, shaking his son's hand instead.

"Brian, it's just great to see you,'' he said heartily. "Son, I want you to meet Pepper Nolan.''

"Hi, Pepper,'' said Brian, in a perfunctory manner.

Gray looked around, frowning. "Where's Lisa?''

"Oh, she's back at the apartment, she's got a deadline to meet.'' Lisa Ortini, Brian's wife, wrote occasional articles for ski and outdoor magazines, in addition to working as a ski instructor at Buttermilk, the area's teaching mountain.

"Well, it's going to be good to see her. How have you been, Brian?"

"I'll be a lot better when we have some good snow," said Brian, walking with them to the baggage-claim area.

Waiting for the luggage, they made stilted conversation, mostly about the upcoming ski season. Brian dropped several strong hints about how he wouldn't mind if Gray bought him some "killer" new skis.

Gray had arranged to rent a Chrysler Le Baron, and he picked up the rental car, then they followed Brian into the posh mountain resort town with its hundreds of shops, restaurants, motels, and condos, overlooked by the huge, looming bulk of "Ajax," as the local residents called Aspen Mountain. This was jet-set and movie-star territory, the "big kahuna" of ski resorts, as Gray told Pepper in the car. Pepper vaguely remembered coming here as a child with her father when she was maybe seven. He'd left her with a baby-sitter most of the time.

Then it was out of town again, to an apartment complex that housed waiters, ski-lift attendants, cooks, ski instructors, and all the other worker bees who made the town of Aspen run. Mountains loomed everywhere, beautiful and snow-capped against a brilliantly deep blue sky. *A perfect setting,* Pepper thought. *How could anyone not be happy here?*

Brian and Lisa lived in a cramped one-bedroom apartment plastered with ski posters and smelling of cigarette smoke and stale cooking odors.

"Hi, Gray . . . Pepper," said Lisa Ortini casually. She was slender, hard-bodied, and had the same kind of deep mahogany mountain tan that her husband did—and the same sort of discontent on her face.

While Brian showed his father a picture of the Salomon skis he wanted in a ski magazine, Pepper attempted to make polite conversation with Lisa.

"You're a writer?"

"I try," responded the girl briefly.

Pepper glanced around but saw no sign of a computer or typewriter. It had to be in the bedroom, she thought.

"Do you write for the ski magazines? It must be very interesting," Pepper plowed on.

"You think ski magazines are interesting? They print the same shit all the time, year after year. We just tweak it around, upgrade it, spit it out in a new form, that's all." Lisa seemed contemptuous.

The conversation went on like that, Lisa talking about her writing, the town of Aspen, and her job in the same derogatory manner. On the other side of the small living room, Brian was talking in much the same way to Gray.

"In another month Aspen will be full of rich turkeys," she overheard Brian tell his father.

"Turkeys?"

"Tourists," explained Brian. "You know."

No wonder Gray was so disappointed in his son, Pepper thought. The pair of rebels didn't even seem happy with their lives here, which seemed to her like the ultimate tragedy.

A purplish dusk had fallen, and old-fashioned light posts switched on to illuminate the picturesque, gentrified downtown. Gray took them all to dinner at Little Nell on East Durant Street, located in the Little Nell Hotel. The hotel, which dated back to Aspen's original incarnation as a silver-mining town, looked as if miners and their fancy women might emerge, laughing, from its door at any time.

"I recommend the pecan-fried oysters," said Gray, smiling and affable. "Shucked to order and flash-fried in a nutty crust . . . It makes my mouth water just to think of them."

They all ordered, Brian and Lisa getting expensive items with equally expensive starters. The young couple raved about the food. But from there it was all downhill, with Brian and Lisa complaining about how expensive the local restaurants were for people who had to work for a living, how Hollywood stars were jacking up all the property values, what poor tippers some of the rich visitors were, what bratty kids they had, and so forth.

Looking over at Gray, Pepper could see him pressing his

lips together and she sensed how much of an effort it was for him to keep his mouth shut and not be critical.

Over coffee, Brian mentioned that he and Lisa had a party to go to later, making it obvious that Gray and Pepper were not to be included. "This party's been in the works for three weeks, Dad."

Gray nodded, disappointment written on his face. But he said nothing, making arrangements to meet his son and daughter-in-law for breakfast the following morning.

"Oh, let's go to the Wienerstube," cried Lisa. "I love their eggs Benedict, but we can hardly ever afford to eat there."

In a few minutes they had dropped off Gray's son and his wife, and were back in the rental car, driving toward the clear, twinkling lights of Aspen. "The evening is still young," said Gray heavily. "What say we explore the nightlife a little, see if we can find some dancing? Since our other plans sort of collapsed."

"Of course," agreed Pepper. She felt terribly sorry for Gray. Both of them had expected to spend the entire evening with Brian and Lisa.

The streets of the Victorian mountain town were still sparsely populated—the town's real action would not begin until around Thanksgiving—but they were able to find a nightclub called the Paradise that featured a live band.

Top 40 music, pounding rhythm, all the couples in their twenties and thirties, everyone deeply tanned and in peak physical condition. The waitress came bustling over to take their drink orders, a sturdily built Amazon who looked as if she were on leave from the Olympic ski team.

When the drinks arrived, Gray leaned forward to be heard over the pound of the band, and said, "I had Brian's life mapped out from day one. I wanted him to attend the U. of M.—that's where I went—and then he was going to go on to med school either there or at Harvard or Yale. Or maybe he'd pick law school. I thought that was a good option, too."

"Big plans," said Pepper, gulping her wine, feeling unusually thirsty tonight.

"Yeah . . . it sounds foolish now, doesn't it, all those plans *I* made for the kid. He rejected all of it, every single damn thing. He told me football was for animals. He threw his dirty laundry over the computer I bought him." Gray sighed. "He deliberately kept his grades down to C minuses and D's . . . then he dropped out in October of his senior year. Nothing could make him go back. Even a therapist couldn't help."

The expression on Gray's face was so tormented that Pepper felt a stab of sympathy. "He is a fine young man," she soothed. "He's still in a rebellious phase. Just give him some time."

"He's twenty-six. When do they stop rebelling? I haven't got that kind of time. I want a second chance at fatherhood, Pepper."

Pepper was so startled that she nearly dropped her wineglass. Yes, Gray had mentioned this before, the first time they had made love, but she'd managed to put it out of her mind, figuring he had said it in the heat of passion.

"Oh, I don't want you to feel pressured, and I'm not saying I want a child any time soon, but looking back, I can see all of the mistakes I made with Brian, and I would like things to be different the next time around. I want to do it right, if I can."

The band had finished their set and was taking a break. Couples filed off the dance floor as Pepper set her glass down on the tabletop. She could feel her cheeks flaming, and was relieved that the dimness of the nightclub concealed her high coloring from Gray.

"A baby? Are you saying you want *me* to have a child, or is this just a general, generic type of conversation?"

Gray's eyes met hers. "I'm just telling you how I feel about fatherhood right now. I'm not pressuring. I hope I haven't offended you."

"No . . . ," said Pepper slowly. Her mind flashed back to her abortion in late August, and she felt a flash of sadness at the ironic timing. "But I'm not ready for this kind of a discussion, Gray. Not now. It's much, much too soon."

"Of course."

Later the band came back, they danced to a heavy rock beat, and Gray seemed to throw off his mood of melancholy. He moved energetically, sweat glistening on his forehead. He was a sexy man who worked out regularly in his home exercise room, able to keep up with much younger men on the dance floor. Pepper, too, began to enjoy herself, feeling rushes of animal pleasure as she danced and moved her body.

Back at the table, she thirstily drank several glasses of wine, then switched to Diet Pepsi so that she wouldn't become drunk. Something about Aspen . . . it made her want to gulp down huge quantities of fluids.

Back in their luxurious hotel suite, which had a Jacuzzi and a closet with a storage compartment for skis, as well as a stunning mountain view, Gray poured them more drinks. They carried their glasses into the bedroom, where they took off their clothes and made love.

Gray stroked and kissed Pepper's body, murmuring over and over again how beautiful she was, how lovely, how he never got tired of her.

"I was so proud of you tonight at that disco," he whispered, kissing her breasts. "So proud to have you on my arm. You were the only woman I even noticed."

"You mean you didn't see Kathleen Turner?" Pepper teased.

"Was she there?"

"Oh, yes, and Fran Drescher . . . Oh, and I saw Christie Brinkley . . . You mean to say you didn't even notice them?"

Gray laughed, pulling her tightly to him. "Even if they were there, I wouldn't have seen them, Pepper. You don't realize how besotted I am with you. I used to think about my business and how I could hire better creative people, make better games, grab more of a share of the market. Now

I think about my beautiful Pepper and how I can get more of a share of her."

As always, Gray was a tireless lover, and he brought Pepper to several orgasms, pleasure flashing through her with such sharp intensity that she cried out loud. Then Gray entered her again and they rocked together, breathless, panting and moaning with their release.

Just as Gray was coming, Pepper suddenly thought of what he had said earlier—about wanting a second chance at fatherhood. A child . . . oh, God. Even the idea made her feel panicky.

Being in Aspen's high altitude, away from her regular routine and sleeping in a strange room, made it difficult for Pepper to settle down. She lay half awake for a long time, her mind moving in and out of strangely disjointed dreams and images. Herself pregnant . . . Gray's hand placed atop the mound of her stomach as he bent down to eagerly listen to the baby's heartbeat . . . *No*. In the dream she pushed him away.

"Are you all right?" Gray murmured about 4:30 A.M., waking briefly.

"I'm . . . fine."

"Are you having weird dreams?"

"A few," she admitted.

"I forgot to tell you, that's an effect of high altitude, that and being really thirsty. Well, you'll be feeling great by the time we get back to Michigan. I love you, Pepper," he added.

She turned to him, snuggling up to his warmth. *I love you.* The words hesitated on her lips, almost ready to come out, but then she could not say them.

As it turned out, breakfast was very rushed because Brian and Lisa overslept, and they ended up gulping down their eggs Benedict. Gray slipped Brian a check, telling him to use it to buy new skis for both himself and Lisa. They said a hasty good-bye, and rushed to return their rental car.

In Denver their connecting Northwest flight was forty minutes late, and they were forced to wait at the gate area. Gray purchased a *Wall Street Journal* and became absorbed in the stock market quotes, his concentration so intense that Pepper began to feel as if she were invisible. Last night's conversation about the baby kept echoing in her mind. *I don't want you to feel pressured.* Bullshit. He did want her to feel pressured, or he would not have said it, she told herself.

Restlessly she got up to roam the gate area, buying several paperbacks and stopping at a snack bar. She returned with two hot dogs dripping chili and onions—a rare treat for her.

"I never eat hot dogs," Gray told her, waving his away.

"I don't usually either, but I got a sudden urge. Come on, these look wonderful."

"The fat content is too high for me."

"Oh, Gray—"

"I do watch my weight."

Pepper felt a sudden spurt of irritation at the priggish way that Gray was acting. *One* hot dog and he was Mr. Healthy? She made a point of walking over to a trash container and dumping the second hot dog inside, untouched. Then she sat down and ate hers, being careful not to drip on her silk blouse. Gray had returned to his newspaper and didn't seem to notice her annoyance, which, perversely, made her feel even more irritated than ever. With sharp clacking sounds of her high heels, she got up and disposed of the paper wrapper.

After several PA announcements giving further delays, they finally boarded the aircraft. On the plane, Gray put his seat back to the reclining position and took a nap. Pepper found this irritating, too. She settled into her window seat, opened up her paperback, and attempted to become absorbed in the thriller by Kate Wilhelm.

Finally she put her book aside and began staring out the window at the layers of fluffy cloud cover, a mood of gloom descending on her. She had to face it. Gray was closing in on her life, wanting more and more of it . . .

*   *   *

Because of the change in time zones, back in Ann Arbor it was already dark, and Pepper was anxious to get into her apartment and make sure that Oscar was all right. Mrs. Melnick had promised to feed her cat.

Gray helped her to carry her suitcase and carry-on upstairs to the apartment. She could still feel the tension simmering between them, and fought a feeling of relief that the weekend was over.

Pepper switched on lights, feeling absurdly glad to be home. She felt as if she'd been gone for a month instead of only one hurried, unexpectedly stressful weekend.

The long-haired, white cat sprang down from the couch and came prowling over to greet them, his tail flying like a flag. Behind him Pepper could see one three-inch-long double claw mark splitting the fabric on the couch back.

"Oscar! Oh, no . . . he's used the couch as a scratching post! He must be mad because I left for the weekend."

"He certainly has scratched it," Gray remarked. "I thought your landlady was supposed to watch him."

"She wasn't supposed to *watch* him, she was supposed to feed him." Pepper walked over to the couch to inspect the damage. "He does claw a little, but I keep a scratching post, and I have another one in the back room of the shop. One time when I was gone for too many weekend trips in too short of a time, he threw up into a pair of my shoes."

"Call an upholstering place and have them come and pick up the couch. I'll have it re-covered for you," said Gray.

"Thanks, but this isn't really a horrible rip. I can mend this. Or I'll put a pillow in front of it and no one will ever notice it."

"Why not let me upholster it? You never would have taken the trip except for me, and I want to do it for you, Pepper."

She felt her chin jut out. "It's really not that big of a disaster."

Gray looked at her, and then knelt down and began examining the rip, while an unrepentant Oscar meowed and crisscrossed against Pepper's calves. "Cat hairs, too," he remarked. "They really show up against this dark blue. Pepper, I don't like to see you living like this."

"Like how?"

"So financially close to the bone. Your cat clawed your couch and now you're going to hide it with a pillow."

She stared at him. "Look, not everyone can afford to upholster the minute there's a tiny bit of damage to their couch. Millions of people have cats that do a little damage once in a while, and they deal with it without spending a ton of money. I prefer having Oscar to having pristine, brand-new furniture."

Gray sighed. "But you can have a reupholstered couch rather than one with a rip in it. You're not alone anymore, Pepper, you have me. I have some very nice financial resources—I've never lied to you about that—and I don't see why they can't be put to a good use."

Were they arguing? Yes, they certainly were.

Pepper walked to the living room window and stood staring down through the curtains at the cramped front parking lot of the building. There hadn't been a real lawn in years. The usual motley collection of residents' cars and vans were parked on the gravel. She could see the scrofulous rust marks on the fenders of Billy Ip's Subaru, and the missing hubcaps on Terry Frieze's VW Jetta.

"You're very generous, Gray, maybe to a fault, but I *don't* want to take anything monetary from you. I shouldn't have even accepted the plane tickets to Aspen, I should have paid for them myself."

"Then you wouldn't have been able to come with me. Honey." Gray came up to her from behind and slid his arms around her waist. "There's nothing wrong if you accept a few plane tickets. I can afford those things; to me they mean very little other than an opportunity for us to be together."

"I won't take your money," she whispered, not turning. "I'm doing fine on my own. My apartment may be small, but I'm happy in it, and if my cat claws my couch, well, he's my cat and I love him." Somehow in the middle of that speech she had started to cry.

Gray turned her around and pulled her into his arms, holding her. She could smell the familiar odor of his aftershave, the clean smell of his body. "Pepper . . . Pepper . . . what's wrong? Why are we fighting about a couch?"

"We're not fighting."

"It sure feels like it to me. Honestly, I didn't mean to hurt you by offering to help pay for some reupholstery. Nor did I mean to buy you, or try to buy you. I promise you that."

Finally she nodded. Of course he hadn't. He *was* a very generous man—she'd always known that about Gray. And he could afford to be generous. From things he had said about his business, and from several articles she had read in the *Ann Arbor News,* she estimated his net worth at over $20 million.

"Darling, you must be terribly tired," Gray remarked at last. "You had a reaction to the mountain altitude, it wiped you out. Look, don't even bother to unpack, just fall into bed and get some sleep, and I'll call you first thing in the morning."

At the door he kissed her tenderly, and after a moment Pepper gave in to his embrace, allowing herself to be enfolded in Gray's arms. But after he left, she went back to the couch and lay down on it, taking Oscar on her stomach and petting the cat until he purred like a small engine.

It wasn't the hot dog in the airport she was angry about, she realized.

Nor was it the fact that Gray wanted to reupholster the couch for her, nor was it even the fact that he had mentioned wanting a baby . . . not entirely. Or was it? Did she even want the kind of life Gray seemed to be offering her so persistently?

That night Pepper dreamed that she was back in Aspen, lying in bed with Gray, and the entire wall of their hotel room had opened up, becoming glass with a view of the looming Ajax Mountain and scattered, twinkling stars.

I will buy all of the stars for you, Gray was murmuring. *Just pick one—pick as many as you want, Pepper. I'll get them all for you.*

But I don't want all of them. I just want one.

You have to take them all. That's the only way it can work.

A phone call awoke Pepper with a start. Sunlight was pouring in her windows, filtered through Battenberg lace, and tiny motes of dust danced in the air. Oscar was wedged up against her hip, his body heavy against her.

"Did I call too early?" he murmured into her ear.

"No . . . I had to get up anyway to answer the phone," she mumbled thickly, making a face.

Gray's laugh was warm, rumbling. "Are you totally wiped out from that trip to the Rockies?"

Pepper struggled to blink her eyes open. "Not *totally* wiped out," she admitted. "I did have some pretty vivid dreams, though."

"You should just sleep in all morning."

"It's Monday," she mumbled. "I have to open the shop."

"Would you like me to stop by and take you out for breakfast?"

She cleared her throat. "I was thinking more along the lines of a frozen toaster waffle."

"How about a Belgian waffle and some freshly squeezed juice? We can meet at Zev's—then you can go right to the boutique and I'll go on to work. It won't take twenty extra minutes and I really need to see you for just a few minutes."

"Deal," said Pepper a little reluctantly. She *liked* toaster waffles.

Pepper rolled out of bed, showered and blow-dried her hair, securing it with pearl clips, and climbed into one of her boutique uniforms, a DKNY jumpsuit the color of smoked salmon.

Another manic Monday, she was thinking as she drove downtown with Oscar, parked in the structure in her usual spot, and dropped off the white cat inside her shop, before walking into Zev's.

Gray was already there, in one of the coveted booths next to the wall. Two cups of steaming coffee had been placed on the table, one with cream the way Pepper liked it.

"I ordered for us," said Gray, smiling. "I got you a Belgian waffle with strawberries on it."

"Great."

They looked at each other. "Pepper . . ." he began, at exactly the same time she was saying, "Gray . . ."

They both reached across the table and then they were holding hands.

"I'm sorry if I overstepped my limits," Gray murmured, his blue eyes searching hers. "Asking for things I had no business asking for."

"You didn't overstep—"

"But I did. I'm such a take-charge person, I sometimes forget that I can be a bit overwhelming. Pepper, please be patient with me. Maybe I need some lessons. In a relationship, I mean."

"Lessons?" Pepper smiled. "You do very well at being intimate, Gray. Maybe a bit too well sometimes. If I got rid of my stuff every time Oscar shed a few hairs on it, I'd be living out of a moving box."

He grimaced. "Touché. Anyway, this isn't about couches and cat hair, is it? I asked for a baby; it was much too early, way out of line. I just don't want to mess this up," he told her. "I've never had this before, Pepper . . . I mean, what we have."

"And I . . . feel the same," Pepper managed.

"Good. Let's not let this relationship slip away from us, okay? We just need time, that's all."

A group of chattering customers entered the restaurant, their noise temporarily drowning out conversation, but Pepper and Gray continued to hold hands until their waffles arrived. Pepper suddenly felt light and free, as if their quarrels and tension of the weekend had somehow vanished in a puff of coffee-shop steam.

"I love you," Gray whispered, as they were walking out of the restaurant. "I do, Pepper. I really do. More than you know."

"And I love you," she murmured, heat rising to her face. She did mean it, she realized with a tick of shock. The admission felt wonderful and yet scary, too. She hoped Gray meant what he said, but she wasn't 100 percent sure.

Five minutes later, Pepper was at her shop, having a long phone conversation with a bra manufacturer in New York who was late sending a shipment.

"I *really* need those push-ups," Pepper pleaded. "They're my most popular line, my customers are begging for them."

"We've had a problem with a supplier, some delays . . ."

Pepper knew what had happened—a big store chain had placed a large order, and because she was small, she was being shunted aside. She begged, pleaded, threatened, and finally was promised a partial shipment within the next two weeks.

Frustrated, she hung up.

"I'll bet Victoria's Secret doesn't have to beg for a few bras," she told Oscar, who was crouched over his food dish, daintily eating. "I'll bet Lord and Taylor doesn't have to plead and whine, just to get a *partial* shipment."

She sank down on the couch in the back room, realizing that she was letting her frustration show. It was a full-time job, running a shop like Pepper's, only she hadn't been working at it full-time since she'd met Gray. She'd allowed herself to become sidetracked by romance. In fact—

The phone rang. Pepper picked it up. "Pepper's Fine Lingerie. How may I help you?"

"Well, *you* certainly picked up the phone fast," said her mother. "And the way you said 'Pepper's,' very chic."

"Hi, Mom." Pepper hid a sigh, knowing that her mother would not be satisfied until she'd talked for twenty or thirty minutes. She picked up a box of hangtags to sort while she was talking to Toni.

They chatted for a few minutes about several recent tropical storms that had swept past Florida. The condo on Sanibel Island was vulnerable to storms, and Toni was forced to evacuate several times a year. Pepper had been urging her for years to buy a condo that was located more inland, or maybe even move to Phoenix or Tempe.

"What about that man you told me about?" Toni Maddalena finally said. "The rich business owner. Are you still seeing him, Pepper?"

"We're still dating," Pepper replied cautiously, bracing for the barrage of questions.

"Well?" Toni demanded. "How is it going?"

"What do you mean, how is it going?"

"Is it progressing? Or is he just using you?"

Pepper dropped the hangtags, her stomach tightening. "He isn't 'using' me, Mom, as you put it. Gray is a very nice, very decent man."

"And he's how old?"

"Well, he's fifty-one."

"And you're thirty-one. Well, you know older men, you know what they want from a woman."

"Really, Mom—"

"It's not just sex, although they definitely want that. They want to use you to prove that they're still able to cut it, that they can still attract a woman sexually. You're not a real person to them, you're just a symbol—a sexy little doll—"

"*Mom.*" Now Pepper was angry. "You've never met Gray. How do you know he's using me as a symbol?"

Toni did not answer directly. "Oh, your father was fifty when I married him, did you know that? And I was twenty-one. I really thought he loved *me*—can you imagine anything more dumb? But what he loved was my body. And as soon as my breasts began to swell up during pregnancy, as soon as my stomach began to protrude . . . well, suddenly my body wasn't so pretty anymore. Suddenly I was used Kleenex, ready to be thrown aside."

Pepper hung on to the phone, recognizing one of her

mother's semiannual "used Kleenex parties," probably brought on by a long weekend with not enough to do, and a bottle of wine.

"Mom," she repeated. "That has to do with Dad and you, it has nothing to do with Gray and me."

"Doesn't it? Pepper, my God, don't you realize? You're even prettier than I was, you're *just* the type that men like him want. Why won't you face it? So you might as well use him, too," Toni concluded.

"What?"

"Tit for tat," her mother said. "He gets something, why shouldn't you get something, too? At least maybe you could get some help with that shop of yours, not have to sit around worrying whether you're going to be able to make your loan payments. Not that I mind loaning you the money, dear, and you have been doing a beautiful job of paying me back."

Pepper had only heard the first part of her mother's speech. "Do you mean that I should get *Gray* to pay my bills?"

"Well," her mother said snippily. "He can afford to, can't he? And you ought to think about, well, seeing if you can get him to start thinking seriously. Rich men aren't that easy to come by, Pepper. Good-looking, heterosexual, generous, and not an alcoholic . . . If you can find all that in one man, you've got a rarity."

Pepper moistened her lips, angrier at her mother than she'd been in years. "Gray Ortini's not my sugar daddy, and I don't want him to be. My bills get paid every month and I don't need a man to help me do it," she went on. "You've been getting every loan payment on time, haven't you?"

"Well, yes, you do pay on the dot, Pepper."

"Well, then. In fact, I have to go, Mom—I have a ton of things to do, and customers waiting up front."

She quickly hung up, and then sat staring at the phone, trying to quell the rage that her mother's phone call had engendered, assuring herself that Toni was projecting her own life and feelings onto Pepper.

Toni was the one who had been used, who had practiced "tit for tat" and married Mason Maddalena for his "generosity," using his resources as greedily as he had used her, continuing to take alimony from him many years after their divorce was finalized, refusing to remarry so that the monthly checks would not stop.

Oscar had finished his meal and leaped up onto the tabletop, padding along the Formica and then making another delicate leap which placed him on top of Pepper's computer. Here he allowed his beautiful, thick, white tail to drape down over the screen like a feather boa.

The cat began purring, the sound motor-loud.

"Oh, Oskie," Pepper sighed. "Why is it all so confusing sometimes?"

The following weekend there was another black-tie dinner, this one to benefit childhood cancer, held at a hotel in nearby Plymouth. Once more Gray's company had bought a table for ten, and GrayCo had also written a big check to the organization.

Pepper wore a dress she had borrowed from Jan, a sky blue gown covered in expensive blue and silver embroidered beading, with a matching cap-sleeved silver jacket. A long slit started at the hip and swept downward, revealing Pepper's long, sleek leg.

The hotel ballroom was decorated with small, twinkling lights woven among swags of ribbons, and there were seemingly acres of flowers. An hors d'oeuvres table was adorned with two large ice sculptures and more of the tiny lights. Each table had a lavish centerpiece, also sparkling with lights.

They circulated among the crowds, saying hello to friends, and one woman came up to Pepper and began saying effusive things about her boutique.

"I just love Pepper's . . . I adore your store. I want to open something like it down in West Palm Beach. I know this is an imposition, but is your cat, well, intact? I'd love to have him father some kittens for me."

"He's neutered." Pepper smiled. "Sorry. And my shop is one of a kind. Best of luck with yours, though."

As the evening progressed, with Gray often introducing her by saying, "This beautiful woman beside me is . . ." Pepper also began to notice something else, the large number of men over the age of forty who had attractive, younger women on their arms.

Trophy wives and girlfriends.

Even now a couple was bearing down on them, the man about fifty-five, wearing evening apparel that couldn't hide his paunchy abdomen. The woman was somewhere in her early thirties, sleek and blond, and she wore a diamond and pearl necklace that Pepper had seen illustrated in a Jules Schubot ad in *Town and Country*. The type of necklace first wives seldom were given, she found herself thinking.

"Gray Ortini! Still making kiddie games?" said the man in a jocular fashion.

Gray grimaced a little. "Pepper, meet Josh and Renee Alvarado."

They talked for a while, and the Alvarados revealed that they were planning to make a trip to the Galápagos Islands. "I want to show Renee a few unusual corners of the earth," said Josh. "Before we're done I'll have her circumnavigating the globe," he added patronizingly.

"Yes . . . we've been to some amazing places," said Renee, gazing at her husband adoringly.

Pepper was repelled by the way Josh patronized Renee. Renee was almost a cliché example of trophy wife—didn't the woman even know it? Or maybe she didn't care. The age difference between Josh and Renee was about the same as between herself and Gray, she realized.

Later, after a dinner that dragged on too long, served with three kinds of wine, Pepper danced cheek to cheek with Gray on the dance floor. As they swayed to the music from the orchestra, Pepper found her eyes roving around the room, cataloging the other couples by their age differences.

"You seem distracted," murmured Gray into her ear, his breath sending soft, warm puffs along her neck.

"I'm fine. How many of these couples do you suppose are original marriages?"

Gray pulled back a little, staring down at her, surprised. "Why would you ask that?"

"Just . . . curious. It seems like a lot of second marriages in the crowd. Older men and younger women. Like us."

"To hell with other couples and their marriages, *or* their ages. I don't care about them. Let's just hold each other and dance," he said, pulling her tight again.

After the party, Gray took Pepper back to his condominium, an elegant, twenty-five-hundred-foot dwelling in a development that had been built overlooking a widened area of the Huron River, offering water views from most of its rooms. He had furnished it with the aid of a decorator, but the effect still managed to be pleasantly cozy, and there were many personal touches, including a magnificent painting of a sunrise over a marsh.

A brisk autumn wind had begun to blow off the river, battering at the French doors that had been placed on either side of a big fieldstone fireplace. Pepper felt a shiver travel over her bare forearms, raising goose bumps on her flesh.

"Cold?" asked Gray, stroking his warm hand down her back.

"A little."

"Let's go in the bedroom and I'll warm you up."

Gratefully she followed him into the bedroom, which was dominated by the view of sparkling lights reflecting on the river, from buildings and houses on the other side. They began one of their usual lovemaking sessions, and within a few minutes Pepper had lost herself in a flood of sensations, her mind swimming in pleasure.

"I love you," Gray said hoarsely as he climaxed.

Within seconds, Pepper, too, was arching her pelvis and moaning, her voice rising in a high-pitched cry. It was one of the most powerful orgasms he had ever given her, and afterward she could feel the pleasure lingering, surfeited and swollen in her tissues. She lay stretched out naked beside Gray, too drained to move.

"I love it that you sometimes scream," remarked Gray in a satisfied tone.

"I don't scream."

"Oh, yes, you do. I think it's quite wonderful. Sometimes I can't believe I'm really with you, Pepper. An old man like me—a beautiful young woman like you. My cup runneth over."

"You're not old," she said vehemently. "Please, don't say that, Gray."

"I am fifty-one," he told her. "Mostly I don't think about my age, but there are times . . ."

Pepper put her arms around him and kissed him, her thoughts at the dinner dance tonight swirling in her head again. Trophy wives and girlfriends . . .

"What are you thinking?" whispered Gray.

"I never want to be a trophy," she blurted.

"What?"

She snuggled close to him, pressing her long, lanky bare legs against his. "Gray, I'm me. I'm not a prize to show off on your arm, which I notice you did quite a few times tonight."

"Did I? It didn't feel like I did that. But I must admit that if you are on my arm, I can't help being proud of you. It's just part of me, honey. Allow me to adore you a little."

Gray was already breathing deeply, and in a few minutes he dropped off to sleep. Pepper lay quietly, willing sleep to come for herself. She had better accept reality, she thought. Nice as he was, decent and kind and loving as he could be, Gray could not completely separate her looks from her inner self.

Her appearance, to him, would always be something to be shown off.

The following Monday brought more roses from Gray, an arrangement of more than five dozen deep red blooms. In the back room, Pepper casually tore off the green and white florist's wrapping, feeling guilty that she wasn't thrilled to get them. She'd asked Gray twice to pull back on the flower arrangements, but he had protested that he loved flowers and wanted to do it for her, making her feel churlish that she had objected.

"Oh!" cried Mandy, the new shop clerk, to whom these extravagant deliveries were still a novelty. "Oh, my God. I can't believe all those roses. I've never seen so many. There's *dozens,* right?"

"Five," said Pepper dryly.

There was a larger than usual envelope with the flowers this time, bulging as if something was inside it. When Pepper opened it, she found a pair of stunning pearl and diamond earrings. *Because you are my sunrise,* read the note. *Allow me to adore you a little.*

"Earrings?" gasped Mandy.

"He's giving you earrings, Pepper?" Jan, too, had crowded around. "These are the real thing," the assistant manager declared. "Look at those diamonds. Those definitely *aren't* CZs."

Pepper took the earrings and held them in her hand, seeing the way the sparkling diamonds caught the shop lights, turning them into rays of fire. She remembered the glittering trophy women at the cancer ball, diamonds dripping from their necks, ears, wrists. And her mother's remarks about getting a "generous" rich man.

Something squeezed deep in the pit of her stomach.

"I can't keep them," she muttered.

"Now, girl." Jan took her arm, guiding Pepper to the back part of the shop, leaving Mandy to attend to two customers who had just walked in the door. "You can't tell the man to take those back—no way."

"Why can't I?"

"Because to him they are just trinkets."

"They aren't trinkets, they are serious jewelry. What do you think they cost, Jan? I have a very good idea. I *can't* take that kind of a gift from him. I don't even want it. I hate the idea of it."

Pepper was already moving toward the phone, dialing Gray's private line at GrayCo.

"Gray, darling," she said when he was on the line, and Jan had tactfully gone back out to the front of the shop. "I received the roses and you shouldn't have done it, but you still keep doing it, so what can I say? But I'm going to have to give you back the earrings. I loved your note, but I won't be able to keep them."

"But the diamonds will look wonderful on you, honey."

"I know, and you're terribly thoughtful, but I can't accept gifts of such serious monetary value," she told him. "Please, don't be offended."

There was a small silence.

"I won't be," he said slowly, but she could tell she had hurt him. "If you'll have lunch with me today. Can you come to the office? We'll eat somewhere nearby."

She didn't really want to take a long lunch hour, but she felt she had little choice since she had refused Gray's gift. Besides, she felt it was necessary to give him back the earrings as soon as possible, to finish making her point.

"I'll be over at one-thirty," she told him.

It was a brisk, glowing October day, sunlight pouring through Ann Arbor's many trees, planted through many years of Arbor Days, charging yellow leaves with molten gold.

A man with a leaf blower was working on the grounds of GrayCo's headquarters, which were located in a white, three-story building off Plymouth Road. It was a striking, California-style building dominated by a big, dome-shaped skylight that rested atop the structure. GrayCo occupied only the third floor of the building; the other two floors had been leased to other firms.

Pepper parked and entered the main-floor lobby, giving her name to a security officer seated at a desk, and signing a guest book. She entered a mirrored elevator that whispered her up to the third floor.

This was the prime floor of the building, the receptionist's desk centered underneath the magnificent glass dome that enclosed the entire third-floor lobby in a bath of sunlight. The floor was white marble, each square laced with faint gray swirls. An elegant sitting area was located to the left, dominated by tropical trees and an enormous arrangement of rust-colored mums. Through an opened doorway Pepper could see blocks of office cubes.

"Gray Ortini, please," she said to the attractive, middle-aged receptionist. "I'm Pepper Nolan." She had been here several times before, but this woman appeared to be new.

"Oh, yes, Miss Nolan, he's expecting you. I'll page his assistant—"

"Pepper," said Gray, emerging from the doorway, smiling. Obviously he had been lurking nearby, waiting for her. This afternoon he was wearing a gray, Italian-made suit and a blue and silver silk tie, his silver hair, freshly cut, making his attire look even more flattering. Gray was a man of power, and every inch of him showed it.

"Look," he went on, "I've got a conference call coming in about five minutes in the small conference room, and after that I'll be free. I'll have Penny take you to my office and bring you some coffee."

"Thanks, but anymore coffee and I'll go on a caffeine jag."

An assistant came through the door, inviting Pepper to follow her.

However, just as Pepper turned to leave, a young, red-haired woman appeared, wearing a leaf green suit with a jacket that had been cut to show off her tiny waist. She trotted up to Gray, her three-inch high heels clacking on the marble tiles.

"Gray—sorry—I was tied up on the phone to L.A.," the woman apologized.

"Pepper, I'd like you to meet Codi Duncan, she's one of my project managers," said Gray cordially. "Codi, this is Pepper Nolan."

"Hi, Codi," said Pepper, observing the woman's fall of

magnificent red hair, which could have appeared in an ad for Pantene, and the cool, green eyes.

"Hi." Codi said it quickly, moving closer to Gray. She touched his arm, her eyes seeking his. "Gray, I've got that games writer in Sausalito really interested in us, but Microsoft has made him an offer, too, and we're going to have to—"

Gray nodded. "Okay, we'll talk about it at our meeting this afternoon. Meanwhile, I have the conference call from Tokyo. Excuse us, Pepper, I promise I won't let this phone call drag on too long."

Lunch was chicken and shrimp fajitas at a new Tex-Mex restaurant located a few minutes from the GrayCo building. As they forked chicken, grilled onions, tomatoes, and other condiments into tortillas, Pepper casually mentioned Codi's name. She knew she shouldn't, but it just popped out.

"Pepper . . ." Gray put down his fork, smiling. "I'm not interested in Codi, not in the slightest. Oh, she's attractive, yes. I can't deny that. But women like Codi Duncan are everywhere—it's just part of the scene when a man has wealth. I told you before, to some women I'm just money on the hoof. Thank God you've never been unduly impressed by my money."

Pepper cleared her throat. "If anything, it's just the opposite. I'm turned off by too much money," she blurted.

"Oh?" Gray looked surprised.

"That's why I have to give you back these earrings," she continued, pulling the envelope with the diamond earrings in it out of her purse and handing it to him. "Please. I just can't take them. I don't want big gifts. I don't even feel really comfortable with all those roses you send me, and I have told you that before."

"Darling, I had fun picking out those earrings for you," said Gray, frowning. "Is that wrong? Should I have gone to Kmart when I can afford Tiffany's? Would you really want Kmart earrings?"

Her eyes filled as she put her shoulder bag back on the

seat of the booth beside her. "Gray . . . please."

He sighed. "I can't win, Pepper. I try to please, I try to do the things most women want, but for you, that's apparently the exact wrong thing."

Pepper bent over her plate and began fussing with her fajita, adding a dollop of guacamole. "It goes back to my childhood, I guess. My father throwing around all that money, buying me this and that, flashing bills in front of waitresses . . ." She stopped. "I don't know why I mentioned it now."

"Honey, I'm not your father. You've already told me what a selfish SOB he was. I'm not trying to buy you like he did. I don't even want a woman if I have to buy her."

"Then why the earrings?" Pepper snapped, feeling like a bitch.

"That was a token, Pepper. I felt good that day. I felt like buying them. Ah, God . . . I just wanted you to have them."

"Your 'tokens' are other women's treasured possessions," muttered Pepper, staring at her filled tortilla without touching it. "Your 'tokens' could feed a family or buy Disney World for a child dying of cancer."

"And sometimes I think you're a reverse snob, Pepper," snapped Gray, his face reddening. "It is not a crime to have a good income, and I refuse to feel guilty about it. And last time I heard, I did donate a very sizable sum to childhood cancer."

Pepper nodded and muttered something like an apology. Gray curtly nodded, accepting it.

It felt awkward as they finished their meal, both of them forcing the conversation to more casual matters, in order to ease the tension.

Pepper felt so confused. *Was* she a reverse snob? Yeah, probably. This relationship with Gray Ortini was really mixing her up. He seemed so charming, so warm and sincere. But was he really? Or somewhere under Gray's handsome exterior, was there another Mason Maddalena, the rich man who used trips, gifts, and flowers to substitute for love?

TREVA

EVEN THOUGH TREVA HAD KNOWN THAT BED REST would be boring and inconvenient, she hadn't been prepared for the colossal discomfort of always having to lie on one side, and always having to ask Wade even for the simplest things. Like fresh paper for her printer, or a bottle of Snapple when her supply in the cooler ran out.

Trips to the bathroom were her big recreation, and she would walk slowly toward the powder room, gazing all around her, trying to see the views from other windows that differed from what she normally saw from the couch. Her rock garden needed raking and covering. She'd have to get Wade to do it . . . A few times she cheated and stood in a shaft of sunlight, just letting it warm her skin. The living room didn't get direct sunlight . . .

Of course, she had visitors nearly every day—Annie, Rhonda, Dr. Rosenkrantz—and Pepper Nolan had visited her twice, once bringing Treva a huge bouquet of roses that she said she did not have room for in her shop. Diedre Samms also came, full of talk about the child custody case she'd been assigned, and worries that the young man she was seeing also happened to be the father of the fetus she had aborted. Pepper found herself growing fond of Diedre. It had been a long time since a young woman had seemed to want her for a mentor.

"So how's it going, Trev?" said Annie Larocca cheerfully, arriving one morning with a big bag of low-fat, low-salt snacks, and some red, seedless grapes she had bought at Kerrytown. "Are you hanging in there?"

Treva thanked her for the fruit and they both began munching the large, sweet grapes with skins still covered with a fragrant white patina.

"Mostly," Treva admitted. "Sometimes I climb the walls a little—like when there was a fly in the living room yesterday and I just had to let it buzz and buzz until Wade finally came home and killed it for me."

"Whew, flies, those are tough."

"Yeah . . . and . . ." But then Treva laughed and stopped. "I shouldn't be complaining, not when I have this guy in my belly." She patted her stomach. "I've been reading aloud to him every day."

Annie grinned. "Have you? What type of reading material does he like?"

"A book of poetry by Shel Silverstein. Shanae had it when she was young, she brought it to me. I try to read with expression, and, Annie, I could swear when I do the voices of the characters, he kicks more."

They settled down for one of their long talks, and Treva wanted to know everything that was going on at the clinic.

"Oh, we had a sad case the other day," Annie said.

"How so?"

"A little girl only eleven years old."

"Eleven?" Such cases were rare, but they did happen.

"She was raped by a so-called friend of the family," said Annie. "I'd like to take him and hold his head in the toilet until there aren't anymore bubbles. She came to the clinic with her mother—and a big old fuzzy teddy bear about as big as she was. We had her specially driven into the clinic, I didn't want Bobbie Lynn or any of those sidewalk people scaring her. I swear, Treva. She was just a baby herself, and the antiabortion people want to force children like her to give birth?"

So they talked about the endless permutations of abortion politics, the latest legislation on "partial-birth abortions," and then a newspaper article Annie had just read about another abortion center firebombing in Boston. Two people had been injured.

"It's not safe," Annie said nervously. "If my husband sees that article, he'll just shit, Treva."

Treva nodded. "*You* hang in there, Annie. It's tough,

working in that field. It burns people out sometimes. Maybe you're reaching that stage . . . and it's all right if you are.''

"Not for a while longer," Annie said after a pause. "Not when I see little girls like that eleven-year-old, Tiffani. If it wasn't for us, and people like us, what would happen to girls like Tiffani? Would she be traumatized by having to give birth at that age? Would her mother or one of her family members try to abort her with some awful chemicals or stick something sharp up into her vagina? What if they killed her?"

They sat for a while in silence, both thinking about horrible stories they'd heard about the old days. The most horrifying story Treva had ever heard was about a seventeen-year-old girl in 1956 whose backstreet abortion had been badly botched. She had arrived in the emergency room with her intestines protruding from her vagina. The girl had died. Even now, thinking about that made Treva feel sick to her stomach.

"I refuse to let myself get burned out," Annie finally sighed.

"That's the spirit, dear Annie."

Shanae arrived for a weekend of laugher and a marathon of movies that she and Wade rented at the video store, accompanied by take-out food and a meal that Shanae herself prepared from scratch, from a *Gourmet* magazine recipe.

Still, Treva felt restless. Sometimes she resented the situation she found herself in, resented her own body for betraying her, her race for making her more susceptible to high blood pressure.

Then guiltily she pushed away the feelings. She was seventeen weeks along now. A book Wade had bought her, *Your Pregnancy Week-by-Week*, told her that the crown-to-rump length of her baby was now between 4.4 and 4.8 inches. It weighed around three and a half ounces, and was starting to put on a little body fat. She'd already felt it move—or a strange sensation in her abdomen that felt almost like thick bubbles popping.

The blues . . . What was she thinking of? She desperately wanted this pregnancy, she reminded herself. The bed rest would only last a few more months and then she would receive her reward, a healthy baby.

One thing that was saving her sanity was the interview phone calls for the abortion study. She made between two and four daily. Kelly Cruz, a heavyset seventeen-year-old who had been too frightened to tell anyone about her pregnancy until she was into her second trimester, was now being pressured by her boyfriend to have sex with him again.

"Kelly, what kind of prescription for birth control did the clinic recommend for you?" Treva asked.

"It was—yeah, the pill," the teenager said. "But I didn't, you know, get the prescription filled or anything, 'cause, well, I didn't want to get pregnant again."

"If you don't take the pills, you *could* get pregnant again. In fact, if you have sex regularly with him without using anything, your chances of getting pregnant again in a year are eighty percent."

"Yeah, but if I don't do it with him—I mean I'm not planning on having sex. I don't want to do it, but he keeps asking and asking, and he wrestled me the other night. I mean . . ." The girl's voice trailed off.

Treva sighed in frustration. The "wrestling" meant he probably had sex with her again—unprotected intercourse since Kelly hadn't filled her prescription, apparently believing, as many teenage girls did, that if she took precautions, it meant she was planning to have sex.

"How long ago was it that you two were 'wrestling'?"

"I . . . maybe yesterday."

"Did he put his penis inside you, Kelly, or near your vagina?"

"Yeah . . ."

"Kelly, there are some new guidelines now about taking higher doses of oral contraceptives up to three days after you have unprotected sex. If you follow directions, there's

about a seventy percent chance you *won't* get pregnant. It's
certainly worth a try anyway.''

Treva gave the girl the clinic phone number, encouraging
Kelly to discuss this with her mother and go in the following
day. Cases like Kelly's—the sheer vulnerability of teenage
girls—made Treva feel sad sometimes. She worried about
Shanae, too; Shanae was such a passionate girl. Reproductive ability could be burdensome and frightening for girls
who were still half children themselves.

When Wade arrived home from the university that night
to prepare their dinner, he found Treva in an odd mood.
''Do you hate having me so helpless like this?'' she queried.
''I mean twenty-four hours a day. You have to cook for me,
take care of my rock garden, and you're sleeping on an air
mattress on the floor.''

''Hate it?'' Wade looked puzzled.

''Fetching. Carrying. Cooking. It's such an inconvenience
for you, even though you're turning into a great cook,'' she
added hastily.

''Almost *cordon bleu* in another month or two.'' Wade
grinned at her. ''Honey, never think you're an inconvenience. You're the center of my life, you and that little mite
of ours in there.'' He patted her abdomen. ''And now what
do you want to eat? I've got a recipe for a low-fat seafood
salad, supposed to be sensational. I even bought the ingredients on the way home, including pea pods. Would you
believe it, Wade Connor buying pea pods?''

Treva laughed, her anxious mood at last dissipating. God,
she loved her husband so much. Maybe they *would* make a
gourmet cook out of him, at that.

Shanae called later that evening as she did nearly every
night. ''Is the baby kicking?'' Treva's stepdaughter asked
when she had finished giving Treva a rundown on her
school day, and a song she said she was writing.

''Well . . . I can definitely feel something.''

''What does it feel like?''

Treva took a sip of the bottled lemonade Wade had put

in her picnic cooler tonight. "Like—I don't know—a wiggling sensation. Or maybe like bubbles when you cook chocolate pudding, you know, the slow way they pop."

"Bubbles?" Shanae giggled.

"Probably its tiny, tiny feet. I can't wait for the good, hard kicks," declared Treva. "I'm going to love every one of them."

"Do you talk to her?"

"All the time. But are you sure it's going to be a her?"

"There's a fifty-fifty chance, right? Anyway, you'll find out soon, won't you? They're going to do that test, I can't remember what it's called."

"Ultrasound," said Treva, feeling a thrill of pleasurable excitement. "But you know, lots of doctors now don't give the baby's sex any longer in an ultrasound, since they're wrong about thirty percent of the time."

"Oh . . ." groaned Shanae.

"It's the baby that counts, not what sex it is, darling."

"But the baby's going to be okay, isn't it, Treva?" The girl's voice sounded anxious.

"Of course, baby. Of course, baby doll," said Treva quickly. "I come from strong stock, sweetie, and so does your father—the strength in this family goes way, way back to slave times, honey. And way before that, dear. We're survivors, all of us . . . you, too, Shanae. This baby is going to be just *fine*."

"Great," said Shanae, too cheerfully.

The phone rang as Wade stood in the big, white-tiled kitchen that overlooked Treva's rock garden, loading the dishwasher, careful to insert all of the forks and knives with points down so that he wouldn't stick his fingers as he'd done the first couple of times.

He quickly reached out and picked up the wall phone.

"Daddy?" said Shanae.

"Honey?" Wade frowned. His daughter had called only an hour ago to talk to Treva. "Do you want to talk to Treva again? I can go tell her to pick up."

"No, Daddy, I want to talk to you."

"What about, cupcake?"

"It's—well, I went to the library today and I got this book. I've just been reading it. I . . . I didn't want to ask Treva about it. She said we were strong, but . . ."

"What sort of book?"

In the background Wade could hear the rustle of pages. "It's called *When Pregnancy Isn't Perfect*," said Shanae. "It's got a whole big chapter on hypertension. That's what Treva has, isn't it?"

"Yes." Wade stopped loading dishes. "What does the book say, honey lamb?"

"Just a bunch of stuff about the awful things that can happen to her, Daddy. I mean really, really awful stuff. Like how she can have these seizures—"

"Honey," said Wade, frowning. "Now, stop. Just stop right there. This is just worry talk, about something that's probably never going to happen. I told you before, Treva's going to be just fine."

"But, Daddy, the book says—"

"Now, Shanae. I want you to take that book back to the library and I *don't* want you to mention anything about it to Treva. You know any kind of worry will push her BP right up."

"I know," said Shanae in a small voice. "Daddy, I can't help it, worrying, I mean. I . . . I love Treva."

"I know, baby. But if you love her, you have to keep cheering her up like you've been doing. You do a terrific job of that. That's what she needs more than anything."

After they had hung up, Wade finished tidying the kitchen, then he made sure that Treva had everything she needed for the evening.

"I'm going to drive over to the racket club, Trev, see if I can get a pickup game," he told her, feeling guilty. "I'll only be gone about two hours, okay?"

"I've got TV and six HBO movie channels and the telephone," she said lightly. "Plus Rhonda's stopping by. When am I going to have time to miss you?"

Wade smiled. "I'll leave the mudroom door unlocked and put out the bell for Rhonda, then. Tell her I said hi."

When he felt stressed, Wade desperately needed physical activity, the tougher and more competitive, the better. Wade drove to the racket club and played a violent game of racquetball that left him weak in the knees and sweating like a glass of soda in hundred-degree heat.

Shanae wasn't the only one doing a little worrying. Wade had been asking around, some of his freinds in the School of Social Work, a woman he knew who taught nursing. He'd heard a few disquieting things, too.

He just wanted this pregnancy to be over with. He wanted his family to be safe again.

Two days later, Wade and Treva drove to the U. of M. Medical Center for her checkup and the ultrasound test that had been scheduled—her second. The first one had been too early to tell the baby's sex, but it had shown that the fetus was developing normally, thank God. Treva had been told to drink eight full glasses of water before leaving the house, in order to inflate her bladder and move the uterus up to where it could be more easily viewed. She was not supposed to urinate.

Whew.

Already her bladder was distended, and all she could think about was peeing.

Well, she'd just hold it back. She'd make a game out of it—a nonpeeing contest, she told Wade, trying to laugh. "But don't drive the car over any big bumps, or there may be an accident."

Treva also made a joke of the fact that she had to put her seat down in order to ride scrunched over on her left side as best she could.

"I'm getting a super view of your hip pockets, Wade," she laughed. "Oh, and your thighs. Very, very nice thighs."

Wade grinned. "Glad you like them, my dear."

"Mmmm, yes, I like them. If things were different, I'd

be groping you right now, honey, maybe even begging you to pull off the road and, well, you know.''

They both laughed. Playful, loving sex was the glue that held their marriage together. Both of them desperately missed that physical contact, making do with kissing and cuddling, which, as Wade complained, was like having ''one bite instead of an eighteen-ounce steak.''

They drove up Fuller to East Medical Center Drive. As usual, the parking structure at the Taubman Center was packed with cars, but Wade decided to utilize the valet parking. He helped Treva out of the car and found an unused wheelchair.

''Your ride, my queen,'' he said in a courtly manner. ''I apologize that I don't have fourteen trotting, champing black steeds.''

''The one I have will be just great,'' she said, holding her abdomen when she started to laugh too hard.

Wade wheeled her toward the area of Women's Hospital where the testing was going to take place. Today the sick patients who thronged the center didn't seem as drawn and sad to Treva, and she spotted several young children with bright, merry faces. Glancing at her watch, she saw that they were around twenty minutes early. Bad news for her bladder, but maybe if they wheeled around a bit, it would take her mind off the pressure on her insides.

''Can we take a little detour?'' she asked Wade.

''Where do you want to go, Your Highness?''

''I'd *love* the ladies' room, but I'll settle for finding a baby nursery. I want to look at babies.''

''At your service, madame.''

Endless corridors connected the complex of medical buildings, and it seemed to Treva as if the hallways went on literally for miles, marked by arrows and signs, and hurrying personnel in various types of hospital garb. The smell of steam-table cafeteria food saturated the halls.

Finally by luck they stumbled upon a neonatal area. Wade wheeled Treva up to a row of glass windows that had been installed in the hallway. Even though she was supposed to sit quietly, she rose to her feet and peered through the glass. Rows of isolettes filled the nursery, mechanized and high-tech looking, each one with a tiny, scrawny infant inside, hooked up to fetal monitors and glowing lights.

"Oh," breathed Treva. "Oh, Wade, these are *preemies*."

"Very preemie, by the look of them."

Treva swallowed, hard. Some of the babies were only around two or two and a half pounds, tiny enough to be cradled in the palm of the hand. One of the neonates looked even smaller than that. It was amazing it had survived at all.

As Treva knew from working at the clinic, fetuses of this exact same size were sometimes aborted, although their clinic did not do "third tri" abortions and few centers did, nowadays.

"Look at that one," she cried. "Look how he's kicking so hard. Isn't that brave? And over there, look at that little one, how he's crying. And that one sucking his tiny, tiny thumb." Treva's voice softened, becoming full of emotion. "Oh, Wade. They are so beautiful. Skinny and scrawny and fighting for their lives."

Wade wanted to leave, but Treva wasn't ready to be pulled away, not just yet. She couldn't get her fill of looking at these tiny scraps of humanity. Would their baby, floating and kicking inside her, be as brave as these infants? Would it fight just as hard for life?

For the first time, she allowed herself to face the fact that their child might be born early, or "preterm" as they called it. If that did happen, their child would have to fight as these infants were doing. That was why she had to carry it inside her for as long as possible, so it wouldn't face lung problems or retardation.

She wanted her baby's survival more than she'd ever wanted anything.

"Ready?" said Wade gently.

"Yeah." Treva lowered herself back into the wheelchair, placed her feet on the support bar, and allowed herself to be pushed back to Dr. Sandoval's office area.

*   *   *

Looking at Treva in the faded, unflattering hospital gown fastened by ties at the back of her neck, Wade was much more nervous than he thought he'd be.

The sonogram room had a hospital bed in it, and a machine that looked rather like an elaborate computer with an oversized keyboard containing many more keys. They were greeted by a technician named Ruth Ann, then Dr. Sandoval walked into the sonogram room, wearing her trademark sterling silver teddy bear pin on her physician's coat.

"Mrs. Connor, Mr. Connor, are you ready for the test?"

"Ready," Treva piped up, and Wade nodded, too, a bit more slowly.

"You both already know that this test does not involve any X rays or injections of drugs or dyes. It just uses high-frequency sound waves that bounce off structures in the womb, producing echoes that are converted into images that we'll see here on this display screen."

Dr. Sandoval went on to explain, mostly for Wade's benefit, that the test would be painless but Treva might feel uncomfortable because of her full bladder. "I promise you can get up and pee as soon as we're done here," she added.

"That's a promise I'll hold you to," quipped Treva, grinning.

Wade felt his stomach tighten as the technician put a sheet over his wife's thighs and pubis, and lifted her gown, rubbing a liquid gel on Treva's rounded abdomen. "This gooey stuff assures adequate contact for the transducer," the technician explained.

Wade watched as an expression of anticipation suffused Treva's face. His wife's black, curly hair glowed with blue-black lights, and she looked to him bronzy and beautiful, almost Madonna-like.

Dr. Sandoval paused. "One thing before we begin, you two . . . Do you want to know the sex of the baby? It's only a rough guesstimate. Sometimes that umbilical cord or an arm or a leg just fools us."

Treva moistened her lips, hesitating, but Wade blurted out, "Yes!"

"Wade?" Treva turned to him, startled. "I thought you said you wanted to be surprised."

"Well, I changed my mind." He spoke in a low voice. "Now that I'm here, I mean. Well, we might as well know, right? So we'll know what color of paint to buy for the baby's room."

"Oh, Wade . . ." She reached out for his hand.

Wade squeezed Treva's hand back. Tears stung his eyes and he stared straight ahead, hoping they wouldn't spill out and betray his emotion. He didn't feel it was dignified to have tears in front of hospital personnel.

As the technician moved the transducer, they began to hear fast, odd, *lub-lub-lub*by sounds, and various shapes appeared on the computer screen.

"See—see that on the screen?" Ruth Sandoval leaned forward eagerly as the technician manipulated the transducer across the swell of Treva's abdomen. She seemed almost as thrilled by the procedure as they were. "That's your baby."

"Where?" said Wade, staring in puzzlement at the unfamiliar lines, bright spots, and movements.

"There," said the doctor, pointing. "That's the head right there. He's moving around very nicely—see—see that movement? Your son just gave a nice, healthy kick."

"Our son? You mean it's a—"

"A boy, Mr. Connor." Dr. Sandoval pointed out some infinitesimal lights and lines which she said showed the baby's genitals. "As far as I can tell at this point, you have about a sixty to eighty percent chance of having a boy. And that's as far as I'm going, prediction-wise."

"Oh, my God." Wade's voice cracked. He barely heard the doctor give the percentages, heard only the word *boy*.

"We have a son. Oh, Wade . . ." Treva's hand squeezed his and they locked fingers tightly.

"We're going to do our best to see this baby through. I do want you to be prepared, though. As soon as he's able to survive outside of the womb, we may induce labor, Treva. The sooner he is out of your womb and on his own, the better it will be for your own health and his."

But Wade and Treva weren't listening. Treva was weeping, burying her face in Wade's shoulder. Dr. Sandoval stepped toward the door of the room, followed by the technician. "We'll leave you two alone for a few minutes."

When they had privacy, Wade again took Treva into his arms. "Treva . . . my God . . . I love you," he whispered. "We have a boy. A little boy . . ."

"I've prayed so hard," whispered Treva. "And now I hate to spoil this wonderful moment, but I'm about to float on out of here if you don't get me to a ladies' room—now!"

Wade wheeled Treva back to the parking structure, and when the valet parker returned with their car, he helped her into the passenger seat and settled her in the lying-down position that the doctor had recommended.

He felt much different now than he had only a short hour ago. The news of their son, the crying they'd done together, had loosened some terrible knot tied in the center of him. For the first time, Wade felt real hope. It wasn't just a case of worrying about his wife's health anymore, no, it was the knowledge that *they were going to have a child*. Why hadn't this sunk into his consciousness until now? He was going to be a father for the second time!

"Today is a special day," he told Treva jubilantly, as he pulled out of the structure and turned left on East Medical Center Drive. "We have to do something to celebrate."

"I'll have to celebrate on my left side."

"Okay. It'll have to be a bed-rest celebration. Maybe we should just drive home. I'll go out and rent a new video. And then I'll make a stir-fry dinner, and after that we'll just lie on the couch and hold each other. I'll light candles. Vanilla scented. I'll play that new CD you bought this summer—the one by Enya that you like so much."

"Oh, yes," murmured Treva.

"I know we can't have sex, but we can cuddle and I'll rub your back as you've never had it rubbed before."

They ate the simple dinner Wade had prepared, but they never made it to the video. Instead Wade climbed on the couch with Treva, carefully positioning himself so that she could still lie on her left side.

Music soared through the living room, a crystalline female voice singing ancient Gaelic ballads. Candles flickered in candelabras throughout the room, giving off wafts of vanilla. The light wavered and glowed, casting moving shadows. Wade felt a sentimental rush of remembered emotion. This was how they had often made love, before Treva's pregnancy.

"Treva," he whispered, touching her face with his fingertips, stroking her temples, her jawline, her beautiful eyes. "I can't believe it. I never thought—I mean, before, it didn't seem real. The baby. Our little guy. And now he's real. He's really in there," he said, tenderly touching her abdomen.

They held each other, laughing and caressing and whispering secret love words. In some ways it was their most tender lovemaking, because it seemed to Wade as if their souls touched. He could feel his eyes again filling with tears of emotion, and giving way, he let them come.

Treva touched the rivulets of tears that streamed from her husband's eyes. She knew him so well and accepted every part of him, as his first wife, Wanda, had never done.

"Babe," he said huskily, holding her, thanking God for this woman he had been so lucky to find at that long-ago university meeting, eleven years back.

"What shall we name him?" Wade asked after a long while.

Candlelight played across Treva's beautiful, caramel-colored face. "Shall we name him after one of our fathers?"

Wade laughed. "Not unless we want him to be called Willie or Rodney."

They shared a quiet chuckle, then Treva said, "Well, how about a black name?"

"Maybe," said Wade. "But not DeShawn or Tyreek, and not DeJuan either. I want something . . . bigger."

"Something with a classical bent? Like maybe Ulysses?"

Wade chuckled. "What about Demetrius?"

"I don't know. How about Moses?"

"Moses?" They both giggled.

It was going to take them a long time to pick out a name, and they were going to love every minute of it.

Finally Treva fell asleep, cradled against Wade's chest, her own chest rising and falling shallowly. Wade lay still, holding his wife, trying not to fall off the couch, until his limbs grew cramped and his right arm went to sleep.

Finally he moved to the air mattress he usually slept on, and adjusted its covers to fit his long body. He stared into the flickering candlelight.

ANNIE

IT WAS A CLOUDY DAY CLOSE TO HALLOWEEN, THE SKY colored a peculiar shade of fish white that promised rain later in the morning, or maybe in the next ten minutes. Most of the trees were bare now, but a few dead leaves hung on some of the trees.

Where had summer gone? Annie Larocca wondered. Now it seemed as if Thanksgiving was almost in the air.

Annie balanced her usual jumbo-sized cup of 7-Eleven coffee, driving toward the women's clinic. She was tired this morning; she'd stayed up late last night to watch a Sean Connery movie on Pay-Per-View. Now the Kevlar vest she wore this morning, at her husband's insistence, seemed to pinch too tightly under her armpits. Not to mention the fact that it made her sweat. The thing was as bad as a sauna suit, she decided. She could hardly wait to get inside the clinic and take it off.

Pulling into the clinic lot, Annie breathed in a quick gasp as she saw the group of demonstrators.

Eighteen or twenty people were huddled at one end of the parking lot around the tailgate of a GMC van, drinking coffee from thermoses. The van had a Massachusetts license plate. She'd heard that a national antiabortion group, No Genocide, had driven into town and was planning to target the clinic.

Glancing more closely at the group, Annie saw that the demonstrators were dressed in old clothes, some wearing jeans that had been padded at the knees, others wearing sports or gardening knee pads.

Oh, shit, she thought. No Genocide was famous for its crawl-ins. Demonstrators would crawl on their hands and knees, sometimes for hours, confounding police officers who tried to deal with them, on the theory that it was very hard to pick up and arrest someone on his or her hands and knees.

As Annie parked, six or seven demonstrators approached her, waving posters. One man was waving a plastic fetus doll, grotesquely realistic. "Don't go in! Don't go in!" they began to chant. "Quit your job!"

Ignoring them, her heart beginning to pound, Annie walked fast toward the door.

"Murderer! Murderer! Murderer!"

Annie picked up her pace, sweat soaking her under the Kevlar. She was relieved to reach the door, where Ramon, one of the security guards, quickly let her in.

"It's gonna be one rough 'n' tough day," he told her.

"Yeah."

"I heard there's gonna be about a hundred fifty of 'em, maybe more."

"Great," sighed Annie, picturing the pandemonium that would result. Patients would drive past, see the demonstrators, and be terrified. The clinic would receive sobbing phone calls. Some of the women would cancel their appointments. "Have the police been called?"

"Not yet. You know the procedure."

"Yeah." From hard experience, the clinic had learned that having the police on the scene usually escalated the demonstration, creating more violence, not less, so they tried to defuse matters by ignoring the demonstrators as long as possible.

Walking inside, Annie took off her Kevlar vest and went around turning on computers, making coffee, performing her usual morning routine. Half an hour later, the rest of the staff arrived, having run the gauntlet of shouting demonstrators.

"Man, I did not need this," said Mei, one of the phone counselors. She dashed for a ringing phone and picked it up.

Within minutes, patients began to flood the switchboard with anxious calls. Which, of course, was the purpose of the demonstrations, to scare patients into canceling their appointments. Some would reschedule, others wouldn't. Pro-life groups considered it a victory when even one woman decided against an abortion, Annie knew.

Annie started making phone calls to arrange for a van and volunteer escorts from a pro-choice group to accompany patients into the clinic. She asked one of the escorts to bring in loads of bagels, doughnuts, sandwiches, and soft drinks in case they were blocked from leaving.

The morning inched by. Noise penetrated the building from the parking lot—the sound of hymns being played over a portable PA system. It was very unnerving. Why was it that ordinary church hymns sounded so menacing when they were used to threaten?

Weeping patients trailed in, scared and showing it. The air began to smell of nervous perspiration. Everyone felt the tension, and briefly Annie wished Treva were here, to help defuse everything. Treva had a way of being calm and centered . . . When she was around, everything went better.

"Just ignore the chaos and let's concentrate on our work, people," said Dr. Ellen Rosenkrantz, striding out of an exam room with her white hair flying out in energetic wisps. "We'll keep on seeing patients as long as we have any to see."

Peering out through a small viewing pane in the glass-bricked front vestibule window, Annie saw that more crowds had gathered, now including TV crews. Demonstrators were crawling on their hands and knees in front of startled police officers, who didn't know whether to grab them or just stand back.

Great, Annie thought.

She soothed anxious patients who were still in the waiting room, promising them they would be safe and would be provided escorts out of the clinic.

At 2:30 P.M., Dr. Rosenkrantz went into her office to eat a sandwich at her desk. She emerged from her office and handed Annie her private-line answering-machine tape.

"Don't tell anyone, but it's another death threat." The white-haired doctor sighed. "Annie, please give this to the police when you have a moment."

Annie was troubled. "I worry about you."

Dr. Rosenkrantz smiled sadly. "In the past three years I've received eight phone threats like this. I've had rocks thrown through the front windshield of my car, and my tires slashed. One time they set my car on fire. That was a sight to behold. And now I'd better get back to work. There's a fourteen-year-old girl in Exam Room Seven who's crying for her mama, and I need to find a rock tape that'll cheer her up. Any suggestions?"

By four o'clock the mackerel gray skies had opened up, pouring a cold, driving rain on the demonstrators—those who hadn't been arrested, that is—who turned off the amplifiers and began putting their posters and other paraphernalia back into their vans. The TV truck left, and the volunteers began driving patients home, with police escorts. Annie had a spare moment to call Treva.

"It's been a zoo here all day," she told her friend. "People crawling around out front like babies. Eight arrests, I heard. Maybe nine. We had a woman who chained herself out in front to a pile of cement blocks. The police sawed off the chain. Oh, and Dr. Rosenkrantz got another death threat on her answering tape. 'Die, you dirty baby killer. You deserve to burn in hell.' "

"It's really a war, isn't it?" said Treva.

"An unfair war," cried Annie hotly. "Because it's the patients who are being penalized. They have a legal right to get an abortion and they're being prevented from exercising those rights. And I know there's free speech, but who says those demonstrators have a right to frighten and threaten? And they'll threaten to kill an abortion doctor—even actually kill one—but they're supposed to believe in saving human life?''

"I know, I know, Annie, it's hell and it's racking this country apart. But the women need us, hon.''

Annie made arrangements to stop by Treva's house after work. She wouldn't stay long—her husband was expecting her—but suddenly she needed a nice, soothing dose of Treva. She needed it badly.

"You don't know how we miss you here,'' she said. "Treva, you just don't know.''

DIEDRE

DIEDRE HAD BEEN SEEING MITCH STERLING FOR A month and a half now, a succession of study dates interspersed with pizza dates, and another visit to one of Cloris Kovaks's parties, where Diedre debated with the others on whether the cloning of human beings was a man-made miracle or a God-awful mistake.

The sexual tension between her and Mitch was growing. Each time they'd kiss and neck before saying good night, the fireworks heating both of them up. She'd felt his erection beneath his jeans a dozen times, always rock-hard.

"I can't,'' she would whisper, when he became too urgent. "Mitch . . . please . . . I know we did it once, but that was sort of an accident and I'm not ready for a sexual relationship.''

Even when she wasn't with him, she fantasized about him.

She was going to have to slow things down . . . or there might be another catastrophe.

One Friday morning in late October, Pam had clipped some coupons and wanted to stop at an Arbor Drugs on their way to campus to buy some conditioner and some other hair products. This was how they ended up driving past the Geddes/Washtenaw Clinic.

A demonstration.

Protesters crowded around a small, black teenager who was with her mother, surrounding the two women as they attempted to enter the building. The young girl began to run toward the building, stumbling, her face rigid with fright. As Pam and Diedre watched, she made it into the building.

"God." Diedre shuddered, staring at this sight, angry tears springing to her eyes. She'd felt like jumping out and defending the young girl. "It's horrible enough to have to get an abortion without being harassed for it."

By now they were past the clinic, turning in to the shopping center. Diedre was still shaking.

"Look, Deeds, it's over, okay?" Pam said. "You got lucky, you didn't have all those demonstrators to contend with, but even if they'd been there, you'd still have gone in, wouldn't you? So forget about it. You made the right choice. Now just live your life, okay?"

Diedre nodded, but as they wandered the aisles of the drugstore, coupons in hand, she couldn't help shivering again. *Was* it over? Sure, she'd managed to put the abortion out of her mind, and she considered herself emotionally recovered from it. Still, seeing those demonstrators, that frightened girl, had brought it all back. And now Mitch was getting so insistent sexually . . .

At eleven o'clock that day Diedre had a spare hour after her Criminal Law class, and had arranged to meet Rodger Halsick at the Lawyer's Club to confer on her child custody case, *Hertz v. Hertz.*

Halsick was full of information about the process of an evidentiary hearing. It would be held in a courtroom, but there would be no jury. The plaintiff, Marcie's husband, would go first with his case, then Marcie would have a chance to rebut his accusations, each calling witnesses if they chose. Often, he said, the judge did not take extra days to consider, but gave her pronouncement then and there.

"Her?"

"Yes, she has a female judge, Judge Maria Alvarez, the same judge that the Hertzes had for their divorce decree. And the hearing will be in Oakland County, where the decree was finalized."

Halsick began telling Diedre about the "moral fitness" part of their case.

"Judges basically want to see June Cleaver in court. You know, modest, respectable, wide-eyed. They aren't at all comfortable when mothers under custodial siege arrive surrounded by supporters, especially female supporters. They find this unattractively aggressive. Women are supposed to arrive in court alone, brave and respectful, the image of the 'ideal mother.' "

"But it's hardly fair," Diedre protested.

"If courtrooms were a hundred percent fair, we wouldn't have appeals, now would we? Also, negative emotions are a real no-no. If a woman displays anger, or 'hysteria,' or 'coldness,' or dares to lose her temper, she'll probably lose her case. I recall a case where a Tennessee judge threw a pregnant woman in jail for twenty-two hours after she uttered the word *hell* during a custody hearing."

"Incredible," said Diedre.

There was more, and Diedre listened attentively, taking notes. They discussed strategy, and Diedre set forth her ideas. She wanted to call the owner of Evan's day care center as a witness, along with Marcie's master's adviser, who would testify that Marcie was on the verge of being able to earn a very good living. Also, she had her eye on a witness who lived in Marcie's former apartment house, to testify that she had not brought men back to her apartment.

"Good ideas," praised Halsick. "Sounds like you're really into this case, Diedre. Just make sure you know what answers your witnesses are going to give in court. We'll talk more about that later as the hearing gets near.''

Still high on adrenaline from Halsick's praise over her handling of Marcie's case, Diedre telephoned Treva Connor after class, and they had a long discussion about custody cases that Treva had encountered during the years before she had joined the Geddes/Washtenaw Clinic.

"I just hope I can win," Diedre worried. "It'll be tragic if I don't."

"The court system can be very capricious when it comes to women," Treva remarked. "And I know Marcie has a great chance with you on her side, Diedre. But if for some reason she does lose custody of her son, you need to tell her that the judge can decide whether or not her son will live with her, but not how much she'll love him. Tell her to just keep loving him whatever happens, and he'll know in his heart he can count on her."

Diedre felt touched by what Treva said, and even more determined to fight back. Why should Marcie be forced to go through that hurt? This was why Diedre was in law school, to help women like Marcie. Somehow, she'd see to it that Evan remained with his mother.

The following Friday night Diedre rushed into the apartment, her hands flying at her blond hair, pulling it out of its braid. Pam had to work late tonight, which meant they'd both been late getting home, and now she had to hurry to get ready for her date with Mitch Sterling. Breaking from their usual study-date routine, he was planning to take her to one of the children's "wheelchair games" he coached.

"Good grief," Pam remarked, watching her rush about. "He's just a guy. If he gets here and you're not ready, make him wait."

"I don't want to make him wait. That's too much like a formal date."

"It is a date, isn't it? I mean, he's picking you up, right? And he's taking you out for dinner."

"A sandwich," corrected Diedre, blushing bright pink.

"Oh, we're quibbling about it, are we? After all those

nights you've come in with whisker burn? What are you planning to wear for this so-called nondate?''

''I don't know. Just my usual clothes.'' Diedre loped into her bedroom and began pawing through her closet. ''I was going to take a load of laundry to the basement and I forgot. Oh, shit, everything's dirty.'' She gazed at her sister in despair. ''I can't wear a sweater with a big spaghetti stain on it.''

''I bought that new vest and blouse at Hit or Miss,'' Pam offered.

Diedre looked up. ''Oh, Pammy . . . could I? I promise I won't spill anything on it. And you can wear anything of mine anytime you want it.''

In the shower, Diedre turned under the warm spray, closing her eyes as it inundated her head and body. Mitch Sterling. She had to slow down their relationship a little . . . or maybe even stop seeing him.

Be sensible, she ordered herself, pouring shampoo into her cupped palm. He was the father of her baby, but didn't know it. And with every passing day, it was getting harder and harder even to think about telling him.

Pam banged on the bathroom door. ''Deeds! He's here! He's ringing the buzzer.''

''Oh, no,'' wailed Diedre.

She finished showering and threw on Pam's shorty robe, covered with a Minnie Mouse print, which was hanging on a hook on the back of the bathroom door. She rushed out of the bathroom, forced to cross the end of the tiny living room in order to reach her bedroom.

''Well,'' said Mitch, grinning. ''Hello, Diedre.''

She froze, embarrassed at being caught in the silly robe that Pam had brought at Disney World one time. Mitch himself looked shower-fresh. He was freshly shaven, his cheeks smooth. He wore jeans and a flannel shirt over a T-shirt, an outfit that made him look very much like a country-singing hunk. All he needed was the hat and boots.

''Hi—I'm nearly ready. Jeans okay?''

''Jeans are terrific.''

Diedre fled down the hallway to the refuge of her bed-room, finding, to her relief, Pam's blouse and vest lying on her bed. She dressed rapidly, finishing up the outfit with a pair of snakeskin cowboy boots she'd had since freshman year at Wayne. She dabbed some pressed powder on her face, applied lipstick and eyeliner, then had to redo the liner because she'd smeared it.

She emerged from the bedroom still smoothing her hair.

"You look great," said Mitch, eyeing Diedre with a heated glance that created a shiver all up and down her body.

"Thanks," she muttered.

"Shall we go?"

Diedre received a shock when she walked out to the parking lot and saw a familiar-looking Le Baron convertible, the same car that she and Mitch had had sex in during their ill-fated one-night stand. On all of their previous dates, he'd been driving a three- or four-year-old Dodge Dart.

"It's the Le Baron," she said, stopping and trying to hide her dismay.

Mitch smiled pleasantly. "Yeah, my dad said I could drive it the rest of the year. Too bad the weather is getting cold so we can't roll back the convertible top."

Didn't he realize what connotations this car had for her? Diedre slid into the familiar, leather-smelling passenger seat, feeling a jolting sense of déjà vu. Here in this car . . . *in this very backseat . . .*

Her stomach clenched, she forced herself to make con-versation as Mitch started the Le Baron and drove toward downtown Ann Arbor.

First they had an early, five-o'clock dinner at a seafood restaurant on Main Street, the same one that Roger Halsick had taken her to. There were only a few diners at this early hour, mostly older couples. Not exactly a sandwich, Diedre thought, looking at menu items such as crab legs, lobster tails, and scallops *Provençale.* And she certainly couldn't afford to pay her share—not at these prices.

"I'll just have salad," she specified.

Mitch raised an eyebrow. "That's all?"

"I'm on a tight budget, you know that."

"I'll buy, Diedre. I expected to buy when we came here. Please, you need more than just a salad."

"I don't."

"Okay, then we'll both have crab salads. And sometime you can bake me a pie or something. Apples are in season—do you bake?"

"Once in a while," she admitted. "With those prepared crusts."

While they waited for their meals, he began telling her about the kids she was going to meet tonight. "They're paras, most of them—that stands for paraplegic, and means they have full use of their arms. Quads are the ones who don't."

"Do they use motorized wheelchairs?"

"No way, not these kids. Anyway, they don't encourage paras to depend on mechanized chairs, it atrophies the muscles they still do have the use of. That's one reason this wheelchair basketball is so good. It keeps the kids moving and active, builds muscles, lets them know there are still plenty of things they can excel at."

He continued to tell her about the kids, while Diedre toyed with her salad, her stomach muscles painfully tight. Mitch's love of kids kept cropping up, over and over.

The wheelchair game was being held in the gymnasium of a grade school near Packard. The school's hallways were decorated with kids' poster-paint pictures, collages made of macaroni, and handprints that were incredibly small and adorable, each one labeled with a child's name. Diedre studied the palm print of a child named Angela, her throat choking up. Why did Mitch have to love kids so much?

The minute they walked into the gym, kids in wheelchairs started rolling up to Mitch, calling his name.

"These kids just adore Mitch," remarked the woman seated next to Diedre on the scarred wooden bleachers as they watched the "Red Dogs" compete against the "Blue

Streaks." "For my Jalessa, the sun rises and sets in Mitch Sterling."

The game was played by regular basketball rules, with traveling penalties called if a player propelled his or her wheelchair three consecutive times without dribbling. Due to the children's ages, the hoop had been lowered, but Jalessa's mother told Diedre that adult wheelchair competitors used a ten-foot hoop, regulation height.

When they finally left the gym, Mitch still seemed exhilarated, replaying the game for Diedre and giving her more details about the kids' lives and disabilities.

Diedre listened, feeling unaccountably sad. These past weeks she'd tried to deny it, but it was *so* plain that Mitch adored children. How would he react if he knew he'd already been a father—for a few short weeks? She just didn't want to think about it.

They got into the Le Baron again. "Where to now, Diedre? Maybe a drink somewhere?"

She looked down at her lap. "I don't know. I still have forty pages of Torts to read tonight."

He laughed, glancing at his watch. "Today's Friday— you don't have class tomorrow, do you? My kids play early, it's only nine o'clock. Relax, Diedre, let law school go for a few hours."

It *was* still early. How could she tell Mitch to take her home at only nine o'clock? So Diedre allowed Mitch to take her to a lounge near campus where they served 101 brands of imported beers, and where there was dancing.

The dance floor was crowded with students, packed in body to body as they gyrated to pounding "techno" music played by a disc jockey who called himself "Cee Jay the Dee Jay." The noise level was high, much too loud for conversation, and Diedre gave herself up to the dancing, excited by Mitch's energetic, sexy moves, and the other young, healthy bodies all around them.

When a slow dance finally came on, Mitch pulled Diedre to him and enfolded his arms around her waist, leaning his face into the top of her head. He smelled of laundered shirt

and clean dance-floor perspiration, a sensuously erotic combination.

"You're definitely the prettiest woman in the room," he
murmured into her ear.

"Oh, stop."

"Well, you are. I'm not lying. See?" He turned her
around so that she could see their reflection in a mirror that
had been installed on the back dance-floor wall. Diedre
stared at the sight. Her. Him. Their bodies fit together perfectly; he was just the right height for her, she thought,
feeling a little thrill of fright.

The dance number seemed interminable, Diedre drawn
into it as if into a vat of thick, sweet honey. She felt the
movement of Mitch's body against hers, the pressure of his
erection against her left hip. She clung to him, feeling dizzied, dazzled. This wasn't supposed to be happening . . .

They finally left the lounge about 1:45 A.M. Outside on the
street they could still hear the music from inside. While they
had been dancing, a chilly wind had started to blow, swinging the traffic lights and exploding drifts of dead leaves
down the sidewalk. Tomorrow was a home football game.
Somewhere Diedre could hear drunken yelling as a bunch
of male students ran through the streets, and there was the
squeal of tires on the next block as someone turned a corner
much too fast.

Diedre huddled her jacket around her, burningly aware of
Mitch's arm placed casually around her shoulders.

"Diedre, come back to my apartment for another drink,"
he begged.

"No. I can't." But the last word burst out small, tormented.

"I care about you. I really care." He put his hand on her
chin and drew her face up, his eyes locking on to hers.
"Diedre, do you think you could have some feelings for
me?"

She did. She had plenty of feelings for him, but not the
kind she wanted to have.

Terror beat wings inside her as she stared into Mitch's eyes. She fought a wild desire to run, or even walk home by herself again, but a serial rapist had terrorized this town a few years back, and this was not a safe hour to be alone on the streets. "I . . . Mitch . . . please, *don't* push me too fast."

They were both quiet in the car as Mitch drove Diedre home. Diedre silently pondered the situation she'd gotten herself into. He pulled underneath one of the carports, preparing to walk her to the door.

"I'll say good night here," she said quickly, afraid he would try to kiss her. If he did, even once, she knew she would be lost; she could not hold out against these feelings forever.

"Fine," he agreed lightly. He carefully did not touch her, but the possibility hung between them for a long, swooping second, dangerously unbearable. "Good night, beautiful lady."

"Good night, Mitch. And, Mitch?"

"Yeah?"

She said it fast, pushing the words out. "Maybe we'd better cool it for a while."

"Cool it?"

"You know." Diedre stared at him, suddenly speechless. Words simply would not emerge. What could she possibly say? How to explain? She solved the problem by jumping out of the car and hurrying toward the apartment building.

"Diedre—" he called, but she was already shutting the door behind her.

Diedre stepped into the familiar hallway. It smelled like cleaning solution and freshly popped popcorn. One of the downstairs residents had left his bike outside his apartment, chained to a wrought-iron railing on the stairs that led to the basement.

She walked up to their apartment, letting herself in with her key. The buttery smell of popcorn saturated the apartment. Pam was sitting on the couch with Bud, both of them cozily watching a movie on the VCR. The couple had their feet propped on the coffee table, and Pam's lipstick was smeared to the point of being nonexistent. A big dish of popcorn sat in front of them, mostly empty except for un-popped kernels.

It was such a comfortable, cozy, warm, and intimate scene that it stabbed at Diedre's heart. How she envied Pam's uncomplicated relationship. Bud might not be a law student, but he earned fifteen dollars an hour as a CAD designer at an engineering firm in Ypsilanti, and was happy and friendly. He treated Pam well. As far as Diedre knew, there was no secret lurking in their relationship, ready to blow it all apart.

"Good date?" said Pam, looking up.

"Oh, it was all right." Diedre forced her voice to sound cheerful.

"Want some popcorn? I can make some more."

"No, I'm fine."

Diedre walked into her bedroom and closed the door. She knew she couldn't see Mitch again. Tonight . . . those wheelchair kids . . . his obvious devotion to them . . . If only she hadn't had the one-night stand with him! If only she hadn't been so careless!

If only she didn't care.

Diedre avoided Mitch for a week, hurrying out of her Constitutional Law class as fast as she could and blending in with the crowds in the hallway so that she would not have to speak to him. Too bad the law school was really such an insular place, with all the classes being held in Hutchins Hall.

When he called the apartment, Diedre let the answering machine take the calls, telling Pam to tell Mitch that she was out. She knew it was cowardly, but she saw no other way, not without hurting Mitch even more dreadfully.

Twice in the library, Mitch smiled at her from across the reading room. Diedre blushed, dropping a book, and then gathered up all of her stuff and fled to a carrel on the lower level. Damn him. She did *not* need this tension, not with all of the other responsibilities she now had, her classes, the Women's Law project, Marcie Hertz.

"Diedre—" Mitch cornered her one noon hour in the basement lounge of Hutchins Hall where the usual students were brown-bagging it or heating up Budget Gourmet meals or Hot Pockets in the microwave. "Please—we have to talk—"

She got up and left, leaving her tuna fish sandwich on the table, untouched in its plastic zip bag.

That night she was in her bedroom, sitting at her computer keyboard typing her Torts course outline, when Pam knocked, then poked her head around the door.

"Well, he's here," her sister announced in a significant manner, as if Brad Pitt had just rung the buzzer.

"Who?"

"Mitch. That guy you like so much. The one who calls here every day. And he's got a pizza with him."

"Pizza? Oh, great. That's so we won't turn him away. He thinks of everything." Diedre saved her document and exited Windows 95, irritation pushing through her as she planned what to say to him. She didn't need Mitch Sterling, she didn't need the feelings he created in her. She didn't need his *complications*.

"Cheese and veggies," announced Mitch, as Diedre walked into the living room. He offered up a large, fragrant Domino's pizza box, smiling dazzlingly as if he had been invited and this gift were expected. "And sun-dried tomatoes, ripe olives . . . everything except meat and anchovies."

He was wearing jeans and a blue denim shirt and looked heart-stoppingly handsome.

"Mitch, I really can't—" Diedre began, her abdomen knotting. But Pam was already brushing past her, taking the pizza box from Mitch's outstretched arms and carrying it to the table in the dining alcove.

"Mmmm," said her sister, greedily opening the box. Delicious odors wafted out. "I've been starving all night. Great . . . this one has tons of cheese, just dripping off of it. I'll cut it. Where's some plates? Diedre, will you get some plates?''

Diedre glared at Pam, then went to the railroad-style kitchen and retrieved three plates and forks, taking down glasses for diet soda. She rattled them noisily. She wasn't going to give Mitch a beer, even though they had a partial twelve-pack that Bud had left. Mitch had no right to drop in on her like this, using pizza and Pam to weasel his way into her life.

They sat around the table. Mitch began telling Pam some funny law-school stories, then some hilarious lawyer jokes, and Pam laughed and encouraged him. However, when the pizza was finished, Pam got up from the table and announced that she was going over to visit Bud.

''Bud? Right now? But it's eleven o'clock,'' said Diedre in a panic. Her eyes implored Pam. *Don't leave me here with him.*

But her sister just grinned. ''Bud had to work some OT tonight and he's just getting off. We might go to a late movie, or maybe we'll go out and get a beer.''

Pam left, banging the apartment door behind her, her ploy so obvious that it was embarrassing. Diedre and Mitch were now left alone. Pam had done it on purpose, playing matchmaker. Diedre gritted her teeth, making up her mind to castigate her sister for this as soon as she got back.

''I'll help you clear away,'' offered Mitch, reaching for the pizza box.

''No, that won't be necessary.''

''Diedre . . .''

''It *won't* be necessary.''

''Diedre, why are you acting like this? What have I done? I admit I was an unexpected guest, but I did arrive with pizza.'' He smiled crookedly. ''Who can turn down pizza?''

''Obviously not Pam.''

''Or you either. I notice you ate a piece. Diedre, you've been avoiding me all week. When I saw you in the library you could hardly wait to grab up your books and get out of the room. And you left a perfectly good sandwich in Hutchins Hall. Is it really that terrible, the fact that we like each other? More than like, at least on my part.'' He brushed away a lock of his glossy, jet black hair and moved closer to her. ''Look me in the eye and tell me you don't care about me at least a little.''

One look into his intense, blue eyes and she'd cry. She backed away, into the kitchen. ''I like you, Mitch, but now I want you to go home.''

He moved after her, turning her against the refrigerator, taking her in his arms. He smelled of clean shirt and clean, faintly musky skin, a familiar, sexy smell that caused shivers of pleasure to traverse Diedre's skin.

''Diedre . . .''

His mouth touched hers, at first softly, then becoming more demanding. Diedre squeezed her eyes shut, her heart hammering. This was beyond her. She had lost control. She couldn't help it; she pressed herself up against Mitch and opened her mouth to his. The kiss was sweetly deep, an opening not only of her mouth but of her heart.

They stood locked together near the refrigerator on which Diedre had taped various law-school announcements clipped from *The Docket* and *Res Gestae*, along with a card from her mother. Added to these were several jokey Hallmark cards that Bud had sent to Pam.

Diedre was totally unaware of them. She was only conscious that she'd broken down . . . she was kissing Mitch . . . she wanted to do more . . . Oh, God, where was this going to lead? What had she done?

They lay on the living room couch, his leg draped over hers, her leg somehow between his. Their chests were pressed so close that she could feel the deep thump of Mitch's heart pumping against her. Diedre felt lost in hot confusion.

Their kisses flamed, repeating over and over.

Warm skin and twining limbs, the push of Mitch's strong erection against her abdomen. Accidentally Diedre touched it through his clothes. Then, unable to help herself, she touched it deliberately. He felt long, hard, urgent. Oh, God

. . . she squeezed him, running her fingers up and down the length of him through the cloth of his jeans. She felt his reaction as if she had touched him with a live electrical wire.

Urgently Mitch began tugging up the hem of the blouse that Diedre wore. His hand slipped inside, found her bra, and cupped her breast, the feel of his skin so warm on hers that she thought she would scream.

"Mitch . . . we shouldn't . . ." Sense briefly returned to her and she drew back, frightened at how quickly this was progressing and remembering the consequences of the last time she had made love to Mitch. Oh, sweet Jesus, she didn't have any birth control. If she became pregnant again, she'd kill herself.

"I have condoms," he said thickly. "Aren't you on anything?"

"No." But then belatedly she remembered that there was a fresh tube of spermicidal foam that Pam had bought with her coupons at Arbor Drugs. In fact, Pam had bought three tubes. She rushed into the bathroom and began rooting through the cabinet under the sink. She could replace the tube before Pam discovered it was missing . . .

Her hands shook as she inserted the messy foam. This stuff was supposed to make sex romantic? But she didn't care about that right now. She was too caught up . . .

Washing her hands afterward, Diedre stared, shocked, at her own face in the mirror. She looked terribly flushed, her lips swollen, her eyes glittering. Her hair was a tangle and there was a red blotch on her neck, rubbed there by Mitch's rough beard stubble.

Oh, what am I doing? But she knew she couldn't stop.

When she returned to the living room, Mitch had taken off his shirt and jeans, and was lying on the couch in his navy blue boxers. He had the smooth muscles of a natural athlete, and a flat stomach adorned with a silky trail of dark hair that disappeared into his boxers. He sat up and reached out his arms to her, pulling her on top of him.

"Diedre . . . I promise it won't be like last time. I won't

desert you again. This time you're stuck with me. I'm going to call you again and again.''

Oh, God. Oh, God.

She mumbled something, closing her eyes, feeling his hands explore her body, lifting her vest and blouse off her, the lacy bra, releasing the snap at the waist of her jeans. Underneath Diedre was wearing some French-cut panties she'd splurged on at the mall after seeing a much more expensive pair at a lingerie shop on Liberty Street.

Mitch held them in his hands and whispered, ''Soft, as soft as you are. Oh, Diedre . . .''

Diedre felt the heat of him underneath her. There was the brief pause while he unwrapped the condom, then the glorious, spreading feeling as he inserted his penis into her, its progress well lubricated by the foam.

She straddled him, rising and falling, throwing her head back, her voice crying out wordless things. They gripped each other hard, intent on the dance they were performing, the steady thrust and return.

Diedre put a finger on her own opened genitals, pulling pleasure out of herself that was fed by his movements and his pleasure. She came suddenly, her hips bucking. Powerful sensations jolted through her, and her cry became a scream, and still she spasmed. Mitch pulled her down on top of him and then he came, too, his orgasm silent and shaking.

Afterward, Diedre felt tears pushing hotly at the backs of her eyelids. He'd taken everything out of her, all of her resistance.

She lay on top of Mitch, too tired to move, perspiration running down her naked flanks. She could smell their sex odors rising around them like a ferny, pungent mist. Belatedly she remembered that this was the living room couch; they had no real privacy. Pam might return at any time.

She climbed off Mitch, hurriedly reaching for her clothes. Good heavens, what if she became pregnant again? The thought horrified her. But she couldn't; they'd used both a condom and foam. She was safe, she had to be.

''Hey, sweetness,'' said Mitch, touching her lazily.

"Don't be afraid now, all right? This was good, it was meant to be. Please, trust me when I say that, Diedre."

"I'll try."

Still, she felt compelled to pick up her clothes and rush into the bathroom again, where she found a package of Massengill douche. She douched twice, washing herself out thoroughly, and then, when she was finished, she felt a squeeze of horror as she realized she had just washed away all the spermicide that was supposed to kill the sperm. Assuming any had made it through the condom, which she hoped they hadn't.

Shaken, she inserted more foam, and then she sank down on the toilet lid, feeling totally drained of emotion.

"Diedre?" called Mitch from outside the room. "Are you all right?"

"I'm *fine*."

She pulled on her clothes, dressing hurriedly. Mitch helped her straighten the living room and kitchen, plumping the pillows and turning over one of the cushions to hide their stain.

"Tomorrow," he said, kissing her again at the door. "The library, for sure."

"All right," she agreed woodenly.

They walked to the apartment door. "*Love*," whispered Mitch, and then the door closed behind him. She heard his footsteps fast on the stairs, then the bang of the outside door.

It was just sex, Diedre reassured herself like a mantra, putting the dead bolt in place. *That's all. All it was. I won't fall in love, I'll make myself not do it. I'll only see him a little while longer.*

She nervously went into the bathroom and added more spermicidal foam, enough to kill a million eager sperm. But how many million were there in an ejaculation? All it would take was one. Could she do anything else to protect herself? Maybe say a prayer. If she was going to continue to sleep with Mitch, she'd have to go to the doctor, get a prescription for the pill.

Yes, and she'd insist he still use condoms, too. Maybe

the foam as well. She wasn't getting pregnant again. No way.

"Well?" said Pam, barging in twenty minutes later, a smug look on her face as Diedre was trying, without success, to return to her course outline. The lettering was just a blur on her computer screen. For once, she could not concentrate.

Her sister went on, "Did you two work things out?"

"We—we did some talking," Diedre said, flushing hotly. "Who do you think you are, Pam, throwing us together like that? What if I didn't want him here? What if it just wasn't working out with us?"

"Well, did it? Work out, I mean."

"I suppose you're asking if we had sex," said Diedre sullenly, using the mouse to exit from Windows and shut down the computer.

"No. I'm not asking that . . ." Pam giggled. "*Did* you?"

"Oh, God!" Diedre exploded. "Really, Pam. I don't ask what you and Bud do when you stay over at his apartment until four in the morning. I wish you had not decided to play matchmaker. I have plenty to do, enough studying for two people, without—" To her shock, she began to cry.

Pam rushed over to her. "Diedre. Deeds. I didn't mean anything. I thought I was doing you a favor. He's so cute. He's nice and he's funny and he's going to be a rich lawyer, which ought to count for something."

"I know . . . I know . . ."

"Hey . . ."

Out in the parking lot, someone was banging a car horn, part of the regular background noise of a building occupied mostly by students. Neither Diedre nor Pam really heard it. Diedre continued to sob. "I *wish* it hadn't happened . . ."

"You wish what hadn't happened? Making love with him? He's a nice guy, Deeds, he's not the type that'll just use you. Did I tell you I saw him on campus the other day? He told me how much he likes you. He told me how beautiful he thinks you are. How smart. He just kept raving and raving about you, honey. So I don't think he's going to dump you."

"Won't he?" sobbed Diedre.

"No. There's no guarantees, but he seems like a nice one, kiddo, a lot better than some of these guys who come on to you and then act like dickfaces."

"Oh, Pam."

"What is it? What is it?" demanded her sister in alarm. "You're acting crazy . . . He *is* nice, isn't he? Oh, God, he didn't try to date-rape you or do anything horrible, did he?"

"No," gasped Diedre. "He was fine."

"Then what? Why are you acting like this?"

Diedre bent over, putting her face in her hands. "Him. He's the one."

"What one?"

"He's the *one,* Pam. The one who got me pregnant."

"No," breathed Pam.

"I told you I had this one-night stand with a guy at that party in July . . . Well, he's the guy. I ran into him accidentally at the law library . . ."

"Let me get this straight. This guy Mitch was the father. He got you pregnant. Does he know this? Did you tell him?"

"No, of course I didn't tell him. He loves kids, Pam. I mean *loves them.* He's great with them."

"So? That's a plus, isn't it?"

"Is it? I don't know what I'm going to do."

Pam grinned at her. "You could end up marrying him and with both of you being lawyers, your yearly income between the two of you would be astronomical. You could afford the best house in Barton Hills. Trips to Las Vegas . . . Acapulco . . . I don't know . . . You could have way cool cars . . ."

"Pam, please." Diedre shook her head. "You sound like a travel agent. I don't care about money or trips."

"Well, what the hell is it?"

"I don't know if I can live with that kind of a secret."

"You mean the abortion?" Pam walked into the kitchen,

which still smelled of pizza. The big, greasy pizza box had been folded in half and was waiting to go out with the trash. She reached in the fridge, grabbed a Diet Pepsi, and popped the top noisily. "Don't be silly. Millions of women get abortions now. It's not a huge, huge shame anymore."

"I know, but I can't tell him," Diedre said painfully.

"Why not?"

"Because it isn't just any abortion. It's ours! I could tell him if I'd had it done, like, in high school. I wouldn't have a problem with that. But, Pam, this is his abortion, too. It affects him."

"Listen to me," interrupted Pam. "Was he there when you missed your period? No, I don't recall him being there. Was he there offering to marry you or pay your bills and be a daddy? I don't *think* so. So how can he object that you did it? Hey, he's around now. He's a great guy. He's crazy about you, I can tell. Right now he'd probably take just about anything you told him, Deeds."

Diedre gulped in a big breath of air. "I . . . I just can't," she said miserably. "You weren't there at the wheelchair game, Pam, you didn't see the way he reacted to those kids. He was so great with them . . . Pam, if he found out about the abortion, he would hate me. I just know he would."

Diedre lay in bed, listening to the familiar night sounds. Someone in the building was playing a stereo too loudly— alternative rock, which Diedre didn't even like. A car door banged, someone laughed. A building door slammed. A siren whined out somewhere on Stadium Boulevard. Nothing was ever totally quiet, no matter what the hour.

She felt restless, unable to lie still. Her skin felt overheated with the memory of Mitch's body, and her pelvis felt thick, turgid with all the blood and sensations that had rushed there, way out of her control.

The phone extension by her bed rang, startling her out of her thoughts.

"Are you thinking about me?" Mitch's voice sounded husky, as if he were lying down.

"Yes," Diedre admitted. "I'm thinking about you. How could I not?"

"What are you thinking?"

"Oh . . . just lots of things," she responded evasively.

"Like what?"

"Like we're both studying so many hours a week and law school has to come first. It's so tough, and I'm on scholarship—I *have* to do well or I'm out of here. I don't have alternatives and I can't mess myself up with romance. We—we got way too serious, Mitch."

"So we'll sandwich a relationship in between classes," declared Mitch cheerfully. "We'll have more library dates. We'll have exam-crunch dates. We'll have moot court dates. We'll go to Aunt Cloris's soirees. And since we're studying so much, we'll even have terrific grades. How can you beat that?"

She said nothing, her breath coming fast. He made it sound reasonable. She didn't want it to be reasonable. She felt terribly scared because she knew it couldn't work.

"Diedre. I didn't plan on this either. I have a lot riding on law school, too. I . . . I think I'm falling in love with you."

She sucked in her breath, closing her eyes.

"Diedre? Are you still there?"

"Yes."

"Did you hear what I said?"

"Yes." Her heartbeat was wild. She felt so hot she had to throw off the sheets, swallowing several times before she could speak coherently. "I . . . I feel the same way," she admitted in a low voice.

PEPPER

THE FIRST WEEK OF NOVEMBER, PEPPER MANAGED TO scrape together enough money to finance a shopping trip to New York. She had to go, really, if she wanted her shop to be top drawer—it was a necessity to keep the list of wealthy customers she was beginning to build.

So she cashed in her remaining IRA account and begged a few more thousand from her mother, adding it to her debt load at 10 percent interest, their agreed-upon rate. She was so handicapped by not being able to go to a bank, and made up her mind to mail her mother something gorgeous, just to say thanks.

She made reservations at a small, older hotel on Central Park South that one of her customers had recommended as being "charming." Now all her IRAs were gone, but dammit, what good was her retirement if she let her boutique slip through her fingers? She'd be working as a clerk in some upscale department store like Nordstrom's until she was seventy-five if she could not make Pepper's successful.

"You mean all you're going to do is shop?" questioned Gray, raising an eyebrow when she told him about the buying trip.

"Yeah . . . shop till I drop. First I have to see what's selling, what's hot. Then I have to see if I can find some terrific, unique things to bring back, and if I can find a couple of new, young lingerie designers who do great stuff but haven't jacked up their prices too badly yet."

"Unfortunately I have two or three meetings I can't miss, or we could fly out there together," said Gray. "We could do some shopping of our own, take in a play, cruise some galleries."

Pepper laughed. "Would you believe I've never done any

sightseeing when I've been in New York? By the time you've shopped all day, you're tired and all you want is room service and the TV set.''

''That's no way to experience New York,'' he murmured.

''Maybe not, but it's reality for me. Anyway, I'll be back Thursday morning, so you'll hardly have time to miss me.''

On the day she arrived, New York didn't look like a city of dreams at all. It was forty-two degrees and raining on the line of cabs parked in the long La Guardia taxi line, a gray drizzle punctuated by occasional bursts of bitter, wet wind.

The cab driver was Israeli by the spelling of his name, and drove his vehicle as if it were a missile launcher he was aiming at the tall, cruel cement city. Yellow cabs choked the streets, and the sidewalks were a bobbing sea of umbrellas.

Pepper had forgotten all about bringing an umbrella—in Michigan she kept hers in the trunk of her car—so she purchased one from a sidewalk vendor.

Big mistake. Within half an hour one of the ribs was broken, sticking its sharp end through the black nylon, and two more threatened to collapse, too. She'd been taken, of course. Probably no native New Yorker would ever dream of buying an umbrella from a sidewalk vendor. However, it still was keeping some of the water off, and she had miles left to walk.

An hour later, caught in a crowd crossing the street, dodging a taxi careening around a corner and spraying water, Pepper felt a burst of exhilaration. She'd visited a twenty-one-year-old Israeli designer who was creating wonderful, witty, hand-painted chemises and panties. She'd placed a modest order, which would be shipped the following week. The young designer had given her several more leads which she intended to follow through on tomorrow, calling for appointments.

Now she planned to browse the boutiques and shops of Fifth Avenue and then the Village, to get ideas, see what was trendy, and pick out some little luxury she could send to her mother in thanks.

The rain let up a little. A frowsy-looking woman wearing a trench coat on which had been sewn over fifteen hundred ragged patches of cloth was wandering ahead of Pepper, her wet, white hair flowing in tangles down her back. The woman had no umbrella and was talking rapidly to herself.

Pepper felt a wave of pity and began walking faster, thinking that she could give the homeless woman two or three dollars. However, just as she drew abreast, the woman began shrieking out a stream of such ugly obscenities that Pepper drew away, horrified.

Her good mood spoiled a little, Pepper stopped in a deli to use the public phone to make several appointments for the following day, then continued to make her rounds of the shops. Her customers were going to love the sexy, beautiful things. Too bad she couldn't buy a lot more. She became absorbed in her shopping and was startled to realize that it was almost five o'clock.

Damn. It was now rush hour, the streets clogged, the sidewalks jammed with ceaseless crowds, thousands of people flowing past. Their sheer numbers made Pepper feel tired. To make matters worse, it had started raining again, even harder. Pepper couldn't get a cab . . .

By the time she reached her ''charming'' hotel, having ridden part of the way on a jam-packed bus, and gotten her butt fondled into the bargain, Pepper's mood of exhilaration had completely vanished. She was in no mood to enjoy the small, refurbished lobby area decorated with mirrors and enormous urns of flowers, where an elegantly hand-lettered sign on a stand announced that tea and scones were served in the afternoons.

She was chilled. She was wet. Her shoes were ruined. Also, she'd rubbed a blister on the back of her left foot, which burned like crazy.

Wearily Pepper took the slow elevator up to the newly remodeled sixth floor of the hotel, where she'd been given a room. Her room was located at the end, nicely wallpapered with a street view.

Entering her room with a key card, Pepper heard male voices on the other side of the wall, speaking loudly in some foreign language. A TV set penetrated the wall on the other side, CNN by the sound of it. Down on the street, taxis were banging their horns. Oh, Lord, and now a toilet was flushing. Then someone hawked up phlegm, making a project of it.

Great. Dispiritedly Pepper sank down on the too soft double bed, wishing by some magic she could transport herself back to Michigan and her small but comfortable apartment, then return instantly in the morning to resume her shopping. She picked up the phone and called down to the desk to complain about the men arguing in the other room, but what could she possibly say about the phlegm-spitter? If they gave her another room, it could be even worse.

The hotel had a room-service menu—definitely on the expensive side—and Pepper read it over, deciding to order herself some penne pasta and a salad. She didn't like eating in restaurants by herself; all too often, a man would spot her eating alone and try to come on to her.

Sitting alone at the round table, trying to pretend that the meal was great, with CNN turned on for company, Pepper felt a wave of depression. If only Gray were here. They could go out together, they could sample the city and find wonderful things to laugh about. She missed him dreadfully, much more than she'd expected. In fact, it was scary just how much she really did miss him.

But quickly she stifled the wave of loneliness. She was here to work, not to enjoy herself. She'd accomplished a lot today and she still had one more day ahead of her.

Pepper finally left a message on Gray's answering machine at his condo in Ann Arbor, then was in bed by eleven, turning the TV set to a station with nothing but static and white dots in order to create enough background noise to drown out any unwelcome sounds filtering through her walls.

The phone rang at 1:30 A.M., or maybe it was 2:00; Pepper was too sleepy to be able to focus her eyes on her watch.

"Pep," said Gray, his voice exceptionally sexy tonight.

"Um . . . mmmm," she muttered, trying to wake up.

"Sorry, I guess I called too late."

"No—it's fine. I'm using my TV set as white noise. I have foreign men discussing business or maybe killing each other on one side of my room, and a man with a bad throat problem on the other side—I mean he's hawking up his guts."

"Really?"

"Well, it sounds like that. But I did have a good day of shopping."

She began telling him about her day, making light of the homeless woman who'd screamed obscenities at her, the men she'd seen sprawled in doorways, the teenager who'd grabbed her buttocks on the bus, the taxi drivers who had sped past her as if she were invisible, the bleeding blister she'd acquired.

"But the stuff I bought, Gray . . . it's fantastic! This Israeli kid is absolutely a genius. He's got Hollywood stars palpitating to buy his stuff." She went on to rave about the designer's tiny showroom, but after a while her voice slowed down.

Finally Pepper felt herself jump, and realized she had fallen partially asleep in midsentence with the phone propped against her chin.

"Some romantic phone call," she said, yawning. "God, I'm so tired, and this hotel room is really the pits. I don't care how pretty their lobby is, they should have insulated their walls."

"Oh, honey," said Gray.

"Oh, don't worry about me. I love New York." Pepper yawned again as another taxi horn blatted upward from the street. "And the best thing I'll love about it is when I get back on the plane to Michigan."

They said their good-byes.

The foreigners next door had lowered their voices, probably because hotel security had stopped by, but they didn't stop talking excitedly until about 3:30 A.M. By then Pepper finally managed to drift off.

The next morning Pepper took great pleasure in running her shower loudly, banging the plumbing and switching her faucet off and on repeatedly, making the pipes vibrate. She flushed the toilet two or three times. Maybe it would wake up her next-door neighbors, if they weren't totally unconscious, give them a taste of the noise they had dished out last night.

Don't be petty, she told herself, but still found herself grinning.

She flicked on the TV set (loud) and ordered coffee, juice, and a basket of pastries from room service that included some miniature scones with golden raisins in them and granules of sugar sprinkled on top.

Walking to the window, she peered out on a blue-sky November morning, as crisp as a freshly fallen maple leaf. Crowds of people had repopulated the sidewalks, and across the street on a park bench, a homeless man was stirring awake, sitting up to breathe in gulps of smoggy city air.

Well, at least the weather was great. She wouldn't need an umbrella. Pepper showered, then guiltily turned the TV down to a normal level and tried to absorb herself in "Good Morning America" while she nibbled on a scone and a miniature banana muffin.

When the phone rang she was watching a segment about Kevin Costner.

"Hello?"

"It's the desk, ma'am. A Mr. Gray Ortini is in the lobby and wishes you to come downstairs to meet him." It was Gray's voice, though, full of mischief—not a hotel employee.

"*Gray*? You're in the *lobby*?"

"Come on down, Pepper, it's too gorgeous a day to waste."

Pepper uttered a squeak of joy. She tore off the bathrobe

she'd been wearing, jumped into a long cotton dress and lace-up boots, grabbed her trench coat, key card, and big shoulder bag, and raced into the hallway. She hurtled toward the elevator. Gray, in New York!

He was standing in the lobby beside a table that held one of the gigantic floral urns, a handsome, silver-haired man wearing a dark suede jacket and casual brown trousers. She saw the look of pleasure spread across his face as she strode toward him.

"Gray!" she cried. "I can't believe this! How did you get here?"

He swept her into his arms, smelling wonderfully of the vanilla-scented aftershave he wore. "After that pathetic phone call of yours last night, I called Northwest and ordered an early-bird ticket. I'm glad I didn't miss you—it was kind of a risk. Darling, you need someone to show you the real New York or you're always going to think of the city as one gigantic blister. Besides," he admitted, "I missed you so much it hurt."

"Oh, Gray . . . but I have a whole day of shopping planned. I made several appointments. I can't afford to miss them."

"Can you reschedule for Friday? We'll change your airline ticket and extend your hotel stay, at a different hotel. No," added Gray, firmly. "Don't argue. Pepper, I know you've sacrificed financially to come here, and I won't interfere with your business trip. I just want you to myself for a day, that's all. Please, let me make the arrangements."

"Well . . ."

Pepper wasn't 100 percent pleased with having to change her appointments, but she could tell a white lie about getting food poisoning or something, she guessed. Most of the smaller design houses probably wouldn't mind. They were too eager to get her business to object much.

"All right. I'll start making my phone calls. Meanwhile, I'm just so happy to see you, Gray . . . I can't believe it, I just can't believe it." She took his hand, nearly dancing around him in her pleasure at seeing him.

''What shall we do first?'' Gray said, smiling broadly. ''How about breakfast at the Hôtel Plaza Athénée? I got us a suite there . . .''

They never made it to breakfast, which Pepper couldn't have eaten anyway, full as she was on scones.

Instead they made love on the king-sized bed in Gray's magnificent suite, into which Pepper's entire hotel room could be placed five times. Brocaded curtains in delicate tints of hammered gold and mist gray covered the windows, and there was matching paisley fabric on the huge comforter and the upholstered chairs scattered around the room.

The sex was at first playful, then passionately devouring, Gray bringing Pepper to several orgasms with his penis and his tongue. When he came it was with a loud cry of pleasure, and Pepper reveled in the sound, wishing she could give him the same number of climaxes he had given her. But one was always Gray's limit, at least for five or six hours until his sexual batteries had recharged themselves.

Afterward they napped in each other's arms, Pepper fitting herself to Gray's body, her arm flung across his chest. Dozing, she listened to the deep sound of his breathing and felt peaceful as if she were floating in a shallow cobalt blue sea.

At around eleven-thirty, Gray stirred, stretching and yawning. ''I can't believe I fell asleep like that. Well, my lady, what do you want to do for the remainder of the day? The city is yours, darling.''

''I suppose lunch first,'' Pepper said. Sex often made her hungry.

''Ah, yes, lunch.'' Gray named several famous restaurants and gave Pepper her pick. She laughed and said how could she ever decide, but then settled on Bice, on East Fifty-fourth Street, because she liked the sound of the name.

They cabbed the ten blocks to the restaurant. Pepper had eaten many times in expensive restaurants, but still enjoyed the sleekly designed interior, fitted with track lights which glowed out of a ribbed ceiling that looked like a work of art. They ate baked crabmeat salad with citrus fruit and black olives, followed by brioches with lobster and scallops.

After that they cabbed to the Frick and spent an hour looking at paintings, and then Pepper said she wanted to go to Chinatown. So they wandered the polyglot streets, with the Chinese signs everywhere, peering in restaurant windows where the corpses of dead chickens hung suspended by their feet, and visiting tiny, crowded gift shops brimming with Orientalia, where the proprietors barely spoke English.

Pepper found a small soapstone statuette shaped like an Oriental cat, and something about it reminded her of Oscar, so she bought it. Then Gray bought her a little lacquered box painted with chrysanthemums. Pepper laughed and bought him one depicting a fiercely undulating dragon.

Finally, footsore, they stopped to buy ginger ice cream cones from a sidewalk vendor.

"I know this probably wasn't what you had in mind when you said you'd show me New York," Pepper said, licking the odd-tasting cone.

"It wasn't. I had a totally different agenda in mind, art galleries mostly, and Trump Tower." Gray smiled at her over the top of his cone. "Pepper, I don't care where we go in this city or what we do, just as long as I can do it with you."

They taxied back to their hotel, and Gray made late reservations at Le Régence, the elegant restaurant in the hotel. Then they took the elevator back up to their sixteenth-floor suite and made love again, entwining their bodies together, full of laughter and perspiration and—finally—sharp, hoarse cries of abandon.

Pillow talk. As darkness filled the room, they began sharing details of their childhoods—a grandmother Gray had loved, a cat named Sparky, Oscar's predecessor, whom Pepper had adored. In a low voice Pepper told Gray about her first marriage, which had lasted all of four weeks, and her marriage to Jack, which had lasted seven years.

"I admit that Jack and I still stay in touch occasionally,"

Pepper said. "In fact, we still have a friendship. Does that bother you?"

Gray hesitated. "Do you still love him, Pepper?"

"No. Yes. Not that way." Pepper gave a low laugh. "No, I don't love him in the sense you're thinking of, Gray. That stopped a long time ago, maybe around the third or fourth time that Jack bounced checks, or the fifth time he flew off to Las Vegas determined to beat the house at blackjack. But there is a part of me that cares for him. I gave him seven years of my life. We had a lot of laughs together, along with the tears."

"I see." Then Gray fell silent.

"It does bother you!" she cried.

"Maybe a little. I don't know. I'm selfish enough to want to be the man in your life who gives you all of the laughs, and who is the recipient of your caring."

"Gray . . ."

He spoke in a low voice. "I suppose I should fill you in on some of the details of my marriage to Madelyn. I know I've told you all of the surface stuff—how we grew apart, how she had several affairs . . . I've already told you all of that. The truth is, there's a bit more to the story."

"Yes?"

"I was the one who had the first affair," Gray admitted.

Pepper felt something inside her freeze. She reached for the elegant linen sheet to cover her nakedness. "When—when did this happen?"

"About five years before we finally divorced." Gray sat up in bed. "The woman was a paralegal who worked at a law firm on the floor below mine. We used to talk to each other in the elevator, and the flirtation progressed to a lot more. One night—well, Madelyn and I had a disagreement and, I don't know, I found myself asking this woman, Kim, if she'd like to go out for a drink. One drink became two . . . then three . . . no big surprise, it was all very sordid."

Pepper nodded, not knowing what to say.

"I came home that night and when I undressed for bed, there were red fingernail marks on my back. Madelyn was furious. She told me she was going to get her revenge, and she did, all right. She had at least twelve affairs. Her anger was colossal, it spilled over to every aspect of our lives, touching our son as well. He grew to hate me, I'm afraid. You saw his behavior in Aspen.''

"Oh, Gray," she said, touched by pity.

"I never again slept with another woman outside of our marriage; somehow the idea sickened me. My marriage fell apart, but I was too busy building up my software business to work on the relationship, and maybe I didn't want to work on it. I was an asshole in many ways,'' Gray admitted painfully. ''Madelyn used to call me an arrogant Donald Trump, and I suppose that's what I was. Worse, I was even proud of it.''

They lay back down on the pillows while distant traffic noises penetrated through the windows of the suite, the big-city cacophony that even a fifteen-hundred-dollar-a-night suite could not entirely silence.

"Then I had my heart attack," Gray went on heavily. ''By then I was divorced. Madelyn didn't even phone the hospital. Brian only telephoned after I'd been home for more than a week. And then he said something that really stuck with me. He said, 'All you are is a businessman, Dad. All you have is work. All you *want* is work.' '' Gray's voice cracked. ''It . . . It changed me, Pepper. In ways I'm still finding out. That's why I want a second chance so badly, why I want a b—''

"Hush," said Pepper, putting a finger against his mouth. ''I'm not ready for this kind of talk. I'm really not.''

All through dinner, even as Pepper was enjoying the gourmet food and attentive service, a tiny, traitorous part of her mind kept returning to the story that Gray had told her about his affair. And the words he had almost said. *A baby.* Why did she have to meet a man who wanted a child? Especially after she'd just had an abortion only a few months previously.

*   *   *

The following morning Gray had to catch a 6:30 A.M. flight back to Detroit. After he kissed her good-bye, Pepper showered and dressed, feeling guilty at the luxury of showering in a bathroom equipped with fresh flowers, Crabtree & Evelyn toiletries, a Frette terry cloth bathrobe, and a phone extension.

She checked out of the hotel, leaving her bags with the bell captain, then started early, returning to the garment district, where she visited a number of small showrooms, keeping her appointments and being seen at several showrooms without advance notice.

Pepper purchased dozens of items and arranged to have them shipped. She couldn't help feeling a broad sense of satisfaction. She'd had to be careful, but she'd bought wonderful, luxurious things. And her mother was going to adore the celadon silk lounging outfit, its long vest covered with intricate, hand-stitched embroidery done in the same luscious shade. She'd had them ship it right from the shop.

At La Guardia she had forty minutes to wait for her flight, and she used her calling card to phone Gray, managing to catch him at his office, between meetings. They could only talk for a little while. "I already miss you," he murmured, cutting off her excited talk about her purchases. "Hurry home."

There was still time before she boarded her flight, and Pepper was still excited, so she phoned her shop and talked to Jan.

"Are you bringing home a lot of goodies?" asked Jan.

"Oh, tons. Major goodies," declared Pepper proudly. She described her purchases in detail. "Wait till you see it all, Jan. I practically broke the bank, but it's going to be well worth it. I want to call all of our best customers and put a big ad in the *Ann Arbor News*. A full page or at least a half page. Really, really elegant."

"A full page? Hmmmm," said Jan. "Where are we going to get the money for this big advertising budget?"

"I saved a little out of what my mother loaned me. Oh, Jan. This business is a matter of taking some risks. If I just sit back and play it safe, buy the same old panties and bras, then I'm going to have just another boring shop, a Victoria's Secret clone. Pepper's has to be special. It has to offer something that Victoria's Secret can't.''

"Oh, we definitely offer that. Well, when can we expect this fabulous stuff?''

"Between five days and two weeks. Some of it's coming FedEx. Oh, Jan. This trip is *definitely* going to put Pepper's on the map.''

They were calling her flight, so Pepper had to end the phone call. She said good-bye to Jan and joined the line of passengers waiting to board the aircraft.

Settling into a window seat, Pepper gazed out of the streaky, scratched plastic window at the prosaic sight of baggage handlers driving around in their segmented carts. She *was* going to make Pepper's a big success. She felt it today, deep in her gut.

All she had to do was keep control of this love affair with Gray, and not give in to Gray's desire to have a child.

On Saturday morning when Pepper arrived to open up the boutique, she discovered a message from Jan on the boutique's answering machine tape. "Pep, I'm sorry to do this to you, but Ed's mother died—we just got the phone call about an hour ago. She had a heart attack. We're going to have to fly to Tucson. I'm really sorry to let you down, but Mandy is scheduled to come in, so you should be able to make do.''

Pepper immediately phoned Jan's house, but only got the answering machine; apparently Jan and her husband had already left.

Saturdays were her busy day, and customers kept wandering in. Pepper smiled and smiled, ringing up over nine hundred dollars in sales. It got a little hectic, with several women demanding her attention at once, and Pepper did her best to juggle the two customers. She felt so rushed she had to force herself to slow down and drink a cup of coffee. Damn . . . where was Mandy?

Mandy finally walked in about 11:30 A.M. with a story of getting leg cramps during the night, which had thrown off her sleep schedule.

"Don't you set your alarm clock?" Pepper snapped.

"Yeah, but I think I forgot to turn it on." The college sophomore had the grace to look embarrassed.

"Well, now that you're here, I can really use you. I have two women in the back trying on slip dresses—can you check and see if there's anything they need?"

The busy morning progressed toward noon, and Pepper didn't have time to stop for lunch. Would Jan be gone on Monday and Tuesday, or even further into next week? If so, it was going to get hectic indeed. And Pepper wanted to start making the calls to her customers about her new purchases.

"Look, I've got a term paper due next Wednesday," said Mandy, when Pepper tried to set up her schedule during a quiet moment.

"Term paper?"

"I haven't done anything on it, I have to really cram. I don't think I'm going to be able to work much," said the college student.

Pepper swallowed back a surge of annoyance. "Will you be able to work eleven to three at least?"

"I don't think so," said Mandy, making a pretty little moue of apology with her mouth.

A group of four customers had just entered the shop, causing the Sarnia bell fastened to the top of the door to begin chiming. "What a pretty white cat!" one of the women exclaimed. "In the window, so cute. What's her name?"

"His name is Oscar," said Pepper, smiling brilliantly. She got dozens of comments about Oscar every day. She didn't have time to argue with Mandy; there was too much work to do.

"Lunch?" said Gray, calling about one-fifteen.

"Oh, lord," sighed Pepper.

"Does that mean no?"

"It means I'm totally swamped here. Jan's mother-in-law died and she had to fly to Arizona. I'm depending on Mandy for help, and Mandy has just informed me that she has a big term paper due next week, so she's not going to be able to come in much, if at all."

"Uh-oh," said Gray. "Does that leave you really short-handed?"

"It leaves me the only one here, basically. I don't know, I might have to call a temporary agency to get some help. Which I really hate to do. They don't know the shop, and I don't want any temporaries driving away my regular customers."

"You might just close early," suggested Gray casually.

"Close *early*? I always close at six on the dot except for Fridays." She felt a dash of irritation. Pepper had nothing but contempt for "hobby" businesspeople, as she thought of them, who ran stores that kept hours based on the owners' convenience.

"Well, it was only a suggestion."

Pepper had to cut short the call—a woman was trying on bras in the back—so she hung up and went to fetch more underwire bras, bringing them to the fitting room.

"I do have a few padded push-up bras that give a really beautiful décolleté look," she said warmly, knocking before entering the fitting room, which she had wallpapered and finished herself.

A busy day. She didn't have time to talk to Gray, or show her annoyance at his suggestion. She didn't have time to go in the back room and dial a temp agency. She didn't have time for anything.

Jan phoned the next morning from Arizona and told Pepper that her father-in-law had taken her mother-in-law's death very badly. They'd be in Arizona at least three or four days, maybe longer.

"I'm so sorry," apologized Jan. "I know I'm really leaving you in the lurch."

"Not to worry," said Pepper firmly. "Just do what you have to do. I'm really fine here."

Hanging up, she considered her predicament. She wasn't doing fine. Mandy was only going to be working a few hours the following week, which meant—God, she'd better phone that temp agency right away.

Yes, the agency had a woman who'd worked at J. L. Hudson's, but no, she couldn't come in on Saturday to be trained.

"When can she come in? I don't want her coming in here cold, I want her to know the stock and know my customers."

Pepper was forced to wait impatiently for the temp agency to call the temp and verify the hours she could work. They called back about forty minutes later.

"She can come in early on Monday morning, if that would be satisfactory."

It would have to be. What other choice did she have? Pepper castigated herself for becoming so dependent on Jan, for not hiring a cadre of part-time clerks as most other stores did.

She worked on Saturday past her usual closing time until nearly 9:00 P.M., and when Gray called her at the boutique and suggested they have dinner, Pepper put him off.

"I just can't," she told him. "I've got a thousand things to take care of since Jan isn't here."

Was it her imagination, or did Gray say good-bye with a slightly sour tone in his voice?

Driving home at last, Pepper stopped to pick up Chinese takeout, and sank in front of her TV set with Oscar on her lap, eating off a TV tray. She picked out all the shrimp from her shrimp with pea pods, giving one to Oscar and eating the rest while watching the made-for-TV rerun of a movie with Lindsay Wagner in it she'd already seen last year.

What a week. She just felt so drained.

Then guiltily she realized that she wasn't *that* drained, she could have made time to spend with Gray if she'd really wanted to. But she must not have really wanted to, or she wouldn't be sitting here wearing an old terry bathrobe that dated back to before Oscar was a kitten, eating Chinese by herself with only a cat for company.

She cleared away her plate and the cardboard boxes the Chinese food had come in, putting the leftover white rice in the fridge for later. Petting the cat, she sighed. Things were confusing. Gray was every woman's dream . . . wasn't he? Even customers in her shop commented on how lucky she was to have someone to send her such gorgeous flowers. "He's a keeper," one woman had put it.

Why, then, did she feel so annoyed with him sometimes?

Gray called just as the movie was ending.

"Are you having a good evening cocooned away from the world?" he wanted to know.

"As a matter of fact, I'm enjoying myself, yes. The movie was good. I really like Lindsay Wagner, she seems real."

"We could have cocooned together."

"I know, but . . ." She hesitated, keeping her voice level. "Another time, Gray. I promise. I think I just wanted to be alone tonight."

"Tomorrow then," he persisted. "Brunch."

"No. It'll take up half the day. I have to go back to the boutique and try to catch up on all the scut work, like putting away stock and doing some pricing. I have a temp coming in Monday morning at eight, and I'm really going to be snowed under."

"Too snowed under to spend time with me?"

"It's only for a few days until Jan gets back. I have a bunch of new stuff being shipped in, and I've got a ton of stuff to do, Gray." Her voice rose a little. "I don't have a hundred assistants and employees like you do. I have to do everything myself."

"Sounds like you're making excuses, Pepper," he responded stiffly.

"They aren't excuses. That shop is my livelihood, Gray, it's everything I've got. It's not a fucking hobby, and I damn well can't lock the door early just because I'm tired or frustrated or want to have a fuller social life."

Now, why had she spoken so sharply? She heard Gray's indrawn breath. "Pepper—"

She tried not to sound strident. "Can't you remember when you were just getting started, at the beginning? When your business was small and struggling?"

"I just asked you for brunch."

"No, you didn't, you asked me for my time, you asked me to put you ahead of my livelihood, and ordinarily I would have been able to do it, but I'm in a crunch this week, which you don't seem to understand or sympathize with."

"Whoa! Pepper, you're overreacting—"

"I am not overreacting. I hate it when men say things like that!" she exclaimed, frustrated.

"Well, I hope you have a very happy weekend marking price tags," he snapped. "Me, I've got tickets to a Bonnie Raitt concert at the Fox. That was going to be after brunch. I intended to surprise you with them, but I'm certainly not going to let them go to waste."

He hung up.

Pepper stared at the phone, surprised and appalled by the swiftness with which their quarrel had escalated. She felt hot tears sting her eyes as she set her jawline. She picked up Oscar, who was meowing at her feet, and stood with her face buried in the cat's silky, white fur.

"I did *not* overreact, Mr. Oscar Cat," Pepper sighed into the animal's warm flank.

Three days passed, and Gray didn't call her. Hurt, Pepper buried herself in work. The garments she'd ordered in New York had begun to arrive, and she had to unpack them, plan a window display to show them off, and start phoning her best customers. Oh, and the newspaper ad. She had to try to work out what she wanted it to say.

The temp, a Mrs. Bickman, was a charming woman of fifty-six, but she kept asking directions to do even the simplest things, and Pepper had to approve all of her checks and returns, which was time-consuming.

Pepper stayed late every night, working her butt off, playing the stereo to keep herself company. As she worked, she brooded. That concert at the Fox . . . Had Gray gone to it by himself, or had he taken someone with him? If so, who had she been? There were hundreds of available women, very pretty women, *good women*, who'd jump at the chance to go out with Gray Ortini. Maybe even Codi Duncan, that woman in his office who had the hots for him.

She was amazed at the spasm of ugly jealousy she felt. A dozen times she'd almost picked up the phone to call him, but then she'd always hung up again. Her pride wouldn't let her phone him.

When Mandy finally strolled back into the shop on Thursday, declaring she'd turned in her term paper and thought she was going to get an A, Pepper was so glad to see her that she practically hugged her.

"I can work now just as usual," declared Mandy happily.

"Good. Oh, more than good. That's just wonderful."

On Thursday night Pepper had dinner by herself at Zev's, feeling blue as she hunched over her plate of chili and garlic bread, memories pouring over her. She could even look eight feet away and see the very table she'd been sitting at when Gray spilled his chili all over her.

My God, Gray hasn't called me since Saturday night. Maybe this is the end. Maybe I've been dumped.

As if to torment her, a man entered the coffee shop, about Gray's age, with hair almost as silvery as his, although that was where the resemblance ended. The white-haired man, obviously a regular, immediately began flirting with one of the young waitresses, who encouraged his attention. Then the man's glance caught Pepper's and he gave her an intent look that made it obvious he'd like to try his luck with her, too.

Men didn't take breakups like women did, all of Pepper's girlfriends said, and she'd even heard Mrs. Melnick repeat this, too. Men took about a day to grieve, then they were out hunting again . . .

Anxiously she pushed back from the table, leaving her chili half eaten, and quickly paid the bill at the cashier's stand, where Zev himself, an enormous, big-bellied, gregarious man, greeted her with his usual wide smile.

"So where's your friend?" Zev asked her.

"He's working tonight," she told the restaurant owner.

"You hope," said Zev, laughing.

Pepper hurried back to her shop, where she let herself in and went straight to the back room.

She grabbed the phone and dialed the number of Gray's condo.

Three rings . . . four . . . then the message tape. Her heart suddenly hammering, Pepper wondered where Gray was. *Was* he seeing that woman at his office, Codi, the one he said had come on strong? Or was he working late, maybe even out of town?

She tried his car phone, but there was no answer, and she only got voice mail on his private line at work. When she heard the beep, Pepper drew in a shallow breath, her throat feeling as if it were narrowing down, closing off her breathing.

"Call me," she finally managed to say. She hesitated, but could think of nothing else to add, and finally hung up.

He usually checked both his home answering tape and his office voice mail several times daily, Pepper happened to know. He didn't call that night. Pepper stayed up until nearly 1:30 A.M., close to the phone, trying to read a book while watching another no-brainer movie on TV.

Lying across her lap, a heavy, warm weight, Oscar purred contentedly as if nothing at all were wrong.

On Friday Jan came back. "Funerals are the pits," she declared. "Every time I go to one, I tell myself I'm never, never going to another one. Oh, by the way," she went on. "There's a florist truck parked in that space right in front of the shop. You-know-who must be letting his fingers do the walking again."

Pepper felt her heart leap like a live animal.

Mandy accepted the delivery, and Pepper watched while the college student excitedly peeled away the florist wrap, revealing another stunning, prohibitively expensive bouquet of roses, these sunrise pink, the outer edges of their petals touched with magenta. A perfumed, spicy fragrance arose from the blooms.

"God," said Mandy. "I can't believe all the roses you get. My boyfriend buys me flowers he picks up at the supermarket for six dollars."

Her hands shaking, Pepper reached for the card.

I don't know what happened, but you are everything to me, Pepper, it said. *Please, another chance? Call me at my office. All I do is work since you're not around.*

She went to the back room and called him immediately. She only got voice mail on the personal line, so she called the company's main number and was passed through the receptionist, then Gray's assistant, before he was finally on the line.

They talked for over half an hour—what amounted to a huge amount of time in Gray's busy, overprogrammed schedule.

"We're still getting to know each other," he told her. "I guess that means a few ups and downs. We'll survive them, Pepper. Would you like to have dinner with me tonight—a late dinner? I have a meeting at five I can't get out of; it should last about two hours, but after that I'm all yours."

She agreed to have dinner with him. She had to speak slowly, so that he wouldn't hear that her voice was trembling.

It was a new little bistro built on the lower floor of a red-brick commercial building north of downtown near the Greek Orthodox church. The architect had stripped the inside of the building down to the original brick, leaving pipes and beams exposed, and the floor was also the original wide oak planking, refinished to preserve its many scars and blemishes. However, very few students were eating here, probably because the prices on the menu were too steep for undergraduate budgets.

"Pepper," said Gray earnestly. "I never meant to push

you or denigrate your work, or treat you—well, the way you said. I can't tell you how sorry I am for the careless remarks I made.''

Pepper shook her head, suddenly unable to remember the exact details of the ''careless remarks'' he was referring to.

''You have to remember,'' Gray went on, ''I'm twenty years older than you, and I guess some of my attitudes might be a little outdated. I've thought long and hard about this. You and your boutique . . . the wonderful things you've done with it . . .'' He moistened his lips. ''I acted like some old dinosaur from the nineteen fifties.''

Pepper felt touched by the admission, but she still wanted to hold the line firm. ''You could never be a dinosaur, but you just have to realize that my work means just as much to me as yours does to you. And I'm trying every bit as hard!''

''I hear you, love. Oh, do I hear you. Point very well taken.''

Their food came, chicken breasts cooked with crayfish tails, Camembert cheese, and a sauce made of pureed apricots, apple juice, whipping cream, and chopped fresh figs. It was beautifully prepared.

Pepper felt herself sag with relief that Gray seemed to understand where she was coming from, and everything was all right again. They held hands across the table, laughed and talked, as if their four days of not speaking had never occurred.

All at once Pepper felt absurdly, unreasonably happy. He was back . . . here, now, with her. She'd had crazy doubts, she'd let them color her attitude, but now she was in such a good mood that all of the doubts seemed to evaporate, leaving only her joy at being with this man.

As they were finishing their entrées, Pepper suddenly heard Gray's name called out in a loud, raucous tone.

''Gray Ortini! And Pepper! What are you two doing here? I didn't know you knew the secret of this little place.''

It was Ron DeNoyer and his girlfriend, Melody. Pepper had met them at one of the black-tie affairs Gray had taken her to. Ron, around sixty, owned a company that sold computer software used by market research firms. Melody, in her early thirties, sold real estate, Pepper remembered.

Ron and Melody sat down at their table for a few minutes while the men talked business. Pepper tried to stifle her annoyance at the interruption of their intimate dinner, hoping that Gray wouldn't invite Ron and Melody to join them, not tonight when they'd finally made real progress in their relationship.

But the conversation grew more enthusiastic, and finally the men decided that the four of them would join forces. Gray glanced at Pepper, giving her a swift, humorous flick of the eyebrows, as if to say, *I'm dreadfully sorry, I'll make it up to you.*

Disappointed, Pepper sat quietly, letting the others talk while allowing her mind to drift. She *did* work as hard as Gray, she found herself thinking. He was going to have to respect her for that.

Just before dessert and coffee arrived, Melody announced she was going to the ladies' room and invited Pepper to go along. Politely Pepper got up to walk with the other woman toward the back of the restaurant, which smelled deliciously of garlic, coriander, and curry.

In the cramped, one-stall women's room, its brick walls hung with color photos someone had taken on the French Riviera, Melody made repairs to her flawless face, while Pepper replenished her lipstick.

"Has Gray taken you anywhere important?" Melody wanted to know.

"What do you mean?"

"Oh, trips . . . Ronnie took me to Africa on safari and it was fabulous," boasted the blond Melody. "The trip cost him an arm and a leg."

Pepper nodded, saying something, and Melody began telling her about riding in Land Rovers and sleeping in a tent with catered meals, visiting a "fabulous game park" and seeing "a really fabulous river gorge."

On their way back to the table, Pepper felt her good mood

of the evening completely bottom out. *Has Gray taken you anywhere important?* The question repelled her, and she felt even more repelled by Melody's frank gold-digging attitude. A young, pretty woman trying to pull money out of an older man.

But what was worse was that Melody had assumed that she, Pepper, was exactly like her.

"Anything wrong?" Gray said, glancing at Pepper's face as she slid into her seat at the table again, Melody still chattering about some people she had met on the safari.

Pepper smiled brilliantly. "Oh, everything's just great. Melody and I were just talking about travel. 'Important' trips. Very interesting."

Gray eyed her, puzzled, but Pepper, her cheeks flushed, pretended to be very absorbed in her dessert.

TREVA

THANKSGIVING MARKED TREVA'S TWENTY-SECOND WEEK of pregnancy and put her square in the middle of her second trimester. The baby's movements were becoming stronger, more easily felt, and Treva's blood pressure had been stable. Best of all, she was becoming an old hand at bed rest, and some of the blues that had plagued her earlier now seemed to be lifting.

From her living room couch, Treva planned Thanksgiving down to the last detail, including a catered feast, complete with turkey and all the trimmings. The high point of the holiday was going to be a four-day visit from Shanae.

However, the moment she saw her stepdaughter walk in the door on the Wednesday night of the holiday weekend, Treva knew the girl's visit was in serious jeopardy.

"Well?" demanded Shanae defiantly. "Do you like it?" She twirled around so that Treva could get a full view of her new, startling haircut. Treva stared, astonished, at the inches of shaved skin over Shanae's ears, the rest of her hair straightened and moussed to the left side. The girl's lipstick was almost black and there were two cubic zirconia studs in her left nostril and one in her lower lip.

Not only that, the girl was wearing a two-piece, leopard-print outfit, with a micro skirt and a long-sleeved top that revealed inches of her flat, brown midriff and another glittery stud in her navel.

Glancing up at Wade, who stood behind his daughter holding her overnight bag, Treva could see the flash of anger in her husband's eyes.

"Do you like it?" the girl repeated with a show of bravado. There were reddened areas of infected skin around each nostril stud, Treva couldn't help noticing, and the skin around the lip stud looked even worse. She didn't dare think about the navel.

"It's a very West Coast look, isn't it?" said Treva tactfully.

"Yeah . . . my mom hates this look. We had a big fight. She says I look like a little rock-video slut. Which is good, that's exactly what I want to look like."

"You're going to go upstairs and wash off that makeup and take those things out of your nose and mouth and belly button before that infection turns serious," said Wade harshly. "And put some antibiotic cream on them. Do it right now, Shanae, before you get blood poisoning. Then we'll figure out what to do about your hair. Maybe it can be salvaged. As for your clothes, I hope you brought some jeans and a blouse or a sweater, because that's what you're gonna be wearing while you're in this house."

"This is my new look, Daddy," protested the girl, her lips tightening. "I have to look like this if I want to be a singer. I can't look like just—some dumb high school kid."

"You're not going to be a singer. Not at age fifteen. And as long as you're in our house, you'll follow our rules," said Wade. "Upstairs *now*, Shanae. Then we'll have dinner and I'll take you over to Briarwood to see a movie."

"A movie?" Shanae's voice rose rebelliously. "Some baby PG-rated movie, I suppose. I wish I hadn't even come over here. Nobody understands, nobody even wants to understand."

"Shanae," said Wade warningly.

"Oh, all *right*. I'll put cream on. And I've got some jeans. But I'm not taking out the studs. If I do, the holes will close up and I won't be able to get them back in again. I have to leave them in for at least two months."

Shanae turned on her heel and stalked upstairs to her room. When she had gone, Wade sighed deeply, looking at Treva.

"When I picked her up at Wanda's I thought I would have a heart attack. No wonder she and her mother had a fight. If she lived here full-time we'd be fighting too, mark my words. I can't stand the way she looks. She's doing it just to shock us, and Christ, has she succeeded."

"I know, darling."

"Talk to her . . . please, Treva. You have a touch with her, she listens to you."

"I'm not sure she'll listen this time."

Wade brushed back his graying, curly hair, looking upset. "You saw her, the way she looks. If she goes into the music business looking like that, they'll eat her alive. I'm serious, Treva. One of the guys in the department had a daughter that ran away from home when she was fourteen. Two years later, she's back, pregnant and with HIV. This is nothing to mess with."

"I'll do what I can, Wade."

Forty minutes later, Shanae sauntered back down the stairs. Her hair had been washed and now hung to chin length, mercifully obscuring most of the shaved places. Her face was scrubbed and she wore a deep coral lipstick. One nostril stud remained, but a glisten of ointment showed she had taken Wade's advice. She wore a pair of wide-legged jeans and a yellow sweater that Wade had given her the previous fall as a back-to-school gift.

"Better," approved Wade, nodding his head in relief.

"Much, much better. Shanae, you are such a beautiful girl when you try to be."

"Being beautiful *sucks.*"

"Shanae—"

"Come, Shanae," said Treva, patting the couch beside her. "I want you to help me look at these new CD-ROMs that Wade bought me. I haven't had a chance to learn how to use them yet." She waved at her husband. "Go put up the Christmas lights or something, Wade. Your daughter and I are going to be busy."

"I'm in the wrong place," said Shanae sadly as they explored a CD-ROM called *Rock It,* issued by a company called GrayCo, watching a film clip of Michael Jackson doing the moon walk. "I should be in California. I should be on that video."

"There's still so much time for you, Shanae."

"No." The girl jutted out her chin. "No, there *isn't.* In music you have to do things when it's the time to do them. You can't just sit around on your butt and hope that when you're twenty-five or thirty, something will happen. It doesn't work that way."

"But there are only a couple of years until you graduate from high school. After graduation maybe you can get started with—"

"*Graduation*! I'll be almost eighteen! I'll be old, it'll be too late by then! Look at Brandy, she didn't wait. And that new country singer, Lee Ann Rimes. Not that I'd ever sing country." Shanae jumped to her feet and began pacing the wide living room. "Treva, can I tell you something?"

"Of course, darling."

"I haven't told anyone, not my mom and not Dad."

"All right, Shanae, I'll keep your secret."

"I met this guy—he works at a record company in California—he said he might fly me to L.A. and let me record a single at the studio."

Whoa, Treva thought. "Who is this man?"

"Oh, some record guy."

"Darling. There are some men . . . bad men . . . who'll talk to young girls and say things to get them to do whatever they want."

"You mean make them into hookers," said Shanae, shrugging.

"Well, yes."

"He isn't a pimp, he's real—you can call the record company if you don't believe me. Anyway," her stepdaughter went on. "The best thing is there're these guys, they've got a band called Cinnamon Slash. They want me to sing lead for them. Well, I'd share the lead with this guy called Slash-Two. Well, that's not his real name, his real name is Eric Dominico, he lives in Brighton."

Cinnamon Slash. As Shanae continued to chatter on, describing this twenty-year-old Eric in detail, Treva tried not to show her alarm. Was Shanae having sex with the boy? She probably was. Dear God, did Wade know this, or suspect it? What were they going to do?

"Eric is *so* cool," the girl kept saying. "Treva, he is. He's real nice. Oh, I hope you're not going to be like Mom and Daddy, always putting me down and everything I want to do."

Treva stirred, again forcing back her unease. Shanae was poised on the cusp of serious rebellion, she realized. One tactless remark, one put-down or argument, could catapult her far away from them.

Then inspiration struck her. "Shanae, look, it's hard for me to visualize all of these things without ever meeting Eric or hearing you sing. And I know your dad would like to hear you sing, too."

"He would?"

"Why don't you bring your band here," suggested Treva rashly. "Since I can't leave the couch, you can play for us right here in the living room. The room is big and the acoustics are really quite nice in here."

Shanae's face lit up. "Really? You'd really listen to us?"

"Make the arrangements," declared Treva. "The Friday after Thanksgiving would be nice. Have Eric and the others come early, so they can set up and have dinner here beforehand. Tell them we'll have a nice buffet with lots of food. And—and we'll pay a hundred dollars for the gig.''

"Would you? Oh, Treva! Oh! This is so cool!" Shanae rushed toward her and began hugging her. "Treva, you are the coolest stepmother in the world. I love you!"

"And I love you, too, Shanae," said Treva, meaning it. Shanae's vulnerability was deeply touching. She had to do something to help her stepdaughter before she plunged off a precipice and ruined her life.

Outside it had begun to snow, tiny, icy flakes drifting down out of a black sky, settling in the treetops along the ravine. The outdoor floodlights turned the bare tree branches to a diaphanous silver.

"You have arranged *what*?" demanded Wade, his mouth shaking with anger. Shanae was in her bedroom listening to CDs with her headphones while Wade and Treva were alone in the living room.

"I've arranged a little party with some music," said Treva calmly. "For the Friday night after Thanksgiving. I can have the buffet catered, so that's no problem. It's time we met these band people and faced Shanae's life head-on."

Wade was practically sputtering. "But what good can this possibly do? It will only encourage her. These band kids are probably drinkers and dopers and God knows what else. And you know how rockers are about sex. Who knows if they even wear condoms. My God . . . my daughter . . ." He rubbed his face with his hands, then riffled his fingers through his hair. "First your pregnancy and now this. Treva, I'm going to have white hair before I hit fifty. It's already a lot more gray than black now."

Treva wondered if she was doing the right thing, but now that she'd mentioned the idea, she was determined not to back down. "Well, we won't get anywhere if we drive Shanae away from us or fight with her like Wanda does. Our only hope is in maintaining communication with her, and I think we'll do a lot better at that if we meet these band people and listen to her sing.''

''I don't know.''

''Wade—please. She loves you so much. She wants you to be proud of her. Maybe if you heard her and gave her some honest compliments, it would satisfy her for a while and she'd let this band thing go for now.''

''Maybe.'' Wade nodded grudgingly.

''Also I could arrange for singing lessons for her at the School of Music,'' Treva went on. ''She's been asking for lessons for months. And guitar lessons if she wants them, too.''

''The School of Music. That's nice and respectable.''

''Of course it is. Maybe her talent is bigger than just being in a rock band,'' suggested Treva. ''Did you ever think of that? Maybe she's got *real* talent, serious talent. But we'll never know, will we, if we don't pay some attention to her?''

The snow had stopped, but a winter wind blew against the windows, rattling the panes and shaking the bird feeders that Wade had hung, swaying them back and forth.

The caterer's crew was in the kitchen, slicing turkey and arranging salads. Wade had a meeting later in the evening with his departmental chairman, who wanted him to help with interviewing a job candidate, so they were serving the buffet at four o'clock. Treva had changed into a teal-colored maternity pantsuit that had beaded floral designs across the shoulders. Like all of her clothing purchases these days, she'd bought it from a catalog.

Lying in the prescribed position on her couch while holding a makeup mirror, Treva brushed highlighter on her cheeks. Her abdomen felt oddly heavy today. In addition, she'd felt unusually thirsty and even, once or twice, a bit dizzy. Still she felt sure it was nothing more than the usual pregnancy symptoms, exacerbated by having to lie still all day, and the blood pressure medications she had to take, which had dizziness as one of the possible side effects.

"You look beautiful," said her stepdaughter, coming to sit beside her.

"Oh, Shanae, I feel like a big, bulbous balloon. Even on my diet I've gained too much weight because all I do is lie here and I don't get any exercise."

"Well, that outfit is gorgeous and you're gorgeous," proclaimed Shanae, her mood ebullient.

The girl had moussed her hair back into the startling "punk" hairstyle, but had softened the look by not wearing lipstick. Tonight she wore a little, cap-sleeved, pink-flowered cotton dress that skimmed her hips and ended at calf length. A pretty, sweet dress, its effect was unfortunately spoiled by heavy, black combat boots worn with white socks. Part punker, part little girl, Treva thought, hoping Wade wouldn't go too wild over the combat boots.

The ringing of the doorbell interrupted them, and Shanae leaped up and ran to the door. Treva heard male voices, bangs and thumps. Then Shanae returned to the living room, followed by four tall, skinny young men, two white, two black. They were lugging big amplifiers, guitars, and drums.

"Eric wants to set up before we eat, so we can just play afterwards," said Shanae excitedly. "Oh, Treva . . . I want you to meet Eric . . . and Kareem . . . Damon . . . and Joel."

"Mrs. Connor," said Eric, ducking his head, and the others murmured polite greetings.

Eric was nearly six feet three inches tall, his square-jawed, handsome face looking slightly incongruous on his gangling body. He had blond hair brushed long on top, and anxious blue eyes. "I hope this will be all right for you, Mrs. Connor," he said. "Our music is kind of loud, you'll see, but Shanae said you wanted to hear her do a solo, too, so she's going to do a song she just finished writing."

"I'm looking forward to it," said Treva.

The band members seemed polite, slightly ill at ease. Treva began asking them questions to relax them a little, and learned that Eric worked at University Hospital in patient transportation, while Kareem and Joel were students at the University of Michigan, and Damon, slim and very dark skinned, went to Washtenaw Community College. These weren't bums, Treva realized. They seemed like decent young men. Maybe Wade would even approve of them. But he was still at the supermarket, buying soft drinks and extra ice for the buffet.

"We really need a good female lead singer," Eric confided. "We've tried a few, but they didn't have strong voices or they couldn't make it to band practice on time. Shanae, well, she's too good for us really. The trouble is, she's so young. It would be a lot better if she were about twenty or twenty-one."

"I see," said Treva, beginning to warm up to Eric.

While the band members were setting up, turning the living room into a shambles of huge amps, cords, and wires, Wade returned home with the ice. Playing the role of the anxious, overprotective father, he began quizzing Eric immediately.

"Eric, what plans do you have for your band?"

"We want to make a demo single. We're all saving our money and when we have enough there's a studio in Southfield that we can use," he explained. "Also, a guy from Sire Records heard us play last month and might be interested."

"You think Shanae would add to your band?"

"We want to include Shanae if we can. Right now she's just practicing with us once in a while. She's really not in the band yet."

"Hmmm."

"If we could get Shanae, it would really make us," Eric went on frankly. "Mr. Connor, her voice is really special. She's as good as Whitney Houston."

Wade looked startled and disbelieving. "Whitney Houston?"

"Wait," Eric said. "Wait until you hear her."

The band members made repeated raids on the buffet table, loading up their plates with slices of turkey and spiral-sliced ham, salad, pasta, buffalo wings, and an assortment of apple, pumpkin, and cherry tarts.

"I don't believe this," said Wade, bringing Treva a plate. "How can Shanae sound as good as Whitney Houston? And if she is that good, why didn't I know it before? I mean, in grade school she sang great at a couple of school programs and she was the best in the church gospel choir, but that was just school stuff. Every eight-year-old is the next Annie."

"She's not eight anymore," remarked Treva dryly.

The caterers cleared away the food and the band members started warming up and sound-testing their equipment, a process so noisy and nerve-jangling that Treva felt the beginning of a sharp headache.

"It's going to be real loud," warned Shanae. "When we rehearsed one time at Joel's house, the band was so loud that some of the pictures fell off the wall."

"You're kidding," said Wade sharply.

"No, really. That's why we practice in a mini storage place, in one of those garage bays, you know, so we don't bother the neighbors. It won't happen tonight, though, the pictures falling, I mean. They're going to adjust the sound so it won't. Daddy, have patience. I'm so excited. I feel like this is a real concert almost. You're so great to let me do this." She nuzzled up to her father, sliding her arms around his neck and hugging him as if this were entirely his idea.

"I guess if I have a singer in the family, I have to hear what she sounds like," said Wade stiffly.

"Oh, Dad. Loosen *up*."

"All right, I'll try," agreed Wade.

Treva was lying on the long couch, her back propped by the usual pillows, with Wade seated beside her, as Cinnamon Slash began playing its first song. The caterer's crew peeked around the corner from the kitchen, curious to see what kind of band this was.

Eric sang lead, shouting out lyrics that were only partially intelligible, drowned out by the pounding bass, the incredibly loud drums and guitars. Treva felt the heavy, vibratory pounding in her viscera and abdomen and realized her unborn infant must be hearing it, too. How could he not? She felt a spasm of dismay. The band was terrible.

"This isn't even music," Wade complained to Treva under the cover of the music. "It's just noise."

"Don't let them hear you say that. Anyway, Shanae hasn't sung yet. Just be patient."

For the next number Shanae joined Eric, each of them at a separate mike. Both yelled and screamed lyrics—something about "cinnamon death." Treva could only understand a few of the words. Beside her Wade was rigid, and she sensed the effort it was taking him not to actually wince. If Shanae did possess talent, how could anyone even hear her in the midst of all the pounding noise?

But when the number ended, she and Wade applauded politely. Then Eric stepped back, leaving the "stage" to Shanae.

"I'm going to sing a ballad that I wrote," Shanae said into the mike. "It's called 'Don't You Ever Cry,' and it's about how it feels to be all alone in the world sitting in a Greyhound bus station and wondering if you're ever going to see your family again."

As Wade reacted, obviously remembering the time when Shanae was thirteen and had run away for a day and a night, Treva also drew in her breath. Then Shanae began to sing.

"My God," Wade whispered.

Treva listened, stunned, to the fifteen-year-old who sounded like a seasoned singer of thirty, her voice pouring out like pure, raw silk as she sang of loneliness, desperation, and despair. It seemed to Treva that she hit exceptionally high notes without flaw. Of course, there was too much sound in too small a space and the acoustics were far from perfect, but to her, Shanae's voice seemed to transcend all of that, finding its own majesty.

When it was over, the last thrilling note draining away into the air, Shanae bowed deeply, then raised her face, brilliant with hope. "Did you like it, Daddy?"

"Oh, honey." Wade was clapping wildly. "Oh, baby— you were wonderful. You were so great. You were terrific."

Treva clapped, and added her praise, and then Shanae whirled forward. A dervish of energy, she hugged Wade, then Treva, then Eric, then every member of the band. She was incandescent. "I'm good, Daddy—I can sing—see, I can really sing."

"Yes, you can, darling," said Wade. "You really can."

"I *have* to have a career. I can't waste myself. Now can you see it, Daddy?"

But Wade, busy hugging his daughter, didn't answer.

Cinnamon Slash packed up their amps and instruments, uncoiling cords and lugging mikes and mike stands out to the van they'd arrived in. Politely they thanked Treva for the food.

After the band was gone, Shanae's high-pitched mood seemed to deflate a few degrees. The teenager restlessly prowled the living room, helping to move furniture back the way it had been.

"Daddy, did you really like my singing?" she kept saying.

"You were great, cupcake."

"Then will you talk to Mom and make her let me sing in the band?"

"I don't know. Maybe that band isn't the best thing for you," said Wade reluctantly. "Honey, they're very ordinary, they sound like garage punk, nothing really special. When you were singing with them we couldn't even hear your voice."

"You couldn't?" Shanae seemed crushed.

"It was only when you sang solo that you really shone," Wade went on.

"Oh, Dad . . ."

"Well, it's true," he said. "Look, we're all overexcited tonight and Treva has to get some rest. This has been a long day for her, planning all of this for you. And I have a meeting to go to. Dr. Weinberger is interviewing a candidate for full professor, and I've been asked to be part of the interview process. He's buying the man dinner downtown."

"Tonight?" wailed Shanae.

"Unfortunately, yes. Cupcake," he added, hugging his daughter again, "you are a wonderful singer. I was amazed at how beautiful your voice is. But please . . . this is too important to misuse. Let's all get together and plan what we can do for you, how we can make sure you get the best chance possible."

Shanae looked at him. "Do you mean that, Daddy?"

"I mean it," he told her. "We'll do something for you, Shanae—it might not happen this year, but it will happen. And when it does happen I'm going to be your manager to make sure you don't get financially cheated."

"*Daddy!*" Shanae hugged Wade, dancing and prancing and whirling about. "*Oh, Daddy!*"

Snow covered the world in a thin scrim of white that Wade declared was barely going to stick to the ground. He left, promising to return as soon as his meeting was over. Shanae sat on the couch with Treva while she picked at some leftover buffalo wings and salad; she'd been too nervous to eat before.

As the girl chattered, rehashing the "concert" in all of its details, Treva shifted on the couch, changing positions several times. Odd . . . she felt a warm moistness between her legs. Glancing down, she was horrified to see a large stain of blood on the couch cushion.

Shanae had seen it, too. "Treva?"

"I think I'd better make a trip to the bathroom."

She swayed dizzily as she walked into the first-floor powder room, which she had filled with her cosmetics and the toiletries she needed, plus a few clothes hanging from an over-the-door hook arrangement. To her horror, Treva discovered she was bleeding vaginally.

The bright red blood was terrifying.

Her baby . . . oh, God, her baby boy.

Treva forced back a panicky cry as she managed to pad her underclothing with a folded washcloth.

"Treva? Are you okay?" came her stepdaughter's anxious voice outside the bathroom.

"I don't know." Treva opened the door and stood swaying and dizzy.

"Look," cried Shanae, pointing in alarm. More blood was running down Treva's legs, staining her beige trouser socks and beginning to pool in her shoes. Looking at it, Treva felt a wave of terror.

"I've got to call my doctor," said Treva heavily, sitting down in the nearest chair. "Shanae, please bring me the portable phone."

The girl raced for the phone. With shaking hands Treva punched in the numbers of Dr. Sandoval's answering service.

"Is this an emergency?" said the operator.

"Yes—please—can you contact her right away?"

"I'll take the message and have her get back to you," said the woman. "Probably within the next ten minutes."

Treva hung up, anxiety filling her. She could still feel the bleeding. There wasn't time to wait. What should she do?

"Treva, you look so pale," fretted Shanae. "Maybe you should lie back down and put your feet up. And I'll get you some pillows. Oh . . . is this bad? Does bleeding mean something really, really terrible?"

"Not necessarily," lied Treva as a deep despair filled her. She'd been living in a dreamworld, minimizing the seriousness of the bed rest, lulled by the fact that she felt well, that nothing untoward had happened. Now would her baby pay the price?

Several minutes passed and still Dr. Sandoval hadn't called back. "Shanae, which restaurant did your father say he was meeting those people at?"

"I don't remember," said Shanae tensely. "Downtown someplace. Oh, Treva—is this my fault? All that loud music . . . Maybe the vibrations did something to the baby."

"I don't think we can blame Cinnamon Slash. Shanae, do you have your learner's permit with you?"

"Yeah, Mom lets me drive sometimes. I drive her van over to her catering things sometimes when I help her serve.

Oh, Treva—'' Tears spilled out of Shanae's huge, brown eyes.

"Hush," said Treva. "We can't have any crying now. I'm going to call Dr. Sandoval's service and leave another message that we're going to the hospital. I want you to write a note to Wade telling him where we're going. Then I want you to go in the kitchen and get the keys to my Grand Am from off the hook in the pantry."

Somehow they made it out to the garage, Treva leaning heavily on the teenager, strange pains shooting through her abdomen. At one point Shanae had to practically drag her. The tall, lanky girl was surprisingly strong. "I've got you, Treva . . . don't worry . . . just lean on me."

But at last she was sliding into the passenger seat of her car. With her last remaining strength, Treva pushed the button that would recline her car seat. Then she lay back, dizziness spinning her. She felt sick with despair.

"Shanae, you know where the hospital is, don't you?"

"Not really . . . but I'll find it."

"Get on Washtenaw," Treva gasped. "Just drive slowly and carefully, Shanae. This isn't an emergency. There's plenty of time to get there."

Snow had coated the driveway in a half-inch layer of white. Shanae put the Grand Am in reverse, backing it out of the garage, leaving a trail of tire prints in front of them. Then she carefully accelerated and sped down the street.

The emergency room was a maze of hallways, doors, exam rooms, with beds placed out in the hall, some occupied, some not. There was an aura of hurry. At one point Treva heard thundering footsteps as staff ran to one of the holding rooms shouting to each other about a "code." Urgent calls came over the PA system, and Treva could hear the whine of an ambulance bringing in another trauma victim.

A resident examined Treva, took her history, and attached a fetal heart monitor, assuring her at once that her baby still had a good, strong heartbeat.

Treva lay in an exam room shared with three others, each

bed separated by curtains, and tried not to listen to the
sounds of distress from her roommates. A toddler screamed
and struggled as two nurses attempted to get a blood sample
from tiny veins. A car-accident victim had come in with a
head injury, and Treva could hear the doctor questioning
her. What was her name? Did she know where she was?
Who was the president? The woman sounded groggy and
thought Reagan was still the president.

Treva fluttered her eyes shut and began to pray. *God,
please keep this little one safe. It's all I ask, all I want. Just
keep him safe long enough to be born. I'll do whatever it
takes to get him born.*

Finally Dr. Sandoval hurried in.

"I'm so worried," whispered Treva to her doctor.

Ruth Sandoval took her hand, squeezing it. "Now, Treva,
let's go down to Sonar and we'll find out just what's going
on. Then we'll know if it's time to worry."

They wheeled Treva's bed to a sonogram room, where
the technician did another slow, careful ultrasound, putting
the gooey fluid on Treva's abdomen and running the transducer up and down her mounded stomach. When Treva
looked at the screen, she saw what looked like a black blob.
Everything else around it on the screen was gray.

"That's blood," explained Dr. Sandoval, her expression
serious. Underneath her white doctor's coat, she was wearing a blue cotton sweater and twill slacks. "Your placenta
is tearing away from the uterine wall. Fortunately, the tearing is only partial."

"Oh, no," whispered Treva.

"It's called a placental abruption, and happens in about
one of every eighty deliveries—we don't know why. Certain
conditions like hypertension can increase the chances of it
occurring, though."

Treva lost it. She'd been brave in the car, and even when
attendants had come rushing out of the emergency area with
a wheelchair, but now she started to weep. "But—am I
going to lose the baby?"

"Not necessarily. The condition is only partial—that is,

the placenta hasn't totally separated from the uterine wall. If it was totally separated, the fetus would receive no blood supply.''

''But—but what can we do?''

The doctor frowned. ''Well, first of all, the baby seems to still be doing fine—I'm not getting any signs of fetal distress, which is a great development. One thing we need to do is increase the amount of blood you have in circulation, so the little guy can get more of what he needs. To that end, we're going to start an IV and possibly some blood transfusions if that doesn't increase the volume enough. Also, you need to be in bed, to decrease the blood pressure at the placental site. And there'll be no more pelvic exams, to decrease the risk of accidentally making the condition worse.''

''But it's too soon!'' protested Treva, panicking again.

The doctor sighed, her face suffused with pity, and answered the question obliquely. ''I know how much you want this baby. This is a relatively mild abruption and fetal signs are still good, Treva, so we're going to try to continue the pregnancy as long as we can. But your hypertension complicates things, so you're going to have to be hospitalized from now until you give birth.''

''*Hospitalized?*'' Everything seemed to be moving so fast, out of her control.

''I'm afraid so. You'll be on constant bed rest—no getting up for the bathroom this time—and there'll be constant monitoring of your blood pressure and the baby's heart rate. Also there'll be blood-pressure drugs and anticontraction medication to prevent you from going into preterm labor, some of which may have uncomfortable side effects. It won't be easy. In fact, it's going to be a long, tough haul.''

''I . . . I see.''

''I've had patients who went through the wringer. Are you game for that?''

''Yes . . . yes . . .'' breathed Treva. ''Anything. Oh, God—''

Ruth Sandoval reached out and took Treva's hand in hers.

"You have a good deal of courage, Treva. But I have to warn you of the fact that this may not have a positive outcome. We're going to do our damnedest, though."

"Take me up to my hospital room," said Treva grimly. "I'll pray until I'm blue in the face if that's what it takes. I'm going to keep this baby no matter what."

There was a half-hour wait while Dr. Sandoval phoned Admitting for a room in Women's Hospital, and the hospital contacted her insurance plan to make sure her stay was covered. Then another twenty-minute wait for a young man from patient transport to wheel her on a gurney to her room.

While she waited, the staff allowed Shanae to sit beside her in the curtained cubicle and the teenager chattered bravely about how big the hospital was, and a program she'd seen on the TV set in the emergency area waiting room. Treva felt touched that Shanae was trying so hard to take Treva's mind off her problems.

Wheeled along with a bird's-eye view of the hallways and ceiling, then being crammed into a steel-walled elevator, with several hospital workers riding with them, the other passengers pushed next to the wall, Treva had a sense of desperate unreality.

From bed rest to hospitalization. Could this really be happening? With every move, the situation seemed more dire. She fought tears, knowing she couldn't upset her stepdaughter, who trailed behind them, carrying Treva's purse. Treva's coat was in a bag, stored underneath the gurney.

The private room was cheerfully decorated. While the attendant cranked up the hospital bed to the same level as the gurney and helped Treva roll onto the bed, Shanae explored the room, giving a running monologue about the small TV set, the little storage closet, the Formica counter with a sink, the tiny bathroom with a small shower, a red buzzer to summon a nurse, and safety bars for Treva to hold on to.

In a drawer Shanae discovered a blue plastic tub stuffed full of hospital goodies, everything from a toothbrush and toothpaste to body lotion and a smaller, curved plastic container.

"What's this for?" Shanae demanded, holding it up.

"To heave in, if I get the urge," explained Treva dryly.

The attendant embarked on a rote speech about paying for the usage of the TV set, how her bed worked, when meals were, and so forth, then politely told Treva to have a good stay and left.

Treva felt herself sink into the uncomfortable hospital mattress, which had a layer of plastic underneath the too starchy cotton sheet. "Thank God you were with me," she told the teenager. "If you hadn't been, Shanae, I don't know what I would have done."

"Oh, you would have called 911," said Shanae lightly. "You're a tough lady, Treva, when you want to be."

"And so are you, girl," said Treva, trying to laugh.

The next forty minutes got busy as a nurse arrived to take another history and explain the workings of the room all over again, instructing Treva exactly how she was to lie, and how she was to position her bed to keep excess pressure off of her uterus and placenta. During this, Shanae paced the hallway and explored the waiting rooms on the floor.

An hour later, just as Shanae wandered back, Wade arrived at the hospital, frantic and disheveled.

"My God—Treva!"

"It's all right, I'm fine, just calm down," Treva told him. "Everything's under control and I have a very nice room and very nice nurses."

"But all that blood . . . I saw it when I got home . . ."

"It's *okay*."

All three of them huddled together, Treva in the bed on her side, Shanae snuggling up with her arms around both her father and Treva. Wade was crying, and Shanae, too, had started to shake and sniffle.

"Hey, guys," said Treva, uttering a teary laugh. "No more crying, huh? The trip is going to be a little rockier than we expected, but we're gonna get there. I promise you. Now, where in the hell do they keep the tissues around this place? I thought all hospitals gave you free tissues and I want mine right now!"

DIEDRE

DIEDRE DROVE PAM'S TOYOTA INTO THE MODEST SUB-division of brick ranch homes to which Marcie Hertz had moved only a few weeks ago. Looking around, she breathed a sigh of relief.

At least Marcie had managed to pick a perfect neighborhood. Small houses had immaculate lawns, basketball backboards positioned in many of the driveways. A group of seven-year-old boys were playing with Tonka trucks on a cement porch.

A grade school was located only a few blocks away, reached by walking through the neighborhood, not on busy streets. Even more perfect! No judge could object to these surroundings.

Diedre drove toward the house Marcie was renting, her heart pounding in anticipation as she remembered her last briefing with Rodger Halsick, when they'd gone over the list of witnesses again and Halsick had briefed Diedre on what she was to say to Marcie.

"Now, I want you to visit Marcie and make sure she's up to dressing for court, and reassure her so she doesn't come to court too anxious. Make sure she doesn't bring any friends or support groups with her—I don't want anyone disrupting the proceedings. No signs, no yelling or other shenanigans, nothing like that. It happens, especially with Ann Arbor people, who can be activists, and I don't want anything to alienate the judge."

Halsick said he wanted to meet Diedre and Marcie early at the Oakland County Courthouse on the morning of the hearing so they could go over last-minute details. "Make sure all the witnesses are there, too. Give them maps to the courthouse if they don't know where to find it."

Diedre found the house, identical to the others except for a snowman picture drawn and cut out by a child, which had been taped on the front window.

She parked in the driveway and knocked at the door, which was answered by Marcie, clad in a pair of skintight jeans and a pink, cropped sweater, her blond-streaked, tousled hair yanked on top of her head and secured with rubber bands. Marcie wore wire-rimmed glasses with this outfit, and no makeup.

"Hi . . . Diedre . . ." said Marcie, smiling nervously at the sight of the law student who was involved in her case. "Do you want to come in? I made some coffee and I have creamer flavored with almonds."

"Sounds great," said Diedre.

They walked into the small living room, where the blond Evan was sitting on the floor playing with a Playskool garage and what seemed like dozens of little cars and beadlike people. He had also run a plastic railroad track over the floor which he was using for roads.

"Evan, say hi to Miss Diedre," instructed Marcie.

"Hi," said the four-year-old boy shyly. He looked at Diedre for a few seconds, then went back to zooming one of his cars.

Marcie took Diedre into the kitchen, where they sat down at a bar area piled high with papers, books, and materials for Marcie's master's thesis, along with a rough draft marked up with a red pen.

"It's the final haul," admitted Marcie. "I've been really crunching because I know I've got to get out there and get a real job—not just waitressing." She looked at Diedre. "All right, so what's going on? What do I have to do now?"

They discussed the courtroom procedure and the witnesses who would be called. Diedre warned Marcie that her ex-husband had requested that Evan be interviewed by the judge and asked which parent he wanted to live with. It wasn't a necessity that a child be asked, but if a parent requested this, the judge had to comply.

Marcie seemed alarmed. "She's going to talk to Evan?"

"Legally she has to, if your ex requests it."

"But he's only four," said Marcie, looking worried.

"The judge will take that into consideration, Marcie."

"But . . . what if he promises Evan toys or a trip to Disney World or something?" the grad student fretted. "That'd be just like Jerry. Jerry would stop at nothing to buy Evan if that was the only way he could get him. Or he might even threaten him. God . . ."

"We'll fix it so that Jerry doesn't drive Evan to court," said Diedre quickly. "Let's take it one step at a time, huh?"

Diedre launched into another issue, what Marcie should wear in court.

"I know, a gray or navy skirt and a blouse," sighed the master's degree candidate and former topless dancer. "Secretary clothes."

"You do own some clothes like that, don't you?"

"Well, not really. I haven't exactly been living that lifestyle. I can borrow some, though. Is it really that important? I feel like I have to dress up in a costume."

"In a way you do. Marcie, impressions are everything when it comes to the courtroom. The judge has to think you're just a plain, loving mother."

"Maybe I should wear a T-shirt with scrambled egg spilled on it then. That would be a lot more realistic." Marcie expelled her breath. "Oh, God . . . this is serious, isn't it? I can really lose Evan." She began squeezing her hands together. "They'll take him away from me!"

"No, they won't, Marcie. You are a very good mother and you also have me on your side, and Rodger Halsick, the member of the bar who's going to be representing you in court. Mr. Halsick has over fifty years in the practice of law."

"But they will! I didn't tell you. My ex-husband stopped by the house last night to see Evan. He said I'm nothing but a little table-dancing slut. He says the judge will never give Evan to a whore." She was shaking all over, rubbing her hands wildly across her face and through her hair.

"Now, let's put that right out of our minds for now,"

said Diedre. "He's just pushing your buttons, trying to upset you so you'll come across poorly in court. Now, let's go over it one more time, exactly what you'll be wearing."

"A navy blue skirt and a white blouse with navy trim, I guess," said Marcie in a distracted manner. "My girlfriend works in an office and she can lend me the stuff."

"Does the skirt have a slit?"

"I never asked."

"Borrow one that doesn't. And wear two-inch heels, no higher than that. Nothing sexy. And you *must* wear a bra."

"Okay."

"No fingernail polish unless it's clear, no rings on the fingers, no jewelry other than small stud earrings. Beige panty hose, nothing dark or with textures. Don't even think of wearing an ankle bracelet, and if you have tattoos, cover them up. And tone down your hair, Marcie. Put it in a twist or a ponytail, and maybe some temporary coloring will deemphasize those blond streaks."

Marcie looked shocked. "I can't even wear my birthstone ring?"

"Just stud earrings."

Marcie winced. "All right, I'll do anything, even look like Hillary Clinton if I have to."

Diedre spent another two hours coaching Marcie, role-playing some of the questions her ex-husband's attorney might ask, especially about the topless dancing.

In the middle of it they stopped for lunch-meat sandwiches served with a banana and Oreo cookies. Diedre asked the child questions about his age and which of his toys he liked the best.

"Computer games," the boy told her, munching his sandwich. "My mom lets me play."

"What do you want to be when you grow up, Evan?"

"I wanna be a Webmaster."

"A Webmaster?" Diedre couldn't help laughing.

"I've shown him the Internet and we've gone exploring and used some of the searches," explained Marcie proudly. "We went to the Disney Web site and he was just thrilled."

Over the plates of sandwiches, her eyes beseeched Diedre.

Later, as Diedre was preparing to leave, Marcie walked her to the door of the immaculately clean house, then suddenly grabbed her hands. *"Please,"* she begged. "Most people think that topless dancers are whores. Well, I'm not. Even the judge, that's what she's going to think, I know it."

"Not if you do everything I told you to do," Diedre said.

Diedre spent the rest of the afternoon visiting Evan's day care center to talk to the owner, making sure that she knew exactly what the woman would testify about Evan's (exemplary) behavior in day care. She made phone calls to the two other witnesses, then rushed back to campus to sit in on her Contracts class, the one she found dullest and most devoid of human interest.

She knew contracts could be a very lucrative field—many law firms made millions with big businesses as clients—but it was not for her. She already knew she'd be working with women like Marcie. Yes, and women like her mother, too, women who had all the strikes against them.

Still, she bent over her notepad, taking detailed notes and paying close attention to a case called *Tripani v. Shell Oil,* involving a dispute over oil drilling. It might be boring, but that meant she should only try harder, Diedre told herself firmly.

That week Diedre received several frantic calls from Marcie, who said she and her ex-husband were arguing about who was to take Evan over to the courthouse to talk to Judge Alvarez. Alvarez had decided she would interview the boy in her chambers before the hearing.

Jerry Hertz was insisting it was his "right," while Marcie angrily contended that she currently had custody of Evan and should do it. The couple were accusing each other of wanting to influence the four-year-old on the way to the courthouse.

Such accusations weren't unusual, Rodger Halsick had

warned Diedre, explaining that the issue of who drove the child to the judge was often a big bone of contention in child custody cases.

Finally Diedre suggested that a neutral party, perhaps one of the workers at the Happy Duck day care center where Evan went, be delegated to do this job.

"Irene?" said Marcie.

Irene Pettis was the owner of the facility, and Diedre and Halsick already planned to call her as a witness.

"No, I think we'd better use one of the other workers," Diedre said. "Remember, Irene is going to be our witness, and your ex-husband might object to that. Is there anyone else Evan especially likes?"

"Yes, Heidi. She's in her midtwenties and is a lot of fun, and I think that could work, if Jerry agrees. I'll call him and see."

So it was arranged after a bit more arguing that Heidi Bolden would drive Evan over to talk to Judge Alvarez.

"This is just getting so tense," fretted Marcie. "Jerry is such an asshole. He just wants Evan so he can punish me. I can't wait until this is over. I've hardly been able to eat right in days."

That evening Diedre had promised to baby-sit Tarik again, and Mitch was supposed to meet her at Lashonda's around eight-thirty. Diedre was really beginning to enjoy her baby-sitting sessions with the bright, appealing little boy.

"Hi, DeeDee," said the two-and-a-half-year-old boy as she walked in the door. "Are you going to read me brontosaurus?"

"Yeah, sure—or maybe even a tyrannosaurus."

"The dinosaur books are all in his room. I don't know what I'd do without you, girl," said Lashonda, gathering up her briefcase and books for the seminar she was attending.

"Oh, I like sitting with him. He's so terrific."

"Wait until he turns cranky and stays up till three in the morning whining and sobbing," said Lashonda, grimacing.

"This angel child has been known to do that. Hey—I'm outta here."

Diedre sat down and read to Tarik about dinosaurs while her mind continued to run over the Marcie Hertz custody hearing. In her reading she'd found cases such as *Lamky v. Lamky* in which custody was awarded to the father on evidence of the mother's misconduct with other men. In *Williamson v. Williamson,* though, the court ruled that "a mother's acts of adultery do not necessarily preclude her from having custody of the children."

Law in practical life, she was learning, was a mélange of cases that had been decided both for and against any issue. Lawyers picked and chose among the judges' decisions to find those that supported their cases, and hoped the court would agree.

Mitch arrived and spent an hour crouched on the floor with Tarik, roughhousing and pretending that the two of them were stegosauruses. Finally they put the excited little boy to bed, and Diedre and Mitch sat on the couch and talked some more about Marcie.

"I'm really nervous about this child custody case," admitted Diedre. "If I screw it up, it's going to affect both Marcie and Evan for the rest of their lives."

"You're not going to screw it up. Remember, you've got Rodger Halsick in your corner, and he's an old hand."

"But anything could happen in that courtroom. She was a topless dancer, and that's a hard battle to fight. People believe those women are prostitutes. Marcie's ex-husband has already sworn to pillory her as a whore."

"You coached her, didn't you?"

"Yes, but—"

"You drilled it into her head, just what she should say and do?"

"Yes."

"You have witnesses, don't you?"

"Yes . . ."

"When's the hearing?"

"The day after tomorrow," gulped Diedre.

"Oh, honey." Mitch put his arms around her. "You've just got a bad case of courtroom stage fright, that's all. I've heard you in class, you're outstandingly fast on your feet. I've also seen you cut a swath through those law professors and third-year students at Aunt Cloris's bashes. As a matter of fact, I heard one of the guys in your Torts class call you 'Diedre the Drill.' "

"Diedre the Drill?" She let out a surprised laugh. "Diedre the *Drill*?" She poked him in the side.

Mitch winked at her. "Well, actually I made that up, but it does fit you, Deeds. You're going to be a force to be reckoned with in courtroom law, I know you are."

Suddenly Tarik let out a high-pitched cry, and Mitch jumped up even faster than Diedre. The two of them rushed into the child's cramped bedroom.

"Mama . . . Mama . . ." the curly-haired tot was screaming. "Heard a noise!"

"What kind of a noise?" asked Mitch, kneeling beside the battered crib in which Tarik still slept. "Was it a dinosaur noise? A sort of rmmmph . . . rmmmph?"

"No . . ." Big tears ran down Tarik's brown cheeks.

"Then maybe a tchk! tchk! kind of noise."

"No . . . want Mama . . ."

"How about a huffer-guffer noise? Sort of like this." And Mitch made an absurd noise, using his upper lip and tongue. Even Diedre had to giggle.

"Well . . ." said the boy.

"A real huffer-guffer noise?" Mitch continued to make the noise, and in a minute Tarik joined him, his "huffer-guffer" sounds on a smaller but no less fierce scale.

Laughing, Diedre began to make noises, too, and then Mitch lifted Tarik out of the crib and put him on his back, crawling around on the floor like a horse while the boy giggled wildly, clutching Mitch's shirt collar and hair for dear life.

Forty minutes later, Tarik was asleep in Mitch's arms, and gently he laid the child back down in his crib. Returning to the living room, he said, "What a kid. He's as smart as a little whip. I'd like to have about a dozen just like him."

Diedre felt her heart give a little twist. Here was the children issue again, never very far from Mitch's mind. "A dozen? Come on. That's more kids than the old woman had in her shoe."

"Oh, you remember that old nursery rhyme? I happen to know she had twenty or thirty kids. Hey, maybe it's because I was a lonely only, but I always wanted a house full of kids. Five or six kids of my own and the rest adopted, all sizes and colors."

"Hmmm," said Diedre, at a loss what to say. "My plan would be to start with one and see what happened after that."

"One? How about starting with twins or triplets? We could take fertility drugs, have multiple births . . . Well, maybe not."

We. The talk turned to a set of quints Mitch had read about in the *Ann Arbor News,* but all the while they were talking, Diedre's mind kept focusing on what Mitch had said. It was obvious that Mitch wanted a big, noisy family. He had made that very plain. And he was saying words like *we,* which meant . . .

"Anything wrong?" Mitch asked. "You seem quiet."

"No, I—I'm fine. Just obsessing about that child custody case I guess," Diedre lied.

Later Mitch took her out for coffee, and Diedre was still quiet. The moment had come and gone . . . again . . . and now it had gotten to the point that she *couldn't* tell him about the abortion. If only she'd done it first thing, that day when they'd seen each other at the law library. Now with every passing day, it seemed more and more impossible to talk to Mitch about this topic.

Two days later, Diedre woke with butterflies in her stomach. Today was the day of Marcie's court hearing—*her first case*! Diedre would miss several classes, so she had gotten two members of her study group to take class notes for her while she was in Pontiac, at the Oakland County Court-house.

Diedre got out of bed, showered, and put on a gray suit, plum-colored silk shell, and two-inch gray high heels, dressing with care for her first appearance in a courtroom. The outfit had cost her over two hundred dollars at Hudson's, but Diedre had managed to scrape the money out of one of the living-expenses checks that the law firm had sent.

Even though she would not be able to act officially as an attorney, she would still be sitting behind the counsel table, and she knew how important it was to make a good impression.

She combed her honey blond hair back from her face, putting it into a French twist, then regarded herself in the bathroom mirror. Too severe. It did make her look like "Diedre the Drill." Nervously she snatched out all the pins and drew her hair back again, into a ponytail. No, that made her look as if she might get carded for liquor. Damn . . . Finally Diedre settled for pulling her hair back and curling the ends under. She added the pair of small, garnet "good luck" earrings she had inherited from her grandmother.

For the thousandth time, Diedre borrowed Pam's Toyota, dropping her sister off at work, then going to pick up Marcie at her home. Marcie Hertz today was dressed for her courtroom role in her navy skirt and navy and white blouse with a faint hint of bra straps showing through the cloth. Marcie had even added a white pearl circle pin to the blouse—God knew where she had ever found it, maybe at a garage sale. Her shoes were new, navy blue business pumps with modest heels.

"How do I look?" Marcie wanted to know.

"Perfect," declared Diedre.

"Perfectly what?"

"Perfectly . . . June Cleaver."

They both laughed, a little too loudly. Evan had talked to Judge Alvarez the previous afternoon and was already in day care, unaware that his fate was being settled today.

"God, I'm nervous," said Marcie, wringing her hands in

her lap as they entered on US-23 north, heading for a series of expressways that would take them to the Detroit area.

"Well, don't be. Evan has already said he wants to live with you, and we're way ahead of the game on that. If he didn't melt Judge Alvarez's heart, I don't know what could."

"Want to live with my mommy 'cause she takes care of me and makes me peanut butter sandwiches and lets me play on the computer," had been Evan's statement to the judge, dutifully transcribed by a court reporter. "An' she sings me songs. An' she gives me big-boy kisses. An' we make Rice Krispies squares."

It was a gray, cloudy morning, hinting at winter. They got caught in morning rush-hour traffic and sat on I-696 near Telegraph, waiting to exit. Marcie was twitching and fidgeting nervously, her fingernails digging a crease in the navy skirt she wore.

"Take it easy," soothed Diedre, although she herself felt just as nervous. "We've prepared well. We've gone over everything a ton of times. We're fine."

Telegraph Road took them north past huge office complexes, the communities growing wealthier as they approached Bloomfield Hills, where the road began to resemble a parkway. Then the roadside trees and plantings abruptly vanished and it was back to the hurly-burly of Pontiac with its crammed-in strip shopping malls.

The Oakland County Service Center was located north of a big shopping mall called Summit Place. It looked like a sprawling university with dozens of buildings spread out on two "campuses."

Diedre drove in one of the entrances, where a pull-aside for visitors had a plastic box that dispensed maps of the complex. Fortunately the five-story courthouse was hard to miss with its large number 1200 emblazoned along the roof. She drove in, passing a community mental health center, an executive office building, and a health annex. Her heart was pounding so fast that she felt almost sick. And Marcie's presence beside her, the woman's obvious apprehension, made Diedre feel even sicker.

Her first case . . . She couldn't blow it. If she did, poor little Evan's life would be changed forever and so would Marcie's . . .

The visitor's lot was three-quarters filled with cars, and as Diedre cruised for a space she noticed the odd mixture of vehicles. An old white truck with its front bumper held on by bungee cords was parked next to a brand-new Cadillac. There were two police cars, one from Sylvan Lake, the other from Troy.

She could see a county sheriff's vehicle cruising for a spot.

"Diedre," said Marcie desperately, as Diedre found a space and started to open her door. "Wait—"

Diedre looked at the other woman, who was dashing tears out of her eyes. "I . . . I have to sit here for a minute," Marcie choked. "I want to pray a little. Right now it's the only thing I can think of to do."

Diedre sat still while Marcie prayed.

Closing her eyes, Diedre added a heartfelt prayer of her own to Marcie's plea.

Finally she reached out and took the graduate student's icy cold hand in hers. "Just stay beside me, Marcie, and please, trust in Mr. Halsick and me and stay as calm as possible while you're in the courtroom."

As they walked up to the building, two men wearing JUROR badges were smoking cigarettes outside the main door, along with a hugely fat woman wearing shorts and no jacket, despite the fact that the outside temperature was less than thirty degrees.

They walked into the tower wing, with its white marble floor, and were forced to go through an airport-type metal detector run by two Oakland County sheriff's officers in full uniform, carrying guns. A sign on the wall listed the judges' names and their courtroom locations.

"Judge Alvarez is in Four Tower," said Diedre, studying the sign.

CHOICES

347

They walked toward the elevators, sharing one with a
well-dressed woman and a man who was apparently her
lawyer. The woman, wreathed in smiles, kept effusively saying, "Thank you, thank you." Diedre wondered if it was a
divorce settlement, and how much she had gotten. The other
occupant of the elevator was a man in a business suit whose
head was shaved except for two tiny, long braids that
sprouted out of the sides of his skull.

The fourth-floor hallway was lined with windows that
gave sweeping views of the service complex and a distant
expressway. Rows of seats had been bolted along the walls,
these occupied by a varied crowd. Lawyers in suits. A startling variety of ordinary citizens who might be anything
from car-jackers to check kiters to concerned parents. Two
black women wore micromini skirts and four-inch, sexy
high heels.

They caught snatches of lawyers' conversations. "You
can't take it up with the mother. The mother doesn't care."
And "Sorry you had to wait, John, but you got that judg-
ment in, and away we go."

Diedre gulped down a thrill of exhilaration. Only a little
more than two years and this would be her world, too . . .
She, too, would pass the bar exam and might be one of the
lawyers walking through these halls.

God, she prayed. *Let this case go well, please. I can't let
Marcie down.*

Rodger Halsick was waiting for them outside Judge Alvarez's courtroom, which had a big sign attached to the wall:
*Do not pass through court to reach chambers. Use rear
hallway. Do not approach bench for any reason. Take all
orders to chambers. Failure to comply causes disturbances
to court proceedings.*

"Well, Diedre, Marcie, are we ready to show them?" said
Halsick, smiling. He looked very natty today in a dark gray
suit and conservative blue and red necktie, his white hair
glistening and soft.

Diedre forced a smile. "Yes."

"A little secret I learned about forty years ago," said

Halsick. "Prepare as if your life depended on it, review what you've done, then put it out of your mind and just relax. Preparation is ninety-nine percent of a case, and if you've prepared well, you have no worries." He gazed down the wide corridor to the row of seats. "Have our witnesses arrived?"

"Yes," said Diedre, now recognizing Irene Pettis, the day care center owner, and George Rudgood, the man who lived in Marcie's former apartment house. Marcie's master's supervisor, Jay Brouwer, was just rounding the corner from the elevator.

"Oh, good. Diedre, why don't you go over and make sure they're comfortable and answer any questions they may have. Remember, the judge will sequester the witnesses, so they'll have to wait out here in the hallway both before and after they give their testimony."

Diedre nodded.

"Meanwhile, Marcie, let's go down the hall a little and huddle," suggested Halsick kindly. He smiled at the frightened woman. "We'll go over a few things, keep them straight in our minds." He glanced at his watch. "We'll be going into the courtroom in around ten minutes."

Court was already in session when they entered, stepping in quietly and taking seats on a hard wooden bench. Dozens of people occupied the benches, the same type of motley collection of humanity they'd seen in the hallway, interspersed with lawyers in suits. In this setting, Diedre couldn't help seeing, the lawyers stuck out like nuns in Las Vegas.

Judge Alvarez was a petite woman in her fifties, with straight black hair beginning to gray at the temples, pulled back from a pleasant face. She had hooded, dark eyes and wore a dark robe. She spoke in a soft voice that just barely traveled to the back of the courtroom, even though there was a mike on the bench. In fact, Diedre found herself straining to hear.

The courtroom bristled with computers and monitors. There was a monitor positioned on the bench to the judge's left, its screen turned toward Judge Alvarez. Halsick had told Diedre that this was a closed-circuit TV set that switched every ten seconds from the judge to the lawyer to the witness stand, so that the judicial clerk could determine a good time to interrupt the judge if need be. Another closed-circuit TV set had been affixed to the ceiling so that those in the courtroom could see it as it switched from one view to the next. A court reporter sat at a lower level beside the bench, also with several computers.

Diedre gazed around eagerly, trying to take in every fascinating detail. The walls were paneled in a dark orangish type of wood that resembled teak, and the ceiling was lower than she'd expected, paved with acoustical tiles.

The judge's bench was gray marble, positioned in front of a large gray marble panel that displayed the United States and Michigan flags. Rows of wooden benches filled the room. There was an empty jury box, and a witness stand with a microphone on it, facing the bench. Two tables stood on each side of the stand, each equipped with two chairs. A long wooden bench set behind this held the attorneys' coats, briefcases, and other materials they had brought to court. This was where Diedre was going to sit when it was their turn to appear before the judge.

Marcie nudged Diedre. "There's Jerry—two rows ahead."

Diedre focused her eyes on Jerry Hertz, the plaintiff in the hearing. He was a man of about thirty-five, with a solid body and a fat, puffy neck. Just as Marcie pointed him out, he turned and glared at his ex-wife. If looks could wound, Diedre thought, Marcie would already be lying on the courtroom floor with blood running out of her.

Twenty minutes later, the bailiff called their case, and Marcie, Halsick, and Diedre filed their way up to the front. Halsick and Marcie sat at one of the tables, and Diedre took her place on the bench directly behind them, a notebook in her lap.

Since this was an evidentiary hearing, the plaintiff, Jerry Hertz, would go first, and Marcie would be given a chance to rebut. She could call her witnesses then. There'd be no jury.

The fireworks started almost immediately.

"Yes," Jerry Hertz told his attorney, a man named Mark Lowe, during questioning. "She had affairs with men all the time. And she danced at a club called the Booby Trap on Eight Mile Road in Detroit—you know, where all the sleazebags hang out."

"Objection!" cried Rodger Halsick. Diedre, sitting behind Marcie, felt her own body tense. "Plaintiff should confine himself to the questions being asked without giving his personal opinions."

"Objection sustained."

"I'm telling it like it is," said Hertz sullenly, glaring at Judge Alvarez. "Dammit, she—"

"Please, Mr. Hertz, you are not permitted to use inflammatory words and phrases," put in the judge, sighing. "As for the use of obscenities, if you utter one more such word, you will find yourself in contempt of court."

"Judge, if I may be so bold, the nature and character of the Booby Trap topless dancing establishment, and Marcie Hertz's behavior there, is an integral part of this custody hearing, and should be taken into full consideration," said Hertz's attorney in a pedantic tone. "I apologize if my client became overexcited, but this is quite an emotional issue for him. We would like to call our next witness, Jeff Bridette, from the Booby Trap."

Bridette turned out to be a small, fortyish man dressed in loose-fitting designer clothes, with the pale, pale skin of someone who is never awake during normal daylight hours. He was extremely thin.

Hertz's attorney established that Bridette had owned the club for three years, and before that had run another, similar club called the Pussy Kat, also on Eight Mile Road in Detroit.

He testified that Marcie Hertz had worked for him for a month and a half, dancing naked except for a G-string on a stage, and at tables for customers.

"How big is a G-string, sir?" asked Lowe, with a smirky little grin that was captured perfectly in the closed-circuit TV camera overhead.

The witness smiled, too, and made a triangle with his hands. The man had small hands and the triangle looked minuscule. Several people in the courtroom tittered. "It's fastened with a string, you know. A string that goes behind."

"Oh, a string that goes behind?"

"Yeah, up the crack of her butt." Diedre watched Marcie cringe, and she felt like cringing herself. But Judge Alvarez didn't indicate by a flicker of expression how this testimony was affecting her.

"How many nights a week did she work?" questioned Lowe.

"Five, six nights a week easy."

"And would you say that she was one of your top . . . er, performers?"

"She was average, I'd say."

"What kind of money could a woman like Marcie Hertz earn in a night at your establishment?"

"Well, uh, we have dancers making upward of two hundred fifty dollars a night in tips."

"And what types of acts would a woman have to perform to get such tips?"

"Well, stage dancing, they all did, and tips for that ran from five to ten dollars—I have girls making a hundred dollars just from a good stage dance. Then table dances are around ten dollars—that's what the men pay to have a table dance. But the girl can be tipped ten, twenty, fifty dollars . . . Depends on how good she is. Then there's lap dances. The guys pay twenty-five dollars for a lap dance and the tips are proportionally higher."

"Now, sir, can you describe a lap dance for us?"

"Well . . ." The man seemed nervous. "It's not an illegal act."

"We know that, but we would like a description of what is actually done to whom and by whom."

"Well . . ."

With each word the owner of the Booby Trap uttered, Diedre could see Marcie tensing up, at one point passing her hands over her eyes. She turned and gave Diedre a despairing look. "I *didn't* lap-dance," she mouthed. "Only twice. He's making it sound like I did it all the time, but I didn't."

When it was time for cross-examination, Rodger Halsick first put Jerry Hertz on the stand and began "clearing up a few points," as he put it in his deceptively mild voice.

"So there was the potential of Marcie earning around two hundred fifty dollars a night, Mr. Hertz, in the topless dancing establishment."

"Well, yes."

"Did your ex-wife tell you why she needed that kind of money, Mr. Hertz?" asked Halsick.

"I . . . I don't understand the question."

"Isn't it true that you were six months in arrears on your child support payments?"

"No. No, I wasn't in arrears. I paid her, I paid her every month."

"Did you?" Halsick leaned over to Diedre, who pulled some papers out of a file folder and handed them to him. "Then why is it, Mr. Halsick, that the office of the Friend of the Court says they have no records of any payments made by you since early December of *last year*?"

"Their computers must of went down," said the man sullenly.

"Is that so? Strange, isn't it, that all these records are computer printouts, then, isn't it, Mr. Hertz?"

The ex-husband flushed an unpleasant shade of red, while Diedre bit back a nervous giggle. Rodger Halsick was making the man look like a deadbeat and a fool. They'd proved one point—that Hertz didn't care enough about his son to support him regularly. But the hearing wasn't over yet.

"Now let's talk about your allegation that Marcie Hertz

was having relationships with men, bringing them into her apartment house. How did you get your information on this so-called fact?'' Halsick asked.

The man fussed with the mike on the stand, looking at his own reflection in the monitor. ''I saw the building she lived in, the apartment house—you know. Men were going in and out at all hours, you could tell what they were there for.''

''Did you personally see any men going in and out of Marcie's apartment?''

''Not personally, but I heard they did.''

''Who did you hear it from?''

''People. A guy I knew.''

''What was this guy's name?''

''I really can't—I can't remember.''

''And you haven't called this 'guy' as a witness, have you?''

''Well, no . . .''

''Thank you, Mr. Hertz, that will be all.''

Halsick called George Rudgood to the stand. Rudgood was a third-year law student who lived in the apartment house with his wife, and had acted as manager for a period of over a year, the entire time that Marcie had lived there. Rudgood testified that he was in and out of the building during the day, and stayed home almost every night, his apartment right underneath Marcie's.

''The ceilings and walls were kind of thin. I could hear footsteps up there, voices sometimes, the TV set. I always knew when she had a visitor.''

''And did she ever have male visitors after dark?''

''Not that I'm aware of. And I would have been aware of it because my wife baby-sat for Marcie occasionally when she went out. And another woman in the building sat for her, too. So I think I would have heard if there'd been a boyfriend.''

''Where did Marcie usually go when she went out?''

''She did a lot of researching at the library. Basically

that's all it was. Marcie's master's thesis was really looming over her head, she really wanted that degree so she could get a decent job.'

Marcie was standing at the witness stand now. Her face was drained white, her fingers anxiously touching the circle pin she wore. She looked so distressed that Diedre was worried she might actually pass out, but apparently Marcie was made of tougher stuff than that, for she answered each question in a low but firm voice.

Halsick had taken her over the fact that she was renting a new house, and gotten her to describe the house, the neighborhood, the nearby grade school. Coached by Diedre, Marcie offered a subdivision newsletter as evidence that the neighborhood had an active association that sponsored yearly hot dog roasts and a pet parade, offering prizes for the best-decorated homes at Christmastime.

They covered the house, and Marcie told the court how many bedrooms it had and what she had done to fix it up.

Halsick now began to zero in on all the questions that would bring out Marcie's devotion to her son, her efforts to read to him, teach him computer skills, and so forth.

Marcie answered in a clear voice, explaining that she had bought several computer games for him, and also let him use the Paintbrush program on her computer, which he loved.

"Do you and your son attend church?"

"We have just started going to a Methodist church," explained Marcie. "I have Evan enrolled in Sunday school and he does love it. They're very nice to him there and he likes all the games they play."

"Where are you currently working, Mrs. Hertz?" asked Rodger Halsick, eyeing Marcie sympathetically.

"I currently work as a waitress at the Red Caboose, in Ann Arbor."

"You're no longer employed as a topless dancer?"

"No, sir. I only did it for less than two months."

"How did you get into that type of a job, topless dancing?"

"I was desperate for money, my car was dying on me, and I had a big doctor's bill from when Evan had an ear infection and they had to put drainage tubes in his ears. Also I was in arrears on my day care bill because my ex-husband hadn't paid any child support in months. And . . . I guess you could say we just needed the money to eat," she explained painfully.

"How did you hear about the Booby Trap?"

"A girlfriend of mine knew someone who worked there."

"And you were told by this friend of yours that you could earn between a hundred and two hundred fifty dollars a night just doing table dances and dancing onstage?"

"Yes." Marcie looked up pleadingly at the judge. "Yes, that's right."

"And that's what you thought would be involved?"

"Yes. Nothing more. I told them that I would not do private parties, and the owner said I didn't have to."

"By the owner, you mean Mr. Bridette?"

"Yes."

"Why did you choose that means of making a living, Marcie?"

"I had to! I had just lost my previous job of waitressing because the restaurant went out of business. I filled out a lot of applications, but Ann Arbor is full of students and they all fight for the jobs."

"How long did you expect to be working at the Booby Trap?"

"Just enough to get a down payment on a good used car and pay up some of my bills."

"But you quit the job after less than two months, didn't you, Marcie?"

"Yeah . . . this guy attacked me and two bouncers had to pull him off me. I—I didn't want to work there anymore. I had my little boy to think of, and I finally got called to work at the Red Caboose. I quit right away."

"And while you were there, for this less-than-two-month

period," emphasized Halsick, "did you have a child care plan for Evan?"

Diedre had carefully planned all of these questions, and she sat intently listening as Halsick asked them, adding his own special emphasis, born of years of experience, to the words.

"Yes, I did."

"What was it?"

"There was a woman who lived in the apartment next door to me, she was a nurse at University Hospital, and she wanted to pick up a little extra money, so she came over and stayed at my apartment while I was gone. It worked out well . . . and she was a nurse, so if Evan had any problems, she could help. Also the people downstairs, the apartment manager and his wife, were friendly. They helped out a couple of times, too."

The judge announced she was taking a break, so everyone rose, and Judge Alvarez filed out from behind the bench, entering an unmarked door to her right.

"I'm so nervous," whispered Marcie, her voice strained, turning to look at Diedre as the door shut behind Alvarez. "Is it going all right? I can't tell. My stomach is killing me."

"It's going great, Marcie," said Diedre heartily. "Just keep up your courage."

In twenty minutes the judge was back, and Halsick brought on the owner of the day care center.

"Evan is a beautifully behaved little boy who is very responsive and cooperative," said Irene Pettis, reiterating what she had told Diedre some days previously. "I wish all our children were like him. It's easy to tell that he comes from a very loving, structured environment."

The last witness was Jay Brouwer, Marcie's master's adviser, who told the court that Marcie was progressing excellently on her thesis, and he predicted no problems with it, or any problems with her receiving her M.A. degree in psychology in June. A pudgy man in his forties, he wore a tweedy jacket and a tie ten years out of date, looking the part of the university professor he was.

"What are her chances of getting a good job with the M.A. degree?" asked Halsick.

"Oh, excellent. In fact, I know several hospitals and clinics that could use someone like Marcie on staff and I was planning to give her my personal recommendation."

Later Halsick grilled Jerry Hertz on the lifestyle he led, the many business trips the man took out of town, totaling as many as three to four worknights per week. His child care plan was going to be his parents, who he admitted were in their midseventies with health problems.

"But dammit—that doesn't make a difference! My mother is the finest person who ever walked the earth . . . A little arthritis won't interfere with her watching Evan—"

"Mr. Hertz, what did I tell you about using obscenities in this courtroom?" snapped Judge Alvarez. "That's a one-hundred-fifty-dollar fine for you, and if I hear the word again, the next step is a jail sentence."

"We rest, your Honor," said Halsick hastily.

The judge looked down at a stack of folders she had on the bench in front of her, her forehead wrinkling in a frown, and Diedre immediately tensed. Halsick had warned her that usually judges in custody cases announced their decisions then and there.

Judge Alvarez cleared her throat.

"In announcing my decision on this evidentiary hearing, I have taken into consideration that the four-year-old child, Evan Thomas Hertz, has expressed a desire to live with his mother because, among other things, she 'sings to him, gives him big-boy kisses, and makes Rice Krispies squares.' Those sound like the kinds of things that a good, loving mother does with her child."

Seated beside Halsick, Marcie stared at the judge, her face blank with terror, as if she'd heard the words but they hadn't yet registered.

"Marcie Hertz has been there for her child, providing a

decent environment and love even under trying circumstances and lack of money caused by the plaintiff's refusal
to pay his court-ordered child support. In the opinion of this
court, his refusal to pay for the support of the minor child
shows that the plaintiff, Mr. Hertz, has little real interest or
fatherly concern for this child.''

Marcie was now trembling violently. Diedre's throat had
closed, her breath coming shallowly.

''The court has heard the arguments and evidence of both
parties in open court and is fully advised of the issues in
this case. Therefore it is ordered that the defendant, Marcia
Eileen Hertz, shall have custody of the parties' minor child,
Evan Thomas Hertz, until he attains the age of eighteen
years or further order of the court.''

There was more, having to do with visitation and the possible moving of the residence of ''the minor child'' out of
state, and Jerry Hertz was also ordered to pay the entire
amount that he was in arrears to the Friend of the Court, an
amount totaling over seven thousand dollars. If he had not
made arrangements to pay this within thirty days, he would
be jailed for six months.

By the time the judge had finished reading this far, the
whiteness of Marcie's face had changed to a bright, shiny
pink, and tears of joy began running down her face.

Suddenly it was over and they were walking out of the
courtroom. Out in the hallway, Marcie grabbed Diedre and
began hugging her, smiles blending with her tears.

''Oh, God . . . oh, God! Evan's still with me! I've got
custody! And you got all that child support money for me.
Oh, I can't believe it! Diedre, you did it! Oh, and Mr. Halsick, of course. I can't thank both of you enough. I can
never, *never* thank you enough.''

It was a sweet moment for Diedre, maybe one of the
sweetest she would ever know as a lawyer. She'd only been
a helper, but this was what it would be like when things
went the way they were supposed to.

The elderly attorney, Rodger Halsick, watched all this

with a benevolent smile on his face. "It does feel good when you're in the winner's circle, doesn't it?"

They headed back down the hall toward the elevator and took it down to the first floor, where new groups of people were being ushered through the metal detector equipment.

Halsick reached into the briefcase he had been carrying and pulled out a package wrapped in red and blue paper. "I have a little something I bought for you to give to Evan, from the Women's Law Club. You said he liked computer games, so we decided to get him one. *Where in the World Is Carmen Sandiego*, I think it is."

Marcie took the game, flushing bright red and gushing more thanks.

"As for you, Diedre Samms, you did a fantastic job and you're to be congratulated."

Diedre looked at the seventy-five-year-old man who had worked with her so generously, answered so many of her questions, guided her through every step, then appeared in court beside her—all without a lick of pay. She knew he had done this, not only for Marcie Hertz, but also for Diedre, so that that a new, young lawyer could be helped along her path.

"Thanks," she whispered, hugging him. "I couldn't have done it without you. I can't tell you how grateful I am that you gave me this chance. I'll never forget today—never."

"There will be a thousand days like today for you, Diedre," said Halsick, smiling. "Only you'll be the one sitting at the table, riding the whirlwind, not an old fart like me."

Diedre thanked him again, smiling and smiling. She felt so great. She didn't care if she tried ten thousand cases, this would always be the best one.

Diedre dropped Marcie off at her house and again Marcie thanked her profusely, declaring that if there was ever anything she could do for Diedre, she'd do it.

The two women hugged each other, but Diedre left with an unexpected sense of sadness. Yes, Marcie was grateful, but the odds of the two women meeting again, or Diedre

really ever calling on Marcie for help, were decidedly small.
This was probably the last she'd ever see of Marcie Hertz.
It would be the same with many of the other cases coming
up in her law career, Diedre suddenly saw. She would become deeply involved, pouring her emotions into a case, but
then the case would be over and the client would go off and
live his or her life, and they wouldn't meet again unless the
client had new legal problems.

As usual, the beautiful, Gothic law library hit Diedre like
a punch to the stomach as she walked in. Its aura of antiq-
uity made her think of all the lawyers who had gone before
her, like Rodger Halsick, and suddenly she was proud that
one day she would be among the alumni of this law school,
able to go before the bench in any court in Michigan, or
maybe even the Supreme Court sometime.

She found Mitch sitting at their usual table, books and
notebooks spread out in front of him. He lifted his head
when Diedre arrived, a look of pleasure spreading across his
face at the sight of her.

"How did the custody hearing go?"

"Oh, it went fabulously. It really went great. Marcie was
wonderful. And the judge was a honey. She ordered Marcie's ex to pay all his back child support or he'd go to jail."
Lowering her voice to a whisper, she gave him all the high
points, ignoring the annoyed stares of several other students
seated at the table.

"I knew you could do it. This calls for a celebration."

"Mitch—I have to study—"

He pulled a Snickers, her favorite candy bar, out of his
briefcase and gave her a charming, lopsided grin as he produced something from his pocket. To her shock, she saw
that it was a small, white birthday candle. "I wish we could
light this, but I'm afraid we'd probably freak out the smoke
alarms in here. This is only your first victory, Diedre—there
are going to be countless more."

She reached out for the candy bar, her throat suddenly
thickening. Mitch was acting as happy as if her triumph
were his. "I was scared," she whispered. "I thought, what

will I do if Marcie loses custody of that little boy?''

''Never, not as long as Dead-Eye Diedre is on the case.''
Mitch's laugh was gentle. ''Go on, snarf down that candy
bar. I've got two or three more where that came from. Also
the rest of the box of candles, if you should care to go
outside and light some, just for good luck.''

Diedre looked into his eyes and saw the goodness there,
the decency, and felt a wave of love flood over her, so powerful that she felt suddenly like crying. Oh, that would look
great, her crying in the library in front of 150 people. Her
day had been a roller coaster of emotions, hadn't it? Hastily
she opened up her Torts book to today's reading assignment.

Okay. She had a secret. She didn't have to tell Mitch.
And she didn't have to think about it either. She could just
let their lives go on as they were. Wouldn't a million other
women make that very same decision? Besides—things
weren't that serious yet. There was plenty of time left to
work this through.

Later, before walking over to meet Pam, Diedre started making phone calls, first phoning her mother at work, where
Cynthia Samms sounded delighted at her daughter's accom-
plishment in court.

''*Great* news, honey—oh, I've gotta put you on hold,
here's a call.''

Still, between the barrage of incoming phone calls to the
engineering firm, Diedre managed to rehash the entire day
in court, with Cynthia hanging on her every word.

''I wish I'd had someone like you, back when you girls
were little,'' remarked Cynthia with regret.

''You have me now,'' said Diedre excitedly. ''Anybody
messes with you . . . you know who to call.''

It had felt great to share her news with her mother, so
Diedre then called Treva Connor at home, learning from her
husband that Treva had been hospitalized with a pregnancy
complication.

''Oh!'' Diedre cried. ''Is it serious?''

''Serious enough to keep her in the hospital, but so far

the baby is doing well," Wade Connor told her, his voice edged with concern. "She's been so worried about that."

"Do you think she would mind if I visited?"

"Well, Diedre." Wade's laugh was as warm and giving as Treva's. "Why don't I give you her private room number and you can ask. She's had quite a few visitors, but they don't stay very long. We don't want to tire her."

Treva immediately answered the phone, her voice sounding a little huskier than Diedre remembered. "Stop by for five minutes, dear, that would be a pleasure. Oh, and could you bring me a bag of hard candies? The sour-fruit kind? I've had such a weird hankering . . ."

So Diedre took time to stop at a drugstore, buy an assortment of candies, and make the drive to the hospital complex.

She found Treva ensconced in a room that was lined with bouquets of flowers on almost every available surface, a bulletin board bristling with get-well cards and funny drawings Treva said her stepdaughter, Shanae, had made on her computer.

Treva acted thrilled to receive the candies.

"How are you?" said Diedre, feeling a spasm of guilt that she was well and healthy and could do anything she wished, while this beautiful, kind woman was trapped in a hospital bed at the mercy of doctors and her own body.

"Well, it's no picnic," said Treva after a minute. "The drug side effects . . . well, I'm being treated to a bunch of stuff, like a rapid heartbeat and headaches . . . I've heaved up my breakfast a few times . . . Oh, and I have low blood potassium, so they've put me on these big yellow horse pills for that. I hate to take big pills, but I've trained myself to let those babies just slide right on down. There's a trick to it, you know. You put the pill in, take a big gulp of water, and throw your head back while you swallow."

Diedre could tell by Treva's expression that the drug side effects were a lot worse than she was letting on, but clearly Treva wanted to keep things cheerful. She began telling her all about Marcie Hertz's court hearing, her enthusiasm spill-

ing over again, even though she thought she'd calmed down
a little.

"Oh, it's wonderful that you were able to help her keep
her child!" exclaimed Treva. "When will you be able to
appear in court yourself on these cases?"

"As soon as I finish my first year, the statutes allow me
to represent a client in court as long as my grades are good
and it's a pro bono case, and I'm supervised by a member
of the bar," said Diedre proudly. "The only time I can't
appear in court for my client is when it's a criminal or ju-
venile case exposing the client to more than six months in
jail."

"Wonderful," sighed Treva. "There was a time when I
might have gone to law school. I thought seriously about it.
But women of color just didn't go to law school then the
way they do now. I was way ahead of my time."

That weekend Mitch invited Diedre to Bloomfield Hills to
meet his father, Ed Sterling, the president of a small company that sold paper medical supplies to doctor's offices,
clinics, and hospitals. Ed had invited them to have dinner
at Mountain Jack's Steakhouse, a place Mitch explained was
a real favorite of his father, who adored big steaks full of
cholesterol.

"Oh, now you're meeting his father," caroled Pam as
Diedre tried to decide what to wear for this occasion. "That
means it's serious, right? Seriousssssss." She stretched out
the word gleefully.

"We're just having dinner," protested Diedre. "Steaks,
by the sound of it."

"Serious, *serious*," teased Pam. "You lucky dog. I
wouldn't be surprised if—"

But something made Diedre put up her hand to stop her
sister's outburst of optimism. "Hey, cool it," she said. "It's
just dinner at Mountain Jack's, not a lifelong commitment."

It was now well into December. Hard dots of snowflakes
swirled in the air as they drove to Bloomfield Hills, about
an hour's drive away. The sight reminded Diedre of upcom-

ing exams and they began to discuss how they'd attack their studies.

Mitch planned to pick up copies of past exams which were kept on file at the circulation desk in the library, hoping these might inspire him to new heights of erudition. Diedre's study group was doing the same thing. But how much could a past question help? Would it only cloud the issue or trap them into studying something that wouldn't even be on the test this year? They debated this most of the way.

In the part of her mind that wasn't arguing, Diedre began to worry that the dress she had chosen to wear looked too summery, that her four-year-old cloth coat was too old to be stylish. She could feel her stomach knotting. This felt like the hour before she had gone into the courtroom, incredibly tense.

The wealthy area where the Sterlings lived had several lakes, each lined by expensive homes. "There's a whole bunch of lakes in here," explained Mitch proudly. "There's Lower Long Lake, and Island Lake, and Upper Long Lake, and Square Lake, and Turtle Lake—and that doesn't even count all the lakes as you drive over to Waterford or Keego Harbor."

Diedre nodded, thinking of Madison Heights, which had no lakes at all.

"My father is still recuperating from the death of my mother," Mitch warned her as he parked the Le Baron in the circular driveway of a huge, rambling house overlooking Lower Long Lake. The lake's surface was choppy with silver-colored waves, an edge of ice forming at the shoreline, and all around it were the big homes.

"He's really not himself, so be prepared. He still occasionally cries when he talks about her."

Ed Sterling turned out to be a gray-haired version of Mitch, with piercing blue eyes that fastened on Diedre with approval. "I'm really happy to meet you, Diedre. I can see that my son has impeccable taste in women."

"Thank you." She felt herself relax a little.

"He tells me that you're both smart and wise, Diedre, and that you're a brilliant analyst of legal cases."

"I would hardly say that—"

"Ah, but Mitch is a very good observer, he gets that quality from his mother, and if he tells me that you are wowing your law-school professors, and winning your legal cases, then I have to believe him."

They drove to the restaurant on Telegraph Road, which was crowded with diners, most of them casually dressed. Ed told them he came here every week for the steak, "even though I know I shouldn't. But what the hell. If God wanted us to eat vegetables, He would have made our skin green."

Over drinks, Diedre found Ed fun and charming, a lot like Mitch, and she enjoyed his humorous tales of the one hectic year he had attended the Wayne State University medical school.

They ordered, Ed selecting a large sirloin steak, and both Diedre and Mitch choosing chicken in a Marsala wine sauce. The waitress brought a big salad cart to their table and mixed each salad individually, sprinkling each bowl with freshly ground Parmesan cheese.

"I passed out in anatomy class," Ed recalled as they munched their salads. "Mitch's mother, Connie, was the one who waved smelling salts under my nose and revived me." His eyes suddenly glittered with moisture. "Maybe that was why I married her. She always did know how to take care of me."

Diedre nodded. "Mitch has told me so many wonderful things about her."

"Yes . . . there is nothing like love. When you have it, it's the most precious thing there is. When you lose it, it's hell. That might not be brilliantly said, but it's totally true. Whoa," Ed went on, breaking the tension. "Looks like that's our dinner coming—and my steak is so rare it might just jump up and start mooing."

Later they returned to the house for an after-dinner drink. Then, while Ed made several international phone calls connected with his business, Mitch and Diedre strolled down to the lake. A flock of Canadian geese waddled back and forth on the snow-dusted lawn, quacking and clucking. The birds were a lot bigger than ducks, and Mitch and Diedre had to watch where they stepped.

"One of the prices we pay for being on the water—goose puckey," said Mitch, laughing.

"Your father is pretty special," remarked Diedre, tossing a handful of stale bread toward one of the birds, who waddled eagerly toward it, trailed by his cohorts making the honking/quacking sound typical of these birds on the ground. "I like him."

"I know. He does miss Mom, though. I hope it didn't embarrass you that he got teary."

"No. I wish I'd had a father like him."

"Well, maybe someday he can be yours—by marriage, at least."

She stared, shocked, at Mitch.

"Is it such a surprise?" he asked gently.

"Yes . . . no . . ." She stopped in confusion, remembering Pam's teasing before they had left.

"This isn't an official proposal, not yet," Mitch told her. "That will come when I give you the ring. I guess I'm old-fashioned, but I want to make a ceremony out of it, I want it to be really special." He slid both arms around her waist, pulling her around to face him. At the sight of them embracing, several of the geese began honking louder.

"I love you, Diedre. That's the bottom line. I think I've loved you ever since that first night."

"You mean the night we saw each other at the law library."

"No . . . before that."

He meant the night when they'd had their one-night stand, she knew, feeling confused. Her throat felt hot, uncomfortable.

"And I love you," she finally whispered.

"Oh, baby. Oh, my Diedre. You don't know what a good life we're going to have together."

Their kiss was long and full-body, totally fiery, and Diedre knew that if they weren't at Mitch's father's house, standing outdoors by a cold lake, they'd be making love.

It was dark by the time they drove home, and Diedre sat in the passenger seat with her left hand enfolded in Mitch's right one, watching the flash and glare of headlights in the opposite lanes.

Mrs. Mitch Sterling. Under her breath she repeated the name to herself. *Diedre Sterling.* Would she use that name for her professional name, or would she keep her maiden name, as many women lawyers did, especially those who had to deal with defendants in a courtroom environment? Diedre realized that her stomach was still hurting, a dull ache in the center of her. She'd have to take something for it when she got back to the apartment.

"Happy?" whispered Mitch.

"Oh, yes," she breathed.

"Well?" demanded Pam when Diedre finally walked in the door, her face flushed pink, all of her lipstick kissed away. "So what happened?"

"We had dinner . . . at Mountain Jack's."

"And?"

"And it was very nice," said Diedre, deciding not to tell Pam what Mitch had said about a "preengagement." Not yet, anyway. In the first place, she just wanted to savor it herself, privately. In the second . . . well, anything could happen, she thought uneasily. She did not have a ring yet. Why embarrass herself by announcing something that wasn't fully certain?

Besides, there was still the secret she held, nagging at her mind, a secret that could explode everything apart. If only it hadn't been Mitch Sterling who was her one-night stand, she found herself thinking. If only it had been some faceless, anonymous guy . . .

The study group that week started off with a sour note. Belinda, whose baby, Rashida, was now eleven months old, arrived at Lashonda's house with red, puffy eyes. The child she cradled in her arms was crying fretfully.

"Rashida's been crying like this all week—and last week, too," Belinda told the group, putting the little girl in a play-pen that Lashonda kept for the babies, adding her to three other tots already playing with toys. She brushed back her short, black hair, and then rubbed her eyes again, the very picture of weariness and depression. "I just don't know," she said tiredly. "I really don't."

"The ear infections again?" said Lashonda. Rashida had suffered from several infections in the past few months, complete with fever and piercing crying.

"Yeah . . . It's the fourth time. The doctor wants to put tubes in her ears . . . It's gonna cost money . . . and my mom can't take care of her anymore, she's not gonna do day care anymore, she's got a job now managing a dry cleaner's." Belinda blinked hard, and it was obvious she was trying not to cry.

As the women gathered around Belinda, showing their sympathy and support, Diedre thought about how optimistic Belinda had been when they'd first formed the study group in September. She'd been making tapes of all her classes, playing them at night, even reading aloud from her Torts textbook to the baby. But as the weeks passed, it had become obvious that Belinda was falling further and further behind. She was not a fast reader, and it took her many extra hours to do her assignments, some of which she just couldn't complete before class. Then she'd been forced to skip classes to take her baby to the doctor. She'd also over-slept several times, due to the fact that she was trying to get by on four hours of sleep a night.

"I . . . I think I've gotta try a new plan," she was saying now.

"What do you mean?" chorused several of the women, while Diedre's stomach tensed in sympathy.

"I mean this plan I have now isn't workin'," Belinda cried. "I mean I can't keep up. I thought I could, but the reading is killing me . . . I can't read fast enough, and whenever I finish, they pile more shit on me, and I'm getting buried in it.''

"Maybe some of us could give you our notes," said Diedre. "I've got a lot of mine typed up. You can have everything I've got.''

"It won't work," sobbed Belinda, giving in to her emotions. "I'm just not smart enough, not for law school. I thought I was, but I can't do it all . . . Now the baby's s-sick, and my mom won't take care of her . . . and I got all those loans to pay off . . .''

All studying stopped as the women began trying to think of solutions, but finally Belinda waved them off. "Look. I know y'all mean well, but I can't do it. It's too much, that's all. I've gotta take a break . . . I'm moving back to Detroit this weekend. Gonna get a job down at the Ren Cen at the new GM center. My sister knows someone down there in customer service.''

"You mean you're really giving up?" demanded Lashonda.

"Yeah," replied Belinda flatly. And nothing they said could persuade her otherwise. Belinda finally left, promising to call, and the women settled back to their studying, their faces grim. Maybe Belinda had given up, but they hadn't, and they couldn't afford to waste this night. Diedre tried to concentrate, ignoring the sudden, clenching pain in the center of her stomach. Why did it have to turn out this way for Belinda, who'd had just as much courage as the rest of them? Belinda had sacrificed so much for her baby . . . sacrifices none of them had envisioned.

After the women left, Diedre lingered at Lashonda's apartment, talking to her friend while they finished the doughnuts the group had brought and cleaned up the kitchen.

"I feel just awful about Belinda," Diedre said.

Her friend nodded. "I know."

"I wish we could have, you know, convinced her to stay.''

"Honey," said Lashonda sadly. "It isn't over till it's

over. Women like her, with her guts, she'll go far. Maybe
not this year, but someday. I know it. Dammit, I know it!''
she repeated, thumping the kitchen counter for emphasis,
and Diedre began to sense just how deeply Belinda's tragedy had affected Lashonda. Belinda's defection had touched
them all.

They discussed their upcoming exams for a while, and
then Diedre said, ''Lashonda, you know I'm still seeing
Mitch and you know he was the father of my baby, the one
I . . . aborted.'' Even now it was so hard to say the word.
''And now he's talking about marriage.''

''So? Are you gonna do it?''

''I don't know,'' admitted Diedre. ''I want to, but . . .''

''Me? Do you really want to know what I'd do, girl?''

''Yeah.''

''I'd jump back fast. From what you told me about this
guy, he isn't going to take the news very well, so why
should you have to deal with that?''

''But I love him.''

''Sure, but there're plenty of guys out there to love. Hey,
girl, you know this whole fetal thing has gotten way out of
control. I heard of this fathers' rights group, they're looking
for a guy who can go to court and sue his girlfriend because
she had an abortion and didn't give him any rights to the
fetus, didn't let him help decide. They want to make it a
landmark case.''

''No,'' whispered Diedre, appalled.

''Yeah, oh, yeah. Better pray your Mitch boy doesn't hear
about *that*. And sperm donors, they're getting on the band-
wagon, too. A couple of them have sued for paternal rights
to the children they fathered. You really want to open yourself up to that kind of bullshit?''

Feeling sick, Diedre stared at the plastic coffee mug she
held in her hand. Slowly she set it down. Her stomach had
begun to clench in familiar knots. ''But how can I marry
him with this hanging between us? What if I do, and he
somehow finds out?''

''Dump the guy, that's my advice. Then he's gone, and

nobody cares whether or not you had an abortion last summer. Grow up, girl. This Mitch might be a good-looking guy, he might have great prospects, but so what? Hey, the divorce rate sucks. Why marry some dude if you've already got one factor setting you up to fail? Think about it, Diedre.''

Diedre drove home, a headache beginning to throb in her temples. Why did she have to be faced with this issue when she was in law school and supposed to be devoting all of her time to getting through?

Arriving back at the apartment, she found a message from Mitch on the answering tape. ''Meet you outside Torts tomorrow? I love you, Deeds.'' The sound of his sexy chuckle penetrated clearly over the recording. ''Hope your sister isn't listening to this message or I'd say a lot more. Guess I'll just have to tell you in person.''

Diedre began studying, her headache and stomachache continuing to worsen. She didn't want to take Lashonda's advice and break up with Mitch. No way did she want to do that. But if she kept on seeing him, if she married him . . . she wouldn't be able to tell him, would she? She'd have to keep her abortion locked away inside herself forever.

PEPPER

PEPPER'S EX-HUSBAND, JACK, CALLED HER FROM CALIfornia, catching her at the boutique just as she was vacuuming the carpeting, preparing to go home. As always, Oscar had fled into the back room and squeezed himself behind the couch, getting as far away from the noisy roar of the vacuum as he could.

''Hey, beautiful lady, how's the market in nighties? I'm sure you've cornered it by now.''

"Very funny." Pepper hugged the phone to her shoulder while fussing with the cord to her Eureka.

"Seriously, is everything going all right?"

"Everything is great, Jack." She had sent a card to Jack some months ago, telling him he was still fertile, but had received no acknowledgement.

"Well, it's pretty terrific here, too. Our business is going great guns and the clients even paid on time—at least a couple of them did. I've met an heiress . . . cosmetics, my dear. She's got megabucks and she's beautiful, an unbeatable combination."

Pepper found herself stifling just a tiny pang of sadness. "Well, that's very nice for you, Jack."

"Now, what is this, sour grapes from my gorgeous Pepper? Honey, no one is as beautiful as you—that goes without saying. When they made you, they broke the beauty mold. Now can I tell you about my heiress?"

She laughed. "I guess."

"She's forty-eight—well, I didn't say she was a spring chicken, did I? She goes to all of the good parties, and yours truly has accompanied her to a party where Sandra Bullock and Sally Field rubbed shoulders with, let's see, Sly Stallone and, oh, Christ, about ten other celebrities who would knock your slippers off."

"Jack, Jack," she sighed. "Don't tell me you've been sucked up into all that Hollywood fantasyland stuff."

"A bit," he admitted. "Maybe just a skosh. I'm having a little dental work done. You know that dark-looking tooth in the front of my mouth . . . I'm having it capped along with about five or six others. I'm going to have the whitest grin west of the San Gabriel Mountains."

Jack continued to rattle on about his life in L.A., the woman he had met. "I told her the truth about me. I told her I was undependable and that I'd drive her crazy with my whims, that I'm a real screwup about money, but she just tells me how refreshing I am. She loves my honesty. Can you believe it? I guess all it takes is a little California sun to turn a bum and a wastrel into a desirable escort.

"Still dating the rich guy?" Jack asked. "I heard via the grapevine that you've snagged a live one."

"You mean Gray? Yes. But I wish you wouldn't use the word 'snagged.' It makes me feel icky, like I'm some sort of a predator," Pepper blurted.

"Aha." Jack laughed.

"Aha?" She was indignant. "What's that supposed to mean? Jack, I'm not after him for his money, no matter what people may think. I don't care about his money, I really don't."

"I'm sorry, chicken. If a man takes you out to Mc-Donald's on the first date, then you really fall in love with him, but if he dares take you to Lutèce, well, then you find him questionable. And Lord help the man who actually boasts about his income—you'll really set him back on his rear."

She was angry at Jack's accusations, yet they held a horrible sort of truth that even she could recognize. "Am I really a reverse snob?"

"Whoa, are you ever. Hey, if I'd had a fat bank account when we met, you probably would have given me the heave-ho."

"No."

"Oh, yes, my lady."

Pepper laughed uncomfortably.

"Look, seriously," Jack went on. "Don't be so worried about being a trophy wife or whatever. What do you think is going to happen if I get lucky and marry my cosmetics princess? I'm probably going to be her trophy husband. Or some might call me her boy toy, but what do I care? I still have my life, my business, my self-esteem. And my self-esteem is going to be a whole lot higher if someone in the family has a five-million-dollar bank account—and a couple of nice, fat mutual funds."

Pepper felt herself redden. Jack hadn't changed an iota. "Oh, Jack, you're so incorrigible."

"No," he informed her. "I'm just me. I've had enough of being poor, of bouncing stupid two-hundred-dollar checks.

I want to live life with a little style, I want to be on the A-list at parties. Larry Fortensky didn't have it all that bad, I'm coming to see. He should have stuck with La Liz, seen her through her brain surgery. And watched himself on those stairs. What the hell."

The first big snow of December blanketed the ground with a fluffy layer of white, and Pepper's shop began doing its biggest business of the year. She hired a friend of Mandy's as additional help, decorated her windows in luscious holiday lingerie, and put Oscar into his festive red and green Christmas ribbon.

December 12 was Pepper's birthday. She would be thirty-two, and that morning, after her shower, she found herself peering into her bathroom mirror, searching for signs of lines, crow's-feet, and sagging skin. Then she pulled away from the mirror, ashamed because this was what Toni Maddalena had always done on the morning of her birthdays, crying and bemoaning every small sign of aging.

Gray had invited her to stay the weekend at his condo, insisting that "just this once" Jan, Mandy, and Heather could fill in at the shop on Saturday. "If it's not going to put your business in a bind," he was careful to add. "I want to pamper you all weekend."

"We don't have to do anything special," she said.

"Of course it will be special."

"Nothing very expensive, Gray, please promise me."

"All right, if you insist."

First they had dinner at the Italian restaurant next to Pepper's shop. Then they walked around downtown, where the local merchants had turned the rows of trees that had been planted along Main Street into a holiday fairyland of white lights. Falling snow softened the lights, giving them a halo effect, while shop windows, dusted with triangles of snow, resembled Christmas cards.

Pepper found herself oohing and aahing like a child, caught up in the magic. In Florida, when she was a little girl, Christmas lights had been garish, not like this. Amazing

. . . How had Gray known this would please her more than just about anything?

They finally retrieved Gray's car from the structure where he had parked and returned to his condo, making love in front of the flickering fireplace, wrapping themselves in a faded red and brown quilt that had belonged to Gray's grandmother, stitched in the log cabin pattern. Pepper fell asleep in Gray's arms and only half awoke as he carried her to bed around 3:30 A.M.

She must have been extra tired, because she slept deeply, a sleep without dreams. She awoke to the smell of Canadian bacon frying, and the sound of Gray's stereo playing softly, a Wynton Marsalis song. Snow whirled against the windows, enclosing them in their safe world.

"I hope you like eggs Benedict, honey," he said, coming into the bedroom dressed in a pair of knee-length paisley boxer pajamas that showed off his muscular legs, kept trim by exercise equipment he kept in the basement of his condo.

"I love them."

"And fresh strawberries with sinfully rich cream?"

"Yes . . . Gray . . . are you making *breakfast*?"

His smile lit up his whole face. "You thought I couldn't cook?"

"Well, I . . ."

"And now that you're awake, sleepy face, I'm going to bring in your coffee and some freshly squeezed orange juice. No store-bought squeezed, I did it all myself. I have a juicer I've only used about once, and now thanks to you, I'm getting it back into condition again."

"Gray . . . this is fantastic."

"Just lie back and enjoy. I am a good cook," he told her. "I'm even making the eggs Benedict from scratch—none of those canned sauces for me. I hope the lemon does what it's supposed to."

Pepper got up and used the big master bathroom with its whirlpool tub, black marble tile, and skylight which currently was covered with a layer of snow, letting in diffused white light. She found another pair of the paisley pajamas in a drawer, and pulled on the top.

Gray brought breakfast to bed on a black-lacquered tray and they ate leisurely, talking and laughing, while the snow-flakes batted against the windows. "For the most beautiful woman in Ann Arbor," said Gray, feeding her a strawberry, fan-sliced so that it looked like a picture in a book. "When I'm with you, I feel like a million dollars."

She fed him a strawberry in return, slice by slice. "What if I were the ugliest woman in Ann Arbor?"

"You could never be ugly."

She grimaced. "Even with my hair all bed-messy and no makeup?"

"I've never seen you not look beautiful. That's the truth, Pepper."

Thoughtfully Pepper forked up another berry, pondering what he had said. Always it was her looks, she found herself thinking reluctantly. How could she, the person within her, be separated from the outside packaging? She couldn't. So she'd never know, would she, whether Gray loved her for herself or her appearance? At least not until she was very old, and wrinkles took over her face and body.

"Pepper," Gray said, when they'd finished the lavish breakfast. His eyes fastened intently on her. "Did I tell you I'd like to go on eating breakfast in bed with you . . . for the rest of my life?"

She nearly fell back on the king-sized pillows. Panic stabbed her. "It all just seems to be happening so fast," she stammered.

"It is happening fast, I suppose, but I won't push it if you don't want me to," Gray said, although she could tell that his feelings were hurt.

"I'm just going through so many feelings," she excused herself. "And we've really only known each other for a few months. But I do love you. I just need . . . time."

As soon as she said it, Pepper bit her lip. What was wrong with her? Nine million women would all say she was crazy for not leaping immediately upon Gray's declaration, getting him to finalize a commitment. Even Jan had been making noises like that recently, and she didn't have to ask her mother to know what Toni Maddalena would think.

"Time you'll get, then." Gray put the lacquered tray on the floor and reached over for Pepper, enfolding her in his arms and beginning to kiss her passionately. She started to respond to him. Was he the man for her? But how could she possibly know in only a few months? Already he had laid such heavy expectations on her. A child. If she were to marry Gray, she knew she would have to give him a baby.

And she'd be a trophy wife. Oh, no matter what her personal opinions, her protests, there would be no getting around that. Gray just could not separate her from her looks.

Later that day, Gray gave her her birthday present, a beautiful, yellowed, hand-woven lace coverlet that dated from the early 1800's. It was in perfect condition, and he said he had been searching for it for weeks, alerting five antique shop owners to be on the lookout for something of its quality.

Pepper could only touch the intricate lace with her fingertips, astounded. The coverlet was nearly two hundred years old. It was the kind of extraspecial gift she had never expected from Gray.

Monday night. The snow flurries had become a snowstorm, and it was a doozy. Outside on the street, cars spun their wheels on the icy pavement, and a salt truck rumbled by.

Pepper closed up her shop at six o'clock and spent several hours getting some materials together to give to her accountant, while Oscar curled up on the couch beside her, his rough purring keeping her company.

Once a power flicker dimmed the shop lights for a fraction of a second, but then the lights came on, warm and cheerful again. When she had the papers finished, Pepper gathered them together and put them in a folder, then put on her coat and a pair of winter boots she kept on a shelf in the back bathroom, and spoke to Oscar.

"Can you hold the fort here for a half hour or so, Mr.

Oscar Cat? I'm going to stop by the bank, then run over to Zev's for some chili. I promise I'll be right back to take you home. By then the streets should be pretty well salted down. I hope.''

Oscar came strutting up to her, wrapping himself around her legs and meowing insistently. "Hungry?" she said. "Mr. Oscar is hungry? Well, let's see if I have any cat treats. If I'm having chili, the least I can do is leave you some nice fish bits.''

She returned to the back room where she opened a can of Oscar's favorite cat treats, putting it appetizingly in his bowl. He meowed again and began delicately eating, as if this delicacy were only his due.

"Greedy guy," Pepper murmured. "To you I'm just a food carrier, huh? Devoted servant to a fuzz ball.''

Shaking her head and smiling, Pepper cleaned out her cash register except for fifty and put the money and checks into the bank envelope to be dropped into the overnight slot. She exited her shop, walking into a swirl of snowy wind that lifted up the hem of her coat and blew her hair sideways.

The bank was only a block away. Because of the storm, the downtown street was nearly deserted, although she did see a group of young men—students by the look of them—on the next block, running along the sidewalk, whooping and yelling loudly. Then they disappeared into a doorway, probably a bar. Undergrads, she thought ruefully. Too many of them thought college was merely a time to party. End-of-semester grades would soon cure a lot of them of that idea.

Pepper dropped her envelope in the night depository slot, then proceeded two blocks over, where she went into Zev's and got her usual chili, salad, and garlic bread. She lingered over her food, content to sit at a table and look outside at the snowy street, pondering Gray's wonderful birthday gift and his proposal of marriage.

Part of her wanted to . . . but part of her did not.

It was after nine o'clock when Pepper returned to her shop to get Oscar and go home. Immediately she knew that something was wrong. When she'd left, there'd been a security light on in the store, dimly visible through the display windows. Now that light was off. Had another power flicker caused her lights to go out? she wondered as she unlocked the shop door.

Anxiously she stepped inside, reaching for the security pad to disarm it. But it hadn't been armed. Dammit . . . she'd gone back for Oscar's treat and forgotten. She noticed something white and cold on the floor.

Snow tracked in!

She fumbled for a wall switch. Light blazed into the shop, and Pepper stepped back in horror.

The shop was a disaster. The drawer of her cash register had been yanked out. Drawers had been pulled out and thrown in a heap on the floor. Tables were overturned, a glass top smashed and destroyed as if by a hammer. Lingerie had been pulled roughly from drawers, delicate bras ripped in half, slips torn down the middle, strips of silk and lace lying every which way. A vase of Gray's roses was overturned, long-stemmed red blooms scattered all over the carpet.

In fact . . . was that a pile of *human excrement* on the floor? Oh, God! Pepper drew back with an indrawn shriek of anger and revulsion. Who had done this? Vandals! Oh, God . . . how much of her New York stock had they destroyed?

And then, still in shock, she remembered Oscar. There was no sign of the cat. Usually he came prowling out to greet her, his tail waving.

"Oscar! Oskie!" Crying, she raced through the shop, nearly tripping on a flung drawer, dodging around it and plunging into the back room, where she found more chaos, her computer pushed over onto its side, the keyboard smashed on top of it, a smear of feces rubbed into the wall.

"Oscar!" He wasn't on the couch, he wasn't in his cat bed. Pepper could feel her stomach clenching as she pulled out the couch, looking behind it where he sometimes hid. She began searching nooks and crannies, trying to find her

cat. If they'd done anything to him . . . Oh, Jesus, if they had hurt Oscar, she didn't know what she'd ever do. She'd had him since he was a kitten. Jack had given him to her. He'd seen her through a lot of loneliness, she'd poured a lot of emotions into him.

"*Oscar!*" she screamed. She could feel her breath heaving in and out of her throat as she rushed toward the front of the shop again and began looking in the two front display windows, which, by some miracle, had been left untouched, probably because they were visible from the street.

He wasn't there. Only the two silver mannequins, dressed in their elegant holiday slip gowns, white fake-fur boas flung around their shoulders, frozen smiles molded on their faces.

"*Oscar!*"

She ran around the shop like a woman possessed, lifting up fallen drawers, peering in the holes where those drawers had been, shoving aside a pile of camisoles, expecting any second to come upon the broken, white-furred body.

And then she heard a sound, and whirled, trying to figure out where it came from. "Oscar? Oskie? Where are you, boy? Oscar?"

Pepper followed the faint meow to the bathroom. Her heart hammering, she shoved open the door. This room, too, had been demolished, shop supplies dumped all over the floor, packages of paper towels ripped open, air freshener slammed into the sink, which had been partially ripped away from the wall.

Why? Why would anyone do this? What did anyone have against her? How had she hurt anyone?

And then she saw Oscar, his plump body squeezed into the small hole in the wall that contained the water pipes, so that he was actually inside the wall.

"Oscar? Oh, honey. You're all right!" Pepper was unashamedly crying as she reached in and gently took the cat in her hands, pulling him out of the narrow aperture. He was so plump he almost wouldn't come, but she smoothed his fur and coaxed until he was out.

"Oscar . . . oh, Oscar . . ." She swiftly slid her hands over his fur, checking to see if he'd been injured.

Nothing broken . . . no blood . . . only a little dirt and spiderwebs from inside the wall. Thank God. He was all right. Pepper sank to the untidy floor, holding the cat in her arms as her relief gave way to sobs.

A few minutes later, still cradling Oscar, Pepper reached for the phone and dialed Gray's office. He had told her he would be working late tonight.

Animals! she thought.

It was animals who'd broken into her shop, arrogant little human monsters who'd done it only to hurt and destroy. Maybe even those same kids she'd seen running along the street earlier. Her new purchases, what was left of the one-of-a-kind lingerie she'd bought in New York—some of it had been ripped and damaged. She didn't know how much yet. She felt sick with the waste of it. Thank heavens she had good insurance.

A sudden feeling of nausea overcame her and she had to grit her teeth, forcing it back.

"Gray," she choked when he answered the phone.

"Honey? Is everything all right?"

"No, it isn't. Oh, Gray, they broke into my shop!"

"What?"

"It's a wreck. Everything . . ." Her breath was coming fast. "I thought they'd done something to Oscar . . . There's human . . . there's stuff smeared all over the walls."

"I'll be right over," he said quickly.

Within fifteen minutes Gray was at the shop door and Pepper let him in. He entered, stamping snow off his feet.

"Jesus!" he exclaimed, glancing around at the damage.

"I can't believe it," she said brokenly. "Why? Why did they pick me? I just can't believe this. I forgot to arm the security system. *Just this one time.*"

"Who's your insurance agent?"

"Why, it's—" Pepper's mind suddenly went blank. "I have Johnson-Tennyson."

"We'll call them right away—they'll send someone out, hopefully tonight. Meanwhile, what's missing? Did they get the cash register? How much did you have in it? And the stock . . . We've got to start making a list. Oh, and the police. Why don't you call them right now; you'll have to file a police report."

Gray took charge, helping her to deal with the police officer who arrived five minutes later, and the insurance agent who showed up forty minutes after that, assuring Pepper that every effort would be made to have her back in business by Wednesday morning.

"We'll have a plumber in here to fix the bathroom sink, and you'll need a drywall man," said the female adjuster, making notes on a pad of paper. "You'll have records showing the price you paid for the stock you lost, correct?"

"Yes. I want the walls washed, then I want them painted," Pepper insisted. "And the carpeting cleaned . . ." She shuddered.

Pepper still felt dazed, as if she'd been physically attacked. Forcing herself to pick up a pile of panties and inspect them for damage, she gritted her teeth and squeezed the tears back.

"Honey, it's all right," Gray said, pulling her close. "No major structural damage was done, and insurance will take care of the clothes and things they damaged. Fortunately you only had fifty dollars in the cash register."

"Yes . . ." She was still shaking. "Gray, this feels like such a violation."

"Yes, well, you're okay. They only violated things, Pepper, they didn't violate you."

Finally, when all of the damage was noted and assessed, the insurance agent left, and Gray helped Pepper to put Oscar back into his carry-cage, which they'd found stuffed beneath an overturned display rack. He drove her back to her apartment through slippery streets.

"I might not be able to open on Wednesday," Pepper worried. "It might be more like the end of the week, or even Saturday. I'll lose three or four good shopping days."

"Your customers will understand. Pep, I know this has been a terrible shock to you, but you don't have to worry about running out of money. I'll give you an interest-free loan for as much as you need. So you can go back to New York and replace whatever you need."

She felt too drained to argue. "Thanks, but I'm okay for now."

"And you've got to think about moving your location," he continued as he pulled his Infiniti into the snow-covered parking lot in front of Mrs. Melnick's Victorian apartment building.

"What?"

"That downtown location lacks for safety measures. It's not very secure, being on the street like that, especially with kids roaming around and being so close to the campus. Oh, you have the security system and that's fine, but a mall location would be much safer, both for you and for your merchandise. There would even be security guards when you worked late. I worry about you alone there at night, Pepper."

Pepper thought of the evenings she'd spent working in the boutique alone, the way her heart pounded when someone knocked on the door after hours. She remembered the crowds of drunken students who thronged the streets after a home football game, especially when it had been a close one.

"I don't want to move to the mall." Her voice rose. "It would turn Pepper's into just another glitzy mall store . . . just a run-of-the-mill shop—it would take away all of the specialness."

"Why can't it be just as special in a mall?"

"Because it couldn't, that's all. I won't even consider it," she said sharply.

"You're overwrought, this has been a terrible night for you. We can talk about it tomorrow, sweetheart," said Gray, coming around to the passenger side to let Pepper out of the car.

"No, we won't," she snapped, her anger rising at the way

he was patronizing her. "Gray, you're wonderful and I really appreciate your coming to my rescue like this, but it's my shop. I had the idea, I took the financial risk, I run it, I make the decisions. And I am not moving to any damn sterilized mall location, thank you very much."

She reached into the backseat and grabbed Oscar's carry-cage, lifting it out of the car. The animal meowed indignantly when he felt the cold. Why did men always have to act like this? Pepper thought. She hadn't asked for advice, she'd just wanted a shoulder to cry on, someone to listen!

"I'm sorry," Gray said as he walked her up to the front porch where an inch or so of white snow was balanced on the railings and gingerbreading. "I guess that wasn't what you wanted to hear, was it? Me taking over like some arrogant Donald Trump."

From somewhere, Pepper summoned the energy to smile. "I guess you *were* being a little Donald Trumpish at that."

He walked her upstairs, stayed for about ten minutes, helping her to make sure that all of the doors and windows of the apartment were locked and bolted shut. Oscar followed Pepper everywhere, staying within inches of her feet so that she nearly tripped over him. Then he spotted one of his cat toys and pounced on it like a miniature tiger.

"No one is going to come here," Pepper protested. "Not with this attack cat on duty."

"Wish he'd functioned as an attack cat a little earlier tonight. Do you want me to stay the night?"

"No," she admitted. "I really don't. I just want to make myself some hot chocolate and stand under a hot shower. I feel as if I have to scrub myself clean . . . ugh. Those people dirtied a lot more than just some carpeting. They dirtied me."

Gray smiled. "Hot chocolate, the very best medicine for disaster. Ah, God, Pepper, I want to be your medicine for disaster, too."

"You are," she said dutifully. "You certainly have been tonight."

He kissed her good night, long and passionately. After he

had left, Pepper rebolted the door, then wandered to the kitchen to find the ingredients for hot cocoa. But when she had assembled them, the sharp chocolate smells of the cocoa powder seemed to upset her stomach, making her feel slightly queasy, so she put the box back on the shelf.

The stress of being robbed and invaded had certainly affected her entire body, she thought.

Exhausted, she sank down at the dinette table, a mood of gloom sweeping over her.

Gray. So easy for him to offer a loan, she found herself thinking. He had millions at his disposal. Then her thoughts scattered in confusion. He'd meant well . . . he was trying to help her. This was the only way he knew to do it, and yet she was so ungrateful, always thinking there was an ulterior motive.

She didn't know anymore. She didn't know what to do about Gray Ortini and his persistent demands for her to be a part of his life.

TREVA

SOMEONE'S TV SET, TURNED ON LOUDLY IN THE NEXT room, was playing Christmas carols from a holiday special with country singers. Treva had fallen asleep to the pleasant sounds and they had followed her into her dreams, so that she was reliving Christmas back when she was a child in Detroit. An orange, some Hershey's kisses, and sticks of licorice in her stocking, and she and her sister got a blue bicycle. It was not new and they had to share it, but it was the best gift ever . . .

"Treva, baby?" said Rhonda, walking into the hospital room as Treva lay napping in the dark. "It's me, Rhonda."

"Hi." Treva stirred, opening her eyes. For a moment she was still seven, still in Christmas in the mid-1970's. But then she heard the sound of the hospital PA system, voices in the hallway and the rattle of a cart being pushed past her door, and became reoriented.

"You okay, honey? This is a real bitch, having you in the hospital like this. I don't know how you stand having some nurse sashaying in here about every half hour." Ronda picked up the plastic container that was supposed to hold ice water. "And your ice has melted again. Dammit, the least they can do is give you ice for your water, baby."

"They're busy people. I'm surviving it. I'm gonna have this baby, Rhonda. I don't care if I have to do the Macarena on the roof of the hospital, or bungee-jump into the middle of the U. of M. stadium." Treva rubbed her stomach, under the layers of hospital sheets and thin covers. "This little guy's gonna be *born*."

"That's the spirit, honey. But hey, it'd be great to see you doing the Macarena on the hospital roof. I bet we could get ourselves an audience."

Rhonda pulled up a chair, looking around the room with eagle eyes to see if there was anything else she could do, or complain about when she went back by the nurses' station again. It was Rhonda who'd battled with the TV rental company when Treva's bedside television had been turned off for no apparent reason, and Rhonda who'd made sure Treva had enough extra blankets when she got the shivers.

"I brought you the latest issue of *Essence*. Anything else you need?" her sister said.

"Just chocolate," Treva laughed. "And I can't have it. Oh, let's see . . . maybe a *TV Guide*. They give us TV here, but there's never a guide and I hate just clicking when I don't know what the programs are. Oh, and could you smuggle me in some Snapple? That's another thing they don't have. I'm so tired of apple juice and orange juice that I could spit." Was she sounding too testy and irritable?

"You want it, you got it. I'll even bring a small cooler for you, honey lamb. So you never have to worry about getting a cold one."

They talked for a while about Treva's health, Treva trying

to put as good a face on her condition as possible. She was now twenty-five weeks along, and her baby weighed about 1.5 pounds, according to Dr. Sandoval. It actually had a chance of surviving if it were born now, but the chance was only about 43 percent, and in this weight range, most of the babies who did survive were handicapped.

"If you get bored, remember, just call me," said Rhonda, patting Treva's smooth, brown hand as she got up to leave. "Any time, girl. Even if I'm at work, I'll slip out for a quick phone call. I'll raise hell around here any old time."

"Oh, honey . . ."

"I love you, Trev," said Rhonda, leaning over the bed and giving her sister an awkward caress.

"And I love you, Rhonnie."

"Don't you get crazy on me. Don't you do anything really stupid," said Rhonda in a low voice, and Treva nodded, her eyes moistening. They both knew exactly what she meant.

Another hospital morning, identical to all of the others. Treva had applied makeup from the little tray in her bedside stand, adding bronzy lipstick and blush, just to make herself feel better. Yesterday Wade had even sent in a hairdresser to do her hair, in order to keep her spirits up.

"And how are we doing this morning?" A nurse, Patrice Daly, bustled into Treva's room, bearing a tray on which a little paper medicine cup had been arranged. The slim, twenty-six-year-old nurse had a husband who was serving on a nuclear submarine, as Treva had learned during her three weeks here. She knew all the regular nurses by name and even many of the housekeeping staff, who loved to talk to her about their problems.

"Just fine," Treva said. "More than fine. This little fellow is so active I think he's tap-dancing in there."

"Great. We love to hear that he's tap-dancing. And how about you, Treva?"

"Oh, just fine. A few hot flashes. Feels like I've been

dipped in Tex-Mex barbecue sauce and they're getting ready to grill me.''

Patrice laughed. ''Hey, those are just side effects, they'll disappear after you stop taking the Apresoline.''

''I hope before I burn myself up to a crisp.''

Obediently Treva swallowed the pill, thinking that she was getting tired of side effects—feeling flushed and hot, having a stuffy nose, headaches, dizziness, and jittery feelings. When she didn't have the symptoms, she *imagined* she was having them. She was turning into a total hypochondriac!

The truth was, despite her jokes and quips, and all her visitors, and Wade's tender care, she was having a struggle keeping her spirits up. Each medical test became stressful. Was the baby having problems? Was she? But Treva was determined not to force her blood pressure up by imagining symptoms. Fear was her worst enemy. So she played relaxation tapes, she read calming books, she laughed a lot, and she clung to her visits from friends and family.

Wade often came at noon to sit while Treva ate her lunch, and talk to her about his day, or some problem with his students. When no one was in the room, they'd kiss and cuddle a little. After hugging Wade, Treva always felt calmed and more peaceful.

However, she had been forced to drop her interviews for the abortion study for now. Making the calls was too difficult in the hospital setting, and Dr. Sandoval had worried the stress might be too much. Treva was still in contact with two of the women, though, Diedre Samms and Pepper Nolan. Somehow they'd become friends.

Now the nurse bent over to empty the bottle of urine that was draining from Treva's indwelling catheter, another discomfort she was forced to tolerate.

''We've got you scheduled for another ultrasound this morning, honey.''

''This kid is going to appear on more TV screens than Oprah,'' joked Treva.

She chatted for a few minutes with Patrice, then the nurse asked, "Any headache today?"

"Not really," responded Treva, although her temples were throbbing slightly, but that often happened. Her medications caused side effects, and she tried to tolerate them without complaining.

"Any changes in your vision?"

"No."

Patrice went through the usual list of questions that were asked every day, then helped Treva to briefly stand on a doctor's scale that she brought into the room.

"Well, am I chubbier?" she had to ask.

"You're a pound up."

Treva nodded and sank back onto the bed, already feeling tired again. This pregnancy was a colossal project, like signing herself to live inside an iron lung for months at a time.

"Hey," said Patrice, smiling. "And now the good news. I've got a big florist's bouquet that was just delivered out at the nurses' station and it has your name on it. I'll have someone bring them in."

Treva brightened. Maybe Wade had sent her flowers today. His were always special, with little presents attached to them . . . a new tube of lipstick, a gold chain, a paperback she hadn't read.

This morning it was mixed daisies and carnations, and a book on tape, a Faye Kellerman novel.

"That man—I think he spends half his waking hours trying to figure out what present to put in my flowers."

"You're so lucky," said Patrice, smiling. "In fact, if Wade didn't wear a wedding ring, and if I didn't wear one, too—well, I'd probably chase after him."

"Don't you *dare*," laughed Treva.

That night after Treva's early tray dinner, her friends began crowding into her room, lugging gifts. Annie, Rhonda, Mei, Dr. Rosenkrantz, some of the off-duty nurses, even Dr. Sandoval, who said she had to keep an eye on Treva. It was far more than the maximum number of visitors she was al-

lowed, but all the nurses made special concessions for
Treva.

"What?" said Treva, shifting position slightly in her bed.
"What's going on?"

"What do you think?" cried Annie Larocca. "It's a baby
shower!"

"Here? Now?"

A few more arrived, clinic staffers, Wade's secretary, and
his sister, Dinah, until women were standing against the
walls three deep and a pile of presents filled the center of
the floor.

"Oh, my," said Treva, surprised and laughing. "Oh,
my."

"You can thank your stepdaughter for this," said Rhonda
with a grin. "She somehow convinced the nurses to let us
all in, and she organized the whole thing."

"Well, you didn't have anything for the baby," cried
Shanae, rushing in with a blue-wrapped box. The teenager's
face seemed flushed, her eyes glittering almost too brightly.
"This baby needs *stuff*. Pacifiers, Pampers, one of those
pretty mobiles to hang over the crib—all sorts of things."

Treva laughed. "That box you're carrying is big enough
to have a crib in it."

"A crib? Whoa! But maybe there's a surprise or two. Oh,
Treva, isn't this going to be fun? I baked two cakes, and
some cookies, and they're sending up fruit punch from the
hospital cafeteria."

Shanae seemed so proud of herself that Treva laughed
again, leaning back on her pillows and beginning to relax.
She and Wade hadn't bought anything for the baby yet. And
now it just felt wonderful to be surrounded by her friends.

They laughed and gossiped, and Ellen Rosenkrantz told
some outrageous stories of when she'd been a female resident at Florence Crittenton Hospital in a world of male doctors. Treva had everyone in convulsions as she told about
being given a bath when a handsome male visitor blundered
into her room looking for his mother. "He just stopped and
stared at my enormous, bare stomach and then he blurted

out, 'Well, I guess they don't make hospital gowns like they used to,' and practically ran out of the room.''

Everyone roared.

"Presents!" cried Shanae. "You've got to open your presents!"

Shanae stood by the bed and helped Treva tear off the paper and lift the box covers. Treva exclaimed as she lifted out newborn-sized gowns, a tiny pair of OshKosh B' Gosh bibbed blue jeans, a Detroit Tigers T-shirt, crib pads and bumpers, a set of plastic baby bottles with little blue teddy bears printed on them. These were from Shanae.

"Do you love the bottles?" her stepdaughter asked eagerly.

"I adore them."

"I want to give him his bottle—lots of times."

"You will," said Treva, holding back tears of happiness. All of these gifts made her feel as if her baby was going to be a reality, as if the suffering she was undergoing now could pass in the wink of an eye, leaving her a normal mother holding a normal child in her arms.

The party ended a few minutes later, though, with Dr. Sandoval starting to shoo them all out, saying that Treva was tired. Annie and Rhonda volunteered to take the gifts to Treva's house.

"What a party," breathed Treva, not wanting to admit she was tired, just a little. "I can't believe this. It was just a total, total surprise."

"We all love you, dear," said Annie.

The women gathered around the bed and joined hands, including Treva as they formed a circle. Rhonda led the women in prayer. "Dear Jesus, please bless this woman and this child, and shed Your precious light on them, Your mercy and goodness, and keep them safe from harm."

As the prayer continued, Treva could actually feel the energy surrounding her, the hope and prayers of her friends becoming something physical, as real as the nosegay of ribbons Rhonda had made, or the paper plates covered with cake crumbs. Even the child within her seemed to thrust and kick more vigorously.

Then Treva glanced to her left and saw that tears were rolling down Shanae's cheeks.

After the rest of the women had left, Shanae lingered, waiting for Wade, who was supposed to pick her up.

"Anything wrong, cupcake?" asked Treva.

The teenager suddenly looked pensive. "That was so fun. I just wish . . . I hope . . ." The girl bit her lip, all of her happy mood suddenly gone.

"Shanae, honey?"

"I'm okay," said the fifteen-year-old quickly. "Aren't you afraid? About the baby, I mean."

"Of course I'm afraid. But I've decided to 'let go and let God,' " said Treva slowly. "You know we have to trust in Jesus and He'll take care of us."

"Yeah, I know. I hope," said Shanae. She picked up the ribbon nosegay that Rhonda had made by threading ribbons through a hole in the center of a paper plate, and began twirling it so that the hanging ends of the ribbons fluttered. Treva felt a twinge of alarm. The teenager's mood at the shower had been too revved up, too hectic.

"Is something wrong, Shanae?" she repeated.

"I don't want to worry you, not now."

"I can take a little extra worry, no problem," said Treva.

There was a long silence while Shanae sat fussing with the nosegay. "I . . . I can't tell my mom," she whispered. "And Daddy . . . he'd kill me."

"What is it, Shanae?"

"I . . . I didn't get my period when I was supposed to."

"What?" For an instant, Treva just lay there blankly, hearing but not hearing.

"I said my period. It's four days late, maybe five. I should have had it by now." Miserably Shanae played with the ribbons, tears starting to roll down her cheeks again.

"Honey?"

"It's Eric, Eric from the band. I've been, you know,

having sex with him. Please," begged Shanae. "*Please* don't tell Daddy. Eric is a nice guy. Really. I—we—we used condoms and all of that. It was supposed to be safe."

Shanae began to weep, her back shaking.

Treva caught her breath, and then she took Shanae's hand, clasping it between both of her own. "Baby, oh, honey, you might be crying all for nothing. Periods aren't always regular, especially when you're still only fifteen. It takes a few years to get on a regular schedule."

"But we did it!" wept Shanae. "I could be pregnant! I even feel as if my stomach is bloating out—I'm bigger already!"

Treva couldn't help suppressing a smile. "Darling, even if you were pregnant, you wouldn't show a thing yet. Look. If you are really worried about this, why don't you go out and get a pregnancy test kit? Bring it back here tomorrow and I'll be with you when you take it."

"Would you? Oh, would you?" Shanae threw herself into Treva's arms.

"I'll be happy to be with you, Shanae. Now, why don't you take one of those tissues and blow your nose and wipe your eyes. And you might go to the vending machine in the lounge and see if you can find us a couple of Diet Pepsis."

Shanae jumped off the bed. "I've got change—I think."

"If you don't, Wade left me some. Scoot now, Shanae. And when you come back, we can have a nice woman-to-woman talk."

Shanae was back in five minutes with the cans of soda.

"Eric says he hates rubbers," Shanae said, sipping her Pepsi.

"All men hate them; it's like having a sheet of plastic between them and their sensations," said Treva. "But that doesn't mean you shouldn't use them, especially when the alternative could be death."

"Death?" Shanae looked uncomfortable. "Oh, you mean AIDS. But Eric isn't—I mean he's safe. I was the first girl he ever, you know, did it with. And I was a virgin, too."

Treva couldn't help feeling a twinge of doubt about Eric

being a virgin, too; after all, he was twenty, and much more likely to be experienced. Still, he'd worn a condom, hopefully put on properly. At least Shanae probably hadn't been exposed to HIV. But pregnancy? Over the past five years, Treva had seen so many young girls just like Shanae at the clinic. *Oh, please, God, don't let Shanae be one of them.*

"Are you mad at me, Treva?" her stepdaughter was saying in a small voice.

"Mad at you, Shanae? Never."

"But I—we did it four times. I was so dumb."

"No, you weren't dumb. You were just having a big surge of hormones. But at the same time, you aren't ready to have a baby, and neither is he."

"No way," said Shanae, shivering.

"Once you're having sex, Shanae, you probably won't stop. Life just doesn't work that way, I'm afraid. So you need to take precautions so that you won't have a baby until you're ready to raise one."

"Will I have to have an abortion?"

"Let's just take it one step at a time," said Treva.

Shanae moistened her lips. "I'm scared."

"So am I," admitted Treva. "But we'll get through this. Your dad and I will always love you, regardless of whether or not you are pregnant or decide to have an abortion—or aren't pregnant at all."

After Shanae and Wade finally left, Treva sank back onto the bed, her heartbeat pounding. Despite her calmness in front of her stepdaughter, she was still worried. Abortions were so tough for teenagers, many of whom had never even had a gynecological exam before.

She didn't want that traumatic experience for Shanae. Shanae was too bright and sweet and fresh and loving. Although most women recuperated well emotionally from their abortions, Shanae didn't need the lingering guilt, the years-later wondering: *Was it a boy? A girl? What would it have grown up to be?*

Patrice padded in on ripple-soled shoes to take Treva's blood pressure.

"That was quite a party, huh?"

"Yeah . . ."

"Anything wrong?"

"Nothing that a little attention from God wouldn't fix," said Treva. "How's my BP?"

"Up a little. No more parties, Treva, it does affect you."

Treva smiled, eyeing Patrice slyly. "I saved you some cake. Would that change your attitude?"

"Maybe. It just might."

They sat together while Patrice nibbled at a small piece of chocolate cake. "You say your stepdaughter made this? From scratch? She is one hellacious cook."

"And a lot of other things," sighed Treva. "Oh, Patrice. Thank God we're not fifteen anymore. I don't think I'd go back and be that age for anything. Not even for a brand-new body."

"I know what you mean. Oh, *do* I know what you mean."

The next afternoon, Shanae slipped into Treva's room as she was watching "Days of Our Lives," a little habit she'd acquired during her bed rest. Now she was semiaddicted to the program and followed all of the story lines.

Shanae told Treva that Eric had driven her to the hospital and was waiting out in the lounge for her—she'd ducked out of school a little early. She brandished a plastic drug-store shopping bag. "I have it in here. You know . . . the test."

"Does he know?"

Shanae looked uncomfortable. "I didn't tell him. He thinks it's, you know, toothpaste or something. If I have to have something done . . . I don't know . . . I guess I'll have to tell him then."

Treva spoke cheerfully. "Hopefully you won't have to say a word and this will just be an interesting experience that you and I are having today. Would you like to open the kit and read the directions?''

Nervously Shanae looked around. Several aides were walking down the hallway, chattering about something. ''Can I close the door?'' she whispered.

''Of course.''

When the door was shut, Shanae reluctantly came back to the bed and pulled the test kit box out of its sack. Then she just sat and looked at it.

''It's your body and your test kit, Shanae,'' said Treva gently.

Shanae tore away the cardboard flap and lifted out a plastic piece, a small plastic dipstick, and a printed set of directions. ''It's in about four languages,'' she said in wonderment. ''Look, Treva. Spanish and French and I think maybe German. Oh, here's the English one.''

Carefully she read it, while Treva waited. ''If it turns pink . . .'' The teenager lifted her head. ''It means . . . Oh, Treva . . . I'm so scared . . .''

''I'm with you, Shanae. You don't have to be scared. You can do the procedure in the bathroom and wait there for your results by yourself, or you can bring the test kit in here and we'll wait together.''

''Together,'' decided Shanae, swallowing.

She walked into the bathroom, closing the door behind her, and Treva waited tensely on the bed. A minute passed, then two, then three. What was the girl doing in there? Rereading the instructions, Treva thought. Trying to overcome her nerves and panic. Well, this was something she would have to get through. Being sexually active meant responsibilities, and now Shanae was facing them.

''I . . . I did it, I dipped that stick thing in my pee,'' said Shanae, emerging from the bathroom. ''Oh, Treva. There's going to be results in four minutes, it said. *Four minutes* and I'll know. I'm gonna die!''

''I'm here. Sit down on the bed. I have a watch, we can look at that.''

Shanae was close to tears. ''I could have a little baby

inside me right now. No bigger than a pin. I don't even know if I want it. I don't know if I could be a mother. How would I finish high school? And I'd never be able to be a singer.''

Treva took the girl's clammy, cold hand in her own. ''This is a terrible way to grow up, isn't it?''

''Yeah.'' Shanae swallowed loudly. ''Yeah, it is.''

Time seemed to inch by, and Treva began talking lightly about today's plotline for the soap, anything to keep the girl's mind off the ticking of the clock.

''It *has* to be time now!'' cried Shanae, jumping up. She ran in the bathroom and returned with the plastic indicator piece, her eyes wide.

''It's—it's blue, not pink! Treva! Oh, I'm not pregnant! I'm not! Treva!''

''Congratulations,'' said Treva warmly.

''Oh, God. I *thought* I was pregnant. I could feel it, my stomach, it just felt so fat, and I knew . . . I knew it had to be true. I'm only fifteen,'' said Shanae. ''I can't have a baby right now . . . How could I? What would I ever do?''

''Nothing,'' said Treva, allowing relief to sweep over her as sweet as spring rain. ''You don't have to do anything, darling. You're all right this time.''

''Will you tell my dad?'' whispered Shanae.

''I don't know. Should I? Shanae, if you are going to keep on seeing Eric, you have to have some reliable method of birth control. You can go to the Geddes/Washtenaw Clinic and see Dr. Rosenkrantz, or you can call Planned Parenthood, they'll give you a prescription, but you have to do something, dear.''

Shanae nodded, resigned. ''I didn't think,'' she said quietly. ''I mean, all of the things there are to think about. I just did it. And now I have to pay the consequences, don't I? Or I'll get pregnant. Not now, not this month, or this year, but sometime.''

''Yes.'' Treva said it sadly, but she was also proud. Shanae *was* growing up, taking this experience to heart. Oh, she loved her stepdaughter so much, never more than today.

DIEDRE

EXAM WEEK. THE FEAR HAD BEEN BUILDING ALL SEMESter, and now it emerged for the first-year law students in nervous mannerisms, stomach problems, sleeplessness, anxiety attacks, and hives.

After class the students milled around in the hall, trading horror stories of previous exams. It was whispered that yesterday a guy from Florida had already dropped out of law school rather than face the rigors of an exam for which he was not prepared.

"*I'm* going to drink gallons of coffee," declared Lashonda during one of the group's late-night study sessions at her apartment. "I'm just going to keep on drinking it until I either pee myself to death, die of caffeine overload, or ace my finals. Preferably the latter."

Already the study group was even smaller, missing another member. Mariel, mother of one of the toddlers, had dropped out, deciding to return to work as a paralegal. The doctor had diagnosed her with a stomach ulcer, and Mariel had said a tearful good-bye the previous week, promising to come back and visit, although they all knew she never would.

Diedre shivered. "I'm praying for A's. Everything depends on me getting them, or at least mostly A's."

"Just push that out of your mind," advised Lashonda, and some of the other women murmured agreement. "You're pressuring yourself too much."

"But I have to pressure myself. If I fail even one course, my scholarship is gone."

The women looked at each other, their eyes showing the same fear that Diedre felt. Mariel's leaving had shaken them badly.

"Look, you've gotta break up your life into tiny pieces right now," said Lashonda. "Make a list of the things you've gotta study. Then just start doing them, girl, one at a time. Don't think about *any* consequences or it'll screw you up good. Oh, yeah, and don't pull any all-nighters. They'll screw you worse than anything. That was Mariel's worst habit. Then her ass'd be dragging in the morning and she'd go into a panic."

Diedre's mother called the next morning while Diedre was in the shower. Pam had stayed overnight in Bud's apartment off Eisenhower Parkway, so Diedre ran naked and dripping to the phone extension in her room.

"I only have a minute, I have to go to work," said Cynthia. "I just wanted to see how you're doing. Have exams started yet?"

"Not for two more days." Diedre shivered, wishing she'd had the sense to grab a towel.

"DeeDee . . . I know you're going to do great."

"I hope so," sighed Diedre. "People are getting crazed around here, though. Two women in my study group already quit, and I've heard of other people who've quit, too. The pressure is just so intense. None of us have had any real feedback yet as to how we're doing. So we don't know whether we're going to ace our finals or fail them."

"Diedre, you've got so many brains and so much drive," said her mother. "I'm sure you're not going to let a few exams stop you. Anyway, I mailed a gift to you. You should be getting it today."

"A gift?"

"A little care package. Some of my chocolate chip peanut butter cookies."

"Oh, Mom. My favorites." Diedre felt absurdly touched. Cynthia worked so hard at her job, often putting in overtime on Saturdays, and was usually too tired to fuss much in the kitchen.

"Honey, if I could drive over to Ann Arbor and study for you, I would. But I know you're going to do great. Look at the way you aced your college courses. Even with your job you still did better than nearly all of them.''

They talked for a few minutes longer, Cynthia continuing to sound optimistic about Diedre's abilities, and then Cynthia said she had to leave for work, so they hung up. Diedre went back in the bathroom and finished her shower, her skin hot with a flare of sudden nerves. Cynthia Samms had sacrificed a lot to raise her two girls. Her belief in Diedre was so naively wholehearted. What if she disappointed her mother?

Well, she just couldn't.

Her first exam, Torts, was the following day. A tough class, taught by a tough professor who demanded a lot from his students—and usually got it.

Diedre had gone over and over the material, rereading her notes a dozen times, trying to soak up the principles behind every case, from the one in which six workmen had been killed in a gas explosion to the one in which a woman using an outhouse at a county fair had fallen through the rickety seat and plunged into the human waste beneath. The class had giggled a lot when they were discussing that one, but now Diedre forgot about the humor and just tried to absorb every pronouncement of the judge into her brain.

Mitch and Diedre went to the law library, where they planned to study until the reading room closed at 2:00 A.M.

''Look,'' she said to Mitch as they walked up to the library, seeing the stained-glass windows aglow with orange light as if this were a medieval cathedral. ''Look . . . It's . . .'' She couldn't describe how she felt.

''Awe-inspiring, isn't it?'' he said.

''Yeah—it chokes my throat up,'' Diedre admitted. ''I want to stay here, Mitch. So badly. It'll just kill me if I fail the semester—or even one course.''

''You won't fail,'' he assured her.

''I'd better not!''

Bent over her books, with Mitch seated only inches away from her, Diedre concentrated so hard that she found herself lost in a world of plaintiffs, defendants, judges' decisions, and legal memoranda until they took on more reality for her than the room she was in. Suddenly she began to feel exhilarated. Things were coming together . . . she was beginning to make connections she had not made before.

She was amazed when 2:00 A.M. arrived and people started gathering up their books to leave.

"I was totally in another world," she told Mitch.

"I wish I could have been. I was in the world of wondering where to get my résumé typed up and whether I'd like being a management trainee somewhere." He laughed, but she could hear the tension in his voice. Mitch was an above-average student, but not stellar.

"Oh, Mitch," she said contritely. "I'll help you study for Con Law tomorrow—we can go over my notes together. You're a good student, you just have exam fever, that's all."

"No, I have Diedre fever," he murmured, sliding his arm around her and kissing her with puffs of warm breath on the back of her neck. "Good luck tomorrow, honey. I'll be thinking about you—and if you need some notes written on your hand, well, I can write awfully small."

They both laughed, and Mitch drove her back to the apartment. Pam had left her a note on the kitchen counter, along with a giant-sized Hershey's Cookies 'N' Creme candy bar. *Chocolate for you. Burn midnight oil. Kick some butt. Love ya, Pam.*

Diedre smiled, went into her bedroom, switched on the light, and peeled off the wrapper from the candy bar. Munching on segments of chocolate, she cracked open her textbooks again. Her eyes felt red, swollen and sore, but she forced herself to study until 4:30 A.M., almost but not quite an all-nighter. She had to! If she failed, there were too many people she would disappoint.

Diedre finally fell asleep about 5:00 A.M., so exhausted that her eyes had stopped processing the print in her textbooks. Thank God her exam wasn't until one-thirty. She tossed and turned, briefly woke when Pam left for work, and then again around seven forty-five when some jerk in the parking lot kept beeping his car horn to pick up a car-pool rider.

Finally at noon she struggled out of bed. She took a fast shower, then breakfasted on the remainder of the Cookies 'N' Creme candy bar, along with an eight-ounce glass of Five Alive juice.

At twelve-thirty she threw on a favorite pair of worn, jeans, a U. of M. sweatshirt, and her "lucky" garnet earrings. Pam arrived home at twelve thirty-five, during her lunch hour, to drive Diedre back to campus. As they pulled into the staff parking lot Pam used, her sister said, "Are you nervous?"

"Horribly," muttered Diedre.

"But I thought you studied."

"I did. But it's all swimming in my mind like some horrible kind of alphabet soup."

The first thing Diedre had to do when she reached the law quad was find the women's room and pee. She'd urinated before leaving the apartment, of course, but as soon as she'd gotten in the car she'd had to go again. In the bathroom mirror she stared at her pale face, licking her lips nervously. She touched the garnet earrings again, trying to draw their good luck into her fingertips.

The room in Hutchins Hall was filled with about eighty-five students who all looked as anxious and strung out as Diedre felt, with the exception of a guy named David Weinstock, who had worked in his father's law office for three years and played the role of class "expert" all semester. Diedre knew several people were hoping that David would get cut down a peg or two, but she wasn't counting on it.

The air seemed to crackle with nervous tension.

They were permitted to bring electric typewriters, if the machines did not possess any electronic memory, but Diedre didn't own one, so she had brought three blue books, leaflets of lined paper with a blue cover, and would write everything out by hand. To assure anonymous grading, she was given a ticket with a student exam number.

As she waited for Professor Cury to arrive, her hands were so cold from nerves that she could barely hold her Bic. The pen's plastic felt sticky from her clammy sweat. The breakfast she'd eaten of candy and orange juice now burned in her stomach. And she had to pee again. God . . . but she couldn't get up and run to the bathroom now. They might lock the doors.

Then Professor Cury walked into the room, his heels making sharp noises on the floor. Wearing wrinkled khaki pants and a baggy, heather-colored sport jacket, he looked cheerful and efficient. In his hand he carried an expandable file folder.

He began passing out exam sheets, while giving out instructions.

"Don't just scribble some memorized crap, take the time to think, to draw conclusions, to compare and contrast . . . Remember, you're not simply regurgitating what you've learned, you're *solving problems*. That's what we're assessing here today, your problem-solving ability."

Diedre's heart contracted. Right now all she could think of was her pinching bladder. Desperately she recrossed her legs and hoped the sensation would go away.

When the question sheet was passed to her, Diedre stared at hers in panic.

There was only one question and it took up a whole page.

Printed single-spaced, it cited several cases and quoted from several judges' decisions. Diedre's eyes fastened in panic on the closely spaced typing, but her eyes refused to read the words.

They made absolutely no sense.

Oh, God. All her concentrated studying last night— zapped into outer space! Her brain had locked down. She couldn't remember one case she'd read, one decision. All those brilliant answers she'd given in class . . . forgotten. It was as if she hadn't gone to law school at all, as if she were coming to this test off the street, absolutely ignorant.

She struggled not to cry. All around her she could hear rustling as people opened their blue books, beginning to write. A few students were tapping on typewriter keys. Those people were going to end up lawyers, while she . . . And her mother, Cynthia, who had such total faith in Diedre . . .

What would her mother say when Diedre called to tell her she'd failed her exam?

For a wild, panicky moment Diedre thought of lunging up out of her seat and running from the room, but she gasped in a few deep breaths and forced herself to remain where she was. Even if she didn't know the answer, she refused to humiliate herself by running away like a baby. Oh, Christ. She was going to fail the exam.

Nervously she glanced down at the exam sheet again, and this time a few of the words caught her eye. Diedre blinked; some of them actually made sense. She reread the question, and gradually her heartbeat slowed down to normal.

Suddenly Diedre felt as if Lashonda, her study-group friend, were standing over her, smiling crookedly. *Hey, girl, what did I tell you? Do it one little bit at a time. It's just an exam.*

Diedre shook her head, then stared again at the exam sheet. She read it for the third time, and this time she could see the logical sections of the question.

Yeah, girl . . . you're getting it. Now just start writing.

Diedre sucked in a deep breath and began to write.

As soon as she'd finished, Diedre handed in her three filled blue books and left, heading straight for the ladies' room, where she sat on the john and peed, seemingly for minutes. She felt physically drained, shaken, and exhilarated, all at the same time.

Afterward she went downstairs to the lounge, where crowds of students, some glum, others euphoric, were drinking sodas and rehashing their exams. Diedre did not see Mitch, who was still in his Civil Procedure exam.

"How'd you do, Deeds?" asked Lashonda, nursing a Mountain Dew, which many of the students swore gave them extra energy.

"I think okay," Diedre responded cautiously. She ripped open a vending-machine package of "ranch style" chips, her body suddenly craving fat and junk food.

"You aced it, kid. Don't give me any of that 'okay' bullshit. And now let's go to the movies this afternoon."

"What?" Diedre stared at her friend as if Lashonda had suddenly started quoting Howard Stern.

"There's that new, hot Sandra Bullock flick. Eileen and some of us are going, just to clear our heads. My granny's driving out from Detroit to baby-sit Tarik, and I have to get away from the law quad or I'm going to start screaming and they'll have to drag me away with a net over me."

Several hours later, sitting in the darkened theater with a tub of popcorn in her lap, Diedre felt the tension drain out of her body. The most hellish part of that exam had been the anticipation. Maybe she could just get through the rest of them without panicking.

After her last exam, Rodger Halsick bought Diedre lunch again, taking her to the same seafood restaurant downtown, where she was careful this time to order a seafood salad, not crab claws with the potential for squirting juice. She ate hungrily, her body rebelling against the junk-food diet that had kept her going through finals.

"So," he said. "I guess we can assume you got through finals with flying colors?"

"I did my best," Diedre said simply, unwilling to confess how badly she'd panicked that first time.

"Good. We'll expect to see your grades as soon as you receive them, but I'm sure they'll be great," he said, smiling. "You did such a good job on the first case we gave you, Marcie Hertz; are you game to try another one?"

"Why, yes," she said, pleased.

"She's a nursing student, twenty years old, who's being stalked by a former boyfriend. He calls her up to sixteen times daily, and he's also been harassing her girlfriends and her family, following her around. We're going to help her file under the stalker laws, Diedre. There'll be a petition to file, and he'll have to be served. Hopefully we're going to put this young man in jail. Sound interesting?''

''It certainly does,'' said Diedre, getting some of her old enthusiasm back.

Diedre hadn't even thought about her Christmas shopping, but after the lunch with Halsick, she drove to Briarwood Mall and tried to make two hundred dollars stretch to cover gifts for her mother, Pam, and Mitch, along with small presents for Tarik and Lashonda.

For her mother and Pam, she purchased sterling silver picture frames, in which she planned to put a family snapshot she'd taken at Thanksgiving. Then she bought each a fuzzy knit hat in candy-box colors. For Mitch, she ended up buying some software for his computer. Tarik got a dinosaur book, Lashonda a gift certificate to the movie theaters at Briarwood.

She decided to send a beautiful foil card to Rodger Halsick, thanking him for mentoring her. She bought a few more cards, for Treva Connor, Professor Kovacs, and all the women in her study group. Oh, and a card for Marcie and Evan.

She and Pam drove back to Madison Heights where Cynthia, who had three days off, was planning to have a full, festive Christmas dinner with all the trimmings. Cynthia's boss had given her an eighteen-pound turkey and a hundred-dollar gift certificate at Hudson's. Pam was very talkative, almost overexcited, and kept hinting at a ''secret'' she planned to reveal as soon as they reached home.

The apartment building in Madison Heights looked just the same, made of dulled gray bricks and in need of maintenance touches, such as new shutters. However, their mother's apartment was immaculately clean, draped with evergreen branches trimmed with red bows. The artificial Christmas tree they'd had since Diedre was ten had been covered with brightly colored balls and silver ropes of beads. Strings of miniature lights twinkled on and off. Hanging from the branches were holiday decorations that Pam and Diedre had made as children. A few gifts were already under the tree.

As soon as they walked in the door, Pam burst out with the news that she'd been given a promotion at work, and she and Bud were talking marriage.

Both Diedre and Cynthia screamed and threw their arms around Pam, who blushed and hugged them back, hard. "We want to wait to get married until a year from June," Pam said proudly. "So we can save up for all the furniture and stuff we'll need. Deeds, after the wedding you can keep the apartment and get a new roommate. Not that you won't miss *me*."

"How was it? How were exams?" her mother wanted to know, after the excitement of the announcement died down.

"Rough, but I'm hoping I did well. I panicked for a couple of minutes at my first one," Diedre admitted. "I mean I *really* went brain-dead."

"But not for long," insisted Cynthia proudly. "Not you. You always come through, Diedre." Something flashed in her eyes. "I wish in a way your father were still alive so I could show him both of my daughters, and tell him we did it without him and he didn't have a damn thing to do with it."

Christmas turned out to be a warm time, with plenty of food and laughter. Cynthia had needlepointed pillows for both of her daughters, and Pam had a romantic-looking, lace-trimmed blouse for Diedre. Bud came over for Christmas dinner, with more presents, and a few moments later, Mitch arrived. He also was lugging a big shopping bag full of gifts, plus a larger box he said was for Diedre. While the turkey was roasting, Diedre tore off the wrapping paper and found an elegant desktop set with a gray granite finish, complete with in and out trays, pencil holders, a matching desk pad, a rack for storing legal-sized folders, and more.

Down at the bottom of the big box was a Dilbert calendar.

"But—but—" Diedre stammered. "Isn't this a little premature? I mean I'm not a lawyer yet."

"Didn't you have your first case? Didn't you win it? This

is your lucky desk set," Mitch declared. "Use it now and everything you do at your desk will turn to magic. They told me that at OfficeMax and I believe them. As for the Dilbert calendar, that's just to keep you humble, my dear."

She laughed and hugged him, feeling lighthearted and hopeful. God—she did love him. His sweetness never ceased to draw her in. If only—But she didn't want to think about that, not on Christmas day.

They pigged out on dinner, everyone washing and drying dishes as Cynthia had no dishwasher, then they played Pictionary and watched a holiday special on TV.

Later, after the men had left and Cynthia had gone to bed, Diedre and Pam went to the bedroom they had shared as girls, putting sleeping bags on the floor, since both twin beds had been moved to the apartment in Ann Arbor.

"This thing smells like ten-year-old dead leaves," complained Pam, eyeing her sleeping bag with distaste.

"You can have the couch if you want," offered Diedre. "I don't mind."

"You sure?"

"Positive." Diedre drew in a deep breath. "Do you think Mom looks thinner?"

"Maybe a little," said Pam.

"She works too hard. She told me while we were clearing up the dishes that they've got her doing overtime almost every Saturday now. She needs the money too much to refuse. And she's doing typing on the side now, for some psychologist. I think it's just shitty that they can't pay receptionists more money. It just sucks."

Later Diedre lay on the sleeping bag, staring at the familiar pattern of car headlights from Eleven Mile Road as they flared across the bedroom ceiling, over and over again. It had always made her angry that her mother gave so much to that engineering company she worked for, yet even with her recent raise, only made $10.50 an hour. Even the maintenance man at Cynthia's company made more than she did.

Just one more reason to get through law school with flying colors, Diedre told herself. After she did, maybe she would send her mother to school to become a paralegal. Cynthia had talked about it several times. And she'd supplement her mother's monthly salary, maybe buy her a house . . .

Her eyes fluttered shut.

She drifted off to sleep, thinking about Mitch. He'd spent such care picking out their presents . . . and that silly Dilbert calendar . . . and he'd kissed her at the door, whispering to her how much he loved her. Even as her mind relaxed its hold and fell toward sleep, she could feel her stomach muscles tighten.

Ann Arbor had just recovered from a January blizzard that had dumped sixteen inches of snow on the city in the space of two days. Plow trucks had done yeoman service, piling heaps of snow on the sides of roads, and in some cases dumping big piles down the center turn lanes as well.

One of the residents of Mitch's apartment house had made a snowman in front of the building, providing it with a GO BLUE sweatshirt, carrot nose, and carrot genitals.

Mitch's bedroom smelled slightly rank and salty, the odors of their recent lovemaking mixed with the greasy fragrances of a large, thick-crust Domino's pizza that sat on the bedside table, decimated to one remaining piece. The brief respite of Christmas break might never have occurred. Law books were again stacked everywhere. A bottle of Advil sat on the bedside table, along with a container of Tums.

"Grades," sighed Mitch, lying naked in his bed with his arms behind his head. Tufts of dark hair curled out of his armpits. "Jesus, they're going to arrive any day now. This whole semester has been like living with the ax over your head. I just hope it doesn't fall on me."

"Oh, I'm positive your grades are going to be fine," Diedre reassured him.

"Deeds, I'm not the student you are. I know I can be a competent lawyer—I'm aggressive enough and I'll go the extra mile—but I'm going to have to sweat. I knew that coming in."

"I'm sure your grades will be more than fine."

Mitch reached toward the side of the bed and flipped open the pizza box lid. "Another piece? One more left. Can I tempt you?"

"No way. I'm going to get fat."

"You? Never."

Diedre flushed, thinking that if she hadn't had the abortion, she would have been six months pregnant by now. And Mitch thought she'd never be fat. His ignorance about the secret she carried seemed to haunt her almost daily.

"I'm going to have this last piece then," Mitch declared. "And after that I'm going to have another bite of you."

Sex. They never could get enough of it. The hot, sweaty kind, or the tender, loving kind, or the kind where they attacked each other greedily, devouring each other until they both cried out in ecstasy.

"I love everything about you, Diedre," Mitch said after a long while. "Those two cute dimples on your butt just on either side of your spine. That funny long toe of yours. The way you can't sing, and don't even know it. That little, tiny, golden fleck in your right eye. The little mole on your thigh there—"

He pushed up the sheets and went nuzzling under them, kissing the mole in question, then licking it, then kissing other places until Diedre was again gasping with pleasure. Oh, she loved him. She wanted to keep him so badly that she lay awake sometimes at night, terrified she would lose him.

"Deeds?" he said, after they had made love again for the third time, rocking together in slow, familiar harmony. "Honey, you seemed kind of quiet. Is everything all right?"

"Everything's great," she insisted.

"I want our life to be perfect. My dad and mom had a great life together . . . It's what I want for us, too."

Diedre smiled bleakly and hugged him close, squeezing her eyes shut and praying he wouldn't see the fear on her face. She was going to have to tell him, clear the air—and soon. She couldn't go on much longer like this, her stomach constantly tied into knots of worry.

Several days later, Diedre stood at the bank of small, metal mailboxes in the lobby of the apartment building, staring down at the computerized report card printed with the name of the law school. She'd been too excited to wait until she got upstairs before ripping it open.

Her eyes scanned the figures over and over again, searching the ink that had been printed too lightly.

A's. All A's. It had to be a mistake!

She read the card for a third time, just to make sure, then rushed up the staircase back into the apartment, where Pam was exercising in the middle of the living room floor to a Susan Powter video. "Pam," she said in a strange voice, holding out the report card. "Read this and see if it says what I think it does."

Pam stopped kicking and wiped her sweaty, blond hair off her forehead. "Sure, okay . . . Holy shit, Deeds—these are all A's!"

"I thought so." Diedre sank down on the couch, waves of shock pouring through her. She'd hoped for this . . . prayed for this . . . and now that it had happened, she felt strange and shaky.

"Hey, jump up and down or something," Pam urged. "Get happy, kiddo!"

"I feel funny," stammered Diedre.

"Why? Jesus, this is it, Diedre, this is so great! You're gonna ace your way through law school! Call up Mitch! Call him up and we'll all go out for a beer!"

"All right," said Diedre, moving toward the phone. She dialed Mitch's apartment, waiting impatiently while the phone rang. "Hey, I'm out, leave your number, wait until the beep."

She hesitated, wondering what to say on the tape. Had Mitch gotten his grades? What had his been? He'd been worried about his Torts exam. The beep sounded, and Diedre said, "Mitch, it's me. Grades came. Call me and we'll all go out for a beer, okay?"

That was general enough and didn't sound gloating. When she hung up, Pam was looking at her. "Well, *I* don't want to wait for Mitch," her sister said. "I want to go and celebrate right now."

"In a minute," said Diedre, happiness finally beginning to fill her like fizzy soda water. "I have to make some phone calls!"

Buzzing with excitement, Diedre phoned Cynthia at work, and then she dialed Rodger Halsick at the home number he had given her, too proud to wait to mail him a copy of her grades.

"Wonderful news," he said. "I expected nothing less."

"I can't believe it—I still feel so stunned."

"With your brilliant mind and the way you've worked, Diedre, you deserve every A and then some. I hope you'll consider being one of our 'summer associates' at the law firm this summer. It would be a tremendous experience for you."

"This summer?" Although she had been told that a summer job was a possibility, she still felt a stir of surprise and joy.

"Believe me, we'll keep you busy and you'll learn plenty of law," said Halsick. "And the pay is excellent."

Thrilled with the invitation, Diedre thanked Halsick profusely, and after they had hung up she dialed Treva Connor's room number at the U-M hospital complex. She just had to tell Treva, too.

Treva congratulated Diedre warmly, and then their call was interrupted by a nurse coming in to take the older woman's vital signs.

"How are you doing?" Diedre said when Treva was back on the line.

"Just trying to hold on to this baby as long as I can," said the social worker cheerfully. "Now, don't you worry about me . . . you go out and celebrate those terrific grades of yours, Diedre. If anyone deserves them, it's you. So just enjoy them."

TREVA

"TREVA? HOW ARE YOU?" SAID DR. ELLEN ROSENKRANTZ a few minutes later, rapping on the door of Treva's hospital room, then walking in. The elderly physician was carrying a pot of forced yellow daffodils.

"Pretty. Very pretty," Treva said with a broad smile. "I just adore daffs—I've got about a hundred of them in my rock garden at home. Wade is going to take pictures of them for me if I can't see them. Oh, and I feel fine."

Dr. Rosenkrantz gave her a long look. "You sure, honey?"

"I'm sure," said Treva, but then her smile vanished. "Okay, it's a little rougher than I thought it would be. All the drugs they've been giving me. I feel depressed, disoriented, sleepy, jittery . . . and that's only for starters. I snapped at Wade the other day. God, Ellen, I hate to complain. I *hate* being a complainer." Tears rolled down her cheeks.

"You're not a complainer, Treva, you're about as brave a woman as I'd ever want to meet," said Ellen Rosenkrantz.

"Brave," muttered Treva. "Maybe to the outside world, maybe to Wade . . . yeah. But some nights I lie awake and I think . . ." She stopped, not wanting to admit to the bleakness to which her thoughts sometimes sunk. She knew it was partially the drugs . . . Dr. Sandoval had told her to expect depression as a natural part of what she was going through . . . Still, in the small hours of the night after they had just awakened her to take her BP and the fetal heartbeat, Treva found herself sometimes fighting off feelings of apprehension so awful that they surprised and alarmed her.

Dr. Rosenkrantz took one of Treva's hands in hers, carefully examining it for puffiness even as she held it. "We all have those nights when we lie awake,'' she said softly. ''Trev, I've been doing some soul-searching of my own.''

''Oh?''

''Yeah. The death threats. I got another one yesterday that I haven't told anyone about, even the police or anyone at the clinic.'' Ellen sighed. ''This was the worst threat I've ever had.''

''What happened?'' asked Treva anxiously.

The older woman cleared her throat. ''I got home yesterday from the clinic around six-thirty and I was planning to have a salad and some leftover lasagna and, you know, vegetate in front of the television set for a while.'' Her smile was sad. ''A typical evening at home with the cat in my lap. Only my cat, Butterscotch, wasn't at the door to greet me.''

''Oh, no,'' said Treva, horror growing in her as she was already beginning to see where this story was leading.

''I called for her, and I looked all over, and I couldn't find her. I have a little cat door in back for her to use to go in and out ... I went out back and there she was, Treva. They'd killed her and skinned her and nailed her to my shed wall. With—'' Dr. Rosenkrantz's voice shook. ''With a big sign nailed up next to her. 'You're next, filthy baby killer. We know where you live, we know where to find you.' ''

''Dear Ellen,'' said Treva, shaken. ''You have to go to the police with this.''

''Yes, and they'll do what they've always done before. Tromp around my property, question the neighbors, cruise back and forth around my house a couple of times, and then it's back to business as usual. Nobody ever sees these people. Maybe they *are* my neighbors, I don't know for sure. Treva, I ... I'm going to be seventy-four years old next month. I'm still healthy, but the aches and pains are beginning to creep up on me, and I'm too old to be living under this kind of constant stress. Wondering whether these are just empty threats or whether they really *are* going to kill me sometime ...'' She stopped, her voice quivering. ''I loved that little cat. I think that's what finally broke me, Treva. That they could kill Butterscotch.''

"I'd say their threats are to be taken very seriously,'' Treva said.

"Yes . . . that's what I think, too.'' There was a long silence, punctuated by the usual background of hospital sounds to which Treva had grown so accustomed she seldom heard them any longer. "I don't want to retire, Treva, not entirely. There are too many people in this world who need me, even if I am up there in years.''

Again Dr. Rosenkrantz paused, her face looking sad.

"What are you going to do?'' asked Treva.

"I'm not sure yet. Maybe I'll go to Appalachia. My friend Pete has come back from Haiti, and he's accepted a position with a clinic in the Blue Ridge Mountains near a town called Harrisonburg. I could work there, with him, practice family medicine, do breast exams and Pap smears, deliver babies . . . I'd be needed and there wouldn't be crazed and bitter people constantly hounding me, threatening my life. I'd never have to lose another cat. Not that way at least.''

"So their threats will drive you away after all,'' said Treva, a heavy disappointment settling over her. Dr. Rosenkrantz had been the driving force behind the clinic, the one person who had kept them going through demonstrations, threats, and attacks. Now with her gone, what would happen? Dr. Tallchief only gave eight hours a week to the clinic. They'd have to get another doctor. But who?

"Yes, honey. I'm only human, I'm not Mother Teresa, I react to fear just as much as the next person. Yes, the victory is theirs,'' repeated Ellen Rosenkrantz, heavily. "Because once I'm gone, who will replace me? Dr. Tallchief is a good doctor, but he will have to double his hours to make up for all the procedures I did, and I'm sure that's not going to be possible. *He's* only human. Fear is not a pleasant way to live.''

"But the abortion study . . .'' said Treva anxiously.

"I will keep up with that,'' said Dr. Rosenkrantz. "They have phone lines down in Harrisonburg, and we can send messages back and forth on the Internet, not to mention faxes, so I don't see a problem there. I intend to finish the study and publish; that part of it won't change.''

''When do you think you'll be leaving?'' asked Treva, fighting sadness.

''I have already put my house up for sale, dear. The real estate woman informs me that houses like mine with a big, wooded lot are going at a pretty good clip, so it shouldn't be long. Pete and I want to find a nice house overlooking the mountains—or maybe we'll build one of logs. I've always been partial to the idea of a log house. Only I want a big one with huge, sweeping views of the mountains.''

Treva continued to talk with Dr. Rosenkrantz about her plans, but all the while she was fighting a tight sorrow that welled up into her throat. They'd all worked so hard—had such big plans—believed in choices for women. But it all depended on workers, and in this abortion war, the other side was gradually scaring away the abortion workers who made everything possible.

''Do you have any ideas on who we could get to replace you?'' she asked at last.

''There's another woman who's still in Haiti, Marilyn Curtiss. She's a very good doctor, but she's been diagnosed with diabetes and wants to slow up a bit. Maybe she could put in a few days at the clinic doing the procedures, and you could get someone else for the routine exams . . . you know, the Pap smears and so forth. That person wouldn't be doing procedures at all.''

Treva nodded. It wouldn't be the same, but it would be something, and the clinic would continue—somehow. They would limp along as long as a doctor could be found to volunteer.

After Dr. Rosenkrantz had left, Treva had a hard time getting settled again, her mind constantly going to all of the things the tiny, white-haired doctor had done for the women of Ann Arbor. She had faced death for them on a daily basis, smiling and with good courage, all so that they would be able to take advantage of their legal choices. In a hundred ways, Ellen had given that extra bit of cheer so that a frightened woman could get through her procedure. She had never flagged, always encouraging the other staff members.

There weren't any medals in the abortion world, but if they gave any, Treva would pin a gold one right on Dr. Rosenkrantz's lapel. Tears welled to Treva's eyes, and she let them come, feeling sad for the world.

How could people be so split on this issue? Cruelties and crimes were committed in the name of saving human life. Treva found it so hard to grasp, so hard to see. Yes, clumps of dividing cells and fetuses were being extracted, but were girls and women supposed to be forced to carry a child they did not want or could not take care of, simply because it was in their bodies? The pro-lifers acted as if women had absolutely no control over their bodies or their destinies. What would men do if they were suddenly informed they had a child growing within them that they would have to rear for the next eighteen years? *They* would do something about it . . .

Troubled, Treva closed her eyes and drifted off to a half sleep. While she was asleep she dreamed that a man with a knife was attacking Dr. Rosenkrantz, inserting the tip of his blade in the older woman's neck, then drawing the blade swiftly down. He was trying to peel off her skin, as he'd done the cat's.

She awoke, crying out hoarsely. A nurse came running, answering her buzzer and injecting her with a sedative.

DIEDRE

TEN MINUTES AFTER DIEDRE SPOKE WITH TREVA, MITCH called. "Hi, sweetheart, I was coaching a game with my wheelchair kids. Those kids are terrific, they just tear me

up. That little Jalessa is a sweetie. I take it your grades
came.''

"Yeah . . ."

"What'd you get?"

"All A's," said Diedre quickly.

"All A's? Deeds, that's fabulous news. Jesus, I knew you
could do it. See, your new desk set already brought good
luck. That's super, super news." Mitch was generous in his
congratulations.

"What about you? Did yours come, too?"

"Yeah, mine were a little less stellar, I'm afraid. Two B's
and the rest C's.''

"Oh, Mitch, but that's great! Congratulations."

"I admit I was worried for a while, but I guess I made
it.''

They discussed his grades for a while, and then Mitch
said, "Look, your straight A's deserve a lot of attention,
and I want us to go out and celebrate big time. What about
tomorrow night?" There was a curious note to his voice.

"All right," agreed Diedre, picking up on the note in his
voice right away. He had something planned . . . something
special, she realized. She hoped it wasn't what she feared it
was.

"Wear something smashing—a really dressy dress. We're
going out on the town."

"Out on the town?"

"Dinner, dancing, romance, the works. We've hardly
done anything this past semester besides eat pizza and study
in the library, and I think it's about time we changed that."

Dinner? Dancing? And the anticipatory sound in his
voice. What were his plans? Oh, God . . . Diedre felt a stab
of apprehension, a sudden feeling that life was pushing her
along much, much too fast. "I'll borrow something from
Pam to wear," she decided.

"Make it something sexy."

"Sure."

*   *   *

All day Saturday, Diedre could barely concentrate on her studying. She just kept reading the same paragraphs over and over, her mind constantly flicking back to Mitch. His love of children. His expectations of a life filled with them.

Tonight *had* to be the night. The night she confessed the truth. She just wasn't a person who could nurse an important secret to the grave, which was exactly what she'd have to do if she married Mitch.

Pam returned from shopping, and the two sisters ransacked their closets, pulling out dresses and laying them across Diedre's bed. There were a couple of bridesmaid's dresses, worn at various weddings, and a black cocktail dress that Pam had purchased at Winkelman's to wear for the previous New Year's Eve. It had a flirty little bias-cut skirt, and spaghetti straps ornamented with black rhinestones.

"Whoa, this is the one you should wear, Deeds," declared Pam, holding up the black dress. "And it's stretchy enough so it'll fit you even if you're a size smaller than me."

"Are you sure? You've only worn it twice."

"As long as you don't spill steak sauce all over it."

"I won't even order steak."

Pam nodded. "Okay . . . and how do you want your hair braided?"

Diedre hesitated. She hadn't even thought about her hair. She was going crazy with nerves . . .

"I don't want to braid it tonight. I'll wear it down. I could use your curling iron, though."

Nervously she went in the bathroom to take a shower, under the spray rehearsing all the possible scenarios of Mitch's reaction. None of the scenarios she imagined were pleasant.

Under running water, Diedre squeezed her eyes shut. *Please,* she prayed. *Let it be all right. Let him understand.*

But she was terrified he would not.

* * *

Diedre stared at herself in the mirror. Pam's dress had been an inspired choice. The flirty skirt made her legs look endless, and the three-inch high heels she'd chosen were incredibly sexy. Mitch was a "shoe man," so she felt sure he'd like these.

Mitch arrived exactly on time, carrying a floral arrangement from a florist near campus. He was dressed in a dark charcoal suit and a red tie with a black paisley design on it, classy and expensive-looking. He looked so handsome that new fingers of fear stroked up and down Diedre's spine. *I might lose him. God, I'm going to lose him. I know it.*

"You look so beautiful," he breathed, his eyes riveted on her. "You look like a movie star in that dress."

Diedre felt herself start to perspire lightly. "Let me put the flowers in a vase or they'll die."

She hurried to the small apartment kitchen and began rummaging in the cupboards for a vase. She found a common green vase, but as she was about to put it on the countertop, her shaking hand slipped and the vase crashed to the floor.

"Oh!" she cried, jumping back as broken glass flew.

"Are you all right?" Mitch rushed into the kitchen, followed by Pam.

"I'm—fine. The vase s-slipped." Diedre was so rattled that she was stammering.

"Don't touch this glass. I'll clean it up. Where's a broom?" asked Mitch, looking around.

"We don't have one," said Pam.

"You don't have a broom? What do you use then?"

"We vacuum everything," said Pam. "We also have a Dustbuster. Welcome to the millennium, Mitch. Deeds, go and get the Hoover."

Diedre headed for the coat closet, where Pam kept a vacuum cleaner jammed among the coats. She pulled it out, only to find that Mitch had followed her there. He took her in his arms, kissing her gently on her left temple.

"My beautiful Deeds, all dressed up and looking absolutely killer. You don't have to vacuum. You sit down here in the living room and wait; I'll handle the mess. I don't want you getting cut on glass."

Mitch kissed her again and walked back into the kitchen. In a few seconds Diedre heard the whine of the Hoover.

Dully she sat in the living room, feeling her pulse hammer up into the hollow of her throat. He was vacuuming up broken glass for her. He adored her; that was obvious. What was her horrible announcement going to do to that? Would he even be speaking to her by tomorrow?

Finally the roses were arranged in another vase that Pam had found, and Diedre slipped into her black, dressy coat. On her lapel she wore an old-fashioned rhinestone starburst pin that Cynthia had given her years ago. They said good-bye and left, walking down to the parking lot.

It was a cold, starry night, the roads clear, although white snow glistened on the lawn area of the apartment complex, interspersed with a maze of paw prints that marked where the dogs living in the development had been let out for their daily runs.

Mitch had just had the Le Baron washed and it gleamed in the parking-lot floodlights, its fenders a glossy, lustrous black. *The car where I conceived the baby,* Diedre found herself remembering uneasily. He made a ceremony of handing her into the passenger seat, and Diedre clenched her hands together in her lap, almost wishing he wouldn't. He was being so wonderful and it was only going to make it harder.

"A quarter for your thoughts," said Mitch, smiling as he inserted his key into the ignition. "Or should I say five dollars to allow for inflation?"

She tried to smile. "I'm not thinking anything really."

"Nothing? On such a great night when you've got those super, super grades to celebrate?"

Diedre started a little. In the turmoil of trying to decide what to say to Mitch, she'd almost forgotten about her straight-A grades.

He turned the car in the direction of Saline, a small town located south of Ann Arbor, where a new restaurant called

Waterworks was drawing hordes of Ann Arborites, along with its adjoining nightclub, named Fountains.

As they drove, Mitch chatted pleasantly about his wheelchair kids, grades, some news about his father, who had started traveling again for his business. Then they were pulling into the parking lot of the restaurant, which had been built out of an old factory, its lot jammed with cars, trucks, and vans.

Four water fountains had been installed in front, their usually flowing water currently frozen into surrealistic sculptures lit by blue floodlights.

"The indoor ones are sure to be running, though," Mitch told her.

He made another ceremony of escorting Diedre inside, taking her coat to be checked, treating her like a beautiful, breakable movie star arriving for the Oscars. At Mitch's suggestion, they threw coins in the lobby fountain, which was already packed with hundreds of dollars worth of change thrown there by previous patrons.

"Make a wish—and wish for me," he teased, as she tossed in her quarter.

She forced herself to smile at him, to laugh and shrug her shoulders, to walk so that the short little skirt twirled. She was so terrified she felt like throwing up.

Tonight. She just had to tell him tonight—or she wouldn't be able to do it at all.

Dinner was incredible—fresh salmon with thyme and red wine sauce, and a spinach and citrus salad sprinkled with slivered almonds. Despite her raw, lacerated nerves, Diedre found herself enjoying the delicate flavors, the food so artistically served that each plate looked like an illustration in a magazine.

Mitch was very attentive, leaning across the table to talk to her. Diedre saw frank, unbridled adoration and it frightened her. *Will he still adore me after I've told him the truth?*

"You seem quiet tonight," he finally remarked, after the waiter had cleared away their plates.

She jumped nervously. "Do I?"

"Yes, very."

"I . . . I've been under a lot of strain lately," she responded, wondering if this was the time she should start telling him, now, before the dancing started. Once the music began, they'd have to shout to be heard.

"Well, I can understand that, with exams and all." But he looked at her strangely.

Before she could think, the waiter was back with a dessert trolley, and Mitch insisted that they get a walnut and banana torte and split it. The act of sharing her food with him, both of their forks digging into the same segment of frosting, was curiously intimate. At one point Mitch cut off a bite of cake and forked it into Diedre's mouth like a bridegroom at a wedding reception.

Surprised, Diedre jumped back a little.

Mitch laughed. "Hey, I'm not going to smear frosting on your chin. I have more class than that."

"I—I was still chewing," she excused herself, flushing.

She still had not found the words when they walked through the lobby, with its splashing fountains, into the adjoining nightclub, where the band had set up and was belting out Top 40 songs. Mirrors reflected a floor-to-ceiling waterfall, colored floodlights turning the water that splashed over rocks into a rainbow of changing colors.

When Mitch led her onto the dance floor, Diedre was relieved to have a respite from the tumult of her thoughts. The dance floor was crowded, almost everyone under thirty, the energy tremendous as couples pumped and gyrated to the pulsating music.

During the rare slow ballad, Mitch held Diedre so close that she could almost feel the thumping of his heartbeat.

"I love you," he whispered. "I'll always remember tonight."

"I love you, too," she whispered back.

She clung to him, wishing they could always be like this, that their lives never had to move beyond these few seconds. But they had to, of course.

When the set ended, they threaded their way through the crowd, back to their table. "Great music, great partner," Mitch said, pulling out Diedre's chair for her. "My straight-A Diedre."

Suddenly Mitch seemed very nervous, his complexion turning red as he fumbled in the pocket of his suit jacket and brought out an elegant-looking ring box with the name of a jeweler embossed in gold.

Diedre stared at it. Her stomach swooped and dove and shimmied, like a dinghy tossing in a windstorm. *"Mitch."*

"Go on, open it. I've been nervous all night," he told her. "I hope you like it. If you don't, we can exchange it. Oh, Diedre, I just love you so much. Will you marry me? I promise I'll make you happy."

Marry him? Oh, God! Diedre had suspected this was coming, yet she still quivered with shock and stress. She loved him, but did they want the same things? Children . . . with him wanting a dozen, and her, one or two. How could they come to an agreement? Also, his family was so much richer than hers. The very car that Mitch had driven tonight was worth more than Diedre's mother, Cynthia, earned in a year.

Diedre's thoughts disintegrated into confusion.

"Well, open the box," Mitch urged.

In a heart-thumping daze, Diedre opened the dark blue velvet lid. Inside glittered a stunning creation of quadrillion diamonds set in diagonal rows, with a larger, central stone that looked like a rock to her. She'd never known a woman who had a diamond that big. In the sparkling lights of the nightclub, the channel-set diamonds glittered fiercely.

"Oh," said Diedre, the breath expelled from her lungs involuntarily.

"Diedre?" His eyes sought hers.

She moved her lips, but could not speak. A few people at other tables had seen him take out the ring box and were watching them, waiting to see what she would say, which made her even more nervous.

"Put the ring on, honey. I want to make sure it fits. I

measured it while you were sleeping one night. Believe me, it was hard getting that little string around your finger while you were tossing and turning. You're a regular little tosser sometimes, especially before exams.''

Diedre's eyes watered. She couldn't stop staring at the impossibly expensive ring. She didn't deserve it. Not now, not like this, not until Mitch knew the truth. A wave of horrified sorrow ran through her. Once she had this beautiful ring on her finger, she knew she'd *never* tell Mitch. She'd marry him, live a lie . . .

''Here, honey, let me help you.'' Mitch reached across the table and began taking the ring out of its slot in the velvet box.

''Hold your hand out,'' he said huskily.

Terrified, she extended her left hand, and felt the cool smoothness as Mitch slid the gold band up her ring finger. It was a perfect fit. Of course it would be. Guys like Mitch never bought a ring in the wrong size.

''With this ring . . .'' Mitch said, his voice breaking. ''Oh, Diedre.''

The people at the next table were cheering. Diedre heard their voices as a buzz at the edge of her consciousness. Mitch's eyes were so full of naked love that Diedre lost it.

''Mitch . . . I . . .''

She suddenly pushed away from the table, jumping to her feet. Tears blurred her eyes and she heard Mitch's cry of consternation as she turned and rushed through the nightclub.

Diedre was crying by the time she reached the lobby, where a line of trendily dressed couples were waiting to get into the nightclub, or tossing coins in the fountains. Mitch had checked her coat, but the coat-check woman was busy with a crowd, and Diedre rushed past, banging into the front door and then shoving it open.

She flew outdoors. The air was freezing, tiny spicules of frost sparkling in the air. On the road, cars sped back and forth, someone blasting on his horn as he passed the blazing lights of the nightclub and restaurant complex.

A winter chill froze Diedre's skin, and she shivered convulsively. The rhinestones on her dress straps felt like tiny ice cubes pressing into her shoulders. Why hadn't she stood in line to get her coat?

Glancing down, she saw the icy flash of the huge engagement ring on her finger, and her stomach again swooped sickeningly with the realization of what she'd done. She'd turned Mitch down. Was she a fool? Or was this the smartest thing she had ever done?

A couple walking from the parking lot paused to stare at her, and Diedre hunched her almost bare shoulders, realizing she was going to have to walk back into the lobby and get her coat or she'd freeze. Then she would find a phone and call Pam, beg her sister to drive out to Saline to pick her up.

She'd think later about what to say to Pam.

She trudged back inside the lobby, which was warm with the convivial press of human bodies, the air slightly humid with splashing water. Mitch was standing near the coat-check window with Diedre's coat draped over his arm, his lips thinned with anger.

She walked over to him. "Mitch, I—"

"I don't want to talk here. Let's go back out to the car."

"Mitch, I know it seems terrible, but—"

"To the car, Diedre."

She put on her coat, the black wool that she'd carefully saved for "best," as she'd been taught. The coat warmed her skin, but not her heart. Her heart was a shrunken ice cube of pain.

They walked out to the crowded parking lot, a horrible silence stretching between them. This time Mitch didn't hold her hand or her arm. He didn't treat her like a movie star, as he'd done on the way in. That was over, probably forever, she thought. He walked stiffly far apart from her, his jaw set grimly.

They got into the car.

Mitch inserted his car keys in the ignition of the Le Baron, starting the engine, but he did not put the car in gear.

"Okay, so tell me," he said hoarsely. "What happened in there? What's going on?"

Panic flooded her, washing away her courage. How could she tell him such a horrid thing? How?

"I . . . I wanted to tell you . . . but I was so confused and it seemed there was never a good time to tell you."

"What's wrong? Apparently you care very deeply for me—apparently you love me. That's what you've told me anyway, on many occasions. We've made plans, Diedre. We've already talked about marriage. My giving you a ring didn't come as any big surprise to you, you must have known it was coming."

His voice was full of pain.

Several couples were crossing the parking lot, arms around each other. One couple was kissing, just as Mitch and Diedre used to do. Diedre stared at them, feeling the sharp, glassy edges pierce her chest as her heart broke.

She drew back against the passenger window. "Please," she whispered. "Just take me home." She peeled the ring off her finger and handed it to him. "I . . . I can't take this."

"Is that a no?" he snapped. "Don't you even have an explanation?"

She stared out the passenger window. Tears stood in her eyes. She wished to hell she had never let it go this far.

"Now. Tell me now, Diedre. Oh, I know something is bothering you. I've known it almost since I met you. You've had something on your mind, some secret that you haven't shared with me. Sometimes you'd get so quiet and wouldn't tell me what was wrong. Those times you seemed moody."

She didn't respond.

"It's some secret that affects *us,* isn't it?"

She opened her lips, moistened them with her tongue, gulped in another breath of chilly air that seemed to give no sustenance. "Mitch . . ."

"It isn't HIV, is it?" he said reluctantly. "It can't be that."

HIV? She uttered a sharp, weeping cry. "Of course not! Oh, Christ . . . Please, just take me home or I'll call Pam."

"Tell me, Diedre, or we're not leaving this parking lot, and I don't care if we have to stay here until morning."

It was here, the moment she'd dreaded. Diedre wished she were anywhere else, climbing one of the foothills of the Himalayas, or teaching schoolchildren in Korea, as one of her college friends had done. She was weeping as she turned to Mitch. "It's not so simple to tell you. I . . . I just couldn't say it."

"I have plenty of time. I can listen," he said implacably. "And you're going to be a great lawyer, so you can manage to get out the right words—trust me."

"I wanted to tell you—part of me did anyway. But I was afraid . . ." She spoke raggedly, her hands clenched in her lap, her fingernails cutting into her skin.

"Just tell me."

"I . . . Mitch . . . when we met . . . that first time at that party on the lake, somebody's party, I can't remember her name now . . ."

"Yes?"

"We made love in the car."

"Yes."

"And . . . something happened."

"What?" His eyes bored into hers. "What do you mean?"

"I got pregnant!" she cried, losing control. "You never called me and I couldn't raise a baby by myself—not and go to law school—it wasn't the right time for me—"

"What are you saying?" Mitch asked in a strangely quiet tone. "Diedre, what are you telling me?"

"Don't be dense!" she cried, her patience at an end, her fear overwhelming everything. "I had an abortion!"

"An . . . *You aborted our baby?*"

She looked down at her lap, at the dashboard of the car, at her own knees, anywhere but him. "Yes," she whispered. "I had to, Mitch. I was going to law school in two weeks— on a full-ride scholarship. I couldn't risk that . . . I couldn't ruin my life. *I couldn't raise a baby and go to law school, it would have been too hard.*"

"*My* baby? It was *my* child?"

"Of course it was your child! I would never have told you this if it wasn't. You were the first guy I'd had sex with in over a year."

Mitch shook his head from side to side. "Jesus, I can't believe this, Diedre. *Why* didn't you call me? *Why?* Even with all the stress with my mother dying and all, I would have done something. I would have stood by you, I would have helped you figure it out. *I would have married you.*"

"Oh, sure," she said, her voice rising. "Sure you would have married me. We had a one-night stand, Mitch, that's all it was. Face reality. We didn't even know each other then, and we certainly didn't care about each other. All we did was screw in the back seat of this car. Five minutes of screwing!" she cried. "So don't lie. You'd never have married me!"

"But I have rights." He gripped Diedre's shoulders, his voice raw. "I'm the father. I *was* the father. And now it's— it's dead. Who knows what it might have been if it'd lived . . . Oh, Jesus . . ."

Horrified, Diedre shrank back against the passenger door. This was even worse than she'd expected. Mitch was alternately crying and scraping the tears away from his face, shaking his head like a man possessed.

"I was *alone*," she whispered. "I had to do something! I made a decision. I had a legal right to make that decision and I did it."

"How could you? *How could you*?" he kept repeating. "How could you let me go on like that, month after month, not knowing that I lost my first child? I would have paid child support. I would have tried to get to know you better. I would have ended up marrying you just like I want to do now. Diedre, if only you'd decided not to kill it."

Kill it. The accusation reverberated inside her head.

"What gets me is that you didn't even give me the chance to do something. Not one fucking chance. *You totally obliterated me from the decision.*"

He shoved the gear lever in reverse and began to back out of the parking space.

"But I did tell you!" she shouted. "I just now told you!"

"A few months too late. I'm going to drive you home."

"I am telling you," she yelled furiously. "I didn't want to live a lie. I didn't want to have any secrets . . . I guess I should have kept quiet, huh? Then it could have gone on, then it would have been okay, right? As long as you didn't know," she sneered. "You could put your head in the sand and forget all about our one-night stand and your stupid condom with the stupid, stupid hole in it!"

He did not respond to her tirade but drove the car out of the parking lot and turned right, taking the highway back to Ann Arbor. The hour was late and only an occasional set of headlights flared toward them, to be swallowed up by the darkness. Diedre huddled in the passenger seat, too stunned and exhausted even to think.

It was exactly what she had feared would happen, exactly! She had done the honest thing in telling him and now he was punishing her, and it was over.

Damn her abortion! Damn it! She should have been braver, she should have had the baby, as Lashonda had. Confused, Diedre again clenched her hands in her lap, pressing her fingernails into her skin until her flesh felt raw. She hated Mitch and she hated herself. She'd fucked up. She'd totally fucked it up.

Diedre stood on the cement stoop of her apartment building and numbly watched Mitch's taillights disappear down the street.

That awful Le Baron—where they'd conceived the baby she'd aborted, where they'd broken up forever and for good. She hated the car! She would like to kick its tires, dent its fenders, take out her rage upon it! Tears began to crawl down her cheeks, burning her skin.

She went upstairs. Inside the apartment she found her sister lying on the couch, a *Terminator* movie on TV. Pam had fallen asleep and was snoring lightly. In sleep, her sister's face looked soft and slack, and held an innocence that Diedre remembered from when Pam had been a little girl. She was not yet wearing an engagement ring. She and Bud planned to shop for it together.

Diedre tiptoed past her toward the kitchen. Suddenly she was terribly thirsty. She wanted a drink of water, and then she would go in her bedroom, close the door, and crawl in bed to cry for the rest of the night.

Mitch had been sweet, funny, wonderful, he had been everything she ever wanted. But it had been all just a fantasy, she realized now. Reality was that morning in late August when she had gone to the clinic and lain on that exam table, listening to the horrible whine of the suction machine, suctioning out her baby.

The narrow kitchen was lit by one light over the sink, creating dim shadows on the canisters of flour and sugar, a plastic towel rack, some snack dishes Pam had left out. Diedre found a clean glass and poured herself water from the faucet. She drained it in three or four gulps, feeling the cold liquid all the way down her throat.

It was the only thing to do, she thought dully. *I had to do it. I couldn't have had a baby—then.*

"Have a good time?" said Pam, coming sleepily into the kitchen, knuckling her eyes. Then she caught a glimpse of her sister's face. "Diedre? Deeds?"

"I told him," confessed Diedre brokenly.

"Oh, Jesus. Oh, shit."

"It's over. And don't tell me 'I told you so,' because I don't want to hear it," said Diedre, wearily setting down the glass and starting through to her bedroom.

"You really screwed up, but I won't say a thing. Oh, Deeds—are you all right?"

"No. I'm not. I'm just going to bed. I don't want to answer the phone if it rings . . . but don't worry, it won't be him calling," she added bitterly. "He's never going to call me again."

* * *

The dream. Diedre was in a huge nursery, frantically running between the endless rows of pink and blue bassinets, searching for her own infant. She raced from crib to crib, reading name tags. But none had her name on it; her baby wasn't in the room. She hurried into another room, lined with hundreds more cribs, and raced up and down, searching. She got confused and had to retrace her steps and by now she was sobbing.

A church bell began to ring and then a nurse, very stern-looking in her starched white cap, came into the nursery and told Diedre to get out.

You have no right to be here, she said in an odd, cawing voice. *You're not a mother.*

Please . . . my baby is here!

You have no baby. You have nothing.

Diedre woke up, quivering. It was 6:30 A.M. Sunday morning. Despite the winter chill, sweat had soaked her body and dampened her hair. She struggled out from under the covers, her heart hammering.

Mitch, she thought, feeling the loss again. *Oh, Mitch.*

She sat on the edge of her bed, feeling disoriented. In the glow of the small night-light, Diedre could see the dress she'd worn last night flung across the dresser top, its rhinestoned straps glinting. Her panty hose lay crumpled on top of that, her little evening purse hanging by its strap from a drawer pull. Her party shoes lay on the floor where she'd kicked them off.

Just a few hours ago she'd been loved and in love, and Mitch had asked her to marry him.

But that was in some other lifetime.

Diedre dragged herself up and pulled on a pair of old, much-washed jeans and a WSU sweatshirt that had been new when she was a freshman at Wayne State.

She padded out into the kitchen and fixed herself a slice of toast, but didn't even bother to spread it with butter and jelly. Instead she dropped it in the disposal. If she ate it, she knew she was going to throw up.

I wish I'd never met him, Diedre thought. *I wish I could go to sleep for about a hundred years and wake up and everything would be great.*

She slumped down at the dinette table. She felt so alone. She had to talk to someone, had to pour out her feelings or surely they would choke her.

She stumbled to her feet and reached for the wall phone, dialing Cynthia's apartment in Madison Heights. Her mother often rose early to watch early morning news shows, even on weekends.

"Hello?" came Cynthia's soft voice over the wire.

"It's me, Diedre." But instead of saying more, Diedre began to cry. Her tears became sobs. The sobs grew in volume.

"Diedre, are you all right?" her mother kept repeating anxiously. "What's happened? Is Pam all right?"

"She's fine. It's all over," wept Diedre, when she could finally talk. "He . . . Mitch . . . I . . . We broke up."

She began to pour it out, the whole evening from beginning to end, the beautiful ring that Mitch had slid on her finger, her own confession which had turned a wonderful evening into a nightmare.

"Oh, honey. Oh, baby. But are you sure it's over? He was taken unawares last night and he reacted emotionally. Once Mitch has had a little time to sort through things, he may very well change his mind."

Diedre's sobs were bitter. "He won't. I know him."

"Diedre, I know that love is very hard to extinguish—if it is real love."

Diedre blinked her burning eyes. "He *doesn't* want me. Not after knowing about the abortion. I knew he wouldn't and he doesn't. I never should have told him—I should have just let him go on thinking everything was great!"

"But it wasn't great, was it?" whispered Cynthia. "Not for you. Honey, emotional honesty is part of love, acceptance of the other person, unconditionally. Just hang in there, DeeDee. Give Mitch some time. You've had six months, he's only had a few hours to adjust to this development."

"He's gone," said Diedre dully. "I knew he would be gone and he is."

After her talk with her mother, Diedre felt exhaustion fall over her again. She crept back into her bedroom and fell into bed, sleeping fitfully for several hours, until she was finally awakened by voices yelling in the building's parking lot as several renters tried to back up a U-Haul truck to one of the doors.

Diedre crawled out of bed, feeling as if she'd been beaten up by a car-jacker. Her skin actually felt bruised and her eyes ached. All of her joints were stiff.

She made her way out to the kitchen like a woman of seventy. Her sister had left a note on the kitchen table saying that she and Bud had gone out for Sunday brunch and then were going to see a movie.

Call him, her sister had scribbled on a piece of notebook paper. *Make up with him right away and it will be all right.* She finished the message with a line of Xs and Os, as they'd done when they were twelve and thirteen. As she read the message, Diedre's eyes watered. It was not that simple. This was not just some little spat that a sweet phone call, a few flowers, and a box of candy would fix.

A light was blinking on the answering machine, but Diedre was afraid to play back the message.

Maybe he wanted to talk, tell her he was sorry. *Yeah, right!*

Finally she pushed the button to play the tape.

But instead of Mitch's baritone, it was Lashonda's warm, buttery voice. "I just got home, just got my grades. Man, I got three A's and the rest B's. I'm taking Tarik to Thirty-one Flavors to celebrate. Want to come with us? We're leaving at two-thirty if you get home by then. Call me."

Lashonda's was the only message.

Diedre stared fixedly at the answering machine, thinking how ironic it was that it was Lashonda who had left the message. Lashonda could have had an abortion, too, but she hadn't. She was doing the very thing that Diedre had thought she could not do alone—going to law school and raising a child, making sacrifices every day to achieve her goals.

She dialed Mitch's number, waiting tensely while it rang once, twice, three times. Diedre was about to hang up, knowing that his answering machine kicked in on the fourth ring, when suddenly he picked up the phone.

"Yes?" His voice sounded thick, raspy.

"It's me," she whispered. "Mitch—we have to talk—"

"Diedre, don't, don't do this. I'm going to find out about transferring to the University of Detroit. I can't be here in Ann Arbor anymore with you. It just won't work."

He's leaving Ann Arbor? Diedre felt herself reel in shock. It was another blow, almost as great as the first.

"I have to keep my apartment until the lease runs out unless I can get a sublet, but after that I'm out of here," Mitch was saying. "Do you have any expenses connected with the—with it?"

"You mean the abortion," Diedre said, dazed. "No, Pam loaned me the money."

"How much was it? I'll send you a check to cover it. It was partly my responsibility and I never intended for you to pay the price for 'five minutes of screwing,' as you say." His voice was cold. "And then, Diedre, I guess we're out of each other's lives."

Weakness overcame her. "Mitch," she begged. "It doesn't have to be this way. We love each other. I haven't stopped loving you. And I know you love me. Please—"

There was a long silence during which she could hear Mitch's thickened breathing. "I love you, too," he finally said. "But what will I think from now on when I look at you? I'll think of what you threw away. Got rid of. You stole something from me, Diedre, something more precious than rubies."

"Oh, what a guilt trip!" something made her cry out, defiance that spurted up in the center of her like a geyser. "Really, Mitch, more precious than rubies? You were happy enough to have sex. Well, weren't you?"

"I took responsibility."

"Responsibility? Wearing a little rubber from your bill-fold that probably had a hole in it, which was why I got pregnant in the first place?" Her anger ripped out of her. "You were so 'responsible' that you never even phoned me, you just dropped me into thin air. If we hadn't run into each other at the law library, you *never* would have called me, would you?"

"Don't twist things. It wasn't like that."

"Wasn't it?" But Diedre was tired of arguing, tired of her anger and pain, tired of it all. She wasn't the only one involved in this. "What would you have done if *you* had been pregnant, Mitch? Would *you* have made the sacrifice and gone to law school nine months pregnant? I don't *think* so. You'd have run straight to the clinic and had the procedure done. Just like every other man I know."

"This isn't—I'm a man, I can't—"

"Listen to him hem and haw," she said sarcastically. "Life is so damn much easier if you're a man, isn't it? You don't have to make these tough decisions. Well, I had to decide, and it happened, and you're not going to lay a big guilt trip on me over this. I offered you love, plenty of love. Everything was okay, wasn't it, when things were going well? But as soon as we hit a rocky place, then you back off. Your love was *conditional*." Tears streamed down her cheeks. "Well, fuck you, Mitch! Just fuck you! I don't want you, I don't need you."

She slammed down the phone.

MITCH

MITCH FELT SHAKEN AS HE SLOWLY LOWERED THE phone.

Diedre's words lashed at him like those medieval whips

with spiked metal balls on the ends of them. *If we hadn't run into each other at the law library, you never would have called me, would you?*

And more, battering at him. *What would you have done if you had been pregnant, Mitch? Would you have made the sacrifice and gone to law school nine months pregnant?*

Blindly Mitch walked across the room, grabbing his jacket, shoving his arms into the sleeves. His car keys lay on the table and he scooped them up, not caring where he went or what he did, knowing only that he had to do *something*.

Within a few minutes he had gunned the accelerator, aiming the Le Baron out of his apartment parking lot. He just drove. North of town on US-23, then west on North Territorial Road, a rural area beginning to be dotted with $450,000 homes. Then north onto more rural roads, trees, woods, and farmhouses flashing past him. Snow covered the fields, blown into drifts by last night's wind.

Somehow he found himself in a village called Pinckney and drove around, looking for a bar, but none seemed to be open.

His baby.

His child, blood of his blood.

Lost forever. And he hadn't even known, hadn't been given any choice in the matter at all, his rights totally disregarded. One moment Mitch was angry, the next he was full of roiling self-pity, then it was grief so painful that he felt his throat might explode with it. How could she have done it, not even telling him? She'd acted as if he didn't exist.

He stopped at a 7-Eleven for a can of soda, and somewhere near the bottom of the can it occurred to Mitch that *he'd* acted as if *she* didn't exist, but then the thought disappeared on a wave of sorrow again, and he finally got back inside the Le Baron and kept on driving.

Family . . . it was all he'd ever wanted.

ANNIE

IT WAS A RAW WINTER MORNING, THE SKY THE COLOR OF old ice. There had been a sleet storm the previous night, and Annie Larocca nearly skidded her Dodge Shadow while making the right turn into the parking structure. She hated parking here, but today she got lucky; a woman in a Ford minivan was leaving a space just as Annie approached.

Annie strode down the maze of hospital corridors, heading for the Women's Hospital area, where Treva Connor was.

It was her lunch hour and she had to hurry, but she wanted to stop and see Treva. She was getting worried about her friend, although she couldn't really put her finger on exactly why. Maybe it was that Treva hadn't sounded like herself on the phone for the past few days. Her voice had sounded flatter, duller, and she hadn't laughed, even once.

When Annie walked into the room, she found Treva lying on her side with her lunch tray on the wheeled tray table. Vegetable soup, it looked like, and a pasta dish, typical hospital fare. Treva looked up as she entered.

"Annie, love! What a nice surprise. I didn't expect to see you here."

"I took a long lunch hour. How are you, Trev? How are you holding up?"

Annie pulled up a chair and sat down beside the bed, gazing sharply at her friend. Did her face look a bit puffy? Compared to the last time she'd seen her, that is. Why hadn't she examined Treva more closely during her visit the previous week? Then she'd have something to compare her to.

"I'm fit and feisty," declared Treva, although her voice didn't sound feisty at all. "Dr. Sandoval says I'm holding on just great. Just the usual aches and pains.''

''Such as?''

''Oh, you know. Side effects from all the medications mostly. But let's not talk about that,'' said Treva.

They began talking about the clinic, and Dr. Rosenkrantz's sudden announcement that she would be leaving in May. Both women were convinced that the heart of the clinic would be gone with Dr. Rosenkrantz's departure.

''She's just burned out,'' said Annie. ''She's too old to have somebody threaten to kill her—not that anybody is ever prepared for that. Oh, I hear No Genocide is back in town, and I hear they could be picketing us and also a clinic in Royal Oak. Aren't we lucky to be the recipients of their attention? They're going to screw up the patients for days.''

''I remember the first time I saw those people,'' Treva reminisced. ''Hundreds of them, shoulder to shoulder, all of them waving posters, singing hymns. Unbelievable. I was so scared. This woman chained herself by the neck to the clinic's door. It seemed so bizarre.''

''*Invasions,*'' said Annie. ''They're what's really scary. When I was in Worcester, this twenty-seven-year-old man broke into the clinic and went on a rampage. I mean he went berserko, totally violent, smashing up two evacuation machines with a baseball bat, yelling and screaming. We all hid behind locked doors and under desks until the police finally arrested him.'' Annie shivered.

After a while Annie looked at her watch. ''Hey, I've gotta get back to the clinic. Nancy is covering for me.''

''It was great seeing you—as usual,'' said Treva.

''Yeah. Hey, you still putting on water weight?''

''Not that much.''

''You sure? Your cheeks look a little chipmunky to me.''

''My whole body is chipmunky,'' admitted Treva ruefully. ''I've gained so much weight from just lying here and never getting any exercise.''

They embraced and then Annie left, hurrying back to her car in the parking structure and driving back to the clinic. Her heart sank as she pulled into the parking lot. The No Genocide group had arrived—forty or fifty people, standing around several vans and an old church bus. They were singing a hymn, "Jesus Loves the Little Children," substituting the word *babies* for *children*.

Annie sighed, noticing their crawling jeans and old clothes, suitable for wearing to jail. Damn . . . Was it going to be another all-day-long hassle again, as it had been the time before?

Today, almost as soon as she got out of the car, a middle-aged woman with salt-and-pepper gray hair came charging at her, breaking past the legal fifteen-foot line, waving a grisly poster of a fetus killed by saline injection, a procedure not even practiced at this clinic.

"Don't kill a baby today . . . please! Your baby has a heartbeat! Your baby is alive! Please don't kill it!"

"She works here! She works at the clinic!" someone called. "I saw her walk in this morning."

Annie strode faster. Damn . . . she didn't have her vest on again, she'd been in a hurry to visit Treva and she'd forgotten to put it on. When was she going to learn to wear it regularly? It was just such an inconvenience. In winter its bulk would barely fit underneath her coat.

She had almost reached the clinic door when something hard hit her in the right upper arm, stinging her with such pain that Annie uttered a cry of surprise. Horrified, she glanced at her arm and saw a splotch of red.

She'd been shot! *Oh, God!* And then she smelled the red fluid and realized what it was. *Paint.* She'd been hit by a paint ball.

Her breath catching, Annie stumbled toward the clinic door and threw it open, rushing inside the outer lobby. Ramon, one of the security guards, let her in.

"You okay? Jesus, they hit you."

"Paint bullet," gasped Annie.

"I'll get Dr. Rosenkrantz."

"I'm all right," breathed Annie, beginning to feel the aftereffects of shock. "My arm just hurts, that's all."

Ramon helped her in, and someone else helped her to a chair. Mei Rosario helped Annie take off the red-soaked jacket she wore. Underneath, a raised welt was already turning black and blue on Annie's skin.

Annie couldn't seem to catch her breath. She'd heard of several paint-ball game places in the Detroit area, where people stalked and "shot" each other with paint-ball guns amid a background that simulated a high-tech inner-city environment. And now the horrible game was leaking its aggression into the outside world.

"Oh, God," said Mei in revulsion. "They did this to scare you. If this had been a real bullet . . . and if their aim had been different . . ." She stopped, clapping a hand over her mouth.

I'd be dead, Annie thought in horror. Just like those two women at the clinics in Brookline, Massachusetts, and other abortion workers who had been murdered at other clinics.

Dr. Rosenkrantz came hurrying up. "Paint balls now. What will they think of next? Let's see that arm."

Obediently Annie held it up. She was shaking.

"You have a very nice contusion," said the white-haired doctor. Something in her eyes was sad. "But it isn't serious. Why don't you take a short break, Annie, clean up, and calm yourself a little. If you want, you can go home. I'll have Ramon escort you out to your car."

In the waiting room, a woman of about seventeen was sobbing softly while her boyfriend held her hand, on the verge of tears himself. Four women were being called to the conference room for their orientation talk, their faces solemn.

The patients.

Annie hesitated. Maybe Carl was right, maybe it really was time for her to get out of this business, take a nice, safe job in a gynecologist's office or something. After all, Dr. Rosenkrantz was going to do it. But how could Annie when the patients needed her? Annie knew that she had helped hundreds of women. That talk she gave, reassuring them. By holding their hands, hugging them, giving them a little extra caring, being there to listen.

Of course, no one was irreplaceable. Still, if she did go

home, and never came back, then Annie was afraid that more staffers might do the same thing. If too many staff deserted the clinic, if they couldn't find replacements, then the clinic would have to close. Already there was a serious shortage of clinic workers, especially doctors. Every defection affected everyone.

"I'll stay," she said, getting to her feet. "Does anyone have an extra uniform that'll fit me?"

"I do," said Nancy, from behind the counter. "It's in my locker—I'll get it."

Five minutes later, Annie had washed off her arm, taken two Advil, and changed into the fresh uniform. Putting a smile on her face, she walked into the conference room to explain to another group of women just what the abortion procedure was all about.

She was damned if she was going to allow terrorist tactics to stop her from helping women.

PEPPER

THE CARPET-CLEANING PEOPLE DID THEIR THING AFTER the vandalism of her boutique, along with an army of other workers, and when they were all done, Pepper herself scrubbed and scoured. Fortunately, her insurance covered full replacement value—an extravagance she was now glad she'd purchased.

Several of the design houses and factories she used were very cooperative, FedExing her new stock. Meanwhile, she had a sale, and customers snapped up the bras, panties, robes, and gowns that the intruders had tossed around but not damaged.

Turning her attentions to Oscar, Pepper took him to a cat-grooming center and had his fur meticulously trimmed,

washed, and combed into white silk. Seeing him so fluffy
and beautiful made her feel comforted.

Oscar was so much more than just a cat to her. He was
a security blanket, a talisman, a baby. If he had been murdered, which was how Pepper thought of it, she felt she
might actually have cracked emotionally.

She also upgraded her security system at Gray's insistence. "I know you can't afford all the bells and whistles
right now," he told her one Thursday night after he had
picked her up at the boutique. They planned to see a romance movie with Salma Hayek in it. "But I can, and I
want to do this, and I'm not going to listen to your protests,
Pepper. What if something had happened to you?"

They drove toward the Briarwood Mall, which had a theater complex.

"Nothing did happen to me. They weren't even interested
in me. All they wanted to do was shit on the floor and throw
things around. I don't want to take your charity, Gray. I
don't like being dependent."

Gray frowned. "In the first place, it's not charity. I'm
doing it for myself, Pepper, don't be so dense. I don't ever
want to get another frantic phone call like that again. Would
you relax a little about this money issue and allow me to
do this?"

Pepper wrinkled her forehead. She knew she was going
to have to give in on this one item, much as she hated to
do so. "It just bothers me when you spend on me. I can't
explain it. I don't like it when—"

*I don't like it when I feel that men are using their money
and power to affect me,* she'd been about to say, but she
cut off the words. Still, Gray had certainly sensed what she
had not said, and his frown intensified, drawing his dark
brows straight together across his forehead.

"I wish I could have met your father," he said evenly.
"I think it would have been very educational."

"What do you mean?"

"You've told me a few things about him, vacations at
dude ranches and swimming outside hotels on Maui, all the

gifts he used to buy you. And I think the operative phrase is 'buy you.' He really did a number on you, honey.''

"Please," Pepper said, flushing. "I . . . I don't want to talk about my father right now.''

"If not now, then when, Pepper? He has something to do with your attitude about men and money, doesn't he? He's why you're so prickly when I try to do something for you. You think I'm trying to buy you, don't you?''

"Please." She felt a surge of anger. "*Please* don't analyze me. And please let me pay for my business when I can. Don't try to take it over, Gray. You have your own company, I have my boutique, so just let up on me, okay?''

They were pulling into the mall parking lot now, using the entrance closest to the movie complex.

Gray came around to the passenger side to let Pepper out, but she had already jumped out of the car, her face hot. They started toward the marquee entrance, walking several feet apart from each other like an old married couple having a spat.

Pepper sighed. It did seem that she and Gray were squabbling more and more lately, usually about money or her independence. Maybe because they were getting too close, making her feel slightly trapped.

Gray could be controlling, and sometimes it just got to her.

The strong smell of popcorn greeted them as they walked into the theater area. A huge line of people snaked back into the mall, most of them here to see the newest Brad Pitt movie. A theater employee walked up and down the line, announcing a cutoff point for the sold-out picture. People groaned and those cut off began walking away.

Finally Gray bought their tickets for the romantic comedy.

"Lighten up, darling," he told her. "I won't bug you about your father anymore, honest. I just want you to know I'm not like him. I love you. Really and truly I do, and if I was a convenience-store clerk and you were a cashier at Kmart, I'd still love you just as much.''

They stopped at the concession stand to buy a tub of popcorn and two Diet Pepsis; Gray always insisted a movie wasn't a flick without popcorn. But the buttery, pungent popcorn smell seemed nauseating to Pepper. She stood back behind Gray as he purchased it, averting her eyes from the sight of fat, orange hot dogs turning on spits and large, greasy chocolate chunk cookies covered by a plastic bell.

As the previews began for a new Chris Rock comedy, Pepper fixed her eyes on the screen, refusing popcorn when Gray handed her the tub.

"Sure you don't want any? This is the best. The air-popped kind slathered in butter."

She shuddered. "Please, no."

So Gray ate most of the popcorn himself, while Pepper stared at the screen, gradually allowing herself to become caught up in the movie plot, which involved feisty women standing up to the men in their lives. She could really identify with that.

Gray laughed, and so did the other men in the audience, but Pepper thought she could detect a note of unease in their mirth. She found herself thinking about her mother, Toni. In fact, Pepper suddenly remembered, Toni had once gone to Mason Maddalena's home in Sarasota and smashed windows, running her car into his garage door, totaling it.

Her attention segued away from the movie, and Pepper sat there miserably, thinking that she had really come from a very unhappy background, hadn't she? Her mother had been so angry at her father for his rejection of her. Hating him for his money, even as she spent it. Saying poisonous things to her young daughter, making sure Pepper knew her dad's gifts were only ploys, not real.

"Pepper? Pep?" To Pepper's astonished surprise, the movie was over and the lights were going up. She felt a rush of saliva to her mouth, and swallowed it back.

"Come on," said Gray, gently taking her hand. "We're going back to your apartment, Pepper. I think we have some talking to do."

*   *   *

But when they got to her apartment, Oscar jumping down from the couch to wind himself, meowing, around her calves, Pepper felt suddenly, totally exhausted.

"I'm sorry," she muttered. "I think I'm going to have to crash. I really can't keep my eyes open much longer."

"I'll make us some coffee," offered Gray.

"No. Really." She gave him a light kiss on the cheek. "Not tonight, Gray."

"You're still angry."

"No." God, she hated their fighting, hated the idea that most of it came about because of her balkiness. Suddenly she felt penitent, and she threw her arms around him, holding him close and smelling the vanilla odor of his aftershave, the deeper, musky, sexy odors of his skin and hair. "I love you, Gray."

"Do you?" His voice sounded oddly sad. "I hope you do, Pepper."

She felt a flash of horrible guilt as she hugged him. She did love him . . . she did! And yet . . . all the negative thoughts she'd been having, her feeling of being too tightly pressed . . .

At the door they kissed again, holding their bodies close. Not a passionate kiss, but a sweet one. But suddenly even the scent of Gray's aftershave seemed too rich and cloying, and Pepper unobtrusively pulled back.

"Good night," she whispered.

Later that night Pepper woke from a sound sleep with a strange, clutching feeling at the center of her stomach. She staggered out of bed and barely made it to the bathroom before she was violently sick.

She spewed up her dinner and then it was just dry heaves, over and over again. Perspiring, she sank down onto the floor on her knees, remembering that there was a flu bug going around Ann Arbor. Jan's husband had it, and Jan had taken a morning off to be with him.

Maybe Jan had brought some germs to work and Pepper had caught them.

Miserably she rinsed out her mouth, washed her sweaty face, and shuffled back to bed. That was all she needed, the flu. Oscar, who'd stayed well away from the bathroom while she was being sick, now padded back into the bedroom and leaped up on the mattress beside her.

"Oskie," she murmured. "Do you think what I need is chicken soup? I couldn't eat any chicken soup, not even if the chicken itself were clucking and begging me. I couldn't eat anything."

Her queasiness continued in the morning, but Pepper forced herself to have a bowl of bran flakes and skim milk, with a banana sliced up in it. Once she started eating, the nausea went away and she decided to go in to the shop.

It was one of those sunny, glaringly bright February mornings when the harsh sun bounced off the white snow and hurt the eyes. Pepper put on her big, new, round glasses which made her look like a movie star. Peering through the windshield, she assured herself that last night she might have had just a touch of the twenty-four-hour variety of bug. Hopefully it was gone today.

As always, she was the first to arrive at the shop, and she went through her morning ritual of disarming the new security system, which had to be done within thirty seconds or the alarm would sound. She let Oscar out of his cage, switching on lights and doing all the other small chores she usually performed.

One of the bouquets of roses that Gray had sent this week was getting a little overblown, she noticed. She would keep it one more day, then toss it. Her customers often commented on how her place was always full of roses. It was becoming part of the shop's mystique, Pepper knew. People had come to expect stunning roses, along with a white cat, when they walked in.

Casting a critical eye over the shop, Pepper made a mental list of what replacement items from New York were still due to be delivered. She needed to make another buying trip to New York as soon as she could.

In fact, Valentine's Day was coming up—where had her mind been? Suddenly she longed for wild brightness and color. Magenta. Fuchsia. Ruby. Scarlet. Vermilion. Black to set it off. Slutty, sexy colors . . . oh, yes! That was what her customers wanted this year, Pepper decided.

She began prowling through drawers and shelves, pulling out sexy little nothings. Absorbed in what she was doing, she barely noticed Jan coming in the front door.

"Whoa," said Jan, grinning. "Looks like it's going to be a sex-kitten Valentine's day."

Pepper looked up. "You're absolutely right." She held up a ravishing bra and matching panties made of fuchsia lace. "What about these? Aren't they just to die for? I'm going to have a completely fuchsia window display. Even Oscar gets a fuchsia bow. And red and fuchsia everywhere in the shop . . . nothing pastel anywhere."

Jan waited on customers while Pepper, having a sudden creative spurt, climbed on a stool and began arranging stock on the elegant plastic display grids she used to show off her merchandise.

Standing on the stool, she suddenly felt a wave of dizziness. She clutched at the wall hook, dropping an armload of frothy panties. The panties scattered to the floor.

"Hey, klutz, you all right?" called Jan.

"I just got a little light-headed. Maybe it's that flu bug. I could be getting it."

"Better get down from that stool, then. Come on, you've been working like a horse all morning, Pepper. Why don't we sit down and have some coffee? I made a fresh pot—Swiss chocolate, just the way you like it."

"Swiss chocolate," Pepper repeated. She rolled the words around on her tongue, feeling another twinge of the nausea. Strange . . . usually she loved Swiss chocolate and regarded it as a treat.

"You okay?" inquired Jan when she had brought out a steaming mug printed with the lavender Pepper's logo.

"I'm fine. More than fine." Pepper pretended to sip the

coffee. Actually, even the smell was making her feel nauseous.

"But you were dizzy up there on that stool. We're lucky you didn't take a nose dive, Pepper."

"Heights bother me."

"But the stool is only a foot high."

"Low heights."

Pepper grinned crookedly and changed the subject, and they began arguing about which colors were really traditional for Valentine's Day. Red, of course, but what about magenta, or white? Was purple too sleazy?

Later Pepper put down her cup still almost full, and went into the bathroom to rinse it out.

"Lunch?" called Jan from the other side of the partition. "Shall I send out to Zev's or do you want something from the deli?"

Pepper caught her breath, again experiencing another twinge of nausea. The thought of a plump deli sandwich stuffed with greasy, fatty meat was enough to make her feel sick. The smell of rye. And a big lump of potato salad . . .

Oh, shit, she thought as she turned around and threw up in the toilet.

A repeat of last time.

Again? It seemed some cruel trick of fate, the gods laughing at her. Pepper leaned toward the bathroom mirror, staring at her pale face, her eyes wide with terror. Could she possibly be pregnant again?

Oh, yes, definitely she could.

She sank down on the closed lid of the commode, swallowing back her fear.

Their social life was often stressful and there were plenty of late hours, a few nights when they'd been out until after 3:30 A.M. at one black-tie affair or another. Then lovemaking for several hours after that. In fact, hadn't she forgotten her pill compact on one of the weekends at Gray's condo? She had missed two pills, but had assured herself two wouldn't really matter. God, what had she been thinking?

She could run her shop to perfection, but when it came to a simple little compact of pills . . . *Oh, shit!*

Pepper rubbed her hands over her dry eyes, blinking back a sudden headache that pounded at her sinuses and extended into her temples. Even birth control pills had a failure rate, they'd told her at the clinic, especially if a woman skipped a pill or two . . . Wasn't it something like .7 pregnancies per a hundred women under ordinary use?

She uttered a soft moan. The nausea. The dizziness. And hadn't she noticed, just this morning in the shower, that her nipples felt full and tender? She'd been so tired recently. Weepy.

Oh, shit, shit, shit! she thought, pounding her palms into the sides of her skull.

What am I going to do?

On the occasion of her last pregnancy crisis, Pepper had gone out and bought a pregnancy test kit, confirming her condition, then confiding immediately in Jan. Now, for some reason, she didn't want to do that. She wanted time to think. To plan.

This time was different. This time there was Gray. He'd want to marry her for sure as soon as he knew.

She was afraid she knew exactly what Jan would tell her—*marry the man.* Oh, yes, that was *exactly* what Jan would say, along with every other girlfriend Pepper had, and her mother, and her ex-husband, Jack, and her landlady, Mrs. Melnick . . . *Every woman in Ann Arbor would tell me not to be a fool, to take this opportunity and marry the man.*

"Pepper?" called Jan from outside the bathroom door, in an eerie repeat of last August. "You okay?"

"Just a little stomach bug," lied Pepper. "Those germs do travel around. Maybe I'll go home a little early if you wouldn't mind closing. I much prefer urping in the privacy of my own home."

"I'll close; I don't mind. You sure you're okay, honey?"

"Right as rain." Pepper winced at the blatant untruth. "Actually," she called through the door, "I feel like a goat's dinner. All I want to do is go home, lie on the couch, and turn on the cable. I think there's a Danielle Steel movie on the tube tonight—it's about all I'm going to be capable of watching.''

"This isn't like you," commented Jan.

Irritably Pepper poked her head outside the door. "Even workaholics get sick, Jan. I have to get three times as sick as everyone else, but eventually even I throw in the towel."

"I didn't mean—"

"I know. I'm just grumpy. I hate getting sick. I don't even like chicken soup that much. Actually what I do like is ice cream. I think I'll buy some on the way home . . . Häagen-Daz's vanilla."

Pepper put Oscar into his carry-cage and started giving Jan last-minute instructions, which Jan waved away with a laugh. "How many times have I closed up, or helped you close, Pepper? Just go home and get a big spoon and sit in front of the TV with your Häagen-Daz. And stay home as long as you have to. I'll open in the morning if you're not in."

Pepper nodded, and felt another wave of dizziness as she lifted the cat. But she wasn't about to tell Jan about it, and by the time she was walking through the door, the dizziness was gone. She'd been dizzy before, too—last August she'd even fainted, she now recalled. In front of her landlady. Christ.

There was a convenience store near Pepper's apartment, and she drove into the parking lot, suddenly possessed by a real craving for ice cream. Inside the store, she pawed through the ice cream case, discarding Ben & Jerry's Chunky Monkey, various flavors of yogurt, and ice cream with nuts, cookies, swirls, or toppings in it. Only plain vanilla would do.

Finally she found a pint container of vanilla Häagen-Daz at the back of the case, its surface dotted by ice crystals, and she took it up to the counter. Then she left it there and returned to the back of the store, to the women's sanitary section, where she rooted around on the lower shelves, hoping to find a pregnancy kit. Convenience stores never had what you wanted, she thought in annoyance as she searched among boxes of super tampons and curved pads.

Whoa . . . one lone little kit on the back shelf, an E.P.T. brand. Hiding there, just waiting for her, or some other worried-insane woman. Pepper grabbed it up and took it to the checkout. The clerk, a woman in her early twenties, glanced curiously at the E.P.T. box.

"Just checking," said Pepper inanely. She thrust the ice cream and the pregnancy test onto the counter and fumbled in her purse for a twenty-dollar bill.

"Me, I take an ovulation test every month," said the clerk. "I'm trying to get pregnant."

"Hope you make it," snapped Pepper. She paced around until the clerk had put her purchases in a bag, then fled the store.

Somewhere in the big, Victorian apartment house, one of the tenants was playing crescendoing, classical music. Probably it was Billy Ip, who sometimes went on a classical binge that lasted for weeks. Pepper wished he would use earphones but didn't have the energy to go downstairs and request that he do so.

Wearing her old terry bathrobe, sitting in front of her TV set with a big, cereal-sized bowl in her lap, Pepper slowly spooned the sweet, rich ice cream to her mouth. But after only a few mouthfuls she lost her appetite and put the dish aside.

Oh, God . . . she had a problem on her hands. She'd taken the pregnancy test just as soon as she'd arrived home, and it had been positive, just as she'd known it would be. She had missed one period . . . Had it been two weeks? Three? God, why hadn't she kept better track? She just blithely went on about her busy life and never even thought about her menstrual cycle until it came.

Gray. She had to tell him—it was his child; he had to know.

However, Pepper made no move toward the telephone, but continued to watch the TV set, where beautiful, blond women and handsome men lived lives of emotional turmoil. She didn't want to talk to Gray, not yet. She had to hold on to this news for a while, had to think about it by herself. Because once he became aware of her pregnancy, he'd be all over her, proposing marriage, telling her what to do, taking charge.

Marriage. Oh, God. She just didn't know.

And yet another alternative, abortion, didn't sound that great either. Her third. Was she just going to keep on going back to the clinic twice a year, like taking her car in for service? Using the clinic as "birth control," for heaven's sake?

An hour later, Gray called. Pepper told him merely that she'd had some flu symptoms and was under the weather.

"Poor baby. Want me to come by and make you some chicken soup?"

"Oh, you make soup, too?" She forced a laugh. "Honestly, I don't even like soup that much. I'm just going to veg out in front of the TV. There's a Danielle Steel tearjerker on."

"Two can veg out," he suggested.

"Yeah . . . but not tonight."

As Gray made a sound of disappointment, Pepper explained, "I've got on an old terry bathrobe that has threads hanging from every hem and holes in the elbows. Plus it has old chocolate stains that probably date back to 1985."

Gray laughed. "A truly memorable garment."

"Trust me, you wouldn't want to see me in it. I keep the remote in the side pocket," she improvised. "And I put my Milk Duds in the other pocket, so they'll be handy. I'm truly a pig."

"Well, I certainly won't interfere with you and your Milk Duds. Honey, are you sure there isn't anything I can do for you? By the way, I hope you're not taking any aspirin. You know aspirin really upsets the stomach."

Pepper made a face. There it was, him giving her un-

wanted advice again. He always said he wouldn't, but then
he did. If she married him, would she have a lifetime of
that? But she didn't have the energy to challenge him right
now.

"I have Tylenol and Advil. I can manage. As long as the
power doesn't go out, and the cable box still works, I'll be
in seventh heaven."

Pepper felt better by the next morning and managed to
go in to the shop, where she had small portions of saltine
crackers and Pepsi throughout the morning, then treated herself to a skimpy bowl of ice cream at noon. If she ate ice
cream every day, she was going to balloon up, but it was
the only food that really tasted good to her right now.

When Jan went out at noon for lunch, Pepper went in the
back room and dialed the Geddes/Washtenaw Clinic, asking
for an appointment. The clinic did many women's services,
she knew, and they would be able to counsel her on this
pregnancy.

She didn't want to call her regular ob-gyn, Dr. Jewett.
She just couldn't face that big bulletin board he had with
all the baby pictures on it. It seemed like all baby doctors
had them.

Coming back to the Geddes/Washtenaw Clinic was a strange
experience. Pepper sat in the waiting room surrounded by
women, some in varying stages of pregnancy, some who
had brought small children with them. The clinic only did
abortions on Mondays, Tuesdays, and Thursdays, Pepper
had learned, so these women might be here for Pap smears,
breast exams, or any other female problem.

Still, when the nurse called her name, she rose nervously,
going into the back office area with a feeling of trepidation.
If she decided to abort, this was where she'd find herself
again, lying on a table once more with her legs suspended
from stirrups . . .

She felt another spasm of the nausea and had to quickly
ask the nurse where the rest room was. Rushing inside, Pep-

per leaned over the toilet and coughed up foul-tasting stomach acid.

Finally she emerged, and was shown to an exam room, where she was given a paper gown to put on. A nurse came in—she didn't recognize the face—and the woman took a detailed history. Pepper told her everything. She was perspiring heavily. This time it was not like the previous time. This time her options were so much different . . .

"Congratulations, Pepper. You are definitely pregnant," said Dr. Ellen Rosenkrantz, smiling at Pepper across her desk, which was piled high with papers and folders. The tiny, white-haired doctor was wearing jeans and a T-shirt underneath her physician's coat, attire that gave her a disconcertingly young-old look.

"Oh," Pepper said in a small voice, a second wave of shock pouring over her, even though this wasn't exactly a surprise.

"I take it this pregnancy isn't a hundred percent wonderful news," said Dr. Rosenkrantz.

"It isn't," she managed to say. "I . . . I have questions."

"Go ahead and ask them, dear."

"Well, for one thing . . . I've been on the pill. Will that affect the baby if I—if I do have it?"

"Well, the chances are excellent that it won't, Pepper. At first it was feared that there might be problems in babies exposed to oral contraceptives, but later studies have failed to confirm this," explained Dr. Rosenkrantz.

"I'm thinking—I'm thinking of terminating the pregnancy. Just considering," she added quickly.

There was a pause, then Dr. Rosenkrantz cleared her throat. "Pepper, there are a few things I do want to mention. Your medical history—the two abortion procedures you've already had, one here at this clinic, and the one in Miami fifteen years ago."

"Yes?"

"You said that you had some bleeding after your first abortion?"

"Yeah. I had to go back to the doctor, he took some stitches."

"Your uterus was probably mildly perforated," Dr. Rosenkrantz said, again frowning.

Pepper clenched her hands in her lap. "I-I was crying too hard to know what happened. They didn't tell me. I just got through it, that's all. Oh, and I had a fever, too. They had to give me antibiotics."

"You could have had a pelvic infection—it can be very serious."

"But I recovered fine."

"Yes, and I know the correct procedures were used on you here at the Geddes/Washtenaw Clinic—because I absolutely insist on them. Still, you've had two pregnancy terminations now, Pepper, and it's possible that a third one wouldn't be such a good idea. The truth is that multiple abortions *can* damage the reproductive organs. Not in all cases, but sometimes."

"I . . . I see," said Pepper, wetting her lips. "Multiple abortions." Even the words seemed terrible, carrying with them a stigma.

"Don't feel badly, Pepper, when I tell you this. You made the proper choices for you at the time, but I'm just telling you that the more procedures you undergo, the greater the risk that at some future time you may find it difficult to become pregnant. Would you like to arrange for further counseling? We have very good counselors here, and maybe one of them can help you work this through."

"I . . . all right," mumbled Pepper, getting to her feet.

She stopped at the desk and paid for her visit, but instead of making the appointment to see the counselor, she fled out of the building, hurrying to her car. Multiple abortions! Oh, God, if that meant what she thought it did, then maybe she didn't have infinite chances to give birth. Suppose she got another abortion now, and screwed her body up so that it would be harder to get pregnant again later when she wanted to? Also, she wasn't getting younger. She was already over thirty.

Gray.

He was part of this now . . . or he could be, if she decided to tell him.

She didn't know what to do. If she told him, it would be like jumping into the river just above Niagara Falls. He'd sweep her down the current so fast she'd never be able to swim to shore before tumbling over the falls.

DIEDRE

MITCH DIDN'T CALL—NOT THAT SUNDAY AND NOT THE following week. There were moments when Diedre felt horror at the words she'd hurled at him, the terrible accusations they'd both made, and wanted to call him up and take them all back, beg him to love her.

She forced herself not to. She'd known all along it would end, and it did. End of story. Maybe a part of her had even wanted to test their love, or she wouldn't have insisted on telling him as she'd done.

Grimly she settled down to her classes, forcing herself to excel, but without any real enjoyment. She went to the meetings of the Women's Law Club, and started working on the stalker case that Rodger Halsick had given her. The nursing student, Yasmeen Mammoud, was young and frightened, very grateful for the free help the club was giving her.

Diedre spent time writing up a stalking petition and filing it with the court in Washtenaw County. Now if the man continued to stalk Yasmeen, he could be arrested. It did help—to have something to do that didn't involve Mitch in any way.

Still, every time she walked into the reading room of the Law Library, where she and Mitch had spent so many happy hours, her heart constricted. She started taking her books to the Harlan Hatcher Graduate Library, just a short walk away, on the "diag" that crisscrossed the main campus. At least that library wasn't contaminated by painful memories.

She didn't want to see Mitch's smiling, handsome ghost.

A few days later, Yasmeen called Diedre and told her that Tonio was continuing to call her—she thought. Now, however, instead of getting his voice on the phone, she was getting dozens of hang-ups. So were her mother, roommates, and sister.

After advising Yasmeen to order Caller ID, which would provide a record of all callers, Diedre borrowed Pam's car and drove up to the hospital to visit Treva Connor. She still felt very much drawn to the older woman's serenity and courage, and wanted to discuss Yasmeen with her, and find out if Treva had any ideas on how the nineteen-year-old nursing student could deal with her stalker.

She found Treva lying on her side, attached to an IV line and a discreet tube that snaked out from under the covers. She wore a teal blue cotton shift trimmed in lace, her stomach mounding underneath. A bedside tray held a jumble of objects: books, a plastic water pitcher, tissues, cosmetics, pens, pencils, a half-eaten apple. A small TV set was playing a PBS program. And of course, there was the telephone. Diedre knew that even though she'd temporarily tabled the abortion-study interviews, Treva still lived for the phone.

While they were talking, a nurse came in to check the fetal heart rate and take Treva's blood pressure and other vital signs, so Diedre had to wait in the hallway for a few minutes.

"Everything's great," announced Treva when she reentered the room. "The little guy's heart is a hundred thirty beats a minute, just what it's supposed to be." She was now in her thirty-first week, she told Diedre. "We're just hoping I can carry for a few more weeks—even three or four would be great."

Treva's suggestions on how Yasmeen might deal with her ex-boyfriend were all good ones. "Caller ID is a terrific idea. You know, any time she talks to him, about anything, she only encourages him to bother her again," said Treva. "These people obsess, and any slight contact, they take as an invitation. Even an answering-machine tape feeds their neurosis. Yasmeen might consider getting a new, second phone line that she can give out to her friends and relatives, and take the answering machine off the old line. Turn off the ringer so she doesn't have to hear it all the time. Eventually he'll tire of hearing nothing but rings. She should also start keeping a diary of everything he does, every contact she or her friends or relatives have with him."

They discussed this for a while, then Treva said, "How's your young man?"

Diedre burst out with the story of their breakup.

"I'm very sorry to hear it," said Treva softly.

"I wish I'd never met him!" Diedre burst out. "If it hadn't been for him, I'd be happy right now in law school, everything would be going so great for me."

"But everything *is* going great for you," Treva pointed out. "Your grades . . . your future . . . losing Mitch won't change that if you don't allow it to."

"Oh, I'll study. I'll keep up the A's if it's the last thing I do," said Diedre grimly. "I'll get over the damn abortion. But I just wish—I wish I hadn't gotten drunk that night. I wish his condom hadn't had a hole in it. Isn't it crazy? One tiny, pinpoint hole, and one tiny sperm—oh, and a little egg—and people's lives can change forever."

That weekend was Tarik's birthday, and Lashonda was giving a party for him that would include her study-group friends and several of their small children, along with Lashonda's granny, who was driving over from Detroit for the celebration.

The party turned out to be a raucous, lively affair. Women and children crowded Lashonda's small apartment, toddlers laughing and shrieking, occasionally wailing as someone tripped and fell, or had a toy snatched away. There was cake, ice cream, and strawberry Kool-Aid. Tarik was adorable in a new outfit, his brown eyes shining.

"You bring present, DeeDee?" he wanted to know.

"I certainly did. I brought that blue box right over there."

"What inside? Is you giving me a dinosaur?"

Diedre couldn't help smiling. Actually, she'd been able to find a realistically painted, plastic replica of a diplodocus.

"You'll just have to wait and see, Tarik."

The little boy ran off to join the other children, and Diedre couldn't help noticing that all the other toddlers were equally cute. Tiny, dark-skinned girls with their hair corn-rowed and beaded, wearing fluffy party dresses. A chubby little boy with a crown of loose, dark curls who looked as if he could appear in a Huggies ad.

So cute. In her present mood, Diedre could scarcely bear to look at them.

Lashonda's granny, a woman named Jovita Beauchamel, turned out to be a slender, chocolate-colored woman of only fifty-six, an accounting clerk who worked at Ford Motor Credit in Dearborn.

"So your man dropped you, honey?" Jovita said to Die-dre, as they watched six young children playing on the floor with Tarik's toys while several of the other mothers were cleaning up the cake and Kool-Aid mess.

Diedre flushed. "Lashonda told you?"

"Don't worry, nothing Lashonda tells me ever goes any further. I help her, I've always helped her, and we're close. Don't you let a man make you feel guilty for what you did."

"Oh . . . I won't."

"Hey, how old is a girl when she gets her first period? Mine started at eleven. And I went through my change at forty-five. How many months is that to get pregnant? More than four hundred. And how many times do you have sex in that time period? Maybe more than six thousand times! And that's only doing it every other day."

Shocked at these statistics, Diedre could only stare at the older woman.

"Men aren't gonna agonize about that, nosiree," Jovita went on. "And they're not going to count months either. You think you can have sex six thousand times and not have your birth control slip up at least once? No matter what you use. I had three abortions back before they were legal. I nearly died from one of them. It was either get the abortion or lose my sanity. I chose sanity. You choose it, too, Diedre girl. If that man of yours can't take it, then he's not worth your time.''

Diedre nodded, trying to be polite. Just what she needed, advice from Lashonda's granny. She wished she hadn't come to this party, with all of the cute children running around. Her head ached, a set of bellows squeezing in her temples.

"I guess Granny was kinda nosy, wasn't she?" said Lashonda as Diedre was preparing to leave. "Sorry, she can be pretty outspoken. She'll say anything to anyone."

"It was all right," said Diedre.

"If that man of yours asks you about your abortion, you tell him how it really was. Don't leave anything out. Make him see it. Make him *feel* it. That's the only way you're going to get him back," declared Lashonda.

When Diedre got back to the apartment that evening, she studied for six more hours. She had to. Her heart might be breaking, but she couldn't let her grades slip.

The call from Lashonda came at 5:30 P.M. the following night, just as Diedre had finished eating her Budget Gourmet microwave dinner and was getting out her law books to prepare for yet another night of studying.

"It's—oh, G-God—it's Tarik!" Her friend's voice was so high-pitched that Diedre could barely understand her.

"What? Lashonda? Is that you?"

"Blood all over. Oh, sweet Jesus, I can't believe it, that damn day care center, I'm going to sue the *shit* out of them." Lashonda started to weep.

"What is it? What's wrong? Talk to me, Lashonda!"

"Tarik ran through a glass door in day care. I'm in emergency right now. St. Joe's. He cut one of his arteries . . . almost bled to death . . . He's in s-surgery . . ."

*   *   *

Diedre grabbed the car keys off the coffee table, threw on her coat, and ran out of the apartment, taking the stairs two at a time. Gunning the accelerator of the Toyota, she sped to St. Joseph's Hospital off Huron River Drive, bucking rush-hour traffic as she ran several stoplights. *Tarik!* Such a sweet, bright boy. If he died . . . *But he can't die. God, please.*

Visiting hours were still in session and Diedre had to cruise the crowded hospital parking lot, growing desperate before she finally found a space. Getting out of the car, she ran full tilt toward the emergency entrance.

Lashonda was sitting in a lounge, bent forward, her arms crossed in front of her chest as if she were chilled to the bone. Her eyes were reddened and her milk-chocolate skin was drained of its gloss, looking ashy in the overhead fluorescent lights.

"Lashonda!" Diedre rushed forward, and the two women hugged. Lashonda was trembling, and an acrid, peppery smell of fear came from her. "Is he all right?" Diedre demanded. "Is he still in surgery? What happened?"

"Those frigging day care people, I'm going to sue their *asses* off," cried Lashonda. "They had this stupid *door* that led outside. The kids were playing and Tarik was running back and forth and a kid pushed him or something. He went right through the door. He had a cut in his artery—what's it called?—femoral artery. Almost bled to death. Jesus sweet Christ. If this aide hadn't come running and put pressure on the cut, he would have . . . would have . . ."

Lashonda broke into tears as Diedre patted her and murmured and fumbled in her purse for a tissue, finally finding a very crumpled but clean one. Lashonda took it, blew several times, then balled it up in her hand.

"He's in surgery now," said Lashonda. "They said he'd be okay, but I guess I'm just falling apart. He's my life, Diedre. He's why I do so well in law school, he's why I have my dream. If I never had him, I probably wouldn't even be here."

Lashonda continued to talk, telling her that Jovita was on

her way over, but part of Diedre's mind kept repeating what her friend had said. *He's why I have my dream.*

Diedre fought confusion, trying for the dozenth time to make sense of her own decision, so different from Lashonda's. Would she have been like Lashonda, centering all of her dreams around her baby, or would the child have been the encumbrance she'd feared? She'd never know now, would she? Her choice had been so final.

She only knew that now she wanted Mitch so painfully that she ached all over. And she wanted his children. She wanted a little boy like Tarik. But would she ever have one, at least with Mitch? The possibility seemed terribly unlikely.

A sobbing woman entered the emergency-room lounge, accompanied by two other women, also crying. A sixteen-year-old boy was in critical condition after a car accident. The women's crying infected everyone else in the room, and Diedre felt her own chest heaving, tears about to surface.

Life was so capriciously unfair. The pleasure, the pain, it struck everyone and no one was immune, she thought. You could think you had it all, and maybe you did, but then something would happen . . .

About fifteen minutes later, a doctor in green scrubs spotted with bloodstains—a young Asian woman with a name tag that said D. WU.—came into the lounge and told them that Tarik was in recovery and was going to be fine.

Lashonda started to weep with relief. "You mean he'll be able to walk and run and everything?"

"Fortunately, yes. It's a miracle he's here with us, though. If that woman at the day care center hadn't put pressure on the wound, he wouldn't be here," said the doctor.

"Will there be scarring?" Lashonda wanted to know.

"Black skin does scar, I'm afraid, but the scars shouldn't be too noticeable. As soon as he's conscious, you can go in to see him. Then we'll be taking him up to his room. Kids recover from trauma amazingly fast. He'll be lively and feisty by tomorrow morning probably."

"Oh, thank you," said Lashonda, in her emotion hugging

the doctor. Then she hugged Diedre, whirling her around.
''Oh, thank God.''

By the time Diedre left St. Joseph's Hospital, she was feeling drained, and full of a sudden longing to tell Mitch about
her feelings while she'd been sitting there with Lashonda
. . . *all* her thoughts. But of course, that wasn't possible anymore, was it? He hated her now.

She left the emergency area, finding her car in the parking
lot. It was a bitterly cold night, frozen ice from a previous
thaw glittering on the parking lot, making it slippery in
places. She turned her car in the direction of home, her
mood at an all-time low. But instead of returning home, she
found herself driving toward Mitch's apartment.

Located on Plymouth Road, it was one of Ann Arbor's
nicer apartment complexes, brick buildings set back behind
expensive, professionally landscaped shrubbery. A big club-
house offered a well-equipped weight room, plus a small
indoor pool and a Jacuzzi, all of this touted by a big sign
that said LIVE THE LIFESTYLE! Mitch's unit was toward the
back.

Diedre slowly drove through the complex, her heartbeat
beginning to thud painfully. One unit, blazing with light,
held at least fifty people having a party—not a common beer
party but one with mixed drinks, she could see by the
glasses that most held. She passed two or three people walking dogs, a pizza delivery car with a big Domino's sign lit
up on the roof of the vehicle.

She shouldn't be doing this. What was she going to do,
ring Mitch's doorbell, beg to come up? He didn't want to
talk to her, and she'd only humiliate herself. Still, as she
rounded the corner near a covered carport marked with code
numbers for the tenants, Diedre couldn't help lifting her
eyes to the second floor.

Mitch's lights were on.

Which meant he was home—he had to be! Unless he'd
already sublet his apartment and a new tenant was inside,
but she didn't think it was possible to transfer to another

university that fast. He'd undoubtedly have to wait until June, she surmised.

She drove slowly past the unit, hoping to catch a glimpse of Mitch. Vertical blinds hung carelessly open just as Mitch usually left them. She saw a big poster of a World War II fighter plane which Mitch had hung on the wall of his dining area. Its familiarity tore at her heart.

And then she saw a shadow move on the wall near the poster, and in a second there was Mitch, wearing a white sweater, his dark hair falling over his eyes. She was too far away to see his facial expression, but she didn't have to. The way he walked, the set of his shoulders, the way he moved his arms, told her how unhappy he was.

Diedre gulped in a big breath, expelling it fast. Even seeing him like this tore at her emotions. She'd thought she was starting to recover, but now she realized that she wasn't.

Diedre accelerated fast, speeding out of the complex, her tires peeling rubber as she made a left turn on Plymouth. Another car pulled out behind her, but Diedre was too upset to notice it. She pushed her foot on the gas pedal, breaking the speed limit as she started home.

It was only as she slowed for her third stoplight that she noticed the car still behind her. A Ford Sunbird with a crumpled front bumper. Hadn't it pulled out of the apartment complex behind her? She hadn't been paying attention.

She drove two more blocks, the Sunbird directly behind her. A streetlight allowed her to see, in her rearview mirror, that there was a man behind the wheel. Diedre quickly turned off on a side street and the car didn't follow, but then when she turned back on Plymouth it was there again, two vehicles behind her.

Shit!

She pulled into another apartment complex, where Eileen, one of the members of Lashonda's study group, lived with two roommates. Speeding through the maze of buildings, she popped out of an exit that took her to Nixon Road and a subdivision of homes.

This time she had lost him, she felt almost sure.

She clenched the steering wheel, narrowly avoiding a skid on an icy patch caused by melted snow running over the road. A light sheen of perspiration coated her forehead and upper lip. If only Mitch had been with her—Suddenly she needed to see Mitch, talk to him, touch him, the need so desperate that she felt as if she were strangling.

On Washtenaw Diedre pulled into a small strip mall where a telephone kiosk was positioned out in the parking lot of a hardware store. She fed in the coins, then dialed, shivering in the bitter cold as trucks rumbled and roared past, only about a dozen feet from where she stood.

"Hello?" His voice was as deep and resonant as she remembered, its sound stabbing lancets of pain through her.

She had to shout over the sounds of traffic. "Mitch . . . it's Diedre. I—I was followed by a car!"

"You were what? Diedre, I can't hear you."

She yelled it louder. "Some guy in a car followed me. I . . . Mitch . . ."

"Diedre, where are you? Are you calling from a phone booth? Is he still following you?"

She gripped the phone, realizing she couldn't tell him she'd just driven past his apartment building.

"I was just out driving. Driving around. I ducked into some apartment complex and left by another exit. I'm pretty sure I lost him."

"Only pretty sure? Jesus, Diedre. Where are you? I'll come and get you. We can go to the police station and make a report."

She bent closer to the phone, trying to hear his words over the roar of traffic. "What? Mitch, I can't hear you."

"I said I'll come and pick you up. What phone are you at?"

She gave him directions, adding that the strip mall was closed, so she couldn't go inside any of the stores.

"Stay there, keep your car doors locked, and if anyone approaches your car, bang on the horn and use your flashers."

Diedre muttered an assent. Her heart was hammering. She

couldn't think anymore, couldn't think clearly. Mitch was coming to help her, but it didn't mean anything personal, she knew. It certainly did not mean that they were getting back together again.

She waited inside her car with the door locked, her thoughts accompanied by the whoosh of traffic on the nearby multilaned road, until she saw Mitch's Le Baron pull up beside the Toyota. Mitch got out of the car, wearing a brown leather jacket, wind blowing at his hair.

She unlocked the Toyota's passenger door and he slid inside, bringing with him the scent of cold snow and leather.

"Are you all right?" he demanded.

"It was just pretty scary, that was all."

"You sure he's not around here anymore?"

"He's gone—I drove around quite a bit until I was sure."

They looked at each other and Diedre thought that Mitch's cheeks looked slightly more hollow than she remembered. Had he lost weight? She remembered the discouraged set of his shoulders as she had glimpsed him in the window.

"Well," said Mitch awkwardly. "Why don't I follow you to the police station and you can report this incident? You can give them a description of the car, can't you?"

"It was a dark car. Maybe a Sunbird. It had a crumpled bumper. Oh, Mitch—" But her cry subsided into silence. The harsh, businesslike way he was looking at her, his brows furrowed together, his jawline knotting. It terrified her, the way he was now. He wasn't the Mitch she knew, but a stranger.

"Are you really transferring away from here?" she dared to say.

"I'm still investigating that," he told her. "My father is pulling some strings."

"But will all your courses transfer?"

"We're looking into that."

Two people who had loved each other, and now they sat only a few feet away, a barrier stretched between them like bulletproof glass. Diedre wanted to break through that impenetrable glass, but she didn't know how and it was obvious he didn't want to try at all.

"Mitch," she whispered.

"Don't," he said hoarsely. "Diedre . . . just follow me to the police station. Make your report. And we'll go our separate ways. And next time don't go driving around aimlessly at night—it attracts too many jerks and weirdos."

Numbly Diedre waited while Mitch got out of her car, got into his own Le Baron, and started its engine.

We'll go our separate ways.

What had she expected?

Diedre didn't go to the police station—she just didn't have the heart. If the stupid guy who was following her chose to follow her home, at this moment she certainly didn't care. She drove back to the apartment, her heart clenched with grief.

Driving into the parking lot, she noticed Bud Clancy's Ford 150 pickup truck parked near the building. Pam's fiancé had a bumper sticker on his truck that said HONK YOUR BRAINS OUT—IT WON'T TAKE LONG. Bud thought this was the funniest bumper sticker he'd ever seen.

Dully Diedre let herself into the building and walked upstairs.

"So how's Tarik?" asked Pam as Diedre entered the apartment. "Yo," added Bud. "How's the kiddo?"

Pam and Bud were watching TV, the coffee table littered with cracker boxes and crumbs, soda cans, tortilla chips, and salsa dip. Bud had his arm around Pam and was playing possessively with a strand of her blond hair. Diedre felt a sharp stab of envy at their intimacy.

"Tarik's going to be fine." Diedre stalked through the room and dropped her shoulder bag on the dining table in the alcove near the kitchen. "He came out of surgery just great."

Bud got up and ambled toward the bathroom, leaving the sisters alone, and Pam came over to the table. "You don't act as if he's fine. What's the matter?"

"It's just—I waited with Lashonda while Tarik was in surgery—the doctor said he's going to be okay—that's not it—" Diedre slumped into a dining chair. In a low voice she told her sister about calling Mitch from the phone booth.

"Oh, shit, you called him?" cried Pam.

"A car followed me. I got away, but . . . I had a weak moment."

"Oh, Deeds, let him call you."

"He won't. He'll never call me. He's transferring out of here. Pam, it's over. *Over, over, over*!" Diedre pounded with her clenched fist on the tabletop. She got up and stumbled into her bedroom, where she closed the door behind her and threw herself on the bed.

Pam peeked in the door. "You okay?"

"Yeah," sobbed Diedre. "Yeah, I'm just great. I love breaking up, it just feels so g-good. I hate him! He's such an asshole! Men think they know everything," she wept. "They do, Pam! *He* wasn't there. *He* wasn't anywhere in sight at the time! He just plain disappeared! But now he's telling me what I should have done! *It wasn't his decision to make, Pam. It wasn't his damn choice!*"

"This young woman is being pursued by a stalker," said Rodger Halsick at the Women's Law Club meeting the following Thursday in a room at the Lawyer's Club. He was summarizing Diedre's case, Yasmeen Mammoud.

"The ex-boyfriend has telephoned her over five hundred fifty times in a ten-day period alone." Halsick consulted some notes. "Eighty-eight phone calls to Yasmeen's mother in the same time period. Thirty calls to one of her girlfriends, seventeen to another. Seems totally incredible, doesn't it? And now he's doing hang-up calls. When does this man have time to eat and go to the bathroom?"

Everyone tittered.

They discussed the new stalker laws for a while, the proliferation of people, both male and female, who were now signing complaints against ex-spouses, exes of every sort, and other annoying types.

"The number of stalker petitions has quadrupled in the past year or two. It almost seems fashionable to file," said Halsick. "Still, when the stalking is serious, or when the person is endangered, these laws do have some teeth to them now. We can make them stick and we can put people in jail. As soon as we prove those hang-ups belong to him, Yasmeen's ex-boyfriend is going to find himself looking out through the bars of a jail cell."

When the meeting was over, many of the students trailed out of the room, heading toward a lecture on "Gender and the Law," being given by a visiting woman professor of law emeritus, who had written several books on the topic.

The lecture hall wasn't going to be filled—Diedre could see that immediately—but the crowd would be reasonable. This year, she'd heard, 45 percent of the law students were women, with 24 percent being students of color.

"Diedre—Diedre, wait up." A masculine voice called to her as she was walking down the aisle.

Diedre paused, her heart jumping into her throat, a thought of Mitch instantly flying into her head, as it always did. But of course, it wasn't Mitch. Instead it was a man named Allen Huber who was in several of her classes.

"Oh, hi, Allen."

"Would you like to sit together?" he asked.

"I guess we could," she said, trying not to sound too ungracious. Since she and Mitch had split up, a few of the male students were beginning to hit on her.

Allen was nearly six feet four inches in height. He'd been a star quarterback, she'd heard, at the University of Wisconsin. Before she'd met Mitch, Diedre might even have been interested in him. Now his husky good looks didn't appeal to her. He seemed too bulky in comparison to Mitch's lanky slimness.

They found seats halfway back, and Allen began telling her about a travel fellowship he was thinking of applying for, to study the international legal issues involved in water resources development.

Diedre listened, nodding politely. Although she did recycle soda cans and paper, environmental law didn't interest her much. And Allen was pretty long-winded about it, she decided after a few minutes, her thoughts glazing over as he continued to talk.

Just then the speaker walked up to the lectern, a woman with iron gray hair clipped short in a modified bowl and no makeup, although some makeup would have helped under the small spotlight that had been trained on the podium. But as soon as she started to talk, Diedre forgot about the woman's plainness.

An hour later, Diedre clapped enthusiastically with the rest of the audience, and reached to the floor for her shoulder bag, preparing to leave for the graduate library.

"Would you like to get some coffee, Diedre?"

She turned, startled. She'd become absorbed in the lecture and had forgotten all about Allen sitting beside her. "Oh—I really should get in some studying."

"Just a quick cup," he pleaded. "You'll need some caffeine, anyway, to jack you up for the night."

She hesitated. She supposed she had to start dating again—sometime.

"I heard that you and Mitch Sterling broke up," Allen pressed her. "That's what everyone is saying."

"Oh, are they?" she said, annoyed that her personal life was being bandied around school like this. "I'm sorry, Allen—not today. Another time maybe."

She left the lecture hall alone, walking fast toward the library.

Later, Diedre took a study break and walked toward South University Street. Students were everywhere, bundled up in winter jackets; even an Indian woman wearing a sari was equipped with a good Michigan down jacket. However, the atmosphere was no longer idyllic, as it had been in the fall when Diedre had first arrived in Ann Arbor. Now many walked with heads down. The first semester had taken its toll, and now they were well immersed in the second one, which for some students would be the last. Each year's classes had an attrition rate; already Diedre's law classes were smaller than they'd been in the fall.

Passing a campus bookstore, Diedre noticed a sign in the window saying that a professional storyteller was going to appear at the store on the weekend to do "interactive reading" to children. The topic was dinosaurs.

Diedre stopped to read the poster, making a note of the times. Maybe she'd bring Tarik to hear the stories. Tarik was out of the hospital, back in a new day care center—the same place Evan Hertz attended—running all around as if he'd never had the accident at all.

She had turned to leave when she saw a familiar-looking figure cross the street by the corner, clad in a brown leather jacket of a texture she knew intimately.

Mitch.

Her chest squeezed and her breath started coming fast. She started walking away, then her walk turned to a half run. She *didn't* want to see him . . . not anymore. She finally saw that now; it could never have worked between them, it had been doomed from the start. A pity it had taken her more than a semester to realize this.

TREVA

TREVA'S HOSPITAL ROOM NOW LOOKED AS IF SHE'D LIVED in it for at least a year, colorful with get-well cards and crowded with her personal possessions, everything from a portable CD player to stacks of books and the latest issue of *TV Guide*.

Home away from home.

Treva lay curled on her left side, listening to the sound of snowflakes tapping against her window, and the distant blat of the hospital PA system, calling for doctors and residents whose names were now very familiar to her. Right now they were calling a "code blue," and she fluttered her eyes shut for a moment, saying a prayer for whoever the code was for.

She tried to think about Diedre Samms coming to the hospital tonight to visit her for a short while. The young law student had called only a few minutes ago, and Treva had told her she could stop by. It cheered Treva up to talk to Diedre and she enjoyed the young woman's idealistic eagerness. Once, she'd been a lot like Diedre, totally wrapped up in her work and the women she helped, and Treva enjoyed having the chance to help another woman move along the path of life.

Still, even the prospect of visitors tonight somehow wasn't doing the trick of pulling Treva out of her funky mood.

"Does your head ache?" Patrice, her favorite nurse, had asked this morning, quizzing Treva about her symptoms as she did every day—the same questions, repeated until Treva had committed them all to memory.

"Not really," Treva had lied, not wanting to admit even to herself that she'd had a headache for days. It was probably a side effect of the Apresoline, mixed with the other drugs she'd been given. Every drug had its side effect, Treva knew. And when you mixed more than one drug, you created a whole grab bag full of aches, pains, hot flashes, dry mouth, you name it.

Now she just felt trapped inside her own brain by the headache that kept squeezing. She longed to get up and walk around, thinking maybe that would alleviate the discomfort, but of course, she was forbidden to leave the bed. Any activity could raise her blood pressure too much. Besides, how far could she go with a catheter and an IV pole?

Glancing down at her hands, Treva saw with a stomach-twist of alarm that her fingers were puffy again. Weeks ago she'd taken off all of her rings, and even her watch had seemed uncomfortable recently. The skin of her feet also felt tight, as if they might burst. Even her eyes felt tight. And . . . didn't her upper right side and shoulder ache?

Oh, Jesus. She was becoming a total hypochondriac. But who wouldn't, with people asking her about her symptoms two and three times a day?

Then, making a tremendous mental effort, Treva thrust the uncomfortable physical symptoms out of her mind. She'd stood everything this long, she could do it a few weeks longer. Dwelling on her physical condition was only going to raise her blood pressure—just what the doctors didn't want.

She'd signed up for this, hadn't she? She knew it would be tough, but she'd made the decision, and now, she told herself, no complaining was allowed.

She felt a healthy kick on the left side of her abdomen, followed by another one in quick succession. She imagined she could feel little toes wiggling.

Hey there, little guy, she said to the infant swimming around inside her uterus. *We're gonna get you out of there healthy and happy. You're gonna be just fine. And Mama already loves you so much. You'll never know how much.*

An hour later, Dr. Sandoval walked into the room wearing a set of green surgical scrubs, her shining, light brown hair pulled to the nape of her neck with a tortoiseshell clip. She looked fresh and crisp, and smelled faintly of lemon-scented soap.

"How do you feel today, Treva?"

Treva looked up from the paperback she had been reading, a new Mary Higgins Clark thriller that Wade had brought her the previous day. "I feel great," she said, smiling. "Well, medium great."

"Or medium poor? Treva, you've gained two pounds of water weight in the last day," the physician said after taking Treva's blood pressure, looking into her eyes, and carefully examining her feet, legs, hands, and face.

"That much?"

"Plus the proteins in your urine have gone way up. Your face is swollen, too. Your eyelids have taken on fluid. How bad is your headache?"

"It's . . . bad," admitted Treva, ashamed because she'd ignored it for so long.

"Any blurring of your vision? Even a slight blurring? Strange lights, strange sensations?"

Treva hesitated, her heart sinking. "I'm not sure. When I woke up this morning I had to blink and blink before I could really see well."

She gazed pleadingly at the doctor. She knew what this meant, of course; her preeclampsia was progressing toward eclampsia. Dammit . . . She'd tried so hard not to complain, to put the seriousness out of her mind. But they'd get it under control, she assured herself. That was why she was in the hospital. She had the best doctors in the state, maybe the country. They could make miracles, and she wanted one for her and her baby.

Ruth Sandoval expelled her breath, pressing her lips together for a second before she said, "Treva, your condition is worsening. I'm sorry. I'd like to induce labor tomorrow. We have to get that baby outside of you."

Treva felt her heart thud and she put her hand over her chest, as if to contain its wild-wing beating. "You mean . . . I'm going to have my baby now? But isn't it way too soon?"

"At thirty-three weeks he has a good chance of survival with medical assistance. He'll be somewhere in the four-and-a-half-pound range. Fortunately, preemies of mothers with hypertensive disorders do a lot better than regular preemies. It's almost as if they sense the problem and their lungs develop sooner than other babies. That's one good point in our favor."

"Couldn't we wait a few weeks more?" Treva begged. Her eyes filled. "I want to keep him inside me as long as I can. I want to give him the best chance."

"Which is exactly what you've been doing," said Dr. Sandoval. "Treva, you're a real trouper, and you've gone through stresses that a lot of other women couldn't have handled. But now we have to think about *your* health, too.

We're going to do everything we humanly can to get you through this. *And* the baby.''

Dr. Sandoval went on to explain how they'd be giving her oxytocin intravenously, in a gradually, increasing manner until contractions began. The amount of medication would be controlled by a pump, so she'd receive only a certain, safe amount of it at a time.

Treva only half listened to the explanation. She felt a wild swing of emotion. She was going to be giving birth . . . at last.

After Dr. Sandoval left the room, Treva lay very still, fighting the waves of elation and terror that sped through her body. It was time . . . She'd be having her baby soon . . . This ordeal was almost over. But was it too soon for the baby to have a fair chance to live whole and healthy? She remembered the preemie nursery full of incredibly tiny babies struggling for life, all of them attached to fetal monitors. *Four pounds?* That was tiny, really.

Good chance of survival with medical assistance, Dr. Sandoval had said. She replayed the words in her mind, trying to relax. The baby had a fighting chance; that was why they'd waited this long . . . She was just going to have to trust in Jesus, that was all.

Treva brought her hands up and clasped them together on her chest. *Dearest Jesus,* she prayed. *Please, let my baby live. Let him be fine, without any problems. It's all I ask of You. I'll do anything, give anything, if only You will save my little boy.*

Treva used the bedside phone, dialing Wade at the School of Social Work, but only got his voice mail. Then she called home and got the machine there. She left messages on both tapes, telling him to call her as soon as possible.

Restlessly she shifted around, trying to find a comfortable position in bed without violating the left-side rule. Maybe Wade was playing racquetball—something he now did four or five times a week, relieving his stress through physical activity.

She dialed the racket club and was told that Wade had reserved a court but hadn't arrived yet.

"Please, could you have him call his wife at the hospital?" she asked the young desk clerk.

"Sure," said the girl, giggling as someone spoke to her in the background.

The lobby of the racket club was dominated by a glass display court wall, behind which two men were ferociously whamming a small, black ball at around a hundred miles per hour, popping it into the back wall with explosive sounds. Their yelling, the popping of balls, multiplied by the same noises emanating from the nine other courts, was a loud cacophony.

When Wade walked up to the desk to register and pay for his court time, the young, blond desk clerk was busy laughing and chattering with a group of her friends, and barely glanced up at him as she ran his card through a machine and took his money.

He went in the locker room, put on a pair of shorts and a much-washed GO BLUE T-shirt, and then trotted to the court he'd reserved, where he spent an hour practicing his serve, gradually working up a sweat. Then finally pushing himself.

A woman peered into the small, square glass window, waiting to use the court.

It had been a rough hour. Wade leaned against the front wall, his knees bent as he breathed heavily, sucking in air. The woman tapped on the glass, indicating it was time for him to vacate the court. She was in her early twenties, with a lean, olive-skinned face and jet black hair pulled back into a scraggly ponytail.

Reluctantly Wade took off his sweat-soaked headband and gathered up his racket, tube of balls, and bag, exiting the court. He was tired, but he hadn't released all of his tension yet—the worry that ate at him now corroding his gut. Treva, her health, the danger that she and her child were in.

The young woman was looking at him assessingly. "Want a game? I have this court for two hours."

Wade was tired from his workout, but still said yes.

"I'm Meliza Fernandez," she told him. "I've seen you around here before."

Meliza wanted to warm up, so they hit a few volleys. Then the shit hit the fan. Within five minutes, Wade was in racquetball hell. He forgot she was a twenty-two-year-old female, forgot everything except the smash of balls, the hard running, the loud echo and pong of balls hitting the wall, the squeak of court shoes, and his own guttural shouts.

Suddenly Meliza lunged for the ball just as Wade was lunging. They slammed shoulders and went down in a heap, her hard, bony knee hitting him in the jaw. He rocked flat on his back, nausea welling up inside of him. He turned his head to the side just in time for a spew of bile to pour out of his mouth.

"Oh, shit," he groaned.

"Are you all right?" Meliza unfolded herself, easily springing to her feet. She gazed down at Wade as if he'd turned into an old man right before her eyes. "Should I get someone?"

He gasped, wiping his mouth, dizziness causing the court to tilt up and down. "No—I'm okay."

"Well, you'd better rest, guy."

"I can play. Just give me a couple minutes."

"No way. You're down for the count. I'll go get the janitor or someone."

Humiliated, Wade pulled himself to his feet and hobbled to the locker room, where he opened his locker and pulled on his street clothes, feeling too dragged out to shower. He'd do it at home, he decided.

By the time he was in the car, Wade had cheered up. Hell, he was in great shape, he'd just fallen down, that was all. Racquetball was not a game of niceties and manners; everyone fell down, got shoved, banged into the wall. If you couldn't stand the heat, get out of the kitchen.

He went home, found Treva's message on the answering machine tape, and called his wife at the hospital.

"I have good news," she told him, her voice trembling slightly. "*Very* good news."

"Oh? What's that?"

"Dr. Sandoval wants to induce labor tomorrow. We're going to have our son."

"Tomorrow?" He felt as if he'd just been hit by a spinning ball going 150 miles per hour. "You don't mean, as in . . . *tomorrow*? The day that comes after this one?"

"That's exactly what I mean."

"Oh," he managed. "Oh, my God."

"Isn't it great news?"

"Terrific," Wade said. "But, Treva, you're only thirty-three weeks. Isn't that too soon?"

He listened to her explain what the doctor had said about the baby's survival chances. Shanae had weighed seven pounds when she was born, not four. To him it sounded iffy, but the doctors were supposed to know what they were talking about.

"Great," Wade responded as heartily as he could. "Trev, it's great. I'm getting sick of these microwave dinners. Watery broccoli, rubbery pasta, disappearing shrimp . . ."

Her laugh on the other end of the line was warm and rich, the old Treva laugh he loved so much. "Microwave dinners? I thought you were the new Paul Prudhomme. Making everything from scratch. Broiling and sautéing and chopping."

"Only if I have someone else to consume the food with me. Otherwise I nuke everything. I'd better start working on the nursery," he added hoarsely. "I haven't even set up the crib yet. I'll do it tonight."

"And unpack all the shower gifts," said Treva. "Maybe Shanae can help you with it, Wade. Why don't you go up to Brighton and get her? I promised her she could help with the baby's room."

"All right," Wade agreed. "I'll bring her up to the hospital later tonight."

They talked for a while about how Treva wanted the baby's room arranged. It was all positive, upbeat, and Wade didn't tell Treva about the incident at the racket club. Why should he worry her? After a few minutes his own anxiety began to decrease. They were two normal parents, planning the birth of their baby. This was the way it was supposed to be all along, the comfortable planning they'd been cheated of.

It was going to be all right.

Snow was falling by the time Wade reached Brighton, big, soft, wet flakes. He had to keep his windshield wipers going in order to clear the slushy stuff from the glass. Shanae was waiting for him, her overnight bag already packed.

His ex-wife, Wanda, was in the kitchen baking a batch of caramel pecan swirl cheesecakes for a party she was catering. The rich smells that emanated from her double ovens were almost overpowering.

"So I hear you're going to be a daddy again, like tomorrow," Wanda said. She was fifty but looked much younger, and wore her jet black hair in fashionable braids, her jeans also in the latest trendy style. Wade would still be married to her if she hadn't started having affairs, but thank God they'd been able to cooperate enough about Shanae so that the young girl hadn't been emotionally damaged.

"That's right."

"But isn't it a little early?"

"A little," Wade admitted.

"Daddy, how is she? Is she really going to have the baby tomorrow?" Shanae wanted to know.

"That's right, honey. They'll give her stuff, it'll start the labor."

"Can I spend the whole week with you, Daddy, so I can be here when she has the baby?" The girl turned to her mother. "Mom, can I?"

Wanda smiled. "If you want, Shanae. It isn't every day a girl gets a new half brother."

But Wade demurred. "I don't know, Shanae. You have school."

"Please!" The girl turned her pretty face intensely to him. "I could just stay with you now, and go back Wednesday. I have all of my homework caught up, honest. This is important, I want to be there, Daddy. I want to see my little brother."

"You'll see plenty of him, honey." Then Wade gave in. "All right, baby doll. You won't be in the delivery room, but you'll be in the lounge and you'll see the baby right after it's born."

Wanda walked them to the door. "If there's anything you need . . . just call. I don't know what I could do, but tell Treva I'm thinking about her."

"I will."

"And, Shanae, you be a good girl, hear, and help your father and stepmother out. If your dad tells you to do something, you do it."

"Yes, ma'am," said Shanae, meekly for once.

Wade and Shanae drove back to Ann Arbor, going to the house and getting started on the job of unpacking boxes and getting out the soft, small baby garments, which the girl kept exclaiming over in pleasure. Happily the teenager unpacked boxes of baby wipes, Q-tips, baby oil, pacifiers, and other infant paraphernalia. However, there wasn't time to take the beautiful oak crib that Wade had bought out of its box.

"I put together a crib once before, and it's not a job you can do in half an hour," Wade told his disappointed daughter. "Don't worry, honey, there'll be plenty of time to set it up before the baby comes home. We'll have it ready to go, mattress, sheets, blankets, crib bumpers, the whole nine yards."

They grabbed a roast beef and cheddar sandwich at a nearby Arby's and drove up to the hospital. By now it was after 7:00 P.M., snow still falling and beginning to coat the streets. Wade's daughter could not contain her excitement as they pulled into the hospital complex behind a plow truck.

"I wonder what he'll look like," she said. "The baby, I mean. Do you think he'll look like you or Treva?"

"Better pray he looks like Treva," Wade said.

"Oh, Daddy—"

Wade used valet parking, as he usually did, and they walked along the hospital corridors, Shanae chattering happily about a baby mobile she wanted to buy with teddy bears hanging from it. She'd seen one at Hudson's and thought it looked cute.

The Women's Hospital area was filled with the usual cheerful bustle of nurses and aides walking back and forth, fathers-to-be pacing around, fathers and grandparents arriving for visits. By now Treva's hallway was very familiar to both Wade and Shanae, and Shanae said hi to one of the floor nurses she recognized.

Treva's door was standing halfway open, as was usually the case. However, Wade noticed that the room was in heavy shadow. Usually Treva had the lights on by this hour of the night, he reflected uneasily.

Well, maybe she was napping. She'd been drifting off to sleep more and more often, taking mini catnaps several times a day.

They walked in, finding Treva in her usual position, lying on her left side, eyes shut. Wade stood staring down at his wife, feeling a tug of unease. Something about her looked different, even alarming. Her face looked swollen; that was it. Really puffy.

"Treva," he said anxiously. "Trev?"

"Wake up, Treva," said Shanae excitedly. The teenager walked over to the wall by the sink and flicked on the overhead fluorescent light. "Treva, we're getting the baby's room all fixed up. We couldn't set up the crib yet, but it's gonna look awesome."

Treva moaned and stirred awake, opening her eyes and staring at them as if she didn't quite see them clearly. A muscle on her face was twitching, Wade noticed. Even as he watched, the twitching spread over her features, involving her whole mouth and cheek.

CHOICES 483

"Treva?"

His wife's body suddenly contracted, becoming rigid. As Wade watched in horror, the rigidity continued for about twenty seconds. Then Treva's body relaxed and again convulsed violently. Her torso bucked, nearly propelling her off the bed.

"Daddy! Daddy!" Shanae screamed.

Wade ran into the hallway, shouting, and in a few seconds nurses were converging on the room, pushing Shanae and Wade aside. Shanae was sobbing. Wade knew he should take his daughter out of the room, but horror held him pinned where he was, a helpless, terrified observer as Treva convulsed over and over, foaming at the mouth.

The IV line crashed over.

Two nurses struggled to keep her from falling out of bed. Treva thrashed cruelly; it was a scene from a nightmare.

Dazed, Wade realized that Shanae had him by the arm and was dragging him out of the room. They stumbled into the hall, nearly knocked over by more medical personnel who were running into the room, one woman pulling a cart loaded with medications and equipment.

"Daddy, come on down the hall, there's a waiting room," Shanae begged.

"No. I can't leave her."

"Daddy . . ." Shanae began to cry again. "Is she going to die, Daddy? What happened? Is she dying?"

"I don't know."

Treva floated in a dark void totally without sensation or feeling. She didn't even know she was in the void. She didn't know anything at all.

She had been sleeping when it began, dreaming about her baby. She was giving birth outdoors, in the woods, squatting over a birth stool, and there were wild flowers growing everywhere and she could smell them as she labored. Then a black cloud came, blotting out everything.

She didn't know that Wade and Shanae had entered the room, or that her facial twitching had turned to convulsions so violent that it took five nurses to hold her on the bed. She didn't know that she had bitten her tongue and blood was flowing out of her mouth. She didn't know that she had stopped breathing for over a minute.

There were shouts—nurses calling to each other. A doctor came pelting into the room, another one on his heels. Frantically they worked on her, calling out in sharp voices for medications, for airways, for this and that. Treva was not aware of this.

The spasms gradually decreased in intensity.

Finally Treva became motionless.

She was breathing, but she had gone into a coma.

DIEDRE

THAT DAY DIEDRE HAD SPENT AN HOUR HAVING COFFEE with Yasmeen Mammoud, the nursing student whose exboyfriend was stalking her. He'd started following her around again, and Yasmeen had called the police, but they had not caught Tonio, and now he was denying he had been anywhere near her.

"He's ruining my college education," said the nineteen-year-old, her eyes brimming with tears. "He knows when my classes meet and he follows me. Even when I have two friends go with me, I'm so nervous I can barely concentrate. And my roommate says if he doesn't stop calling, she wants me to move. I want him stopped!"

They discussed Yasmeen's options for a while, and Diedre urged her to keep calling the police and eventually Tonio would be picked up and jailed.

Later, feeling unsatisfied with what she had accomplished, Diedre borrowed the Toyota from Pam and drove over to the University Hospital complex.

Diedre couldn't wait to tell Treva this latest development

about Yasmeen's boyfriend. What should Yasmeen do if she reported Tonio again stalking her but couldn't prove it and he denied it? Diedre was also looking forward just to talking to Treva. Being around her made her feel better inside.

At the hospital she found an elevator and made her way through the maze of corridors and directional signs to the floor Treva was on. However, when Diedre reached Treva's room she was shocked to find it empty, the bed neatly made, the cards taken down from the walls. Even the vases of flowers were gone, as if they'd never existed. Shocked, Diedre sucked in her breath. Had something happened to Treva?

Alarm filling her, she walked out to the nurses' station.

"Has Treva Connor been moved to a new room?"

"She's in ICU, honey."

"What?"

"The family is in the lounge down the hall if you want to talk to them."

Diedre stepped backward. *The ICU?* "But—but she's going to be all right, isn't she?"

"You'd have to talk to the family, dear."

Frustrated, Diedre turned on her heel and walked down the hallway to the lounge. Looking inside, she saw six or eight people sitting in a lounge where a TV set was playing an old "Baywatch" rerun. Among them was a handsome, older, African-American man—Treva's husband, Wade, whom Diedre had met before. There was also a pretty black girl of about fifteen or sixteen, and a black woman of about forty with a tear-streaked face. There were several other women as well, including a plump, freckled redhead vaguely familiar in appearance, wearing surgical scrubs.

Annie, that was who it was. The PA at the clinic.

"Daddy," the teenager was saying anxiously, patting Wade's hand. "Daddy, she'll come out of it, I know she will. Treva's strong! She's not some wimp. They're giving her that medicine. The mag . . . mag whatever, the stuff that dilates the blood vessels. Any minute now they'll come to tell us she's waking up."

Treva's husband looked utterly grief-stricken. He bent

forward, rubbing his hands along the graying curls of his temples. "Ah, God, Shanae," he said brokenly.

Diedre caught her breath, unsure whether to intrude on this family scene. Finally she stepped into the lounge. "I'm Diedre Samms," she said. "I'm a friend of Treva's—that is—is she going to be okay?" she blurted.

The older woman got up, a necklace of silver beads jangling around her neck, her face a slightly darker version of Treva's. "I'm Rhonda Smith, Treva's sister. And, honey, we don't know whether she's going to be okay. We think she is, we're praying she will be, she and the child. We've been doing a lot of praying here."

Diedre swallowed. "But what happened?"

"She had a massive seizure. They're giving her mag sulfate, it's a medicine that's supposed to work wonders, and as soon as they bring her out of it, they're going to induce labor. Getting the baby out will do more than anything to cure her."

"Oh."

"Would you like to sit with us awhile? The more prayers the better."

"Yes, sure." Diedre sat down on a couch. She hadn't been to church in two or three years, and she wasn't really religious, although she did believe in a supreme being.

"Let's all join hands again," said Rhonda, in a rich, warm voice that closely resembled Treva's. Diedre found herself gripping Shanae Connor's hand on her right, and Rhonda's hand on her left. Eight of them, clasping hands.

"Dear Jesus, we ask it in Your name, please give our brave sister, Treva, the strength to survive just a little longer. Watch over her and keep her safe, keep her and her child warm and safe in Your love . . ." There was more, a repetition on this theme, and several times someone said "amen" or just murmured assent. Diedre had never held hands while praying before. It was a curious sensation, giving her a sense of peace.

More people came into the room and joined the prayer circle. One was a tiny woman of seventy-three or seventy-four, with white hair pulled back in a bun, and tears in her eyes. The doctor who had done Diedre's abortion.

"Please," Diedre whispered under her breath, closing her eyes intensely. "Please, help Treva."

After a few more minutes, Diedre left, giving Shanae Connor her phone number scribbled on a scrap of paper, and telling the girl to call her if there was anything Treva needed—anything at all. And . . . would Shanae call her with news about Treva and the baby?

The teenager said she would. Impulsively Diedre gave the young girl a hug. "It's going to be okay," she whispered. "I just know it."

She drove home, her mind on Treva and the woman's heroism. She desperately wanted to share the events of today with Mitch, but of course, she could not. How odd it was, she thought, that the part of Mitch she missed most was the sharing they'd done, the talking. The way he would listen to her so intently, paying attention to every word, nodding and smiling and asking quick, smart questions.

When she got back to the apartment, Pam was out, probably on another date with Bud. Diedre wandered the empty apartment, feeling restless and out of sorts. The scene in the hospital lounge had left her feeling confused and over-emotional. Why did bad things have to happen to people you cared about?

Diedre mopped at some tears she hadn't even realized she was shedding, and then grudgingly switched on her computer. She entered her Microsoft Word program, forcing herself to continue on her course outline for her Torts class. But somehow she couldn't get into the typing. In fact, she didn't want to do it at all. She didn't want to do anything.

Where had it all gone, the zest, the joy she'd first experienced with her studies? Now the backbreaking hours of study, almost the equivalent of two full-time jobs, seemed like an awful chore. Only the women's law cases seemed to be holding her interest, but if she flunked the rest of her classes, she wouldn't be able to help anyone, would she?

By 2:00 A.M. the letters on her computer screen were beginning to blur and Diedre realized that she had just typed in a huge chunk of text without remembering any of it.

She exited the program and shut off her computer, again pacing the apartment. Wind and snow were blowing against the windows. She heard the metallic thump as the building's furnace switched on, then the rattly rumble of the blower motor. The refrigerator made some clicking noises and then its blower switched on. The kitchen faucet was dripping, as it had been doing for several weeks. Pam had called building maintenance, but thus far no one had come to fix it.

Lonely sounds, alone sounds.

Treva Connor in the hospital, in a coma, battling to survive.

Mitch out of Diedre's life now, gone forever . . .

Desperate to push away the unfamiliar feelings, Diedre switched on the radio for company, but her favorite station had gone to a lower frequency and there was too much static. A strange disc jockey pattered mindlessly about rock groups Diedre had never heard of, probably because at age twenty-three she was getting too old, too busy, and too out of touch. She got up to change the station, but she didn't like that format either.

Diedre thought about her mother and dialed Cynthia Samms's apartment in Madison Heights.

Her mother sounded sleepy, and Diedre guiltily realized she had awakened her from a sound sleep. "I'm sorry, I didn't mean to wake you," she apologized.

"It's fine, honey." Cynthia sounded bleary. "I was so tired that I fell asleep on the couch. I just got up and went to bed and I guess I'm not really all there right now."

"It's Treva, my friend," Diedre sobbed. "She—she's in a coma."

She told her mother about the events at the hospital, and Cynthia roused herself and began asking questions. Diedre poured out the story of her visit.

"I don't know if she's going to be okay," said Diedre. "I joined a p-prayer circle. Oh, Mom, you should have seen her husband . . . his face . . . He looked so awfully sad."

"But they accomplish miracles in hospitals these days," said Cynthia. "Especially in pregnancies. And I'm sure Treva has the best doctors. The U. of M. hospital is wonderful."

Diedre wanted to believe this so badly, and Cynthia's words did cheer her up for a few minutes. There was so much else she wanted to say . . . She also longed to pour out her heart about Mitch. But she'd woken up her mother. Reluctantly she said good night, knowing her physically fragile mother needed her sleep.

"Call me tomorrow," instructed Cynthia. "You just sound so down. Honey, I'm sure everything will be fine."

"Sure."

But after she had hung up, Diedre's mood fell again, and she felt as if she was right back to where she'd been before.

I wish I could sleep for a long time, she found herself thinking. *And when I wake up, everything will be different.*

Diedre wandered into the kitchen and opened the refrigerator, finding a frozen Sara Lee cheesecake with strawberry topping. She pried off the lid with a knife and found a fork, carrying the entire cake with her to her bedroom.

She undressed and climbed into bed, still holding the cheesecake. Propped up against two pillows, she began digging in to the dessert. The strawberry topping had shards of freezer ice in it. It tasted cloyingly sweet. After about ten minutes she had finished one-third of the cheesecake. Diedre got out of bed again and went to the refrigerator, where there was a half bottle of cheap Chablis that Pam had bought one night when she made Bud dinner. She unscrewed the top and padded to the bathroom, where she began rummaging in Pam's half of the medicine cabinet and vanity drawers.

There—there it was, a nearly full bottle of Darvocet left over from when Pam had twisted her knee last year while sledding.

Diedre took the pills and the wine back to bed, and popped two Darvocet in her mouth. She washed them down with wine. Outdoors it was still snowing, wind blowing against the window. Traffic out on Pauline Street sounded muffled, and for once, there were no noises in their own parking lot.

I'll just sleep for a day, Diedre told herself, eating more cheesecake while waiting for the Darvocet to take effect. *One little day. Then I'll get up and face life again. But for tonight, I don't care anymore.*

"Deeds! Diedre! Jesus!" Pam's voice came from very far away, full of panic. "Diedre! Wake up!"

Diedre moaned and turned to one side, vomit rising up her throat. She threw up onto the pillowcase, hot acid stinging her throat tissues.

"Christ!" exclaimed Pam. "Throw it up, that's a girl, throw it all up."

Diedre obeyed, making ugly sounds. The empty cheesecake tin lay on the bedspread, scraped down to the crumbs. There was a damp patch of spilled wine, and the fork she'd used was lying beside her, greasy with filling.

"How many of these did you take?" demanded Pam, holding up the amber-colored Darvocet bottle.

"Don't . . . don't know," said Diedre between heaves. "I think two."

"Two? Are you sure?"

"Yeah . . . Just two."

"Shit! I can't believe you did that. Bud and I had a fight, that's why I came home early. If I hadn't, would you have taken the whole bottle?"

"Don't know . . ." croaked Diedre, slumping down on the pillow as waves of tiredness rippled through her. "Just wanted to take a little vacation. Sleep for a day. Just sleep."

"I'm going to call 911."

"No!" Diedre begged. "Please—I'm okay! I am. This is not a 911 case. I only took two pills, honest!"

"Well . . ."

"I'm okay . . . I just got crazy for a while . . . I wanted to go to sleep for a long time."

Pam looked at her. "You mean like forever? *You tried to kill yourself?*"

"I don't know," said Diedre. "I don't think two pills would have done much."

"Oh, God." Pam shook her head, her expression white and strained. "It's that Mitch asshole, isn't it? He's the one who caused all of this."

"Mitch is not an asshole." Diedre lay down, feeling wobbly and woozy, but sane again. "I'm the asshole, Pam."

"You?"

"I knew he wouldn't be able to deal with it and I told him anyway. Maybe I was the one who wanted to wreck it. Punishing myself," Diedre said bitterly. "Because I got the damn abortion."

Even to say that much had exhausted her. She lay there while Pam took the sheets, pillowcase, and bedcovers off the bed to be washed. Had she really wanted to die? Or had she wanted only temporary relief? She would have been the first person in the world to commit suicide with cheesecake, she told herself, laughing hollowly.

She heard Pam rummaging in the hall closet, and then her sister came into the room again carrying some old, faded twin bedsheets that Diedre remembered from their childhood. Pam must have taken them when she got her apartment.

"Get off the bed and I'll make it for you." Pam's eyes were wet. "Diedre, if you ever die on me, I'm going to kill you. I mean that. I'll hate you forever and ever."

Diedre sat up and Pam came and sat beside her, and they hugged each other for a long time. "Remember that dollhouse we made out of cardboard?" Pam said. "We used to make all the little furniture for it? We could play with that thing for ten hours a day."

"Yes . . . and remember the pink Barbie dress we made . . . with the tulle . . . And we glued all those beads on it. We had beads all over the room and you had them in your hair . . ."

They clung together. "Hey, you're my sister," said Pam shakily. "No man is worth this, Diedre. Never, never. I don't care how much you loved him. Screw him."

Pam finished making the bed, and then Diedre lay down again. She stared at the ceiling, feeling as if somehow— through cheesecake or pills or Pam's love—she had changed.

She was going to have to live, wasn't she? Without Mitch, in a world where little boys could be cut by flying glass, expectant mothers could die, in a world where nothing was really secure, not really, not in the long run.

Except love, the thought came to her suddenly.

She remembered the people in the hospital lounge, Treva's friends and family, their hands linked, a subtle energy connecting them, the energy of prayer. And finally she was able to relax a little and then sleep came.

PEPPER

A THIRD ABORTION?

Pepper had spent the past four days in an agony of indecision. One moment she had made up her mind to have the baby and raise it herself, give up her dreams for the shop and move to the mall, as Gray suggested, and settle into mediocrity and a small margin of profit.

The next moment she was reaching out her hand to call the clinic, make an appointment for a "procedure." But always something stopped her before she could actually dial the number.

Her third choice was marrying Gray.

Marriage. She hadn't even talked to him about it, had she? But she knew that he would jump at the chance to give her a ring and have the second chance at fatherhood he'd been longing for. But was that what *she* wanted? A luxurious house in Barton Hills, a semi-jet-set life, all the trimmings, the clothes, jewels, fresh flowers every day. She'd have roses in every room of her house if that was what she desired.

Stuff. The external, material things that had been so important in the lives of both her mother, Toni, and her father, Mason Maddalena. If she married Gray, wouldn't she be selling herself for the gifts, buying in to the whole "contractual" aspect of marriage in which the woman provided the looks and the sex, and the man provided the money? Or was that just her own idea, born out of her dysfunctional childhood? Anyway, the idea bothered Pepper—a lot.

And what about respect? Pepper thought, rubbing her eyes tiredly. She had her boutique, which she loved. It was as much a part of her as the color of her hair, or her eyes. What if Gray, once he was her husband, tried to take that over big-time, trying to make her syndicate it, or turn it over to a full-time manager so she could stay with the baby, or travel with him? He was a powerful man, used to making decisions . . . How could he resist thinking of Pepper's shop as being under his control? She'd have to fight him about that, all the time.

A surprise phone call from her ex-husband, Jack, startled Pepper on Friday morning. "Hey, Pep, would you believe I'm calling you from thirty thousand feet up?"

"What?"

"Yeah," her ex-husband said. "I'm flying into Detroit, got some business to transact with a guy I know who's been working with some of the youth gangs here. We're gonna be touching down in about half an hour. How about if I take you to lunch, Pepper?"

"Lunch? Today? Oh, Jack—" She'd had nothing this morning but Pepsi and saltine crackers, throwing up twice in the shop bathroom. Finally she sighed. "All right. Where do you want to meet?"

"I'll pick you up at the boutique. You pick the restaurant. Something small, quaint, and expensive. I'm modestly rolling in bucks, Pepper, so I can afford it for a change, and God knows you deserve the best."

"It'll have to be the restaurant next door," she told him.

"We're having a busy day here and I can't take an hour and a half to go on lunch break."

Jack looked the best that Pepper had seen him in years, his skin suntanned to a burnished toast color, his eyes clear, his haircut shorter and younger-looking. He was wearing jeans and a loosely structured Armani jacket, and looked, she thought, very California.

"Pepper, Pep," he said, reaching across the table at Ristorante Antonio, which was full of dark, wooden booths and exposed beams, a gas fireplace flickering not far from their table. The place was crowded with downtown people grabbing lunch.

They ordered, a plain salad and bread for Pepper, ravioli filled with Fontina cheese for Jack. The hard roll came with a dish of olive oil sprinkled with herbs, in which Pepper was supposed to dip the bread before eating it. She gave the sickening-looking bowl a push toward Jack's side of the table. Ugh. One bite of olive oil and she'd definitely heave.

Jack's romance with the cosmetics heiress was going splendidly, he told her.

He went on at length about his new ladylove, the $2 million house she owned in Hollywood, her swimming pool with a black granite bottom, a party she had given at Spago's. But then he frowned. "Pep, you look wonderful, as always, but are those a few new worry lines at the corners of your eyes?"

"Worry lines?" Pepper couldn't help touching her face.

"A figure of speech. You look perfect. But I do sense something about your mood, dear. Anything you want to share with good old Jack?"

Pepper hesitated. She had barely eaten one piece of lettuce from her salad, and only two bites of the plain roll. "Oh, Jack . . ."

"There is. There is something wrong. Does it have to do with that guy in your life, that Ortini guy?"

"I don't know—no—yes—"

"A problem, huh?" said Jack, gazing at her with warm affection. "Anything I can help with?"

Him, helping her? As he'd helped her before, having sex with her before he'd had his vasectomy medically checked to be sure it was safe? She laughed, the sound coming out wrong and becoming a half sob. Glancing around the restaurant, she stifled the noise with her hand. "I don't think so . . . Oh, Jack!" She swallowed, pushing away her roll, and then whispered, "I'm going to have a baby, Jack."

"My God." He flushed, perhaps remembering the card she'd sent him.

"I don't know what to do, what to decide."

"What's there to decide? Ortini's the father, isn't he? The guy with the bucks? You'll marry him and live happily ever after, happy and rich. That's the way it's meant to be."

She scrunched her napkin into a ball. "I love him, but I have these feelings . . . It seems as if he's just pushing me too hard, pushing me into a role I can't play."

Their waiter sidled over, wanting to know if everything was all right, and Jack waved him away. Looking at Pepper, he raised an eyebrow. "Don't tell me you're still on that trophy-wife bullshit. Trophy wives live a great life, kid, a lot better than most first wives, all things considered."

Pepper reddened. "You're no help!" she blurted. "You never were, Jack. You're the most selfish man I've ever known. All you want to do is throw money around and have some woman take the responsibility."

She threw her napkin down and pushed back from the table, digging in her purse for enough bills to pay her share of the meal.

"You leave the tip," she snapped.

She marched down the aisle to the lobby and exited onto the street, Jack hurrying only a few feet behind her, calling her name.

"Jack—please, just go back where you came from. Maybe in Hollywood your way works, but this is Ann Arbor, Michigan, and we live real lives, not fake ones."

"Well, don't blame me," he said, sounding miffed. "You

could be missing out on Prince Charming here. Or at the very least, a knight in shining armor.''

''Oh, could I? Jack, back in the Middle Ages the knights in shining armor were only about five feet tall and they probably hadn't bathed in a year. When they wanted food they said 'ugh,' and some poor woman ran to cook a cow. They didn't know love from a serving wench!''

She walked inside her shop, shutting the door in Jack's face. To his credit, he didn't follow her in, but walked away, moving lightly, confidently, just as he always did. Out of her life again, and this time she was very glad to see him go.

Rushing straight through the shop to the bathroom, Pepper heaved up her meager ''lunch'' into the commode, tears running from her eyes even as she threw up.

Prince Charming. Like hell. Even Gray Ortini didn't qualify for that title.

Pepper worked in a fury of concentration all the rest of the afternoon, her nausea alleviated by eating dry cereal and crackers and sipping Diet Pepsi. She helped a bride-to-be select her honeymoon lingerie, assisted a woman choosing a gown to wear for a glamour photograph, and advised a man who wanted to pick out panties and a camisole for his wife. The bride-to-be promised to send her friends to the shop, and the glamour-photograph woman was thrilled with the sexy gown Pepper had found for her to wear, praising Pepper to the skies. The man merely bought and paid, completing his entire purchase in ten minutes.

Ringing up the last sale, for $79.95, Pepper reflected that her shop was finally beginning to show a decent profit. Despite the heavy loans from her mother and uncle, the break-in, the problems getting enough help, the time she'd spent socializing with Gray, she was still beginning to make it.

Gray had said he planned to work late tonight, but as Pepper locked up her shop, arming the new security system, she realized she couldn't wait until their dinner date on the following night to talk to him about her pregnancy. She was throwing up all the time; it wasn't exactly something she could hide.

She and Oscar drove back to her apartment house over streets beginning to be covered with a half-inch slick of new snow. As Pepper carried the cat upstairs she could hear screams of laughter coming from Mrs. Melnick's apartment. The seventy-five-year-old landlady was entertaining her friends again for cards. Pepper felt a brief, unexpected twinge of envy. Life seemed so simple for Mrs. Melnick, who appeared to have nothing more important to do than shop for jogging outfits, gossip, and play cards.

Whereas she . . .

Three abortions, she found herself thinking again as she let Oscar out of his carrying case, petted his fur, and made sure his food dish was filled. *How can this be happening? Can I really do it again? How can I? Everything's the same . . . but it's all different.*

She changed into a pair of jeans and boots, throwing a white sweater tunic on over the jeans, the fabric shot through with tiny metallic threads. She wasn't anywhere near showing her pregnancy yet, but somehow the voluminous sweater made Pepper feel more secure.

She stopped in the kitchen for a few spoonfuls of vanilla ice cream, scooped right out of the pint container—the only food that really settled well in her stomach now. Then she locked up the apartment and clattered back downstairs, going back out in the cold to her car.

More snow, wet, soft flakes, had begun to fall as Pepper drove into the parking lot of the GrayCo Building. It was after seven o'clock. The bottom two floors of the building—the ones leased out—had only security lights on, but the top floor, occupied by Gray's company, was still brightly lit, the huge, rounded skylight casting a glow into the winter night. The parking lot only held two or three cars, their hoods beginning to be coated with a frosting of white.

Pepper recognized Gray's Infiniti parked in his reserved spot, and pulled into an empty slot opposite from it. She walked toward the building, and showed a special pass that Gray had given her to the twenty-something, white, female security guard who sat at a desk in the lobby.

"Miss Nolan? I'll phone upstairs, tell Mr. Ortini you're on your way."

"Thank you."

"You're gonna have to sign the after-hours book. And when you leave you'll have to sign out on this line, here, and put down the time."

"Sure." She scribbled her name and the time of her arrival, then waited impatiently while the guard called. "He said it's okay, ma'am. Just take the elevator up and he'll meet you in the lobby."

Beginning to tremble, she took the elevator up to the third floor. The elevator car had a mirrored interior, and as she rode up, Pepper stared at her own reflection, seeing the shininess of her eyes, the way a few snowflakes had caught themselves in her glossy, dark hair, which she had piled on her head and secured with clips.

She was scared. So scared. Why did a baby have to screw her life up now, just when she was getting her shop off the ground and everything looked so great for her?

But she'd said all that before, hadn't she? Way back at the end of the summer. And now Gray was about to complicate everything.

"Pepper? Is everything all right?" As she stepped off the elevator into the elegant, marbled lobby, Gray was waiting for her. The empty receptionist's desk looked ghostly, and the overhead skylight was obscured with a film of white. "Are you okay?" he repeated anxiously.

She smiled woodenly. "I just wanted to see you, that's all."

"Well, you know I'm always happy to see you. Come on back to my office, I've got a pot of coffee on."

They walked through the lobby into the main work space. A network of empty cubicles stretched out before them, computers turned off, here and there a sweater slung over the back of someone's chair. Pepper saw family photos, calendars, colored posters of national parks; even a Smurf doll decorated one of the cubes. Cardboard boxes on the floor held recycled papers.

"It seems so ghostly here at night, so different with all the people gone," Pepper murmured.

"Yeah, as soon as the staff leaves, it's not the same place. But I'm used to it. I was planning to work until about eleven tonight, and I'm having Thai food sent up—do you want me to call and increase the order?"

"I'm not very hungry," Pepper murmured, feeling a horrid, clutching twinge at the kindness written on Gray's face, the pleasant smile, his pleasure at seeing her.

Even Gray's big, luxurious office looked different at night, the two corner windows giving views of the sparkling lights of traffic on Plymouth Road and the glitter of Ann Arbor, seen through a scrim of snow. Gray's laptop had been set up on his desk, its colored screen showing an Excel spreadsheet. He had a Mr. Coffee machine sitting on his credenza, and the aroma of freshly ground coffee permeated the room.

Pepper drew in a shallow, frantic breath. The coffee smell was partially pleasant, partly nauseating . . .

But Gray didn't seem to notice her distress, pulling a ceramic mug imprinted with the GrayCo logo out of a lower shelf in the credenza. He filled the cup, adding sugar as Pepper liked it, and handed it to her.

She sank into a leather chair, quickly placing the cup on a table. Her stomach felt tight, tense and queasy, and she was afraid if she even held the coffee cup, she might have to jump up and run for the bathroom.

Oh, God—

"What is it, Pepper?" Gray asked quietly. "You pushed away that coffee cup as if it were poison, and your face is as pale as a ghost. Are you sick?"

"I'm . . . fine."

"No, you are not fine. And you never drop in at the office unexpectedly like this. Your schedule is as tight as mine. What is it?"

She sat very still, pressing her lips together, her pulsebeat seeming to throb in her ears. All she had to do was say the words and her life would immediately change forever. It was like turning on a faucet at Boulder Dam, knowing a flood of water would spew out, sweeping you off your feet, sweeping you into a river gorge.

"I'm going to have a baby," she finally whispered.

Gray's face went white, then red, then white again. "A baby? Are you sure?"

"Oh, very sure. I took a pregnancy test and I went to the doctor and I've been throwing up all the t-time . . ."

"Pepper! Ah, God! Oh, Pepper!" In three steps Gray had reached her, and he put his arms around her, lifting her out of the chair, sweeping her into his arms, pressing her close. "Pepper . . . you can't imagine how happy this makes me! Our child. A baby! This seems—" His voice broke. "This seems like a miracle."

"Is it?"

He pulled away for a moment. "Aren't you happy? Pepper, we'll get married right away. We'll sell my condo—it's too small to raise a child in, and we'll buy a big house with plenty of room. Or we can build. There are still some good building sites around here if you look. But we won't spoil this baby." Now Gray was laughing, his eyes glittering with emotion. "We won't make the mistakes I did in the past. We'll raise him with moderation. We'll—"

"Oh, Gray." The way she said it caused Gray to stop in midsentence.

"What's wrong?"

"I'm not sure—I mean, I don't know if marriage is what I want."

He stared at her. Something in his face crumpled. "You don't want marriage?"

Pepper got up and went to stand at the windows, staring down at Plymouth Road where an ambulance was just passing through, with lights blinking but no siren. Behind the ambulance was a police car. She wondered who was inside the EMS vehicle, what had happened, if the person was going to die.

"I don't want to be your trophy wife," she explained in a low voice. "I've told you this before."

"My trophy wife?"

"I love you, but it just sticks in my craw. Being your ornament, the pretty woman who's on your arm, the one you show off when you go to parties, the symbol of your achievement, your—your virility as a male."

"What? *What*?"

Pepper pushed on, afraid to stop talking. "Do you realize that you seldom compliment me on my business acumen, or the fact that I've got my boutique in the black, when around fifty percent of start-up businesses fail? If we do marry, you'll try to take over everything—"

Gray came up behind her, took her by the upper arms, and turned her around. "What in the *hell* are you talking about?"

"I'm not a trophy!"

"Whoever said you were? And whoever said I'd try to take over your business, for God's sake?"

"You did. Oh, maybe not consciously, Gray, but you were always so quick with the advice, so quick to tell me how you'd do things. Well, I've been running my shop just fine even before you came on the scene. And instead of respecting that, you try to get me to close my shop early so I can go off and have fun with you . . . It's all surface with you," she burst out, unable to hold back her anger any longer. "Looks. A pretty face. A thin body. Yeah, I was born with those, but it was only an accident of the gene pool. I count for a whole hell of a lot more than that!"

Gray's face darkened. "This is total, total bullshit, Pepper. I *never* considered you a trophy, an ornament, a decoration, a prize, or any of that sexist shit. I fell in love with you, plain and simple. I just showed you off because I adored you so much. Was that wrong? I wanted everyone to see how much I loved you."

Pepper pressed her lips together, confusion overwhelming

her. "But you did show me off," she persisted.

"Of course I showed you off. Maybe it's male posturing, macho bullcrap, I don't know. But I didn't consider you a *trophy*, for God's sake. You mean like Donald Trump and that woman he married—Marla? Or ninety-five-year-old what's-his-name and his twenty-four-year-old wife with the enormous—? Jesus Christ, I'm better than that, or I want to be. I love you for *you*, Pepper. Maybe I didn't say it enough. Maybe I didn't say it with the right tone of voice. You're a great businesswoman. Smart and sexy. You—"

"See?" she cried. "There you go again! You can't resist adding the word *sexy*."

She wrenched herself away from him, returning to the window, where she put her finger on the glass, touching a drizzle of snow that slid down the other side of the glass, then dropped away into thin air. *Like this relationship,* she thought despairingly.

Gray's voice was thick. "Pepper, this is totally crazy. You're pregnant with my child, I want to marry you, we both love each other—what is the goddamn problem?"

"I just told you."

"Look, there's a baby to think about now. Our baby. We have to think about it now."

"I am thinking about it!" she snapped. "I've got several alternatives. I can raise it myself, or I can—"

"Struggle to raise a child by yourself with all of the pressures on kids today? Or get a—You *wouldn't*—God, no, Pepper. I know you wouldn't do that. Please," Gray begged. "Please marry me."

The speck of snow had slid down past the window level now, dropping to the ground. Pepper removed her finger from the glass. There seemed to be a cold knot at the center of her, as cold as the clump of ice she had just watched fall. She couldn't believe she was here, having these feelings, saying these awful things. Why couldn't their love have been perfect? But then, with a stab of horror, she realized that she didn't know what perfect was, not when it came to her and a man.

How had she ever had the chance to learn?

"I won't marry you, Gray. I can't."

"Jesus—but why not?"

"Because you can't separate beautiful and sexy from the rest of me. Because I'm going to grow old and I want somebody with me who'll love me when I have wrinkles and won't trade me in on some new cookie-doll who raves about taking 'important trips.' "

"Important trips?" he said, bewildered.

Pepper lifted her chin. "I'll raise the baby by myself. You can have fair visitation—but you're not going to be buying the kid a lot of fancy gifts—I'll have that written into our visitation agreement. You'll give me child support, I assume. I won't ask for much. I do have my shop, I'm not totally financially dependent."

"But you're pregnant! That's going to impact your shop. Having a newborn baby will. Pepper, this is foolhardy! You aren't even thinking! I'm a man of means, I want to be a full-time father. I'll be a good father this time around. Are you so selfish that you would deny this for your child? I love you! I always have and I always will! *You, Pepper!* And you want to toss it all away like garbage."

How she wished she could believe him—it would be so easy to knuckle under, accept his proposal. But Pepper knew her marriage to Gray would be flawed.

Tears burning inside her, she pushed past him, hurrying out of his office. Walking fast, she proceeded past the cubicles to the third-floor lobby where the vacant receptionist's desk looked like an eerie marble sarcophagus.

She reached the elevator, which was still standing open. She stepped inside. She felt lonely and icy and scared. Millions of women would call what she'd done stupid and shortsighted. Giving up a rich, desirable man like Gray, "the most eligible bachelor in Ann Arbor"—all for a principle. But she just could not go into a trophy marriage. She was a full person, with a full, rich life of her own, and she didn't want to lose that to "Prince Charming," who would lay all of his own expectations on her. Maybe he wouldn't say,

"Ugh, go cook cow," but the idea was the same.

The door took a long time to close, so she reached out to push the down button, but before her finger could reach it, Gray was in the elevator with her.

"Don't push that floor button!" snapped Gray. He took her roughly into his arms, holding her so tightly that she almost couldn't breathe. With one hand he stroked her hair, with the other he pulled her face up so that her eyes were looking into his.

"Pepper, I love you," said Gray brokenly. He squeezed her so closely to him that their chest bones pressed together. "I have no words for it other than that. You're not a trophy—not to me. I swear it. I swear on all that is holy. I know I have things to learn. I'll learn them. I will. I'll do whatever it takes. I do respect who you are. I do. You can dress in long, baggy dresses and cardigan sweaters if you want . . . sloppy sweat socks . . . you can have BO . . . You can be fifty, or seventy, or ninety-two . . . I'll still think you're beautiful. I'll love your face forever. It's *you* I want. *You* I love. How can I convince you?"

His gaze was so intense that she closed her eyes, tears stinging behind her lids. What was she to say? She wanted him . . . but she was so frightened.

"Pepper," he went on. "Marry me. I repeat that. Please, just give me a chance to prove my love. We could be a family. Don't throw that away." The sound of his swallowing was thick in his throat. "Pep, I had a heart attack a while back, I told you that. They said I'm fully recovered, but I'm older than you, which means—our lifetimes might not totally coincide. I'll die first. Which doesn't make me that great a bargain from that standpoint. But I want the years I have left to be with you. There's no other way I want to spend them." His voice cracked again. "Waking up every morning with you . . . *every* morning . . . I'd give ten years off my life just for that one privilege."

He was crying now, openly; she could hear his breath catching.

She opened her eyes. In the mirrored elevator wall she

could see both of their reflections, Gray's arms around her, his face wet with tears, lines deepened in his skin so that he looked much older than his fifty-one years. In the glass she could see the way Gray would look in another fifteen or twenty years, the lines and crevices deepening, flesh loosening away from the bone structure.

Seeing Gray that way, as he'd look in the future, made him seem so vulnerable, so human. Pepper's throat closed. Yes, he did love her, she felt sure, but much male machismo was wrapped up in that love, and he would always want to show her off because that was the way he was, and how could he ever completely change? He couldn't. So if she wanted him, she would have to live with that. When she was sixty, he'd still proudly introduce her at parties, and when she was seventy-five, there was a slim chance he'd still be around, and he'd probably still show her off then, too. And by then she would love it. None of what she felt today would matter by then.

"Well?" he said, holding her, wiping at his streaming eyes. "Well, Pepper?"

"Don't buy me jewelry," she said fiercely. "Not one damned piece except maybe some costume jewelry. I want your solemn promise, Gray. No trophy-wife diamonds, no gold, no pearls, no little gold watches."

"Yes, if that's what you want."

"And never put my business down, or try to tell me how to run it, or take it over, or make me feel you think it's just a hobby."

"God forbid," he said. "I promise." A smile had begun to tug at his mouth. "Anything else?"

Pepper's mind had suddenly gone blank. "I'll think of other things, but for right now that's all. All right," she agreed shakily. "We'll get married."

"Thank God," breathed Gray.

She signed out in the book in the lobby, carefully entering the time under the scrutiny of the young security guard. Gray walked Pepper out to the parking lot, talking about

weddings and where they should have theirs. Her car was
coated with a layer of snow, so Gray reached in the backseat, found the plastic brush, and began cleaning off her
windshield. Should they find a little chapel someplace,
should they be married by a judge, should they fly to Maui
or somewhere beautiful and get married there?

"Let's . . . talk about that tomorrow," Pepper managed to
breathe. Stress was making her feel tired. She needed to get
home, crawl into bed, try to think about the momentous
change her life had just taken.

Gray kissed her tenderly. "Pepper, I just can't say how
glad I am this is happening. I could get some tickets for
Hawaii, you could wear plumeria in your hair for the wedding, we could be barefoot on the beach . . ."

"Whoa. Just give me a little time." Pepper got into her
car, starting the engine. "I have to go," she told Gray, starting the car's engine. "I have a whole lot to think about."

"Think of me. Think how I love you."

She pulled out of the lot, aware of him standing there
without a coat, a chilly wind buffeting the designer necktie
he wore, ruffling his silver hair, his expression both exalted
and still somewhat worried.

Oh, jeez, Pepper thought, swallowing hard as she drove
onto Plymouth Road. She'd just said she'd marry him—
exactly what she had not wanted to do. A quick, snap decision, but was it the right one?

He did love her. She felt that deeply within her bones.
He would try hard, by his standards. There would never
been another woman for him but her; she did believe that.

Why don't I feel happier?

By the time Pepper reached her apartment, she was trembling, and she didn't even bother to shed her jeans and
sweater tunic before crawling into bed, where she sat huddled
and shaking, her skin cold all over.

The lovely words he'd said. The way he'd cried. Yes,
he'd be a good father to her child, and she would have no
serious financial worries. There would be a cushion to fall
back on in case—God forbid—her boutique did fail. Her

mother and uncle's loan money would never be in jeopardy.

But now panic was beginning to fill her as she remembered her mother's marriage to a man much like Gray Ortini. Mason Maddalena had been repelled by the natural changes of Toni's body as her pregnancy progressed. He'd looked at his wife with revulsion. Divorced her within eight weeks of Pepper's birth.

Had Mason, too, promised to *love Toni's face forever*?

She rubbed her burning eyes, fighting to get control of her fear.

TREVA

THE HOSPITAL PA SYSTEM SOUNDED IN THE BACKGROUND, calling for a Dr. Shoushanian. A man from Housekeeping slowly rolled a cart filled with garbage bags down the hall. An elderly couple wandered past the lounge, appearing lost.

Just another day in the hospital.

"Daddy," said Shanae. "You haven't even had any coffee in hours—you have to drink something or you're going to get sick."

"Coffee?" said Wade, as if Shanae had suggested that he jump from the hospital roof.

"Yes, Daddy, *coffee*. And maybe a sandwich. Let's go over to the cafeteria. I've got some money, I'll buy."

"In a while," said Wade.

Shanae sighed. Her father had been acting like this ever since Treva's seizure, so caught up in his anxiety that he seemed to have forgotten about his own bodily functions.

The ICU lounge was now empty, the TV set on the wall playing the original *Die Hard*, with Bruce Willis, constantly interrupted by commercials. Shanae had seen the movie six times. Although visiting hours were over, the nurses, most of them Treva's friends, had permitted Wade and Shanae to continue to wait.

Maybe she'd be coming out of her coma soon.

Shanae fluttered her eyes shut and said another prayer, sending it up to Jesus. She'd prayed so much in the past day that the words came automatically, without her even having to think about them. *Please save Treva. And the baby. Amen.*

A commercial was coming on, for Arizona Jeans. Shanae was wearing a pair right now. Her eyes flicked dully to the screen where she watched several attractive young people doing wheelies on bicycles in front of a stunning, tan-colored mesa.

Shanae rubbed her hands together, fussing with a birth-stone ring that Wade and Treva had given her last year for her birthday. If Treva died, what would they do? She might be only a stepmother, but she'd been so much a part of Shanae's life that the girl could scarcely imagine life without her.

And the baby . . .

Beside her, Wade put his face in his hands. He muttered, "I should have been with her more. I wasn't here enough—I should have seen this coming. Instead I was at the racket club trying to forget."

"Daddy," whispered Shanae, touching his shoulder. "You were here plenty. You came twice a day most of the time. Treva loved it when you came for lunch. And the gifts and things you tucked in the flowers. She loved those so much. She said you—she said you p-pampered her . . . Oh, Daddy . . ."

The last words emerged as a thin cry and Shanae threw herself toward her father, and Wade enfolded her in his arms. They both cried for a long while.

Suddenly Shanae looked up to see Dr. Sandoval walking into the room, wearing a slightly rumpled hospital coat, looking sallow and tired, as if she'd spent too many hours in the hospital environment.

"Mr. Connor—Shanae. At the nurses' station they told me you were still here."

"We wanted to stick around just in case," said Wade.

"She's still in the coma—no change."

"But how long?"

"We don't know how long she'll remain comatose. In cases of eclampsia, the length of the coma varies from individual to individual and can last as long as a week or more."

"A week?" Wade had already been told this, but he must have been too upset to hear it, because now he stared at Dr. Sandoval as if this news were raw and fresh.

"As you know, we've already started her on mag sulfate. It'll stop any repeat seizures, we hope. And we're going to bring out the baby as soon as possible. That more than anything will help, although she won't be out of the woods yet by any means."

Wade looked stunned. "She won't? I thought having the baby would clear this up."

"Possibly. We hope it will. If seizures occur after birth, they're usually within the first forty-eight hours, but they can set in from ten days to two weeks after delivery."

"Jesus," said Wade. He shook his head.

"Mr. Connor, I know this sounds placating, but take my word for it, your wife is a very strong woman, and if anyone can survive this, it's her. I got to know Treva fairly well over the past several months or so, and I can tell you she has a very strong life force."

"She's got to live. Please, call in more doctors if you have to. I don't care what they cost. Do everything."

"We are doing everything, Mr. Connor," Ruth Sandoval said quietly.

Shanae phoned her mother, Wanda, starting to sob over the phone. "Mom . . . it's awful. She's still in this coma, and Dad's, like, out of it."

"Oh, honey. What do the doctors say?"

"They think they can bring her out of it . . . with that

medicine they're using.'' Shanae's voice shook. ''It's something they call a vaso—vaso something. It, like, dilates the
blood vessels. So when she does come out of it she's going
to feel real hot.''

''You just have to believe she's gonna get better, honey,''
said Wanda. ''Tell your dad to hang in there. You, too, baby
doll. Maybe you should come home, rest for a while. I can
drive down and pick you up. This sounds like an awful lot
for you to handle.''

''It isn't. I can take it. I want to be here,'' protested
Shanae. ''Dad needs me.''

Later, another movie started running on the TV set, one
of the first *Highlander* flicks. Wade leaned his head back
on the couch and fell asleep, making sounds that were halfway between snores and gasps. A man came down the hallway pushing an empty hospital bed. Down the hall, Shanae
could hear someone moaning. The sound was scary, giving
her thoughts she'd rather not have.

In fact, the hospital at night was very creepy, and if they
slept here in the lounge all night, they'd be exhausted by
morning and would *still* have to put in another day waiting
in the lounge.

Sighing, she tapped her father on the shoulder. He awakened with a loud snort.

''Daddy. Wake up. This is ridiculous. You have to go
home, get some rest, and so do I. The nurses will call us
just as soon as there's any change.''

''Can wait—no problem,'' Wade insisted groggily.

''*Daddy,*'' said Shanae, feeling like the mother. ''Get up.
Drive us home. I promise you, Treva wouldn't want us sitting around here like this. You can bring her some more
flowers in the morning. Bring her some roses. Put something
cute in it, maybe a teddy bear.''

''Roses, yeah,'' said Wade, rubbing his eyes. He came
awake fast, his face showing lines of strain. Then he smiled
at Shanae. It was Wade's old, jaunty smile, the one that
crinkled his eyes and put double vertical lines at the corners

of his mouth. "She's going to make it," he told his daughter.

"Sure, Daddy."

"I mean I *know* she's going to make it. I feel it here." Wade tapped his chest. "By tomorrow morning she's going to be coming out of it. I feel it in my gut."

DIEDRE

THE NEXT DAY DIEDRE PHONED THE CONNORS' HOME, BUT I got only the answering machine. Then she called the hospital, where she was connected to a patient information office and given a very brief, stilted message that Treva's condition was "stable." Whatever that meant. It sounded like she was better, though.

Since it was Saturday, Pam and Bud were off in his truck, visiting friends in Plymouth. Diedre borrowed the keys to Pam's Toyota. She'd promised to take Tarik to the bookstore reading today, and if she didn't hurry, she'd be late.

For a change, it wasn't snowing. It was one of those cold, bright winter days when the sun glares down on car windshields and reflects off every shiny surface, hurting the eyes. Piles of snow glittered white at the edges of driveways, and icicles hanging from rooflines were silver daggers. Kids playing in a yard were making a snow fort, their faces red with cold.

Diedre drove to Lashonda's house, her mind still on Treva Connor.

When she arrived, she found Lashonda and Tarik sitting in the middle of the living room floor surrounded by a stack of giant-sized plastic blocks. Lashonda had a law book open, one finger marking her page while she helped Tarik to balance a block.

"DeeDee!" the child cried, running toward her. "I want

to hear the dinosaurs! I want to hear the dinosaurs!''

"He's been talking about nothing else all morning," said Lashonda, grinning. "Take this child and get him some tyrannosaurs and get him out of my hair."

"Well, Tarik, let's go and get in the car then," said Diedre, smiling. "Can you put on your own jacket?"

"My own jacket, yeah," said the cute little boy. "An' my hat. An' my gwubs."

"Gwubs?"

"His gloves," translated Lashonda.

"Gwubs," repeated the child.

As they drove toward campus, Tarik chattered about a dinosaur doll he wanted to get. They passed a little Pakistani shop where Mitch had bought Diedre some silver earrings, a restaurant where they used to get *huevos rancheros*. Then the pizza place where they'd eaten after that first encounter in the law library's reading room.

Diedre averted her eyes, forcing herself to talk to Tarik. Everything in Ann Arbor was now tainted by Mitch memories; she couldn't go anywhere without something popping up that reminded her of him.

As always, the parking problem on campus was monumental, and Diedre had to drive around for a long time before someone finally pulled out of a space. Probably because of the sunny day, the sidewalks held a holiday gaiety. A student wearing a sandwich board marched up and down, advertising some comedy event on campus. A group of Central American students with brown skin and jet black ponytails had formed a street band and were playing lovely, plaintive music with wooden instruments.

The bookstore was huge, selling textbooks, computer software, University of Michigan sweatshirts and memorabilia, remaindered books, and current fiction. Students browsed remainder tables, poring over the books. An area in the children's section had been set aside for the reading. The professional storyteller was already there, a middle-aged woman wearing a caramel-colored jumpsuit, wooden

ethnic jewelry, and a hand-woven shawl—an outfit very typical of a certain type of Ann Arbor woman who had come
out of the sixties.

Tarik hung back at first, clinging to Diedre's legs, but the
storyteller spoke to him, and soon he joined the other children, a rainbow mixture of races, even a tiny girl in native
Guatemalan dress.

As the storyteller began telling a story about a little boy
who woke up and found himself in the Jurassic era, with
dinosaurs for pets, Diedre stood with the other parents,
watching at the edge. Tarik's laughter rang out infectiously.

A mood of sadness overtook Diedre. She'd screwed
everything up. No, that wasn't true. She and Mitch had *both*
screwed it all up. And it was too late to start over again
now. Their relationship was permanently scarred by too
much truth, too late.

She felt someone coming to stand beside her and instinctively turned.

"Diedre," said Mitch, his voice hoarse. "Oh, Diedre."

Shock spun through her. *"Mitch."* She widened her eyes,
unable to believe she was really seeing him now when he
had been at the forefront of her thoughts. "Why are you
here? How did you know I—"

"The other day I saw you looking at the poster, writing
down the times. I came here yesterday for the session and
I was here for the morning one, too. I wanted to talk to you
in person, but I didn't think you'd talk to me, and I guess
I can't blame you. I've been pretty shitty to you."

Several of the parents had turned to stare, so they walked
to the other side of the store and stood by a rack that sold
books on Microsoft Office, CorelDRAW and Aldus Page-
Maker. The rack, positioned in front of a wall, gave them a
bit of privacy.

"Oh, Mitch. Oh. I don't know what to say." She shook
her head, her eyes drinking him in. He looked dearly familiar, yet different, as if she were seeing him anew, freshly.
Yes, he *had* lost some weight. His hair needed a trim, she
saw. He'd cut himself shaving and there was a tiny scab on

his chin near the scar. His eyes looked naked, tired, pleading.

"Don't say anything. Just agree to marry me."

She froze. "What? You can't be serious."

"I am. I can forgive you, Diedre. For everything. You don't know how it's been—the strain it's been. I can't think about anything except you. Your sweet face, the way you'd always be waiting for me after class, the way you—"

She couldn't believe this. He could "forgive" her?

"Look." She kept her voice low and fierce. "What about all the things you said? You made me feel horrible, Mitch! You made me feel wicked, you treated me as if I were a murderer! Well, you weren't there. You didn't have something growing inside your body, you didn't feel the fear, you didn't have the *responsibility*."

"I did have the responsibility, or I would have if you'd bothered to let me in on it," he snapped.

Diedre was breathing fast. "You don't get it, do you, Mitch? You just plain *don't get it*. You were not there. You were nowhere in sight. You didn't even call me. So what 'responsibility' were you taking? Absolutely none! Then suddenly, six months later, with the brilliant view of hindsight, you accuse me of committing some kind of a crime because I didn't inform you that I was pregnant. Well, I did what I had to! It was my body, my uterus, my life. And damn you for making me feel guilty!"

Totally disgusted, too angry for tears, she started to turn away, but Mitch put a hand on her arm and stopped her. "There's no use discussing it anymore, is there, Diedre? I thought we could get past all of that bullshit. I thought we could start over again, forgive each other, but we can't, can we? It's too late."

"Sure it's too late," she cried. "Because you're selfish and male and all you want to do is lay a big guilt trip on me. Well, if men had to have the babies, there'd be a big change around here. Oh, yes!" She was fighting not to cry. "*Men* wouldn't pussyfoot around about the ethics of abortion. Oh, no way!"

Mitch stepped backward, offended. "You're lumping me with other men. I'm not like other men."

"Oh, I think you're *very* much like them," Diedre snapped. "You want to take charge of my womb. That's all you want to do. Well, you'll never control mine. Not ever."

She stalked away from him, going toward the edge of the storytelling area, where the kids were giggling as the storyteller spoke in a growly dinosaur's "voice." Diedre waited for the story to be finished, her heart pounding and thumping inside of her. She didn't turn around to look, but she felt sure Mitch had left the bookstore, as angry at her as she was at him.

It really *was* over.

How had she expected or fantasized anything else? They had foundered on the issues of guilt and her control of her own reproductive ability—yeah, that was exactly what it was. His right and her right. Her choice. A child that never was.

Diedre expelled her breath in a big, shaky sigh. She'd never thought she'd ever sound like a feminist tract; it was the last thing in her mind. But that was how she was beginning to think. Amazing.

And then, just as the storytelling session was beginning to break up, kids starting to stream back to their waiting parents, Diedre felt the first hot, ugly sob begin to choke its way up her esophagus. Grimly she swallowed it back. She couldn't cry—not here in the bookstore, not in front of Tarik.

It seemed a lifetime, but finally she had helped Tarik to buy a copy of the same book the storyteller had read, Diedre's gift to him. He clutched the store bag happily. Then they were on their way out of the bookstore. It felt as if someone had died, and Diedre knew that someone was part of herself. The Diedre who loved Mitch, who would have stayed married to him until she was very, very old. Well, she'd axed that scenario, hadn't she?

Forever.

They started in the direction of the car, Tarik still chattering about the little boy who had a dinosaur for a pet. Suddenly Diedre spotted an unusual sight. A Pontiac Grand Am parked a block away from the bookstore had been festooned with several dozen helium balloons, which bobbed and dipped merrily in the slight breeze that swept across campus.

Some campus high jinks, Diedre supposed dully.

"Look!" cried Tarik in delight, pointing. "Look, DeeDee. Look, the balloons have writing."

Diedre stopped short, narrowing her eyes. The child had better eyesight, but now she could see it, too. Even as she watched, one of the balloons slipped its mooring and floated up into the sky.

WILL YOU MARRY ME? it asked in gala lettering, paper streamers dangling.

All of the balloons had been imprinted with the same message, obviously left there for someone who would innocently emerge from some campus shop or restaurant, only to find herself the recipient of a marriage proposal. Diedre stared at the rampant balloons, feeling as if a knife tip had ripped across the chambers of her heart.

The happiness of strangers, she thought.

Well, it certainly wasn't going to be hers.

"So what's wrong with you, girlfriend? You look as if you've got the entire Western Hemisphere balanced on your shoulders and it's sinking you fast," said Lashonda when Diedre returned Tarik. She was still studying, almost exactly as Diedre had left her several hours previously.

Happily clutching his new book, the little boy ran into the kitchen, and Diedre slumped onto the couch, rubbing her throbbing temples. "Mitch was in the bookstore, Lashonda. Wanting to apologize to me and forgive me . . . *forgive me.* Like everything was my fault."

"Oh, honey, you got a problem with that man."

"I don't have a problem anymore," said Diedre miserably. "Because he's not around anymore. I really told him where to go. End of story. The end. And all of that."

"It's never 'the end,' " said Lashonda slowly. "Until you both want it to be."

"Well, I want it to be. And so does he. I can't imagine that I spent all of this time being fascinated by Mitch Sterling. I never should have dated anyone at all," declared Diedre. "Not while I have all of this studying to do. Who needs men anyway?"

"Ah," said Lashonda. "You feel that way now. Wait until a few months from now." She chuckled. "Then see how you feel. Even when we hate 'em, we want 'em."

"Not me."

"Bullshit," said Lashonda. "You have the same weak spots the rest of us do, and one of those weak spots is spelled M-E-N."

Mitch Sterling drove aimlessly around the outskirts of campus, his head pounding with wave after wave of pain, as if all the confused emotions he felt were trying to pound themselves out through the very bones of his skull.

Diedre's accusations in the bookstore rang in his mind, ugly with truth. Yeah, what if men did get pregnant? Not that Mitch would ever want to be pregnant. But if . . . Oh, Christ, what would he have done in Diedre's shoes? He'd read a quote once; it had made him grimace at the time, but now it seemed serious and awful. *If men could get pregnant, abortion would be a sacrament.*

Part of him wanted a drink, but he knew that a drink wouldn't solve anything, so instead he just drove, out past the University of Michigan football stadium where generations of students had cheered their favorite gridiron players. As a sixteen-year-old, Mitch had dreams of being a college player, but a damaged knee in the October of his junior year had ended that particular dream. Besides, he'd never been able to put on the weight.

A family. Lots of kids. Another dream of his.

He pounded the steering wheel in frustration. He'd fucked that up royally, hadn't he?

He found himself turning on Washtenaw, passing the

usual subdivisions, strip malls, and side streets, but then something caught his eye, a one-story, Colonial-style office set back from the street, with a security guard standing in front of its entrance.

Mitch narrowed his eyes. An abortion clinic—in fact, he had read about it a while back in the *Ann Arbor News* when demonstrators from some weird pro-life group had picketed the place, with a lot of them crawling around on their hands and knees before getting arrested.

Is this where Diedre had the abortion done?

Mitch took his foot off the accelerator and slowed down, reluctantly fastening his eyes on the building. It looked like an ordinary medical-type office except for the glass-brick windows and a few people walking up and down in the parking lot, carrying posters. Mitch couldn't read all the lettering from here, but he thought one might say something like DON'T KILL YOUR BABY.

An icy sensation slid up from his stomach. It was very likely that this *was* the place where Diedre had come to have the procedure done. Maybe that same woman had been in the parking lot when Diedre arrived, maybe with the same sign. Mitch swallowed down metallic-tasting acid. How would it have felt, to know you were going to have an abortion and then be forced to read that sign?

Sheer hell.

That was what it must have felt like.

There was a turnaround up ahead, and Mitch pushed his foot on the brake, swerving around to head back the way he had come. Suddenly he had the urge to see the clinic up close. To see whatever it was that Diedre had seen on that day.

He drove into the nearly full parking lot. As he parked, a middle-aged woman dressed in a dowdy down coat and fur hat came rushing over to meet him, staying about fifteen feet away.

"Are you going inside? Do you work here? Quit your job! Don't go in. Don't kill another baby!"

The woman pushed closer, waving the poster. Horrified,

Mitch stared at her. She was dressed like a teacher or librarian, but her eyes were hard little dots of blue, her expression grimly fanatic. A name tag on her coat read MY NAME IS BOBBIE LYNN. WORKING FOR THE LORD.

"Don't kill another baby!" Bobbie Lynn shouted.

Annie Larocca was in a rush, slightly behind schedule because Nancy, the other PA, was home sick and everything had gotten off kilter. The usual 10 or 15 percent of no-shows had all decided to show up today, and every chair in the waiting room was full, some of the men who'd arrived with the patients sitting on the floor or standing.

She looked up hurriedly as Ramon approached her in the hallway.

"Annie, there's some guy outside, wants to come in, says he's an ex-boyfriend of a girl who had an abortion way last summer."

"Don't let him in," ordered Annie. "He could be somebody from No Genocide, wants to chain himself to the men's urinal or something. We've had more than enough of those people."

The security guard flushed. "He doesn't look like that kind of guy."

Annie had changed since the paint-ball incident, becoming much more suspicious, and she wasn't about to let a strange man in, especially one unaccompanied by a patient. "Well, he can't come in. Tell him that. If he won't move away, Ramon, call the police."

"Sure."

But Ramon was back in two minutes carrying something in his hand. "He said to give you these."

Annie gazed in surprise at the two objects that Ramon placed in her palm. A Michigan driver's license and a University of Michigan Law School ID card. These were both in the name of Mitchell Sterling, age twenty-three. She stared at the driver's-license photo of a good-looking young man with a shock of black hair and clear, honest-looking eyes. *A law student.* Some of them were flaming political activists, but those types usually cultivated long hair, ponytails, and earrings, and didn't have such a clean-cut appearance as this one.

"What does he want here?"

"I don't know. Something about his girlfriend's abortion. He wants to understand it, he said. He just wants to talk to someone. He looks all upset, ma'am. Doesn't act like a protester."

Annie hesitated. *Shit, why did he have to pick such a busy day?* But Annie knew that husbands and boyfriends of patients sometimes felt powerless, caught in a dilemma of life and death, yet shunted aside from the decision process.

"Tell him he can have a couple of minutes, Ramon. But that's all. We've got eighteen women here today."

Ramon nodded, and in a few minutes he was back with a tall young man wearing an expensively cut leather jacket, his hair windblown. Mitch's face looked tight, a muscle knotting at his jawline, as he spoke directly to Annie.

"I have to know. What she went through. Everything. Is that impossible, or is there something you can show me that will help me to understand?"

His eyes beseeched her.

Annie felt a burst of sympathy. An ex-father, lost and guilty, trying to make sense of something that could seem cruel and senseless. "Okay," she said. "I can give you a fast tour. If that's what you really want to do. Many people find it disturbing."

"I want to do it," said Mitch, breathing fast.

Soft-rock music played over the clinic's PA system, Whitney Houston's hit from *Waiting to Exhale.* Mitch gazed into the waiting room, which was jammed with young women staring at magazines or at the TV set, their faces pale with anxiety. One girl sat with tears rolling silently down her cheeks. Another sat with her arms clenched protectively around her abdomen. She couldn't have been any older than sixteen.

Mitch shuddered. Sixteen-year-old girls . . . and that one

in the corner looked even younger. Maybe even as young as thirteen! What had it been, rape, incest? Mitch felt his heart pulsate.

Annie led him along. "Now, we can peek in an empty exam room—if we can find one that's empty."

Mitch peered in a room that had cheery wallpaper, equipped with cabinets, Formica-topped counter, the usual medical stuff, and an exam table with big metal stirrups coming up at a wide angle, covered with blue terry cloth.

"The terry cloth is to keep their feet warm," Annie told him cheerfully. "And we also have slippers we can give them."

He swallowed as the purpose of the stirrups sank into his mind. It was one incredibly vulnerable position that men rarely faced in their own physical exams. He pictured Diedre spread out like that, exposed, scared, fighting tears.

Mitch heard a whining roar coming from the hallway, rather like a vacuum cleaner. "Oh, that's the suction machine," explained Annie. "That's what's used to suction out the POC—product of conception—into a tube called a cannula."

"Does . . . does it hurt?" he asked.

"We do sedate our patients, but we don't use a general anesthetic because we want to keep the operative risk as low as possible. They do feel some pain and a cramping sensation. It doesn't last for long, and most patients feel a very strong sense of relief when the procedure is finally over. By the way, our clinic has a terrific safety rate. We've never lost a patient. In fact, studies have shown that abortions are actually much safer than giving birth."

"I see," said Mitch, feeling a further queasiness in his stomach.

"Here are the instruments used for abortion," said Annie, looking at him sharply, then opening a drawer. "They aren't pretty, but they all have their use. This is the speculum. Have you heard of that before? It's used to penetrate the woman's vagina, holding the walls apart so that the cervix can be examined . . ."

Mitch was feeling more and more uneasy, but he forced himself to look at each and every instrument, forced himself to think of what they really meant. What had Annie called it? A euphemism. Oh, yes, the "product of conception." He felt sick. But this was what Diedre had had to deal with—this was the end result of the choice she had made. How desperate she must have been, he found himself thinking for the first time. To come here and do this. She must have been totally frightened.

And she'd had to do it alone, without him.

Because she was right, he had not called her, had not made the effort to find her again. He could have driven to Madison Heights, driven around trying to find her apartment building, knocked on doors, but he hadn't done it. True, his mother's dying was an excuse, the lost phone number was truth, but the end result was that Diedre had been left in the lurch. So who was he kidding when he said he would have "supported" her?

"Are you all right?" queried Annie. "You look a bit pale. You're not going to pass out on me, are you?"

"I'm fine."

"Well, I can let you peek in the recovery room, just a quick look, and then—"

The suction machine whirred again, the sound louder this time. Mitch winced. He didn't hear the rest of what Annie said. Sudden wooziness swept over him, black and white dots and an odd, metallic humming sound.

Then somehow he was lying on the floor, gazing up at the white, perforated ceiling tiles.

"Jesus," he groaned. "What . . ."

Annie loomed above him, her freckled face kind. "It's nothing serious, Mitch, you've just fainted, that's all. If you'll just lie there for two or three minutes, the blood will return to your brain and you can get up. Abortion clinics aren't for everyone."

Mitch sucked in a breath of air and sat up. He was sweating profusely. "I'm sorry."

"Don't be. This is not a place for the fainthearted. Sometimes we have patients who faint, too. Or their relatives. This decision is a tough one, Mitch, the toughest in the world. And it has to be made by women who are feeling ill and frightened and pressured—by society, by their families, by their husbands or boyfriends, or by the absence of same; by drugs and money and multiple other problems."

Annie's eyes bored into his, as if trying to force him into some sort of realization.

She continued, "Mitch, you have to understand that although there are people at work trying to take away women's rights to choose abortion, or to set further limits on those rights, currently women *do* have those rights, Mitch. Nothing has been done inside this clinic that wasn't legal. If the pro-life groups would spend as much effort on educating women about birth control and family planning as they do in hassling abortion clinics . . . if they would take care of the unwanted children we already have, instead of fighting to bring more of them into the world, the world would be a better place," she added sharply.

Mitch nodded, feeling numbed. He hadn't even kept up with abortion issues. When an article appeared in the paper, he usually just skipped over it, feeling it didn't affect him.

"Now I really have to get back to work," said Annie. "I have some booklets I can let you have—and there are books in the library. Most abortion books are very one-sided, a lot of them twist statistics, but a few of them do give both sides of the controversy. Oh, and a few books tell what it was like in the forties and fifties, back when women died in some dirty abortion mill, or aborted themselves and perforated their uteruses. That's what we'll go back to if abortion is banned again—trust me on that."

"Thank you," he managed to say, as the sound of the suction apparatus assaulted his ears again.

He stumbled out of the clinic, pushing his way past Bobbie Lynn. Getting into his car, Mitch sat slumped behind the wheel, too exhausted to start the engine.

While he'd been leading his own life, trying to deal with his mother's death, while he'd forgotten about Diedre and the one-night stand they'd had, Diedre had been going through . . . *that*.

TREVA

TREVA GROANED, THRASHING HER HEAD FROM SIDE TO side. Something was caught in her throat, giving her a panicky, choking sensation. She fought it with her hands, trying to pull it out.

"It's all right, it's a respirator, Treva. Just relax, it's helping you breathe," said a female voice at her shoulder.

Something had happened . . . She couldn't remember . . . It was all a blank . . . She thrashed again, and then consciousness seeped away from her. She slept.

The waiting room smelled stale, of perspiration and anxiety. The TV set had been playing a Ricki Lake show that featured delinquent, promiscuous thirteen-year-old girls who smirked as members of the studio audience stood at microphones and scolded them. One girl was so hated by the audience that Ricki herself had to intervene.

"Daddy," whispered Shanae. "You can't just sit here . . . Come down to the cafeteria with me. It'll be a good walk, and you have to eat something."

"No. I don't want to leave in case her condition changes."

"It will only take a few minutes, Daddy," begged Shanae.

"What?" he muttered.

"The *cafeteria*. Daddy, haven't you been *listening*? We have to have something to eat. We have to keep our strength up."

"Get me something from a vending machine," said Wade. "I have to be here for her, honey. It doesn't matter if I get a little hungry . . . I've been hungry before. What matters is her."

"All right," agreed Shanae in a small voice. "I'll try to find a sandwich that isn't bologna. Maybe roast beef. And I'll get coffee. Oh, and a piece of pie."

After Shanae had left, Wade sat quietly planning just how he was going to welcome Treva back to the land of the living. A gift. Yeah. Maybe another diamond, bigger than the one he'd given her for "ring day," the biggest, gaudiest, shiniest stone he could afford, a chunk of solid ice.

Ice. Yeah. He would freeze the ring in an ice cube and put it in her drink, wait with bated breath until she was almost down to the bottom of the glass and the ice had melted. Wait to see the surprise spreading across her face, then the shriek of delight . . .

Sadness filled him as he remembered all of their "anniversary" days, the fun, secrets, and laughter. Once Treva had hung a tree in the backyard with new pairs of Jockey low-rise briefs for him. There'd been an extravagant number of them, twenty at least. He couldn't remember which anniversary that was supposed to celebrate . . .

He started. Shanae was already back, carrying a sandwich wrapped in plastic, a piece of pecan pie wrapped in plastic, and an orange, along with a container of coffee.

"Daddy," said his daughter softly. "I hope you like tuna. The roast beef looked kinda dry."

"I do, baby doll."

"There's plastic forks . . . Oh, Daddy." Shanae's laugh was high-pitched and ended in a choke. "I was going to get a sandwich for myself and I forgot."

"So we'll split this one," Wade said.

Treva awoke again as they were inserting a tube down her nose, pushing it all the way down her throat. It hurt, and it made her gag. She weakly raised a hand, attempting to push it away. Her skin felt burning hot, as if her body had been plunged into a scalding bath.

"Don't fight it, Treva. This tube is so we can feed you. That's it . . . that's good. You're doing great, Treva. Everything is okay."

Somewhere in the background she heard the beep of a monitor, and some nurses talking.

"*Hot,*" she tried to croak.

"That's the mag sulfate we gave you. It'll help stop you from having another seizure. It dilates the blood vessels. As time passes your body will become accustomed to it, and it should get less uncomfortable."

She felt black unconsciousness swirling around her again, trying to roll over her. She fought it, trying to talk, but the tube blocked her speech.

Then she passed out again.

An old woman's voice moaned repetitively, calling out to God. "Take me, Lord! Take me, Lord!" she kept begging. A man coughed a deep, phlegmy cough that wouldn't stop. There were the multiple beeps of monitors, the squeak of rubberized shoes on tile, voices. Treva heard a bed being wheeled past. "His blood ox is eighty-nine," someone said.

Treva blinked open her eyes, fastening them on the dials, screen, and spiky lines of a heart monitor—her own. God . . . she must be in the ICU. Her skin burned, especially the tender skin of her scalp, where it felt as if she were a candle being dipped in flame.

Her baby! Was it born yet, or had she lost it? Treva fought panic, struggling to get her hand down to her abdomen so she could find out if she was still pregnant. But something held her hands down so she couldn't move them.

"Treva? Are you awake?" It was Ruth Sandoval, standing by her bed. "We took the feeding tube out so you can talk now, but you're still being restrained because of the seizure you had."

"Yes . . . My b— Is my baby all right?"

"He's still in there. His movements are a little sluggish but still within normal range, and his heartbeat is fine. You had a seizure. You were drifting in and out of consciousness for two days, but you're a lot better now. Listen to that monitor. Your vital signs are improving by the hour, just what we'd hoped.''

''Two . . . two days?'' She felt so groggy, fragmented memories giving way to the fear again.

''We'll be inducing labor tomorrow, Treva. If that doesn't work, we'll do a cesarean, but it's a lot better for you to deliver vaginally, so we're going to give you a trial labor.''

''Please.'' Treva's hand reached out and somehow found Ruth's warm, smooth fingers. She could smell the antiseptic soap the doctor had used to scrub her hands before she came into the ICU unit. ''Please, I . . . I want to ask . . . save him first.''

''We'll save both of you, Treva. Just rest now.''

After Dr. Sandoval left, Treva fluttered her eyes closed, shutting out the sights and sounds of the ICU, trying in her mind to grasp what had occurred. She remembered drifting off to sleep, and then she was in intensive care, struggling with the respirator down her throat. Or was it the feeding tube? Between those two points of time, her life was a blank.

The old woman stopped calling out. But now a thick male voice was complaining, something about a mask that had slipped. More nurses' voices, soothing, and the man quieted. Everyone here was hurting, scared, Treva thought. The ones who knew they were here at all. Had she come close to death? She felt sure she had. It was a terrifying feeling.

Treva's back ached from lying in one position for so long. She tried to shift her position a little, to ease her burning skin. She felt a sudden, weak urge to cry, to say, *Stop this, stop all of it, I want to get off now.*

But of course, she couldn't.

They'd let Wade inside the ICU for a five-minute visit.

''Baby,'' whispered Wade, holding Treva's hand tightly. ''Oh, baby. Oh, Treva. I can't believe this is happening to us.''

She looked at her husband. Wade was rumpled, a physical wreck. His shirt was crumpled and smelled of perspiration.

He had not shaved in several days, and his beard was growing in white around his chin. There was a wild, bloodshot look to his eyes.

"I'm going to have the baby tomorrow," she whispered.

"Thank God. Thank God. I want this nightmare over with."

"It will be. As soon as he's out, I'll feel a lot better, Dr. Sandoval said."

"If I had lost you." He spoke brokenly.

"But you didn't, Wade. I'll get through this."

"I hope the baby is worth it."

"He will be." She brought Wade's hand down to her baby bulge, and guided it to the area where the tiny feet thumped. "He's feisty today."

"A little linebacker in about sixteen years," said Wade. "First a high school gridiron player, then college. Then who knows?"

From somewhere she summoned the strength to laugh richly. "Oh, a football player, is he?"

"All-American," said Wade, smiling for the first time in days. "And maybe, in his spare time, he can be a doctor."

DIEDRE

DIEDRE HAD BEEN ENGROSSED IN HER LAW BOOKS FOR hours, lost in a chapter about medical malpractice. A doctor who had cut off the wrong leg, another doctor who had been drunk in the operating room. The buzz of the apartment doorbell startled her, causing her to lose her place.

"Pam? Will you get it?" she called, but then remembered that her sister had gone out with Bud to help him buy a new TV set at ABC Warehouse. Sighing, she got up and went over to the intercom grille, pressing the speaker button. "Who is it?"

"Mitch," came the staticky, disembodied voice.

"Go away! Please."

"Diedre, let me come up."

"There is no *point*,"she told the plastic grille. "If you don't leave, I'm going to call the police. You are *history*, Mitch."

"Diedre, I'm going to stand on the steps down here until you buzz me in."

She didn't bother to reply, just turned and walked away, returning to the living room couch where she had been sprawled with her books and notes in front of her. Frowning, she found her place and started to read a sentence, but then the buzzing sound came again, loud and annoying.

Damn him! Couldn't he leave her alone? Maybe she really should call the police.

Diedre snatched up her books and marched into her bedroom, closing the door so that the doorbell buzzing wouldn't penetrate. She and Mitch had already parted company—he'd made that very plain. What could happen now except more arguing, more accusations, more pain? She was tired. She didn't feel like suffering anymore emotional pain. Now she had to finish her first year of law school . . . That was where her goal lay at this point.

She forced herself to concentrate, but part of her was still listening for the buzzer. *Damn him!* Diedre clapped her textbook shut and walked over to the window, where she looked down at the parking lot. Mitch's Le Baron was still parked in front near the long, black-roofed carport.

Then she heard it—the pounding at the apartment door itself. With a start of dismay, she realized that he must have just rung other doorbells until someone buzzed him in. Now he was at her door, and she knew he'd bang until she either let him in or called 911.

"All right, all right," Diedre muttered.

By the time she had pulled open the front door, she had worked up a good anger. There he stood, disheveled-looking, his features drawn with anxiety. Well, she'd suffered a little anxiety, too. She hated him. Oh, she did. Why had she opened herself up to him and his love?

"Diedre," he begged. "Diedre, we *have* to talk."

"No, we don't."

"Five minutes of your time."

"*No.*"

Mitch's smile was brief and sad, revealing the new hollows of his cheekbones. "You'd give five minutes to a salesperson on the phone, so please give that amount to me. Diedre, I was wrong."

She stared at him suspiciously. "Mitch—"

"Wrong, wrong, *wrong*. I was, Diedre. I was selfish, judging you for something I knew nothing about. You were right—I judged you on hindsight. I've been a total jerk."

She didn't want the whole building to hear this. Diedre stepped backward, allowing Mitch to enter the apartment. She closed the door but did not offer to take his jacket.

"What is this, another way to get me to feel terrible about making the only decision I felt I could make at the time? About a million women get abortions every year just in this country," she insisted. "It's legal. *Legal*, Mitch, do you get it? I was alone and I had to decide."

"Honey . . . baby . . ." Mitch's forelock of glossy dark hair had fallen over his face, and he tilted his head backward, rubbing the hair out of his eyes. It was a gesture of weariness and sadness, and Diedre felt her heart give a small, unwilling squeeze.

She whispered, "Mitch, why are you here? Why now? Why this big change of heart?"

"I went there," he told her hoarsely.

"Where?"

"The clinic. The Geddes/Washtenaw Clinic."

Diedre felt as if he'd slammed her against the wall. She caught her knees unlocking, and had to steady herself. "But what . . . why . . . ?"

"I was driving past and I decided to stop. I wanted to—to know more about what it felt like, how it was. And I found out." Mitch walked into the living room and sank uninvited on the couch. After a moment Diedre followed him, sitting down at the other end, safely out of touching reach.

"Diedre, I didn't know. That place. Oh, it's clean and modern—safe, they said—but—what you went through. Those machines. The—the instruments. Jesus." He rubbed his head again. "I saw girls sitting in the waiting room. I heard the sound of that machine they use. I passed out, Diedre. I passed out on the floor."

"Oh, Mitch." The thought tore at her. "Why did you go there? To see how your child was lost? To rub your face in it, see the tragedy firsthand?" She spoke bitterly. "So you could *really* hate me?"

"No. Not that. I swear it."

"Then what?"

"I told you. I wanted to see what you went through. And I saw. Will you . . . will you tell me more about it?"

The abortion, he meant.

"You want me to tell you," she repeated.

"As much as you can. I wasn't with you. I should have been, and now I want to know everything you can tell me."

Diedre sat rigidly for several minutes, her mind in a turmoil. If she told him, wouldn't he just hate her more when he learned all the details? But wasn't it time for some honesty? *It had happened.* He had made half of the cells that had been washed away. Let him bear part of the responsibility.

Someone was walking up the stairs in the building's communal hallway, the sound of footsteps, followed by the slamming of an apartment door. Diedre said, "It was . . . it started when I had to go and buy the test kit. I was so terrified, I could feel the sweat on my face from fear. And then I found that the drugstore had put the kits on the same rack as the condoms!" She gave a dry, hard laugh. "It was sort of like before and after . . ."

She stopped. Did he really want to hear this?

"Go on," said Mitch in a low voice. He moved down the couch and his hand crept out to take hers. After a few seconds Diedre allowed her fingers to clutch his.

She talked, reliving it all.

On and on, for more than forty minutes, telling him everything, from the sleepless night, to the few minutes on the
exam table, sedated but fighting cramps and fear, to the hour
and a half she had spent in the recovery room listening to
the radio and the nurses' chatter. And then the hollow feeling of walking out of the clinic, knowing she'd changed
something—forever. Knowing that what she'd done was
irrevocable.

Sometimes he cried.

Sometimes she cried.

At other times she was dry-eyed, her voice sinking to a
whisper as she answered Mitch's questions, going over the
same territory again, wanting him to understand. She could
see by the paleness of his face that this was hard for him—
well, dammit, it had been hard for her, too! Biologically,
men got the easy, pleasurable, ten-minute end of procreation. Women were faced with the pain, the blood, the agonizing decisions, the unrelenting responsibility.

Maybe she had actually said that, for Mitch was staring
at her in a strange way.

"I guess you're right," he said. "Deeds—you were right.
You were in a situation and I was nowhere in sight. I *was*
just a one-night stand . . . at that time. You did what you
had to do. What can I say? I know we've been through a
tremendous amount, we've been to hell and back—but I
don't want it to be over between us."

He didn't want it to be over?

She pulled her hand away, feeling confused again. All the
things he'd said on the night they'd gone to the nightclub,
the accusations he'd made, flared up in front of her like
Fourth of July sky rockets. He'd accused her of killing their
baby, of willfully destroying it. How could he take those
words back so fast? How could she forgive so easily? It just
wasn't realistic. How could she trust that he wasn't just saying these things, motivated by loneliness or some sort of
misplaced, mistaken love?

Love that would turn on me later.

"Deeds?"

"But it *is* over." Her voice rose. "Mitch, *too much* has happened. That abortion will always hang between us. It happened. It'll always be there, and nothing we can say or do will make it go away. That's reality. I never should have become involved with you and we both know it."

"We'll never know if we don't try, will we?"

"Oh, you make it sound so damn simple!" she flared. "Just say some magic words and everything goes away, all the things you said and I said, everything just erased! Well, what if it doesn't work that way? What if I can't stop remembering the way you treated me? What if *you* can't stop remembering—"

"I just want us to start over again, Diedre. That's the bottom line as far as I'm concerned. Can we?"

She hesitated, her cheeks flaming. Finally she got up from the couch and paced uneasily over to the big window that overlooked the parking lot. Gazing down, she saw that one of the other building residents, a grad student's wife from India, was pushing a baby carriage along the sidewalk. Inside was a four-month-old baby boy, all bundled up for the cold with barely his nose sticking out of his jacket, hood, and blankets.

Diedre narrowed her eyes at the sight, feeling tears sting them. "Mitch. I'm looking outside and I see a woman with a baby carriage. How are we going to feel later when we see a—"

"Stop it," he said. He came to stand beside her, not touching her, but holding himself just a few inches away. "I can't promise what the future will hold, Diedre. I don't own a crystal ball. All I know is that I love you. It's been hell without you—sheer, utter hell. I want to try to see what we can make of our relationship."

"I don't know." Diedre fought tears. "I'll fall in love with you again."

She could hear the low, strained rumble of Mitch's laugh, so dear after she had thought she would never hear it again. "So be it," he said. "I can't make radical promises—"

"Don't."

"Just don't shut me out, Diedre. Talk to me. Always make me a part of the decision process—don't shunt me aside, because it's the one thing I can't bear."

She heard herself agreeing, her voice turning into a sob. Blindly she turned to him, ran headlong into his arms, almost bumping him in her haste to be enfolded.

She cried, harder and harder, clutching him. He held on to her until the emotional storm dissipated.

"I haven't got a tissue," he said.

Her voice was tear-thickened, barely intelligible. "On . . . on the kitchen counter."

He fetched her a generous handful, and she blew her nose and cried again, and used up the rest of the tissues, giving some to Mitch, whose eyes were also wet.

"Ah, Mitch," she whispered into his collarbone.

He kissed her on the neck, nuzzling the kiss into the damp side of her face by her ears, his breath soft on her skin. "I do love you. I'm helpless with loving you. I hope you know that."

"And I love you," she finally sighed, giving up most of her anger. She could feel warmth spreading through her. Was it a traitorous warmth? Was she headed for more heartbreak, a relationship that seemed healthy for a while, then cracked apart again, based on an act in the past that neither of them now could change?

She'd have to see.

They would have to see.

But for now she wanted to move ahead into the future, wanted to see what it held. With Mitch.

TREVA

IT WAS 6:30 A.M., AND TREVA HAD BEEN WHEELED INTO a labor room that had been equipped with special monitors. Because it was a high-risk pregnancy and the baby would be premature, she would not use a regular birthing room.

"I'm Lani, I'm going to be your nurse throughout your labor and delivery," said a pleasant-looking Chinese-American woman of about forty, wearing green surgical scrubs. "We're going to set you up with the oxytocin drip right away. Do you have any questions, Treva?"

"How long before I start having contractions?"

"Maybe a couple of hours, maybe sooner. They'll be gradual. We'll continually be monitoring both you and the baby."

Lani attached a belt with a receiver to Treva's abdomen, explaining that it used a principle similar to ultrasound to detect the baby's heartbeat. "Later we'll be using an internal fetal monitor, where an electrode is placed directly on the baby's scalp. It's connected by wires to a machine that records the baby's heart rate. But we'll have to wait to do that until your membranes are broken and you're dilated to at least one centimeter."

Lani continued to fill Treva in on what she could expect, while Treva fought to keep her sense of excitement down. Outside the hospital windows it was still pitch-dark. The exaggerated *whap-whap-whap* of helicopter rotors could be heard as a copter came in for a landing on the helipad located on top of the Taubman Center.

"How do you feel, Treva?" whispered Shanae, slipping into the room, leaning over the hospital bed. The teenager wore a fresh blouse and clean blue jeans, and looked bright and excited.

"Wonderful," said Treva, smiling.

"Are you ready to have a baby now?"

"Oh, dearest, I'm more than ready. I can hardly wait. It feels like the culmination of so much—not that I don't already have a wonderful, wonderful stepdaughter," Treva added, hugging the teenager.

Shanae reached across the bed, wrapping both arms around Treva and resting her head on the pillow near Treva's. Her voice shook as she said, "I was so worried when you—when—you know. That coma thing.''

''I guess I was floating off somewhere, but part of me was worried, too.''

''You were still thinking when you were, you know, in your coma?''

''In a way,'' said Treva, feeling a dark mood suddenly come over her. She shook her shoulders, making an effort to push it away.

''I brought you something,'' said Shanae. ''Here.'' She pulled away, dug into her battered black leather shoulder. bag, and thrust something into Treva's hands.

Treva looked down. It was a plush teddy bear small enough to hold in the palm of her hand. The color of the fur was medium caramel, almost exactly matching the color of Treva's skin, and the eyes were bright buttons.

''Hon, he's perfect!'' exclaimed Treva in her rich voice.

''It's the baby's first toy. It's little, just like he's going to be,'' explained the teenager. Then she lunged forward, burrowing into Treva's arms again. ''Treva . . .'' she choked.

''Don't say it, honey. Just don't say it. I love you,'' murmured Treva, holding her stepdaughter. ''I could never have a better daughter than you.''

After Lani set up the IV drip and checked Treva's blood pressure, she left the room for a few moments and Wade came in, carrying a bag filled with several paperbacks.

''Honey . . . you mean the world to me,'' he began emotionally.

''Hey, no waterworks, I'm just having a baby,'' said Treva, her brown eyes sparkling. ''In a few hours, I don't know how long, we're gonna have a—''

Wade gulped. ''I just want you to know—''

''Don't talk like that or I'm going to start sobbing and I won't be able to stop.''

Then she did sob for a while.

They loved each other so much. She'd come to the marriage late. They'd only had ten years together; she wanted fifty more.

''Ah, babe,'' said Wade, stroking her hair.

* * *

After Dr. Sandoval came in and broke Treva's water membranes ("Lordy, I never knew I could release so much water all at one time," Treva laughed), a few small uterine cramps began.

They were going to use an epidural for pain, Dr. Sandoval explained. "We'll start a nice little continuous epidural block in your lower back, and leave a plastic catheter in place. That way we can administer anesthetic either with a pump that injects a small amount at a time, or an anesthesiologist can administer it as needed."

"Sounds . . . great," Treva said, grimacing a little as a cramp came and went.

"We're also going to keep plenty of fluids running through you with an IV, to make sure you don't get dehydrated. We want plenty of oxygen getting through to that little fellow in there." Dr. Sandoval touched Treva's hand. "You're going to do just fine, Treva."

Wade sat with her, laughing and joking, trying to keep her spirits up. He had brought a new Carl Hiaasen novel with him, and spent several hours reading aloud to her, trying to add life to his reading by taking on the voices of the spicy, disreputable characters. In Wade's deep, baritone voice, it sounded irresistibly funny.

"You sound like James Earl Jones in drag," quipped Treva, smiling during a rest between contractions.

"You mean I'm not yet ready to record for Books on Tape?"

"Don't quit your day job, honey. Uh . . ." She grunted as another one gripped her pelvis.

"You okay, babe?"

"I'm doing great," she mumbled. "Maybe you could start doing that back-rub thing."

She hadn't been able to take any childbirth classes, but Rhonda had found one on video, and now Wade's large, strong fingers felt wonderful as they made their way down the knobs of Treva's spine, alternately squeezing and stroking.

"The baby has a very good heartbeat," announced Lani, checking the fetal monitor, which they had now been able to insert internally. "A nice hundred thirty-four beats a minute. We couldn't ask for much better than that."

Five hours had passed. Wade had long ago stopped reading the paperback aloud, and back rubs didn't help anymore. She was now on the epidural, the medication being administered in small doses by the pump. Her body was numbed from a few inches below the incision line in her back near her spine to a few inches above, although her legs felt heavy, too. She was dilating right on schedule, Dr. Sandoval said.

"It's a textbook labor so far, Treva. And the baby's vital signs are all within normal range."

Treva glanced over at the machine that was recording a tracing of the baby's heart rate and her uterine contractions on a long sheet of paper. "I guess I'm having a high-tech birth," she said. She felt a change inside her, a sensation of something pushing down. She might have been on an epidural anesthetic, but she just knew.

A few minutes later, she said to Lani, "I think . . . I think it's coming—I think it's—*this baby is coming!*"

"Honey?" said Wade.

Lani was already moving around the room, phoning for Dr. Sandoval. "I think we've got ourselves a baby on the way," she said over the phone.

"I love you, Trev," said Wade, gripping Treva's hand.

She lay on the delivery table, her legs suspended high in stirrups. Her hand gripped Wade's, both of their palms sweaty. He stood at her head, watching the delivery on a mirror suspended from the ceiling. Dr. Sandoval hadn't wanted to let him in, but Wade had begged, promising to leave the room if there was the slightest problem. "I swear to God I won't faint. Never passed out in my entire life, and I did see a little blood when I was in 'Nam."

Treva heard the muffled crying as if from a long distance away. "Is that my baby?" She managed to grunt out the words.

"He ... yes, but he isn't quite born yet," Dr. Sandoval said, bending over her.

He was crying inside the birth canal. Was that usual?

"You'll have to try to push," said Lani, on her other side. "I know it's hard, but do what you can."

Then Treva was pushing, forcing her whole being, every particle of her, every muscle and fiber, into the effort of expelling her son. She pushed, grunting like an animal, shameless in her need to eject this child. There were seven or eight people in the room, but there could have been a whole audience, a thousand people, and she wouldn't have cared. This was what she'd been born to do.

Suddenly the crying was in the room with them. A loud, bratty squall.

"Is that ..."

"A very nice little boy," said Ruth Sandoval. She held up a small creature covered with blood and white, cheesy material, its mouth wide in an amazingly healthy cry. The umbilicus extending from his abdomen still attached him to her, looking huge compared to his tiny body. He was scrawny and feisty.

Treva caught her breath, laughing, then crying, then laughing again. Wade was openly weeping. His sobs filled the delivery room.

"Oh," she wept. "Oh, thank you. Oh, I have my baby. Oh, thank you."

Dr. Sandoval had clamped and cut the umbilical cord, and then Lani and another nurse bent over the tiny newborn, suctioning out its mouth and nose. Its crying continued.

"Weight four pounds, six ounces," someone said. It was Dr. Livoti, the neonatal specialist whom Dr. Sandoval had brought in on the case, and who would be overseeing the baby's care once it was born.

"Okay, the Apgar," said Dr. Sandoval.

"Heart rate, two," said Dr. Livoti. "Respiratory, two.

Muscle tone, two. Reflex, one. Color is one. Score is eight.
That's a good score, Treva. Most babies in a normal, healthy
delivery score somewhere in that range. We're going to do
another one in five minutes and the score may go up.''

Treva lay back, tired but smiling broadly.

"Treva. Trev.'' Wade bent down and kissed her, brushing
away her tears with his thumbs. "Thank you, darling.
You've just been . . . so . . .'' He broke down.

"Hey,'' she whispered. "What about a name for this kid?
We've discussed this one and that one—now it's time to
really decide.''

They looked at each other. "You choose,'' he said.

"Wade, Junior,'' Treva said tiredly. "That's his name.
How could it be anything else?''

Treva sank back, her strength seeping out of her. Her head
was aching again, but she barely felt it.

"I want to hold him,'' she said.

"Just for a minute, Mother,'' said Dr. Livoti. "Then
we've got to whisk him to a nice, heated bassinet in the
NICU.''

That meant neonatal intensive care unit, as both Wade
and Treva knew. The baby's weight, a bit over four and a
half pounds, meant he would have a much higher survival
rate than the tinier babies, but he would still be in the hospital for several weeks, until his size and physical condition
became optimal for release.

They let her hold her baby only for a minute. But that
minute for Treva was ineffable, the incredible joy of holding
a scrap of herself, a pale caramel-colored baby with dark
eyes that seemed to stare directly at her, wide open.

"Hi, little Wade,'' she whispered softly, between tears.
She touched the infant's miniature hand with its perfect,
curled fingers. The hand kept moving toward his mouth and
finally it made it. She watched her four-pound-six-ounce son
suck his thumb. A true miracle. He kicked his skinny, brown
legs vigorously. He had minuscule, perfect toes. Another
miracle. Even his tiny penis was perfect.

"Thank you,'' she whispered.

"Mrs. Connor—we need to take the baby now. He's got a great Apgar and he's doing fine. You can come see him in the nursery just as soon as you feel up to it."

Treva felt a sorrowful wrench and reluctantly surrendered her child. She'd visit him in a few hours, as soon as they allowed her to. She'd go down in a wheelchair. And later she'd try to breast-feed. She'd expel her milk, using a breast pump, and they'd give it to him in the nursery.

She was a mother now. Nothing had ever felt so wonderful.

They had wheeled Treva out of the delivery room and she was lying on a gurney in the hallway, still holding on to Wade's hand. Lani, the nurse who had stayed with her through the whole labor and delivery, was on her other side, telling her how vigorous and healthy the baby looked.

Treva felt warmed, suffused with gratefulness for all that she had been given. "Oh, Wade," she whispered. "I took a risk, but it turned out all right after all. It was worth it, every hour in that hospital bed. And little Wade . . . I can't believe how beautiful he is."

"*Beautiful* is for girls. This guy is handsome."

She said, "Yeah . . . in about eighteen years he's gonna be a hunk. Just like his daddy."

Treva was still on an emotional high. She had brought life into the world, she had brought forth a son. He would be with her all her life. There would be grandchildren and great-grandchildren, her descendants reaching down through the millennia. She was part of a life flow so profound that it was the most powerful thing on earth.

Wade gripped her hand, smiling euphorically. "Now, I know he's got to stay in the hospital for a while, but do you think they'd let him have a teddy bear while he's in the incubator? Shanae showed me the bear she brought him. Maybe they'd let us put it next to him so he'd have something to look at."

"Only sterile things in the isolette," said Lani, smiling. "But later, when you bring the baby home—"

Treva started to say something, but it came out slurred.

She felt something electrical buzzing in her head, like a horrid short, and then—

She no longer heard Wade's voice, yelling at her now. She plunged into unconsciousness so deep that it was as if a light were being turned off in her head.

"Help! Help us!" Wade yelled. "Nurse! Doctor!"

Lani and Wade gripped Treva's thrashing body, practically tackling her so she wouldn't throw herself off the gurney, while Lani managed to push an emergency button located in the hall. Treva writhed under her husband's hands, arching her pelvis upward with such violence that he could barely keep her from rocking off the side of the bed.

"Treva! God! Oh, God!" His cry of anguish echoed down the hallway.

Nurses came running, technicians, Dr. Sandoval. Someone dragged a "crash cart" full of instruments and medications. They pushed Wade aside and began ministering to Treva, crowding around her as she thrashed, making ugly, inhuman sounds.

"Get an airway! We're going to lose her!" someone cried.

"She's arrested! V fib!" someone else yelled.

"Oh, Christ." Wade didn't even know he had said it aloud.

Someone pushed Wade farther out of the way. He watched with horror the massive efforts to resuscitate his wife. It was a nightmarish repeat of last time. This was a much worse seizure than the other one, he sensed; she had already gone very far away. She was dying . . . At least, she was poised at the brink of death. Maybe she'd had a heart attack. Something awful.

More medical personnel came running up and Wade stumbled farther away, afraid he would impede someone and it would mean Treva's death. But at the same time he wanted to hold her hand. He didn't want her to die alone.

He wanted to be with her—protect her—cherish her till the last.

Treva, oh, Treva.

Wade stumbled back out to the waiting room, finding Shanae as she sat watching "Oprah" on TV.

The girl took one look at his ashen, wretched face and jumped to her feet. She rushed over to him. "Daddy?"

"She had the—the baby is fine. She had another seizure. It's bad," choked Wade. "They told me to wait here. They'll call us when they get her under control again."

"Daddy," whispered Shanae, horrified. She had been in the waiting lounge all this time, waiting to see her new baby brother. "You mean she had *another* seizure?"

"Yes, cupcake."

"Oh, Daddy."

They clung together, the man and the teenager, leaning against the wall, partly shielded by the bulk of Wade's arms. They cried together, their grief so naked and affecting that passersby, walking down the hallway, gazed at them in sympathy.

"I can't believe this," sobbed Shanae.

"She'll make it," said Wade, choking. "She came out of the other seizure, she'll come out of this one, too."

But he had a dreadful feeling.

"She was willing to sacrifice herself," wept Shanae. "She did all those things—lying on her side for all that time—those horrible medicines and stuff—the catheter—"

"I never should have let her do it," said Wade brokenly.

Shanae hugged him, her slim body as strong as iron. "But it was what she wanted. It was her happiness, Daddy."

Treva existed in the void, where there was a great spray of white light so transparent that she could see layer upon layer of it, shimmering like folds of lustrous silk. Behind the light was an even more concentrated source of power, so bright that it blinded her eyes.

She floated toward that light, drifting like golden dust.

She heard voices, like strings pulling her back toward the earth, and she struggled to become free of them, to float ever higher. Such happiness. So blinding. So free and full. Secrets floated in front of her, secrets of life, and she swam toward them, shaking herself free of the voices, the cords that held her to earth.

Wade stood up when Dr. Sandoval walked into the lounge. The doctor's face looked lined and weary, her hospital coat crumpled. One look at Dr. Sandoval's face and he knew the answer.

"No," he whispered.

"I'm afraid that Treva didn't make it. I'm so sorry. So very sorry. She was such a fighter."

"No," whispered Wade. "Please no."

"She was a very courageous woman."

But Wade had turned away, sobbing bitterly.

ENDINGS AND BEGINNINGS

TREVA

WADE FELT NUMB AS HE AND SHANAE WALKED through the hospital corridors toward the NICU unit where the baby, Wade, Jr., had been taken. Windows looked out on a huge parking lot, more buildings visible behind it, everything part of the dauntingly huge hospital complex where people were born and died daily.

"Daddy, please," Shanae kept saying as she touched his arm. "Daddy, talk. Say something."

But there was nothing more to say. Treva was gone forever, leaving him behind to spend alone all the years they would have had together. An attendant came toward them, pushing a young woman in a wheelchair. The woman, wreathed in smiles, held a newborn in her arms, and behind them walked a man carrying a suitcase and a vase of flowers.

Wade averted his eyes. He was angry, cheated. He didn't want to see others' happiness.

"Here . . ." Shanae was saying as they passed several small nurseries, then a bigger one. "It's this one, I think, Daddy. Look." She went over to the window and leaned toward it, staring in. "Look at the babies."

Wade stood still, then forced himself to walk closer to the window. The day had turned sunny—sometime around the time Treva had died, he imagined—and now shards of sunlight hit the nursery glass, sending off bright reflections.

Reluctantly he leaned closer and gazed inside. Rows of isolettes, each holding a small bit of humanity, some of the infants so incredibly tiny that they could be cupped in the palm of a hand. A gowned and masked nurse tended to one

of the preemies, reaching into some sort of orifice in the
incubator with gloved hands.

"Daddy." Shanae had hold of his hand. "There—there
he is! Back there, the second from the end."

They walked along the glass, their reflections appearing
in the window wall, moving as they moved. Just then a
cloud must have moved away from the sun, for the reflections became brighter, and for a second or two Wade
thought he saw a third reflection in the window, a female
figure dressed in a white hospital gown. It was hard to tell—
the image was blurry—but it almost seemed as if she was
smiling, her body yearning toward the sheet of glass as if
she longed to pass through it but could not.

Treva? He turned, startled, feeling a brief warm touch on
his neck, as if a furnace blower might have started up
nearby. But when he glanced around he saw no furnace
vents, nothing to explain the odd sensation of warmth.

He looked again and the reflection of the woman was
gone.

"Daddy, look, he's sucking his thumb," said Shanae
softly. "Looks like he's trying to eat it up."

Wade turned his gaze toward the nursery again. The baby
inside the incubator was skinny, not much fat on its bones.
However, it was amazingly lively, kicking vigorously, its
thumb fastened in its mouth. Suddenly its own movements
caused it to lose suction, and the child opened his mouth
and began to wail.

"Daddy, look, now he's crying. He wants his thumb
back."

"I see."

Shanae tugged urgently at his hand like the small girl she,
too, had been only a few years back. "Look how active he
is. How much he kicks his legs. He's going to be okay,
Daddy. He is. I bet we can take him home soon."

Take him home. It was the first time Wade had thought
about this. He shook his head, feeling some of the fuzziness
leave his mind. Jesus, the nursery, all fixed up the way Treva
had wanted it, the blue and yellow wallpaper, the carved

wooden crib she would have thought so beautiful. He still had to set it up. Still, most of the baby's room was ready, from baby wipes to safety pins, boxes of Huggies and Pampers, even a nursery clock shaped like a bear which Dr. Rosenkrantz had given Treva at the shower.

"He's so cute," said Shanae.

There . . . to the corner of his eye. A suggestion of the reflection again, mostly white, and fading as the sun changed angles. Wade looked at his daughter again, seeing her tear-streaked cheeks, her earnest expression.

"I know, pumpkin."

"And she got him, too, didn't she? The baby she wanted so much. And we have him now."

"Yes, we do," said Wade. The thickness that had been caught inside his chest for hours slowly began to shift and dissolve. He slid his arm around Shanae and they both looked through the glass at the newborn child. "Yes, he's ours," said Wade.

It was a redbrick church that had been built in 1860 by a group of African-Americans who had settled in Ann Arbor, lured north to work at Willow Run during the war. Stained-glass windows in simple colors let in the winter light. Its floors were made of wood and squeaked when someone stepped on them, the painted pews immaculately clean.

Treva's casket had been placed at the front. It was covered with a blanket of red roses, and surrounded by so many fan-shaped arrangements, many blazing with roses and white lilies, that the air was thickly perfumed.

More than 150 mourners crowded into the building. Treva's sister, Rhonda; Annie Larocca, Dr. Ellen Rosenkrantz, nearly all of the clinic workers, plus women from Treva's church, some of the Connors' neighbors, Wade's secretary. A cadre of staff members from the hospital were also in attendance, including Treva's favorite nurse, Patrice, and Dr. Ruth Sandoval.

The singing had already begun, a group of women in white choir robes, their bodies swaying as the rich gospel

Abigail Reed

notes belted out, filling every last inch of the church. Shanae Connor was singing with them, her voice ringing out over the others, pure as rich wine.

Pepper Nolan took the printed program someone handed her and slipped into the church, picking a seat at the back. She hadn't known Treva well, but oddly, she had come to depend on her in the past few months, and she wanted to say good-bye. She and Gray had decided to be married at a judge's office the following afternoon, and they'd be taking a two-week honeymoon on Maui. A mistake, marrying Gray? Pepper didn't know, couldn't tell, but the terror still clutched her. She had wanted to discuss this with Treva, get her take on it.

Now she'd never be able to. She felt the harsh pang of regret.

Still, maybe in the quietness of the church she could somehow take some time to think, to decide if she was making the right decision.

Glancing to her right, she saw that a young, blond woman had slid into a pew, a woman who looked oddly familiar.

Diedre Samms sat down, clenching her shoulder bag to her chest. She couldn't believe it, just couldn't believe it. Treva Connor had seemed so young, so vital, despite her hospitalization. She'd had such spirit and life. Now that life had been quenched, and she'd left a newborn baby behind.

The gospel choir had taken their seats and now an organ was playing something rich and flowing. Shanae left the choir and went to sit with the family in a pew at the front of the church. Her father, Wade, slipped an arm around her. From underneath her white robe the teenager took a small, caramel-colored teddy bear, cradling it as if it were a living infant—it was probably meant to represent Treva's new baby, Wade, Jr., who was still in an incubator at the hospital.

Treva had lived a life full of love, Diedre mused. While she . . . What lay ahead for her?

I want to have someone love me like that, Diedre thought. *Like Wade loves Treva. It's so obvious. The look on his face*

... Will anyone ever have that look on his face for me? Will Mitch?

Then the answer came, partially out of her own mind but also out of the peace that seemed to radiate out of every floorboard in the small church, and the altar, simply decorated with wall hangings, massed with white and red flowers.

Yes. Yes.

Sitting there while various friends and relatives testified about ''Sister Treva,'' Pepper thought about the woman they had come to mourn, and she shed hot tears. But then her thoughts inevitably turned to her own life. The choice she'd made. She still wasn't sure why she'd agreed to marry Gray so quickly. Doing it tomorrow afternoon at the courthouse was really cutting it fine.

Still, it all seemed so reasonable. Get married fast, save the hassle of flowers and a reception, while she still had the nerve and the courage to go ahead with the ceremony, then go off on a honeymoon.

Gray had already told his son, Brian, about their wedding. Brian had mustered up some congratulations but told his father he wouldn't be making it to the ceremony because he was going to ski in a giant slalom tournament.

Oh, Lord, she thought, nervously folding her hands together so tightly that her fingers trembled. *I'm really doing it, aren't I? Tomorrow. Marrying him. I really said I'd do it. Am I crazy? What if it falls apart in a year or so? What if—*

She felt a stir beside her and looked up to see Gray sliding into the pew on her left. He was wearing a dark business suit. As he settled himself on the hard seat, she caught a whiff of his vanilla-scented aftershave.

''Gray.'' She mouthed his name, turning to stare at him in surprise. He'd told her he had several important meetings to attend today.

''Thought you might want some company,'' he whispered in her ear. ''Funerals are incredibly sad to go to all by yourself. Especially one like this, when the person was so young.''

She gazed at him, his blue eyes surrounded by crow's-feet and creases, his skin comfortably aged by years of living.

''I mean it, Pepper,'' he whispered, leaning toward her ear again. ''I'm going to be there for you—I am. It's a solemn promise.''

Up at the speaker's podium, Shanae Connor had just taken the mike to deliver her eulogy, still clutching the teddy bear, which wore a blue bow around its neck. The girl was slim and beautiful, her brown eyes reddened now with tears.

''Treva was good,'' Shanae was saying into the mike. ''Maybe one of the last really good people around. She wanted her son so bad. She would do anything to have him. Even d-die . . . She was my hero . . .''

Sobs filled the church.

Pepper closed her eyes, deeply affected, then opened them again as Gray's hand crept out and enfolded hers. His palm was warm and dry, his fingers gently squeezing hers. It was the most companionable handhold that Pepper had ever experienced. Maybe it was her imagination, but she could feel the love in him, rushing like energy from his flesh to hers.

''Pep,'' he whispered again, leaning toward her. ''I know I've made a lot of promises, but I mean them—every one of them. I love you. I'll be with you for the rest of my life, so I hope you're prepared for that.''

Pepper started to smile. Even though it was a funeral, she couldn't help herself. The smile spread across her face, opening her lips, and she knew that somewhere Treva Connor, perhaps floating above them in the church, disembodied as a beam of sunlight, would totally understand and approve.

''I'm prepared,'' she said, gripping Gray's hand.

She sank back, feeling warmth spread through her, a warmth she could not stop and did not want to stop. A warmth she prayed would last as long as their lifetimes were woven together.

*   *   *

In the family pew, Wade Connor dabbed at the tears that ran openly down his cheeks as he listened to his daughter's eulogy for the woman he had loved so deeply. Treva had been his hero, too. He didn't know why God had chosen for her to die, but he did know there was a reason . . . There was always a reason.

He began to think about the small, brown child still at the hospital, attached to fetal monitors, vigorously sucking his thumb. Wade, Jr., their son. The infant was thriving, Dr. Livoti had told Wade this morning. Every day he grew more active, and was rapidly putting on weight. Soon Wade could bring him home from the hospital.

Treva, he thought, speaking to the spirit of his wife, which he felt just had to be hovering near, somewhere in the church. *I'll raise him right. I'll make sure he's a fine young man. For you, for us.*

The tears burned again as he thought of the years ahead.